Morning's Gate

Louisa Elliott

ANN VICTORIA ROBERTS

Morning's Gate

William Morrow and Company, Inc.
New York

Copyright© 1991 by Ann Victoria Roberts

First published in Great Britain in 1991 by Chatto & Windus Ltd under the title
Liam's Story

The lines from "Little Grey Home in the West" are by Hermann Lohr and Dorothy
Eardley-Wilmot © 1914 Chappell & Co. Ltd (assigned 1988 to Marlow Lynn Ltd
trading as the Chappell Recorded Music Library), reproduced by permission.

It is the policy of William Morrow and Company, Inc., and its imprints and affil-
iates, recognizing the importance of preserving what has been written, to print
the books we publish on acid-free paper, and we exert our best efforts to that
end.

Library of Congress Cataloging-in-Publication Data

Roberts, Ann Victoria.
    Morning's gate / Ann Victoria Roberts.
        p.   cm.
    ISBN 0-688-11074-6
    I. Title.
PR6068.O1414M6   1992
823'.914—dc20   91-24424
                                                                              CIP

Printed in the United States of America

First U.S. Edition

1 2 3 4 5 6 7 8 9 10

BOOK DESIGN BY A. DEMAIO

For Peter Scott Roberts
with all my love

Author's Note

$\mathcal{M}$orning's Gate was inspired by a diary written by a young Australian soldier in 1916. In the novel, all that relates to the First World War is based upon that diary and extensive research undertaken to verify it. The rest of the novel is fiction, and except with regard to public figures, none of the characters is intended to bear any resemblance to real people, either living or dead.

I am indebted to my friend Bill Mulholland for his knowledge and assistance with research; and to my husband, who willingly relived some harrowing experiences in the Persian Gulf in the cause of authenticity. In Melbourne, Jenny Carew worked hard on my behalf with a very vague brief indeed; and two people, Carol and Gary Matthews, were very kind in helping a complete stranger in her quest for information about old Dandenong.

It remains to be said that I could not have written about the Australian Imperial Force without referring constantly to several books: *The Official History of Australia in the War of 1914–1918* by C.E.W. Bean (University of Queensland Press), *The Anzacs* by Patsy Adam-Smith (Nelson), *The Broken Years* by Bill Gammage (Penguin), and *Pozières* by Peter Charlton (Leo Cooper).

ANN VICTORIA ROBERTS

Breathless, we flung us on the windy hill,
    Laughed in the sun, and kissed the lovely grass.
    You said, "Through glory and ecstasy we pass;
Wind, sun, and earth remain, the birds sing still,
When we are old, are old . . ." "And when we die
    All's over that is ours; and life burns on
Through other lovers, other lips," said I . . .

from "The Hill"
by Rupert Brooke

I

*A*ll over England the year was dying in a blaze of glory. The shortening days were blessed at noon by cobalt skies and brilliant sun, by a warmth which belied early morning frosts and chilling mists at twilight. Tempted by the weather, groups of late tourists ventured forth to enjoy some lingering views before winter quickened everyone's step and made the cosiness of tea shops more attractive.

In York, Americans with cameras exclaimed before the Minster, backing into the road for better shots of the famous twin towers, while a party of Japanese, with the stoic expressions of dedicated tourists on a tight schedule, brushed past as they left by the west door. Clutching her guidebook, Zoe Clifford paused, debating whether or not to go inside. It was not yet twelve and she had the rest of the afternoon, but four or five hours might not be enough to do what she had planned, and the Minster deserved an hour or more to itself, an hour which might be regretted later in the day.

Reluctantly she stepped back, joining those transatlantic cousins on the pavement's edge, staring up with them at fine stone tracery and those soaring white pinnacles, two hundred feet above the ground. In full sunlight and against a cloudless blue sky, the effect was dazzling. And magnetic: she did not want to leave. Half regretting her decision, she contented herself with a walk around the outside, astonished by the cathedral's length and size, the way it dwarfed everything nearby. With the massive east window at her back, Zoe stood for a moment in a clear triangle of space, contemplating the long, half-timbered building of St. William's College, the line of trees that faced it, and a medieval archway that led into the street beyond. What seemed a dollhouse scale of chimney stacks and irregular rooflines marked that narrow thoroughfare, and she thought how satisfying it must be to gaze up at the Minster every day from one of those tiny windows. As she turned, a huge bell began to toll the dozen strokes of noon, the deep, sonorous note reverberating against her breastbone. Its solemn grandeur was like a knell for the dying year, underscoring the glorious, golden day, and the fact that she was alone.

For a moment she stood quite still, eyes closed; as the last stroke died away, she wondered why it was that beauty perceived alone should be so sad, and why it made loneliness so much harder to bear.

On a deep breath she turned away and completed her circuit of the Minster, glancing up at repairs being done to the roof of the south transept before cutting across to a paved walkway that led into the city's maze of medieval streets. A cup of coffee and a sandwich went some way toward restoring her emotional balance, and with her mind set on more immediate matters, she consulted her guide again.

Gillygate, the street she wanted, ran, according to the map, just beyond and parallel to the city wall, not far from the Minster. She checked the number of the house against her notes and mentally prepared herself for disappointment. For all she knew, Gillygate might well have been a slum, razed to the ground decades ago, or crushingly redeveloped in the brave new world of the 1960s. Anything could have happened; the chances of finding her great-grandmother's birthplace intact were very slim, but looking for that house was one of her reasons for being here.

According to a birth certificate obtained some weeks ago from St. Catherine's House in London, Zoe's great-grandmother had been born in the late summer of 1897, the year of

Queen Victoria's Diamond Jubilee. She was named Letitia Mary Duncannon Elliott, which was something of a surprise, as no one in the family could ever recall Letitia using the name Duncannon. It did not even appear on her marriage lines, although one Robert Devereaux Duncannon had been a witness at her wedding. Was there a mystery there, Zoe wondered, stuffing notes and guide back into her capacious shoulder bag, or was it simply that the Elliotts had wanted to impress wealthy relatives at the birth of their only daughter?

Zoe inclined toward the latter theory, although her mother always maintained that Letitia—who was never called Grandmother—had been a walking mystery until the day she died.

Mysterious perhaps, aggressively independent, and more than a little eccentric she certainly was. As a child, and contrary to the rest of her immediate family, Zoe had always rather liked her, probably because the old lady had never given a damn for anyone's opinion and frequently said so. She had possessed an amazing ability to confound people, Zoe's mother particularly, reducing that strong-willed but intensely conventional woman to tears of abject frustration. And as a child, subject to her mother's arbitrary decisions, Zoe had admired that quality. Even now, when time and the beginnings of maturity enabled her to understand something of Marian's problems, there was still a strong bias toward Letitia.

She was, after all, the only member of her family with whom Zoe felt any affinity at all. Mother, father, a couple of aunts and a few cousins on her father's side, none of them shared anything in common with Zoe. She liked her father and, had it not been for the divorce, might have been closer to him; but it could hardly be said that they understood each other. And Marian would never be any different, Zoe thought, regretting, not for the first time, that she could not like her mother better.

For a few brief weeks, albeit for very different reasons, she and Letitia had been like allies resisting a common foe. The ten-year-old child and the woman of seventy-three had both liked and understood each other, and Zoe's biggest regret was that Letitia had not lived long enough to share the secrets of her past and the family she had left behind in York. Some deep-seated instinct—or was it mere wishful thinking?—pressed Zoe into the conviction that her identity lay here in York, among the long-dead members of Letitia Elliott's family, rather than with her father's line of Surrey stockbrokers and businessmen. And she needed to discover that identity, needed to know why she was the odd one out, the willful, creative, unconventional child of such conservative parents. Perhaps, understanding herself, she might then learn to understand other people.

Crossing the road before the great square mass of Bootham Bar, Zoe made her way around the corner and into Gillygate. Unconsciously slowing her step, she was aware of a smile touching her lips as it dawned on her that structurally speaking the street had changed little in the past hundred years, and shop fronts had been restored to something approaching their original faces, despite the variety of bijou goods they displayed. She quickened her step, counting numbers as best she could. Most were missing, which was frustrating, but then she saw the house she was looking for, its number clearly displayed on the door. Three stories high, broad-fronted, windows and doorway compatible with the 1850s—Letitia's birthplace was still there.

Not merely intact, but a guesthouse, clean and bright and apparently newly furbished, with Austrian blinds at the upper windows and draped lace at street level. Zoe could scarcely believe such good fortune. For maybe half a minute she hesitated, staring up at rusty-pink brick, gleaming paintwork, and a bright brass knocker on the dark blue door. The temptation to be inside that house was too much. She had her checkbook and credit cards, and her return train ticket would be just as valid tomorrow as it was today. On a surge of anticipation she rang the bell.

A middle-aged woman answered, inviting her into a narrow hall. The reception desk was no more than a half-moon table with a vase of chrysanthemums and a visitors book, but after a cursory glance at her register, the woman said yes, she could offer a single room. It was small and on the second floor, but, she added with a smile, it had the advantage of quietness and an excellent view of the Minster.

The stairway ran across the house, dividing front from rear, and doubled back on itself at a half landing. On the first floor the corridor was broad, with a modern glass fire door leading to a second staircase. On the upper floor the landing was tiny, with just three doors opening off.

"Here we are. You'll be nice and quiet, there's nobody to trouble you next door, which is a family room, and children can be a bit noisy. Bathroom across the way, here—and all to yourself." The landlady, who had introduced herself as Mrs. Bilton, opened the door of a single room and went across to a low-silled window, bending her head to look out. "There, you can see the Minster now the leaves are falling. Somebody complained the other week—said we were contravening the Trade Descriptions Act! The trouble is, in summer the trees form too thick a screen. I keep telling my husband we should have them cut down."

Zoe was horrified by the idea. "Oh no, you mustn't do that! Just tell people to come in the winter, instead."

Mrs. Bilton laughed. "Well, perhaps we should have them thinned out—then everybody's happy!"

Warming to that unforced amusement, Zoe was almost tempted to reveal the significance of her visit, but to start talking now would waste too much time. Confidences, with perhaps a tour of the whole house, would be better left until later. While the sun lasted, she wanted to be out, seeing as much of the city as possible. Above those grassy, wooded ramparts, the white city wall divided Gillygate's backyards from the Minster precincts. It was hard to believe that she was only a few hundred yards from where she had stood at noon.

"Can you walk on those walls?" she asked, noticing for the first time the heads bobbing between the crenellations.

"Yes, of course—but I should hurry if you want to do it this afternoon, dear. They close the walls at dusk."

Descending the stairs, Zoe was given the times of breakfast and a front door key should she happen to be out late. With a cheerful wave, she set forth down Gillygate, hardly able to contain her elation.

Although from street level, the picture was a close and detailed one, from the height of the city walls it was the broad sweep of the canvas which took the eye. Above a sea of roofs and chimney pots, the Minster rose like an enormous ship in full sail, catching the falling light of late afternoon, and shadowing the narrow streets around it. Couples passed her on the wall, and a large party, complete with a guide, politely excused themselves as she lingered, entranced by the views. There was fascination on every side, from the undisguised age of the backs of houses on Gillygate, to the elegant expanse of the seven-teenth-century Treasurer's House within the walls, its tree-shaded grounds carpeted in bronze and gold. Autumn was a season for nostalgia, she always felt, the scent of dying leaves so evocative of the past. As the shadows lengthened she thought of Letitia, leaving this place for London and her tragi-cally brief marriage, could not help wondering why she had settled for Sussex and a house her parents-in-law had ensured she would never own, when York in all its beauty was here, waiting. Her family, too. The parents she never talked about, the brothers she had mentioned but once. Why did she leave, Zoe wondered; and why had she never come back? And what had happened to those brothers of hers, two handsome young men in a photograph sent from France in the summer of 1916?

In a cloudless sky, the sun was setting, no more than a fiery rim of gold low down in the southwest. There was a damp chill in the air, and above the chimney stacks and pantiled roofs, an orange haze was deepening to red.

As she came to Monk Bar, a uniformed attendant was waiting, looking out for stragglers on the walls before he locked up for the night. With a sigh of resignation he held the heavy oak door and, as she stepped inside the stairwell, closed it behind her. It was very dark, and the limestone walls within the Bar were smooth and cold, like those of a dungeon. The sound of the attendant's feet in heavy boots echoed behind her. With no light but that of the tiny doorway below, Zoe felt her way gingerly down those well-worn steps, and with some relief emerged into the everyday bustle of the street.

Goodramgate was busy, homebound shoppers edging carefully along narrow pavements, avoiding traffic which passed alarmingly close along that ancient and idiosyncratic thoroughfare. A chemist's brightly lit window, already dressed for Christmas, reminded her that she had brought no luggage; pausing to buy toothpaste and a brush, she went on to purchase a couple of items of essential underwear, cramming the parcels into an already bulging bag. Weaving between traffic and pas-sersby, she tucked the bag beneath her arm for safety.

In the darkening sky, a vestige of natural light remained, and above the jettied buildings of that winding city street, it had deepened to an astonishing color, like the French blue in Renaissance paintings of the Nativity. Gazing up as she walked, Zoe stopped as she reached a junction, arrested by an unexpected view of the Minster, the whole of its east end floodlit against the dark blue sky. White and perfect as ivory, intricate as lace, it stood in mighty Gothic splendor, dwarfing all that stood before it.

With some surprise, Zoe realized that she was facing the spot where she had stood at noon, and across the street was the little archway that led into Minster Yard.

Standing beneath its shelter, she simply stood and stared, knowing this to be a rare and perfect moment and wanting to preserve it in her memory. The traffic had eased and the flow of pedestrians dwindled to a few hardy strollers, who paused to look for a moment before passing on. It was numbingly cold, but Zoe hardly noticed. Her keen artist's eye was absorbing color and light, the vastness of the picture and its tiniest details; intent upon the whole, she suddenly noticed a strange phenomenon. What appeared to be thick white smoke was billowing from the Minster roof and curling around pinnacles and piers. Recalling the fire which had wrought such damage to the south transept a couple of years before, she was alarmed, darting forward at a run along the cobbled path. Before St. William's College she stopped short. There was no smell of burning, no sign of flames, but like smoke from some bloody but silent battlefield, the moving cloud drifted slowly toward her.

Roofs and chimneys which had stood in stark silhouette moments before were rapidly obscured. The carved relief of Gothic masonry faded, insubstantial as a dream in that swirling mist. Images of death replaced it, so real she could almost hear the boom of the guns, smell the cordite. Men advanced and fell before her eyes, their silent cries an obscenity. She cringed, screwing her eyes tight shut against it, and when she dared to look again they were gone. White light dazzled her, and all over her body, her skin was tingling with tiny shocks. Surrounded by that drifting mist, the whole of the east end seemed to be moving, advancing and receding, pulsing with some great inner power. In the silence nothing else moved, time was irrelevant, past and present were one, divided only by the pitiful awareness of five human senses. And it seemed those limitations were melting . . .

For a moment, drawn forward, Zoe was convinced that if she walked into that mist, she would simply be absorbed by it, that she would cease to exist. For an instant the idea was tempting, but on the verge of acquiescence, she hesitated; she shivered, and the moment was gone.

The touch of the mist was like a cold, damp shroud; trembling violently she turned away, fighting weakness and an urge to sink to her knees. Her eyes were stinging and her steps uncertain as she retreated toward the reassuring bustle of Goodramgate. A tall man, wearing a light raincoat, gave her a searching glance as she hesitated beside him at the curb; meeting his eyes, Zoe lifted her chin and glared, every muscle tensed against inner trembling and a ridiculous desire to flee.

With another quick glance to the right, Stephen Elliott took in the line of high cheekbones and dark, tumbling curls and, despite the fierce look she had just bestowed, thought she was the prettiest girl he had seen in a long time. The road cleared and she stepped across before him, a determined set to her shoulders and aggression in her stride.

Watching her round the opposite corner, he was momentarily intrigued. He had seen her standing there, watching the mist curl across the Minster roof, as fascinated by the evening's freak weather conditions as he was himself. Most people paused briefly and then walked on; but she had watched for several minutes and seemed unnerved as she returned.

Amused by his own fancies, Stephen turned and headed for home, and a moment later was climbing the stairs to his own flat in Bedern. Glancing at the time, he stacked his purchases on the kitchen table, knowing he would have to hurry to finish his packing and meet that appointment for dinner with friends at Strensall.

He picked up the telephone, calling first an old acquaintance with whom he usually left his car when going away, and with the arrangements made for its collection, dialed his sister's number in Harrogate.

Assuring Pamela that he was all packed and ready, he

repeated his destination, told her the ship's name, and said no, he was not at all sure where he would be over the festive season.

"It might well be West Africa, since the ship's been on that run for a while, but it's impossible to say for sure. From Philadelphia we really could go anywhere—it all depends on the charterers, and the price of oil . . ."

Suppressing a sigh, Stephen listened impatiently while his sister indulged in the usual exhortations regarding correspondence—which with her was infrequent—and healthy eating, in his opinion a contradiction in terms when applied to most of what came out of a ship's galley. But he said nothing: To point out what she already knew was a waste of time. When she launched into the subject of sexually transmitted diseases, however, Stephen held the receiver away from him, staring at it in disbelief.

"For God's sake, Pamela," he interrupted sharply, "I'm thirty-six, not sixteen! And if you'd seen what I've seen in twenty years at sea, you'd realize that this conversation is totally unnecessary . . . Yes, I know you only have my best interests at heart," he conceded, glancing at his watch, "but I do keep abreast of current affairs, I've heard about AIDS, and, believe it or not, I do know what condoms are for . . ."

That blunt sarcasm prompted further outraged protest. When her voice had settled to a more bearable level, he said, "Look, Pam, I'm going away in the morning, I might not be back for six months. Let's part friends, shall we?"

Reluctantly, she gave her assent. He visualized her tight little mouth and wondered whom she resembled. Certainly no one in the immediate family. At last, having soothed her ruffled feathers, he was able to end the conversation and rescue his underwear from the dryer. Adding those final items to his suitcase, Stephen ironed a couple of shirts, then went to shower and shave. Twenty minutes later he was backing his Jaguar XJ-S from its garage and wondering how soon he could decently say his farewells and return for a good night's sleep. By six in the morning he must be on his way to Philadelphia, and by this time tomorrow he would be taking over command of the M.V. *Nordic*.

2

As she lay in bed at the top of the house on Gillygate, Zoe's thoughts kept returning to the Minster, to the deep blue sky above, and the fog billowing around like smoke. In the intervening hours, with a hearty meal and a couple of brandies under her belt, she had regained both nerve and logic, realizing that natural phenomena had created the rolling mist, and floodlights that illusion of light and movement. Better than any theatrical effect, she told herself firmly, although there was no escaping the conviction that there had been rather more to it than that. Much more. That vision of death, for instance, which could have had no bearing on weather conditions, freak or otherwise, and that tingling sensation, warming her blood like a caress . . .

The rest she shied away from, not wanting to examine her own reactions too closely, but she had to admit that she had been moved by the experience, whatever it was.

With something of an effort, she pushed it to the back of her mind, concentrating instead on the pretty little bedroom with its daisy-patterned wallpaper and matching curtains. She wondered what it had looked like ninety years ago. Considerably more austere, she decided. On the top floor and without benefit of a fireplace, it had probably been part of the servants' quarters, and in a house this size, servants would have been essential.

Mrs. Bilton, sadly, knew little of its history, but her interest had been aroused by Zoe's questions, and she had obligingly shown her guest all the unoccupied rooms. Extensive alterations had been made to the kitchen some ten years before, when the stove had been ripped out, together with massive shelves and deep, floor-to-ceiling cupboards. The last owners, however, had seen the novelty of retaining the open fireplaces elsewhere, and Mrs. Bilton was particularly pleased about that.

Admiring the polished mahogany mantelpiece in the front sitting room, and imagining Letitia's family gathered before a blazing coal fire, Zoe had asked, only half jokingly, whether the house was possessed of any ghosts.

Her reply was in the negative, but Mrs. Bilton had gone on to mention ghosts she did know about, from the well-documented Roman soldiers in the cellars of the Treasurer's House and the theater's Grey Lady, to other, less publicity-conscious apparitions. There was a story about children playing in Bedern, and one of the shops down Gillygate often had the sound of heavy footsteps crossing an attic floor; to the rear of another shop, the assistants sometimes saw a little old lady dressed in black—"as solid-looking as you and me, they say"—crossing the yard . . .

With her own strange experience still fresh in her mind, Zoe had shivered a little at that but made no comment. Brought up between divorced parents and the hearty, no-nonsense tenets of an Anglican girls' school, she tended to be wary of revealing too much to strangers, especially on this particular subject. Although in the past she had never actually seen anything untoward, she was always aware of place and atmosphere, sometimes acutely so, which could be disturbing. She tended to think that places absorbed events, in the manner of a sponge, and that strong emotions leaked back into the atmosphere, slowly, over hundreds of years. But it was no more than a feeling which put into words sounded silly; although no more so than the idea of ghosts clinging to one place, perpetually reenacting one moment from long and human lives which must have contained far more dramatic events than pacing an attic floor, or crossing the yard to bring in the washing.

But York was old, with almost two thousand years of history behind it. Perhaps, as Mrs. Bilton claimed, the city was a place where the past had no means of escape. If ghostly figures were indeed as commonplace as she maintained, then possibly that experience by the Minster was less strange than she imagined. Part of the city, part of the place itself.

Except that the last pitched battle York had witnessed was during the Civil War, some three hundred years ago; and the images that had come to Zoe were not those of Roundheads and Royalists, but of men more modern than that, in uniforms of the Great War . . .

Three weeks later, after several hours closeted within the jumble-sale atmosphere of St. Catherine's House, Zoe fought her way home through the misery of a wet London rush hour. There was fine, drizzly rain in the wind blowing off Kensington Gardens, but she lifted her face to it in gratitude as she stepped off the bus. Despite the chilliness of early December, for her it had been a hot, crowded, frustrating day, in which she had learned far more about sharp elbows, territorial rights, and the extent of human obsessiveness than she had so far learned about the Elliotts.

Scorning her umbrella, she slowly walked the few hundred yards down Queen's Gate, enjoying the rain and unhooking the neck of the old nurse's cape she had purchased last year from Oxfam. It was warm and serviceable, and she liked its freedom, but it still had the power to shock her father and prompt him to offer something better from Harrods. His disapproval could still raise a wicked smile.

The policeman on duty at the Middle Eastern embassy was one she knew. He said good evening as she passed and touched his cap. Zoe continued smiling as she climbed the steps to her own door, knowing that she should not flirt so obviously, yet with no intention of discontinuing the habit. Such old-fashioned manners seemed to match the dignity of these elegant, stuccoed terraces. She loved Queen's Gate, loved the broad pavements, the porticoed houses, the tall plane trees, and the sheer Victorian grandeur of it all. It was such a pity, she often thought, that the air of ease and confidence it exuded was no more than a lingering breath from another age. Family houses, with servants by the dozen, had mostly been split into apartments decades ago; and since then had come hotels and offices, and most recently of all, the embassies. Diplomats from oil-rich Middle Eastern countries now occupied the former houses of men who had ruled an empire. Zoe found a certain irony in that.

Four flights of broad, shallow stairs led to her flat, and it was a matter of pride to run all the way up, even though she usually fell through the door, gasping. This evening was no exception. As usual, she filled the kettle, switched it on, then collapsed on the sofa to recover herself while it boiled.

As she considered her scribbled notes over a pot of scalding coffee, it became apparent that the day had yielded little in the way of fresh information. The reference library in York had proved a gold mine, while St. Catherine's House seemed full of dross where the Elliotts were concerned. Expensive dross too. The birth certificates she had ordered were several pounds each, and she had ordered those only in pique at being unable to find the two she had set her heart upon.

"So where *were* you born?" she demanded of the sepia photograph on the bookcase; but two half smiles returned her frown, and two pairs of eyes regarded her with silent amusement, as though they shared a private joke.

The two young men in the photograph were Letitia's brothers; Zoe knew that because Letitia had said so, once, a long time ago. Without that information, however, she might never have guessed. To begin with, they were not very much alike; and second, they were wearing the uniforms of different countries. In what seemed to be standard British infantry issue, one was seated in an armchair, a peaked cap resting against his knee, while the other, dressed in the uniform of the Australian forces, leaned against the arm. By comparison, he looked crumpled and scruffy, leather gaiters and boots appearing white and dull, as though covered in mud. His distinctive bush hat, caught up at one side, was pushed back, lending a slightly rakish air and revealing hair and brows which were much lighter than his brother's. He might even have been blond, whereas the other was dark, his hair close-cropped above a slender handsome face.

In spite of that youthful perfection, however, Zoe found the Australian far more attractive. Less obviously handsome, his features were broader, stronger, the mouth more full. It was the kind of mouth she would have liked to see drawn back in a hearty laugh. She had the impression that his smile in the photograph was a shade quirky, suppressing amusement which longed to burst forth over that studiously casual pose. As though the two of them had had a great day together, rounded off by a few drinks and a decision to have their pictures taken for the folks back home.

She did not have to remove the frame to know what was written on the back of that cheap postcard sent from a small French town in the summer of 1916, it had been committed to memory years before. *"Found each other at last! Congratulations on the wedding, Tish—wish we could have been there—Yours, Robin and Liam."*

But which was which? And had either of them survived the war? Letitia had never said, and Zoe had no way of knowing. Having possessed that photograph for more than half her life, until recently she had not given it much practical consideration. Hidden away for years among schoolbooks and ancient treasures, it had been resurrected only a few months ago while searching for something else. Strange, she thought, what a turn of the heart it had given her, like some forgotten memento of an old love affair.

Although the simile made her smile, it was apt enough. At an age when the other girls at school were screaming over pop stars and busy joining fan clubs, Zoe had been sighing over this very photograph and reading Rupert Brooke. A strange passion for a young girl, some might have said, although in terms of accessibility, the two were about equal, and the war poets were as young and blighted as any chart-topping rock group. In those days the brothers had been her own secret fantasy, part of a necessary insulation against the very public, overwhelming, and lonely life of boarding school. They had fulfilled the roles of lovers and guardians, coming to her in the quiet times before sleep, listening to her thoughts and comforting her tears. To Zoe at that time their presence had been unquestionable; only now, remembering, did she find that certainty faintly disturbing. To appease herself, she put it down to adolescence and a peculiarly vivid imagination, which she had thankfully managed to harness to better use.

It was odd, however, that the discovery of that old photograph and its companion—one of Letitia when she was in her twenties—should have set her wondering about the Elliotts as a family. Questions never before considered leapt to mind, becoming more insistent as the answers continued to elude her. Marian apparently knew nothing, and the more Zoe pressed, the more annoyed her mother became. She could not understand why Zoe wanted to know these things; the Elliott ancestors were as remote to her as aboriginal tribesmen, and what they did, whether they were the landed gentry Letitia had once been known to claim or paupers dying in the local work-house, Marian neither knew nor cared. They were dead and gone, so what did it matter? What possible use could knowing about them be to people living now? Zoe should concentrate instead upon improving her social life, which was nonexistent as far as Marian could see, and let the dead rest in peace.

That pious sentiment cut no ice with Zoe. Marian did not wish peace upon the woman who had reared her after her parents' untimely deaths; indeed, Zoe suspected that her mother liked to think of Letitia suffering in purgatory for her sins. And that irritation at being questioned only served to make Zoe more determined than ever to unearth the answers. Family history was a popular hobby apparently: There were books on the subject, offering guidelines to research in archives both accessible and remote. She would have the answers eventually; and if the frustrations were frequent, the satisfaction of discovery was equal to that of solving a complex detective story, with the added pleasure of knowing that the story went on . . .

Backtracking from Letitia's marriage lines, Zoe had found it easy to establish her birth, but her brothers were proving something of a problem. If not born in England—and Zoe was almost certain they were not—then it was possible that their parents had been living in either Scotland or Ireland at the time. Or even, she thought wryly, Australia. Nevertheless, wherever their travels had taken them, the Elliotts were living in York by 1897, the year of their daughter's birth.

Pondering the possibilities, Zoe reached for the notebook in which she had neatly written up all the information gleaned so far. At the top were listed details taken from Letitia's birth certificate: father Edward Elliott, Bookbinder; mother Louisa Elliott, formerly Elliott. Zoe had added a note that Edward and Louisa were possibly cousins, a supposition borne out later by information gathered in York.

Before leaving the city three weeks ago, she had made a visit to the reference library and, with the aid of a keen young assistant, managed to establish the tenancy of the house on Gillygate. Not all the street directories had survived, but of the half dozen extant between the years 1880 and 1898, one Mary Elliott was listed as the householder. Having expected to see a man's name, Zoe had been rather surprised. Even more so to find that the house was described as a commercial hotel. Not a private residence at all, which rather deflated her illusion that the Elliotts had been living there in some style. In fact with an entire family resident there, servants and guests as well, it sounded very crowded indeed.

She was struck, too, by the coincidence of the house having been a hotel then as it was now. Only for the past ten years, but still . . .

By 1902, however, Elliott's Commercial Hotel was in the possession of a Mrs. Eliza Greenwood, who offered lodgings. Zoe could only assume that the Elliotts had left for larger premises.

Intrigued by the identity of this Mary Elliott, Zoe had then bearded the young assistant afresh and been delighted to discover that a look at the local census returns might throw light on the matter. The hundred-year block on those ten-yearly returns was something of an annoyance and meant that the year 1881 was the latest available. She waited for the relevant microfilm to be found and watched in fascination as it was set up for viewing on a large television screen; then she had the problem of finding Gillygate for herself. It was a time-consuming, eye-straining task, but eventually the street came to light, and at last she found the hotel.

There, for one night in April 1881 were all its residents. Not only their names and ages, but their occupations, relationships, and places of birth. They were all there: Mary Elliott, head of household and a widow, her three daughters, her nephew Edward, one servant, and four guests. It was so exciting she wanted to jump up and shout the news aloud, but repressed by the silence in the library, she simply left the screen and found her helper. "I've found them," she had whispered, grinning delightedly from ear to ear, and the girl had smiled with genuine pleasure.

She had written down exactly all that the census divulged. Mary Elliott had been born in Lincolnshire, while her three daughters, of whom Louisa at fourteen had been the eldest, were all born in York. Edward's birthplace was Darlington, and he was twenty-six in 1881, and a bookbinder. As a family, Zoe reflected, they had certainly moved around, which destroyed facile assumptions that only in recent times had people become truly mobile. So, they had traveled, and to have been in business presupposed a certain intelligence. In that day and age, widowed, with three young children to bring up and no social security as a safety net, Mary Elliott must have been both capable and astute. Also determined and strong. Zoe admired that. Recalling Letitia's second name, Mary, she wondered whether her great-grandmother had favored the old woman, and an image came to mind of a smart, plump, gray-haired woman with shrewd blue eyes and a slightly cynical smile. For all her eccentricities, Letitia had been nobody's fool, and Zoe rather suspected Mary Elliott of being a similarly tough character.

What had really intrigued her, however, and continued to do so, was the relationship between Mary's eldest daughter, Louisa, and her nephew Edward Elliott: first cousins with a gap of twelve years between them—she a young girl, ripe for romance, and he a grown man. Living in the same house, or just visiting? It was impossible to say, but Zoe could not help wondering whether he had taken advantage of close proximity, perhaps made Louisa pregnant, and then had had to marry her. There may have been a family row occasioned by disapproval of the situation and their close blood relationship—perhaps they had moved away from York, yet for some reason been forced to return and eat humble pie at Mary Elliott's table.

It was a tempting theory, but no more than supposition. With such slender facts in hand, a dozen different interpretations were possible. Sighing, Zoe wished that her great-grandmother had not been so close-mouthed, wished she could have been an elderly woman who delighted in talking about her own and her family's past. That she had not made Zoe wonder whether she was ashamed of those comparatively humble origins. Her claim to be descended from landed gentry seemed to bear that out, but Zoe was determined not to reveal Letitia as either liar or romancer until the full story was known. And for that, what she needed were some other Elliott descendants, people who had known Letitia, Liam and Robin, and understood something of their background.

It was a tall order, she realized that. The carnage of the First World War could have wiped out one or both of those young men, and it was quite possible that she was the only descendant of that family left alive.

But no, she would not allow herself to believe that, or admit defeat before every avenue of research was exhausted. Besides, something deep inside kept urging her on, something more vital than just the thrill of the chase.

Hunger impinged upon those considerations, together with the realization that in less than an hour Philip was coming to collect her, and they were meeting Clare and David at yet another little bistro that David had discovered.

The glow of pleasure she experienced at seeing Philip Dent again was not entirely unalloyed. She had always found David rather overbearing, and the thought of another evening in his company—the third in short succession—was not one she relished. Which was a shame on more than one account. He had recently become engaged to Clare, who was one of Zoe's oldest friends. Not the closest by any means, but the two women had somehow retained their connection since school days, while most of the others had fallen by the wayside.

Naturally, they had seen much less of each other once the romance with David became serious, and a small kernel of cynicism in Zoe was aware that these recent invitations were prompted largely by David's desire to set up his old friend Philip with a girlfriend. He had been working in Brussels for the past two years and was rather out of touch these days. But it was also to Zoe's advantage, and for that she was grateful. In recent months she had become something of a hermit, too taken up with a sudden rush of commissions and her own desire to consolidate her reputation as an illustrator to pay much attention to a social life.

So it had been a pleasant surprise to meet Philip, and to feel that mutual attraction. He was really very good-looking, if a little unsure of himself with women, which Zoe found charming. And with the shyness in abeyance, he could be amusing, full of fascinating anecdotes about life in the European Community. If he were away from his friend David's shadow, Zoe felt that he might be more interesting still.

Musing happily on the possibilities, she showered and changed into a flowing calf-length skirt and silk blouse, its dark emerald lending a touch of green to her clear gray eyes. For once, her hair was behaving, with little tendrils of curls framing her face. Surveying her reflection, she had just decided, as Philip arrived, that her outfit needed something else . . .

Spotting the shawl she wanted as he waited in the hall, Zoe whipped it off the sofa back, shook its silk folds vigorously, and arranged it around her shoulders. Her companion looked on in some surprise.

"Isn't that part of the decor?"

It was her turn to be surprised. "Well, yes . . ." She gave him a consciously winning smile. "But it goes rather well with what I'm wearing, don't you think?"

He smiled and nodded, but she had the feeling that he did not quite approve. She sighed. Perhaps his mother was a woman whose possessions were static rather than fluid, or he was afraid that the shawl was dusty after weeks on a sofa back. Well, maybe it was, but to Zoe that mattered less than the fact that it completed her outfit.

For a moment she hesitated, wondering whether she should give in to his sense of propriety and discard the prettily patterned shawl in favor of something more respectable; but no, that would be like shedding part of her personality, and Philip must learn to accept her as she was, warts, shawls, dust, and all.

At the last moment, as she was locking the door, he managed to save her mood and the evening by telling her that David had come down with laryngitis and, as the rising young barrister was due in court on Monday morning, felt he must stay at home and save his voice.

It was excellent news.

Next morning, with dust still on her mind, the searching rays of low winter sun revealed layers of it, along skirtings and cornices, and in a considerably grayer film on the gray-and-white marble hearth and mantelpiece. There were cobwebs, too, in corners and along the bookcases. With her mother threatening a visit, Zoe knew she should set some time aside for cleaning, and the sooner the better.

What it really needed, of course, was redecorating, but that would have to wait until the spring. Four years since its last fresh coat of paint, and the memory of weeks of backbreaking work beforehand was enough to make the idea of starting again feel like masochism. But the place had been filthy before she moved in, the victim of years of neglect and sooty coal fires, requiring more effort in dedication and elbow grease than anything she had undertaken before or since. Then, however, it had been the kind of challenge she needed, an effective cure for postexamination blues, and a broken love affair.

With her first sight of the flat, however, in spite of the dirt and mustiness, Zoe had been aware of its beautiful proportions, and a sense of welcome, somehow, as though people known to her had lived here once.

That first impression had never changed. It still gave Zoe great pleasure to return whenever she had been out, and in this room particularly she worked better and more consistently than anywhere else.

With breakfast cleared away, Zoe sat at her work-table, and glancing through a series of sketches and illustrations, she was aware of a strong sense of satisfaction. It was good, after years of study, struggle, and a few professional blind alleys, to be doing what she had always wanted to do, and to be doing it with a certain amount of success. The illustrations before her were in different stages of completion for a new, expensive edition of Hans Christian Andersen's fairy tales. It was her most lucrative commission so far and the kind of work at which she excelled—exotic, highly detailed, subtly colored, reminiscent of another age.

Among her favorite books as a child had been some first editions illustrated by Arthur Rackham; and as a student she had been influenced by the sure, bold lines of Beardsley and Eric Gill. Her style as an illustrator reflected that early partiality, and a resurgence of interest in art nouveau had recently put Zoe's work in some demand.

It was immensely gratifying. At last she could think of paying her father a more realistic rent, although true to form, James Clifford said she owed him nothing, that her success was enough and she should enjoy it. Zoe could not forget that he owned the roof over her head, however, and while he might be a wealthy man with several more profitable leases in his possession, it was no excuse to take his generosity for granted. To counter her protests, he often said that he might be thinking of selling the place now that it was so desirable, but she knew he had no intentions of doing so. Since her abortive affair at college with Kit, James Clifford had been delighted to see his only daughter progress, emotionally and materially, into independent adulthood. Other than her friendship, he wanted nothing more.

Thoughts of Kit made her smile, particularly when she compared him with Philip. It was like standing a scruffy mongrel beside a well-trained pedigree gundog; while the mongrel might be fun to play with, at least the gundog was well mannered and reliable. It was such a pleasant change to be treated with deference and respect after some of the egocentric characters she had known in the past; and rather a surprise, she had to admit, to realize that Philip wanted to impress her.

An expensive restaurant, a nightclub afterward: These things had been flattering and enjoyable, especially as he had turned out, unexpectedly, to be more than adept on the dance floor. Zoe loved to dance, and so it seemed did Philip. With that shared enthusiasm warming them, the evening had been a success and opened a range of possibilities for the future. Possibilities which need not include David and Clare.

3

---

*I*n the Gulf of Guinea, just south of the Equator, the sun was making its rapid descent into the sea. The heat on deck was phenomenal, every steel plate throwing back what it had absorbed during the course of the day. In crisp white shirt and shorts, Stephen Elliott was taking one of his apparently casual strolls along the raised catwalk, sharp eyes taking note of maintenance done and yet to do, assessing the progress made by his Chinese crew and balancing it against overtime claimed.

He climbed up to the fo'c'sle, noting patches of rust which demanded attention, and cast his eye over winches and mooring equipment checked that afternoon. He peered into the anchor housing and leaned over the bow, visually assuring himself that all was secure; and then he relaxed, enjoying the breeze which gave an illusion of coolness, the silence which soothed his ears. The bridge, his cabin, all the after-end accommodation, suffered constant noise, incessant vibration from generators and engines, twenty-four hours a day; these few minutes, while the crew were below and most of his officers in the bar enjoying a drink before dinner, were Stephen Elliott's moments of luxury.

The sun's lower edge touched the horizon; within a moment or two it was gone, leaving night clouds streaked with red and gold below a purple sky. The high drama of a tropical sunset never failed to please him, expanding his mind beyond the mundane, beyond ship and cargo and the weight of his responsibility for twenty-six lives. For a few minutes he could forget who he was and what he was, and stand outside himself, at one with the sea and the sky.

But that kind of freedom was all too brief. Behind him stood the mass of his everyday life, and before his eyes the light was fading. Sighing, he made his way back down the shadowy deck, his mind returning to more practical matters. In a little over twelve hours they would be arriving at the West African port of Cabinda, or, more precisely, mooring alongside a single buoy fifteen miles off the coast. And a day later, having loaded eighty thousand tons of oil, the *Nordic* would sail on to Muanda, at the mouth of the Congo, and load some more. With a full cargo, worth something like thirty million dollars, the ship would make its return journey to Philadelphia, eighteen days away across the Atlantic. In the way of light relief, the round trip did not have much to recommend it. Six weeks without mail or shore leave, of absolute and utter boredom punctuated at three-week intervals by the madness of pilots and port officials, essential repairs, ship chandlers, agents, surveyors, bills of lading, notes of protest, all designed to keep every last man on his toes from dawn through till dawn, and maybe the dawn after that. The personal test, Stephen always felt, was whether he could stay awake for thirty or forty hours, keep his good temper, forget nothing and no one, and still get his ship safely to sea at the end of it. So far he had never failed, but with every voyage the demands were increasing, the ships getting older, the personnel fewer. What had once been a challenge was becoming for him an endurance test.

As ever, almost halfway through the trip, he found himself wondering what it was that kept him at sea, what streak of masochism drove him back time after time, when all the fun had long since gone. Habit, he supposed; money, certainly; and perhaps a residue of hope that the next ship would be better. This voyage, however, was as boring as a bus trip up and down the same stretch of road, except that this particular bus was old and cantankerous and liable to stall at the least convenient moment. And it was no good, he reflected, saying that the engine was somebody else's responsibility; when you were doing the driving, you were the one held responsible for accidents.

On a deep breath before he went inside, Stephen tried to stop worrying, looked for something, anything, to lighten the boredom which was always his chief enemy. There was nothing in Cabinda, less in Muanda . . . but Philadelphia might, just *might*, prove interesting next time around. He smiled suddenly, remembering the attractive divorcée who was acting as water clerk for the agent. If he could only steal a few hours away from the ship, he might take her out to dinner, and then . . .

But over a month later, when the ship arrived back in the States, Stephen's intentions seemed doomed to remain fantasies. The pretty redhead flirted discreetly, stayed to lunch on board, and accepted his invitation to dinner in town; but there was a discrepancy with the cargo figures, arguments with marine surveyors and representatives of the receiving company which went on half the night. He phoned her at eight, and then again at half past ten; she agreed, very gracefully, that there was no point in waiting for him. Disappointed and frustrated, Stephen returned to his office sharp-tongued and prepared to give no quarter on those cargo figures; his temper was not eased by knowing that he was right and the receiving company wrong.

She arrived the next morning before they sailed, looking fresh and maddeningly sexy in a crisp white shirt and thigh-hugging black trousers. Despite his lack of sleep and the presence of her superior, all it needed was one regretful, conspiratorial glance and Stephen was well aware of all that he had missed the night before.

"I'll be taking a vacation next time," she whispered as her boss stood talking to the chief, "but give me a call anyway—maybe we can fix something."

"I'd like that," he murmured, wondering whether the ship would allow more than an hour's respite. Only after she had gone did Stephen realize that next time in Philadelphia he was due for relief; it was a measure of the effect she had on him that he had forgotten. In the course of the next six weeks, however, the M.V. *Nordic* managed to erase all such considerations from his consciousness.

After dark off Cabinda, before they began their approach to the mooring buoy, the engines suddenly failed. Ordinarily that would not have been much of a problem; but while they were drifting, the engineers slaving below in intense heat and humidity to root out the cause of this too-frequent occurrence, another ship appeared on the radar, apparently on a collision course and taking no evasive action.

Called to the bridge, Stephen waited a moment to allow his eyes to adjust to the darkness. From the direction of the radar console, the Third Mate addressed him, his voice squeaky with nerves. "Ship on the starboard beam, Captain—getting very close."

"Have you called him up?" Stephen asked, glancing at the radar plot and picking up the binoculars. The other ship was indeed right on the beam, and in these circumstances a little too close for comfort.

As he reached for the VHF radio, the Mate arrived, curious as ever, clad in flapping sandals and a pair of shorts. "What the hell's he playing at?" he muttered, gazing out over the bridgewing. "Is he blind or what?"

"Probably gone to sleep." The engine room telephone began to ring. "Answer that, will you, Johnny? Should be the Chief." Ignoring what was going on around him, Stephen started to transmit on Channel 16, the hailing frequency, anxiety controlled beneath a veneer of calm.

"This is the Liberian ship *Nordic*, in position five degrees, three minutes south, and nine degrees, fifty-two minutes east, bound in a southeasterly direction, calling the northbound ship on my starboard side."

Releasing the transmit button, he waited for a reply. For perhaps half a minute he inwardly fumed, wondering whether the watchkeeper on the other ship had abandoned the bridge altogether.

Eventually, a thickly accented voice replied, obviously irritated by the interruption. "*Nordic*, this is the Greek ship *Lemnos*. I receive you."

With fury edging his voice with ice, Stephen called again. *"Lemnos*, this is *Nordic*—I receive you too, but can we please *get off* Channel sixteen? I suggest Channel six."

"Okay, *Nordic*, with me that is fine. Channel six, going down."

Changing channels, requesting confirmation that he could be heard, Stephen declared with cutting emphasis: "I am without power. I am *not under command*. I request you give me a *wide berth*—do you understand?" English was the language of the sea, but sometimes that understanding was severely limited, and this was no time to be wondering whether the message was clear.

"Okay, *Nordic*, I understand fine. I alter my course to port."

"Sensible, sensible," the Mate whispered.

"Lemnos, this is *Nordic*. Thank you. Have a pleasant voyage. Over and out."

With another response, the transmission was over. Returning the VHF to channel 16, Stephen let out a long, pent-up breath. "Just make sure he does turn to port."

"Bloody fine seamen, the Greeks," Johnny commented, "when they're actually on the bridge and remembering to keep a watch." As the *Lemnos* visibly changed course, he laughed to release the tension. "That's it, Nick—you can do it. Left hand down a bit, and you'll be clear, mate!"

Stephen gave a dry smile as he watched the other ship come around the stern, wondering why its name should seem familiar. Eventually it came to him. "Lemnos—that's in the Aegean, isn't it?"

"No idea—the only Greek island I know is Crete. The girlfriend dragged me there last leave. In August—she got sunburned."

"Hmm." Stephen pondered for a moment. "Anyway, what did the Chief have to say?"

"Main generator's packed in—number two failed to start for some godforsaken reason, and number three is lying around the engine room in bits. They've been working on it all day, he says."

"Wonderful. And what's the prognosis?"

"Didn't want to have to commit himself at this stage."

"Well, he's going to have to." Anxiously, Stephen glanced

at his watch. Almost eight, and the pilot booked for first light off Cabinda about half past five. With time in hand, Stephen had been planning to slow down for the next few hours; but could the repairs be done in that small margin? If not, it meant canceling the pilot, canceling their slot in the queue of ships waiting to load; and cancellations cost money. A lot of money. He would not be popular with his managers sitting tight in their London office. Nor with the charterers in Hong Kong.

On the sill below the bridge windows were matches and a pack of Marlboros. "Thought you were giving up?" he remarked to the Third Mate, and at the young man's sheepish grin, took a cigarette and handed the pack back to him. Then he telephoned the engine room.

"We've got about an hour and a half. Two if we really push it. But after that we'll need fifteen knots out of her to get there in time. Can you do it?"

The reply was brief, the other phone slammed down. With raised eyebrows but no comment, Stephen replaced his receiver with exaggerated care and went out on to the bridgewing. With no generators to power the air-conditioning, it was becoming hot and sticky, even in the wheelhouse; in his cabin, with no opening portholes, it would be worse. He dreaded to think what it was like below in the engine room.

"Johnny, get one of the stewards to take a couple of cases of something down, will you? Coke, lemonade—they won't want beer while they're working. Charge it to the company account."

Unbuttoning his shirt, he breathed deeply, watching the lights of the *Lemnos* receding safely into the distance. Scarcely a breeze touched his skin.

"Well," he remarked softly as the Mate joined him, "thank God it's a calm night."

As the big American jet lifted off the tarmac, Stephen could see the *Nordic* alongside the berth, just yards from Philadelphia's main runway. That ship, he reflected, had been a bitch before he met her, and that she continued to be so, despite the ministrations performed by a succession of engineers, should not have depressed him. But it did. Her unpredictability worked in ways both subtle and crude, until by the end of his five-month tour of duty, Stephen Elliott hated her and prayed never to see her again. A steel hawser had parted at one tie-up, narrowly missing three of the crew—an inch or so closer and it might have killed them. And despite making their appointment with the pilot of Cabinda with minutes to spare, those generators had continued to give trouble, cutting out when most needed, and for no discernible reason. He was reminded of an Indian electrician who had once claimed that a motor was perfectly all right, he had checked everything. "The only trouble with it, sir, is that the bally thing will not work."

But that had been funny; the *Nordic* was not.

And the night before last, coming up the Delaware, Stephen had seen the *Nordic* as his nemesis. In the last moments of delicate maneuvers, with the pilot asking for half astern as they made the turn to come into the berth, the engine had cut out again. For several terrible, palpitating minutes, as the ship's momentum carried her bow first toward the berth and the airport's main runway beyond, Stephen had visualized catastrophe: a ripped and twisted bow embedded in concrete, a full cargo of oil spilling out into the river, fire hoses, foam detergents, and a courtroom full of federal lawyers baying for his blood.

Then, as he tried to contact the engine room, the phone had chosen that moment to play up too. With one man transmitting questions and orders through the emergency connection, himself operating the telegraph, the Third Mate feverishly scribbling all orders and times for the logbook, and the pilot as rigid with anxiety as Stephen had ever seen a man, the scene was like something out of a badly staged melodrama. At the last minute, however, with the engineers below performing miracles, the engines had jerked into life with a resounding thud and cough of thick black smoke; and on full astern, the tugs had managed to pull the *Nordic* around into position for the berth.

With no accidents, no catastrophes, and with his Master's Certificate still intact, he had managed to joke about it as they came safely alongside. "You know, for a minute or so," he remarked dryly to the pilot, "I thought I wouldn't need a taxi to the airport." And the Chief, staggering up to the bridge in an oily, sweat-streaked boiler suit, had spluttered with appre-

ciative laughter. The Delaware pilot, however, had seemed to find such levity in bad taste, for he left with a very curt goodnight.

As customs and immigration officers went through the ship's papers in his office, Stephen had shut the cabin door and tossed down a very large whisky; but he was sweating and trembling for more than an hour afterward. By the time the relieving Master arrived, Stephen had calmed himself sufficiently to perform an adequate handover. And after that he had downed the best part of a half bottle of scotch. Fortunately his replacement was a man he knew well—they had sailed together as Master and Mate a couple of years previously—and Stephen's cautionary tale of the *Nordic*'s tendency to perform circus tricks was taken seriously.

Only as the agent mentioned Stephen's flights home did he recall the pretty water clerk and her invitation. Under the expansive influence of the whisky, Stephen said he was in no particular hurry; he would fly home the following afternoon, and in the meantime see something of Philadelphia.

Well, he acknowledged wryly, he had certainly seen something of the place in the last twenty-four hours, visiting the Liberty Bell and Independence Hall, walking the Quaker City's checkerboard network of streets and admiring the fine restoration of Georgian town houses. He was a little surprised, however, to read on a plaque that the city had been laid out according to the Roman grid system of York, England. It bore no resemblance, as far as he could see, to the York with which he was familiar. He saw nothing at all of the attractive redhead. Having tried her number several times that afternoon, he had finally resigned himself to the fact that she was out of town this spring weekend, having taken up, no doubt, some more recent offer.

It was annoying, but he was far from brokenhearted. It had been many years since he had had the opportunity to play the tourist in foreign ports, and there was a quaint, old-world charm about much of Philadelphia which appealed to his sense of the past. He had dined that night with the ship chandler, a pleasant highly cultured man whose family could be traced back to the original Quaker settlers. His wit and hospitality had rapidly doused any lingering embers of disappointment.

With the spring sunshine winking back from the waters of the Delaware, Stephen craned his head to take a last look at the *Nordic*. As the aircraft swept away to the northeast, he breathed a sigh of relief; she was somebody else's problem now, and with any luck he would never be asked to take command of her again.

Leaving Kennedy just after six in the evening, he arrived at Heathrow in plenty of time to catch one of the midmorning flights to Leeds-Bradford. His long limbs were aching and cramped from confinement, his eyes stinging from too little sleep and the effects of warm, dry, processed air; but as soon as he stepped out onto the tarmac, a bracing blast of March air whipped exhaustion away.

The sun was shining from a china blue sky, fleecy clouds scudding across that high, unprotected plateau, and way below in the Wharfe valley, it would be a mild, slightly breezy morning. He knew because he had lived there once. Just three miles from the airport, convenient for a commuter, which was how he liked to describe himself, and perhaps a mile from the school where Ruth still taught.

Five years, he thought as the taxi sped down Pool Bank, taking those steep, snaking corners with contempt. A tunnel of trees not yet green, and on another bend, the Avenue des Hirondelles, its name carved so incongruously into a classical arch of millstone grit. Its unexpectedness caught the imagination. The setting was beautiful, and possibly swallows did return there each spring, but what inspiration of allegory or affectation had caused it to be built? He had never explored that muddy lane, and now probably never would. It was part of his past, like Ruth. Five years since their parting, and a journey like this, so familiar, so unchanging, could make it seem like yesterday.

He wished it were otherwise, because in a strange way it still hurt, even after all this time. Was she happy, he wondered, with her new, safe, reliable husband? Secure in the conviction that he would come home each evening for his dinner, be there every weekend to dig the garden and put up shelves? Whenever he thought of her, Stephen always wondered that. No children, however, and that continued to surprise him. She had wanted children. It was one of the reasons she gave for wanting to end their marriage. With children, she claimed, her life would have been that of a single-parent family, and that was not good enough for her or her putative offspring. It was a hypothetical argument, and from Stephen's point of view, also unfair; she had known what he did for a living before she married him. Known also that he had no intention of giving it up. Known his intention, but not believed it. Like many a good woman before her, Ruth had imagined that love and marriage would change the man in her life, that she, with all the power at her command, could persuade him that her ideas were best. And her ideas, being the most conventional, had to be right.

Quite simply, it seemed wrong to her that he should go away and leave her for months at a time, when she hated being alone. Stephen had countered that by saying she could give up her career and travel with him, as did many other wives; but her first voyage, undertaken during an extended summer holiday from school, had proved such a failure she refused to repeat it. Ruth had been immensely bored, had missed friends, family, shopping, days out; even missed her own cooking. Admittedly, the food that trip had been appalling, and the long journey across the Pacific notable only for its sunbathing hours, but she had not *tried* to enjoy it. Unlike Stephen, she read very little for pleasure, while he could sit for hours with any kind of book and frequently did. It was such relaxation, such a perfect escape. But Ruth had even accused him of escaping from her.

Although at the time he had convinced himself, out of love for her, that it was not her fault, looking back he knew he had secretly resented her attitude. Now he wished he had tackled it there and then, brought it out into the open. Wished too, with the clarity of hindsight, that he had been less enthralled by physical need, but that had always been his vulnerable point. Now that he was older, more self-controlled, he could admit it, even laugh at the antics of his youth.

What he could not laugh about was his wife's betrayal. Stephen had remained faithful throughout the period of their marriage, wearing his virtue like a hair shirt and expecting a loving reward for his pains, yet that last couple of years had provided few rewards, loving or otherwise.

When Ruth told him she had met someone else, he was

stunned. When she admitted to a long-standing affair and said she wanted a divorce, his rage was uncontrollable. He had had to leave the house; had gone to his sister's, which was a mistake, but Stephen had known with a terrible clarity that to stay would have been to hit his wife. What made things worse was Pamela's lack of real sympathy; she could see the situation only through her best friend's eyes, and for that Stephen had never really forgiven her. Even now he was careful in conversation with his sister, in the old days she and Ruth had told each other everything, and he had no reason to suppose their habits had changed.

At that time, he remembered, he had sorely missed his parents, whose deaths in a Bank Holiday car crash, a year after his marriage, had occurred while he was away at sea. He had been unable to come home until well after the funeral, and then, being so used to not seeing them, he was left strangely unmoved by their absence. With the ending of his marriage, however, Stephen had suddenly felt like a thirty-year-old orphan, and that joint grief had been difficult to bear. That painful recollection made him think of his mother, a gentle and affectionate woman, devoted to husband and children, easy to be with, easy to love; and although his father's stern exterior had made him harder to know, as far as Stephen was aware they had enjoyed a good and happy relationship. With a sudden flash of insight, he realized that he had rather naïvely expected all marriages to be like that.

He envied his parents' past contentment, the easy companionship which had sustained them for so many years. For him, marriage had obviously been a mistake, yet he still missed having a wife to come home to. Such loneliness, unlike the pain of immediate loss, did not abate with time; and like every other awareness, it was so much more acute when he was returning home.

There had been several women since Ruth, and one or two he had been extremely fond of, yet while he remained at sea, Stephen knew he would not marry again; it was too hazardous a course to attempt twice in one lifetime. Nor, on the other hand, would he consider giving up his career simply for the sake of marriage. If he ever did give up his present career—and it was an idea which pressed him more and more with every voyage—it would have to be for something better, something he really *wanted* to do. And as yet he had not found it. He wondered whether he ever would.

There was no answer to that. Banishing the question, he shook his head. The day was too new, too brilliant, to waste on impossibilities. Instead, he gave himself up to the pleasure of the journey: winter wheat, fresh and green, the dark richness of plowed fields and lacy pink blossoms in gardens on the way. All a delight to eyes starved of such beauty for five long months. But with the Minster towers in sight against the horizon, he found himself thinking about his grandmother. A few weeks previously, after a short illness, she had finally succumbed to old age and died. A stiff, reserved woman, his father's mother had managed to inspire more respect in the family than whole-hearted affection, but over the years she and Stephen had been on good terms, and that he would miss her was indisputable.

Although he had telephoned his aunt via the satellite to express his sympathy, and again yesterday from Philadelphia, he knew he should see her soon. Joan Elliot, his dead father's sister, was by far his favorite blood relative, and he owed her much in gratitude.

She had obviously called at the flat within hours of his telephone call. Beside the mail stacked neatly at one end of the breakfast bar, was a note telling him that electricity and water were turned on, fridge and freezer stocked with basic essentials. A postscript informed him that she had spent twelve pounds and a few pence.

Stephen made himself some coffee, smoked a cigarette, and spent a good ten minutes deciding whether to defrost something in the microwave or eat out. Ultimately, the thought of having to make conversation with anyone, even his favorite lunchtime barmaid, was too much. Instead he reached for the frying pan and cooked himself the most satisfying English breakfast he had tasted in months. Within an hour he was in bed, sleeping the sleep of the utterly exhausted.

When the alarm rang at six, he was drowsily tempted to ignore it; eventually, however, good sense prevailed. The rest he had had was not enough but would suffice for the time being, enabling his body clock to adjust more naturally. With mind still numbed and body sluggish, he forced himself out of

bed and into the shower; afterward he felt much better but
decided the unpacking could wait until morning. Pulling on an
old pair of jeans, Stephen went into the sitting room, a towel
still draped around his naked shoulders. He bent to light the
fire, a modern compromise with the genuine coal flame he
would have liked, and slipped a tape into the stereo. The music
of Dire Straits, almost Spanish in its passionate cadences,
swelled to fill the room, while beyond the window Goodramgate's black, uneven rooflines stood dramatically against the
floodlit Minster. Its purity touched his soul as always, while the
music stirred longings not entirely spiritual. He found himself
remembering his last night at home, the strange light and sudden, swirling mist, and a girl, silhouetted against it. The memory was as clear as yesterday, but all that was long gone. The
daffodils were in bloom again beneath the city walls, and it was
time for him to pick up the threads of his other life.

Lighting a cigarette, he poured himself a drink and sat
down to flick through the collection of mail, immediately con-
signing a whole bundle of circulars to the wastepaper basket.
Bank and fuel statements were pushed to one side for later
perusal, leaving a few letters, mainly from friends abroad,
which had arrived too late to be sent on to the ship. There was
a note from the shipping company, querying his report on an
injured seaman, which raised a muttered oath, and another,
addressed in a neat, italic hand, which made him frown.

The postmark was London, dated just after Christmas, and
for a moment Stephen wondered why his aunt had neglected
to forward it. Then he saw her message scribbled in pencil on
the back: "We had one of these, so no point in sending it
on—Joan."

Intrigued, he extracted a single sheet of typescript from the
unsealed envelope. The message was photocopied, a fact that
was apologized for in the first sentence.

As there are fifty-two Elliotts in the York phone book, and
no gender indicated, I trust you will forgive the impersonal
nature of this letter, and understand that it is prompted
simply by my desire to know something about the family
to whom I am related.

I am the great-granddaughter of Letitia Mary Elliott,

who was born in York in 1897, and died in Sussex in 1972. I understand that Letitia, whose nickname was Tisha, had two brothers, known as Robin and Liam, both of whom served during the First World War. I would very much like to contact anyone who might be descended from them.

Obviously this is very much a shot in the dark—not all the Elliotts in York will be related. But I sincerely hope that someone is—and that one of you will reply.

The signature was bold and clear—Zoe Clifford.

Bemused, Stephen read it through again, and then a third time. Letitia Mary Elliott was a name that meant nothing to him at all, but his grandfather, Robert Elliott—known variously as Bobby or Robin—had certainly served during the First World War. As had his brother, William Elliott, known as Liam.

At first it struck him as very odd. Then he recalled a friend of his sister's who was heavily involved in researching her family history, and realized this young woman was probably doing the same thing. Privately, he thought Zoe Clifford was wasting her time; apart from Liam, who had emigrated to Australia, the Elliotts had done nothing remarkable that he was aware of. No royal bastards, no fortunes in chancery, not even a poacher sentenced to be hanged.

Turning the envelope over, scanning Joan's message again, Stephen picked up the telephone. For perhaps half an hour they talked about his grandmother, and the illness which had developed so rapidly after Christmas. They talked about the short period in hospital and her peaceful end. Joan had been with her, and although she did not break down in the telling, Stephen could hear the rough emotion in her voice.

Then with a sharp cough, his aunt changed the subject. "Anyway, I'm glad you're home, love, because I want to see you. I'm buying a flat. Putting this ark up for sale any day now. Never could abide the place, and now Mother's gone, I can't wait to get out. The sooner the better."

Stephen was taken aback. "Are you sure? That you're doing the right thing, I mean? A flat will be very small after Gran's rambling place."

"That's just what I want. Something small, easy to clean—and above all, Stephen—*warm*. My arthritis isn't getting

any better, you know, and so much wants doing here. Quite
frankly, love, I can't afford the maintenance, not on one pension. So I've taken advice and I'm selling. Buying a nice little
one-bedroomed affair off Walmgate."

"Walmgate?"

"Oh, don't sound so snotty," the brisk voice in his ear
said reprovingly. "It's handy for town and these new flats are
lovely—central heating, double-glazing, fitted kitchen, the lot.
Nearly as smart as yours," she added archly.

Stephen laughed. "Listen, you don't have to sell it to me.
I think it sounds fine. You're the one who's always been so
disparaging about Walmgate."

"Well," she conceded, "it was dreadful before the war. But
it's come up in the world since then, you know—and with the
price of property the way it is, beggars can't be choosers."

Smiling to himself, knowing full well that his aunt was in
a far from beggarly situation, he told her she would get a good
price for the old house. It was as sound as a bell, and both
size and situation made it a desirable property. Sounding less
convinced than her nephew, Joan said she was also intending
to send most of the furniture to the salerooms, so if there was
anything he particularly wanted, he must say so.

"I thought I'd call and see you tomorrow, anyway," he
told her. "Maybe I can have a look then."

"Come for lunch—I'll cook you a decent meal."

Just in time, before she put down the 'phone, Stephen
remembered to ask about the letter.

"Oh yes—I want to talk to you about that as well. She
came to see us in January. Nice girl. Anyway, I'll see you tomorrow, about twelve." And having given her nephew plenty to
think about, she hung up.

The house, a short walk from Stephen's flat, was only a few
hundred yards outside the city wall. From an attic window the
top of Monk Bar could be seen, which would, Stephen thought,
prompt some keen young estate agent to describe it as having
views of the city's north-eastern gateway. It was, however, a
pleasant late-Victorian house, with deep bay windows and an
imposing front door. Apart from a first-floor bathroom installed

during the early fifties, and a kitchen of roughly the same era, the house had escaped much modernization. Fireplaces, picture rails and dados were all intact, together with doorknobs, cast-iron coat pegs in the hall, fancy floor tiles, and stained glass in the porch door. For someone with sympathy and plenty of money to spend on rewiring and damp-proofing, the place would be a delight. If he could bear to give up his view of the Minster, Stephen thought, he might be half tempted himself . . .

Joan was in the kitchen, preparing a meal which promised to be substantial: Soup was bubbling on the stove, and from inside the oven came the tantalizing smell of a meat and potato pie. Kissing his aunt's rosy cheek, Stephen whipped a bunch of daffodils from behind his back, laughing at her surprise. The flowers were instantly put into a cut-glass vase and set upon the dining table.

A large, round woman with clear skin and thick, peppery hair, Joan Elliott looked as though she should have been a farmer's wife with a brood of grown-up children; her hands, however, were unadorned by rings. Having served with the ATS during the last war, she had lost her man at the D day landings, and in her eyes there had never been another to replace him. Returning home to an austere peace, she had taken a job in the railway offices, moved in with her mother and simply stayed on, the two of them sharing the costs of that large family house. It could have been a sad tale, but in respect of his father's only sister, Stephen never thought so. Kind but immensely shrewd, she was one of the least pitiful women he could think of, and also one of his favorites. Faced with the wreck of his marriage and delayed grief for his parents, when Stephen was eventually able to talk rationally about it, she had listened; and more than that, she had been able to tell him things about his father that Stephen had never known, so that he was able to think of that rather stern, reserved man in a more kindly light, and thus shed many of his own regrets.

If he were able to repay her in any small way, Stephen knew he would not hesitate. There was indeed a problem, and during their meal she approached it in her usual, straightforward way. Her new flat was small and there were certain items for which she had no room at all. They were of no intrinsic

value, and it seemed no one else had either space or inclination
to give them a home. Stephen had time on his hands and a
spare bedroom, so would he oblige?

For a moment he was totally bemused, and mentally assessing the contents of his "spare" room, asked what these
items were, and could he see them first.

Joan led the way to the attic, climbing steep wooden steps
with little grunts of effort. With her hand on the narrow, half-
glazed door, she paused to catch her breath. "It's all up
here—including Father's photographic equipment. But all
that's going to the museum, so don't panic."

"Thank heavens for that." He laughed, but in the midst of
his curiosity came an involuntary thrill of excitement which
transported him back to childhood. On certain rare occasions
he had been allowed to come up here, not to play, but to look
at the giant camera and tripods and huge glass negatives which
had been part of his grandfather's life. Robin Elliott had trained
as a photographer before the First World War, and afterward
had run his own business on Monkgate. Hundreds of photographs, not all of them mounted, lay in boxes and drawers
beneath the eaves.

But he had forgotten the trunks. As soon as Joan pointed
to them, however, memory came flooding back. The big black
metal one, with its brass studs and clasps, had books in it,
he was sure. Tomes from the last century, bound copies of
illustrated journals, old bibles, and history books. And photographs—albums of them—which he and Pamela had been allowed to look at when they were very young. For a moment he
was a child again, hushed and expectant, wondering at the
treasure hidden within. And then he smiled, recalling disappointment: Books and photographs had seemed dull stuff indeed when his imagination painted strings of pearls and gold
coins. But the other trunk, smaller, leather-bound, with its over-
sized padlock, had always remained closed. Gran had invari-
ably said the key was missing.

Surprisingly, after a very short search, Joan produced a key
from the top drawer of a painted chest.

Before he could stop the words, Stephen said, "I thought
that was lost."

His aunt gave him a very old-fashioned look. "She always

said that." The key turned without too much effort, but the catch refused to give until Stephen wrenched it. The hinges were stiff too, squeaking in protest as he lifted the heavy lid.

"Lord," he muttered, thinking of his own lightweight luggage, "to think people traveled with these things. No wonder they needed porters!"

There was a layer of old newspapers covering the contents, and beneath, a sectional drawer with several small boxes and three very tiny pairs of children's shoes. The leather was stiff with age.

"And who did they belong to, I wonder?" Stephen softly asked.

"My father," his aunt whispered, "and his brother and sister." After a moment, clearing her throat, she said, "Granny was so sentimental—couldn't bear to part with anything, especially letters. Just take out that drawer—"

He hesitated. The sight of those little shoes, Stephen felt, was ridiculously disturbing. They were such an intimate part of someone else's past he did not want to touch them; nor, suddenly, did he want to see the rest. Time was telescoped alarmingly, the gap of a hundred years no longer existed; it was here, beneath his hand, and it made him shiver.

Leaning over his shoulder as he crouched before the trunk, Joan released the catches and tugged at the wooden drawer. Reluctantly, Stephen helped her to lift it out. Beneath, in bundles tied up with bits of ribbon, were what must have been hundreds of letters. The uppermost ones, with envelopes yellowed and brittle, were directed to a Mrs. L. Elliott; one, Stephen noticed, was clearly postmarked Dublin, the year 1922.

"Did you know these were here?" he asked. "But of course, you must have. Have you ever been through them?"

Joan shook her head. "No. I never could, somehow. I remember her very well, you see. She was my favorite person when I was a little girl—a *real* granny, cosy and cuddly, the sort of person you could tell your troubles to." Joan smiled, a regretful, affectionate smile, and then she sighed. "She came to live with Mother during the war—the last one, I mean—and she died here, just before D-Day." There was a pause in which Stephen well recalled the significance of that date to Joan, and then she said, "I really missed her."

"Was she very old?"

"She was seventy-seven—a good age." She paused again. "Poor Granny."

"Why do you say that?" he asked gently.

There was another sigh, a compressing of the lips which seemed to indicate that all had not been well at the end. "Well," she said slowly, "she outlived most of her own family—apart from that daughter of hers, who never bothered—and she was a bit confused toward the end. It got on Mother's nerves, I'm afraid. I remember her standing in the kitchen, only the day before poor Granny died, wringing her hands and saying she wished she would stop it. *'She'll have me believing this house is haunted,'* she said, *'and I know it isn't!'* " With a rueful smile, Joan added, "She thought they were still here, you see . . ."

A shiver touched Stephen's spine. With a deep breath, he said, "But your mother kept her things?"

"Well, they were precious to Granny, and I don't think Mother could bear to dispose of them." Lifting one packet of envelopes, she spotted another with familiar handwriting. "Just a minute—I think some of these are Father's letters. Yes," she said slowly, scanning the addresses, "they are. His letters to Mother. She must have put them here for safekeeping." For a moment, overcome, she held them against her breast. "I'll have to keep these—you don't mind, do you?"

"No, of course not," Stephen said, surprised. In truth he wanted none of them but was afraid to say so. He supposed he would have to store the trunks, but he could not imagine wading through the contents.

Downstairs again, with the kettle on, his aunt became her practical self, ticking off the problem of the attic on a lengthy list. Watching her tuck pen and paper behind a china ornament on the high mantelpiece, he said, "Now then, are you going to tell me about this letter?"

It was a strangely inconclusive tale, which, like the house and those possessions of another age, Joan seemed to want cleared up. The letter from Zoe Clifford had arrived at the beginning of January, and Joan had written back within a few days, saying yes, they were related through Letitia's brother Robin; but owing to Letitia's leaving York such a long time ago,

it was doubtful whether they could be of much help. The girl
had telephoned a couple of days later, sounding so grateful for
the letter Joan had immediately warmed to her. Having clarified
present-day relationships—Joan would have been first cousin
to Letitia's daughter who was killed in 1942—Zoe wanted to
know something about Robin and Liam, when and where they
were born, and where their parents had been married. Joan
could give their respective birth dates, but that was all. For the
rest she would have to ask her mother, who was not very well.
The girl then said that as she had to be in York for another
appointment in a few days' time, could she call on them?

"Seeing no problem, Stephen, I said yes, of course she
could. I fancied to meet her, and thought Mother would be
delighted to meet a long-lost relative, somebody young and
new, who wanted to talk about the past. She hadn't been well,
and I thought it would buck her up a bit." Joan made a face at
the memory of Sarah Elliott's reaction and reached for the tea-
pot. "It never occurred to me that there might be anything
wrong, or that Mother *wouldn't* want to see her—but she was
furious. Of course, by then I couldn't very well put Zoe off."

"What was it?"

"Well, it was Tisha, you see—Letitia Mary, if you please,
was my father's sister. A no-good baggage if ever there was
one, according to Mother. She'd known her as a girl—but I
never met her, so I can't comment." Sipping her tea, Joan added
thoughtfully, "Apparently Zoe had a look of Tisha, that was
the problem. Mother took one glance at that girl and simply
clammed up. Wouldn't tell her anything, bar the barest essentials. And I didn't want to upset the applecart by mentioning
the boxes in the attic—I'd never have heard the last of it."

"But *you* liked her?" Stephen said, knowing his aunt to be
a generally good judge of character.

"Yes, I did," she replied emphatically. "She was a nice,
cheerful, honest sort of girl. *Very* well spoken. I got the impression there was plenty of money somewhere in the background—she certainly wasn't after sponging from us.

"No," Joan added a moment later, "all she wanted was
what we could tell her. And in the end, it wasn't much. Mother
gave her a few names and places and dates of birth—very

grudgingly, might I say—and that was that. What she *wouldn't* tell her—and she could have done, I'm sure of it—was why Tisha left York and never came back."

Stephen smiled and helped himself to more tea. In the manner of the worldly-wise, he said, "The old, old story, I suppose. Got pregnant and ran away."

Joan Elliott shook her head. "No, I don't think so. That's too simple. And Mother would have said—to me, at least—if it'd been that. When I tackled her about it afterward, she just kept on about what a dreadful little snob Tisha was, how cruel she'd been to her mother, and how it served her right that she died alone, and without friends."

Faintly shocked by that unexpected vindictiveness, Stephen said, "That doesn't sound like Gran."

"No. But she obviously detested Tisha—and I'd love to know why."

"Gran asked the girl plenty of questions, then?"

"Oh yes. She got Tisha's life story, practically. And she lapped it up, I'm sorry to say. Like an old cat with a bowl of cream."

With an eye for the passing afternoon, Stephen asked whether she had been in touch with the girl since her visit, but his aunt said no, she had been too busy hospital visiting, and then her mother had died. Since then, Joan explained, there had been so much to attend to, letters were the last thing she could think about. But she had not forgotten the girl and, with Stephen due home, had hoped he might get in touch with her.

"But what can I tell her?" he demanded.

"She's very nice," his aunt insisted, "and very pretty too. I think you'd like her," she added with an arch smile.

"I'm too old for young girls," he told her, laughing. "She'll think I've got one foot in the grave. And what's the point, anyway? I can't tell her any more than you can."

"But I've given you the boxes, haven't I?"

4

*C*linging to the top of a step-
ladder, Zoe arched her back and swept the paint roller back
and forth, struggling to reach the corner and leave no faint
patches. The ceiling and two walls were done and looking good,
and already she was feeling better, working the aggression out
of her system, making a clean sweep in more ways than one.

Three wasted months, she kept thinking, and that was
what made her angriest of all; that and the realization that she
had been a fool to think it could ever have worked between
herself and Philip Dent. He just wasn't her type at all. Well, it
was over; she had told him so, and the sooner he accepted it,
the better.

The telephone rang, a muffled, pathetic chirping that
brought forth curses as she struggled to regain her balance. "If
that's him *again*," she muttered furiously, "I'll kill him." For a
moment she considered not answering; but it might just be a
business call, and decorating or not, she could not afford to
miss those. Hurriedly, she climbed down, peeling back dust-
sheets and cushions to reach the buried telephone.

Suspicion edged her voice. "Hello?"

A man's voice bade Zoe good afternoon and asked for her by name. Not Philip, obviously, and with that realization her hostility faded; this voice was deeper, richer, with faintly northern undertones. Even as she wondered, he gave his name as Stephen Elliott, mentioning his aunt and York in explanation for the call. A little shaft of surprise cut through her; she had not expected to hear from the Elliotts again.

Sinking down onto the sofa, she listened while he briefly outlined the situation. At news of his grandmother's death, she expressed the proper condolences but could not keep the excitement out of her voice when he mentioned the contents of boxes which were now in his possession.

"But that's *wonderful*. Have you been through them?"

"Only a cursory search," he said. "There hasn't been time for more. There are a lot of photographs—some identified—which might be of interest to you, and what looks like hundreds of letters." He laughed briefly. "I haven't been through those. But what you will find interesting, I'm sure, are the birth and marriage certificates." He paused at that point, and she wondered why. Old Mrs. Elliott, Robin's widow, had reluctantly told her that the brothers were born in Ireland, which was a severe disappointment. Zoe had read enough books on genealogy to know that few if any state records had survived the Irish Civil War, and felt that her research had come to an abrupt and frustrating end. But perhaps she was wrong.

"You've found the original certificates?"

"Yes."

"Oh brilliant," she murmured approvingly while experiencing an absurd desire to giggle with delight. She took a deep breath. "I'd love to see them."

There was another pause. "Well, if you'd like to come up to York, just say when. I'm available most days for the next few weeks, so we can make it to your convenience . . ."

Determined to grab the opportunity before he could change his mind, she plunged in firmly. "That's very kind of you, Mr. Elliott. I'd like to make it soon, if I may—how about next week?" Ignoring the chaos around her, she added impulsively, "Would Monday suit?"

A little surprised, he said that it would, and the requisite arrangements were made. Zoe would catch the train which arrived closest to midday, and he and his aunt would meet her at the station.

Her excitement refused to be quenched, even by the task she had set herself. If she was planning to be in York on Monday, the decorating would have to be finished by then, even if it meant working every hour over the weekend. But it was a challenge and worth it. After weeks in which the Elliotts had had to take a backseat, she could hardly wait to see those letters and take up the chase again.

With a fresh surge of energy, she climbed the ladder and resumed her painting.

By the following evening—Friday—the walls and ceiling were a delicate shade of apricot, so much warmer than the stark white she had originally employed as a reaction to dirt and grime when she moved in, and she was busily undercoating the bookshelves which filled one alcove beside the chimney. Vowing that she would never again paint anything black, Zoe broke off, irritably, at the sound of the doorbell.

It was Philip. Her heart sank. No matter that she was decorating and covered in paint, that the flat was a mess with nowhere to sit—he had to talk to her. Wearily, she pressed the door-release and let him in. But she was determined not to be held up; leaving the front door open, Zoe returned, somewhat grimly, to her task.

She heard him come in but did not turn. For at least a minute he stood and watched her, his eyes boring into her back. When she could stand it no longer, she wiped her brush and stood it in a jar of turpentine. Immaculate as ever, he looked so incongruous against the dust-sheets and rolled-up rugs, Zoe had a terrible urge to laugh. But the situation was far from funny. His misery communicated itself to her, promoting guilt, resentment, and, ultimately, anger.

"Philip, why are you doing this? We've said all there is to say—and I'm not going to change my mind."

"No, you had your say," he reminded her tersely, "but I was too angry the other night. I've telephoned, and you wouldn't agree to meet me, so I thought I'd better call in person."

That put Zoe in the wrong and made her angrier still. "I can't think why—I've nothing more to say."

"Well I have. Won't you listen to me? Please?"

With bad grace, she dragged some dust-sheets aside and made a space for him on one sofa, brought a couple of cans of lager from the kitchen—no glasses, just to irritate him further—and sat herself down on the other. They were at odd angles to one another, and he had to twist himself awkwardly to look at her. He toyed with the can, but did not open it.

"I'm sorry I lost my temper," he said with an effort at contrition. "I shouldn't have said all those things. I didn't mean them, Zoe, honestly."

"Oh, but you did, Philip, and that's a fact. What you said was unpleasant and hurtful, but it only serves to underline what I was trying to say to you—that we really don't have anything in common."

"I don't agree. We like similar things—theaters, concerts, galleries—we've had some wonderful times together . . ."

"You only like them because you think you *should*—because it sounds good to say you went to see a Chekhov play or the latest exhibition at the Tate. You haven't the first clue what they're about—and neither has your wonderful friend *David*." Zoe took a long pull on the lager and watched him wince.

"Oh yes—that's what it's all about, isn't it? David. You're screwed up with jealousy!"

His childishness did not amuse her. As ever when she was really angry, Zoe's voice dropped and took on a cutting edge. "That's not true. I'm not jealous of David—I just don't like him. I'm sure he must be brilliant in court, but I do wish he wouldn't practice on his friends. He isn't kind, Philip—can't you see that? He belittles you, and you let him. He does the same to Clare, and it hurts me just as much.

"That girl used to have a mind of her own—but not anymore. He says, 'Jump,' and she asks, 'How high?' I don't like it. Nor do I enjoy seeing him do the same to you. If you were a match for him, fair enough—but you're not. You're far too nice to be a friend of his."

He flushed with embarrassment or anger, she was not sure. Eventually, he said, "Look, if that's what you really think, why are you ending it between us? Can't we try again? We've

been honest with each other, we know the problems, why can't
we settle them?"

"I've told you why."

"But Zoe—you mean so much to me. I can't bear it—this
week's been hell . . ."

For a moment she felt sorry, remembering. Guilty, too.
But sympathy would only make it worse. "You'll get over it,
Philip—people do. I'm sorry—I'm not unfeeling, just trying to
be practical. Things just weren't right between us—you know
that as well as I do."

"Forget David and Clare—we don't have to see them—"

"No." His simplicity was infuriating. Once it had charmed
her. Dear God! "You'd never forgive me for coming between
you and your oldest friend."

After a while, he said, "I suppose you feel like that about
David?"

It was not true: She blamed Clare for being such a fool.
"Yes," she lied, "I suppose I do."

Frustrated, guilty, wishing he would go, she stood up,
only to have her pacing intercepted. After a small hesitation,
he kissed her, clumsily. She did not protest, but wondered how
his lips could ever have been exciting. For the sake of all that
had been between them—and on her part it had never been
enough—she kissed him gently on the cheek. "Philip, to be
happy, you have to be able to be yourself—not what you think
someone else expects you to be . . ."

But he was not prepared to accept that and stayed another
hour trying to talk her around to his point of view, becoming
more and more depressed as he perceived the futility of it. In
the end Zoe lost patience and even her pity evaporated. She
told him he would have to go; she had work to do, work that
must be finished, as she was going to York for a couple of days.

"I see. York. I suppose that means you're still chasing a lot
of ghosts. Well, between them and your art, I hope you're
happy. Real life's obviously a bit much for you." He paused in
the hall, his hand on the open door. "Good-bye, Zoe."

After that, she did not even want to work. Pouring herself
a large brandy, she went upstairs to see her friend Polly, but
Polly was out. Hardly surprising on a Friday evening, but nevertheless Zoe was disappointed. Returning to her own flat, she

finished the brandy and grabbed brushes and paint with grim determination. At half past midnight, when her friend came back, she was still busy.

Polly had seen the lights from outside and called in with a friend, fortunately a tactful sort who soon saw that he was not required and left. When he had gone, Zoe poured her heart out, had a good cry because she was angry and tired, and suddenly felt a lot better. Polly put away the brandy bottle, made some coffee, and with a few succinct comments on life, love, and the nature of mankind, ushered Zoe off to bed.

The next day, Clare rang. It was not a pleasant conversation for either of them. Clare, it seemed, was appalled by Zoe's behavior, accusing her of using Philip, leading him on, and—what was worse—trying to destroy his long-standing friendship with David.

Zoe was in no mood to take those accusations calmly. If it was a matter of using people, she said, David had done his fair share while Clare had abetted him; and David was the one who was possessive, resenting any relationship Clare had other than with him.

"You don't like David," Clare said furiously, and Zoe agreed with her; Clare slammed down the phone and that was that.

Cursing roundly, unsure which of the three deserved most odium, Zoe snapped a tape into the stereo; for the rest of the afternoon the flat vibrated to the sounds of a heavy metal band. She worked with angry intensity, and by the time she was ready to fall into bed that night, most of the work was done.

By Sunday afternoon, all of the painting in the sitting room was complete, doors, skirtings, and shelves in a similar color to the walls, the tone slightly deeper. The overall effect was that of a gentle, spacious, elegant room, reflecting none of the anger that had gone into its transformation. For a while, Zoe was not sure that she was in the right frame of mind to appreciate it; but as she sat back to survey her handiwork, the room at least seemed cheerful, and, however briefly, she smiled back.

Although it was impossible to replace books and plants immediately, Polly came in to help clear up. With the sheets put away and rugs unrolled across the polished floorboards, sofas pushed back, and Zoe's worktable standing in its proper place before the windows, the room was acquiring an old familiarity. Pictures were rehung, a couple of examples of her own work, some Beardsley prints, a copy of a portrait by Gwen John, and one small, original abstract, a souvenir of her first love affair. There were small mementos of other men dotted about the flat, but Philip had given her nothing more lasting than a stiff bouquet of flowers.

As well, she reflected, he had given her a sense of injustice done, so perhaps it was fitting that she had nothing material to remember him by. His last words were enough. The Elliotts were important to her, but nobody else seemed to understand that.

Rescuing the framed photographs of Tisha and her brothers, Zoe stared long and hard at those sepia likenesses before giving them a temporary home on her worktable. Her last trip to York had managed to establish, at long last, the Australian soldier's name. "Liam," she softly whispered, and as always it gave her an absurd rush of pleasure to speak his name. Thinking of the next day, she wondered at the extent of the information waiting for her, and where it would lead. The possibilities were intriguing, far more so than Philip Dent, her friend Clare, and the insufferable David.

She remarked to Polly, however, that she was more distressed by the end of an old friendship than by the loss of a lover. But then, as Polly observed, men tended to come and go, while friends were usually more lasting.

Two hours after leaving Kings Cross, the British Rail Intercity locomotive was pulling around the long curve into York. It had been a gloomy morning in London, steadily improving as the train swished northward. York was sunny, with blue skies and cotton-wool clouds, and a strong breeze caught Zoe's skirts as she stepped down onto the platform.

From the overhead bridge which spanned the tracks, she immediately spotted Joan Elliott's generous form and, standing beside her, a tall man with light brown hair. Striking, rather than handsome, he stood looking up at her, his hands thrust deep into the pockets of a Burberry raincoat.

They were obviously together, so he must be the man

she had spoken to on the telephone. Stephen Elliott, old Mrs. Elliott's grandson. He was much younger than she had expected; somehow, with a full generation between them, she had imagined him to be more her mother's age. Noting the deep tan as she came down the steps, and wondering how genuine it was, Zoe suddenly remembered that he had said something about working abroad and gave him the benefit of the doubt. For a moment she was enveloped in Joan Elliott's warm embrace, then he stepped forward, his handshake dry and firm.

He said he was delighted, while his eyes seemed intent upon registering everything about her. Almost before she realized it, he had relieved her of the overnight bag and was steering both women through the concourse. Had she not been so intent upon his aunt's conversation, Zoe felt that she might have been annoyed.

But all irritation fled as they came out of the station. Directly facing them across a broad and busy thoroughfare, the city walls seemed to be smiling above ramparts covered in daffodils. The sight was so unexpected, and so welcoming, it brought smiles and an involuntary halt. Zoe thought that she had never seen anything so uplifting as that waving mass of cheerful yellow flowers.

"Aren't they *beautiful*."

"They certainly are. It's almost worth being away all winter . . ." He left the sentence unfinished, and Zoe glanced up in surprise.

"Yes," she said, "I can imagine that."

His eyes met hers and she was disconcerted, yet again, by that peculiarly searching look of his. "You said you'd been abroad, Mr. Elliott," she reminded him brightly. "Was it anywhere interesting?"

He chuckled as they moved on. "Not really. And by the way, the name's Stephen."

Not a man for conversational gambits, Zoe thought, feeling cross again. Then with a little cluck of mock disapproval, Joan Elliot nodded in her nephew's direction and told Zoe not to be fooled. "He does it all the time, you know—lets people think he's a jailbird, or traveling salesman, or some such nonsense, just because it amuses him. He's not," she declared, shaking a finger at his mischievous grin. "He's a Master Mariner, and I'm very proud of him."

"There now, Joan, you've done it again—just spoiled my best line . . ."

Zoe could not help laughing. "And what's that?"

"I usually say, in answer to the next question, that I travel in oil and steel—it sounds so much more impressive."

"Oh come now, *Captain* Elliott—I'm impressed already!"

Across the gleaming, dark green hood of a Jaguar XJ-S, he smiled at her, a curiously intimate, knowing smile. "Now it's my turn to be impressed, Miss Clifford—most people have no idea what a Master Mariner is."

Years ago, at college, Zoe had known a girl whose father was at sea, but she did not intend to reveal the source of her information. Let him wonder, she thought as she sank back against soft leather upholstery. While Joan pointed out various places of interest, Zoe was mentally assessing the man in the driving seat: probably unmarried, with an eye for the ladies, and judging by the car, as image-conscious as Philip Dent. But was he? She stole another look at Stephen Elliot, noticed that while the Aran sweater was new, his old Burberry wore a comfortable patina of age, and his hair, which was brown with a tendency to curl, would have benefited from trip to the barber's. She smiled and almost forgave him the car.

He dropped Zoe and his aunt on Gillygate, outside the hotel, then drove off to park by his flat in town with an arrangement to meet them there.

"It's so awkward these days," Joan explained, "with all this traffic and foot streets everywhere. I'm glad I don't drive."

Zoe said she did, but it was doubtful whether her disreputable old car would cope with the journey north, which was why she traveled any distance by train. "But it's useful for the odd weekends when I visit my parents."

She checked in and Mrs. Bilton was glad to see her, handing Zoe the usual two keys, and smiling at Joan Elliott's unabashed curiosity. Until Zoe passed on all the information she had gleaned about Mary Elliott and her family, Joan had had no idea that they were in the hotel business.

"So was Granny born here?" she asked, referring to Louisa.

"I don't think so. Letitia was, certainly, but I don't know

about Louisa. She and Edward lived here with their children, and that would include Robin. He was your father, wasn't he? Liam was the one who went to Australia?"

"Yes, that's right." She paused, peering out of Zoe's tiny window at a network of twigs and branches and the Minster towers beyond. "Fancy my father living here, and I never knew. It's strange, you know—Granny often talked about her cottage at Clementhorpe, but never mentioned living here."

For a moment Zoe wondered why, but then Joan remembered that Stephen was waiting to take them to lunch and the two women left.

They shared a satisfying meal at an oak-beamed restaurant in town. Over coffee, the conversation turned from general talk about the Elliotts' past to a more specific matter. Zoe was at first surprised, and then considerably embarrassed. The birth certificates found by Stephen in that box full of letters had a marriage certificate with them. They should have matched—a marriage followed by three children, roughly a couple of years apart—but they did not. Nor did they fit the facts as Joan knew them. It seemed that lies had been told and deceits continued, but by whom and for what reason, Joan Elliott had no idea. Coming so soon after her mother's death, it was obvious that she found the revelations upsetting. In her turn, Zoe was also upset. She did not know what to say.

Refusing a second cup of coffee, the older woman said that she would leave them; she had the estate agent to see and some shopping to do, and she had no real wish to be present while they probed the secrets of Louisa Elliott's life.

"It's not that I mind you doing that," she explained gently to Zoe, "but I couldn't. Tell me what you come up with, by all means—and if I can answer any questions at all, I'll be happy to do so. But I don't want to go through those papers myself—I couldn't bear it."

Watching her retreating back, Zoe was seized with guilt, seeing herself as the harbinger of pain, and wondering what Pandora's box had been opened by those first, innocent inquiries of hers. About to say something fatuous to the man facing her, such as his grandmother had been right, and she should never have come, she was silenced by the brief touch of his hand on her arm.

"Don't say it," he softly advised, "and stop feeling so guilty—I can see it written all over your face. I did ask Joan, a day or so before I phoned you, whether she wanted me to go ahead with this." He paused, seemed suddenly aware that he was touching her, and removed his hand. "She was so shattered I didn't think she'd want anyone to know about it—least of all a comparative stranger. But,"—he smiled—"Joan's obviously taken a fancy to you, accepted you as family, which, I may say, is quite a compliment."

Zoe glanced away, feeling a small rush of pleasure and embarrassment warm her cheeks. "But—"

"But sooner or later one of us would have gone through that box, and we would have discovered the anomalies anyway. You can't just throw out the remains of someone's life without examining it first."

On an indrawn breath, she said, "Well, I just wish I hadn't been the one to force the issue."

Delineated by their fringe of thick brown lashes, his eyes caught the light and warmed into a smile. For the first time she noticed how blue they were. "Don't worry about it."

He rose to pay the bill, and she studied him unobserved. There was something familiar about his features, but she could not decide what it was; she thought perhaps he reminded her of someone but could not think who. He turned and she glanced away, not wanting to be caught staring.

By comparison with the crush of pedestrians in the Shambles, St. Andrewgate was almost deserted, peopled largely by workmen engaged in the process of renovating old property and building new to blend in. Zoe's eyes were everywhere, noting the details of windows and brickwork; Stephen had to touch her arm to direct her through a narrow alleyway between the houses. It opened into a pretty courtyard, and with some surprise she realized they were back in Bedern and that he was searching for the keys to his flat.

"It's a strange name, *Bedern*—what does it mean?"

"Oh, I forget now—and there's a plaque over there, I must pass it nearly every day. 'House of Prayer,' I think—from the Anglo-Saxon."

For the first time she noticed the ancient limestone wall, punctuated by lancet windows, which bore the plaque. Stephen said it had once been part of the college of the Vicars Choral. The rest of the buildings—no more than a collection of medieval houses like those in the Shambles—had disappeared long ago.

"It was handy for the Minster, just across the street, but the young priests were turned out in the Reformation—not that I think anyone was very sorry," he added ironically. "From what I can gather, they were no better than a bunch of medieval lager louts—drinking, brawling in the street, terrorizing the local residents . . ."

Warming to him, she chuckled at the image he created, but it was hard to believe such things had gone on within the precincts of this modern development.

". . . and then there was a ragged school here in the last century—not nearly so amusing. The children were badly treated." He paused, looking up at the sunlit walls, the pretty little gardens full of spring flowers. "They're still here," he said softly, "sometimes you can hear them at night, laughing and playing . . ."

Suspecting him of teasing, she glanced up quickly, but he seemed unusually serious. "Have *you* heard them?"

"Yes, I have. Just once, coming home late one night. I'd never heard the story and honestly thought a bunch of kids were messing about—I walked right round the place but couldn't find them. It was only later, when I asked one or two of the neighbors, that I found other people had heard it too—right here, in this courtyard. And at different times."

She shivered. "York seems to be full of ghosts . . ."

"I'm sure it is." He smiled. "I used to scoff at things like that . . ."

Beyond the limestone wall with its lancet windows was a deep archway; watching people pass, she asked the name of the street. When he said it was Goodramgate, a sudden, sharp memory drew her toward it. She paused in shadow, looking across the way to another arch, the one that led into Minster Yard. The east end of the cathedral was perhaps a hundred yards distant. Zoe shivered again, remembering that night of the mist, the strange images conjured against a shifting wall of light.

Aware of the man beside her, she glanced at him, and for

a second he seemed taken aback. For a long moment neither of them said anything, then as she looked away he asked her, quietly, whether she had been in York the previous autumn, one evening about six when mist was billowing around the Minster.

It was as though he had read her mind; Zoe was so startled she was tempted, inexplicably, to deny it. But as she nodded, he explained that he had seen her, standing for several minutes by St. William's College.

"And then you walked toward me, paused on the corner, and *glared* at me before you crossed the road." Somewhat shortly, he laughed. "You know, ever since you stepped off that train, I've been trying to think where I'd seen you before."

"What an extraordinary memory you must have . . ."

"Not at all. It's just that it was my last night at home—I remember the mist, and obviously I remembered you too. The only extraordinary thing about it is that I have these gaps in my life—often of five or six months' duration, when I'm away at sea. I leave—and a few months later I come back. But to me, it's as though those months have never been." He paused. "It's an odd sensation."

She thought it must be, and said so; but, grateful for such a prosaic explanation, Zoe could have hugged him. It struck her, too, that perhaps it answered that nagging feeling she had, that she should know him too. Obviously, they had seen each other that night, but she retained no conscious memory of it.

They went back to the courtyard, and as he unlocked his door, Stephen stood back for her to enter; at the top of a flight of stairs, several doors opened off a skylighted landing. She caught a glimpse of a very tidy kitchen before following him into the sitting room, but then, with no more than an impression of books and pictures and modern furniture, Zoe's attention was caught by the view. Tall chimney stacks, pitched roofs of weathered slate and pantiles, mellow bricks and tiny windows, the whole formed a foreground for the fairy-tale magic of the Minster itself. The picture was framed by the window itself, and she knew without doubt why Stephen Elliott lived here, and she both admired and envied him.

He was watching her face, her reactions. She made no

attempt to disguise her pleasure, because the man who lived here deserved to know that she appreciated it too. Laughing, she said, "You're a lucky man."

He laughed too, telling her to sit down and enjoy the view while he made some coffee. A little while later, sharing the window seat with the tray between them, Zoe was suddenly aware of feeling relaxed and happy. Stephen Elliott was very easy to be with, a man who was used to listening as well as speaking. His questions never seemed to probe, and yet almost without realizing it, Zoe found that they had moved from neutral topics to far more personal ones, that she was revealing far more about herself than she usually did, certainly on so short an acquaintance. Conversation flowed back and forth between them, as though they had known each other for years. He talked, briefly, about his marriage and divorce, and while he did not dwell upon the reasons for its ending, she understood immediately how betrayed he had felt, and by her own intuition, why he had not remarried, despite his apparent liking for women. He spoke affectionately of his aunt, and of the wives of close friends, and Zoe could see why his social life was not limited to a few drinking cronies, but encompassed a broad, if scattered field. He was often away for weekends, visiting old friends on leave, and that was why he enjoyed his car. It was an extravagance, but it transported him about the country in comfort, and it was such a pleasure to drive. Besides, he admitted with a disarming grin, the Jag was something he had always wanted.

What a change from Philip, she thought, glancing around as Stephen went to make more coffee. Philip's flat was smart to the point of sterility, with a few coffee table tomes, one enormous picture, three large ornaments, and furniture that was designed for utility rather than comfort. She would be hard-pressed tomorrow to recount Stephen's bits and pieces. Books almost filled one wall, a collection of unusual pictures and ornaments were displayed haphazardly, while things like letters, a calculator, and keys were dotted on various surfaces about the room.

The ashtray, she noticed, was almost full. He smoked too much, but she could understand it; after a year without cigarettes herself, passing cravings could still catch her unawares.

He came back with the coffee in two steaming mugs, all pretensions at gentility, with cups and cream and sugar bowls, had disappeared, for which she was thankful. It was good to know that he felt as relaxed as she did. Outside the light was falling, and between them lay the softness of dusk.

Only as he moved to light one of the lamps did either of them notice the time and then Stephen was all concern at having wasted it, inquiring as to her plans for the evening.

"Well," she said easily, "apart from having to be back at the hotel sometime to sleep, I don't have any plans. And after that excellent lunch, I'm not even hungry. Perhaps we could have a look at those papers this evening? That is, if you don't have any plans?"

"No," he assured her, "I don't. There's salad and things in the fridge—if you like, we could share something later."

On that agreement he went to fetch a thick, decorated album from an open shelf on the bookcase. It was old, the ties and tassels faded, its embossed and gilded cover shabby with use.

"Before we take a look at those certificates, I thought you might like to see a few photographs. Just to show you who it is we're talking about."

Flicking through the first few pages, he came to a pair of portraits, the first of a young woman with cropped, curly hair and a rather challenging set to her chin. She had a lovely, rounded face, intelligent eyes, and a well-shaped, generous mouth. Stephen said that her smile fascinated him. Like the Mona Lisa's, he could not decide whether it was amused, disdainful, uncertain, or downright sexy, although as a man, he preferred to think the latter.

Zoe laughed and shook her head. "Wishful thinking. She looks proud, to me—and just a shade disdainful. But she does remind me of someone"—Zoe gazed intently for a moment, shading the lower half of the face—"It's her eyes and the shape of her forehead . . ."

His mouth twitched with amusement. He glanced quickly at Zoe, and then back at the album. "Forget what I said about her smile, and ignore the hairstyle—who does she remind you of?"

"I'm not sure—I think it's Letitia, but—"

"She reminds me of *you*. Oh, not feature for feature," he amended hastily, "I don't mean that. But you do have a look of her—at least *I* think you do . . ."

For the first time, Zoe was lost for words. He seemed to regret that impulsive statement and was about to pass on to the next portrait, but she stayed his hand. "Who is she?"

"Louisa Elliott. My great-grandmother."

"And my great-great-grandmother," Zoe mused, trying to sound calm and reflective to dispel the sudden tension that was between them. "Well, she was Letitia's mother, and I was always supposed to be like Tisha in looks, so maybe that explains it." She smiled. "I can't see it, myself, but as you say, resemblance isn't always a matter of matching features.

"But I must say," she went on, "that I'm surprised. *She* looks as though she knew her own mind—she's not a bit the simpering victim I imagined."

Amused by her use of the word, he said, "Why *victim*?"

"Well, it was just my interpretation of the facts—or what seemed to be the facts. However, it seems I was wrong on both counts." Indicating the other portrait, that of a youngish, bearded man in a frock coat and soft cravat, she inquired who he was.

"That's Edward Elliott, Louisa's husband. He was also her cousin, I gather, and I'd say it was taken some years before they married. By my calculations she was thirty-two when they tied the knot, and he must have been forty-four."

"*As old as that?* But—"

"Yes I know. The reason you couldn't find any record of their marriage is that you didn't look far enough. I have the original certificate—they didn't marry until 1899."

"But what about the children?"

"Good question," he observed dryly. "Hang on to it for a minute, will you, and take a look at these."

Stephen produced two more photographs, ones he had found inserted loose between the pages. One was an informal group photograph taken in a garden; the other, which he now laid before Zoe, was a seated portrait of a man in military dress uniform. By its style and insignia, he was an officer, possibly in his early thirties. He was well built, and long legs gave an impression of height; he had a mustache, crisp black hair, and a strong-featured face. On the back of the stiff card mount was the photographer's name and Dublin address. Turning it over again, looking at that slightly arrogant smile, Zoe experienced an irrational feeling of disquiet.

"And who, pray, is *he*?"

Stephen pursed his lips. "Well, I haven't proved it yet, but I'm almost sure his name was Robert Duncannon."

Zoe bit her lip. "Witness at Letitia's wedding."

"The writer of many letters."

"A rich, close relative?" She looked to Stephen for the answer. "Or something else?"

He raised a single, quizzical eyebrow. "You tell me."

5

$\mathcal{M}$usic was playing softly, and the dining table was covered with papers and photographs. Stephen leaned back and stretched, aware of tender amusement as he surveyed Zoe's bent head, the intent expression on her face. Her skin made him think of Ireland and misty mornings, and it was impossible not to smile as he imagined its softness against his lips.

They had been working for hours, and he was beginning to wonder whether she would go on all night, following every little item like clues in a treasure hunt. The handful of letters they had looked at raised more questions than they answered, generating curiosity and enthusiasm, provoking reactions that had already revealed more of their true selves than weeks of normal acquaintance might have done.

He liked her. Tremendously. No edge, no affectations, no artifice. Despite the perfect vowels and privileged background, she was no spoiled brat. And she was sharp and funny and oddly vulnerable and—oh, be honest, Elliott, his practical self said, you want to go to bed with her, you know you do, you fancied her from the minute you first laid eyes on her . . .

She looked up, her clear gray eyes wide and questioning,

as though his thoughts had somehow changed the atmosphere between them, as perhaps they had. He did not look away and nor did she; he saw her expression change, a quick rush of blood color her cheeks. Intense physical awareness crackled between them like a sustained electric charge. The letter she held trembled; she bowed her head and a fall of dark curls hid that sudden warmth but did not obscure the sharp rise and fall of her breasts.

Breathless, tense with desire, Stephen forced himself to his feet. "I'll make some coffee," he said, but could not resist touching her, very lightly, as he passed.

Leaning forward against the sink, he took a long, deep breath and released it very slowly. Within a moment or two he was once more in control, although the blood in his veins was still running hot, eager, after months of enforced abstinence, to grab at this prime opportunity. Which would not only be a mistake, he told his reflection in the glass, but a breach of good manners. Calm down, he ordered silently, take her back to the hotel, give her time; even if she leaves York tomorrow, she'll be back, you know she will . . .

And anyway, he told himself as he returned with the coffee, it was always possible to suggest a meeting in London.

Before she could remark on the time, he said easily, "It's late, Zoe—and you must be tired. Why don't we have this coffee and call it a day? I'll walk you back to Gillygate, and we can begin again tomorrow."

She was instantly contrite. "Oh, I'm sorry, I've kept you—I wasn't thinking—"

"Not at all." With what he hoped was a disarming smile, Stephen took her hand and briefly squeezed it. "I'm a night owl—always have been. It's you I'm thinking of—all that decorating you were telling me about—it's a wonder you're not on your knees."

There was gratitude in her response and something of understanding. That reinforced his confidence, made it easier a few minutes later to fetch her cape and make arrangements for the following day.

"It's a nurse's cape, isn't it? How on earth did you come by it?"

Laughing, she told him the tale of the Oxfam shop and her

father's horror at such an object, his conviction that it must be flea-ridden and therefore consigned to the dustbin. "But you know, I had it cleaned and there's not a break in it. I've had it two winters now, and I've become so fond of the thing, I hate wearing anything else. Which is silly, since there must be three coats hanging in the wardrobe in my flat."

"I like it," he said, draping the cloak around her shoulders. His hands lingered for a moment beneath her hair, then, as she turned to face him, traced the line of her jaw. She thought, for one breath-taking moment, that he was about to kiss her.

But all he said was, "It suits you," before opening the door.

It was no more than a few steps to the place of that first, brief meeting. Through Bedern, beneath its dark archway, across Goodramgate to that second arch which led into Minster Yard. Sheltered from a searching night wind, they paused for a while beneath ancient oak beams that supported the upper story of a quaint halfhouse. Once, as Stephen said, it had been the connecting part of a long row, but since the demolition of its neighbors to one side, it stood forlorn and somewhat redundant, with a new, wide access beside it.

There was an old photograph of that part of Goodramgate, framed on Stephen's sitting room wall; even so, Zoe found it hard to reconcile image and reality. She turned her eyes to the Minster, its floodlit tracery framed by the night and the trees and the long, low building of St. William's College. There was no mist, nothing was moving, and apart from the faint sounds of revelry coming from a nearby public house, all was silent.

As though sharing her memory of that night, he said again that he remembered seeing her as he paused to look at the curling mist, hurrying forward toward it; then she had halted, standing so still, so entranced, that he had been intrigued. "Then you turned suddenly, and came hurrying toward me. I didn't want to be caught, like some sinister Peeping Tom, so I moved out of the shadows here and pretended to be waiting to cross the road."

She chuckled, squeezing his hand. "I didn't see you . . ."

"No, you didn't. Your mind was on something else. Tell me," he added, searching her face intently, "what was it that unnerved you?"

Startled by his perception, Zoe shook her head, looked away. "I'm not sure." For a moment she hesitated. "It's hard to explain. Something—I don't know what it was—in the mist. Like your children in Bedern, except I didn't *hear* anything, it was more . . ." Her voice tailed away. The more she sought for words to describe it, the more they eluded her. And although she wanted him to understand, she was afraid, irrationally, that he might think her mad. "I can't explain," she said finally, glancing up with mute appeal. "Perhaps I might try when I know you a little better . . ."

"I hope so," he whispered, and in that least unexpected moment, Stephen bent his head and kissed her. It was very tender, very brief, but in that moment she felt she needed his strength, his solidity. Involuntarily, she clung to him, burying her face against the lapels of his coat. For a little while he held her very close, sheltering her between himself and the old oak timbers of the little arch. When his lips met hers again they were warm and sensual, seeking her response but not demanding it, until the touch of his tongue set her senses aflame, obliterating everything in a dizzying surge of emotion. Passion flared then, and she was aware of his hunger and her own desire to satisfy it. It was like a physical shock when he detached himself, standing back to grip her hands with painful force.

"I'm sorry," he whispered, "this won't do, will it?"

Still breathing raggedly, he cupped her face between trembling fingers and kissed her on the forehead, then with grim determination led her on through Minster Yard.

She had difficulty keeping up with his long, rapid strides, but he swept her on, regardless. In a state of shock, Zoe hardly knew what to make of him, still less so when he stopped before the south transept, and said tersely, "If you do decide to stay another night, will you stay with me?"

She faltered at his abruptness and could not immediately reply. Images of the recent past—fleeting but clear—flashed through her mind. Philip and his inexperience, the innate prudery which had left her wondering, ultimately, whether he really liked or approved of women. His hero worship of David suddenly assumed different proportions, and she shivered. She suffered a moment's dread for that little trio and was relieved to be out of it. By contrast, Stephen's reassuring masculinity was reassuring. Almost without thinking, she nodded gravely. "Yes, Stephen, I will."

A smile twitched the corner of his mouth. "Good," he murmured, slipping an arm around her shoulders. "On a promise like that, I might just get some sleep tonight . . ."

But he did not sleep well. The stimulation of mind and body left him restless, his thoughts a jumble of Zoe the desirable woman, and Zoe his blood relation, descendant, as he was, of all those other Elliotts. Seeing her enter that house on Gillygate had given him the oddest feeling, as though he knew the place, and all this had happened before.

Déjà vu, of course, as common as it was inexplicable, yet disturbing enough to set his mind running over the evening's facts and suppositions, and the mass of detail still contained in that little trunk. As much as Zoe, he wanted now to discover the truth behind those birth certificates.

Waking early, with chores done and those old letters gathered together in their original order, he went to call for her just before ten. As Zoe paid her bill, he glanced around the guests sitting room with interest, an interest which prompted Mrs. Bilton to ask whether he would like to look at the rest of the house, as his cousin had already done. Agreeing, Stephen found it an extraordinary experience. His own people had lived here for more than twenty years, and climbing the stairs to those elegant rooms on the first floor, he felt as he had when opening those boxes for the very first time: that the past was a little too close, touching emotions and responses of which he had been previously unaware. Having thought of himself as a man of the present day, shaped by circumstances and environment into solitary independence, Stephen found it hard to come to terms with this new awareness, this feeling that he might be no more than a link in a very long chain.

And that chain had unexpectedly coiled back on itself, bringing him face-to-face with earlier Elliotts, people who shared the same name and the same genes, whose lives had been shaped in this house, this city, whose eyes had looked out on streets not immeasurably different from the ones he saw today. More personal, more immediate, was the awareness that at the crossing of the chain stood Zoe Clifford, a woman as much a part of the Elliotts as he was himself. The progression of that thought was daunting. So much so that he was glad to abandon it, sighing with relief as they said their good-byes to Mrs. Bilton and stepped out into the brisk morning.

"What did you think?" Zoe demanded as they rounded the corner into Lord Mayor's Walk. All along the moat, beneath the high walls, daffodils were dancing in the stiff breeze, echoing her own lively spirits.

"It was certainly interesting," he said cautiously. "Before you told me, I'd no idea they were in the hotel business."

"But how did you *feel*," she pressed, "being there?"

With a short laugh, Stephen squeezed her hand. "Later," he said, "when I know you better."

Her eager smile turned into a grimace. "Oh dear—bad as that?"

"No, not bad, more—disturbing, I think. Difficult to explain, though."

With a sideways glance, Zoe sought to reassure him. "It's all right—I understand."

Back at the flat, he was all practicality, setting bundles of letters on the table, together with notepads and pens. The albums were set out too, each with a sheet of paper inside the flyleaf, giving the approximate dates. Although the letters had been grouped by Louisa Elliott into years and correspondents, it was important, Stephen said, to be organized themselves, otherwise vital points could easily be over-looked. And surely, now that they had a fair idea of the family's circumstances while they were living in Gillygate, it might be as well to turn to the earlier letters first, instead of reading haphazardly as bundles came to hand.

Listening, agreeing with every word, Zoe realized that for a man who only yesterday had confessed his reluctance to invade someone else's past, Stephen Elliott was being very efficient about it. Given her limited time in York, did his desire to help her conflict with other, more personal needs? Remembering last night, she thought it must, but he was making such a concerted effort to give her a firm base for further inquiry, she had not the heart to distract him.

But even with Stephen working in the other room, it was hard to concentrate. As it had last night, she found her mind going back over that intense moment of physical awareness. Warmth and liking had blossomed almost from the first, and had it been no more than that, Zoe would have been immensely grateful for this meeting with someone who shared not just her ancestry, but humor, outlook, and even certain reservations. He said he knew nothing about art, but he was interested in photography, so understood more than he claimed; and he was extremely well read. What touched her most of all, however, was his unprompted confession that he too had always felt an odd one out. To his immediate family, Stephen's boyhood passion for ships and the sea had seemed an aberration, and his desire to travel the world for a living was viewed with a mixture of indulgence and mild disapproval. "My sister," he said, "still treats me like an elderly Jim Hawkins—as though she's constantly wondering when I'm going to get a proper job and settle down." It appeared to amuse him, but Zoe had sensed an underlying resentment; she knew it well, having experienced much the same with regard to her own chosen career. And not just from Marian.

But the sexual attraction had been something of a shock. She was glad that it had not been pursued immediately, that he had tried to give her time. Even so, recognizing his impatience, feeling its echo in herself, Zoe was still faintly aghast at her own reactions. In the past, such things had been very much a matter of time, and never, ever, had she fallen into bed with a man on the very first date; yet last night she had been more than willing. That kiss had shaken her, both physically and emotionally, exciting her in ways she could not recall since—well, since Kit. She had been in love with Kit, but never since. Very fond of one or two, emotionally involved, cer- tainly—but not head over heels in love.

It was a little daunting to realize that it was happening again. But it was too late to back out, and, besides, she wanted him. With an effort, Zoe forced her mind away from Stephen and back to Louisa Elliott's letters.

Deciphering the idiosyncrasies of other peoples' handwrit- ing was slow work, but after an hour of establishing names and dates, Zoe had deduced that in the move from Gillygate in the

late 1890s, Louisa must have destroyed much previous correspondence. It was frustrating, because by that time the children
were already born and there seemed to be no reference to their
parentage. The earliest letters were postmarked Dublin in the
spring of 1899, all from someone called Letty, who seemed to
be a friend of some standing. From her correspondence, which
was full of gardening advice, Zoe quickly saw that the two
women had shared a common passion, and that Louisa was at
that time setting up her kitchen garden. Letty had apparently
visited them, with a child named Georgina, because later missives referred to Louisa's cottage and its delightful setting by
the riverside.

Could that cottage have been the one in that group photograph? Zoe wondered. Needing Stephen's opinion, she crossed
the carpeted hall to the sunny room where he was sorting books
from the larger trunk. Intent upon something, unaware of her
presence, he was crouched with his back to her, sweater discarded, shirtsleeves rolled back over tanned and muscular forearms. Shadow made a deep indentation of his spine, a long,
pleasing curve from shoulders to haunches, which the artist
longed to record and the woman to touch. Something, perhaps
the intensity of her gaze, made him turn.

Poised there, regarding her steadily, for a long moment
Stephen did not move. When he did it was slowly, in one
smooth movement, the little book which had taken his attention
still in his hand. She felt its cover cold against her neck as he
kissed her, and the kiss was quick and hard with suppressed
desire, his breath coming short as he crushed her against him.

Lying in bed with him afterward, warm with love and satisfaction, Zoe was beyond speech. They had come together so
quickly, it made her heart race to think of it. Wanting to recapture something of that first touch, she ran a hand over his chest
and the flatness of his stomach, seeing, through half-closed
lids, the perfect lines of his body. After years spent working
under a southern sun, he was lean and hard and bronzed, and
beside him she felt soft and deliciously fragile.

Unprepared for the depth and range of her own responses,
Zoe was also astonished by his. She wondered, last night,
whether a man so absolutely in control of himself would make

love as though painting by numbers; that he had not only relinquished that iron control but made love with such unself-conscious abandon was something that brought a smile to her lips. And when he felt that little curve of happiness and drew back to look at her, she saw the same delight in his eyes. Wonderment, too. He looked at her for some time before he spoke.

"I do believe," he sighed, "that for the first time in my entire life, I've been granted a reward for good behavior." Enveloping her in a warm bear hug, he chuckled softly and kissed her. "And at the risk of sounding like a philanderer, I have to tell you that this is the point where I'm usually apologizing like mad and promising to do better next time!

"But on this occasion," he whispered against her mouth, "I really do have the feeling that there's no need to apologize at all . . ."

A little bubble of laughter escaped her, but as she gave herself up to his embrace, Zoe was thankful that he had not inquired as to her period of abstinence. But that had been a depressing encounter, and she would not think of it now . . .

It was quite some time later that he felt for his shirt and the cigarettes which lived in his breast pocket. He smoked in silence, caressing her gently as he might have done a child. Zoe felt oddly separated then, as though his thoughts had abandoned her. Hesitantly, she ventured to ask what he was thinking and was not entirely reassured by the wry smile her question prompted.

"A great many things," Stephen said softly, "mostly concerned with you."

"What things?"

"I should have thought it was obvious. In twenty-four hours, this little research project of yours has developed along lines neither of us could have envisaged." There was a long pause, and then he said, "But tomorrow, you're going back to London."

The statement hung between them ominously, a cloud heralding responsibility and separation, which should perhaps have been taken into account; yet all had fled before that urgent physical need, and Zoe could not regret its initial satisfaction.

Tracing the line of her cheek, he ran a finger beneath her chin, making her look at him. The conflict she felt was mirrored in his eyes.

"I don't want you to go."

"But I shall have to. Sooner or later, if not tomorrow. My work's there." For the first time she half regretted it. The work she had loved and striven to do, which had been all in all until a moment ago, was suddenly something she wanted to lay aside, if only temporarily. There had to be a way of resolving the problem, of reaching a compromise, but it would take time and thought and planning.

"Don't ask me to think about it now," she begged, laying her lips against his shoulder, his cheek, his mouth. "I'll try to work something out, even if I have to go back to London to do it."

"But you'll come back?"

"Of course," she promised with a suddenly wicked grin. "I haven't got through those letters yet!" She gave a little yelp as Stephen pinched her, rolled over, and saw the time in red digital numbers on his bedside alarm. It was nearly one o'clock. "What time did you say your aunt was coming over?"

"After lunch."

"Then I think we'd better get dressed—"

With a muttered exclamation, he agreed with her. "Joan's a broad-minded lady, but I don't think she'd appreciate finding us like this!"

Fully clothed, with her hair brushed and fresh makeup enhancing eyes that were perhaps too revealing, Zoe returned to the bedroom to pick up her watch. On the bedside chest was the little book Stephen had been holding before they undressed. Bound in scuffed black leather, it had the initials W.E. embossed in gold on the front cover. Curious, Zoe picked it up. It was a diary dated 1916, each page closely written in tiny copperplate script. The owner, she saw at last, had been one William Elliott, serving with a machine-gun company of the Australian Imperial Force . . .

William Elliott—Liam. *Liam*! His name ran through her like a shock, bringing startling flashes of memory—his face on a dozen photographs, that strange vision in the fog . . .

Stephen's voice called to her as she sank weakly onto the bed. A moment later he appeared in the doorway, smiling, saying they had better eat before Joan arrived, and what would she like for lunch?

She looked up, seeing him as though for the very first time, knowing that smile, those eyes, recognizing the familiarity which had hovered on the edge of memory for the past twenty-four hours. In eyes, mouth, and shape of face, Stephen was so very like Liam Elliott. He was a modern man, older in years than the young soldier had been, but with two generations between them, the likeness was still there. Was that what had attracted her to him? The possibility passed over her like an icy wave.

Alarmed by her expression and that sudden, violent shiver, Stephen went to her immediately, touching her cold face, kissing it, chaffing her hands. She was like someone in a trance. Then abruptly she pulled away from him.

He saw the diary and picked it up. As she rose and moved away, he said hesitantly, "I found this in the bottom of the small trunk. It—" Stephen broke off, wondering how to describe the sensation which passed through him as he opened it. He supposed excitement must have caused that physical tingling, like a series of small shocks spreading up from his fingertips.

And then he had turned and seen Zoe.

Just remembering that moment, the look on her face, the feel of her as they embraced was enough to make him want her again. Releasing a long, pent-up breath, he went to her and made her face him.

"Did I do something wrong? Did I hurt you?" She shook her head but kept her eyes averted. Stephen held her close, nuzzling her hair, stroking the silky curls, touching his lips to her temple. "Then tell me what it is."

She stiffened for a moment, then relaxed, burying her face in his neck in a negative, bemused sort of way. "I don't know—I think I'm going mad."

It was so ridiculous, he almost laughed. "Don't be silly, why should you think that?"

"The queerest things keep happening—I don't know how to explain them, or even where to start. Just now, I suppose it was that diary, realizing whose it was—it gave me a shock. And then, seeing you . . ." Her voice faltered, became even more muffled, so that he had to strain to hear the rest, something about the Minster and that evening in the fog . . .

The doorbell rang shrilly. With a low expletive Stephen gripped her shoulders, asked whether he should make some excuse, put off Joan's visit until later.

"No—no, I'm all right," Zoe said, straightening her shoulders and pushing back her hair. "We'll talk later."

"We *must*," he insisted.

But Joan's visit prompted discussion of births and deaths, intricate family relationships and house moves, past and present. She was in better spirits, having come to terms with the job they were doing, and although none of their suspicions could yet be confirmed, her attitude was one of rueful acceptance. Having had time to mull over the anomaly of her father's birth certificate, various other things had apparently sprung to mind, like odd bits of jigsaw which suddenly slipped into place with ease. Those revelations prompted more questions until the afternoon slipped away, and Zoe's moment of disturbance seemed very much a thing of the past.

Fascinated by the older woman, at ease with her, Zoe was amused by the conspiratorial smile she gave Stephen as she was leaving.

"I told you you'd like her, didn't I?" was uttered in a stage whisper, which left both Zoe and Stephen laughing and slightly embarrassed.

Afterward, when she had gone, Zoe said, "I feel as though I've been adopted—as though I really am family, instead of a total stranger . . ."

"She likes you," Stephen said simply, "and so do I."

But as though his aunt's warmth reminded him by contrast of other, less generous family members, he went on to warn her about his sister. "If you ever meet Pam—and you may, she has a habit of dropping in when she's in town—you must expect a very thorough going-over. She'll disapprove on principle, I'm afraid, whether she likes you or not. My ex-wife was—and is—her best friend. It doesn't seem to matter that I was the injured party—according to Pamela, it was all my fault in the first place for not buckling under, staying at home, and taking a shore job . . ." He sighed. "For all she's my sister, we have very little in common."

"Have you never considered working ashore? Seriously, I mean?"

"I didn't in those days. Now, I think of it more and more. But"—he shrugged—"I'm faced with the eternal problem of what does Jolly Jack *do* once he swallows the anchor? Short of marine surveying, which would bore me to tears, I can't think of a thing."

"You could always write your memoirs," she said wickedly, "I'm sure they'd be fascinating!" Warming to the idea as he laughed and shook his head, she added, "And what about Joseph Conrad? He wrote some wonderful novels, didn't he?"

"Be careful, my love—you're treading on my heart!" And with that he fetched her cape and told her they were going out.

He took her to a quiet restaurant down one of York's quainter back streets. Stephen's avoidance of the subject begun before Joan Elliott's arrival was, she felt, deliberate; but as he regaled her with stories of his early life at sea, characters he had known, places he had visited, she forgot that unnerving moment in laughter, and the likeness which had seemed so uncanny receded. He was himself, no other—warm, vital, alive, and with eyes that told her she was beautiful and very much desired. Face-to-face, looking into those eyes, so light and blue against the gold of his skin, Zoe knew that it was Stephen she wanted, would have wanted, whatever his name, whatever his ancestry. The rest was just coincidence. In that context she could deal with it, and when the time came, talk about it with some degree of detachment.

It was dark when they left but not very late, the city quiet and left to itself in midweek solitude. York was a different place at night, Zoe sensed immediately, as though unrestricted by the crush of visitors, the city was breathing in satisfied calm. Old streetlamps cast gentle light on older buildings, which in their age and lack of vanity were immensely reassuring. Like old eyes, the windows dozed, having seen everything before. This city, she felt, could be neither shocked nor surprised, and current interest in all things past was simply another phase in a long and ongoing history.

Passing old doorways, traversing a series of ancient alleys on their walk through town toward the riverside, Zoe was aware of feet which had trodden these paths before, found herself wondering, at every turn, whether those other Elliotts had walked this way, seen that beautifully turned corner, noticed a church's perfect tower. And the river itself, reflecting lights, its bridges graceful, staithes still cobbled, could have changed little in the intervening years.

Saying nothing, Stephen simply drew her closer. She knew, however, that he felt as she did; knew too, that even without their shared ancestry, he would have understood her growing affinity for this place. With some reluctance and on a promise to return, they moved away.

Walking back up Stonegate, with the great central tower of the Minster illuminated above the chimney stacks, Stephen pointed to a ship's figurehead supporting a jutting upper story; and a little farther on, paused to show her Coffee Yard, where Edward Elliott had once been in business as a bookbinder. It was innocently said, yet reminded them both of that return address in Liam's diary; the quietness of separate thoughts descended in that short journey home to Stephen's flat.

He poured a drink for them both and lit the fire; found the tape of an old and very English film sound track by Richard Rodney Bennett and slipped that into the stereo; then stood for a moment watching Zoe framed against the window. The haunting, plaintive melody echoed something inside him, a tenderness for her that was impossible to put into words. Almost hesitantly, he placed his hands on her shoulders and laid his cheek against her hair; beyond them both, standing dramatically against the night sky, was the floodlit Minster.

With Liam still on his mind, Stephen wondered what she was thinking, and whether she really wanted to tell him what the connection was between his diary and that night in the mist. Her very quietness seemed a prelude, as though she was trying to marshal thoughts and words for something that eluded both. Then, as though it was vital to explain all that had happened to her that evening, she began by describing her walk and the sky's intense, remarkable blue. Her voice was low and clear, a lyrical counterpoint to the music; but as the melody strengthened, building up to a storm, her words became shorter, sharper, describing that battlefield in the mist with staccato clarity.

He almost wished she had not told him. The strangeness of it sent chills up his spine. He remembered the shock of touching that diary, reading random pages of Liam's meticulous script written amid the mud and horror of the Western Front. And he recalled with acute intensity that sense he had had of holding someone else's life in his hands.

He drew Zoe closer, breathing in the scent of her hair and skin, and then, so strongly that he almost uttered the words, he wanted to tell her that he loved her. Overcome by the unexpected power of those words, he struggled for mastery, telling himself that love was the last thing he wanted to feel. Love meant involvement on a total scale, the pain of parting, the dread of betrayal; love meant anguish, jealousy, and the heart-chilling realization that it is a word of variable meaning.

It passed. The words left him. Shaken, he buried his face against her hair, looked out at the floodlit towers above the silhouette of Goodramgate, and told himself not to be a fool. He wanted her companionship, yes, and the pleasure her body offered was enticing, but the rest he was willing to forgo.

She turned, clinging for a moment before drawing back to search his eyes; he did not look away, but on a slow release of breath, said, "Come to bed now—I need you."

With that first, feverish disrobing in both their minds, they undressed each other slowly. Lingering over the fragrance of her skin, his hands tenderly explored every curve and hollow, lips teasing, reaching down to the fullness of her breasts and the soft, rounded curve of her abdomen. He wanted to appreciate her, to take his time, despite the urgent need, to please them both to the full. And she knew his intent, he could see it in her eyes, in the parting of a smile, feel it in her touch. Desire and acquiescence, and a constant, flickering excitement which found its echo in himself.

They embraced and held apart, touched lightly and gripped with passion, explored each other fully until it was impossible to hold back. With urgent satisfaction they came together; and thrusting deep into the soft moist heart of her, he rolled, bringing her over until she was astride him and he could feast his eyes on the sight of her. Winter-pale skin, almost translucent in the lamp's glow, and rosy-pink buds of breasts shadowed in a dark fall of curls as she shook her head. He touched her gently, reverently, entranced by the different textures of hair and skin, by his own bronzed hands against her breasts; and then she smiled and began to move against him, and all else was forgotten in that deep, seductive, obliterating rhythm.

It was as astonishing as the first time, better, he decided; and finding unexpected reserves in himself, Stephen took her again, this time pushing every response to the limit. Only afterward, as she lay exhausted against him, did he wonder why. What was he trying to prove? That she was bloody good in bed, or that he was better than all the other men she must have slept with? Or was it simply that he was trying to eradicate with sex the powerful emotions she aroused.

If any of that were true, he thought painfully, then it would appear to be something of a pointless exercise. Caressing the smoothness of her back, listening to the gentle sighs of her breathing, Stephen sensed that every encounter drew them closer together. She was exciting and beautiful and generous, and he wanted all that she could give; but for the first time he found himself considering what the cost might be to her.

It was probably as well, he reflected, that she would soon be on her way back to London. Once she had gone, perhaps it might be better not to encourage too speedy a return.

It was one thing to reach that decision in the dark hours of the night, quite another to implement it. Although Zoe stayed another day, when it came time for her to leave, Stephen could hardly bear to see her go. At the very last moment, with laughter and kisses and the knowledge that they were both acting crazily, he stuffed a few things in an overnight bag while she grabbed bundles of letters and photographs and they set off for London in the Jaguar.

An atmosphere of truancy pervaded that journey; they laughed a lot and played rock music very loud, arriving at Zoe's flat just as dusk was falling. The air, as she opened the door, was pungent with new paint, and apologizing for it, she rushed across to raise the tall sash windows and disperse the smell. Books were stacked all over the floor, ornaments and photographs on a long white table, while a draftman's drawing board rose at an angle beside it. Obsessed by the chaos, for a few minutes she dashed about, beginning one task and then another; eventually, Stephen caught hold of her, told her to pour them both a drink and then he would help her to straighten things out.

But with her drink only half consumed, Zoe remembered Polly. "I must go and tell her I'm back—she's been keeping an eye on things for me, and she must be wondering why I was away so long . . ."

She dashed off, leaving Stephen bemused. Where she had begun to replace books on shelves, he thought he would continue, trusting that the stacks corresponded with certain places. If he were wrong, he reflected, then Zoe would have to reorganize them, but in the meantime, they would be off the floor. Intrigued by her taste in literature, and enjoying the task, he was startled by the asthmatic buzzing of the doorbell. For a moment he wondered what it was, then having established its source, he was faced with operating the ancient intercom.

"Yes?"

A woman's voice answered. "Philip? Is that you?"

"No. This is Zoe Clifford's flat."

"Well yes, I know it is." There was an anxious pause. "Is she there?"

It seemed odd to Stephen to be conducting a conversation like this, so he explained Zoe's momentary absence and invited the woman in. Wondering who Philip might be, he pressed what he hoped was the door-release button, left the door to the flat open, and returned to the books.

He felt rather than heard Zoe's visitor enter and turned to see a young woman whose smart clothes and cropped, ultra-fashionable hairstyle went oddly with the look of uncertainty in her eyes.

"Why don't you sit down? She shouldn't be long. I'm Stephen Elliott, by the way—Zoe's cousin."

"Oh. Thank you." Her glance flickered over him and away, then wandered nervously back again. "I'm Clare," she said, "an old friend of Zoe's." There was another pause in which Stephen read her suspicion, the thought processes which were casting back for any mention of male cousins of his name or description, and the unspoken demand as to why he was there.

He continued replacing books on their shelves.

"I've been trying to get hold of her for days." It was almost an accusation.

"She's been in York."

"Oh. York . . .?"

"Chasing up some family history. I've been helping her."

"Oh, I see . . ." And with a quick glance, Stephen saw that she did, that the topic suddenly answered many questions and opened a slot into which he might fit. Suspicion was replaced by hostility.

Seconds later, he heard Zoe's voice, light with laughter as she called her thanks to Polly. He wanted to warn her, although he could not have said why: Watching her expression change as she came in, he wished he had been able to.

Greetings between the two women were cool, despite Clare's explanations and the halting apology for some row they had evidently had over the telephone. Embarrassed, Stephen asked whether he should disappear for an hour.

"No—no, Stephen, there's no need for that." But she was embarrassed too, torn between different loyalties.

"In that case, perhaps I should make us all a cup of coffee." And with that he escaped to the kitchen, leaving the women to settle their differences alone. Although he closed the door firmly, it connected with the sitting room, and he could still hear what was being said. He ran the cold tap, clattered a few items of crockery, turned the gas up full, and lit a cigarette, but in his mind's eye he could still see Zoe's face, closed and still, feel her restraint in the pauses. Whatever the other woman had done, it had managed to upset Zoe mightily, and she was not ready to forgive, that much was obvious. It seemed to him that she was accepting the apologies in order to get rid of Clare.

But Clare was bent upon confession, admitting to certain problems with someone called David and begging Zoe's understanding. Zoe seemed ready to go along with that, even to the extent of suggesting another meeting so that she and Clare could talk things over. That was agreed, and the voices faded a little as they moved into the hall, then he heard Clare say something about Philip. Clare felt sorry for him, she said, and still felt Zoe had behaved badly; she supposed it was because of this new man, and thought she might at least have been a little more honest, instead of blaming David for everything . . .

Zoe's voice faded to a murmur, as though they had stepped out on to the landing. It was frustrating: He would have liked to hear her reply to that. If the demise of this man Philip was as recent as it seemed, he wondered whether Zoe would feel able to admit that she and Stephen had only just met.

Initially, he was not unduly concerned, although as the minutes ticked by he did begin to wonder why she had omitted to mention it. Had it been some months past, he could have understood, but something so recent?

He shrugged, told himself that he preferred not to know. He had told her briefly about Ruth, and she had told him with equal brevity about the married man she had met at college, some mad artist with a passion for women and booze. A fiasco, apparently, but, like his marriage to Ruth, it had been important. And with a similar time span between those events, they were relegated to their proper place. It struck him that just as he would never think of giving her a list of his previous affairs, so he would not want a list of hers. But still . . .

Who the hell was this Philip, anyway?

Zoe came running up the stairs, upset and apologetic. Waiting for her to calm down, he handed her a cup of cooling coffee and lit another cigarette.

"I suppose you heard most of that?"

"I did, yes. Hard not to."

"And I suppose," she went on heavily, "you must be wondering what on earth it was all about?"

With a dry smile, he nodded. "But only if you want to tell me—don't feel you have to."

That she did feel he merited an explanation was something of a mixed blessing. Stephen discovered far more about her relationship with Clare—and by association, her fiancé, David—than he did about Philip. From what she did say, he thought the man sounded inadequate, but he refused to comment. Or to probe. She was young yet, and women were attracted to men for the oddest reasons. Whether she had slept with Philip, whether there had been emotional involvement was something he preferred not to know. He told himself it was over, that it had been over even before he spoke to her on the telephone. Nevertheless, it bothered him.

In truth, Zoe was ashamed. She would have given almost anything for Stephen not to have witnessed the scene between herself and Clare. It was so hard to explain old ties, harder still when any sympathy she might have felt had disappeared in the face of Clare's blatant tactlessness. In retrospect, of course, she did feel sorry for Clare and was more convinced than ever that her engagement to David was a mistake. But how on earth did anyone explain suspicions like that? Quite simply, it was impossible. The most she could do was to stay in touch occasionally and hope against hope that Clare saw the pitfalls for herself.

But because of the connection with Philip, Zoe did not feel able to explain her suspicions to Stephen. To say, yes, I slept with Philip but he was pretty hopeless in bed, and to be honest, I think the person he really fancies is David, except he's not aware of it, was impossible. What would he think of her? She thought pretty badly of herself. Could not imagine how blind she had been not to see what appeared so obvious now. But if her suspicions were correct—and there was no way of proving them—then he was more to be pitied than judged. What a situation! The trouble was, for long enough, Zoe had thought she could help him, boost his confidence, wean him away from the abominable David. But that was the last thing he wanted, which was why she had made so little headway.

Her own overweaning confidence appalled her. And her mother would never understand: She had liked Philip, knew his family in Sussex. But Marian was Marian, and Stephen was a different matter altogether. Zoe felt that she had behaved both badly and stupidly, and somehow damaged her standing in Stephen's eyes. Oh, if only Clare had stayed away, or telephoned, then they could have met privately and saved all this.

Awake in the small hours, with Stephen asleep beside her, she castigated herself far more severely than ever he would have thought to do. She prayed with anxious fervency that this

incident would cast no further shadows; her mood this evening
had been abstracted enough to concern him, and while he asked
no questions, she knew he was wondering.

Zoe's answer to anxiety had always been work. Needing a
similar distraction now, she slipped out of bed and lit the lamps
in the sitting room. With a hot drink and a bundle of Louisa
Elliott's letters, she settled down to read. As ever, more questions were raised than were answered, but she jotted them
down in a notebook, occasionally breaking to look at photographs, particularly those of Liam. Having now seen pictures
of Stephen as a young man, she was more than ever struck by
the likeness between them, but her studiously casual comment
the other day had caused no apparent surprise. Oh yes, he had
said, his grandmother, Sarah, who had known Liam as a boy,
had often remarked on it. But Zoe thought that light response
as careful as her own comment. Stephen's interest in Liam's
diary was now as great as her obsession with the letters.

Among Louisa's photographs was a head-and-shoulders
portrait of a young nurse, probably taken during the First World
War. Although her hair was mostly covered by a winged white
headdress, Zoe was convinced she was the young woman who
also appeared in the group photograph taken perhaps a year
or so earlier. From the later correspondence, Zoe had deduced
that she must be Georgina, Robert Duncannon's daughter.

And Robert Duncannon was now identified positively as
the young officer photographed in Dublin before the turn of
the century; almost certainly he was also the man at the center
of that much later family group. In a dark civilian suit he was
older, grayer, heavier, but the strong lines of nose and brow
and jaw were unmistakable. Relaxing on a garden seat, smiling
at the camera, he dominated the picture as he had probably
dominated the people in his life.

To one side of him sat Louisa, her expression sweeter,
softened by life and experience into kindliness, and on her
other side was Edward, less relaxed, frowning against the light.
He had been more difficult to identify, having abandoned the
beard of earlier portraits. For all the passing years, he was still
remarkably handsome, his features fine, the mouth gentle. In
his younger days, Joan had said, Edward was something of a

poet, an image that suited him better, Zoe felt, than that of a bookbinder with a business of his own.

Before them on the grass was a girl in white, a girl with rounded cheeks and slanting, dark-fringed eyes. Zoe's own photograph of Letitia showed a sophisticated young woman in her twenties, but there was no mistaking those eyes, or the thick, unruly hair that Zoe herself had inherited.

On Robert Duncannon's right, sat the young woman identified as his daughter, Georgina. She sat straight-backed, hands folded neatly in her lap, smooth blonde hair swept back from a delicately boned face. The posture, the simple, dark dress, made Zoe think of a nun. A very beautiful nun. No wonder Liam gazed at her so attentively; she would have turned heads, Zoe decided, wherever she went.

Yes, they were all there, with the exception of Robin, and as Stephen said, he was probably the one taking the photograph. The Elliotts and their wealthy relatives from Dublin, the Duncannons. A happy family group, captured in the garden of a pretty cottage on a summer's afternoon. But Zoe wished she could establish the exact relationship between them. It really was too bad that the Irish records were lost.

6

*M*ellow pantiles, uneven in places, roofed an elderly cottage of rusty-pink brick. The projecting scullery was not quite central, and the windows, half hidden beneath encroaching ivy, were set with even less regard for balance; yet overall the effect was charming, the impression that of a place which was loved, despite its idiosyncrasies. To the north, a high wall flanked by Lombardy poplars gave shelter to fruit trees and an abundance of vegetables, while a screen of roses divided kitchen garden from a broad strip of green lawn.

With his back to that mass of pale pink roses, Robin Elliott peered through the lens of his borrowed camera and wished his brother would try to look as though he belonged to the group instead of standing so tall and uncompromising behind them. Frowning, too: He was bored and eager to be off, but Robin was determined to have one more picture, and to make it a good one. Calling out to Liam to bend, kneel, or otherwise shrink into place, he waited while Georgina organized him. Liam leaned forward, resting his elbows on the seat back, his face turned toward her, smiling; she turned to the camera, folded her hands, and Robin pressed the shutter release.

Immediately, they all began to move. "Oh, don't rush away," Robin pleaded. "Let's have just one more."

"But you've taken half a dozen already," his mother pointed out. "And we can't sit here all afternoon posing—I've got tea to make, if nothing else. Come on, Tisha," she added, taking her daughter's arm before she could disappear, "we've got things to do."

There was an audible groan from the girl, and a reluctant droop to her shoulders as she headed for the kitchen. Turning to their hostess, Georgina Duncannon asked whether she needed more help.

"No, dear—you sit and talk to your father. I know you don't see him very often."

But Robert Duncannon was apparently more interested in examining the photographic equipment, demanding to know how it worked and what the time exposures needed to be. Flattered, Robin was only too keen to share his knowledge, to talk about the career upon which he had so recently embarked. He was even more impressed by Colonel Duncannon's interest in his other activities, particularly his part-time membership of the local volunteer force.

"If you should ever change your mind and decide to make the army your profession," Liam overheard him say, "do get in touch with me, first. I have a little influence at the War Office and might be able to do something for you."

Just for a moment, with their heads together, the two struck Liam as being very much alike. And the resemblance was more profound than that of shared height and coloring. Very briefly, he was disturbed by it, and then his brother moved and the similarity was gone.

It seemed, as he glanced around, that there was something dour in his father's steady observation of the pair, and Liam wondered why. Was it Robin's obsession with photographing anything and everything in sight? Or could it be that their father was less than pleased to be entertaining this wealthy, distant relative with his fine clothes and expansive manner? Their mother, certainly, had been quite overcome by that unexpected note that arrived as they were sitting down to Saturday dinner, thrown as close to panic as he had ever seen her. And since the

Colonel's arrival with Georgina an hour ago, she had been smiling and chattering like a young girl. That too was unusual. Perhaps his father was jealous?

The thought crossed his mind fleetingly and was as quickly dismissed. After all, he reasoned, married couples with grown children had no cause to be racked by emotions like that.

On the seat before him, Georgina was also alert to that conversation between her father and Robin. He could see tension in her spine and the set of her smooth blonde head, and thinking she was hurt by her father's careless neglect, Liam was ready to condemn the man forever. As he moved, however, she glanced around at Liam, and the eyes which met his softened into a smile.

"What a pity," she remarked lightly, "that photographs can't show color. Those roses are so beautiful."

Although he knew it was not the roses which had claimed her attention, Liam went along with the fiction, suggesting she should return to paint them one afternoon. At that she laughed, saying her expertise was too limited, she could never do them justice. He denied it, having seen some of her botanical drawings and the painting she had done for his mother, which now had pride of place in the parlor. They argued, amicably, and as she stood up he straightened, ready to fall in with whatever she wanted to do, wherever she wanted to go. He liked her immensely. She was so easy to be with, quiet and self-effacing, so gently humorous that sometimes it was a while before her wit was appreciated; and she had such an attractive lilt to her voice, with a little bubble of laughter in it. Although she often teased him for his seriousness, from her he did not mind; unlike his sister's barbed wit, Georgina Duncannon's held no tinge of cruelty.

Although as a girl she had visited them occasionally with her aunt, it was hard for Liam to align those distant memories with what he knew of her now. For the last three months, since arriving in York to nurse at the Retreat, she had been visiting regularly, spending most of her days off at the cottage, helping his mother in the kitchen or the garden, and joining the family for their evening meal. That affection for his mother always surprised Liam; he tended to forget that they were related, and that Georgina had known them all for years. And that she remembered him as a small child, far more clearly than he remembered her, was sometimes embarrassing. It also underlined the gulf between them, the great divide of age and class. She could, he knew, have spent her life in Dublin considering nothing more strenuous than her social obligations, but she had chosen instead to become a nurse; and having completed one training, she had recently embarked upon another at the Quaker hospital for the mentally ill.

Physically, Georgina worked harder than he did, and his heart ached at the sight of her ungloved hands, often red and chapped from the zealous use of carbolic. In that respect at least, Liam could understand the Colonel's anger at his daughter's choice of vocation; she tended to laugh about it, but to defy her father's authority must have required a matching strength of will. That seemed hard to credit now: Touching pretty shrubs, pausing to lean close to a full-blown rose, she seemed no less fragile than they.

Newly painted railings guarded the front garden like a row of bright green spears, and recalling recent hours spent chipping at rust, Liam flushed with pleasure at her praise. He was particularly proud of having cured the gate's long-lasting squeak, despite his father's claim that it would not be cured for long. For now, however, the gate was opening easily, and at Georgina's suggestion that they should walk a little way along the riverbank, Liam readily agreed.

In one direction, the sandy, tree-shaded path led past allotment gardens and a boat-building yard and ultimately into town. To the right, however, it meandered past woods and open meadows where he and his brother and sister had played as children. Liam always thought how well placed they were, within a few minutes' walk of the city, yet having miles of open countryside at hand. He had learned to swim in the river, learned to row too; and now, when he needed to escape, he had his bicycle, handy for riding to work but handier still for exploring outlying villages on his own. Unlike Robin, his interests were solitary ones, and except when Georgina was around, Liam much preferred his own company.

As he closed the gate, the sound of catcalls and whistles reached them from the far bank. Beneath the trees on New Walk, Liam caught sight of a group of girls in colorful finery hurrying along before a bunch of soldiers from the nearby barracks. In some embarrassment, he remarked that the girls should know better: New Walk was notorious in that respect. But Georgina smiled impishly, saying she thought the girls were heading toward the fairground on St. George's Field and were determined to have some handsome escorts.

"Does a uniform make a man handsome?"

"Well"—she grinned—"it improves an ugly one!"

His assent was grudging. For a moment they stood and watched the progress of that unsubtle courtship, and sure enough, the girls slowed down, introductions were made, and the group moved on together toward the fair. They could hear distantly the sound of deep base notes from a Gavioli organ, overlaid by tantalizing snatches of a popular melody. They looked at each other, then looked away. After a short pause, Georgina said she had never been to a fair. Liam, who had been to several over the years, was surprised. His sense of decorum, however, made him point out that fairs could be rough and rowdy, hardly fit for a lady. Looking crestfallen, Georgina said yes, Aunt Letty had always thought the same, then, unable to contain the impulse, declared that she would love to go.

"I know I shouldn't," she said wistfully, "and particularly today . . . But they'll be gone by my next day off, and I might never get another chance."

Liam looked upriver, toward Skeldergate Bridge, assessing the time it would take to walk around to St. George's Field. Then he glanced back at the house, thinking of her father, and his mother making the tea. Suddenly he remembered the old rowing boat which was often moored by the slipway, and stepped down the bank to see if it was there.

"Wait a minute, I haven't got my hat!"

"If you go back for that, they'll want to know where you're going," he told her. "You can forget the fair."

"You're right," she agreed, feeling reckless, infected by a desire to be young and silly and happy, instead of the serious, dedicated woman she had become. She felt guilty, too, remembering the reason for her father's visit; the guilt, however, merely spurred her on.

With incongruous formality, Liam handed her down the bank and into the boat. In one neat movement he took his place by the oars, and with long, smooth strokes soon had them across the river. As they passed beneath Blue Bridge with its massive Crimean guns on either side, and into the stream of the Foss, Liam explained his intention. He would moor in the Foss Basin, where the boat would be safer and the facility of steps made alighting easier. From there it was but a few yards to the fairground.

Georgina admired his capability, was even touched by the overprotective, very formal way he escorted her. At home among his family he was usually very relaxed, saying little but happy to be in her company. It was easy to treat him like a younger brother, which was what she wanted, and he made no objection to that. For the first time, however, they were out together in a very public place, and that seemed to have set every sense on the alert and made a young man of the boy she usually teased and joked with. Watching Liam as they pushed through the noisy, laughing crowd, she suddenly became aware that he was behaving as he might have done with a girl he was courting. Silly though it was, the idea was so appealing, yet so utterly impossible, it brought a lump to her throat. Very quickly she looked away, exclaiming at the stalls and side-shows, the music and the crowds.

There was an enormously fat, bearded lady, who looked stronger, Liam said, than the so-called strong man in his tights and leopard skin, and a shooting gallery doing excellent business with the young soldiers present. At one of the stalls he bought her a bag of pink-and-white coconut ice, presenting it with a shyness she had not thought he possessed, and refusing to take any for himself. Then, among the gaily colored stalls and that dazzle of noise and movement, they found the source of the music, the biggest crowd. A huge merry-go-round with pairs of painted wooden horses going up and down, and here and there a carriage for two following on to the music of the great Gavioli fair organ. It was such a delightful sight, Georgina clapped her hands like a child, saying that they *must* have a ride, she could not possibly leave without trying it. In the end they had two turns, once in a carriage and next on the horses, going around and around until she was dizzy. It was like dancing, she said, only much, much better, more like flying, and she loved it. Her delight was infectious, and as he helped her

down, Liam was laughing too, eyes sparkling, teeth white
against the smooth summer gold of his skin. She was so happy
and he was so beautiful, she wanted to hug him. But as his
hand lingered on hers she drew it quickly away, pushing on
through the crush before he should notice her silliness getting
out of hand.

"It's time we went," Georgina reminded him, and as they
stood to assess their bearings, she noticed a tight knot of men
behind one of the tents. There was a scuffling within the ring,
and at first she thought it no more than rivalries that had developed into a fight. Then a dog yelped and another squealed, and
she saw a sheen of lustful eagerness on faces that were turned
toward her, money changing hands.

"Whatever's happening over there?"

Liam's smile faded. "Dog baiting. But they won't be at it
long," he added gruffly, "here's the constable." Even as he
spoke, the warning was given and the ring broke, men scattering in all directions. Slavering and bleeding, the dogs were
dragged apart and leashed, their keepers feigning outrage and
aggression in an attempt to cover their guilt. Georgina was
struck by a horrible similarity between them: evil, predatory
eyes and snarling mouths. The men, she thought, were more
repulsive than their dogs.

She was glad to be led away. They walked back in silence
to where they had left the boat, saying little as they recrossed
the river. That sickening scene had taken the edge off the afternoon, reminding Liam of a reality which could never match up
to his dreams, and Georgina of unpleasantness waiting in the
wings.

Tying up, walking the few yards back to the cottage, she
would have preferred to stop, sit for a while on the quiet riverbank, and tell him why her father had come to York today.
But it was a long, sad, complicated story; and stupidly, she had
a feeling that once she began she would cry. That would never
do. "People don't want to know your sadnesses," Aunt Letty
always said. "If asked, you're *very well, thank you*, and you must
never complain."

Aunt Letty was good and she was kind, and Georgina
loved her dearly, but, oh, she often longed to be honest, to tell

someone how she really felt. Especially now, with her mother dead only two days and the funeral to face, and the past welling up like a tidal wave, threatening to engulf her. Stoic to the last, Aunt Letty would never understand, and her father, Georgina knew, was simply glad to be free of that poor mad woman who had haunted his life for twenty-five years. It was impossible to be honest with him when so much of her sadness was tied up with his abrupt comings and goings and lengthy, interminable absences.

Louisa was the only one who might understand; yet how could she talk to her now? It would have to wait until after the funeral, when she came back from Dublin. Her next day off, however, could be a fortnight away.

But Georgina had been well trained. She was a little quieter than usual when she and Liam returned, but among the constant buzz of conversation it went unnoticed. They were just in time for tea, and some instinct kept Liam from admitting where they had been, so Georgina did not enlighten anyone. It would be their secret, she thought, catching Liam's eye as he sat down, and no one could be shocked at that unsuitable entertainment when she should have been grieving.

In the parlor, the table was out to its fullest extent and set as though for a banquet, with white damask and silver cutlery, china plates, and a centerpiece of midsummer flowers. Three varieties of pie graced the setting, with salads and cold meats and eggs in mayonnaise, and on the dresser stood a crystal dish of ripe crimson strawberries, with a matching pitcher full of cream.

Even Georgina was amazed at the speed with which this unexpected visit had been catered for. In the kitchen, however, Louisa admitted she had baked a larger amount than usual that morning; the rest was quickly put together, and the strawberries and salad were fresh from the garden. With a smile, she handed a tray to Georgina and turned to the stove to rescue a boiling kettle.

"Did my father say why he'd come to York today?"

"Well no," the older woman admitted, looking slightly puzzled. "I imagined he'd come to visit you for a few days. Was there something else?" she asked keenly.

"It's not important just now—I'll tell you later."

The fine eyes shot her a look of inquiry, then with a sympathetic smile, Louisa patted her arm. "Make it soon."

With another ridiculous lump in her throat, Georgina went into the parlor and took her place next to Liam. Her father was immediately opposite, with Tisha and Robin on either side, and Edward at the head of the table. As Louisa took her place at the foot, Georgina thought how little she had changed. More matronly, of course, and with fine lines around her eyes and mouth, but the beauty of her expression had not diminished, and that was what made her so attractive. And at that sparkle of amusement in Louisa's eyes, Georgina observed, her father responded with even more gallantry than usual. She had watched him in recent years with various women and knew enough about him to detect the slightest insincerity, knew also what he wanted and from whom. Once it had appalled her, but nursing had taught Georgina the simplest, most basic facts of life, and experience with the mentally deranged had inured her to shock. Now, she accepted that her father had strong physical desires, and in the absence of a wife, must seek satisfaction where he could. Not that it had ever been difficult for him; when it suited, Robert Duncannon could be both generous and affectionate and, even at fifty, was still an attractive man.

Watching him, remembering the years between—nine or ten, surely, since his last brief visit here—Georgina was astonished to realize that her father's inclinations toward Louisa were still unchanged. Despite Edward, despite the gathered family in this haven of domestic peace, he could still want Louisa, and be stupid enough to let it show. Darting an anxious glance around the table, she noted Edward's studiously blank expression and burned for him. Robin and Tisha were arguing amicably, noticing nothing, but Liam beside her was tense with all the alertness of a young male in the presence of a threat.

Beset by a furious sense of panic, she wished her father would simply *go*, get on the next train to London and not come back. She would tell him so as soon as they were alone. It was unfair that he should come here, after all this time, charming Louisa, making her remember things that were surely best forgotten.

With sharp frustration she moved, accidentally scattering cutlery from her plate. The knife shot across Liam's lap, depositing blobs of mayonnaise as it landed by his feet. Exclaiming, apologizing, Georgina seized the distraction. Grabbing Liam's arm, she almost dragged him into the kitchen, handing him cloths and instructions, hurrying back to deal with the other damage. It was with great satisfaction that she saw she had broken her father's spell. While Louisa bent to wipe the mess from the carpet, Robert Duncannon remembered his manners and turned his attention to Edward.

In the kitchen, Liam was ruefully surveying the state of his best suit. Regretting the action which had caused the damage, hoping it was not irrevocable, Georgina apologized again. He glanced up from beneath a lock of thick fair hair, his mouth twisting into a wry grin.

"It's all right," he murmured, "there's no need to fuss."

Straightening, he held her gaze, seeming suddenly much older; in the depth and shrewdness of that glance, for the first time she saw a likeness to her father. It unnerved her and she did not know why.

Dismissing the idea, she told herself that Liam was nothing like Robert Duncannon. In looks he was his mother's son, in character he was Edward's. Sensitive, something of a dreamer, he was a boy still trying to find his feet. A boy who turned to her for advice, because to voice his uncertainties to either of his parents would have hurt them. A sharp memory of that stolen hour at the fair, however, his protectiveness, and a hand which might have lingered on hers caused a sudden apprehension. Sternly, she told herself that he regarded her as a sister, there was nothing more to it than that.

Although she repeated the litany several times in the course of the next hour, Georgina found herself taking surreptitious glances for confirmation. With similar looks, Liam seemed to be keeping an eye on her father, who was now behaving himself admirably, engaging the younger members of the family in conversation. If anything, Tisha was the one who was flirting. Just sixteen and working as a clerk at the new confectionery works outside town, she was full of her own achievements. Conscious, too, of a pretty face and blossoming figure, she angled unashamedly for compliments. And laughing, Robert Duncannon indulged her, just as Edward did.

She was the kind of girl, Georgina thought without envy, who would always have men on her side. The pity of it was that Tisha had so very little compassion in her heart. She was so acquisitive and materialistic, and it was hard to think which side of the family she favored. It seemed that all she wanted were the trappings of wealth and no doubt one day would find a man to provide them. It galled her that the Elliotts continued to live in this humble riverside cottage, employing no more than a daily girl, when their means would allow them a handsome town house, with at least one live-in servant. That her mother enjoyed gardening, selling excess produce to neighbors and casual passersby, was another source of embarrassment for Tisha. In her eyes, Edward Elliott was a man of some substance, respected both socially and professionally: His wife should not demean herself by selling fruit and vegetables like any common market trader.

In short, the girl was a snob. Robin might ignore it, find excuses for it, sometimes even sympathize, but Liam never would. Idealistic and uncompromising, he found it hard to forgive his sister for the dissensions she caused, and most particularly for the pain she inflicted on his mother.

He must learn to bend, Georgina thought anxiously, learn to give a little, before life dealt blows which could break him. In some ways, not least in height and coloring, Robin resembled her father, sharing a certain resilience of spirit which marked them out as survivors. But Liam was different. Liam worried her because in that very upright stance he was vulnerable, and as things stood at the moment, danger walked too close to him.

The sun was setting as they said their good-byes at the gate, farewells that were a little too prolonged for Georgina's taste, and Edward's too, she thought, reading his expression. Keen to put some distance between him and her father, she hurried along the sandy path, slowing only as her feet touched cobblestones by the bridge. Reminded of Dublin, here she often paused to look along the river, at the warehouses and flour mills, the busy staithes with barges and keelboats tied up alongside. She could still hear the jolly fairground music, and with her mind on what had driven her there that afternoon, rather than the joy of it, she spoke more sharply then intended.

"You know, you could have written. There was no need to travel all this way."

Robert paused, a little out of breath at her youthful haste, and a little hurt that she should address him so. "I haven't seen you," he slowly pointed out, "for several months. Is it unnatural that I should want to see for myself how you are?"

Her profile, beneath that uncompromisingly plain hat, reminded him of his sister's in one of her more intransigent moods. Indeed, as Georgina grew older, he could see the likeness more and more. Fair where Letty was dark, nevertheless his daughter had the same fine bone structure inherited from Robert's Irish mother. And Letty too had been beautiful in her youth. For a moment, he was tempted to be cruel, to tell his blonde and willowy daughter that if she was not careful, she would end up a prickly, angular old maid like her aunt.

But he was fond of Letty, and was it entirely her fault that she had never married? Letty could have had any one of a dozen suitors, even in her thirties. Instead, she had taken care of a newborn baby and turned her back on society. Despite Robert's pangs of guilt, she had never reproached him on that score; indeed, when pressed, she always said Georgina had given her the chance of knowing something of motherhood without having to suffer the inconvenience of a husband. That always reassured him, always made him laugh.

He was not laughing now, however. Letty had managed to instill too many of her own unconventional views into this child of his, denied her too many frivolities. With talents both musical and artistic, and looks remarkable enough to set any red-blooded young man after her hand in marriage, Georgina evinced no interest in anything but nursing. She cared not a whit for clothes, jewelery, social diversions; instead, she had demanded, persuaded, cajoled, and virtually blackmailed him into agreeing to this further nonsense. As if nursing the physically sick were not enough, Georgina now insisted on caring for those poor mad souls at the Retreat. With her background, he would have supposed such a place to be abhorrent to her, but her letters were full of compassion for her patients and praise for the Quaker staff. Looking at Georgina now as she strode so disapprovingly beside him, Robert could imagine her marrying some dour Quaker doctor and producing serious Quaker children. The thought depressed him.

But at least, he told himself, apart from her delicate coloring, she was nothing like Charlotte, and that was something to be eternally thankful for. Once, he had been horribly afraid that Georgina would turn out like her mother, but there seemed little fear of that now. Unconventional she might be, and even obsessive when it came to her vocation, but his daughter was also warm and affectionate, which was something Charlotte had never been.

Now her mother was dead, Robert had ensured that she would inherit most of Charlotte's wealth. That is, most of what was left. It never failed to astonish him how much had gone in medical bills and nursing home fees, how much had been swallowed by structural repairs to the family home in Waterford and his house in Dublin. Then, a few years ago, there had been some ill-advised investments, reducing the income, making huge inroads on the capital, so that the remains were pitiful. Although he regretted it, Robert could say, hand on heart, that little had been diverted to his own personal use. Never forgetting how cleverly he had been trapped into that farce of a marriage, to him, Charlotte's fortune had always seemed like blood money.

Sighing, he remarked, "I thought the news I had to impart was better *said*. However, I'm glad to see it hasn't been too distressing for you."

It was not said unkindly, but the observation hurt her nevertheless. Saying nothing, she looked away, over the stillness of the river in the soft glow of evening. Perhaps her father detected something amiss, for they had not gone far when he took her hand and tucked it into the crook of his arm.

Concerned at the tight expression on his daughter's face, he wondered what she was thinking, whether in fact she was more distressed by her mother's death than he thought possible. It was, however, such a difficult topic, he chose what he considered a safer one, telling her she was working too hard and that he had arranged a week's leave of absence with the Superintendent of the hospital. He felt her displeasure at that, the defensiveness which came into being whenever her independence was threatened. It was not entirely dissipated by their walk back to the Retreat. As they climbed the hill toward it, however, he discovered something of her thoughts, and they were at such a tangent to what might have been expected that Robert was taken aback.

"You won't go back to the cottage, will you?"

"What? Tonight? No, of course not."

"Tonight, tomorrow, *anytime*," she said tersely. "Don't go back, please."

Astonished by her temerity, Robert stopped. "Why ever not?"

"You know why. It's not fair—to any of them. Not after all these years."

"Georgina," he said heavily, "it's *my* business, not yours, and I'll thank you not to interfere. You have no right to—"

"I have *every* right!" she declared with force. "They mean as much to me as they do to you. Probably more, if truth be known. I was *curling* with embarrassment for Edward this afternoon—and while you may not have noticed, Liam was watching you like a hawk!"

"Was he, by God? I didn't realize . . ."

"No," came the quick reply, "you were too taken up with Louisa. *You* might be free, Daddy, but she's not!"

Guilty color flooded his face. Aware of it, Robert took refuge in anger. "Watch your tongue, miss!"

At once contrite, Georgina shook her head. "I'm sorry. But if *I* don't remind you, Daddy, who will?"

That unexpected maturity startled him, as did the power of her observation. Momentarily humbled by it, he squeezed her hand. "Do I need such reminders?"

"Not usually," she conceded, "but this time it's important."

"In that case, I'll try to remember it."

A porter opened the gate for them, and Robert walked with his daughter up the drive. It was a fine house, he thought, with a mellow, comfortable air to it, more like a gentleman's country residence than a hospital. Which was surprising since the place had been built specifically to house the mentally ill and was less than half a mile from the edge of town. From the outside it was not unlike that other place in Ireland where Charlotte had been confined for the past fifteen years, but its interior was different and infinitely preferable. Here there were no nuns in rustling black robes, no colored plaster saints, and the fine paintings which graced the Retreat's walls would not have been out of place in Robert's Dublin home. The staff were approachable too. Pleasant, ordinary people, with no great air of piety. Robert's chief difficulty was in distinguishing one from another, for as Georgina explained, rank, both social and authoritative, went unstressed and unadvertised. With its array of doors without name or number, it was a mystery to him how people found their way about. Used to the clear-cut structure of army life, he wondered also how order was kept so effectively. The principle of mutual respect, as explained by his daughter, sounded a fine aim, but in his experience human failings generally made mincemeat of such ideals.

That it worked here, however, had been obvious to Robert that morning as the superintendent showed him around. And reading the words of its founder, that the Retreat should be a place *in which the unhappy might obtain refuge*, he was reminded of similar words spoken by the Mother Superior of that obscure little order of nursing nuns in Ireland. Only after remarking on that to his daughter did Robert learn that the Irish doctor in charge had spent a considerable amount of time at the Quaker hospital and, influenced by its success, had gone on to spread those excellent principles elsewhere.

How strange, he thought as he saw Georgina to her door, that so many things came full circle, and that the line should so often begin and end with York. Leaving her, he stood for a moment outside on the crest of the hill on which the hospital was built, gazing out over the darkening grounds. On one side he could see the Minster's towers catching the last residue of light from the west, while below him, beyond grounds and grassy strays, he could just make out the barracks. A few lights were twinkling there, reminding him with sudden, but not unwelcome nostalgia of his own tour of duty at Fulford.

Savoring the memory and its banishment of the twenty years between, for a moment he was thirty again, impulsive and hot-blooded, and with Charlotte on his mind, just a little crazy too. Living too hard, drinking too much, searching for a panacea which always eluded him. And then, unexpectedly, at her mother's little hotel on Gillygate, he had met Louisa, and she had changed everything.

Not materially, of course. That travesty of a marriage did not go away, nor did it cease to plague him; but Louisa banished its morbid fascination, and once free of that, Robert's life regained its balance, became bearable, even enjoyable at times. He supposed, looking back, that it should have gone no further, yet even under the closest examination, he could not see where he had forced the issue. He had put his situation honestly before her, and she had rejected him; and taking the honorable path, he had stayed away. Fate, however, seemed to have had other plans in store. Never, if he lived to be ninety, would he forget that summer's evening—so like this one!—when Louisa had made that unexpected visit to his lodgings at Fulford. That, for him, was where it had *really* begun, the point where honor and pain and loneliness assumed the aspect of unwanted baggage on life's hard road, and having abandoned them, he set out quite deliberately to take her.

With all he knew now, and all that had happened between, Robert would not have changed those two years even if he could. Like a many-faceted jewel, that time stood out, its dark depths and shafts of light still glowing in his memory. Nothing since had matched it.

It was all very well, he thought, for Georgina to tell him what he must and must not do. She knew too little, and her perspective was different. Seeing Louisa again was a revelation for which he had been largely unprepared. After all these years, he had expected her to seem older, unattractive against the picture he held in his heart. He should have known better. The warmth of her smile had not changed, nor the light in her eyes, and she had matured with grace. Yes, he thought, smiling into the darkness, Louisa Elliott was still a lovely woman, natural and artless as ever, but that had always been her attraction.

Wanting to see her again, he knew he would return. Next time, however, he would not make the mistake of calling when the family were gathered. Next time he would ensure that he saw her alone.

7

*I*n the house there was no-
where to talk. Nowhere, that is, with sufficient privacy. Tisha
was helping in the kitchen and would soon be going to bed,
where the upper walls were too thin to allow much more than
a hushed whisper. By the window's fading light Robin was
writing a log of photographs taken that afternoon, and slumped
on the sofa with an oil lamp already lit, Liam was absorbed by
a book. He looked set to stay there all night. Irritated by that
calm family scene and unable to feign interest in anything,
Edward waited with gnawing impatience for Louisa to finish
clearing away.

Able to stand his thoughts no longer, he went outside to
pace the length of the garden until she should join him. Against
a low band of pink, the trees seemed no more than black paper
cutouts with a random pattern of holes here and there. A pretty
illusion, he thought, life imitating art, masking its three-dimen-
sional reality. He looked back at the cottage, all quaint angles
and lack of symmetry, and knew it rested on insecure foundations; yet in the last rosy glow from the west, it presented a
delightful picture of rural peace. He wondered whether the
years of happiness beneath its roof had been a similar illusion,

resting on equally insecure foundations, maintained with ease only while Robert Duncannon stayed away.

It was a bitter thought, and a frightening one. Loving Louisa as he did, for him the years of their marriage had been the happiest of his life. Not usually given to jealousy, where Robert Duncannon was concerned Edward found it difficult to be rational.

She came at last, pausing to remove her apron and reaching up to hang it on a peg behind the door. He stood beneath the trees in the orchard, watching her maddeningly slow progress along the path, loving her beyond everything. The pauses she made, her comments on the vegetables and burgeoning raspberry plants—quite audible in the stillness—illustrated her reluctance to air the subject which tormented him.

And she was aware of his torment. Brightly determined at first, her smile became uncertain as she discerned his face, then faded altogether. Choked by the sheer volume of words that begged for release, for a moment Edward could say nothing, and in the silence she stiffened half turned her back before uttering the briefest apology.

"And so you *should* be sorry," he muttered fiercely, taking her arm. "Come on—we can't talk here—every word will carry back to the house."

Not until they were a good hundred yards down the towpath did he speak again, and in his anger and apprehension the words were staccato, his phrases short and disjointed. Not trusting Robert Duncannon, Edward's accusations came out badly, making his wife the guilty party, the one to blame for that brazen flirtation in front of the children, the one who had encouraged a man who stood to ruin them all. In her turn, Louisa was furious, accusing him of irrational and unreasonable jealousy.

"It's not every day we have visitors," she declared hotly. "Would you have me sit like a specter at the feast, ignoring him?"

It was an unfortunate analogy, one that prompted bitter sarcasm from Edward, who had been informed of Charlotte Duncannon's death only as their guests were leaving. " 'Specter at the feast,' " he repeated with a harsh laugh, "is a curiously apt phrase in the circumstances. Except the *specter* should have been *his wife*, don't you think? She's the one so recently dead! Not that anyone would have suspected it—he was giving an impression of an extremely happy man!"

"Given those circumstances, Edward," she retorted, "I doubt whether you'd be heartbroken, either!"

"I'd at least try to observe the decencies!"

Biting back a cutting reply, Louisa turned away, gazing through the purple shades of evening toward the river's far bank. In the distance streetlights twinkled, and beyond the houses flanking Fulford Road stood the barracks. Even after all these years the place drew her eyes like a magnet. And yet she had been happy with Edward, contented and peaceful. Only in the last year or so had they argued at all, and that was mainly over Tisha. Usually Louisa was the one who was hurt and accusatory; it was painful to be on the receiving end of Edward's resentment.

Wanting to placate him, she said with forced calm, "Robert said nothing at all about Charlotte until after we'd eaten—and he explained then that he hadn't wanted to spoil our day with news of her death."

But Edward's anger was not to be diffused so easily. "How very thoughtful of him! A pity he didn't consider how his visit might spoil the rest of our lives."

"Oh, Edward," she sighed, "don't exaggerate."

On a deep breath he paused, taking his wife's arm, making her turn to face him. With an effort he calmed his temper, put stays on the fear and jealousy which threatened more destruction than even Robert Duncannon could accomplish.

"Louisa, I'm not exaggerating. He hasn't been near us for years and suddenly he turns up, out of the blue, all charm and good humor. And quite apart from the fact that you welcomed him like the prodigal returned"—he broke off, letting that accusation sink in—"what worries me is the effect on the children—they must be wondering who he is, and why he's come."

"He's Georgina's father, for goodness' sake. She visits us—why shouldn't he?"

Her attempt at a nonchalant shrug irritated Edward further. "And she's another one!" he exclaimed. "Oh, I know she's a delightful girl, and you're very fond of her—but in her own way, Louisa, she's as dangerous as he is. Can't you see that?"

"What?" she demanded. "See what?"

"She's young and beautiful and exceptionally charming—to all of us. We're all very fond of her, wouldn't you say?"

"Yes, but—"

"But one of us is more than just *fond* of the girl. One of us is quite besotted by Robert's daughter, or *hadn't you noticed?*"

Louisa's breath caught in her throat. For several seconds she absorbed the grimness of her husband's expression, the angry glitter of his eyes in the half-light. "Who?"

With chilling abruptness he turned, seemed about to leave her standing there, but then he paused, and on a sharp release of breath shook his head. Suddenly, all that uncharacteristic fury was gone, and in its place was sadness and perplexity, and a deep, loving compassion which in that moment was as unwelcome as his jealousy.

"So you haven't noticed," he said softly, "I didn't think you had. I've been trying to tell you for weeks, trying to find the right words."

"Which of them?" But there was no real need to ask. With his wide range of interests and string of friends, Robin hardly had time to eat these days, much less to fall in love. Anyway, she thought, he was far too young. But so was Liam. Perhaps he did admire Georgina—she was, after all, an admirable young woman—but it was no more than that. Could not be more than that.

"I suppose you mean Liam?" she said derisively.

"I do indeed." Before she could interrupt, however, he went on quickly. "Puppy love it may be, I don't dispute that—nor am I suggesting for a moment that Georgina's encouraged him. She's probably not aware of it. But she does like him, Louisa—and he's flattered by that. What young man wouldn't be? So, he imagines himself in love. Spends his time daydreaming about her instead of getting on with his work. He never was the most diligent apprentice," Edward added with bitter humor, "but recently his concentration has been nonexistent."

A tight band seemed to be squeezing Louisa's heart. Liam

in love at eighteen? The idea was ludicrous. And with *Robert's daughter*? It was unthinkable. "What nonsense!" she exclaimed. "I've never heard anything so silly in my life."

"There's nothing silly about it. Tragic, yes—especially if he should try to show how he feels."

That was too much. "He *wouldn't*!"

"But he's young, Louisa—he *might*."

"*She* wouldn't—"

"No, I'm sure she wouldn't. But," he added heavily, "the situation mustn't be allowed to get that far."

In the gathering darkness Louisa paced up and down, six paces along the path, six paces back, arms folded and hugged into her body as though holding a grievous hurt. "You're making something out of nothing," she accused, her voice harsh with pain, "finding reasons to stop Georgina from seeing us. Liam isn't in love with her at all—he's just unhappy in the business. He's not cut out for that kind of work—have you considered that?"

"He was happy enough in the beginning," Edward said defensively. "I gave him every opportunity to choose what he would do."

"He didn't know what he wanted to do—you talked him into it."

Desperately hurt by that, Edward was nevertheless aware that she was steering him away from the heart of the problem. Having comfortably avoided the subject for years, now when danger threatened, she was ill prepared to face it. In many ways, Edward reflected, he was just as much to blame; but with Robert Duncannon apparently content to let them be, it had been difficult to press Louisa into action. The time had never seemed right. Now, however, some kind of action was essential. And if she could not be persuaded that truth was the only armor, then he would have to defend his family with the only weapons at his disposal.

"I think you must explain to Georgina that her frequent visits are not desirable. And you must tell her why. She knows the situation—she wouldn't wish to hurt us further."

"But, Edward—"

"And as for her *father*," he stated grimly, "I'll not have him over my doorstep, Louisa. You're *my* wife, and the cottage is *my* home—I won't countenance his presence again."

Burning beneath that implied mistrust, she asked scathingly, "After all these years, do you trust me so little?"

Angrily, he turned on her. "I don't trust *him*. But even if I did, I still wouldn't want him in my house. Not now—not after all this time. His presence gives rise to too much speculation—and people have long memories. Do you want the gossip to start again?"

She did not reply to that, but he could see resentment in her stance, in the outward thrust of her chin. She did not want to believe him, did not want to accept that what he said might be true. Searching for something to convince her, he recalled a painful moment from the turmoil of impressions which had attacked that afternoon. Watching young Robin with Robert Duncannon, their heads together over that borrowed camera, Edward had been stricken by a marked similarity of height and posture and coloring, and the almost mirror image of their profiles. Georgina, he was sure, had also noticed the resemblance. How long before someone else remarked on it?

Louisa's anger and frustration burned for most of the following day, taking her through a vicious attack on the kitchen cupboards and a later assault on weeds in the vegetable plot. By late afternoon, however, her fury was spent, and although she wept a few tears over an old photograph kept with her private things, she was sensible enough to admit that Edward was right. Washed and changed into a clean cotton dress, she felt better, more able to think. With the dangers so evident, it seemed sensible to point them out to Robert; and if anyone was to do that, it must be herself, not Edward. That was the easiest part. She had learned to live without Robert long ago, and despite the excitement of seeing him yesterday, Louisa was well aware of the trouble another visit could cause.

Having made that decision, and forgiven Edward for his jealousy, her doubts and heart searchings were largely reserved for his other suspicions. She could not believe that Liam entertained anything more than a brotherly affection for Georgina and, until she was convinced of it, would do nothing to hurt the girl. Because she would be hurt by such action as Edward proposed, of that Louisa had no doubt. In seeking to protect his own, Edward's loyalties were clearly marked, while hers were sometimes confused, particularly with regard to Robert and his family. Guilt came into it as well as love. The three years she had spent in Dublin before her marriage cast long shadows, and having loved Georgina as a child, she could not forget the pain of parting, or the fact that Robert had similarly abandoned his daughter immediately afterward. With his regiment safe in Ireland, there had been no need for him to volunteer for the Sudan; even now, she could not view that war as anything more than an excuse for his leaving.

Although she had seen the girl rarely over the succeeding years, Louisa felt she knew her better than Robert, and she treasured this new, adult friendship, finding a sympathy and understanding which was sadly lacking in her relationship with Tisha. Her own daughter, Louisa reflected unhappily, was a chip off another block, reminding her of her sister Blanche, and her mother's sister, Elizabeth. How odd it was, she often thought, that Edward should love Tisha so blindly, seeing few of the shortcomings which in those other women had grieved him so much.

That particular bias never failed to be baffling. Georgina's choice of vocation, however, was not. Unlike Letty and Robert, she could quite understand why the girl had decided to become a nurse, and why she had chosen that most difficult aspect, the nursing of the mentally ill. That passionate concern for life's unfortunates had been instilled by Letty, although the older woman could never see it, and from there it was no more than a step to Charlotte Duncannon, who had been strange when Robert married her and beyond redemption after Georgina's birth. Having always visited her mother, the girl was no stranger to madness, or its various treatments. It seemed logical to Louisa that being the person she was, Georgina Duncannon should feel the need to care for those who shared her mother's afflictions.

Nor did it surprise her that the daughter of a woman so irredeemably insane should have made a vow never to marry. That had come out during one long and very serious conversation, and she had asked Louisa not to repeat it. She was, she said, afraid of developing the same brand of insanity: Too little was known about heredity, and she would not wish to pass a similar affliction on to her children. Although Louisa understood and admired the sentiments involved, she did wonder whether that decision would hold if Georgina ever fell in love. From her own experience, Louisa knew how hard it was to stick to principle where passion was involved.

If the girl had gone to Dublin for the funeral, they would not see her again for a while. In the meantime she would drop a few questions subtly and watch Liam's reaction. The real test, however, would be to see them together. Armed with those warnings of Edward's, then she would know the truth of the situation.

Over the next few days, Liam fielded her questions admirably, but a slight heightening of color beneath his summer tan was revealing. Louisa began to think Edward might be right in his assumptions, and she was full of foreboding. Sensing it, trying to press a decision, at every opportunity Edward talked of nothing else. Those hushed whispers created a tension of their own.

With the extraordinary perception of those who hold a secret passion, Liam was alerted by his mother's inquiries, to the extent that he dared phrase no direct questions with regard to Georgina's continued absence. It also seemed to him that the tension at home was connected to his father's touchiness at work, and on pure instinct he attributed all of it to his unsuitable and unrequited love for Colonel Duncannon's daughter.

Unhappy, missing Georgina to distraction, Liam did try to submerge his anxieties in the work at hand, but his heart and mind were elsewhere, and his forgetfulness brought constant recriminations. At the end of ten days, convinced that something was wrong, he took to cycling past the Retreat each evening in the hopes of seeing her. By the third occasion, desperation had fueled enough courage for him to write a note in which he said he *must* see her and would wait for an hour in case she might be free, and again the following evening.

It was one thing to write the note, quite another to persuade the porter to pass it on. It was more than his job was worth, the man said, to pass *billy-doos* to the nurses. Liam's offer of a tip would persuade him only to leave the note on the board by the nurses' quarters, where Miss Duncannon might find it in the morning; he would do no more.

Liam had to be content with that. Disconsolate, he went home, but when he returned just before seven the following evening, Georgina was already watching from a high point within the grounds that overlooked the road. He caught the movement of something white beneath the overhanging trees, looked up, and realized Georgina was signaling to him. A moment later she came out of the drive on a bicycle and, with barely a glance in his direction, started pedaling away toward the village of Heslington. Bemused for a moment, he simply stood with his bike by the roadside, but as she disappeared beyond the crest of the hill, he remounted and went after her through golden light and lengthening shadows. Not too quickly, however. He had sense enough to keep some distance between them until they were clear of the village.

She cycled with confidence, quickly gaining speed, so he had no difficulty in following at what was for him a natural pace. With the last house behind him, he pressed a little harder, intending to overtake her; but as the gap between them shortened, Liam found himself fascinated by the shape of her back, her narrow waist, and flaring, womanly hips. In a simple straw hat and white blouse, she sat forward on her seat, navy skirt pulled tight under a neat, provocative bottom, while her thighs moved rhythmically with the pedals. He was unable to tear his eyes away.

A moment later, his thoughts were shaming him; with an effort he forced his eyes upward and himself to overtake. It was none too soon. Rounding the next bend she slowed, stopping as he drew level. Flushed with exercise and agitation, he thought she looked more beautiful than ever; but her words were sharp and very concise, telling him he must *not* pester the porter with notes, nor must he make demands to see her unless it was a matter of life or death. She would be in serious trouble, she said, if anyone suspected her of meeting young men outside the hospital gates.

Crushed by the tone of that reproof, stunned by its unexpectedness, for a moment Liam stared in disbelief. Then he turned his bicycle, intending to ride away. He was stopped by the pressure of her hand on his arm.

Struggling to regain her breath and composure, Georgina apologized. "I'm sorry—that wasn't fair. It must be something vital, of course it must, and you weren't to know the rules." She sighed, studying his averted face, then tugged gently at his sleeve. "Come on—we'll park the bikes out of sight and walk a little way. I've got an hour or so before I go on duty."

There was a dry, rutted cart track just a few yards up the road, leading between fields of ripening wheat. Dog rose and honeysuckle threaded the hedge, while tall spikes of foxglove pierced the shadows beneath. Along the border of the field a few early poppies reared silken scarlet heads. The air was full of mingling scents of earth and grass and flowers, and in the low evening sunlight all was somnolent and still. As they walked, Liam's tension began to ease, but his first words to her came out badly.

"Where have you *been*? It's been so long since your last visit, I thought there must be something wrong."

It was clear she was surprised by his vehemence. "Didn't your mother tell you I was going to Dublin? She knew, I'm sure she did."

"Nobody tells me anything," he said bitterly. "But why Dublin? I think you might have *said*, since you knew you were going!" Georgina stopped at that, her frown deepening, and Liam realized the mistake in showing his anguish. "I thought we were friends," he finished lamely.

"We are friends," she said quietly. "And it's obvious I owe you an apology, Liam. At the time, it wasn't something I felt I could talk about—and I just assumed it would have been explained later after we'd gone."

For a while they walked on in silence, and Liam waited with some impatience for her explanation. When it came, in short, wrung-out sentences, he was at first incredulous and then ashamed. He could only imagine her loss in terms of losing his own mother, and that she should have bottled up her grief to the extent she had was astounding. That he had taken her to the fair that day, and had absolutely no idea of the news her father had come to impart, was also rather hurtful. He wished she could have confided in him and said so.

"Just then, Liam, it was too painful—and there wasn't time."

Her voice was firm, but he was beginning to know her, to realize the hidden depths. That reassessment was difficult for him. Six years his senior, Georgina had seemed mature and somehow invulnerable; he had talked to her, confided in her, trusted her with his problems, and listened to her advice. For the first time he was forced to see her as a suffering human being with problems far greater than his own, forced to place himself in the role of comforter, which was new to him and awkward.

Imagining his own mother incarcerated for fifteen years in a mental hospital, Liam winced; it was hard to grasp the other concept, that Georgina had never known Charlotte Duncannon as a mother in the true sense, yet he felt the tragedy of never knowing warmth and comfort as a child. He declared, with some feeling, that it must have been worse than being an orphan.

"Yes," she said thoughtfully, "I suppose it was. Of course, we visited, my aunt and I, over the years . . . but I doubt she knew me."

"But that's terrible . . ."

"It certainly wasn't easy." Locked into her own thoughts, memories of a past that did not include him, Georgina stared unseeing over the still, golden fields while he ached for her, wishing he could know her feelings, experience her emotions. The gap of inches which separated them as they walked might well have been miles. Liam was painfully conscious of all that divided them: age and gender, circumstances and experience. He had long been convinced that to kiss her would be to transform everything, that joined in a passionate yet tender embrace he would absorb all that she was, just as she would know him, feel as he felt, love as he loved.

The sheer impossibility of it made him sigh.

Georgina turned to him and smiled and, with a touch that was all too brief, pressed his hand. "Oh, Liam! I didn't mean to make you sad too. Let's change this awful subject, and talk about you instead. What have *you* been doing while I've been away?"

With a short laugh, he shook his head. "Nothing of any moment. In more trouble than ever with my father, I'm afraid."

"Oh, I'm sorry to hear that. What's wrong this time?"

"Nothing specific. It's just his attitude." He laughed again.

"I can't seem to do anything right, and yet when I try to tackle him about the accounts and keeping them up to date—which he's terrible at, he leaves things outstanding for *months*—he tells me not to be clever and to mind my own business!"

"Oh dear."

"I don't know why it is, Georgina, but I can't talk to him anymore. We used to get on so well, but recently, all he does is *bite*. To hear him talk, I'm no good at the job, I'm mean to Tisha, I don't help in the garden anymore, and I go out too much. But if I stay in," Liam added bitterly, "he accuses me of reading too much and going to bed too late. But Robin comes and goes as he pleases, and never a word to him. And as for Tisha—well, she might not get away with much when Mother's there, but she winds Dad around her little finger. She can do no wrong, while I can do no right!"

"And it's not fair," Georgina chided with gentle humor.

He grimaced at that. "No, it *isn't*, and it's driving me mad. I don't know what to do. Maybe I'm not as good at the job as I should be—and I must admit I find it tedious at times. I didn't think I would, but I do. And I must admit I hate being inside all the time. That's why I go out in the evenings—I need the fresh air."

"Have you tried talking to him—outside work, I mean?"

"No, but I don't think I could at the moment."

She tried suggesting that Louisa's help might be the sort to enlist, but he explained his mother had also been peculiar with him recently, and the atmosphere at home was taut in the extreme. "I mean, she didn't even see fit to tell me that your mother had died!"

After that, they were both silent for a while, each considering possible motives. A grassy bank by a gap in the hedge looked too inviting to ignore. Liam flopped down dejectedly, chewing a piece of grass, while Georgina stood looking down at him, deep in contemplation. Youth was so terribly painful, she thought, remembering her own, and harder still when things were never explained, when you had to struggle alone in the dark. A wave of love and compassion swept over her, and she wished he was still a little child to be fussed and petted and coaxed back to smiles. Instead he was tall and broad-shouldered and self-consciously tragic, sprawled there on the grass: handsome enough to break a young girl's heart. How easy he would be to fall in love with, she thought, envying the girls he might choose. With his straightness and honesty, he would never betray, never abandon the ones he loved. Thinking of the honesty he deserved, she longed to tell him why things were as they were at home, but the secret was not hers to divulge, and the pain of keeping silent was bitter indeed.

"So," she said firmly, sitting down beside him, "what *would* you do, given a totally free rein?"

For a moment he glanced up, startled by that abrupt change of subject. Then a smile began to play at the corner of his mouth, and throwing away that chewed piece of grass, he rolled over onto his stomach. With his face in shadow, he said, "A totally free rein? No ties, no apprenticeship?"

"No ties," she stressed, wondering why it was so important, and why she should wait with baited breath for his reply.

"If I had money as well, I'd travel the world," he said softly, aware that with this confession he was trusting her with his most cherished dreams. "Travel until I got tired and found a place to settle. And then I'd write about it." He glanced at her again, half afraid she might be laughing; but she was gazing intently into his face, willing him to go on. Suddenly smiling, he said, "But if I hadn't any money—which I haven't—I'd simply go abroad to work. Canada, Australia, America—somewhere new and untouched. Farming probably, but it wouldn't really matter."

"And then you'd write?"

"Eventually. When I'd lived a little, had something to write about."

Stunned by the simplicity of it, by its very obviousness, Georgina wondered why no one had thought to ask him before. He was a young man who loved the outdoors, not the sort to welcome being cooped up in a small, airless space, making books for other people to read, ledgers for other people to enter columns of tiny figures. Writing books, yes, she could see that, eventually. Writing about adventures and foreign lands he might have had a hand in conquering. With all the undercurrents at home, especially now her father was taking such belated interest, Liam would be better away from it.

"Why don't you?" she asked with breathless intensity, but even as the words left her lips, she thought how much she would miss him.

"How can I?" Liam whispered, aware he could never leave without knowing her fully, never say good-bye until she knew him too.

"But you *can!*"

He looked away, hurt that she did not understand. "I have my apprenticeship to finish," he said abruptly, gathering himself together. "Perhaps after that . . ."

He stood up. She looked at her watch, realizing simultaneously that she had failed him in some way, also that she had to go. The sun dipped below the horizon as they returned down the rutted track, and the golden light was gone, the land a uniform shade of gray.

8

As he had to be in Ireland for his wife's funeral, Robert's superior at the War Office had asked whether he would mind staying on an extra few days to attend to some official business. Knowing that it would save another journey immediately afterward, Robert agreed, but not without some degree of concern for his daughter. She had borne up well during the small, private ceremony that accompanied her mother's interment, but, as he had expected, she was exhausted by the whole affair. He hated having to let her make the long journey back to York alone.

The War Office business kept him in Dublin for several days. Several days in which he was forced to listen to his sister Letty's catalogue of anxieties regarding her niece, also her admonitions on his role as her father. With his conscience suitably nagged into life, on his return he wrote to Georgina, but her reply was not as reassuring as Letty would have liked. Even to him the letter seemed flat and depressed, leaving much apparently unsaid. With a couple of days at his disposal, Robert decided to pay her another visit. The decision cheered him, especially when it came to him that if he timed it carefully, he might also spend an hour or so with Louisa.

A telephone call to the Retreat's superintendent established his daughter's free time and a suitable appointment. The
following morning he took a cab to King's Cross and caught
the express for York. Depositing his bags at the Royal Station
Hotel, Robert was immediately reminded of other visits in other
years, particularly that summer of 1899, when Kruger's antics
in the Transvaal had kept everyone in suspense. Knowing what
was coming, seeing too the sheer impossibility of family life,
Robert in that year had finally relinquished his ties with Louisa.
It was what she had wanted for a long time, but it had taken a
war to make him see the sense of it. Even so, it had not been
easy.

As he approached the riverside with its unchanging vistas,
the flourishing trees, and soft, sandy path, he remembered all
the old passions, and the jealousy that had made it so hard to
accept her marriage to Edward. Even now he found it difficult
to believe that Louisa had really preferred a quiet life with
Edward to the heady emotion she had shared with him. Their
relationship had been passionate, perhaps too much so, heaven
and hell at times; but recalling the sparks that had flashed
between them so recently, Robert knew that the magic was still
alive, stirring the embers of that old affair.

There had never been anyone to match Louisa, and the
thing was, he was still inordinately fond of her. He always had
been despite the other women, the years abroad, the stupid
things he had said and done. She was a loving and lovable
woman and he still wanted her, that was the hell of it.

With the cottage in sight, a frisson of nervous anticipation
made him pause. Screened by trees and the lie of the land, it
stood no more than a few hundred yards from busy riverside
wharves and the spread of new housing off Bishopthorpe Road,
yet in the nearby meadows cows munched contentedly, giving
an illusion of deepest countryside. It was peaceful and perfect.
On the river a couple of barges were idling their way downstream, and in Louisa's front garden the subdued buzz of bees
foraging among the flowers was almost the only sound.

Outside the gate, in dappled shade, Robert noticed a
wooden board, listing various fruits and vegetables—*all fresh
from the garden*—and their respective prices. His euphoria suffered considerable evaporation as he realized that the afternoon

might not be as uninterrupted as he had envisaged. With a sigh he pushed open the newly painted gate, hoping his walk would merit a cool drink and a shady seat if nothing else. A light tap on the front door produced no answer. At the back of the house the kitchen door stood open, but there was no sign of life inside, and even the garden seemed deserted. A moment later, however, with her sleeves pushed back and wearing a sunbonnet, Louisa emerged from behind that screen of glorious pink roses, bearing a gardening basket full of lettuce and soft fruit.

He felt his breath catch. Seeing her like that, he was instantly transported back twenty years, to an afternoon when they had walked across broad meadows, she in a pretty cotton dress and flapping sunbonnet, he minus jacket and tie, to that wood outside Blankney. And there, under an oak wreathed about with mistletoe, they had made love for the very first time . . .

The memory was so clear it was almost painful, and although she was older now, she was as graceful as ever. And just as desirable. Meeting his gaze she paused, pushing back a few stray tendrils of hair which had escaped the loose chignon beneath her bonnet. As a young woman, he recalled, she had worn her hair cropped short like a boy's, a mark of independence that in those days had suited her very well. Now, however, he preferred the softer image.

As the fact of his presence sank in, Louisa's expression hovered between pleasure and dismay. It settled, ultimately, into a wry smile. Her step was resolute as she approached, as though she had decided to make the best of things. It was not an encouraging beginning, he thought, and as he kissed her cheek, it seemed to Robert that her eyes weighed him rather too well.

"You shouldn't be here," she said. "Although, having said that, now you are here, I have to admit I'm pleased to see you."

"You don't sound it," he said with light reproof.

"Perhaps *pleased* is the wrong word," she observed cryptically. "*Thankful* would be nearer the mark."

He started to follow her inside, but she stopped him with a firm hand. "Edward said—after your last visit—that he wouldn't have you across his doorstep again. And you can't blame him for that. So don't make me lie to him. Stay there," she added, "and I'll fetch you something to drink."

She came out a few minutes later with a tray of glasses and a jug of lemonade, setting it down on a stool before the long garden seat. "I said I'd write to you and explain the situation," Louisa began, "but since then something else has been worrying me. Something you should know about since it concerns Georgina."

Sighing heavily, she glanced up at him, and he saw anxiety and apprehension lurking there. Then, quite unexpectedly, she slipped a brown, work-roughened hand into his. Robert was far from sure whether she was seeking comfort or giving it.

"I should have written," she murmured huskily, "but I've been putting it off, simply because it would have been so hard to express in a letter. So, although Edward will be furious if he knows you've been here again, I'm very glad to see you." Her eyes met his and pleaded with him. "We have to talk—and very seriously—about our children."

At the age of fourteen, Edward had begun his working life in Fossgate, apprenticed to a firm of printers and bookbinders. He had stayed with the same firm for twenty-five years before opening his own business in the maze of courts and alleys which in those days constituted Piccadilly. Eight years later, in 1901, he had moved on, and the old premises had recently disappeared under a new, broad thoroughfare constructed between Fishergate and Pavement. Walking down the new Piccadilly, Edward could no longer distinguish the place where his old business had been. It seemed very strange.

York was changing and growing, particularly outside the city wall. Much of the change was needed, but he found it hard to accept and even harder to like what he saw. It was, he suspected, a symptom of age. He was growing old and becoming entrenched in his attitudes, finding safety in familiar things, resenting the turmoil brought about by progress. In the unchanging heart of the city, however, he could close his eyes to much of it. The area of Minster Gates, Stonegate, and its adjacent alleyway, Coffee Yard, was the traditional home of publishing in York, and although his premises were ancient and even less practical than the old ones in Piccadilly, it gave Edward a sense of satisfaction to know that writers, printers, and bookbinders had occupied the place for centuries before him.

Coffee Yard was, in reality, no more than a paved shortcut leading between tall medieval buildings, past a walled court-yard and beneath the upper floors of two timbered houses, emerging eventually into Grape Lane. Edward's premises were nearer Stonegate, traditionally narrow on the ground floor and opening out to more spacious rooms above. The huge oak beams and steep staircases, odd angles and unsquare walls, made the original moving of equipment something of a night-mare; but they were well settled now, with offices below and workrooms on the middle and upper floors. For light and size Edward's favorite was in the middle, where two massive Georgian windows had been installed at the beginning of the previous century. It had drawbacks, however: Freezing cold in winter, it needed a good fire in the hearth, while summer sun often made the heat unbearable.

Sighing as he returned from lunch and a visit to the bank, Edward stood for a moment in the cool alleyway, relishing the breeze and the shade. As his bank manager had suggested, it was probably an afternoon for contemplating the accounts, and at least his office on the ground floor was less hot than upstairs. It was irritating to remember that Liam had been badgering him about the accounts for weeks; in that respect at least the lad was more methodical, but Edward still wished he were a better bookbinder. It would come eventually, he supposed, and as apprentices went, Liam was not a bad one. But if only, Edward thought, he would stop making such careless mistakes! It was lack of application that afflicted him, not lack of ability, and his carelessness was increasing. It was all attributable to puppy love and the uneasy proximity of Georgina Duncannon, and the sooner Louisa saw that and took steps to get rid of her, the better.

In an irritable humor, Edward went inside. Among the clutter on his desk was the lunchtime mail.

In the rear ground-floor room, Liam was using the guillotine, cutting boards for a set of twelve books. Remembering an earlier mistake when he had cut a complete set fractionally short, he checked every one against a template. As the outside door banged and Edward went into his office, Liam marked the time with some resentment. An hour and a half for lunch, he thought bitterly, knowing anything over his own half hour would be an occasion for criticism. Wearing no more than a thick apron over his shirt and trousers, he was still sweating, his shirt damp with it despite its open neck and rolled-back sleeves. Wiping his forehead, Liam gathered the boards together and went back up the winding staircase to the next floor.

Heat, and the pungent, sickly smell of horse glue hit him as he entered the workroom. Angrily, he reached across a wide bench to force up the sash another two inches. With that sharp movement the cord snapped, bringing the lower window crashing down. He swore roundly, not caring whether his father heard him, and a moment later Edward's foot was on the stair.

Liam ground out an apology between gritted teeth. "It's so bloody hot in here, I was only trying to get a bit more air into the place! It's broken—I'm sorry."

But Edward's attention was not confined to the window. In his hand was an opened parcel. In an overly dramatic gesture, he peeled off the paper and flung it aside.

"What do you call this?" he demanded, holding out a large tome expensively bound in leather.

Recognizing it as one of a set he had been allowed to help with, Liam took it resentfully, wondering what minor blemish had been found. While Edward looked on, he turned it over and over, examining spine and engraving, the smooth gold edges of the paper.

"I can't see anything wrong with it."

"Open it!"

Liam did so and his heart sank. He had bound the book upside down.

The ensuing row was explosive, fueled by the heat and a score of festering resentments. For Edward, the book was the last straw in a pack of other stupid mistakes, while Liam, who had rarely answered back before, countered the charges of incompetence with a few of his own. He brought up the subject of the neglected accounts, telling his father that if he did not pay more attention to outstanding bills, bankruptcy would be the next step. Grossly insulted, Edward grabbed a heavy bookbinding manual and flung it into the boy's outstretched arms.

"And if you paid less attention to young women beyond your age and station," he snapped, "and more to your *work*, you might have a job to look forward to in ten years' time!"

Liam's heart seemed to halt in his breast. So I was right, he thought, they do know what I feel for Georgina. Nor do they like it. Hurt more by that shot than he had been by the others, Liam placed the manual carefully on the bench. Without a word he removed his glue-spotted apron and reached for his jacket and tie. Edward watched him, his expression sardonic.

"And where do you think you're going?"

"Does it matter?" Liam asked, fixing his collar.

"The work matters."

"Not to me. Not anymore." With that he clattered down the stairs and into the yard for his bike.

Short of a dignified answer, Edward could only bite his tongue and watch him go.

Smarting from that argument, yet curiously elated by his bravery in walking out, Liam cycled through town in the early afternoon heat, convinced he had done the right thing. If nothing else, it would show his father that he was not prepared to tolerate such constant, belittling criticism, that sharpness of manner which took no account of his efforts or abilities. Admittedly, he thought, that book was a stupid mistake, but it had been committed at the end of a long, hot day, and the thing *was* rectifiable.

No, it was more than that carelessness, more than all the other silly things he had done and forgotten to do, the whole list of which had been itemized for his benefit; it was all a matter of his affection for Georgina, that friendship which for him, at least, had grown into love. She was so far beyond his reach, he knew it could never come to anything, despite all his dreams and fantasies. He simply loved to be with her: Was that so very wrong? His parents' disapproval was incomprehensible yet very hurtful. It seemed to Liam that as they liked and admired Georgina, any fault must lie with himself. He was not good enough for her, which he was well aware of, but it might have been expected that his parents would think otherwise.

He decided to go home and have it out with his mother. Although he had not been in her good graces recently, she could usually be counted upon to see his point of view, and she was generally more forthright than his father. Whatever the outcome, Liam knew that the argument had brought something to a head. With regard to his immediate future at least. Perhaps he should go abroad, as Georgina suggested; it would be hard to leave, but with his leaving she might realize she loved him too and follow, eventually . . .

Still in the realms of fantasy, Liam cycled along the riverbank, glad of the shade provided by the trees. He dismounted at the gate, pushing it open fully, careful not to chip the new paint. In his eagerness to solve a problem, he abandoned his bike by the side wall and walked around on the grass. Within a couple of paces the sound of voices halted him. At first he thought his mother must be talking to a neighbor, someone buying fruit or flowers from the garden; then he heard his name mentioned, and a responding male voice which set every hackle bristling.

Not again! he thought angrily, picturing Colonel Duncannon flirting with his mother over tea on the lawn. The very idea made him want to rush around the corner and put a stop to it, but words penetrated his consciousness, freezing anger and action simultaneously, making him listen almost without breathing.

Entirely unaware of a listener only yards away, Robert and Louisa were speaking heatedly, possessed as much by old passions and grievances as by the immediate problem.

"I'll say it again, Louisa—this situation should never have been allowed to arise. She's their sister, for God's sake, and they should all have been told years ago."

"Half sister," Louisa repeated through gritted teeth, "and I'll thank you not to tell me what I *should* have done. The responsibility of bringing them up was left to me, while you gallivanted around the world playing soldier!"

"You left *me*, remember? To marry another man! I would never have abandoned you, Louisa, and you know that."

With a catch in her voice, Louisa said, "Why do you always go back to that? I married Edward because I loved him, because he needed me and we understood each other in ways you and I never did. It's been a good marriage, and he's been a good father to your children—far better than you ever were or will be!"

"This is getting us nowhere," Robert declared bitterly. "His virtues don't interest me. The point is it's time you stopped sticking your head in the sand, Louisa. Tell Liam the truth, for God's sake. Tell him straight—that he's *my* son and Georgina's his sister. She's always known—she doesn't need warning off!"

Stunned and disbelieving, shocked to the point where he thought he was going to be physically sick, for a moment Liam hunched himself against the wall. *He* was *Robert Duncannon's* son? Georgina, his *sister*? No, it couldn't be!

With his head spinning on those words, he stumbled away. Grabbing his bike for support, he crashed it through the gateway, mounted it with leaden limbs, and rode off downriver. Wobbling dangerously for the first few hundred yards, he fell off twice, eventually regained his balance, and peddled furiously the three or four miles to Bishopthorpe, as though speed could outdistance the pain. Just before the village, too violently distressed to face other human beings, Liam flung the bike aside, stripped off his clothes, and made a perfect dive into the river. He swam almost a mile upstream before exhaustion overtook him, then floated back, staring up at the wide blue sky, at trees dark in their midsummer leaf, and at the larks singing joyously above.

The physical world seemed possessed of a burning clarity, illogical and unreasonable against the appalling destruction of his life. The sun warmed his face, while his body, like his mind, was numb. For a while he imagined drowning, but knew he could not by act of will. It would have to be a cramp, or weeds dragging him under, and either was possible with the river so low and the water so cold. He passed the spot where he had left his clothes, and on the next curve there was the Archbishop's Palace, its graceful walls rising from the river, the mullioned windows glinting like eyes as he floated past. The current was strong there, and swimming back against it took tremendous effort. When he reached the place where he had dived in, it was all he could do to scramble out. Wet and shivering uncontrollably, he pulled on his pants and trousers, lying back like a dead man in the hot afternoon sun.

Grievously wounded but feeling no pain, Liam examined the shreds that were left. Strangely, in that moment, he doubted nothing of what he had heard. It all fitted too well. That extraordinary likeness between Robin and Robert Duncannon—even the names. His mother's reluctance to mention Mrs. Duncannon. Short tempers, jealousy, tension, he almost laughed when he thought of his own innocent, pathetic interpretation. He even felt a queer, detached pity for the man who had been his father. But Edward Elliott was his father no more, and it seemed his adored mother was no better than the women who flaunted themselves after dark on New Walk. No wonder she could flirt so brazenly with the colonel, Liam thought bitterly, he was her lover, the father of her children. The man who sat at the head of her table was simply someone she had married to cover her sin.

And Georgina Duncannon, the woman he had loved and dreamed of making his own, was as forbidden a fruit as ever came out of the Garden of Eden. She was his sister. Her father was his father, and Liam hated him.

After a little while he fell asleep, waking hours later to find that some kindly passerby had spread his shirt over his chest to protect him from the sun. Nevertheless, he was confused and shivering and his skin felt hot and tight. Dressing clumsily, his first thought was to get home for something to eat and drink, particularly to drink, since he had a raging thirst. Then he remembered and was violently sick.

What he had been able to contemplate with such icy calm after his swim was suddenly impossible to face without raging and cursing and weeping. For several minutes he did just that, then fatigue claimed him again and he dropped by the river's edge. He felt alone, bereft, as though his entire family had been wiped out by some freak accident, and like someone so tragically bereaved, could not believe it. Amid all that shock and pain, however, the thing to which he kept returning was Robert Duncannon's claim that Georgina was his sister and had always known it. If that was truth, then it turned his love for her into something abhorrent, perverted the time and attention she had bestowed into sadistic amusement, made him demand with silent, bitter repetition, why she could not have told him. Her knowledge, her silence, had made of him an ignorant, gullible fool. Had she pitied him, Liam wondered, or simply laughed at his obvious adoration? Either way it was insupportable and unforgivable, and he knew he would never be able to face her again.

But it could not be true, Liam thought, could *not* be true. If it was, then his whole life was a lie, without the smallest foundation. His parents had always insisted on honesty—how could people like that have built their lives on deceit? Perhaps he should go home and ask them. Perhaps he would find that it had all been a terrible nightmare: Robert Duncannon had never been to the cottage, his mother had never said those things, and all would be as it was before. But a low, evil voice in his mind kept reminding him that he *had* heard that angry exchange, and because of it nothing would ever be the same again.

Time passed, dusk became darkness, and still he sat there. Rinsing his face in the cool water, Liam's mind grasped at mental straws: perhaps they knew he was there and wanted only to shock him, to stop him from loving Georgina. Perhaps they were rehearsing lines from a play . . .

But *names* were mentioned, the voice replied, his name, her name, his father's name. No, not his father. His real father was Colonel Duncannon, the arrogant bastard, the charmer, ladies' man, the cavalry officer who thought himself so much better than Edward Elliott . . .

"The *bastard*," Liam whispered, repeating the word like an incantation as he dragged his bike out of the long grass. He used it all the way home. It was the only protection he had against the wall of pain that was crashing around him.

Before going up to bed, Louisa glanced yet again at the clock. It was almost eleven and Liam had been gone since two. Where on earth could he be at this time? Robin had been to the drill hall, and on his way home had questioned most of his acquaintances, but nobody had seen him, and Louisa's anxiety was rapidly turning to panic. At his desk, Edward was working, an excuse, she knew, for waiting up for Liam, even though he seemed convinced the boy was worrying them deliberately.

"He's paying me back," Edward had said several times that evening, "for telling him off this afternoon."

Arriving home just after six, he had been irritated to find Liam still missing and with justifiable anger had repeated the tale of what had passed between them in the workshop. "It won't do," he kept saying, "the boy must realize he cannot simply walk out, even though I am his father. He wouldn't get away with it anywhere else, and he must realize he can't get away with it now. I'm afraid there'll have to be some plain speaking when he does come home."

But while he went over the situation several times for her benefit, Louisa began to wonder whether Liam had already been home that afternoon. And if he had, what had he overheard? There had been a noise, enough to penetrate Robert's consciousness, enough to stop him in midsentence and make him look around the corner. They had gone together into the front garden, even glanced along the towpath, but apart from the gate standing open, there was no sign of anyone. At the time it had been disturbing, and inexplicable; shortly afterward, hardly on better terms, Robert had said he must go.

With awful dread that their mysterious eavesdropper might have been Liam, Louisa had tried to find a way of telling Edward, but he was more concerned about the boy's attitude and lack of discipline. She had been reluctant to provoke harsh words over Robert's illicit visit while her other son was in the house, but after Robin had gone out and before she could make her confession, Tisha arrived home with a girlfriend, and they had clung maddeningly to the garden, discussing the latest fashions and people at work in girlish, affected voices. Wishing them gone, Louisa was astonished to hear her garden being praised by the friend, and Tisha saying airily that yes, it was wonderful to have this touch of rural peace, that it was so much pleasanter than living in town. Ordinarily, Louisa would have smothered a laugh at such affected nonsense, but in that moment she could have smacked Tisha for her insincerity and that desire to impress. Usually, she was inordinately keen to keep her friends on *their* home ground, rather than her own.

The friend eventually went home, and Robin returned;

touchingly concerned about his brother, he had offered to go out again, but Liam could have gone in any direction, and Louisa was far from convinced he would return at all. Keeping her voice light, she had sent her younger son to bed half an hour ago but still had not broached the subject to Edward.

At her sigh, Edward turned. "Don't worry," he said gently, "he will be back. And even if he decides to stay out all night, he can't come to much harm. It's hardly the middle of winter."

Twisting a handkerchief between her fingers, Louisa shook her head. "It's not that." She took a deep breath. "Something else is worrying me. I think he might have come back this afternoon, when—"

The sound of footsteps coming up the path halted her in mid-sentence; she dashed into the kitchen while Edward slowly pushed back his chair.

She stood like someone frozen to the spot. As he strode quickly to her side, Edward immediately saw why. In the shadows cast by the room's single oil lamp, Liam stood against the closed door, his eyes glittering feverishly, his face suffused. At first Edward thought he was drunk, but then he moved, and in the light his brows and thick, tumbled hair gleamed in contrast to his sunburned skin.

Without uttering a word Liam went to the sink, turned on the tap, and cupped his hands beneath it, drinking like someone dying of thirst, splashing vast amounts of water over his face and neck. As though a spell had been broken, Louisa grabbed a pint pot from the shelf and, as she handed it to him, touched his head and neck. Her gentle fingers might have been those of a torturer: As he flinched away, Liam told her harshly to leave him alone.

"I won't hurt you," his mother protested, reaching out again, "I only want to feel if you have a temperature . . ."

"What if I have? It's no business of yours. Get away—don't touch me."

Gingerly dabbing his face with a towel, he backed out of reach. But he need not have bothered, Edward thought; holding the sink for support, Louisa was staring as though Liam had struck her physically. For a second Edward wanted to hit him, wanted to grab him by the collar and kick him up the stairs to bed. But the boy was obviously ill, his behavior so completely out of character that Edward knew he must be calmed, not provoked.

"If you're not feeling well, Liam," he said quietly, drawing out a couple of chairs, "why don't you sit down and tell us where you've been?" Ignoring him for the moment, he turned to Louisa and gently persuaded her into a chair. Drawing out another, Edward seated himself and repeated his suggestion.

"Obviously," he went on, "you've been in the sun all afternoon—not very wise, as I'm sure you'll agree. But that's the penalty you're paying for going off half-cocked. Next time, perhaps you'll remember it."

Dropping the towel, Liam started to laugh. It was a harsh, mirthless sound which seemed to hurt him even more than it hurt them to hear it. "Oh, I'm not likely to forget this afternoon," he said with bitter irony. "Rest assured, *Father*, I'll remember it to my dying day!"

"What do you mean?" Edward whispered, his heart plummeting in sudden fear. He glanced at Louisa, ashen-faced with shock, and knew, instantly, that something had occurred that afternoon which had nothing to do with that argument in Coffee Yard. "What does he mean?" he demanded of her, but with eyes only for Liam, she merely shook her head.

"Didn't you tell him?" Liam demanded. "Didn't you tell him who was here this afternoon and what you were discussing? Didn't you say you were talking about me and Georgina—and that he told you it was time you told the *truth*?"

By the ghastliness of their faces, Liam knew he had managed to stun them both, knew he had the upper hand for once, and the knowledge gave him a sense of tremendous power. Outside, the child that remained in him had quaked at the temerity of a frontal attack, but a lover's pain and a man's anger had smothered its mewing voice, and that sense of power killed it outright. He wanted to hurt them as much as he had been hurt and was prepared to give no quarter.

"Tell me," he asked conversationally of his mother, "has the colonel always been your lover, or did you give him up on your wedding day?"

"That's *enough*," Edward hissed, thrusting himself between the two and forcing Liam back. "This is your *mother*, for heaven's sake! Have you no respect?"

There were no denials, he noted. Something else in Liam died. Less than a foot from the man who had been his father, Liam drew himself up to his full height. He had the advantage of four or five inches. Looking down into Edward's face, noting its grayness, its anger and distress, Liam felt no pity at all.

"I have no respect," he declared implacably, "for either of you."

The older man seemed to shrink before his eyes. Sagging backward against the table, he slowly shook his head.

"Oh my God," he murmured under his breath, "what have we done?" Like someone in a dream, he turned to his wife. "Robert was here, then? Today? Why didn't you tell me?"

She answered faintly, "I don't know. I should have—I tried to . . ." With a great effort she rose to her feet, taking a step toward Liam, her hand extended like a beggar's. "I'm sorry," she cried as he jerked away. "Liam, love, I'm sorry! It wasn't intended—we didn't know you were there—I don't know what you heard, but—"

"Spare me your excuses! Try the *truth* for a change. *Why* didn't you tell me before? Why did you let me go on believing something that wasn't true?" His mother winced and he enjoyed it, letting his voice gather power as the words rushed out in a torrent. "Everything I believed in is lies—*everything*. There's nothing left—my life is destroyed. You've taken it all away and made a fool of me. I *loved* you—I loved my father, but he's not my father at all. I loved Georgina too—stupidly, ridiculously, hopelessly, but still I *loved* her.

"But I didn't know," he whispered, "I didn't *know* she was my sister . . ." There was a hard pain in his chest and in his throat, a pain that might have found ease in tears, but he forced it down, determined not to give way.

"She should never have come here," Edward murmured distractedly.

"So your lies could have gone unchallenged?"

"No—so your pain could have been avoided! That was all your mother ever wanted—to spare you and Robin and Tisha the agony of knowing you were the children of a man she could never marry!'

"Oh yes, I forgot," Liam said with something akin to a

sneer, "he was married, Mother, wasn't he? So you added the sin of adultery to that of fornication—and then married your cousin in an attempt to cover it up!" Hating her with intense hatred for being so much less than perfect, for destroying his image of her as a mother and as a woman, Liam never noticed the hand Edward raised against him. The fist which crashed into his jaw sent him staggering sideways, and as he flung out an arm to save himself, brought down a shelf full of crockery.

There was a second crash as Robin burst into the kitchen, sending the door juddering against its hinges, followed by a moment's horrified silence. As Liam gathered himself together, ready to strike back, Robin leapt forward, pinioning his arms, urging him to come away, not to make things worse. Sparing barely a glance for his anguished mother, or his father massaging painful knuckles, the younger boy dragged Liam out of the room.

Tisha was sitting halfway up the stairs, knees tucked beneath her chin, eyes huge in a pale, shocked face. She seemed to be staring at nothing, made no response to her brother's request, and, even as Robin brushed past, pulling Liam with him, did not move.

Gruffly, from the top of the stairs, he told her to go to bed; but for the moment he was more concerned with his brother who, on the point of collapse, was bleeding profusely from a cut lip. In their shared bedroom Robin poured water into a basin and silently bathed his brother's face. With very little assistance he stripped off Liam's clothes and made him lie down on the big bed they had shared since childhood. Although it was many years since they had wrapped their arms around each other in sleep, when Robin climbed in he curled around his older brother.

Tisha did not stir. She listened to her mother's sobs and her father's pleas, his bitter, anguished recriminations, which were directed as much against himself as anyone else. It was frightening to hear her calm, assured, beloved father so distressed, and awful to realize his vulnerability. She heard her mother crying over Liam, repeating his name like a litany; a chair scraped on the stone floor below, there was a scuffle of feet, a cry from her mother, and more muffled sobs. Tisha's heart hardened. Liam was her mother's favorite and always had been. She would grieve for him and less for Robin, but not at all for her daughter.

Robert Duncannon's name was repeated several times, and it slowly dawned on Tisha that the witty, handsome army officer she so admired was in fact her father. She realized too that Edward hated him. For the moment, however, that was less important than her need to be comforted. The secure world she so enjoyed kicking against was suddenly no more: She was suspended in a yawning, echoing void and nobody seemed aware of it. Obsessed with their own misery, her parents cared nothing for Tisha's, while Robin and Liam had each other and would not welcome her.

She heard Edward telling her mother to come to bed. With a cold hand around her heart, Tisha crept silently away.

Overtaken by exhaustion, neither Edward nor Louisa had the heart to face their children then. "Tomorrow," Edward said as he helped her to undress, "we must sort it out tomorrow. Things will seem different in the morning."

"Do you hate me?" she asked as they lay together between the linen sheets.

"How could I hate you," he whispered into the darkness, "when I've loved you from the moment you were born?" He drew her, unresisting, into his arms, wiping away the tears with gentle, loving hands. He kissed her forehead as she nestled against him, knowing, in spite of all that he had said, that Louisa needed him and always would. His bitterness and resentment were reserved for Robert Duncannon, not because of jealousy but because he had always known his capacity for destruction. And now those fears were realized.

Seeking words which would comfort her, Edward looked back over the years. Linked by the closeness of their blood relationship, the two lives seemed one. Brought up together in the same household, their ties had been those of brother and sister rather than of cousins; it was ironic, Edward thought, that those close links should have made his feelings for her seem so incestuous, to the extent that he had not declared himself, and subsequently lost her to Robert Duncannon. That was his biggest regret. And now the appalling irony was that

Liam should fall in love with Robert's daughter, not having known the incestuous nature of his feelings for her.

Sympathizing with the boy's pain, regretting the fury that had prompted him to strike out, nevertheless Edward had to admit to a certain sense of relief. Horrible though that scene had been, now at least things were out in the open. He would not have wished it so, and his regrets were legion when he thought of the past's lost opportunities, but always he had been bound by Louisa's desire for secrecy. Edward knew he should have overridden her, that things should never have been allowed to come to this pass, but they were, after all, Louisa's children, and he their father in name only. However, he had loved them as though they were his own and in retrospect was able to understand the tension which had made him so short-tempered in recent months: a need to speak to Liam, to tell him the truth, conflicting with his loyalty to Louisa.

He did not blame her for the afternoon's sequence of events, or if he did, he blamed himself in equal measure. Knowing the depth of her love for her eldest child, and understanding too her propensity for guilt, he was more deeply concerned for her than he was for the children. He felt for them, for Liam particularly. But they were young and had always been loved, and he was sure their hearts would mend. Where his wife was concerned, he was not so sure. In the old days, before they were married, she had suffered greatly. Edward did not want her to suffer like that again.

Tomorrow, he thought, when the sun was up, would be the time to gather themselves and talk honestly and openly about the past—his own as well as Louisa's—and then, hopefully, they could begin to discuss the future.

Liam awoke with a shaft of sunlight in his eyes, just after half past four. His head was throbbing and his mouth was sore, proving, if proof were needed, that yesterday's events were real. Wincing with pain and unbidden memory, he turned away from the light. On the pillow beside him, innocent in sleep, Robin's face was curiously unmarked by the grief which had broken in the hours of darkness. Although they were very different, and might not have chosen each other as friends, Liam was never more aware of the bonds that existed between them. But that was another pain he did not want to feel. For a moment he acknowledged the debt he owed to his brother. Without his intervention, Liam knew he might have done unforgivable, irretrievable damage. The grief they had shared afterward, the tortured questions he had answered, Liam thrust aside. He would not dwell on that, just as he would not think of yesterday.

With sleep, thank God, the torture had subsided, leaving him cold and empty and capable of thought. Now was the time to go, before claims were made upon him, before apologies and explanations and other people's pain could screw him down with guilt. Liam knew, as surely as the sun had risen and would duly set, that to be forced into Georgina's presence after this would be the most unbearable agony a man could imagine. He saw her eyes smiling at him, imagined her hair loose and tumbling about her face, thought of that supple, slender figure, and knew he would always want her. No matter who she was or what she was, however misplaced his heart, he would always, always love her. But he could not face her pity.

Trying not to wake his brother, Liam rolled out of bed and stifled a groan. He was hurting all over, his muscles aching, skin tender, head throbbing; dried blood had caked his lips together and left his mouth tasting foul. He felt physically and mentally unclean, and surveyed yesterday's stained and crumpled clothes with distaste. Opening a drawer with great care, he found two sets of clean linen and, taking his suit and a spare pair of trousers from the wardrobe, crept downstairs to the kitchen.

His ablutions complete, Liam stuffed the spare clothing into a knapsack together with his razor and a cake of soap. He added half a loaf of bread and some cheese, and slipped his post office savings book into an inner pocket. That, together with this week's unspent allowance, he hoped would pay for meals and a few days' cheap lodgings. He must trust to fortune for the rest. Knotting his tie, he slipped on his jacket and glanced in the mirror to give his hair a final brush. It was wet, but several shades lighter than his skin. Although his lower lip was bruised and swollen, the cut was much less noticeable. All in all, he thought dispassionately, he looked better than he felt, which as far as a prospective employer was concerned was all that mattered. He hoped his journey would pass without incident.

With his hand on the door, Liam remembered something; for a moment he wavered, but need won. He went to Robin's neat stack of photographs on the sideboard, flicked through them, and found a set of postcard-sized portraits of members of the family. They had been isolated and enlarged from the group photographs, and there were several of each. Just one, surely, would not be missed.

Guiltily, hearing a movement above, Liam pushed a portrait of Georgina between the pages of his savings book and rearranged the others into neatness. He hurried into the hall just as Robin came down the stairs. He was fully dressed.

Liam stood for a moment, saying nothing, then jerked his head. "If you want to talk," he murmured, "you'd better come outside."

They walked around the house on the grass, and opening the gate, Liam blessed the fact that he had cured its tortured squeak; it did not occur to him that had he left it alone, his mother and Robert Duncannon might have been warned of his approach and thus not blighted his hopes so abruptly.

Liam led the way to where he had left his bike the night before. Some instinct had made him hide it in the hedge rather than run the risk of having it taken from him and locked away. As he pulled it free of twigs and branches, Robin asked what his plans were.

"I'm leaving York, looking for another job, something entirely different. I'm not going to say what and where, because if you know, as I said last night, they'll worm it out of you and probably come looking. I don't want that. Not yet, anyway," he amended, seeing his brother's crestfallen glance. "Once I get a place, I'll be in touch."

"Why can't we go together?"

Liam looked up, taking in Robin's unruly dark hair, his thin, pale face. He was tougher than he looked, but still Liam knew his intention would not suit the younger boy, and he might well regret it, probably for the rest of his life. "Don't be stupid. You've got a good job, you'll do well at it. I don't think you'd care for what I intend to do."

"And what's that?"

"Ask no questions and you'll be told no lies."

Standing foursquare across the sandy path, Robin gave a snort of disgust. "Then you're as bad as they are."

"Shut up!" Liam hissed. "Do you want to wake the whole house?" He grasped the handlebar of his bike with purpose and told his brother to move. "Let me go before somebody comes out and tries to stop me."

"I shall leave anyway," Robin announced stubbornly. "I was thinking about it last night. I'm going to join up."

"Well, that's a bloody stupid thing to do. You'll get nowhere in the army."

"It'll get me away from here."

"Please yourself then," Liam muttered harshly. "Make your own mistakes, but you're not coming with me."

Pressing forward on the pedals, he edged his brother out of the way. "Say good-bye to Tisha for me." He turned again and paused. "Tell her—tell her I'm sorry, won't you?"

"What for?"

"I don't know. Everything, I suppose."

"What if I see Georgie?"

"Nothing," Liam whispered, turning away. "Nothing at all."

Out there on the towpath, neither of them noticed the face at the window of their bedroom. A pair of blue eyes, fringed with dark lashes, watched their good-byes with a mixture of envy and pain. Tisha had lain awake all night, listening to whispered words and the creaks of the old house. She had waited in vain for someone to come and comfort her. Nobody had come, not even her father, whose favorite she had always been. But he was not her father anymore, so maybe that explained it. She saw her younger brother watching as Liam rode away and was relieved that he was not going too. As Robin came into the house she went back to her own room, determined to pretend to be asleep. Pride would not let her admit to anyone that she had suffered from their neglect.

In warm, early-morning sun, Liam rode past empty cattle pens outside the Walmgate walls, and by the massive barbican turned right on to the broad highroad which led across the East Riding and ultimately to the busy port of Kingston-upon-Hull.

By the side of the road, a scuffed and worn mounting block announced a distance of thirty-seven miles. A long way, but if he were lucky, Liam thought, pushing his hat firmly onto his head, he would reach the port before the sun touched the meridian. A sudden sense of his momentous decision made him turn and look back. The old walled city of his birth was beginning to stir to yet another day; it did not seem the slightest bit dismayed by his defection.

White limestone defenses gleamed in the sun, and the Minster's towers soared into the blue; nearby stood Coffee Yard, and strangely, at the thought of it, Liam could have wept for all that he was leaving behind. But York was part of the past, and for him the past must be a closed book. It was time to press on toward the rest of his life. There would be a berth, no doubt, on some tramp steamer shipping out of Hull; he could work his passage to somewhere. Destinations, at the moment, were irrelevant.

9

*T*he daffodils were almost gone, and what remained of them was being whipped and flattened by the wind. As they left the station Stephen grabbed Zoe to prevent her from being blown into the road. Large drops of rain hit the backs of her legs with the force of pennies. She was glad Stephen had brought the car.

The telephone was ringing as they entered the flat. Dropping her case at the top of the stairs, he hurried to answer it. At a more leisurely pace Zoe followed, tactfully going into the kitchen to make coffee for them both. It was impossible, however, not to catch something of the conversation, and she wondered who on earth it could be on the other end of the line. Stephen's replies were curt, his voice so deep with disapproval, she was afraid it must be his ex-wife.

"Well, it's bloody short notice," he said at last, "but I'll see what I can do . . . Yes, I'll make it somehow, but give me an hour to sort things out . . . You'll phone me back? Good." The sharp release of his breath as he replaced the receiver was eloquent; the single expletive which followed, more so.

At sight of his face, Zoe braced herself, but before she could ask, he took her into his arms, holding her tight and very close.

When he released her, there was a difference in him which she noticed at once. He reminded her of the Stephen she had known that first day: holding himself back, setting deliberate distance between them.

"I'm sorry, love. It seems you've had a wasted journey."

"Nonsense," she said bravely, aware of a hollowness inside. "I'm here and I'm with you—that's not wasted." He lit a cigarette, lost in thought; she was forced to ask for an explanation.

With an abrupt gesture, he apologized. "Sorry—thought you'd gathered it. That was the company. They want me back, tonight preferably. Teesport—Middlesborough. It's a bugger of a place to get to—it'll have to be a taxi."

"*Tonight?*" She was astonished and highly indignant. "But surely they can't do this? Your leave's not up for—how long did you say?—another two weeks?"

Stephen leaned back against the breakfast bar, regarding her steadily, one eyebrow raised in that familiar, slightly ironic way he had. "Believe me, Zoe, shipping companies can do what they like. They're a law unto themselves."

"But why the short notice? Surely they knew the ship was coming in?"

"They did, but the Old Man's not due off for another month. He was thrown across the wheelhouse last night and broke his leg. Heavy weather, and the ship's in ballast—no cargo. She was rolling like a pig apparently."

"Oh."

"Yes, *oh*." Stephen leaned across her to look out of the window. Trees by the Minster were still tossing like cotton candy. Musing on that, he looked worried. "If it continues like this, they'll never get her in tonight. I'll have to keep in touch with the agent . . ."

While Stephen telephoned for a taxi to pick him up at midnight, Zoe inspected fridge and freezer for something with which to make a meal. He had planned to take her out to their favorite restaurant, but with so much to do, there would not be time. He was dialing another number as she defrosted a couple of thick chops and, by the time that call was over, had baked potatoes in the microwave and was preparing a salad. Not very original, she thought, but quick and nourishing; and

with six hours to go, some instinct told her it was better to
eat now, before anguish took hold and appetites disappeared
completely. Hers, if not Stephen's. He was used to this, while
she was not. For the moment, however, she was feeling astonishingly calm and capable.

"There is one blessing to all this," he announced, stealing
a stick of celery. "I don't know if you recall him saying, when
we were up there last weekend, but Mac's joining as Chief."

"Is he?" she asked with genuine pleasure, having an instant picture of the burly Chief Engineer with his big red beard
and beaming smile. MacDonald Petersen's mother had been a
Scot, his father a Norwegian seaman; they had married in Newcastle before the war, and Mac had been brought up in South
Shields. Now, he and his wife, Irene, had a house in Alnwick,
with a view of the river and the castle. Zoe and Stephen had
recently spent two days with them, and Zoe had fallen in love
with the Northumberland countryside.

The two men had sailed together often enough to become
more than "Board of Trade acquaintances," as Stephen put it,
but to sail together now was a rare and unexpected bonus.

"Fate takes a turn." Zoe smiled, kissing his cheek. "It
should be a good trip for you."

"Better than the last one, anyway. And this ship is relatively new, so we shouldn't have too many problems."

They both had cause later to remember those words.

"I expect Irene will be driving Mac down to Teesport," she
said casually, clearing their plates away. Nodding as he lit a
cigarette, Stephen was poring over a list of essentials. "Do you
think," she ventured slowly, "that I might come along too?"

His head came up sharply, his eyes narrowing through a
haze of blue smoke. "To the ship? I'd rather you didn't."

It was curtly said, and Zoe turned abruptly for the kitchen.
To cover her distress she turned on the radio, and as fate would
have it, the voice of Phil Collins filled the air, singing apt and
emotive lyrics from *Against All Odds*.

"Take a Look at Me Now" was a cry from the heart of a
man who had watched his wife walk away; after all she'd been
to him, after all they had shared, he was left with nothing more
than the memory of her face. The singer's impassioned pleading

for her to turn around, to see him as he really was, so echoed Zoe's feelings for Stephen that she could have cried out. Sloshing water into the sink she let emotion flow with it, hoping those words, that music, were saying as much to Stephen as to herself.

She whispered fiercely, echoing the lyrics as she clattered dishes on to the draining board, feeling the truth of every phrase. There *was* much that needed to be said, and a dozen reasons why he would do anything but listen; his going *would* leave an empty space and as for the odds against him coming back to her . . .

Stephen snapped the radio off. The silence, for a second, was tangible.

"*That*," he said roughly, "is why I've always said I won't have a woman standing on a godforsaken quayside, waving good-bye to me!"

He turned on his heel, slamming a door after him. But she could hear him in the bedroom, banging around as he threw things into his suitcase. Her own, she noticed, was still standing in the hall where it had been abandoned earlier. For a moment, she considered picking it up and heading straight back to London. After all, what was the point in staying? He was going away, and Zoe had a stomach-churning suspicion that six months was going to be a long time, and with no guarantee at the end of it that she would see him again. Or if she did, that he would want to resume their relationship.

If he had just said nothing at all, it would have been less hurtful, but Stephen had made it abundantly plain that he did not expect her to wait for him. She was young, he said, and had a lot of living to do; there was really no point in making commitments she was bound to regret later. It did not seem to matter that she was ready to make such a commitment; he did not want it, and that knowledge stopped the words on her tongue. He seemed to read her mind and, whenever sentiment threatened, managed to turn it aside as though he was determined, at all costs, to divert her.

It negated everything that had passed between them, left her doubting every instinct that said he did care, that these few weeks had been as important to him as they were to her. But the last few days alone, while Stephen helped his aunt move into her new flat, had given Zoe a chance to think. It seemed to her, in retrospect, that there had been a subtle change in him, and that it dated back to the first night of their arrival in London, to that scene with Clare and the mention of Philip Dent. Things were never so spontaneous again. It was as though the seed of doubt had crept in, perhaps reminding him of other hurts and the transitory nature of all his relationships; and whether or not he trusted Zoe was immaterial, the barriers were up and likely to remain so.

That he had to go away tonight was galling indeed. She had steeled herself to raise the matter this weekend, to override all his objections and say what was on her mind, and if necessary, to explain Philip Dent once and for all. She had been determined, too, to tell Stephen to stop treating her like a young and inexperienced girl, as though his extra decade and one failed marriage made him an expert on life and love. Perhaps she did have a lot to learn yet, but being the victim of divorce had given her a wisdom of her own; and she was not entirely green where men were concerned. She knew what she felt for Stephen, and his magnanimous gift of freedom was not one to treasure. Surely she had meant something to him, something more than just a pleasant interlude between voyages? And surely she deserved more than just a note of thanks and a quick farewell?

Those thoughts plagued her, so that when he did reappear, looking contrite, she could do no more than raise an abandoned glass of wine in mock salute.

"Cheers," she said sardonically. "Would you rather I left *now*, or do you want to kiss me good-bye first?"

"I don't want to kiss you good-bye at all," he muttered grimly, "because I don't want to bloody well go."

That was heartening, especially when he took her in his arms to prove it; but a moment later, with a brief apology, he said that the thought of going away always made him foul-tempered. It was like looking forward to a six-month prison sentence without privilege of visitors or time off for good behavior.

Despite the gallows humor, she could feel the tension in him, and the conflict; it seemed to Zoe that he could not make up his mind whether he wanted her there or wished her far away. But she wanted him. A kiss that might have developed along more interesting lines was interrupted by the telephone. He swore as he went to answer it. This time Zoe listened unashamedly. It was obviously some hard-pressed worker from the company's London office having to stay late that Friday night to clear things up. Stephen's replies were all in the affirmative this time, although he did express anxiety about the weather. As he listened he jotted down details and instructions. Repeating the agent's name, address, and telephone number, he assured his interrogator that he would meet the ship as soon as she came alongside.

When he came off the phone, he stood for a moment, lost in thought. Then, abruptly, he turned to Zoe. "Do you really want to come up to Teesport? I warn you, it could be a hanging-around-all-night job . . ."

She struggled for nonchalance. "Well, I did think it might be interesting," she remarked lightly. "My previous experience of ships has been limited to cross-Channel ferries."

For the first time that evening, he laughed, heartily, and that glimpse of strong white teeth against his tan made her want him all the more.

"I think you'll find a hundred-thousand-ton tanker somewhat different from a cross-Channel ferry!" He picked up the telephone. "I'll get on to the agent, then, and arrange a dock pass for you." Briefly, he grinned at her. "Can't have you being mistaken for a lady of the night, can we?"

There were other calls to make too. One to Joan, who was obviously being very understanding, and refusing to hold him up. She had a message for Zoe telling her to get in touch soon. Then a call to his sister, who was less understanding and seemed to want to talk for hours. Zoe began to think he would never be finished, and the hands of the clock seemed to be going around like a catherine wheel. The wind, however, was lessening. With a final call to the agent in Middlesbrough, who said conditions on the coast were looking hopeful, Stephen cleared the line and left the receiver off the hook.

With a sigh of immense weariness, he pulled Zoe to his side. "Let's go to bed."

He loved her tenderly, with a long, slow gentleness that

made her sad. Although she swore she would give in to neither tears nor entreaties, the effort required was almost beyond her.

Carefully applied makeup and a fluffy pink sweater gave an impression of cheerfulness afterward. Zoe was glad she had brought a pair of warm trousers and a padded ski jacket; in those she could not imagine being cold. Waiting for Stephen to shower and finish packing, at his suggestion she made sandwiches and a flask of coffee. Which would be welcome, he said, if they had a long wait on an exposed quayside.

He joined her in the sitting room, looking businesslike in a pale gray suit and tie. With his Burberry and a thick scarf over his arm, he peered down into Bedern, looking for the taxi. Zoe's eyes were on the Minster, hazy in the driving rain. Even in that weather, the chimney pots of Goodramgate stood out like theatrical silhouettes. She could not help wondering whether she would ever see this particular view again.

"Well," Stephen said, glancing at his watch, "it's midnight—I hope he's not going to be late."

Almost before his words were out, a pair of headlights arced around the tiny courtyard below; simultaneously, other lights were extinguished, and the Minster disappeared like the good fairy in a pantomime. This was a nightly occurrence, but Zoe had never seen it happen before; it seemed ominous and she shivered. Concerned with more immediate things, Stephen did not notice.

Once they were on the road, however, her spirits revived. It was a strange experience to be setting off at that time of night, when ordinary mortals were going to bed. The A19 was practically deserted, their driver silent in his desire to do his job and get back home again.

Speeding through a sleeping village, her hand enclosed in Stephen's, she suddenly thought of Liam; and in the next moment, curiously, Stephen mentioned the diary, which at the last moment he had slipped into his pocket. He said he would give it some attention while he was away, produce a typed-up version which he could then photocopy and send on to Zoe.

"It will give me something to do between ports," he said dryly. "Several weeks at sea without a break can be mindbending."

"Any idea where you'll be going from here?"

"Mediterranean, I think. But from there it could be any-where."

About to ask him for his address, Zoe bit the question back. He would probably give it to her of his own volition; if not, she would get it from Joan. Inhibited by the driver's presence, she thought it was better to stick to impersonal matters.

"How did Liam get to Australia? Is it mentioned in the diary?"

"Only the anniversary of his arrival date. January 1914. Poor sod—he didn't have much time there, did he? Eight months in Australia—then the war broke out and he was on his way back again."

"Would he have emigrated, do you think?"

"He might have," Stephen said dubiously, "but for that he'd have had to get parental permission. And I get the impres-sion—from one of those letters at least—that he left rather abruptly. No, I think he probably worked his passage."

"Could he do that?"

"Plenty did. In my time, too. Signed on as deckhand, look-ing for a bit of adventure, wanting to see the world, that sort of thing—then found it was a bloody sight tougher than they expected, or they met a girl in one of the ports, or simply thought Australia the land of golden opportunity—which it was. And in those days it was the easiest thing in the world to jump ship out there—if you kept your nose clean for a couple of years, you were all right, Blue, you could stay!" He chuckled, obviously thinking of his own days on the Australian coast. In the late sixties he had been a young cadet aboard refrigerated cargo ships, spending weeks in every port. Zoe had heard something of his early experiences, a seemingly endless round of parties and fishing trips, races back to the ship after being ashore all night, and one memorable occasion when it had sailed without them and they had had to take a train to the next port. But the work had been hard, voyages often lengthy, home leave negligible—and all for the princely sum of five pounds a week.

"When I was a lad," he said wistfully, "you'd see red ensigns by the score in every port of the world. And shipping companies were so desperate for men, just about anybody could get a job on a tramp ship—so long as they didn't want to go home for a couple of years!" He laughed. "But all that's finished, the Merchant Navy's finished. It's been dying quietly since the advent of the EEC, for all sorts of different reasons. Greed, selfishness, government inaction—you name it. And if it's not dead already, it's on its last gasp. Just pray there's never another Falklands, Zoe—because if there is, the government will be hard-pressed to find a fishing boat to supply the fleet!"

Resenting the fact that he had to go back to a job that was no longer what it had been, Stephen seemed to feel the need to talk it out of his system. Pressing his hand, Zoe let him carry on. She had heard the good side; now, when he was feeling low, she might hear the less attractive aspects, and know him better.

She heard tales of redundancies and enforced retirements; junior officers who were forced ashore in search of whatever other employment they could find; old-established shipping companies giving up general cargo in favor of container fleets, road haulage, even travel companies selling holidays in the sun. She heard of takeovers by foreign entrepreneurs, British crews ousted in favor of Hong Kong Chinese, Filipinos, even Koreans. And a few die-hard British companies who ceased to be ship owners in favor of being ship managers, managing for foreign flag consortia registered in the world's tax havens.

"They're no more than box numbers in places like the Bahamas and Hong Kong. They run ships registered in Liberia and Panama. And they employ people like me. I'm a mercenary these days," he added with a touch of defensive arrogance, "working for whoever pays best. And it's a buyer's market out there, Zoe, which is why I don't argue too strongly when I get phone calls like the one I had tonight.

"If I'd refused to go, they might have said okay and gone on to the next name on the list. They might have given me another call in a couple of months' time—but there again, they might not. I can't take that risk—not if I want to go on working for them."

"Is it so bad," she asked, "that you wouldn't get a job elsewhere?"

"Oh no—I'd find another job with another company, all right. But I doubt the pay would be as good. And from what I hear, the conditions could well be a bloody sight worse. At least

I know this bunch. They might be tough, but they're reasonably fair and not likely to go under."

There was tension in him, and an ambivalence Zoe found difficult to understand. She wanted to say, "If you hate it so much, why do you do it? Why not give up and find something else?" He had no dependents, and apart from his car, Stephen's tastes were not extravagant, his life-style modest without being miserly. She would not have said that money was particularly important to him, yet with regard to his job, it obviously was. A flash of insight made her suspect that it was part of the hate: If I have to do it, he might have said, I'll get the best rate there is.

But did he have to do it? She was back to her original question. Perhaps, beneath the resentment, love still existed, desire still burned, as in a failing marriage. The sea had been his first love, and more than that, his refuge; it must be hard to admit that the relationship was over. Stephen Elliott, Zoe began to realize, was a man who liked to succeed, and that might be a clue to his relationship with her. With one broken marriage behind him, he was not about to place himself in a position to lose again.

The road would not have been easy, she reflected, stealing a glance at that uncompromising profile, even if Stephen's career had kept him in York, but to have him regularly away, and for five or six months at a time, made it hard indeed. Surveying the boulders of his fixed ideas, the chasms of widely differing experience, for a moment Zoe was swamped by gloom. But then she comforted herself with the thought that she had always enjoyed a challenge, that her success so far had not been won without taking chances. To let him go without a fight would be foolish and could only confirm her as a weak-kneed woman; but to prove him wrong would be no easy task. Suddenly, however, Zoe wanted to do just that.

The broad acres of North Yorkshire became Cleveland, and from a raised section of motorway Zoe saw Teesport spread out before her like a glittering, spangled carpet. Black night, black sea, and as they drew closer, the man-made mystery of piers and refineries; shadows and shining steel, massive storage tanks bearing the legends of half a dozen oil companies; ships alongside, funnels lit up, decks that were pools of light. There was excitement here and an air of romance which defied the cold commercial heart of it. Merchant ships, by their very definition, Stephen might have said, were always commercial, yet Zoe could not have been more thoroughly besotted, had those prosaic, unlovely vessels been a group of clipper ships or four-masted schooners.

Where are they going? What oceans will they cross? What sights will they see? The questions, unuttered, filled her head, and the words of a psalm remembered from schooldays "They that go down to the sea in ships: and occupy their business in great waters: These men see the works of the Lord: and his wonders in the deep . . ."

This was Stephen's world, and with that first glance she both envied and pitied him, beginning to understand the feelings that drew him back to sea time after time. Like a lover to a fickle mistress, she thought, pressing his hand.

He slipped an arm around her shoulders, leaning across to peer out of the window, trying to get his bearings. There was a light in his eyes that spoke of a challenge accepted, a firmness of speech as he addressed the driver which held nothing of regret.

Although from its smokestack Stephen was able to identify the ship coming in, it took some time to find the entrance to the oil terminal. It was almost half past one when they arrived, with no sign of Mac and Irene. No sign, either, of the agent. The guard at the gate seemed to have little information, and restricted access meant that they could not go through to the berth without an official pass.

Ten minutes later the agent arrived, full of apologies, explaining that the ship was only just alongside, but his information was that they were having problems with the gangway, damaged in heavy weather the night before. With the right documentation and the taxi dismissed, the young man took them through the terminal in his car.

It was so huge, Zoe did not at first recognize it as a ship. It appeared, between two towering gantries, as a sheer black wall of steel some fifty or sixty feet in height. Straight-sided, when she had thought ships' hulls were curved, the foredeck bare like a barge, the after bridge and accommodation rising like a floodlit tower block, after-end, while the name, *Damaris*, and port of registry were emblazoned in huge white letters across the squared-off stern. Men were milling about on deck and quay, and it transpired that a temporary gangway would have to be rigged. While they were waiting for that, another car arrived, this time with Mac and Irene. They exchanged hugs and greetings, and after a rapid assessment of the situation, broke out the coffee and sandwiches. It was like a party, Zoe thought, in the dead of night, in the teeth of a chilling wind, with the biggest ship she had ever seen looming over them. It was so bizarre she could not help laughing, and her laughter infected Irene, until in the end even the men were dryly amused, shaking their heads and muttering that the performance was about par for the course.

"And anyway, whoever joined a ship during office hours?" Mac wanted to know.

But by quarter to three the gangway was rigged, Customs and Excise officers boarding first with the agent. Stephen hoisted his baggage and Mac did likewise, preparing to carry it up that steep and narrow wooden gangway. Zoe eyed the angle and the ropes with horror. It looked like a plank set against the north face of the Eiger. Fortunately, one of the Filipino crew descended halfway to take the luggage, and the two men returned to escort Zoe and Irene to the top.

"Just think," Irene gasped as she struggled to regain her breath, "we've got to go *down* that before long."

"I prefer not to think about it," Zoe replied with feeling. "I might be tempted to stow away instead!"

"Don't," Stephen warned, "else I'll clap you in irons, and feed you on bread and water!"

All jokes ended as they met the Mate. Zoe hung back while he and Stephen discussed the Captain; glancing down on to the quay, she saw an ambulance drawing in between the gantries. Inside the accommodation, they climbed several flights of stairs to reach the Master's cabin. She waited in the office with the agent and a customs officer as the Mate took Stephen into a bedroom. Through two open doors, she could just see the foot of a double bed and a man's legs, one of which was bound into a heavy splint.

"Bad business," the agent commented. "He was on the

bridge, apparently, and a sudden bad roll sent him flying across the wheelhouse. Smashed his leg against the radar."

Zoe winced. She noticed, suddenly, an object on the floor which looked like an instrument of medieval torture; the agent told her it was a stretcher, the type that enclosed a body from neck to foot. The Old Man, he said, would be manhandled off the ship in that. Thinking of that perilous gangway, Zoe did not envy the Captain at the mercy of whoever was carrying him down.

Two uniformed ambulance men arrived at the door and were shown through into the bedroom; two very slight crew members stood out in the alleyway, looking nervous. As well they might, Zoe thought, wondering whether they were the ones designated for the job of carrying the stretcher. Stephen appeared, carrying a sheaf of papers. He had a word with the customs officer and then turned to Zoe.

"I think you should make yourself scarce while they get him out of here. I'll take you to Mac's cabin—you can have a natter with Irene for a little while. I'll give you a shout when we're all clear."

Mac and the Chief Engineer were busy in the office, but the retiring chief greeted Zoe cheerfully and showed her into his dayroom, where Irene was flicking through a magazine, and told her to help herself to a drink. Irene was sipping a glass of cola.

"I'm driving," she explained, "but there's spirits by the bottle there. You have what you want."

Gratefully, Zoe helped herself to a large brandy. Despite the ski jacket, the cold had seeped into her bones, and there seemed to be no heating on the ship. The warming liquid stilled her shivering and dispelled the tiredness, but her conversation with Irene was interrupted by the sounds of unusual activity from the other end of the alleyway. There was a sudden shout, and both Mac and the Chief responded instantly. Hesitantly, the two women went to see what was wrong.

"We need a bit more muscle," Stephen was saying. The two ambulance men were kneeling by the stretcher, obviously unhappy with the situation. Mac was strong enough to oblige, and as though from nowhere another burly figure materialized, oil-streaked and boiler-suited, but with forearms like an Olympic weight lifter. With the stretcher between them they began the journey down those endless flights of steps, past at least half a dozen heavy fire doors, and to the deck. Kneeling up on the fitted couch beneath a large, square window, Irene watched their progress with baited breath. Beside her, Zoe could hardly bear to look. As the stretcher was lifted from the deck to the gangway, and over the side, she pictured that tremendous drop and felt sick. The little group slowly disappeared from sight and Irene turned away, her face blanched of color.

"I think I will have that drink, after all," she said shakily.

Stephen was standing at the top of the gangway, watching; there was tension in every muscle. Eventually, he relaxed and turned with a smile to the Mate standing by, and Zoe knew that they had handled the man on the stretcher without mishap.

"It's all right," she said, and the two women clasped hands in mutual relief.

Despite the chill of the night, Mac was sweating when he returned, his red beard glistening. He dismissed his wife's concern as unnecessary fuss, and pouring himself a beer, he returned to the office and that mound of paperwork.

Zoe's remark that there seemed an awful lot to do was greeted by laughter from Irene. "There is. It's like having a new head of department every five or six months—and only half a day for the handover. After that, they're on their own."

Zoe shook her head. "I couldn't cope—it would drive me crazy."

"Me too, but they seem to thrive on it . . ."

When Stephen reappeared he had changed into smart black trousers and a navy blue, military-style sweater. As though emphasizing his air of authority, the four gold stripes of his epaulets glinted in the light, and Zoe suddenly found herself thinking of Robert Duncannon, wedded far more securely to the army, it seemed, than he had been to any woman. The uniform might be different, she thought, but its effect was the same, completing the change in Stephen which had begun, she realized now, with that telephone call in York. He was colder, harder, detached by some invisible wall that she sensed but could not break, and although he was responding to people and situations with his usual wit and good humor, that ready smile—so genuine before—never quite reached his eyes.

She followed him back to the cabin with the word *Captain* over the door; the cabin that was now his. He closed the door between the office and dayroom, and for a moment leaned against it.

"And so it begins," he said laconically. "But I thought you might like to see what I'll be calling home for the next few months . . ."

There was an awkwardness between them and both were aware of it; but Zoe played her part and looked around, obligingly poking her head into the bedroom, which was beautifully fitted out, finished in teak like the dayroom, with cupboards everywhere and tasteful though unimaginative pictures on the walls. The dayroom even had potted plants growing in a window box.

"Like Captain Bligh," she said in a feeble attempt at a joke.

"Well, let's hope the Mate is no Mr. Christian."

In the ensuing silence, he looked out of the window. "It'll be getting light soon. Irene will want to be going. She said she'd give you a lift to the station."

He reached for her, held her in his arms, but Zoe could not respond. She felt sick and cold inside and was wishing she had not been so eager to come. It would have been better, surely, to have said good-bye in York; in this environment, of which he was so obviously a part, he was a stranger to her. When he had said once that she did not know him, Zoe had thought him callous, the words an excuse for setting distance between them; but now she saw the truth of the claim and wanted only to escape. The vow she had made in the car was folly in the extreme.

Turning away, Stephen wrote something quickly on a piece of paper. It was the ship's name and the company's London address. As he handed it to her, he said tersely, "This will always find me. Let me know how you get on with the letters."

"Yes, I will." Any pleasure she might have felt was neutralized by that request; and although he had given her permission to hold all those letters for as long as was necessary, Zoe wondered whether she really wanted to know what they contained. A catalogue of tragedy caused by at least one unresolved love affair, that was how they were beginning to strike her; and did she really need them to underscore her own particular misery?

IO

*T*he film Stephen had had developed and printed in La Coruña had produced two passable photographs of Zoe and one that was excellent. It had been taken beneath the archway where they had first met, first kissed, on a bright day with light reflecting into her face. Her hair was loose and soft, like a dark cloud about her head, her pale skin and clear gray eyes luminous in the surrounding shadows, and about her mouth a gentle half smile made her more tantalizing than ever. Sometime, Stephen promised himself, he would have the print enlarged and framed, but for the time being the photograph was displayed on a temporary, handmade mount on his bedside chest.

It had been another hot, breathless Mediterranean day, their third spent drifting off Greece, awaiting orders. Showering after an afternoon swim in the ship's tiny pool, Stephen changed into fresh white shorts and shirt and sat down to fasten a pair of sandals over bare brown feet. As always his eyes went to the photograph, and yet again he remembered his last sight of her, the brief wave before she stepped into Irene's car, the bright little smile that was so obviously forced. That determined bravery had touched him far more than tears ever could. By comparison he thought of Ruth, who had wept copiously every time he went away, wringing guilt out of him like blood. That was one of the reasons why he had not wanted Zoe to accompany him to Teesport. Dread, however, had been outweighed by the need to keep her with him to the last possible moment, that and a perverse desire to show off a little, to let her see something of what the job entailed. And in the seeing, perhaps she might understand for herself the impossibility of any lasting relationship. No matter how convinced he was of that fact, Stephen could not help lacerating himself with memory, could no more consign her photograph to the watery deep than he could cast himself overboard; he needed Zoe Clifford in the same way that he had once needed Ruth, and in itself that knowledge was a crippling thing.

He was thankful, however, that he had not given in to that sudden desire to say he loved her. At the time it had come unbidden, before he began to suspect the truth of it, and with such strength that even now he could recall the effort to contain those words. But he had been aware even then that the affair was more than purely physical.

As always, he told himself that it was unfair to impose a lifetime of separations upon a woman he loved, that promises which could not be kept should neither be made nor extracted, that he was being cruel to be ultimately kind. Somehow, though, those fine principles had an empty ring about them when he thought of Zoe, and he seemed to be thinking of her all the time, remembering things she had said and done, her sympathy and tenderness, and the ease he felt just being with her. Stephen had known he was going to miss her, but it was far worse than that: He wanted her so much that he ached with it. The job was usually an antidote to those feelings, sufficiently demanding in the first month to erase most memories of home; but this was a ship that behaved itself, the crew were competent and good-humored, his officers professional. Within days Stephen had come to grips with the paperwork, and things were ticking along with all the ease of a well-oiled machine; he hated himself for wishing problems, but he could have done with a few to take his mind off Zoe.

The nights were the worst. Although he had never been one for spending much time in the officers bar, he found himself

dropping in after dinner, ostensibly with the intention of getting to know them, but really to postpone the moment when
his cabin door was closed and he would be alone. Mac seemed
to suspect what was on his mind, but sensibly forbore to comment. And if he had, Stephen knew he could not have discussed the heart of the problem, the tormenting fear that Zoe
would meet someone else while he was away, someone
younger and more interesting, someone who was around for
365 days of the year.

During the day, he told himself not to be so paranoid, that
if she truly loved him she would be there, waiting, when he
returned; that she would always be there. He told himself that
it was for her sake that he had refused to impose the burden of
his feelings and steered her away from making a commitment
to him in return, but he knew very well that the reverse was
true. And he knew, too, in the dark hours of the night, that it
all went back to that old boyfriend of hers, a relationship that
she had never really explained and which had ended only a
matter of days before he and Zoe met. *Off with the old, and on
with the new*—was that how she operated? While the sun was
up, he did not think so, but shut in his cabin, with only books
and music for company, he thought of his ex-wife whom he
had trusted completely, and he was no longer so sure of Zoe.

She was young and beautiful and extremely talented; and
with such a solitary occupation, she needed a social life. He
could not imagine her being alone for very long. He wished,
however, that he could be more genuinely sanguine about that;
she would never know how much it had cost him to pretend.

Almost his only consolation was the fact that she was so
keen to go on with her research into those letters. It was a
reason for staying in touch, and although he would not admit
it to her, the progress of Zoe's life had become even more
important to him than the questions which brought them together. And he had the diary, which intrigued them both. They
had read parts of it together, but the writing was so tiny, and on
such thin paper, it was hard to grasp the sense of it immediately.
Well, he had promised to transcribe Liam's account of that terrible
year, and that was another reason for writing to Zoe.

Not that he had managed very well so far. A postcard from
Spain, which should have been a letter except that he was

hurting too much to do more than scribble a few innocuous lines; and since then he had wasted innumerable sheets of paper on which he had expressed, far too eloquently, his love and need of her. He thought the trick might be to forget himself—and Zoe too—by concentrating instead upon that point of mutual interest, the Elliotts. Then he could be as eloquent as he wanted to be without expressing personal feelings at all.

But even that had its problems. Halfway through that letter, Stephen found himself thinking of their separate reactions to those cold, brief certificates. The truth, still unproved, seemed more and more obvious: that the father of Louisa's children was Robert Duncannon, not Edward Elliott. Liam and Robin had been born in Dublin and like Tisha, both bore Duncannon as a middle name; and, at that time, Robert's regiment had been stationed in Dublin after a two-year sojourn in York. Edward, meanwhile, according to fresh examination of the street directories, was still conducting his business in York. All the pointers were there, even to the fact of Tisha's subsequent birth at the house on Gillygate. When she was born, Robert was serving in the Sudan; he had even been awarded a medal for bravery at the Battle of Omdurman in 1898. It was not until late the following year that Louisa had married Edward.

Zoe's sympathies were all with those two. She had Robert down for a careless seducer, ready to abandon his mistress for some convenient foreign war as soon as he grew tired of her. "After all," she had said pointedly, "they didn't know much about birth control in those days, did they?"

Rather guiltily, Stephen had felt obliged to leap to Robert Duncannon's defense. It struck him that Zoe was making an oblique reference to their own relationship, its parallels deviating only in that one respect; and, coming after a period of some strain, her comment had bitten deep. As Stephen said, the man was an army officer and he had his job to do, to which Zoe had countered, with the information gleaned from the Public Records Office, that Robert had gone to the Sudan on secondment to the Egyptian Cavalry. His own regiment had stayed in Dublin, and he had rejoined them with the rank of major just in time to earn more medals in South Africa. Presumably, *after* Louisa was safely married to Edward.

"We don't *know* that," Stephen had said, and he had gone

on to point out that Zoe was virtually accusing Louisa of using her cousin as a ticket to security and respectability.

"And if she did," came the sharp response, "who could blame her? In her circumstances, and with three children under five years old, I might have been tempted to do the same!"

That heated exchange, in retrospect, was revealing of both their characters. Nevertheless, he still sympathized with Robert Duncannon. Feeling as he did about Zoe, recalling the power of that initial attraction, Stephen could understand only too well what the man must have felt for Louisa Elliott. And then there was the other side of the coin: ambition. He knew a lot about that too, about the love of the job and the drive to succeed. Ruth had often accused him of having a split personality, of being one man at home and another at sea; well, Stephen reflected, perhaps Robert Duncannon had suffered a similar duality, unable to give up his army career no matter how much he loved Louisa.

He shook his head, slightly bemused by the power of those long-dead forebears. It seemed incredible that they should have, from the distance of the grave, the ability to intrude to such an extent. As though once thought of they began to live again, using the cognizance of their descendants to settle old scores. Or, he thought with progressive and startling insight, to resolve problems which had been outstanding for more than seventy years.

That idea, unwelcome and unnerving, sent a chill up his spine. "Come on, Elliott," he muttered to himself, "don't be ridiculous." Abandoning the letter, he went to have a beer with Mac.

The ship's rare, three-day pause was the chief topic of conversation over dinner in the saloon. In the glorious weather much maintenance had been done, to the imbalance of the overtime chart for the month, and hours of sleep and sunbathing had been indulged in; but it was unsettling not knowing where they were bound and for what cargo. It could, quite literally, have been anywhere in the world. Disliking idleness, Stephen was keen to get on with the job, whatever it might be; keen also to arrive at a port where mail might be delivered. Already he was wondering whether Zoe would have written, and if so, *what*.

An impromptu darts contest enlivened the evening, but with the approach of midnight Stephen left the bar to do his usual rounds before bed. In the dimly lit chart room the third Mate was writing up the logbook, while out on the bridgewing a watchman was looking for his relief at twelve. It was quiet and calm, the ship hardly moving at all. Satisfied that things were as they should be, Stephen left the darkened wheelhouse for the soft night outside.

It was warmer in the open air, and with the main engine shut down, very quiet. On an impulse, he climbed a ladder to the topmost deck above the bridge, breathing deeply, looking up at the dazzling array of stars, like a gem-studded net surrounding the earth. In those latitudes, with no evidence of human habitation to distract the eye, even the tiniest pinpricks of light were visible, from the fine dust of the distant nebulas to the glittering beauty of the nearer stars, like diamonds on black velvet. He picked out the constellation of Orion, the hunter, with Sirius, the Dog Star, close at his heels; Cassiopeia's Chair, and the Plow were far to the north. In England it would be eleven o'clock, on a clear night just dark enough to see the stars in open countryside, but with the lights of London to contend with . . .

He sighed. Did city dwellers ever really notice what was above them?

On thoughts of Zoe his mind drifted for a while again, not happily. Below him the watch changed, and all became silent once more. He felt terribly alone, not a new sensation by any means, but it was suddenly acute. Logically, Stephen was sure he had done the right thing, yet irrational regrets assailed him. Not for the first time, he envied men with faithful, loving wives, envied Mac and Irene their twenty years of married life, the trust which was palpable between them. He was aware that the failure of trust lay in himself, and he wished it could be otherwise, that he could somehow manage to overcome that one area of insecurity. From this distance it seemed a trivial thing, especially in comparison with his daily responsibilities at sea. If he were alone at home, here he was even more so, where the burden of all decisions lay ultimately with him. *Master under God* was how one Old Man had signed himself in Stephen's youth, and the ancient term, valid since the days of the first Elizabeth, had remained forever with him. Never truer than on a night like this, when a man could believe himself the only soul left alive on earth. The stars pressed closer, and it was like looking at the face of eternity.

Once, he had named half a dozen for Zoe, straight off without thinking—Aldebaran, Bellatrix, Betelgeuse, Rigel, Arcturus, and Alphecca—and she had been impressed by the knowledge which enabled him to guide a ship across the faceless oceans of the world. He smiled bitterly at the memory. All part of the job, and what were half a dozen stars among the thousands he could see, the innumerable millions beyond the reach of even the strongest telescope? Awe-inspiring and, without some form of faith, even frightening. Infinity, eternity, a man could go mad just trying to comprehend it. Yet the stars formed their unchanging patterns, the planets moved on their appointed courses, all ordained by a maker whose purpose would always be the profoundest mystery. The only way to retain sanity was to believe in that purpose, even while the ultimate aim remained forever out of sight.

Was there really such a thing as free will, he wondered, or was everything planned to the last detail? Was he destined to go on like this till death reached out and claimed him, or had he just been given his last remaining chance of happiness, and stupidly, ridiculously, turned it down?

If so, it was too late for regrets. With one last, long look at that dazzling array of stars, Stephen told himself that the course was set, the voyage, wherever it led, must be made.

Just before noon the next day a telex arrived. The ship was to proceed with all speed to the Soviet port Odessa for fuel oils. Immediately, Stephen collared the Second Mate, who was just about to go on watch, asking what charts they had for the Aegean Sea and particularly the Dardanelles, that narrow entrance into the Black Sea which had caused such problems for Churchill in the First World War.

On the bridge they checked the charts together. All the necessary ones were present but had not, unfortunately, been corrected for a long time. With a grin at the inches-high stack of Admiralty *Notices to Mariners*, Stephen remarked that the young man would have his work cut out over the next few days. Reaching for the first of them, the Second Mate agreed.

"I wouldn't care, sir," he added with a sigh, "but I've just corrected all the ones for North Africa. The Mate was laying me odds that was where we'd be going."

"Never can tell in this business."

He left him to it, but once the ship was again under way, Stephen returned to discuss courses and distances, and to work out an estimated time of arrival for transmitting to the company's London office and the charterers in Hong Kong. Poring over the various charts, noting the position of several islands which were familiar to him in a secondhand way through his sister's summer holidays, Stephen suddenly spotted the island of Lemnos. It was right at the top of a long chart, and not far from the Dardanelles.

Nor was it far from Gallipoli, the peninsula where the Australians had fought such terrible battles in 1915, and where Liam Elliott must have received his first baptism of fire. Stephen felt chill and grim looking at that long neck of land, wondering, as every one of those young men must have done, what on earth they were doing there when they had joined up to prevent the Kaiser's forces from overrunning Europe and, ultimately, their own mother country.

How the hell did you get involved, he silently asked of Liam, feeling with uncanny surety that soldiering never had been that young man's aim. Had he been caught up in a kind of war fever? Or simply swept along with the rest, a victim of the times in which he found himself? Robin, fully trained by August 1914, would no doubt, in his ignorance, have been excited by the thought of seeing some real action, as many were; while Robert Duncannon must have viewed it all with the caution of a seasoned campaigner. But Liam? Stephen shook his head.

After dinner that evening he refused Mac's offer of a drink in the bar, taking himself back to his cabin instead. With only a few days between here and Istanbul, where mail could be posted, it was time to add something to the typescript that he had promised to Zoe. But first, he thought, he would read a bit more of the diary. Although the year of writing was 1916, Liam had inserted details of important dates in the previous two years. Some were tersely revealing.

January 13, for instance. On that date Liam had recorded in that little black-bound book his arrival at Port Melbourne in 1914. Two days later he stated, *"Left the ship, walked inland."*

I I

*W*ith no specific plan or destination, Liam worked odd days here and there, listening as he went, following suggestions, weighed down by nothing heavier than the pack on his back and the need to eat at reasonable intervals.

Taken up as he was with each day's survival, the journey was too full of interest and incident for him to dwell much upon what had been left behind, and that meandering six-month voyage across the oceans of the world had set mental as well as physical distance between the unhappy boy and the rapidly maturing young man. Work he did in exchange for a few shillings or a meal, finding the food another pleasure, wholesome and plentiful, unlike the weevil-infested victuals aboard ship, or the strange dishes he had encountered in Greece and Lebanon and the Far East. At the height of the Australian summer it was hot and dry, but the outdoor life was clean, the stars making a canopy for a bed far preferable to the cramped and stinking quarters allocated to him in the ship's fo'c'sle. In the tropics water had been rationed, while in foul weather everything was wet, with no facilities for drying salt-encrusted clothes. The bos'n had been a tyrant, the old hands adept at passing all the worst jobs to the least-experienced deckhand, while his peers had found him uncongenial and subsequently left him alone. Nevertheless, Liam had found time to be thankful for quick wits and fingers which had learned to be deft in Edward's workshop. Ignorant to begin with, he had quickly learned the right ways of coiling a rope, holystoning a wooden deck, and chipping at rust. Physically, the most difficult task had been learning to handle the ship's wheel in heavy seas to keep her on the right course, but he had managed that eventually and had a steering certificate to prove it.

There were no certificates to illustrate the rest of his education, however—lessons which taught him to obey orders instantly, without question or complaint and in the worst of conditions, and most important of all, how to stand his ground with men older and more experienced than himself. It was a hard school and there was no escape: A man was confined between ports like a prisoner, forced to tolerate his companions and even form some kind of relationship with them. On occasion, his life might depend on it.

Seasick sometimes, heartsick always, he had been tempted to jump ship many times between Hull and Hong Kong, and only the whisper of Australia, like a ripple of excitement throughout the ship, stayed him. Even then, Liam did not leave at the first opportunity. Having learned the wisdom of consideration, he ignored Fremantle and Adelaide in favor of Melbourne. Escaping into a well-established city would make him less obvious, and the State of Victoria was apparently richer, the climate more congenial to Europeans.

He spent more than a month on the road, traveling first of all toward the northwest and Bendigo. In the thickly forested hills, however, work other than timber clearing was scarce. He moved east after that, laboring at the odd logging camp as he went, picking his way along tracks through magnificent forests of tall, straight eucalypti, their peculiar fragrance a source of constant pleasure. Shady glens full of tall tree ferns, small, whispering streams, and here and there a log cabin or weatherboarded bungalow with wide verandas would occasionally surprise him. The inhabitants were usually friendly and unafraid, finding small jobs for him to do or offering food and drink as a gesture of kindness. Although the people considered themselves British and spoke a rough approximation of his mother tongue, Liam was pleased to discover few other parallels. Like the untamed continent they inhabited, there seemed nothing small about the people he encountered. They had open faces and a relaxed way of moving, a confidence that was almost tangible. And in a land of immigrants strangers were accepted and questions not asked beyond casual inquiries as to where he was headed. Who he was, where he came from, what he had done before, seemed immaterial; no one asked and he never said. In all his time on the road it seemed that only the present and the immediate future were of any importance here. The past was irrelevant.

Out near Yarra Glen, he discovered that he had come in a wide circle around Melbourne, and that if he wanted work of any permanent nature it would have to be on the plains. Unwilling to move closer to the city, he headed south, found work for a few days on a large farm near Lilydale, then crossed another, smaller range of hills whose forests were just as beautiful but surprisingly more populated. Before, he had often walked for a full day without seeing another living soul; in these hills and gullies there were cabins and clearings every few miles. There was even a village with a railway station, a pretty little place hemmed in by flowering trees and giant ferns, but after the solitude of the forests, even Fern Tree Gully was too busy. He soon discovered why. From there it was almost possible to see Melbourne, some twenty miles away, and the Dandenong Ranges were the coolest place within easy reach of the city. In a broad arc between, however, well-watered by creeks which rose in those hills, lay some of the richest farmland in Australia. It was as good for garden produce as it was for grazing; and the railway link between Melbourne and the market town of Dandenong, some ten miles to the south, meant a quick and easy transfer of goods. Everyone he spoke to mentioned Dandenong, and although he was uncertain, a desire to settle for a while, plus a pressing need for money to replace boots and worn-out clothing, made Liam decide to try his luck there. There were many farms and enough local industry to ensure work for a while. If what he wanted proved elusive, he could always move on.

The town was well established, formed mainly around the crossing of the routes between Melbourne and the southeast and from the hills in the north to the coast. The former became a broad main street, shaded from the intense heat of midafternoon by immense red-barked gums, its buildings terminating in an open market area, while at the crossroads stood a very grand town hall, faced by shops and hotels designed to impress by their size and two-storied grandeur. To one who recalled the age and permanence of cities like York, however, Dandenong was no more than a small, brash child; but it was confident despite its rawness, and in his dusty, shabby state, Liam was not sure that he was equal to its demands.

It had been a dry, ten-mile hike from the hills, and he was most of all in need of a drink and a wash. Resting on his haunches with his back against a tree trunk, Liam spent a good while watching the comings and goings from various hostelries, and eventually chose not the smallest but the one whose customers were least concerned with their attire. That decision was confirmed by the approach of a farm laborer from the blacksmith's shop. In dusty moleskins and an open-necked shirt, the man had overseen the shoeing of two sturdy horses before casually taking his leave and crossing the road to the hotel. As he passed, he glanced at the figure beneath the tree and gave him a nod in greeting. A few minutes later, Liam slowly gathered his things together and followed. The man was at the bar, ordering a beer. Liam went through to the washroom, so thankful for the sight of water running from a tap that he dipped his head to drink even before washing his hands and face. In the cracked, fly-blown mirror his reflection was something of a surprise, the face much leaner and harder than he remembered, high cheekbones pared of flesh, jaw revealed as having a grim, determined set to it. His skin, now that it was free of dust, was a rich, golden brown, hardly the look of a recent arrival. That realization pleased him; even the dark gold stubble glinting along his jaw marked him out as a man, not a boy.

Feeling suddenly more confident, he raked the remains of a comb through thick, dusty hair, tucked in his shirt, and slapped a hand over corduroys that were tattered and frayed;

his boots were beyond hope. A moment later he was in the bar ordering a large beer with what little remained of his last day's pay. With luck, he reflected as the cool, bitter liquid slaked his throat, there would be enough to order a meal; if not, he must go hungry. Thirst, however, was not something he could ignore.

The man he had followed into the hotel was still leaning against the counter, having little to do, apparently, but take account of the small company gathered in the dark, bare room. Without bothering to disguise his curiosity, he watched Liam drink, smiling as he set the glass down.

"Looks as though you needed that."

"Been on the road," Liam admitted ruefully. "It's a dry walk from the hills."

"Thought I hadn't seen you around." He fished a squashed pack of cigarettes from his breast pocket and offered it to Liam. "Smoke?"

Trying to disguise the depth of his gratitude, Liam accepted; he had been without tobacco for days, and the beer had released afresh all his longings for a cigarette. Less openly than his companion, he indulged in a little observation himself. Close up, the man was younger than he had thought, late twenties perhaps, much shorter and stockier than Liam, with the walnut tan that goes with near-black hair and dark brown eyes. There was intelligence and good humor in the lines of his face, although Liam noted that the nose had been broken at some time and a deep scar bisected one eyebrow, lending his companion an eternally quizzical look. His expression seemed to be asking questions even when nothing was said, so that Liam eventually found himself talking, about his situation, his most recent travels, and the need for work.

For a moment the other man narrowed his eyes, and the glance that ran over Liam was surprisingly hard and shrewd. "Well," he announced, "I won't pretend you're in clover here, no matter what they told you up north. There's been a bit of a drought these last few months, as you must've noticed, and bosses are laying men off, not taking 'em on." He pursed his lips for a moment. "Still, it's not bothered us too much where we are, and we're a bit short-handed with the harvest coming on. The boss might be willing to take you on, but then again

he might not. It depends. Can't promise anything, but if you
want to come out with me, it's worth a try."

"What's he like?"

"All right, if you're straight. He's a Welshman, came out
here about thirty years back, with not much more than the
clothes he stood up in. He's done well though. His name's
Maddox." The young man grinned. "And mine's Hanley. Ned
Hanley. The old folks—my dad's folks, that is—came out from
Tyneside, way back. Where're you from?"

"Yorkshire."

"Good cricket team, that. You'll be right," he said with an
encouraging grin, and as though the matter had been already
decided, ordered two more beers.

He assumed Liam could ride, and that was a severe embarrassment, as Liam had had no experience with horses. In the
end they both walked, leading the freshly shod mares. It was
a long way, partly back along the road Liam had walked already, the distance a little over five miles.

It was beautiful country, gently rolling grassland interspersed with woody pockets and meandering lines of eucalypts
which followed various watercourses down from the hills. And
on the northern horizon they curved away, deep blue in the
falling light. Every so often there were strands of ghost gums,
trunks and branches white against dark foliage, bent and
twisted shapes reaching out like wraiths across the fields. There
was something beseeching about them, a strange, otherworldly
beauty that Liam felt he would have painted if only he knew
how. And then he thought of Georgina, and how well she could
have portrayed them, how much she would exclaim over this
strange land. A family of kangaroos, disturbed by their approach,
went leaping and bounding away. While Liam stopped to admire
them, Ned cursed his lack of a gun; they were pests, he said,
breaking fences, ruining crops, a nightmare for every farmer in
these parts, although they were slowly being driven out.

Their presence underscored the difference of this landscape, and yet with its lines of trees and well-defined fields,
the cattle grazing here and there and crops ripening into late-
summer gold, it was not entirely strange. It was a land being
tamed by Europeans, and to Liam's eyes it bore an unmistak-
ably English stamp. He was aware of feeling at ease and at

home. This was a place where he could settle, where he could learn to love the land; he was suddenly very eager to be accepted by Ned's boss.

A broad, five-barred gate with the name MADDOX painted across it marked the entrance to the Welshman's land. It was a spread of almost a thousand acres, Ned said, with various crops and a few acres of vegetables, but the main interest was beef cattle. Behind good fences which lined the red dirt drive, Liam saw some of the herd munching contentedly beneath the trees; in a paddock close to the house horses grazed, no thoroughbreds to be sure, but good, sturdy cobs suitable for hard work. Behind a colorful, fenced-off garden sat the house itself, long and low and functional, with deep verandas and a corrugated-iron roof. It was hardly a colonial mansion but it spoke of permanence and solid assets. Ewan Maddox was not a man struggling in the wilderness, he was well organized and here to stay. Liam admired that, knowing, as he weighed all before him, that he wanted the same for himself. One day.

But every man has to start somewhere, and Liam felt, waiting for Ned to find the farmer and explain his presence, that this was the first rung on his particular ladder. Anxiety gnawed at him. He wanted, with an urgency which astonished him, to be accepted here.

Ewan Griffith Maddox was short and heavily built, with thick, iron-gray hair and black eyes that missed nothing. He was also a man of few words, his questions limited to essentials. In return, Liam was as honest as he needed to be, saying he knew little of farming but was keen to learn, and without false modesty claimed to be a good worker. That much he was sure of. He gave his name, as he had done since leaving home, as Bill Elliott. The short, hard, masculine name appealed to him in his new persona, far preferable to the soft Irish diminutive which he had accepted but never understood until that last day. Liam was the name by which his family knew him; Liam resented the Irishness that came from Robert Duncannon, a man he would never acknowledge as his father; and no one else, he swore, would ever use that name again.

Knowing nothing of the young man's background, Ewan Maddox weighed him with shrewd eyes, assessing height and bones and the whipcord slenderness produced by too little of the right food in recent months. Gauging what he might become, the older man asked him to give a hand at shifting some sacks of grain in the barn. Liam performed the task with ease. Maddox told him he was hired on trial for a month.

Delighted, Liam stammered his thanks, but Maddox had turned away, while Ned simply winked his approval and told him to come across to the bunkhouse and settle in.

The men's quarters faced the back of the house, opposite kitchens and storehouses and the quarters where the female servants lived. Usually, Ned said, there were two, but one had recently run off with one of the hands, so if Liam wanted to stay, he advised him not to make eyes at the other girl.

"Mrs. Maddox has had enough of it." He grinned. "So we're all on a promise to keep ourselves to ourselves!" He went on to give a brief history of the family, explaining that the eldest son and daughter were both married and living elsewhere, the son managing his in-laws' farm for them. Another daughter Mary was a nurse at the big hospital in Melbourne, so they didn't see her too often, but she was a decent sort, not stand-offish at all; then there was a son at university, supposed to be studying agriculture, Ned said dryly, although when he was at home he spent most of his time out in the bush, looking at trees and collecting flowers.

"Never make a farmer, won't Lewis, no matter how hard the old man pushes him. He'd rather be a whatchamacallit—he did tell me the name, but I forget—somebody who studies plants, he said."

Liam grinned. "Botanist—was that it?"

"Yeah, that's the word." There was a spark of mockery in the other man's sudden amusement. "Don't tell me you've had an education?"

"Not really—I just read a lot."

"Well, you won't find many books around here—the most we get to see is the weekly paper."

"Never mind—I'll get by." Liam dumped his pack by the wooden bunk Ned indicated. Like the walls it was constructed of solid baulks of timber, roughly planed and pegged together; unlike most of the others it had no bedding, but Ned Hanley explained that Mrs. Maddox kept that sort of thing in the house. In a lean-to outside was a pump with an overhead shower, a

stone sink with a tap, and a couple of cubicles. Mrs. Maddox
saw to the laundry, but she expected the men to wash and
shave regularly.

"If you pass muster, you eat in the kitchen, like family—if
you don't, you eat on your own out here!"

It sounded fair enough to Liam. After weeks of living
rough, he could hardly wait to get under that shower.

It was good to be rid of dust and grime that had accumu-
lated despite his frequent ablutions in mountain creeks; better
still to don the clean if ill-fitting clothes Mrs. Maddox lent him
while his own were laundered. Refreshed and stimulated,
Liam's only problem after that was an empty, grumbling stomach. Shortly after seven, however, that too was taken care of.
In the cool of evening the farmer's wife doled out massive
platefuls of stew and dumplings and vegetables, followed by
hearty portions of fruit pie and cream. Liam ate till he thought
he would burst, grateful for every delicious mouthful. Mrs.
Maddox, he decided, was sharp but kind, as voluble as her
husband was silent, and still with the singsong accents of her
native Wales. With her prematurely white hair and long pointed
nose, she reminded him of a little Jack Russell, lots of bark and
a few nips to the ankles, but basically affectionate. He thought
he would like her, and his feeling that this was a good place to
be was quickly confirmed.

Until they had his measure, the other hands treated the
newcomer with a certain wariness, but in his months at sea
Liam had learned something of tact and diplomacy and the
value of a smile. He said little, kept his past to himself, and
worked hard.

Arriving just as the harvest was about to begin, he was
plunged immediately into an exhausting regime, up at dawn
to follow the reaping machine, stacking the sheaves into neat
pyramids, while the stubble stabbed at every exposed bit of
skin. It was hot, dusty, back-breaking work, yet he enjoyed it,
falling into bed just after dark to sleep the sleep of the just.
Over the harvest period there was little time for anything else;
Mrs. Maddox and Ella, the general help, milked the handful
of dairy cows and worked the kitchen garden, releasing Mr.
Maddox and all six hands to what was essential in the fields.
After the reaping came threshing and winnowing, gathering

oats and barley into sacks and the straw into barns for winter bedding. Hay, gathered well before Christmas, already stood in stacks beyond the yard. The work went on for weeks with hardly a break, but as soon as it began to slacken off, Ned grabbed Liam one morning and ushered him into one of the nearby paddocks for his first riding lesson. Daunted though he was, Liam was secretly elated; it had crossed his mind more than once that Ewan Maddox might have taken him on purely for the harvest and be thinking of some reason to dismiss him. If Ned had been told to teach him to ride, however, the farmer must be thinking of keeping him on.

Smiling as he hitched himself up onto the rails of the fence, Liam watched Ned saddle up. Having tightened the girths, he casually ran his hands down from withers to fetlocks, examining legs and hooves with an expert eye. Memory jerked then, like a sickening physical jolt, and Liam was suddenly a child again, small and suspicious and confused, watching another dark-haired man in boots and breeches perform a similar action.

Words rose from the past: "You don't know what to call me, do you, Liam?" and his mind clamped shut on the question, leaving him white-faced and trembling.

Mistaking the reason, Ned Hanley suddenly laughed, assuring the green newcomer that old Daisy was the dullest, quietest mare ever bred, guaranteed not to shy or rear, even in a thunderstorm. With an effort, that picture from childhood was thrust aside, and Liam managed to concentrate reasonably well on the lesson. Ned seemed pleased with his efforts, however, and before work each day that week the lessons continued. Within a couple of weeks he was pronounced capable of riding out alone, and to his great surprise, Liam found something immensely satisfying about being able to control an animal so much larger and stronger than himself. He discovered, after a while, that he had something of a way with horses and, as he graduated to more spirited mounts than Daisy, that he rode well. That his affinity might have been inherited from Robert Duncannon, who as a cavalry officer had lived and worked with horses all his life, was something Liam refused to consider, but that early, unconnected memory returned to plague him at odd moments. He felt like an amnesiac in possession of one solitary clue to his identity, except that it was an identity he did not want. Several times during that period, he dreamed of a large house with long windows which dwarfed him, and an intricate fanlight above a massive front door. Sometimes his mother was in the dream, weeping; at other times a pretty little girl with blonde ringlets and a blue dress. Both images were oddly disturbing, particularly as he had a strong conviction that the house was real and he should know it, but he could not remember where it was.

To drown those unbidden memories, to smother the questions before they arose, he drove himself to physical exhaustion. March was the season for plowing, and while he was still learning to handle horses in the shafts, he begged to be taught how to drive a plow. Little Nobby, who was the expert, tired of the game long before Liam; he wanted to lie on his bunk after a long day, he said, and teaching somebody was twice as hard as doing it yourself. So Liam practiced on his own with old Daisy, learning to laugh back at the audience which gathered on the rails to watch.

He ate well and mostly slept well, putting on weight and muscle despite the regime he set himself. When Mrs. Maddox remonstrated with him, he said he liked to keep busy, whereas in reality he was afraid to relax. He needed something with which to divert his mind when he did stop for the day, but having read every newspaper and farming journal in the bunk room, what he really longed for was a good book.

Although he liked Ned and found his company by far the most congenial, the other man's weak point was a lack of education and a tendency to mock it, which made inquiries about books difficult. He had never seen Ewan Maddox with anything other than a newspaper or a treatise on cattle, and his wife had no time to read and only listened to what her husband saw fit to relate. Liam's opportunity came at Easter, however, when their son Lewis returned for his vacation. Having expected a pale, bookish youth, Liam was surprised to come face-to-face with a dark, heavily built young man who might have been Ewan Maddox thirty years previously. A keen horseman, he rode out every day, and it was on one of his excursions looking for a particular strain of wattle that Liam's opportunity to speak arose. Polite questions led to a friendly exchange, in the course of which Liam found courage to speak up.

"What sort of books?"

"Well, anything, really—I just like to read."

Lewis Maddox considered. "The Mechanics Institute has a library—it's in the Town Hall. Open most evenings, I think, if you can manage to get down. But I've got all sorts in my room at home—if you're not particular, I'll pass a few your way. And my sister has plenty of novels—a few classics among the romances, I'm sure," he added with a short laugh. "Mary won't mind."

Liam was uncertain about that, but meeting Mary Maddox a few days later, he thought her brother might be right. She was a plain, practical young woman, sure of herself but by no means overbearing. She talked as easily to her father's hired hands as she did to the maid, Ella, seeming to regard all of them as a kind of extended family. Liam supposed that to her that was what they were: old Murphy had been with them since before she was born, and Arnie and Ella, who were brother and sister, had virtually been adopted by Mrs. Maddox after they were orphaned by a bushfire some ten years back. Bert and Ned were more recent, and Ned, although he had all the qualities of leadership required by a foreman, had only been at the Maddox place just over a year. Watching him keeping a covert eye on the daughter of the house, however, Liam wondered whether Ned's ambitions to own his own land someday did not center upon the sturdy, capable figure of Mary Maddox. But nothing was said, and Liam did not ask.

Easter Day dawned bright and clear, and under Mrs. Maddox's persuasion, they all set off in the open wagon for morning service at the Methodist church in Dandenong. It was a long time since Liam had been in any church, and although the service was strange to him with its lengthy prayers and unfamiliar hymns, he thought he preferred it to the set ritual of the Prayer Book. It seemed more sincere. Sitting there with his head bowed, pretending to add his own silent petitions to the words of the preacher, he found himself thinking about God, and wondering about his own faith. He *had* believed, once upon a time; since leaving home, however, he had not spared the Almighty much more than a passing curse. Admittedly, that had been when things seemed at their lowest, but even so, remembering he felt ashamed. Did he believe? He was not sure.

If there was a God, why did He allow such things to happen? He had been happy, and then—

On the trembling edge of pain, his mind winced away. It was better not to think about it, and he was happy enough now, so why bother about the past? Nothing could change it; it was best forgotten. Live for today, he thought, and if you can, work toward a better future. But where God came into that philosophy was something of a mystery.

It was on the way back that Mary Maddox brought up the matter of the books. "Lew says you could do with something to read. I'll sort out a few novels for you and let you have them before I go back to Melbourne."

Her directness threw him a little, forcing a stammer to his thanks.

"It's all right," she smiled. "I'm a keen reader myself."

He caught Ned's louring glance and for a moment regretted mentioning the subject to anyone. If Mary noticed it, she pretended not to, and a moment later was talking about organizing a picnic in the hills for the following day. It was a public holiday and likely to be one of the last fine days of autumn, and she was determined they should all make the best of it. Her father shook his head; he did not want to go trailing miles into the hills, to be faced by crowds of city dwellers. His wife nodded her agreement, but thought it a good idea for the younger ones.

"I'll fix some food for you, if you want to get yourselves off."

Liam glanced at Ned, who was being unusually reticent. Lewis chided him, saying that all he ever did was to go into town to drink in bars, and a day in the hills would be good for him. Ned's scowl deepened.

Lewis turned to the others. "Billy will come, I know—what about Arnie, and you, Bert?"

Arnie was keen, but Murphy and Bert and little Nobby all had things to do apparently. As though he was bestowing a favor, instead of the other way around, Ned eventually allowed himself to be persuaded. Mary teased him unmercifully, and for a while Liam thought he would back out, but on Monday morning after breakfast, he was ready and waiting.

In boots, culottes, and a trim, matching jacket, Mary looked most attractive, Liam thought; so, it seemed, did Ned, who contrived to keep his horse close to hers most of the way. He was wearing his smartest coat and breeches and riding one of Lewis's good hacks, while Archie had had to take the largest but least elegant farm cob. Lighter in weight, Liam had chosen the better-boned but more-spirited mount and was having difficulty keeping him to the rear. The gelding would much rather have been up front with the mares, but Liam had no intention of spoiling Ned's pitch with Mary; the matter of the books was bad enough. He was, however, glad that he had heeded Mrs. Maddox's warning about winter. Only the previous week he had invested in a warm tweed jacket and new moleskin trousers, comfortable enough for riding and ideal for the day. With their food split up in the saddlebags, they continued climbing toward the blue-misted hills.

As ever when he left the farm, Lewis was in his element, pointing out the forest's various species of shrubs and trees to Liam's willing ears, a dozen different eucalypts and as many acacias, from the massive black wattle at almost fifty feet, to the pretty, scented myrtle which grew no taller than a man. And all along the gullies, edging every meandering creek, were the tree ferns, their delicate fronds filtering the sunlight, making dappled patterns across the tracks. It was cool, green, and fresh, alive with the fluttering of bright cockatoos and tinkling bellbirds, and the sudden sharp patter of rain showers on shimmering leaves. And when the rain stopped, as it did within minutes, the aromatic scent of the gums permeated the air, delicate and invigorating, like new green wine.

Breathing appreciatively, Liam started to talk about his first weeks in Australia, the journey, the logging camps, how he had come to the Maddox farm. Although Lewis was fascinated by those experiences, it transpired that logging was an activity he deplored; the native Australian species, he declared with conviction, would soon be extinct unless it was stopped.

"And all that will be left," he added derisively, "will be the precious exotics imported by gardeners for their wealthy and ignorant clients!"

Casting his eyes over the dense woodland which surrounded them, knowing from experience how many thousands of acres there must be in this small area of Victoria, Liam could not repress a smile. It would take an army a lifetime to clear the Dandenongs, and hundreds of years to make the gums extinct throughout Australia. Meanwhile, in spite of Lewis's objections, they set out their picnic in a recent clearing near Belgrave. The severed trunks, he said, looked like amputated elephants' feet, and he would not eat his food among such carnage. They all laughed, but he took his share back into the forest, joining them only as the little party pressed on toward the settlement.

There were campers in tents, and slab-sided huts with bark roofs among more permanent dwellings, and across more than one clearing Liam spied more imposing mansions, but the little town was mainly constructed of weatherboard and corrugated iron beside tracks and roads which ran off into the trees. With the eagerness of a child, Arnie leapt at Mary's suggestion of taking a trip on the narrow-gauge railway which ran to Emerald and Gembrook; the horses were tethered in the shade, their fares paid, and they clambered aboard. Tiny carriages, open to the elements, rattled behind a miniature locomotive which chugged and skidded up seemingly impossible gradients and around tight, snaking bends. City folks, out to enjoy an unex- pectedly fine holiday weekend, exclaimed over unspoiled beauty and the quaintness of some of the dwellings beside the line, while Liam was more intrigued by the feats of engineering necessary to drive it through. Built to encourage settlement in the hills, it was certainly an attraction for people on holiday, especially in the height of summer when fruit growers sold their wares beside every station. He remembered seeing them, and the thronging crowds, on his way down to the plains. He remembered too how repugnant they had seemed to him after the solitude of forests farther north. That recollection made him ponder the truth of what Lewis Maddox had been saying about clearance and settlement. In fifty or a hundred years' time, how much of this unspoiled beauty would be left?

Conscious of the shortening afternoon, they traveled only as far as Emerald, returning by the next train. Even so, the sun was well down in the sky by the time they collected their horses, and it was necessary to make some speed through the darken- ing forests. Abandoning the scenic route on Ned's advice, they took the longer but safer road, arriving home just after dark. Mrs. Maddox was anxious enough to give them a scolding, but her daughter was unrepentant. She had had a wonderful day, she said, and in that, Liam knew, she spoke for them all.

Liam got his books. Mary's selection first, because she had to return to the hospital in Melbourne well before her brother's vacation was over. With her departure and the evidence of her gift on his shelf, Ned's comments became more than usually acidic. In stoic silence Liam ignored him, burying his head in a fat, well-read edition of Dickens's *Bleak House*. Before he had finished that, Lewis came over to the bunkhouse with a dozen or so others, covering a wide range of subjects from the flora and fauna of Australia to biographies of eminent explorers and empire builders. In a few weeks Liam had gone through the life of Captain James Cook, a Yorkshireman like himself, Southey's *Life of Nelson*, and a fairly recent assessment of the wool trade, with its opposite pole in Bradford. He remembered then that his mother's father had been a wool merchant, and that set off a stream of unwelcome associations; after that, glancing at the novels, he skipped *Wuthering Heights* and its companion volume, *Jane Eyre*, and settled for something less emotional.

What he could not avoid, however, were his own memories, which as the fine weather began to break, became increasingly more insistent. Watching bronze and yellow beech leaves scatter across Mrs. Maddox's garden, it came to him that in England it would be spring, and instead of fading marigolds and fuchsias, his mother's garden would be dancing with daffodils. He thought of that mass of golden flowers along the ramparts, and the Minster's towers gleaming against a bright blue sky, and felt an unexpected lump come to his throat. In that moment he would have given almost anything to see York again, to be able to walk beside its broad, slow-moving river and watch the barges unloading along the staithes. It was not that he wanted to leave Australia, Liam told himself, it was simply that he would have liked to reassure himself that York was still there, unchanged. From where he was, it might well have disappeared forever.

Moved by a sense of guilt, a few days later he sat down to write to his brother, fulfilling a promise made so long ago that it had been forgotten for months. The letter was not very long and said little about his journey out, concentrating instead upon his present good fortune and the excellence of his employers.

"I seem to have been accepted here," he added in closing, "and intend to stay for as long as they'll have me. I'm saving as much as I can, though, because I want a place of my own one day."

That was true. Except to the library, Liam did not often go into town, preferring to busy himself in the tack room, polishing saddles or repairing broken bits of harness. On one particularly cold, wet Saturday, however, when the others had gone off on their usual jaunt, he settled down on his bunk to read. Crossing the yard, Mrs. Maddox looked in with some surprise. It was far too cold, she said, to be sitting there; if he wanted to, he could come inside. In the warm kitchen, surrounded by the comforting smell of cakes and freshly baked bread, he was lulled into reverie by the murmur of women's voices. With a book open on his knee, staring into the fire, he was drifting pleasantly, at home in the cottage on a winter's afternoon, his mother rolling out pastry, her wedding ring clicking rhythmically against a hollow earthenware rolling pin.

Comfort and an awareness of affection enveloped him, he was warm and happy and there would be scones and homemade jam for tea. As his mother brushed past to check the oven, she ruffled his hair and told him to move, his long legs were in the way . . .

"Billy, will you move—I want to get to the fire."

Laughter brought him back with a start. Ella, the buxom girl who helped in the house, was nudging his feet; Mrs. Maddox was chuckling as she rolled fresh pastry. Panic-stricken for a moment, Liam stared from one to the other, feeling like a child among strangers whose mother had suddenly abandoned him. Like a child he wanted to cry, was horribly afraid that he might, and with his chest hard and tight with disappointment, left them abruptly.

He heard Ella's sudden "*Well!*" followed by a nervous giggle, and footsteps that halted as he slammed the door. Drenched by rain as he crossed the yard, Liam gave vent to tears he could not control, all the more violent because they had been restrained for so long. But before he had reached the shelter of the bunk room, grief had turned again to fury, to that same impotent rage which had so consumed him a year ago.

Regardless of wet clothes, he lay on his bed for a long time, staring at nothing, while the rain drummed with steady monotony on the corrugated roof. It grew dark, but no sense of urgency possessed him; Ned and the others would not be back much before midnight. Some time later he was startled when the door opened and a solitary figure entered, shrouded by a cape. A woman's voice uttered a muffled exclamation, set something down with a clatter and proceeded to light a lamp.

"Here," Mrs. Maddox announced. "It's some dinner I've brought you. Get it eaten now before Ewan catches me. I've tried to keep it warm, thinking you was coming in for it—"

He took the tray, for a moment too astonished even to thank her. She stood at the foot of his bunk in the long room, regarding him with tense concern. Liam could not meet that gaze. Mumbling his thanks, he began to eat, amazed at his own hunger.

"Homesick, are you? Only natural, you know—I was myself for a long time. But it catches you unexpected . . ." When he did not reply, she sighed with a touch of exasperation, just as his own mother did sometimes. With a sharp click of her tongue, Mrs. Maddox added, "Don't say much, do you? Might do some good if you did. Ah well, you know where I am if you want to talk—and it will go no further."

Liam believed her, but did not know what to say. "Thank you," was all he could manage. Ridiculously moved by her kindness, nevertheless he wished she would leave him alone. As though sensing it, she turned to go.

"Don't forget now."

He did not forget, but gratitude at that time seemed no more than an additional burden he could do without. A small part of him wanted to be mothered and comforted, but his own image of manhood mocked it. There was, too, the deeper fear of what he might say once he began to talk. Although embarrassment made him gruff with Mrs. Maddox for a while after that, she did not seem to notice and treated him no differently. He was, however, glad of the drier weather which kept all of them busy.

* * *

The *Dandenong Journal* came to them once a week, and Melbourne newspapers were brought whenever Lewis or his sister Mary came home. Toward the end of July, the rumors of impending war in Europe grew stronger, setting the whole area agog with excitement. It was all anyone talked about, and the eagerness to get into town to find out more was suddenly stronger than the allure of bars and female company. If Europe erupted, the consensus of opinion was that Britain would not stay out of it, and if Britain stepped in, then so would Australia. Older, and with two sons of fighting age, Ewan Maddox tried to quash the jingoism at his table, and his wife was openly anxious; but the men were obsessed by the topic and would not leave it alone.

Liam was surprised by the evidence of conflicting passions among men he thought he knew well. Old Murphy, whom he had imagined to be as Australian as the outback, gave vent to such invective against England that Liam was almost convinced his list of injustices were personal instead of two generations old. Ned, on the other hand, who could claim a similar inheritance through his Tyneside Irish grandparents, thought Murphy was a silly old fool and said so. Nursing his own secret connections with both England and her other island, Liam was too appalled by what was said to do other than listen in silence while the argument threatened to come to blows. Enraged by the three who were against him, Murphy suddenly forgot his age and would have taken them all on; he danced like a wizened old gnome while Arnie, whose strength was far greater than his intellect, held him back.

It seemed that only Arnie and Liam were neutral, the former because he did not understand what it was all about, and the latter because his own future was more important to him than somebody else's past.

There were plenty like him, but on his trips into town it seemed there was always a fight on somewhere, and it was not always a matter of national prejudice. The Irish, who were numerous and loved a good argument anyway, were the most noticeable; but there were also well-settled Englishmen who professed no love for the mother country which had either kicked them out or provided so little that they felt obliged to

leave. For them, Australia should stay out of the coming conflict. Their opinions were not popular with the overtly patriotic
youngsters who had been brought up on a scholastic diet of
Empire and militarism and absolute allegiance to the British
monarchy.

Liam tried very hard to stay out of it. If a direct opinion
was demanded, all he would say was that it would never come
to war, and they were all being premature. That did not endear
him and more often than not provoked a bit of sniping from
Ned, who accused him of being "bloody clever." When they
were on their own, however, he pressed Liam for an answer.

"So what if it *does* come to it, Billy, what will you do?"

"Look, leave me alone, will you?" Liam snapped back,
exasperated beyond endurance. "I've just bloody well got here,
for heaven's sake, I've no intentions of dashing back at the first
trumpet call!"

Ned was aghast. "Well, of all the—" He broke off, letting
whatever insult had sprung to mind die before it reached his
lips. "You want to be careful who you say that to, mate—them
as don't know you might get the wrong idea."

Liam dropped the harness he was working on and stood
up, his fists clenched. "All right, spit it out! You think because
I'm not waving a flag and backing you up, I'm some sort of
coward!"

"No! No, honest, I don't. But you being English and that,
I can't figure you out. I'd've thought you'd be dead keen!"

"Well, I'm not. For a start, I like it here. I came here to
settle, to make something of myself by my own efforts. I'm not
rushing to throw all that away. And another thing—I've got a
lot of respect for Ewan Maddox. He didn't have to take me on,
but he did, and he kept his word. How's he going to manage
if everybody takes off together? Have you thought of that?"

"Same as everybody else, I suppose."

"And what about *your* grand ideas?"

"They'll just have to wait," came the quick reply. "Do you
think I could sit here, stashing my pay every week while other
blokes go off to do the fighting? Not me, mate! Not me."

That stirred uncomfortable considerations. Lighting a cigarette, Liam went outside. He handed the pack to Ned, who lit
up with a certain grim satisfaction.

"I won't pretend I don't know what you mean," Liam said slowly. "I've got a young brother at home, who said he was going to join up . . ."

That night, remembering the last words they had exchanged on the towpath, he wondered where Robin was now and what he was doing. He thought of Georgina, too, resurrecting the photograph his brother had taken before that precious world fell apart. She was happy and smiling then: Did she smile like that now? He loved her still, knew with absolute certainty that he always would. With a whole year and thirteen thousand miles between them, his feelings for her had not altered one whit; he recalled little things she said, the times they had spent alone together. And it still hurt to look at her captured image.

Ned had no need to be jealous over Mary Maddox. Liam just wished he could tell him so.

A few days later, as he returned chilled and hungry from mending fences on the far border of the property, Mrs. Maddox called out from the kitchen that he had a letter waiting. Stupidly, having had Georgina on his mind for days, he hoped it might be from her, that she might have been given his address from Robin's letter and written something, *anything*, to suggest that she understood what had driven him away, missed him, might once have loved him too . . .

But the letter was from his brother, written from a town with a French name on the island of Jersey. Robin had indeed done as he had threatened that day and, having joined the 2nd Battalion, the Green Howards, was now quartered in the Channel Islands. And having a wonderful time, Liam thought as he read the first page, wondering also how much longer the holiday would last. According to Robin, army life was just the ticket, and he seemed as excited at the prospect of war as most of the youth in Dandenong. Liam shook his head.

But just as Liam had glossed over the agonies of his trip out to Australia, so did his brother skip the immediate aftermath of Liam's departure, except to say that everyone had been upset, their mother especially. He went on to say that Edward had resisted the idea of Robin joining up, right to the moment he went, although his mother had reluctantly given her assent, and that was all he needed.

The next few paragraphs aroused fury, however; Robin

had apparently had an interview with Robert Duncannon in York, and although he had proudly resisted the Colonel's offer of help, it seemed he had in some way fallen under his spell. As he rapidly scanned the following pages, Liam cursed his brother for being a trusting, gullible child. Incredulous at first, he read to the end, then read it again, slowly, anger mounting with every sentence.

> . . . He's not nearly so bad as you make him out, and was most concerned about you. We talked, man to man, which I thought very decent, considering his position. He told me quite frankly that he had wanted to marry Mother more than anything else in the world, but he couldn't, because he was married already. Georgina's mother was ill when he married her, a sort of mental illness that was not so bad to start with but got worse, only nobody told him about it. Her family knew, but they just wanted to get rid of her. Then he came to York and met Mother, and later on she went to live with him and his sister in Dublin. Georgina was very little then, and Mother helped to look after her, which is why she thinks such a lot of Mother, and I must say she was very good to her after you went away. We were all so worried and nobody knew what to do for the best. It took her a few weeks to get over it, but I dare say she will be happy now that she knows where you are and that you are safe. Dad, too.
>
> I expect the Colonel will be relieved as well, because he blames himself for everything. But he didn't blame Dad for marrying her, and his main regret was that he couldn't have married her himself. He said he was still very fond of her, and had never met a finer woman.

I'll bet! Liam thought with bitter derision. As simple as that. Nothing about the lies and the grief, the sheer destruction that ill-begotten affair had brought about. And in the next breath Robin was preaching forgiveness. *Never*, Liam thought, never if he lived to be ninety, would he forgive them for what they had done.

He lit a cigarette and smoked furiously for a minute. Slightly calmer, he read on to the end. There was a line or two about Tisha, who wrote to Robin sometimes, and then Georgina was mentioned again. Her name seemed to leap off the page, and he was so starved for news of her that he read the sentence several times, trying to extract every possible meaning from its casual brevity.

> . . . and her letter arrived by the same post as yours. She is still at the Retreat and working hard, so too busy to write often, but I know she will be as relieved as everyone else when she gets my letter to say you are safe and well . . .

So, she had been worried about him. But so, it seemed, had everyone else. And he had managed to upset his mother for several weeks. He suffered unexpected pangs of guilt at that, guilt that he managed to smother in a fresh surge of anger against Robin. The ease with which he had been seduced into sympathy with their mother and Robert Duncannon infuriated him, and it was some time before he could consider that apparent defection with any degree of objectivity.

When he did, it came to him that Robin had always been the one to sympathize—with everybody. There was nothing treacherous about it, it was simply that he could generally be relied upon to see both sides of every problem. Generous, even-tempered, and with affection to spare, Robin was usually the peacemaker, the one who would always look for the best in people. It was unfortunate, Liam decided, that because of his goodness he could also be manipulated, especially by those without scruples. Tisha was a past master at that, and so, it seemed, was Robert Duncannon.

Forgiving him, trying not to be unduly harsh in his reply, Liam was also consumed by concern for his brother. Several weeks had passed since that letter was written, and war seemed more inevitable by the day. With Robin on his mind, Liam was suddenly just as eager as his companions to know the latest news. And that need to know had become a passion which fired everyone he met. During the last few days, with Austria declaring war on the Balkan state of Serbia, and Russia heaving itself into a threatening position on behalf of its tiny neighbor, it looked as though all the major powers in Europe were on the brink of mobilization. The news took time to arrive, however. On August 3 they read that Germany had sided with Austria Hungary and declared war on Russia, and two days later on France. The Germans' unreasonable demand for free passage through Belgium, in order to attack an innocent neighbor, aroused British passions worldwide. The declaration of war upon Germany was a foregone conclusion.

That declaration, made on August 4, did not reach Australia until two days later. Liam had been detailed to go into town that day, and the atmosphere of tension and excitement struck him instantly. There was a great crowd outside the post office on Lonsdale Street, and another by the offices of the *Journal*, where single sheets were being pasted up before they were dry. Shortly after one, the news they were all waiting for came through from Sydney. Britain was at war, and Australia would back her to the hilt. *"To the last man and the last shilling,"* as one politician declared.

Grabbing one of those single printed sheets as they were handed out, Liam fought his way through the crowd and paused on a street corner to read it. Within seconds half a dozen people were at his elbow, almost tearing the paper from his hands. Their reactions varied from unbounded elation to grim disgust, but most agreed that it was right. Germany should not be allowed to run roughshod over Europe; with her worldwide interests in conflict with those of the British Empire, where would the aggression stop?

There was a report of a German merchant ship scuttling out of Port Melbourne, shots—"the first of the war"—fired across her bow, and a piece about two German warships, the *Scharnhorst* and *Gneisenau*, at large in the Pacific. Suddenly, that war in Europe was no longer half a world away. Seized by emotions both violent and unexpected, Liam did not wait for further news. Mounting his horse he rode some distance out along the Stud Road, then stopped to consider his feelings afresh. He would enlist, he could not do otherwise. He could not stand by while others fought to defend his right to live in this earthly paradise; and if in defending Australia he was also helping to defend England, then so he should. It could not be left to boys like Robin. Besides, Liam reasoned, justifying that abrupt change of heart, his self-respect would shrivel to think that his young brother was in the thick of it while he, Liam, was sitting safe out here.

He thought of Georgina and wondered whether he would see her again; perhaps he would if he returned to England.

Sighing, he carefully folded the paper and tucked it into his pocket. Time to return; all at the Maddox farm would be waiting for the news he brought.

Despite their wholehearted eagerness to support the old country, when faced with the necessity of leaving the farm, most of them felt guilty. While Ewan Maddox stared out at the fallow fields of winter, pondering the difficulties of running his place virtually single-handed, the men finished their supper with unaccustomed speed and loped off to their own quarters to enjoy a freer discussion.

Less eager than the rest, Liam overheard Mrs. Maddox's attempt at reassurance. Murphy would stay, she said, and as for Bert, his teeth were so rotten, an army dentist would faint at the sight of his mouth, never mind sign him up. Let them trail down to Melbourne, she advised her husband, and wait and see who came back.

Hiding a smile, for he was sure she was right, Liam closed the door quietly behind him. In the bunk room there was both argument and a certain amount of heart searching going on. Even Ned, who had declared that he was going to enlist no matter what, seemed less thrilled by the prospect than he had been only a few days ago. Old Murphy had turned sentimental: With tears in his eyes he said he would miss them, but he would stay to keep the farm going with the boss. Arnie was torn between his eagerness for adventure and loyalty to the people who had given him a home, but being less articulate could only find expression for his anguish in violent movement; when not pacing the floor or thumping the walls, he would fling himself into his bunk and pound the pillows. Liam felt sorry for him; Bert and Nobby, however, were full of themselves. According to them, they were going to join up and have a great time seeing England and doing a Cook's tour of Europe while knocking off a few Germans on the way. Liam had a suspicion that it might not be quite as easy as that.

Then somebody mentioned Lewis and his elder brother, the one managing the place out at Warragul. What would they do? And if both sons went, what would Ewan Maddox do? The consensus of opinion was that the older one would stay put, while the boss would probably insist his younger son cut short his studies and get himself home where he was needed. After all, *somebody* had to stay home and keep the country going, so why shouldn't Lewis get his finger out and do something practical for a change?

"What if he wants to enlist, like the rest of us?" Liam asked.

They were nonplussed at that.

If Lewis communicated with his parents over the next few days, nobody heard about it; but they were all astonished when Mary arrived on the Sunday to tell them that she had decided, with half a dozen friends, to volunteer as an army nurse. Ned was overjoyed.

For several days there were no facilities for dealing with the mass of men and women eager to do their bit for king and country; newspapers appealed for patience. Mary had returned within hours to Melbourne, but said she would be home again soon. The men worked badly and found excuses for making frequent trips to town. Mrs. Maddox was anxious about everything and her husband on edge. No one heard from Lewis.

Recruitment began on August 11.

12

*T*hose frequent trips into Dandenong paid off. Even while they were planning their journey into Melbourne to enlist, Nobby returned from town with the news that Dandenong was setting up its own facility. But Ewan Griffith Maddox dug in his heels. He wanted a week's notice, and August 11 was a Tuesday, Market Day, so the only trip into town that any of them would be making was to market with half a dozen young bulls. As far as he was concerned, they were all employed until Thursday evening; after that, they could please themselves.

There was bitter frustration in the bunk room, and talk of mutiny, but in the end respect won through. There was also the possibility—remote, of course—that not all would be accepted, and those who were not would still need a job at the end of the day.

Thursday night saw them polishing boots and shoes, clearing precious possessions from individual shelves, and packing a change of clothes. Over an early breakfast next morning they said their good-byes. Ewan Maddox was very brusque, finding urgent business in the barns, but his wife shed a few unexpected tears over each of them. Ella was inconsolable, weeping floods into the washing up and hiding her face in her apron as they set off down the road at first light. Old Murphy hobbled off to the stables.

Subdued at first, the little group was soon singing down the road to Dandenong, their spirits soaring with the sunrise. Early-morning mist hovered over the paddocks and clung beneath the trees, standing like fog where the creek became marshy near the town. From a distance it looked like a heavenly city, treetops and chimneys and mock-Gothic towers sparkling above a white, sunlit cloud; and only as they drew closer did that impression dissolve into the mundane grayness of mist. People were astir, laborers going about their daily business, one or two women waiting outside butchers and grocers shops, and unusual for that hour, a group of men shifting and fidgeting on the corner by the Royal Hotel. There were perhaps a dozen or so, all waiting for the temporary recruiting office to open.

Liam recognized one of the blacksmiths, and a clerk from the post office; Ned started a conversation with a couple of hands from a neighboring property, while Arnie seemed to know everybody. It was a cold, shivering wait, but they exchanged cigarettes and jokes and discussed the endless possibilities of the war, feeling superior every time other young males passed by. Some, including Arnie, were unable to resist a few jeers. Two boys from a local German family slunk by on the other side of the street, but a couple of Irish laborers were more than willing to make a fight of it, the situation saved only by the arrival of the recruiting party and the speedy opening of the office.

Two burly sergeants ushered them inside, and while a plump young lieutenant shuffled papers at a trestle desk, the men were pushed into something resembling a line. There were grins and coughs and a few self-conscious snickers before one of the sergeants addressed them briefly on their reasons for being there. Then the local doctor arrived, followed by a corporal who had obviously been detailed to assist; after a hurried consultation, the doctor went through into the next room, closing the door behind him. Names were taken, then there was another wait. After what seemed an interminable time, each man was called to the trestled desk to answer a detailed series of questions, and after that came a surprisingly thorough medical examination.

If any of them thought they could sweet-talk that elderly local man into falsifying his entries, they were mistaken. The army had laid down some very exacting standards and he was under precise orders, despite his civilian status, to comply. The corporal measured heights and weights, yelling out each measurement as though across a parade ground; Liam watched the doctor wince. Six feet tall, chest 40 inches, weight 176 pounds, age 19 years 10 months, it was all recorded for the army's benefit. His heart and chest were sound, feet good, genitals normal, eyesight and hearing perfect, and no history of serious illness. His only anxiety was whether inquiry would be made into his means of arrival in the country, but none was. With his signature appended to a form headed "Australian Imperial Force," Liam was in.

That acceptance was not universal. For various reasons, several were rejected. Bert, despite lying about his age, was turned away, his teeth, as Mrs. Maddox had surmised, being the reason. And little Nobby Clarke was two inches below the statutory requirement of five feet six inches. Arnie at twenty-two was fit and strong, with just enough schooling to sign his name; and at a stocky five feet ten inches, Ned sailed through all the examinations with ease to emerge like the victor in a heavyweight contest.

Meeting up with the two rejects outside, they found it hard to find any words of consolation. Hurt, when they had been prepared to give their all, humiliated to find themselves less than what their country expected, Bert and Nobby were like children turned away from the party of the year. There was no point in hanging around. After brusque farewells and exhortations to "knock 'em out" and "give 'em one for us," the two men pushed their way through a thickening crowd to return to the farm.

Relieved by that departure, too full of themselves to contain their elation any longer, the three remaining heroes gave vent to their feelings in an orgy of backslapping and self-congratulation. Returning inside for further orders, however, they were rapidly deflated. Yes, the army was delighted to have their names but, having enlisted its volunteers, did not quite know what to do with them. Victoria Barracks in Melbourne was packed already, so until a decision was made, would they please go home and report back on Monday?

That was not a contingency for which any of them had planned. For several minutes they stood with the other enlisted men feeling very foolish indeed; having left like gladiators, it seemed they must now return like clowns.

And then Ned started to laugh. "Come on," he urged, "let's go and get drunk!"

Arnie was in full agreement. At the risk of sounding like a killjoy, Liam remarked gloomily that as they had nowhere else to go but the farm, they really should try to remember Mrs. Maddox and her feelings about strong drink. Ned cheerfully accused him of being lily-livered, a point that Liam did not dispute; although he had never been much of a drinker, he knew that this was one occasion where Dutch courage was required. They headed for their usual bar, Ned's sense of humor erupting yet again as he spied Bert and Nobby drowning their sorrows in a corner. His laughter was infectious. Within seconds they were all rolling with it, thumping each other's shoulders and wiping tears from their cheeks. One round led to another, and by midafternoon they could hardly stand. It was a very sorry group that eventually made its way back to the Maddox farm that evening.

Fortunately, even Ewan Maddox saw the humor of the situation, and while his wife scolded and commiserated and saw them all to bed, he hid his laughter behind a pipe of tobacco. They could work for their keep over the weekend, he said, hung over or not; and of course he would consider the two rejects as new hands, they had been good enough for him in the past and would be so again, no matter what the army thought.

Well recovered by Monday morning, Liam was able to view the incident with a modicum of gratitude. Leaving on Friday had been wretched, while the farce of their return had injected a much-needed dose of laughter into this second departure. Even Ella was giggling as she kissed them all good-bye. "See you tonight!" she called as they set off again for Dandenong.

But against all expectation they did not return.

* * *

The broad thoroughfare between Flinders Street Station and the barracks on St. Kilda Road was thronged as though for a national celebration. Melbourne seemed to be out in force, whole families moving along with groups of men and boys, children skipping beside them, the atmosphere electric with anticipation and excitement. Paperboys crying the latest war news added to the hubbub, but here and there among the crowds were silent, determined, solitary men, their dusty boots and packs signifying far longer and less convenient journeys than the twenty miles Liam had just made by train.

They reminded him of himself eight months ago, and glancing down at his good tweed jacket, the boots freshly polished that morning, he could scarcely credit the difference, nor the weight in his bag. On the road, the only way to travel was lightly; in settling, things gathered, affections as much as material goods, and they seemed heaviest of all. Beneath the excitement he was conscious of regret, a sadness at leaving the Maddox farm which had intensified with the journey, and a dreadful suspicion that he might never see it again. He glanced up at the girls waving from high windows and flags fluttering in the wind, and thought of the rolling plains and misty blue hills beyond; but he said nothing. The men who had traveled down together on the train were laughing and joking, enjoying a rare sight of the city and the fact that they were part of a spectacle. For them, Dandenong was nothing much, while for him it represented the life he had always wanted. In that moment Liam felt he had been betrayed by his emotions, betrayed by sentimental attachments which he had thought were severed a year ago. With jaundiced eyes he viewed the Dandenong men who had enlisted with him, all, he could swear, at least two inches taller than they had been last week. Most of them were well built, fit in wind and limb, but a motley collection of characters nevertheless. With a sinking heart he feared the army was going to be shipboard life all over again.

St. Kilda Road was probably busier, Liam thought, than it had ever been in its existence, with packed trams rattling one way and empty ones back, and men on foot all heading for the barracks. He could see the tall, bluestone building sitting back from the road, but it was impossible to see the gates for the jostling crowd outside. The army had imagined itself geared and ready for an enthusiastic response, but it was not prepared for this avalanche of volunteers. Although Liam and his companions were already enlisted, they had to wait to be processed and sworn in. The morning passed in endless queues, men keeping places for others who returned into town for food. New volunteers were still crowding in, more than one weeping with frustration as he was turned away.

"At least we're *in*," Ned muttered, "but I wish I knew what they were going to do with us. It's a bloody circus."

With the lines of flimsy trestle desks across the parade ground, it reminded Liam more of a marketplace with impatient customers and extremely harassed vendors, and remembering the army's reputation for efficiency and organization, he wanted to laugh.

Processed at last, they were formed into lines of four into a rough sort of company and, under the guidance of a middle-aged sergeant and a couple of veteran corporals, marched out of the barracks toward an exercise ground at Broadmeadows, twelve miles away. It was a bleak-looking expanse of bush-land, with a few temporary buildings and a lot of tents. Within days, the weather, which had been remarkably dry, changed abruptly. Broadmeadows dust became Broadmeadows mud. The next few weeks were a miserable existence of endless drilling and lectures delivered in the pouring rain—a first taste, although none of them knew it, of what was to come.

Organizing that mass of untrained, authority-hating individuals into a cohesive fighting force was no easy matter, especially as most of the hastily promoted NCOs had no more experience than the men they were attempting to instruct. When asked for volunteers to take the rank of corporal, Liam and Arnie pushed Ned forward; he was older, had always assumed the position of leader at the Maddox farm, and they liked him. Rather Ned than some arrogant stranger, Liam reasoned, and that opinion was reinforced by the other Dandenong men. The post office clerk was designated lance corporal, and while both men were initially reluctant, they took their new positions seriously, particularly once they had their uniforms.

Ned became surprisingly conscientious, attending all the lectures and special courses, and whether it was the fact of those stripes on his shoulder or the weight of a new responsibility, Liam could not have said, but there was a distinct change in him. His laugh was less ready, and his critical streak was suddenly channeled into practical rather than personal matters. Once, after a particularly tough day, he confessed to Liam that he wished he had paid more attention at school.

"You'd walk through this lot," he said, showing a ream of regulations and instructions that he had to learn. "I don't know why you didn't put yourself forward, you'd be a damn sight better at this than me."

Wanting to laugh, Liam confined himself to a wry grin. "But you can tell the blokes what to do and they do it. You've been giving orders for years, you know you have—I wouldn't know what the hell to say. Anyway, they'd laugh as soon as I opened my mouth—my lingo's all wrong."

Ned shook his head and grumbled some more, so obviously overwhelmed by that mass of army jargon that Liam felt constrained to offer some help. "Do you want me to go through it with you?" he asked tentatively. "Two heads might he better than one."

So he read and interpreted, unconsciously absorbing everything; and when Ned did well in his courses, Liam's satisfaction could not have been greater had the success been his own. Although of necessity they spent less time together than on the farm, Liam was pleased to note that he had earned a measure of respect from Ned and in return tried hard not let him down in practical matters. It was not easy. Soldiering struck him as a boring, mind-destroying occupation, a constant struggle on behalf of the officers to replace individuality with conformity, to reduce each man to the level of a cog in a vast, smooth-running machine. And the cogs, at this stage, did not want to be forced into place. Some had poor physical coordination, others deliberately made a mess of drill sessions, turning them into tests of endurance. From past experience Liam knew that in the long run it was easier to conform than to rebel and, being blessed with both stamina and ability, often cursed the less willing.

Arnie was one of them. Not only did he seem possessed of two left feet, he hated what he had to struggle to achieve; his moans of regret wore everyone down. On the day of their enlistment Ned had said to Liam that they must "look out" for Arnie, as he was not one of the brightest; but with Ned having other responsibilities, Liam was left very much alone in that task. Arnie seemed to have a talent for being in the wrong place at the wrong time, and the only thing he liked about being in the army was the uniform. That went to his head. Suddenly he was a success with girls and at every opportunity was away into Melbourne, along with half the camp, ignoring regulations and having a high old time. For a while Liam tried to keep up, steering him away from the worst of the city's attractions, but it was an expensive and exhausting business. Training all day and drinking all night was not Liam's idea of pleasure, and even his stamina was no match for Arnie's. It struck him, too, that most of the girls who made a play for these uniformed demigods were not much better than the prostitutes who haunted seamen's hotels the world over. He tried to explain this but Arnie would not listen, and Liam was too fastidious to enjoy being coaxed and touched by women who were coarse and none too clean. Eventually, unable to curb Arnie's excesses, Liam simply gave up trying. Camp life became no easier, but a full night's sleep reinforced his stoic acceptance.

He had been at Broadmeadows a little over a month when Ned rushed up to tell him that he had just bumped into Lewis Maddox, lacking a uniform as yet, but shortly to be commissioned into the Light Horse Regiment. Apparently his father had threatened to cut him off without a penny unless he came home immediately, but Lewis was over twenty-one and could do as he pleased. And Mary had been accepted into the Australian Army Nursing Service, so with any luck they would all set sail together.

Liam could not make up his mind which piece of information pleased Ned more: the fact that Lewis had managed to outwit his father, or the idea of sailing all the way to Europe with Mary Maddox close at hand. On small reflection, Liam thought the latter. It made him smile.

A few weeks later mail reached him from England, much delayed by the war and having arrived via the Maddox farm and Victoria Barracks. There were two letters, both bearing familiar handwriting, Edward's elegant copperplate and his mother's firm rounded script. With her letter uppermost, Liam paused in drizzling rain to watch the fine drops make a haze of each clear black line. When name and address were almost obliterated, he stuffed both envelopes into his pocket and strode away.

So completely did he erase them from his consciousness, it was a surprise to him later to feel the crackle of paper when he removed his tunic. Most of the men were either away in town or in the canteen; Arnie was for once collapsed and asleep, his phenomenal strength having temporarily deserted him. Lighting a small candle lamp, Liam was tempted to burn those letters unread, his mother's particularly. He even held a corner of it over the flames and watched with satisfaction as it began to brown; a little curl, edged by sparks, peeled away from the tight-packed pages within, but the letter itself refused to burn. The charred edges were like a reproach. Beset by sudden fury, Liam dashed it away; he would not read it, he *would not*! She had no right to intrude upon this new life, no right to impose herself here.

There were voices outside the tent; Arnie moaned and stirred. Hurriedly Liam retrieved that heavy bundle of pages and hid them in his kit. Edward's missive lay unmarked and unopened beside the lamp. The voices went away, Arnie slept on, Liam doused the light and settled himself down. He did not sleep, however. Sometime before midnight he gave up the struggle and relit the lamp. He looked at Edward's letter again, weighed it in his hands, and knew its contents were less than his mother's. Although he wanted to read it, some instinct told him to get the worst over first. So from his kit Liam extracted the other one, sliding the charred pages from their envelope.

If his brother's letter had given Liam an inkling of what to expect, this direct communication from his mother was worse, pouring the salt of guilt and bitter resentment into wounds that had failed to heal. She wrote of love, love which had broken her heart with his leaving, love which had tried to protect and succeeded only in deceiving. And with an honesty that scoured her son, Louisa wrote of her early life with Robert Duncannon. Love again, but a very different kind of love, one which was tarnished, in Liam's translation, by overhwelming lust. No matter how hard she stressed Charlotte Duncannon's madness and the impossibility of divorce, Liam refused to believe it, except as a story attributable to Robert Duncannon. After all, he reasoned, the woman could not have been so repulsive: She had borne a daughter to her husband which presupposed a conjugal relationship and that daughter was very beautiful. Robert Duncannon must have loved his wife, if only in the beginning; that he could abandon her so quickly for another woman said nothing for his morals. It said little for his mother's, either, that with no hope of marriage, she should leave her home and family and go to live openly with him in Dublin. If anything had driven Charlotte Duncannon out of her mind, Liam reasoned, it must have been that.

He read on, his heart hardening with every line. In Dublin, apparently, as the first flush of passion faded, things had begun to go wrong. She said she had become obsessed by guilt, by a realization that life with Robert could never work as a real marriage should; and reading between those lines, Liam guessed that his natural father's attention and affections had begun to wander. Away from home a great deal, driven by the kind of strong sexual needs Liam was coming to understand from the men around him, Robert Duncannon, Liam had decided, had no more idea of abstention or faithfulness than a stallion with his choice of mares in season. And like a willing mare his mother had gone with him, the fact of their continuing sexual relationship obvious from Tisha's birth.

Louisa wrote that she had not known, when she left Dublin, that Tisha was on the way, that she had returned to York simply because she had nowhere else to go. Her mother, their old servant Bessie, and particularly her cousin Edward, had made a home for Louisa and her two sons and supported them. But the hotel on Gillygate, which Liam dimly recalled, had begun to fail as a business, and with Mary Elliott's death it had been necessary to move to somewhere smaller. Bessie had left, leaving Louisa and Edward and the three children. That was when they had moved to the cottage by the river. She and Edward had married ten months later, in 1899, on Liam's fifth birthday.

Astonishingly, Liam's memory of the day was both clear and detailed. He had returned from school to find a party gathered: Aunts Blanche and Emily, Uncle John Chapman, and old Bessie, who had gone to work for the Chapmans in Leeds.

There was a cake and a table groaning with food; everybody was very happy, laughing and talking and congratulating him on his fifth birthday. There were presents too. But his clearest, most vivid memory of that surprise party was of his mother looking as lovely as a princess, laughter dancing in her eyes, and himself wanting to stay with her to be cuddled and fussed over at bedtime. Instead there were tears and disappointment; he and Robin and Tisha were whisked away to Leeds with Aunt Emily and dour Uncle John to endure the nips and pinches of cousin Elsie, who was two years older, and the whining of little Johnnie and Harold, both younger than himself. Despite its size, the house had no more than a tiny square of garden in which they could not play and was hemmed in on every side by grimy terraces, all depressingly alike. Liam had visited the house many times in the succeeding years but never again stayed overnight.

With memory and astonishment came shock at the magnitude of that deception. They had used *him*, and the occasion of his birthday to cover the reason for that family gathering. It seemed such an abuse of innocence that Liam was outraged, unable and unwilling to see, for all his mother's protestations of love and protectiveness, that it had been done in anything but a calculated manner. He was so irrationally hurt by that revelation, he did no more than skim through the rest, which seemed to amount to no more than a lame collection of excuses for her marriage to Edward.

The flimsy tale that they had loved each other all along, yet for some unexplained reason not realized it until that summer of 1899, seemed incredible to him. In love himself, passionately and without hope, Liam was sure that if they had been in love all those years, they would each have known about it. His limited experience did not allow for different levels of love at different times, and between people who had been brought up in close proximity to one another. Disbelieving, sickened by what he saw as self-deception on his mother's part, invented to ease her bad conscience, Liam was also outraged by her temerity in thinking he wanted to know the intimate details of her life. It was enough to know that she had shared another man's bed; he did not want to know that she had done so willingly. Edward was so gentle, so fatherly, it disturbed Liam not at all to imagine him sharing his mother's bed, holding her, kissing her, loving her; indeed he had seen them in bed so often, arms around each other, it was the most natural thing in the world. Or had been. Until that world was shattered. The image of her with Robert Duncannon was altogether different. It smacked of animallike coupling and had become more graphic as his knowledge of other men's sexuality increased.

He could not bring himself to read Edward's letter. It remained unopened in his pocket for several days while his few solitary moments were taken up with self-pity. It seemed he was doomed to be denied all the things which were most important to him: people, places, even a way of life. He missed the Maddox family and their farm with a poignancy akin to homesickness, but he would not admit that he missed York. The army was a poor exchange for all that should have been, and when he did allow himself to dwell on Robert Duncannon, the fact that he had willingly chosen the military life only served to underscore the differences between them.

No solitude, no privacy, poor food, and a succession of days that were full of noise and endless, mindless drilling, that was the army. It amazed Liam that so many of the men seemed to thrive on it. At the end of a crushing week he took himself off into town, eager to shed his depression in any way he could. After several beers in a back street bar, he left the crowd to look for somewhere to eat. Among the maze of dark, wet, ill-lit streets, he found a little chophouse, quiet in the early evening and tolerably clean. The waitress had seen enough uniforms in the past few weeks to be unimpressed, or perhaps, he thought, glancing up into her expressionless face, she had troubles of her own. Either way, she took his order for steak and fried potatoes without enthusiasm and slouched back to the kitchen. He drank another beer while he was waiting, slowly this time; and in the stillness remembered Edward's letter. For the first time in a week Liam felt sufficiently fortified to read it.

Its tone was calmer, less impassioned than his mother's, beginning not with recriminations at his leaving, but hope that his new life in Australia would turn out to be all that he was looking for. There was such unintentional irony in that, Liam almost smiled as he reminded himself that this had been written well before the storm clouds had gathered, and the news about

Robin and Tisha was so old, Liam could not help longing suddenly for more up-to-date information. Especially of Robin. But the letter was not what he had feared. Apart from a passage which begged for understanding of Louisa and that he would read her words with compassion, Edward made little attempt at explanation. For that, at least, Liam was grateful: He could not have borne another lengthy version of what had gone before, and why. Reading the simplicity of Edward's statement that he had always loved Louisa, but that at one time it had seemed wrong to acknowledge it, Liam tried to view it cynically and failed. Instead, he was deeply touched by the older man's loyalty. Even more so when the next sentence went on to acknowledge Liam's feelings for Georgina.

"I could not speak, because I was not free to do so—yet I watched and feared and prayed that I was wrong in what I suspected. That was why I was so short with you, and because of that, my dear boy, I humbly crave your forgiveness. I understand, in part, what you must have felt then, and indeed what you are perhaps still feeling. There can be no greater tragedy in life. I pray that it will pass, as these things sometimes do, and that your memory of this anguish will fade with time. We see Georgina less often now, but she seems well, if much chastened. She always asks for news of you, but I do not think she was aware of your feelings for her and we have not enlightened her. Nor, I think, has her father, but I cannot be certain of that point."

In a sudden mist, the words disappeared. Folding the letter over, Liam coughed to clear his throat. As he found his handkerchief, the waitress reappeared with his meal, and for the moment he set Edward's letter aside. It surprised him that he felt no anger towards his adoptive father, and that those brief lines regarding Georgina should have brought forth such a swell of gratitude. It was little enough, but it was news of her; and while he had longed for her to understand his feelings all those months ago, in retrospect it was probably just as well that she had no inkling. She, at least, would be spared this anguish.

The meal was good and satisfying. Afterward, Liam felt refreshed and suddenly more cheerful. He picked up the letter again and read on. There was not much more, but the last few lines made him glad of his quiet corner with its shadows.

"Although I am not your natural father," Edward had written, "I have loved you all as though you were my own. Remember, too, that I am not a stranger—I am your cousin, and we share the same blood."

The truth of that last statement had not occurred to Liam before. His determination to cut himself off, to stand alone, was temporarily forgotten as the warmth of Edward's words penetrated. He read that letter many times over in the succeeding weeks and derived great comfort from it. Edward's tact and understanding seemed to acknowledge the change in their relationship, projecting them both beyond the narrow confines of father and son and into the realms of equality. Having originally viewed Edward and his mother as partners in a conspiracy against him, Liam was now persuaded to reassess the situation. Edward, it appeared, would have preferred to be honest from the start; and it was suddenly blindingly clear that he need not have taken on three illegitimate children all those years ago. That he should have taken up another man's responsibilities, both willingly and successfully, said a great deal for his qualities as a man. It was also a humbling thought. Liam did not think he would want to do the same. It occurred to him, too, to consider what life would have been like without Edward as their father, and immediately much that had been rich and secure and satisfying fell away. Without him, as children they would all have been so much poorer. Perhaps not in a financial sense, for Robert Duncannon with all his sins would surely not have seen them starve; but spiritually and intellectually they would each have been so much less. Never once, by word or gesture, had he ever intimated resentment of those three children, who were as much Robert Duncannon's as Louisa's; and Edward had little liking for the colonel, of that Liam was certain. Theirs, he reflected, had been a happy childhood, and perhaps it was that very fact which made the truth so hard to bear.

If his thoughts of Edward were increasingly more generous, Liam's attitude toward his mother did not improve. Indeed, she suffered by comparison. In his reply to Edward's letter, he made no reference to Louisa's.

13

*C*hristmas in York that year, Georgina reflected, was going to be a very halfhearted affair. It was midway through December and the war was showing no sign of drawing to any conclusion; indeed, from judicious reading of newspapers and casualty lists, it seemed no better than stalemate: Uniforms in the streets, faces which were either glum with misery or taut with anxiety for absent loved ones, and everywhere a dank, persistent mist. She could not recall a day when the sun had last shone from a blue and perfect sky; she supposed it was in the summer, but summer with its roses and picnics seemed to belong to another age.

The shrouded Minster, as she passed by, seemed shuttered and forlorn, as though God had gone away for the duration. Crossing the road by the south transept, Georgina cut through Minster Gates on her way to meet Louisa for tea. By Coffee Yard her step faltered as she thought of Edward working away at his beautiful books. For a moment she was tempted to stop by and say hello, but their meetings these days were rare, and while his manner was unfailingly courteous, she had the feeling the sight of her pained him. He was so calm, and such a tower of strength emotionally, Georgina often wondered whether

Louisa realized what it cost him in physical terms. His slender, sensitive face was pared almost to the bone, paler than ever, and, Georgina suspected, showing the signs of incipient heart disease. He needed rest and freedom from anxiety, yet the war imposed additional worries.

The cheery welcome of the tea shop bell sounded incongruous to Georgina's ears, but it was warm inside and for that she was grateful. Louisa, sitting by the window, raised a hand in greeting. She was thinner too, but the haggard misery of the last eighteen months had been relieved by Robin's news of Liam; now all she waited for was a direct communication, some sign that he understood and had forgiven her. Georgina, having to listen to that gnawing anxiety whenever they met, steeled herself.

Today, Louisa's smile was tense, but the pressure of her hand on Georgina's was warm with gratitude.

"I'm so glad you were able to come. Edward's had *two* letters from Liam this week—one from Australia, posted over two months ago, and one from Egypt. He's in *Egypt*, Georgina! Goodness me, it seems so strange—imagine Liam seeing places like that. Alexandria—it makes you think of the pharaohs, doesn't it?—and *Cairo*."

Beneath the table, Georgina squeezed her hands together to still their trembling, and while Louisa fished in her small leather bag for the letters themselves, forced her stiff lips into the semblance of a smile. How ridiculous it was, she thought, that news of Liam—from Liam—should affect her in this way. It had been worse the first time. Even now it astounded her how she had managed to control that wild succession of emotions. Exultant at the broken silence, at his safety among good, honest farming people, she was relieved after months of worry. Afterward, in the privacy of her room, Georgina had sobbed like a child, realizing only then how much had been pent up since Liam's disappearance. She had known of it within hours because they came to her first, demanding to know what she knew, and whether Liam had confided anything at all to her. But of course he had not, apart from those tentative dreams of his. It had been a slender clue, too slender to provide much hope, but to that everyone had clung. No one accused her of being to blame for his disappearance, but she felt it nevertheless, knowing in her heart of hearts that his feelings for her were what had tipped the balance so drastically. In retrospect Georgina knew that she had deliberately ignored what should have been obvious, and all for the selfish pleasure of his company.

And because she knew, she did not ask why it was that Liam had reacted so badly to the truth, while Robin had made no more than a token protest and Tisha none at all. And because they were all—even her father—so eaten up with guilt at their own parts in the tragedy, no one thought to question her further.

Past expert that she was at covering her own emotions, Georgina gave nothing away while she listened and comforted and made feeble attempts to reassure. Only Edward had looked askance at her. Dear, kind, shrewd Edward, who might suspect but never accuse.

For the moment, however, there was no need to reassure, Louisa being taken up with Liam's news, albeit as relayed to her husband. She began by reading parts of the first letter aloud, then, as an increasingly quavering voice betrayed her emotions, handed both to Georgina.

"There," she said, dabbing at her eyes, "you read them, I can't. I don't mean to be so silly, and I'm delighted to have news of him by any means—I just wish he would mention me . . ."

Her voice tailed away, and the brilliant eyes stared out over the square. Georgina's heart ached for her, but there was no comfort in empty, unconvincing words. With Liam's letter in her hands she forced herself to relax, to convey an outward impression of calm. There was a trick to it which she had learned as a child and employed to excellent use as a nurse. To herself she labeled it *acceptance*. Accept everything, even the most bizarre situation as normal; don't question it, don't react to it, and above all don't panic. Laugh, weep, rage, or even break your heart, but not until afterward, not until you are alone.

The forward-sloping hand was not as elegant as Edward's, but it formed a pleasing pattern on the page, while words and phrases, stilted at first, soon relaxed into a style far more mature than Robin's, whose letters rushed on, youthful, ingenuous, eager to summarize a situation in as few sentences as possible. But Liam, once in his stride, was possessed of the telling phrase, the vivid description that brought everything to life. Reading his letters to Edward, Georgina cursed the food, sighed over the boredom of basic training, and shared the frustration of not knowing when they were to sail for Europe. The original date, toward the end of September, was constantly put back as the threat of German warships in the vicinity made everyone fearful of losing that vital convoy.

Liam mentioned the fact that his twentieth birthday had been spent in camp, drilling as usual, but that he and a friend had gone into Melbourne that evening for a celebratory meal—"a good excuse," he wrote, "for getting away from the inevitable army stew."

And two weeks later, on October 19, the troopship *Benalla* had eventually sailed from Melbourne to join up with the convoy at Albany, Western Australia, and by November 3 they were preparing to set forth across the Indian Ocean.

"We have a contingent of nurses abroad, most of them from Victoria. One of them is Mary Maddox, daughter of the people I worked for. Her brother Lewis is also aboard, which made for an unexpected send-off when we left Melbourne. Mr. and Mrs. Maddox came down from Dandenong, which nobody imagined they would do, and while they had not approved of Lewis joining up, he had their blessing at the end. It was a great send-off, with streamers, bands, sirens blowing, but also very sad, so many girls and women crying on the quayside. Mary was crying, too, but had her brother to comfort her."

Thanking providence for that, Georgina experienced an irrational surge of jealousy. She told herself that this Maddox family was altogether too good to be true, that they had no right to figure so largely in Liam's affections when his own family were so deprived of him.

Of that letter there was not much more. Concerned lest he should not have chance to catch the post, Liam had finished it hurriedly with a promise to write again soon, and the second was penned largely at sea, relating the daily routines of exercise, lessons in signaling, and an exciting brush with the German cruiser *Emden*. The eventual sinking of the German ship by the H.M.A.S. *Sydney* had cheered them all, making them keener than ever to reach Europe and "get into the thick of it."

After all the excitement, however, the letter ended on a note of disappointment. For some reason they were to disembark at Alexandria, which made Liam wonder whether that unscheduled stop had anything to do with England declaring war on Turkey. He hoped not, "as the lads joined up to be where the real fighting is, not to be used to mop up some side issue out here."

The letters begged for news of Robin and Tisha, and in a postscript gave his new address, which he described as being "in the shadow of the Pyramids." Stricken by that romantic image, picturing Liam escorting some other nurse by moonlight, for a moment Georgina was overcome by loneliness and jealousy. He did not ask for news of *her*, and like Louisa she might have cried, "If only he would mention *me* . . ."

Instead, she slipped the much-thumbed sheets back into their envelopes and remarked that for the time being at least Liam was safe in Egypt. Robin had been in Flanders since the beginning of October, involved in a tremendous battle to defend Ypres, and in the firing line constantly for almost three weeks. His battalion, which had started out at something like a thousand, was reduced to one captain, three second lieutenants, and less than two hundred and fifty men. That Robin had come through it without physical injury was, Georgina felt, no less than a miracle; and while the battalion regrouped they had been moved across the French border to a reserve position. While he was not exactly out of danger, for the time being their collective anxiety was less intense, his letters arriving frequently again, if a little less jaunty than before. But the last few weeks, Georgina reflected, had been ghastly; it was no wonder that Louisa looked so drained.

"And how's Tisha?" she managed to ask, hoping for a little light relief; but Tisha, it seemed, was still behaving as though her heart had been turned to stone, enjoying her new job as a clerk at the barracks and out with friends almost every night. She was at home for meals, Louisa said, but other than that they rarely saw her. She read Robin's letters when they arrived and wrote to him occasionally, but any mention of Liam was a cue for her to change the subject or leave the room. When remonstrated with, she declared cruelly that she was sick of their anxiety for him, he had chosen his own path, and in her opinion was quite able to take care of himself.

"She's young," Georgina observed, "and the young can be very thoughtless." Privately, she wondered whether Tisha simply felt neglected. Quiet and obedient for months, when she did begin to assert herself again, she did so implacably. No argument or remonstration would turn her from her purpose; and looking back, Georgina wondered whether Edward and Louisa had had strength left to exert much discipline. Tisha, it seemed, was intent on going her own way.

As ever before leaving, Georgina mentioned her father, passing on the love and contrition that Louisa always refused to accept.

As expected, she shook her head. "If he had only stayed away . . . But your father has never understood anything but *military* duty!" With a sharp sigh she looked away, and for a few moments silence stretched between them. Then, unexpectedly, she asked about him. "What is he doing, these days? I don't suppose they've sent *him* to the front," she added bitterly.

"No, to his regret. He's been requesting it for months, ever since the war began. *But* . . . His special sphere is Ireland, and they don't seem to want him to abandon the work he's been doing for the past few years."

Again, the silence. With a visible effort, Louisa tried to contain her curiosity and failed. "And what *has* he been doing there?"

"I don't know," Georgina confessed. "He doesn't talk about it. I don't think he's allowed to."

A smile which was more derisive than amused passed Louisa's lips. "Oh, so secret, is it? Ah well, Ireland was always dear to his heart. I wonder," she added a moment later, "whether his masters at the War Office know how he *really* feels about Ireland? If they did, they might be glad to send him to the front!"

"What do you mean?"

"Ask him, my dear. Ask your father, not me."

"Yes, I will," Georgina promised as they parted on Coney Street. Afterward, however, Louisa's insinuations seemed no more than the product of bitterness, a deep-seated resentment that a man who had made the army his life—and at the expense of so much else—should be kept away from this terrible war, while innocent boys suffered and laid down their lives.

Afterward, too, she allowed herself to think about Liam, writing down that new address at the back of her diary beneath two others she had remembered and transcribed. With what remained of her afternoon off she sat down to write to him, an oft-repeated exercise that had yet to reach her own exacting standards. In trying to achieve the perfect balance between detachment and affectionate concern, Georgina always erred. She was either too cold, sounding like an elderly governess issuing reprimands, or else her warmth set fire to itself, becoming an impassioned interrogation. *Why* had he gone away like that without a word? Surely, after the friendship which had existed between them, he could have confided in her. She would have understood, whatever he had to say, and could have helped and comforted him. Knowing the situation, having suffered herself as a child because of it, she was in a better position than anyone to sympathize . . .

Begging for some communication, even a few words on a postcard, then Georgina would remember that his feelings had been those of a boy approaching manhood, and consequently less platonic than hers. Not knowing she was his sister, mistaking her affection and interest for something more, Liam had imagined himself in love. Although in his letters to Edward he asked for news of the family, like Louisa's name, Georgina's was significant by its absence. He had adored his mother, and now it seemed he hated her; perhaps his feelings for Georgina had undergone a similar metamorphosis.

It was the same that afternoon. After an hour of flowing, anguished prose, she was devastated by her own misery and the realization that this was another letter she could never send. Only if they were to meet could this thing possibly be put right between them. Only face-to-face could she say what had to be said, explain the past in terms that he would understand and help him to accept what could not be altered. If only, she prayed, he might survive that long. She could not bear to think that he might die with hatred in his heart. Whatever Louisa's sins, which were surely those of omission rather than intent, she was a good woman and a warm and loving mother: She did not deserve the treatment Liam was meting out.

And if it should prove to be that I am guilty of more than I suspect, Georgina thought, then I, too, need to be forgiven.

A week later, with Christmas a matter of days away, Georgina finally came to a decision about her work. As the war gathered pace in those early weeks, she had wondered whether she should volunteer to serve in a military hospital, and certainly the idea of escaping from York with all its emotional pressures and responsibilities was very attractive. The latter fact was so insistent that she hesitated; it did not seem a valid reason for leaving such rewarding work and a situation so suited to her talents. Several nurses and attendants had left already, and with each publication of casualties from the front, Georgina imagined that one of them might be Robin, or her Irish cousins from White Leigh, both of whom had lately volunteered. Liam for the moment was safe in Egypt, but with the war lurching along into another year, eating up young lives with obscene relish, those Australians would be needed somewhere sooner or later. She had heard of horrific injuries, and young men driven almost mad from the noise of those heavy bombardments; if she could bring the separate disciplines of her training together, she might save lives, comfort shattered minds, return some of them whole to their families when the war was over.

Fired by that idealism, Georgina was able to recognize the stalemate of her personal life and set it to one side. She had done all that it was possible to do, and now that Liam was writing regularly to Edward, at least, the Elliotts as a whole knew of his movements, and could communicate with her and with each other. Her presence in York, as far as she could see, was no longer vital, whereas elsewhere, her abilities might do great good.

14

*T*hirty-eight transports arrived in Alexandria, by degrees discharging company after company, battalion after battalion, on the hundred-mile journey to Cairo. From the city's railway station to their destination on the fringes of the Western Desert was a hot, uncomfortable march of several miles, and when the first of those eighteen thousand men arrived, there was nothing but the looming pyramids and a cluster of buildings around a country house hotel. The Mena House was requisitioned, and from that, Mena Camp took its name. Tents began to sprout like mushrooms, vast numbers of them, rapidly taking on all the aspects of a city. A city full of men.

It should have been obvious from the beginning that there would be a certain amount of trouble; perhaps it was, but the somewhat brutal attempts to squash it before it began were, in the end, both inept and provocative.

Although Liam had glimpsed Egypt briefly during a passage of the Suez Canal the year before, at close quarters it made an impact for which he was no more prepared than the thousands who had never seen anything but Australia. Bleached by centuries of sun and scoured by sand, Egypt, he found, was possessed of a vivid degenerate beauty that both excited and repelled him. There was light and color everywhere, and the most appalling poverty he had ever seen; scented flowers in formal gardens competed with the stench of decay in the streets, while marble palaces on grand avenues fronted a maze of fetid alleys in the native quarters. Electric trams and gleaming motorcars moved alongside other forms of transport that were positively biblical; donkeys and camels nudged each other and brayed while their owners screamed unintelligible insults at passing, goggle-eyed soldiers.

Compared to the streets of Cairo, the open desert was, for the first day or so, something of a relief, but Liam never quite learned how to deal with the nights spent on guard duty. With moonlight bathing the pyramids, the desert managed to exercise its own terrible fascination; the empty tombs of those long-dead pharaohs seemed alive with whispers and laughter and moving shadows and the wraithlike kiss of the wind. It was unnerving.

With the camp complete, however, there was no time for idle dreaming, little time at all for anything but work. Those eighteen thousand men were immediately plunged into an excess of drilling and marching and trench digging that was intended to bring them to a peak of physical fitness; in effect, after the relative inactivity of their sea voyage from Australia, it brought them virtually to their knees. Had the hours been less punishing, had they been well nourished and allowed even one day off a week in which to relax, the gathered troops might not have fallen like flies from heat exhaustion and a plethora of minor but debilitating illnesses. But even Sundays were marked by early calls and church parades and several hours' drilling in the heat of the afternoon. To begin with, few of the men, Liam included, had energy left to go into town after a day spent marching through sand with no more than a bread roll and a tin of sardines to sustain them; but resentment breeds its own particular energy, and after almost three weeks without a break, trouble was building like a thundercloud.

Physically exhausted and mentally adrift, Liam listened to the rumble of discontent and felt it echoed in himself. He too began to question the sense of things, not least the reasons for their stay in this outlandish place. With Christmas practically upon them, all he could hear were the calls of the muezzin from distant minarets, a far cry from the clamor of church bells at home in the city of York. Swept by a tide of homesickness, he found himself longing for sights and sounds not thought about in months, while the patriotism he had privately scoffed at was burning inside, fueled by letters from his brother, lucky enough to be in France and doing his bit for England in a more positive way. Stuck in Egypt, doing nothing but march and drill, drill and dig, Liam was possessed by an envy he would not have thought possible on the day he enlisted. Here and now seemed such a terrible waste of time, while that noble cause, repeated in every lecture, of freeing the world from German imperialist aggression seemed hollow indeed. Pointless while breaking their backs digging useless trenches in the desert, pointless in the face of endless hours on parade, when every missive from England contained news of great battles in France and Belgium. It was agreed among the men that they had not joined up to listen to uplifting speeches by officers who had no more idea of war than themselves; they had come to fight, not to learn a set of petty rules and regulations laid down by pen pushers back home.

Bored and tired and viciously frustrated, with day leave denied, the troops began to depart each night in ever-increasing numbers, with leave and without it, for the fleshpots of Cairo. At five shillings a day, the Australians were the best-paid of all the allied armies, and Liam, particularly, had never been so well off. Even with half his pay allocated in Edward's name to a York bank, he had far more than Robin and was determined to make the most of it. Perpetually hungry as he was, Liam always thought first of food and in Cairo the choice was vast, from the glittering restaurant of Shepheard's, to cheaper but less salubrious establishments in the narrow back streets. To begin with, a decent meal with a few beers was all he indulged in, but like many more he was soon infected with the atmosphere of excitement that pervaded these illicit trips into town. After weeks of confinement, the realization that it was possible to break the rules and get away with it rapidly went to everyone's head.

Those nightly forays became wilder, tinged by an atmo-

sphere of hysteria as large groups of men gathered to drink and
gamble and fornicate their way through the streets of Cairo.
Out of sight of families and employers, with respectable com-
munities left way behind in Australia, they were let loose on a
land that had seen everything before, a city old in sin and well
used to catering to every conceivable taste. And many of them
took full advantage.

Although Liam had been away from home a long time,
grief and revulsion had, for him, kept temptation at arm's
length. But the licentious atmosphere was beginning to blunt
his discrimination. To begin with he stuck to Ned on their
legitimate nights out, but his friend frequently disappeared
without explanation, leaving Liam and Arnie and the rest of the
crowd. They assumed, of course, that Ned was being secretive
about sexual assignations, that he had discovered a good
brothel, and as a corporal was mean enough not to share its
delights with them. Liam had other suspicions that he kept
to himself, but either way those abrupt departures put more
distance between them than rank ever could.

Feeling snubbed, he threw himself all the more into enjoyment. Exhausted through the day, at night he seemed to float
on a tide of exhilaration, buffeted backward and forward against
an exotic, lotus-strewn shore. And that shore seemed to be
peopled by half the women of Europe and Asia. Dark and fair,
bold and shy, they inhabited the shadowy back streets in seedy
rooms and opulent houses, guarded by ancient, painted
Frenchwomen or homosexual Egyptian men. There were shows
which featured eastern belly dancers and young girls with fans,
and there were others that were much less innocently seductive. On every street corner were postcards for sale and the
kinds of books that could never have seen the light of day
in countries where Victorian morality had gained any kind of
foothold. It was a land where sex was for sale, a land where
every persistent and importunate native had a "sister" who
would love to entertain each fine, wealthy, good-looking soldier
before he went to the war. The fact that such offers rapidly
reached saturation point made them easy to resist, but the
atmosphere, loaded with sexual invitation as it was, impinged
upon them all. As far as Liam was concerned, much of what

he saw produced nothing more than embarrassment or disgust; nevertheless, it was also illuminating, larding both dreams and fantasies with an eroticism that had been absent before.

On innumerable occasions he watched Arnie and those of like mind leave the bars to take their pick of the girls along the Haret el Wasser. Oddly enough, while he was prepared to drink and gamble with the best and take his part in the wild dashes back to camp via any form of transport, hired or stolen, the one thing he could not bring himself to do was join them in this nightly ritual. Most of the time he wanted to, and could not understand the reluctance that had survived the loss of almost every other inhabitant. But regardless of either drunkenness or sobriety, and in spite of the good-natured baiting he endured from the bolder spirits, something stopped him. To begin with it was thoughts of Georgina, constant comparisons which sprang unbidden whenever he thought some girl or woman might be vaguely attractive; then he would look again and find that she was not. It became a habit. He told himself that if he could just find a girl who looked like her, then everything would be all right; but Georgina's true, pale fairness was as rare among these rich, dark plums as snow upon the desert's face. And the fair European nurses at Mena and in the Cairo hospitals were as unattainable as women in purdah—certainly to humble private soldiers like himself, although he did suspect that a few pips at the shoulder might have made all the difference.

Nevertheless, he had his suspicions about Ned, although his old friend still infuriatingly refused to be drawn out, tapping his nose as he smartened himself up for the evening and telling Liam to mind his own business. Liam saw Mary Maddox a few times, and she was as cordial as ever, coloring only slightly when he mentioned their mutual friendship, and he bumped into her brother quite frequently. Rank made it impossible to engage in more than a few minutes conversation, but it was always heartening to see the pleasure in Lewis's eyes, and to know that this desert training was as tough on the young mounted officers as it was for the infantry. Lewis had not lost his intensity, but it seemed to Liam he had grown up a great deal. Catching the sight of him one night among a group of officers and nurses on the steps of Shepheard's Hotel, Liam thought how relaxed and sophisticated he seemed. Envying him, imagining his dark and not unhandsome friend as a smooth and successful Lothario, Liam wished he could be so fancy-free, that he had never met Georgina Duncannon, or having met her, that he could release himself from the obsession she had become.

She was both forbidden and unattainable, and nothing was ever going to change that. He told himself that he was being ridiculous and several times swore he would tear up that tantalizing photograph of her, but it was impossible. In the end, it seemed the only cure was to find a girl who looked nothing like Georgina Duncannon and put into practice what he so frequently dreamed of doing. It was not, however, as easy as that. The first time, the sheer squalor of the room quelled his passion. Even as the woman lit the lamps Liam walked out, pursued by shouts and curses. Some were plain enough, others he understood the gist of. It was a little while before inclination and opportunity combined again.

The second time he went about it with more care, choosing a better-class brothel instead of a casual pickup. Swallowing his initial nervousness, Liam explained to the madam that he wanted someone young and clean, with fresh sheets on the bed. The woman was old and fat and grossly painted, and for a moment, as her eyes took in his tall, straight frame and the shock of fair hair falling across his forehead, she seemed about to suggest something else; then with a shrug she turned away. A girl was brought forward. Small and pretty in a childish, undeveloped fashion, she had beautiful eyes and smooth olive skin. Briefly Liam hesitated; this was not quite what he had envisaged. He preferred women to young girls, but any protest might be misunderstood. Recalling the look the madam had cast over him, he thought it more prudent to take what was offered.

The room was hardly as fresh as he would have wished, and the noise from the street outside was distracting, but it was prettily furnished and the sheets were tolerably clean. The girl quickly slipped off her evening dress and lay back on a wide feather bed, legs spread and awaiting him. As Liam glanced at her, slowly removing his tunic, she reached across to a bowl of fruit and began to peel an orange.

That hardened lack of interest in what they were about to do was off-putting. He paused in the act of unfastening his shirt, aware that his edge of excitement was gone. Nothing about her stirred him; she might have been no more than a slab of meat displayed on a butcher's window ledge. He pictured all the men who had used her and was no longer surprised by her attitude. Why should she care? He was just one more, and plenty would follow when he had gone. There was a moment's regret for the money already spent, but it was impossible to claim what he had paid for. With a sigh, he donned his tunic and left.

Back at camp, however, with his pity for the girl dispersed, he called himself a fool and a coward, wondering what was wrong with him that he could not perform the act that other men found so simple. In an agony of frustration, he flung himself down and gave way to self-pity. Ned, returning refreshed from his night out, indulged in a burst of knowing laughter.

"There's nothing wrong, you bloody idiot," he declared. "Nothing a decent woman couldn't put right in no time flat. And for God's sake don't start comparing yourself to Arnie—we all know where he keeps his brains, and one day he'll know about it! Besides," he added with a cryptic grin, "you can take it from me that most women prefer quality to quantity, and on *that* score Arnie's got no more idea than a second-rate ram!"

"It's all very well for you to talk," Liam complained bitterly, "you've got no problems that I can see! It is Mary Maddox you're meeting, isn't it?"

Ned tapped the side of his nose. "Like I told you before—ask no questions, you'll be told no lies."

With a derisory gesture, Liam sat up and lit a cigarette. "Well, I just hope nobody finds out, that's all. She'll be packed off home, and you'll be on fatigues for the rest of the bloody war!"

Ignoring that, Ned simply laughed. "Find yourself a cute little nurse," he blandly advised, "and keep clear of the bloody Wasser. Nothing but trouble there, mate."

But Liam's chances of meeting up with any nurse, unless

he were ill, were remote; they both knew that. Mary Maddox broke every rule in the book for Ned, but only because theirs was a relationship which had begun long before. Perhaps not openly acknowledged, but Liam had been aware of it. He did wonder, however, what Lewis would say if he knew; and indeed, how Mr. and Mrs. Maddox would view such an alliance.

After that, he did steer clear of the Haret el Wasser, but not for the reasons Ned listed. In truth, Liam's fear of humiliation temporarily outweighed his desire for sexual experience; and in the meantime severe lack of discipline throughout the Australian forces meant that changes were about to take place.

Just after Christmas, when three hundred men had been posted absent without leave, and one battalion had been forced to abandon a parade for the simple reason that there were not enough men to hold it, a strong picket line was placed across the road from Mena to Cairo and all passes rigorously checked. Training was intensified, longer marches into the desert became the order of every day, and some units were exiled to garrisons along the Suez Canal. Although the food still consisted largely of bread and jam, sardines and bully beef, it was just adequate, and Sunday became at last a day of rest. Church Parade was still compulsory, but apart from that the men did have a free day at their disposal. They began to behave more like tourists and less like vandals, and the numbers falling sick from exhaustion dropped dramatically. There was another problem, however.

Until one of their number went down with it, venereal disease had been something of a joke among Liam's unit, but after Arnie reported sick they never saw him again. Despite feeling that he, more than most, had "asked for it," all were shocked by the treatment meted out. Under military guard he was taken to join the increasing numbers who had "willfully" contracted the disease, and as per the regulations, his paybook was stamped accordingly and he was forced to wear a white band on his arm "like a leper's bell," as Liam put it. Arnie had been a fool, that was agreed, but the disease could have been contracted just as easily by a man who had succumbed to temptation only once. Liam felt sick when he recalled his past intentions, and guilty that he had not tried harder to keep Arnie away from prostitutes. Conscious of having abandoned the boy, Ned felt worse. They went down to the barbed-wire compound the next Sunday afternoon with fruit and cigarettes.

They were turned away. No one was allowed to speak to the patients, not even their guards. As Ned and Liam stood outside in the burning sun, all they had from Arnie was a halfhearted wave. He looked like a dog that had been tethered and penned without knowing why. Liam took a long, bitter pull on his cigarette, then stubbed it viciously into the sand.

"A fine way to make an example of us!"

"Come on," Ned murmured, "there's no point in standing here, staring. They're like animals in a bloody zoo."

It was a harsh lesson and one that sobered them all. Rumor had it, correctly so for once, that the VD cases were to be repatriated to Australia along with some of the worst criminal offenders. It seemed an ignominious end to what had begun so hopefully a few months before, and the bulk of general opinion gave one reason: Egypt.

With the initial novelty worn away, even rebellion lost its attraction and the troops settled down to something approaching acceptance, although life continued to provide its irritations. Desert sand, much coarser than anything found on an ocean-washed beach, made its way into eyes and ears and noses; it was in their food and in their bedding, and the frequent dust storms were misery for man and beast alike. After four months Liam began to wonder, along with everyone else, whether they would ever leave the dirt and grit to get on with the job for which they had left Australia. Those eight-and ten-mile marches out into the desert with machine guns and rifles and heavy packs seemed just as pointless and pitiless as ever, but it began to be noticeable even to the least enthusiastic that they were pulling together under their officers and NCOs. For the first time they were beginning to feel like fully trained fighting men, instead of an ill-directed rabble. Liam particularly, who had always been something of a loner, was discovering the tactical advantages of teamwork, the necessity of reliance upon others. He was also finding pride in himself. Training and a seemingly natural ability had made of him an excellent marksman, the best of his platoon, while four months of trench digging had developed a muscular strength more than equal to his height. He was twenty years old, lean and fit, and he could not wait, as he wrote more than once to Robin, to see some real action.

By the middle of March, with the issue of new rifles, rumors began to fly. Some said they were about to leave for France, others that the canal was to be defended against an attack by the Turks. But with the naval bombardment of the Dardanelles having failed, there was also talk of an infantry campaign in that area, the object being to capture Constantinople and thus knock the Turks out of the war. Success would release Britain's Russian allies from the Black Sea, where they had been blockaded for months, and seal up Germany's back door into the Mediterranean. With stalemate on the Western front, it was a success the Allies badly needed.

With the men keyed up by the knowledge that they were going somewhere, and soon, by the end of the month the atmosphere at Mena was taut with anticipation. Within days their destination was known: It was the Dardanelles after all, their jumping-off point an island in the Aegean, Lemnos, which nobody seemed to have heard of before.

It was the cue for a wild, final fling, sparked off on Good Friday by an incident in the Haret el Wasser. The story went that a soldier had been stabbed and robbed in one of the brothels; this was hardly unusual, yet it served as an excuse for revenge on the pimps and prostitutes of the area. Several houses of ill-repute were attacked, furniture and bedding thrown over balconies and into the street, even a piano was heaved out to a jangling, smashing end, the applauding troops setting fire to the heap. In that narrow thoroughfare the fire soon spread, and what should have been no more than a small, if violent, incident rapidly escalated into a full-scale riot, with military police, a Cairo fire brigade, and British troops sent to restore order, all drawn into the fray.

The first refugees from law and order flew back to the camp with the speed of swallows to the nest. Many who had not been in town earlier suddenly went to see what it was all about, returning with embellishments to the saga, of fire hoses cut up and used as weapons, shots fired into the rioters, British territorials standing by with fixed bayonets, and military police retreating wholesale from the fight. Few were seriously hurt and fewer still arrested, and no one seemed prepared to give evidence against the perpetrators. It was like the last night of term, so exactly the kind of party the Australians loved, every aspect appealing to their rambustious sense of humor, that Liam could not help laughing. Wishing he had been there, he listened by the campfire that night while stories were repeated, embroidered, and retold, and laughed until his sides ached. It was, he felt, the best send-off they could have had. There was an element about it of an obscene but eloquent gesture: the derisive final word in a long-running argument with the land of Egypt and the hard-pressed military authorities.

Leave for Liam's battalion had been canceled prior to moving out. Along with a thousand others he had spent the day packing guns and ammunition in preparation for their departure. It was to be within thirty-six hours, and after four long months of waiting, the news came both as a relief and a shock. Different units had come and gone, many, including Lewis's band of Light Horse, to the area of the Suez Canal; but Liam's battalion, the 8th, was one of the first to receive its true marching orders. Others would follow by train to Alexandria, and thence aboard ships sailing singly across the Mediterranean. A convoy would have attracted too much attention.

In a wind that stirred the atmosphere over Mena into the consistency of soup, the men in the 8th packed their tents on the morning of April 4 and marched the ten miles into Cairo, none of them sorry to be seeing the last of it.

"And if I never see them bloody pyramids again," Ned remarked bleakly, glancing over his shoulder, "it'll be too bloody soon."

At the station, however, it was a different tale. On one of the platforms, surrounded by a small group of nurses, Mary Maddox was waiting to say farewell. Her kind, plain, distressed face touched Liam's heightened emotions, especially when she came to speak to Ned before they climbed aboard the long line of open trucks. Liam tried tactfully to move away but was stayed by the light pressure of her hand and a half-whispered plea. Bemused for a moment, he suddenly realized that Mary needed his presence as cover. He too belonged to the Maddox farm, sufficient reason for her saying farewell to both of them but not to Ned alone.

Amid pithy comments from all sides on the standard of accommodation for their hundred-mile journey to Alexandria, Mary exchanged a few words with Ned, before turning to Liam. To his astonishment she reached up and kissed his cheek.

"God be with you," she whispered.

He did not catch what she said to Ned, but their lips met, and for a second he embraced her passionately, then, as though ashamed of that weakness, abruptly turned away. Nervously, Liam glanced around, afraid that someone might remark on that obvious and unapproved of alliance, but the group milling around were all of Ned's platoon. A couple of winks and sly grins told Liam all he needed to know, and with a sigh of relief he turned to tell Mary not to worry, he would look out for Ned, but she had turned away.

From the vantage point of the truck he could see her with the other nurses, all come to wish "their" battalion good luck. Practically all the men of the 8th were from Victoria, and for many of the nurses at Mena House the interest was very personal; the little group with Mary Maddox all looked stricken. So did Ned. Wanting to sympathize, Liam found it hard to say anything at all. A sudden longing for Georgina overwhelmed him, and he was envious of the scene he had just witnessed. Watching the nurses taking shelter from the dusty wind, he wondered whether Georgina would be wearing a red cape too; according to letters from home she was no longer in York, but nursing the wounded in some unnamed military hospital in London. That knowledge made him bitter about not going to France and dulled the edge of his excitement now. He wondered whether he would ever see her again and sighed, remembering the cheerless words of the brigadier, who had told them that in a month's time, most of them would probably be dead.

He envied Ned the hours he had spent with Mary, and even the enforced brevity of their parting. With sudden insight, he realized that outside the peculiar circumstances of Egypt and wartime, Ned might never have pursued Mary Maddox, and outside the bonds of marriage, such intimacy as they had shared would have been impossible. Was that a good thing, or was it as morally wrong as he had always been led to believe? It was an uncomfortable question, one that opened avenues he did not wish to explore. Amid that noisy, jostling throng, Liam suddenly felt alone and horribly uncertain. He was glad of the locomotive's shrill whistle and the lurch that set them all scrambling and laughing. They were off, and a cheer went up immediately; hats were waved and thrown into the air, and the little band of nurses smiled bravely, handkerchiefs waving, red capes flapping like flags against the wind.

They left Alexandria four nights later, in winds which were strengthening to gale force. The old troopship rolled and pitched its way across the Mediterranean in some of the worst weather Liam had ever experienced. It was no consolation to the seasick men that the weather was just as bad for enemy submarines. Quartered in cargo holds, packed as close and tight as sardines in a can, the sick groaned and vomited for two days and nights and prayed for death to claim them. The stench was enough to turn the most hardened stomach, and despite the coldness of the nights, Liam spent as much time as possible on deck, huddled in a greatcoat. With the second night the weather subsided, and they arrived off the island of Lemnos to a glorious April morning. Liam thought he had never seen anything so beautiful. Against a curving sweep of grassy, flower-strewn hillsides, the sea was a calm, pale turquoise, reflecting the simple whitewashed village of Mudros at the head of the bay. A vast array of ships lay at anchor, dreadnaughts and destroyers which had taken part in the earlier attack, and among them were the flagship *Queen Elizabeth* with the *Agamemnon* and *Lord Nelson*. Between them were black-hulled cargo boats, white hospital ships, and little sailing vessels whose design must have been old, Liam thought, when the ancient Greeks were young.

It was impossible to set up camp ashore, there being too little water to satisfy the thousands of men gathering for the coming assault on Gallipoli, so they lived aboard their transports in the same cramped and unsanitary conditions that had been their lot from Alexandria, and waited for others to join them. During those two weeks, training was continued, although much of it was novel enough to pass as fun. Every single day they practiced climbing up and down rope ladders with full packs, over the ship's side and into lifeboats. The best rowers were trained intensively, races across the bay being one of the highlights of the week, while trips to Royal Navy ships were organized for afternoons off. Route marches, however, were not crossed off the agenda. Thankfully, in the rest periods, they were also allowed to bathe. After the dust and dirt and stench of Egypt, Lemnos was like a holiday, with warm sun, fresh breezes, and shy but hospitable islanders. Curiously dressed, like characters in some eastern fairy tale, they seemed bemused but friendly, selling food they could spare at a fair price, while none of them, Liam noted in a letter to his brother, had "sisters" for rent.

In the warm, gently lapping sea, Liam swam and dived like a porpoise, reveling in its clean, salt taste, enjoying the fresh tingle of his skin in the sun. His body was hard and brown, his spirits elated once more by the thought of the coming action; keyed up by expectation, he had no fear of dying. Apprehension, such as it was, concerned his likely behavior if wounded. The pain of serious physical injury was something he had not experienced, and having nothing to measure it by, hoped he would behave with dignity and not be a whimpering burden.

On the evening they left the safety of Mudros Bay, however, he was suddenly beset by doubts. So, it seemed, were the majority of those aboard. Everywhere men were scribbling notes and in quiet asides asking their particular friends to be sure to pass on certain possessions if they "bought it on the way in."

"Bet my sister'll be checking out the will when she reads this," Ned joked, showing Liam the envelope with a Melbourne address. "Who you giving the benefit?"

"My people in York," Liam said shortly, pen poised over a blank sheet of paper. Ned carried on talking about his sister and her family, about the broad acres they had left behind in Australia. It was a topic that had drawn them closer, a shared ambition to own land one day, to farm a spread like Ewan Griffith Maddox. Now he gave vent to hopes for a future with Mary, if she would have him once the war was over.

"'Course, her father might not approve, me being just a hired hand, but she's not a kid. Old enough to make up her own mind, Mary is. And I think she'd have me . . ."

He continued to muse aloud while Liam wished he would be quiet; then, taking a sealed envelope from his breast pocket, he nudged his friend. "Just make sure Mary gets this, will you? You know, if anything should happen to me. I don't want to *post* it," he added with a surprisingly bashful smile, "in case I come through—I mean, I'd look a prize dill, saying all that and not a scratch on me."

With a smile, Liam nodded. He thought Ned should post it anyway, but part of him understood that reluctance: After all, he had already written something to Georgina that he did not intend to send through official channels. That letter, addressed via Edward, lay between the pages of his notebook, and if he should survive, it would not be sent at all.

His pen still hovered. As Ned lapsed into reverie, Liam sighed, leaning his head wearily against his pack. Lights were dimmed to a minimum, and in the unaccustomed quietness the steady pulsing of the engines was like a heartbeat, the slight roll of the ship across calm water no more than the gentle rocking of a cradle. The faces all around him were heavy with apprehension; some men were still writing, many were smoking as they lay propped against packs and equipment.

It took no great leap of the imagination to suspect that most, like himself, were thinking of homes and families so far away. It was months now since he had received that first letter from his mother, and there had been others since, innocuous enough, as though she realized her mistake. But he had never replied. Now, with the unknown awaiting him, conscience was dictating its own terms. In truth, Liam knew that given his time over again, he would not—*could* not—have behaved in any markedly different way; but he did regret the pain he had caused. Ever since Robin's letter, he had always regretted that. And if he were to die with the dawn, her pain would be even greater; it would be too cruel to add silence to the burden, to let her feel that he had gone to his grave not forgiving her. He just wished that he could find true forgiveness in his heart, but even now it eluded him. There was still that hard lump of anguish whenever he thought of her, and to mention the reasons for his going would have brought forth a flood of recriminations. That would not do.

In the end, he wrote only a few lines, begging her forgiveness for the grief he had caused and telling her that she was in his thoughts. He added that she was not to worry about him, as he was not afraid of dying, and anyway, he had some good friends, and they would stand or fall together.

Hurriedly, before he could add more, or change his mind completely, Liam folded the single page and thrust it into an envelope. Come what may, his mother would have something from him, and if it was only halfway to reconciliation, then it was better than nothing.

Just after one o'clock, having slept fitfully for a couple of hours, Liam went up on deck. Sailors were moving silently between the troops, handing out mugs of cocoa; he accepted one thankfully. Beneath a moon which shone a path across the glassy sea, he could make out the hulking shapes of other cargo boats; the group of warships and destroyers that had passed them at sunset would be well ahead by now, poised and ready for the landing. Those warships carried men of the 3rd Brigade, those who would be first ashore; Liam envied them. They would have the advantage of surprise, while the 1st and 2nd Brigades must face a roused and implacable enemy. As far as he understood, the 8th Battalion would be one of the last to land. It was a daunting thought.

Time passed with dragging slowness. By three o'clock they were passing the southern tip of Imbros Isle, with possibly a dozen miles to go to the peninsula. They were to land where it was not much more than four miles wide and the long, mountainous backbone was broken by gentle uplands, push inland, and cross the peninsula to a high point commanding the narrows. At the same time the British would be landing at Cape Helles on the southern tip and the French on the Asian shore directly opposite. Hearing the objectives put as simply as that by their CO, Liam thought it sounded deceptively easy, but there had to be hidden snags, else why that dire warning before leaving Egypt?

The moon was setting behind a thick veil of mist. Orders came from the bridge to extinguish all lights, and Liam reluctantly nipped out a cigarette lit only moments before. It must have been his tenth since coming on deck. As he returned the stub to its pack, he noticed his hands were trembling. In the pit of his stomach, the hot breakfast eaten too recently was churning, threatening to disgorge itself. Then a murmur distracted him from that unpleasantness. There was a light, white and hazy, behind land away and to the right of them. Someone said it was a searchlight. The light moved jerkily to left and right, then disappeared. The men around him began to fidget. Liam craved another cigarette; beneath his greatcoat, despite the night's chill, he was sweating profusely. In the first, faint, greenish light of dawn, he could see the high, broken ridge of the land, make out the shapes of three other transports around them moving into line. In a whisper, someone asked the time: It was half past past four. The suspense and the silence were terrible. Liam found himself longing to get there, for something to happen, anything to break the tension.

It came a few minutes later in the form of a bright yellow light, way to the south. A moment later there was a peculiar sound of knocking, isolated small-arms fire which rapidly became continuous. They must have landed! The first wave was there and fighting! The awareness rushed over and through the men like a sigh. In the brightening dawn, faces were suddenly smiling, fingers clenched around rifles, all eagerness to be where it was happening.

The knocking grew louder, brilliant flashes began to appear from a point on the shore; a shower of rain made the sea boil on the starboard side. With surprise Liam realized it was too local for rain: shrapnel falling. From one of the battleships close by, a thunderous explosion rent the air. He saw the gun's recoil, the great curl of smoke that followed, and wanted to cheer. Destroyers that had been close in to the beach began to come alongside the transports, ready to collect the next wave of men.

"Must be our turn next," a man beside Liam muttered, "the jolly jacks are here with the rum . . ."

Shells were falling near the ship while the massive naval guns retorted, flash and boom, flash and boom; a whistling scream and a great fountain of water rose beside the old *Clan MacGillivray* making her roll and sag like an old woman. Liam staggered; the sailor beside him almost lost his footing but saved the rum, handing it out with twice his previous speed. Liam downed his tot in a second, coughing as the thick, treacly spirit hit his throat and burned its way into his chest. He felt better for it, however, and had cause to be doubly glad when their destroyer moved in alongside. In the first rays of the early morning sun, her decks were like a scene from hell, littered with maimed and wounded, and running red with blood. Liam was aghast at the numbers, he could not believe so many in so short a time. Waiting while those poor souls were transferred was torture, and like all the men around him he tried not to look, tried not to hear the cries of pain so clear against the scream of the shells. The platoons gathered in position; the routine of scrambling over the ship's side and down the ladders, so assiduously practiced, went without mishap. Tension again as the destroyer sped toward the beach, men packed like toy soldiers on her decks; then down rope ladders and into the boats, more like barges, Liam thought, wondering how the rowers would handle such large, unwieldy craft.

They were about two hundred yards from the shore, with shrapnel bursting around them; an oarsman was hit and lost his oar, another fought to take his place, pulling out of time with the rest. "*In*, out—*in*, out," their officer yelled, for all the world like a coxswain in a boat race. Liam wanted to laugh.

The boat grounded on pebbles. "Right, chaps, this is as far as we go—everybody out!"

Overboard into four feet of water, Liam gasped with the shock, holding his rifle up and clear, determined not to lose his footing with the heavy pack on his back. On the narrow strip of beach, he saw huddled shapes like bundles of rags and wondered what they were; then bullets danced in the sand and more fell. Something sang past his ear, the sea was suddenly hissing around him; a man with two stripes turned at the water's edge, urging his platoon on. Liam saw that it was Ned and struggled to join him as a shell burst on the rocks ahead. He had time to register the blinding flash before the shock wave knocked him flat; deafened, half-drowned, aware of nothing more than a need to reach the shelter of those cliffs beyond the beach, he lurched forward. A man behind caught his arm and dragged him on.

Liam looked for Ned and could not see him. From the shelter of the cliffs he scanned the beach with mounting panic. Wallowing at the water's edge was a body; soldiers from another boat tripped over it, revealing the stripes on the sleeve.

It was Ned. Liam knew it was Ned. Shedding his pack, he staggered to his feet, only to be grabbed by the man beside him. What was he thinking of, the stranger wanted to know; they had to get *off* the beach, leave casualties to the stretcher-bearers.

"There aren't any bloody stretcher-bearers. And he's my *friend*, for Christ's sake—I can't just leave him to *drown!*"

He leapt forward, and to his credit, the other man followed. Between them they hauled Ned out of the water, getting in the way of the next boatload coming ashore. Liam cursed them as he tried to cut Ned's pack free. He was alive but only just, blood pumping from a wound in his neck. Amid a hail of shrapnel they dragged him to shelter.

Conscious enough to recognize Liam, Ned smiled. Seconds later, with his blood seeping through a hastily applied field dressing, he died in Liam's arms.

Wet through, with seawater dripping from his hair and clothing, Liam was not aware of the tears he shed. His companion's urgent demand as to what they were supposed to do now went unheeded for the moment. From the back of his numbed mind, Liam recalled instructions dinned into each of them on exercise. "Report to the nearest officer. Remember the dead man's position and report."

"Sod that! We'll be dead ourselves if we don't get off this bloody beach. God knows what's happened to my mob—they'll be halfway to Constantinople by now. Come on!" The stranger started to scramble upward, then looked back. "What the hell are you doing now? Let's get *moving*."

Liam was searching Ned's pockets. "There was a letter he wanted me to post . . ."

"In *this* lot? Are you crazy?" He slithered down to Liam, grabbed his arm just as Liam found the wet and crumpled letter, and dragged him upward. "Get moving, you stupid bugger, before you get us both killed."

Numb with shock, his mind operating on a different plane altogether, Liam did not resist again. He was only vaguely aware of scrambling upward among a group of gasping, cursing men; his hands and knees were gashed and scraped on sharp rocks, but he was not aware of it.

"Where the hell are we?" a voice demanded from the left.

"This ain't the place we was supposed to be. Flat, they said—they said the sodding landing place was *flat*!"

"Tide rip," somebody else gasped, "took that first lot north, I reckon, before they could see where they were. Should be down there, where that bloody fort's firing from."

"Stupid bastards," another voice commented, without rancor. "You'd have thought the navy could bloody navigate!"

For the first time, Liam looked down the way they had come. The narrow strip of beach below them was still in shadow, curving from a peaked headland on the left to a smaller one on the right. Beyond that it broadened considerably, reaching gently inland to where a distant wheat field looked like a patch of pale green silk. A rocky headland overlooked that longer beach, and from the promontory came a series of flashes which indicated the source of those shells exploding with such deadly accuracy over the landing craft still coming ashore. Privately, Liam thought they would not have been any better off had they landed down there; the Turkish defenses were obviously concentrated at that vulnerable point, any attacking force likely to be mown down immediately.

From the sea, at least two of the destroyers were pumping shells at the fortress in an attempt to silence those deadly guns; it was a heartening sight for the men on the cliffs but did nothing to halt the equally deadly machine-gun fire coming sporadically from above.

Just below the summit they came across a group who had paused to gather breath. Some of them bore the shoulder flashes of Liam's battalion, but none was of his platoon. He wondered what could have become of them. An officer of the 9th, whose men were scattered in a ravine to the right, was trying to organize all the odd members of other battalions who had been separated in the chaotic advance. He kept saying it was important to reinforce the line, while Liam wondered how he could know where the line was. Men were still landing, still being fired upon; the dead lay huddled among discarded packs at the water's edge, while a few brave souls struggled to get the wounded back into the boats and off the beach. Seeing the terrible numbers, Liam forgave the man who had dragged him away from Ned; Ned was gone and nothing more could be done for him, except the decency of burial. That was not possible here and now, but Liam swore he would not rest until he had found his own company and an officer to whom he could report the details.

If that had been me, he thought, Ned would have done the same.

Looking to right and left, for the first time he realized they were not alone on the cliffs. Half-hidden by the thorny scrub, working their way up in groups of three or four, were scores of men. Every now and then one would fall; with a shock, Liam realized they were being picked off by snipers hidden among the dense, low-lying vegetation.

The officer was talking quietly, rallying the scattered force for a concerted attack on the machine-gun post above them. As they fixed bayonets, Liam kept thinking of maneuvers, the rushing and yelling before the carefully balanced thrust into the gut; but when it came, the reality was nothing like that. It was far from easy to rush the crest through that terrain, over rocks that crumbled and rolled with every footfall, but somehow they achieved it. On the right flank, Liam stumbled into the hidden trench, almost on top of a Turk struggling to escape, and for a second he hesitated. The man leveled his rifle and Liam went at him awkwardly; there was no room for the balanced thrust, the bayonet juddered as it went in and the Turkish soldier fell forward, his scream ending in a froth of blood. Shocked, Liam jerked back, narrowly avoiding a bullet. A sergeant silenced that man while others loaded rifles and shot at the retreating enemy.

The men were jubilant at their success, putting forward a dozen ideas as to what their next move should be. The officer thought they should man the gun and use it against the Turks; their own guns had yet to arrive and would no doubt be the very devil to move up from the beach, but no one knew how to operate the one they had captured, so it had to be disabled. Liam drank from a Turkish water bottle and tried to avoid looking at the man he had just killed. In little more than an hour he had watched his best friend die and killed a man at close quarters. He was shaking so badly he could hardly light a cigarette, and beneath the constant whine and crump of shells to the right, his ears were still ringing from that explosion on the beach. With an effort he forced himself to concentrate on what the sergeant was saying. They were to make their way carefully across the ridge and down into the next gully, where some sort of rendezvous was being set up. From there they might find their own units.

It was vicious, unfriendly country, full of jagged rocks and hidden holes perfect for snipers, a country ideally suited to defense but hostile to attack. Unexpected scree slopes sent the unwary careering down into thorny, dried-up streambeds, and in a couple of hundred yards Liam counted three exposed ridges and as many hidden gullies. Reaching the rendezvous in the deepest and broadest, which ran at an angle up from the beach, was a nightmare journey, unrelieved by what seemed even greater chaos when they arrived. Hideously wounded men were being ferried by stretcher-bearers down that rocky slope while active companies struggled to climb it in an attempt to reinforce the thin line spreading out along the ridges. Brigadiers were holding hurried meetings beneath the rocks, messengers were dodging stray bullets, adjutants looked worried, while the NCOs of a dozen different companies transmitted garbled orders to their men.

Liam and the man from the beach searched for the red-and-white square of their battalion and found several others in the same position as themselves but no NCOs. During that short delay on the beach and their subsequent scramble for the first available cover, it seemed as though the main body had advanced without them. Accosting a harassed adjutant, Liam asked where they were likely to be. With a vague gesture, the man indicated the hills to the right, and equally vaguely gave Liam permission to go in search of his missing company.

"Might as well," one of the men said in answer to Liam's question, grinding out a cigarette. "Feel like a pack of bloody dills, standing here."

The man who had dragged him off the beach was less keen. In the gully they were far from safe, but the odds against survival on the ridge were vast; he was for waiting on direct orders. Impatiently, Liam took a vote and found that they were evenly divided. Sadly, for he felt he owed the man something, Liam said good-bye and, squaring his shoulders, set off with his small group.

Implicitly they followed his lead up and across another

series of crests and gullies, benefitting from a lull in the firing. Within the hour they spotted a large body of Australians ahead of them on the next ridge. Without field glasses it was impossible to tell whether they were men of the 8th, and a sudden increase in shelling over the beach made shouting useless. Scanning the intervening valley, Liam paused for several minutes. It seemed to him that the body ahead must have come this way, and the absence of gunfire below suggested that any lingering Turks had been flushed out. The greatest danger, as Liam was beginning to realize, would inevitably come from above. Nevertheless, it was a chance that must be taken.

Exhausted from their exertions, with little water and no food since well before first light, the others wanted to stop and rest. Liam, sweating just as freely in the hot sun, was anxious to press on before the group ahead moved out of sight. He pointed to the scree slope and told his companions to dig in their heels and slide down; from there it was but one more climb.

"Yeah," the most aggressive of his companions muttered, "just one more fucking climb through that lot!" His hands were torn and bleeding, his breeches, like Liam's, already in tatters. "I say let's rest—we can catch them later."

The rest were wavering; hesitation, Liam felt, might well prove fatal for them all. The bayonet that had wrought such damage a short while before was in its sheath; threateningly, he pulled it free. Although not aware of it, he was a daunting figure with blood all over his breast and sleeve, face scratched and filthy, blue eyes glittering beneath the broad-brimmed hat jammed firmly over his brow.

"If they're advancing," he said tersely, "they need every man they can muster. I say we go now—and we stick together. Right?"

"All right, mate, keep your hair on. You want to go now, fine, we'll go now."

"We will indeed—you first!" With that he shoved hard and sent the other man careering down the slope. The others went of their own free will while Liam followed, bullets from some hidden point flying around his head. The others scrambled for shelter in the gully, but Liam had grown immune to the noise. It seemed to him there was little point in being afraid of bullets, it was more important to discover their source. From the cover of a scented myrtle bush he looked for the hidden sniper; a movement from above brought forth two more flashes from across the gully, only a hundred yards or so from where they had passed. With great care he leveled his rifle and waited; not long and there was another flash and a report. An instant later he pressed the trigger and, as the butt thudded back into his shoulder, had the satisfaction of seeing the barrel of a gun jerk upward through the scrub. He fired again and a body fell like a broken puppet. Gripped by elation, he wanted to jump up and cheer at his own success; instead he kissed the barrel of his Lee Enfield and scurried to join the others. For a moment they were speechless, then, clapping him on the shoulder, resumed their climb. There was a sly whistle and one of them dropped like a stone; shocked out of his complacency, Liam realized that another sniper was at work, something he should have known from the shots that had rained around him as he came down the scree. This time, however, the sudden fire attracted attention from a company above them. Within minutes a regular battle was going on, while the four remaining men climbed like beings possessed to reach their group.

They found men as shattered and exhausted as themselves, almost unrecognizable as the smartly uniformed troops which had mustered on the boat decks before dawn. Of the gathered companies, one was Liam's, but of his platoon, only a handful remained. His arrival caused a stir among them because the shell that had killed Ned and several others had been thought to have finished Liam too. The young officer who had exhorted them all to pull together for the beach had met his end beneath a burst of shrapnel fire in the first gully, while others had been killed or wounded by snipers and machine-gun fire in the subsequent advance. Among so many, Ned's death made little impression, and it struck Liam strangely that his own survival should be the cause of such rejoicing. He had not thought himself so popular.

There were, apparently, several companies of different battalions gathered on that long southerly spur, separated by thick scrub, and under the general command of Colonel Bolton of the 8th. Although orders seemed to be confused and conflicting, it filtered down that the advance had been stopped by concerted enemy fire, and that they were to dig in and hold the heights as the extreme right flank of the line.

During a break in the trench digging, Liam shared water and biscuits with the remaining men of his platoon. It was hardly a feast, but the food and the respite from constant action put renewed heart into them all. It was pleasant, suddenly, to be there. The sky was blue above and birds were singing, and in the noonday warmth they were surrounded by the mingling scents of myrtle and thyme. Before them and to the left, where the hilltop widened before dividing into another ridge, was a small wheat field scattered with scarlet poppies, the field Liam had seen in his original climb from the beach. With familiar faces around him, for the first time that morning he felt safe. Relaxing with a cigarette after that small but satisfying meal, almost idly he watched a destroyer closing into the long beach below them. Peace was abruptly shattered as the *Bacchante* fired shell after shell at the fort of Gaba Tepe on the promontory. The men cheered as shells exploded into great bursts of flame, cheered louder still when one of Gaba Tepe's massive guns was flung into the air and broken like matchwood.

The cheering came to an abrupt end, however, when shelling from inland interrupted their high spirits with crumps and booms close by. A company of the 6th Battalion ordered to dig in on the wheat field had been spotted by the Turks. The pale green wheat made an easy target, and salvo after salvo descended on that small patch of ground, while those who watched were helpless to defend the men lying low before them.

Ducking into a trench while those shells thudded into the soil and scrub around them, Liam was close enough to the command dugout to catch something of their officer's frustration. As yet they had no artillery, but with those huge naval guns so close, if that Turkish battery could be located, it could be stopped. Runners were sent out to make contact with the forward lines to the north, but none returned. Meanwhile, every time troops moved on or near the wheat field, the enemy reopened fire. Other runners were sent back to headquarters in that gully off the beach, returning with the anxious news that the forward line was opening as it continued to advance across the main plateau. The main body must be reinforced if it were to hold, and therefore some of Colonel Bolton's men must be relinquished in support.

Overhearing some of these exchanges, and shrewd enough to guess the rest, Liam began to wonder if he was in the right place. He watched a man detach himself from the party in the wheat field and sprint up the hill toward them, attracting another salvo as he did so. Wincing, he ducked again, while the man fell in a gasping heap beside him. Even as Liam tried to help him up, he was scrambling away to deliver his message.

Permission was granted for the men below to advance; anything was better than lying prostrate beneath those shrieking salvos. Orders were hurriedly given and as hurriedly carried out. Together with several other sections of the 8th, Liam's platoon was detailed to accompany that party in their attempts to reach the forward line. They had to cross the open field while shells screeched and thudded beside them. Knowing the Turks had the range wrong did not ease that nerve-shattering dash: Although the shrapnel was not bursting overhead as it was designed to do, at any moment one of those shells could land on a man and cut him in two. With no casualties, however, they reached the body of men under the command of a young lieutenant, from there wriggling forward on their stomachs until they reached the scrub at the field's far edge. From there it was a steep drop into the gully below.

At the far end of the next spur, they came across another remnant of the 8th with only one surviving NCO; they had been hard-pressed in their advance from the beach, losing many men on the way, and their morale was nonexistent. Somebody asked whether they had eaten—in the heat of battle food had been forgotten. Again, as had happened with Liam, the combination of food and friendly faces put new life into them. After a short spell they set to work digging themselves in.

It was essential to keep on the alert, but apart from the shells still screaming overhead, it was a surprisingly quiet afternoon. Liam found himself counting the salvos, pitying the men still holding the ridge behind them, for the Turks knew exactly where they were. Detailed for this party, he had been convinced he would not survive that dash across the field, but he had, and this was a better position by far. But it seemed a strange sort of battle to him, a series of mad dashes with no more than rifles and bayonets against an enemy entrenched with artillery and machine guns. As yet the Australians had neither.

At about five o'clock, large numbers of Turks were seen on the skyline, advancing from their positions on the highest ridge toward the pine-covered spur immediately in front. Silhouetted against the sky, they were a perfect target but as yet too far off to be reached by rifle fire. Suddenly shells screamed over from one of the warships, but although many men went down, more continued to come on. The joint company prepared themselves for action, and within the half hour, as the Turks crept through a line of pines across the little valley, they opened fire. Heavy and continuous, it was also unexpected, and the enemy fell back; elated, the Australians yelled and whooped for joy. The young lieutenant leapt to his feet, directing fire, and a Turkish bullet felled him. Badly wounded, he could hardly speak but insisted his company hold on until nightfall. They did so, defending their position, losing many men, but determined to hold back the Turkish advance. As the light began to fail Liam could hear isolated battles going on all around, but it was impossible to tell friend from foe. At last the enemy seemed to fade away, and after dark the runner who had gone to report their situation returned with orders to retire to the ridge overlooking the wheat field.

Liam had never envied any officer, never wanted to be one of them. In his mind they were associated with Robert Duncannon, and as such to be held in some sort of contempt. But that day he conceived an admiration for this man, who was no more than his own age yet had managed to keep his head under what, on occasions, had been terrifying conditions. More than that, the young lieutenant had been cheerful and enthusiastic, he had seemed to know what to say and when to say it; he had, in effect, held the men together. His only mistake had cost him dearly. After the unremitting ordeal of a day which had begun some twenty hours before, they were all exhausted to the point of collapse, many sleeping in the shallow trench, rifles clutched beside them. With the return of the messenger, Liam went forward to their acting commander, a corporal he remembered from Cairo. He was a big, muscular Queenslander, and a badly broken nose testified to more than one vicious pounding from fists as big as his own. But he and Liam were of a similar height, bigger than most of the other survivors; it seemed only sensible that they should carry the lieutenant between them.

They made a seat for him from their crossed hands, and with great difficulty descended into the valley. Although he was not particularly heavy, in their exhausted state his weight seemed like lead, and the sheer awkwardness of negotiating a steep slope in darkness, over loose rocks and spiny scrub, called for strength and control that drained them both. By the time they reached the narrow valley, Liam was sweating and trembling in every limb, his arms burning in their sockets. Faced with the scree slope, terrified of dropping the lieutenant and making his injuries worse, Liam suggested carrying him across his back.

Between bouts of agony, the lieutenant objected thoroughly and colorfully, insisting they leave him. But rumor had it that the Turks mutilated their prisoners and that was a risk that Liam was not prepared to take.

Still gasping for breath, the corporal ordered Liam to hold the lieutenant upright. With difficulty he did so, wincing at the groans of agony, easing him as gently as possible onto the other man's shoulders. With Liam guiding and pulling, they managed perhaps twenty paces. Taking over the burden, with another man pushing and the corporal guiding, Liam managed half the slope. As he collapsed, his lungs on fire, he heard voices raised in argument above. The corporal heard them too, identifying himself before they could be mistaken for marauding Turks. Thankfully, help came quickly. Relieved of his burden, however, Liam found himself incapable of movement. To his shame, he had to be carried up the rest of the incline and supported across what appeared to be a plowed field. With something of a shock he realized that it was the wheat field dotted with poppies that had looked so beautiful in the rising sun.

15

$\mathcal{H}$aving checked the course for the Dardanelles, Stephen took his coffee outside, yawning in the warm air, pleased by the touch of the sun on his face and arms. It was another limpid blue morning, with the azure hills of Imbros Isle poised between sea and sky. It was the kind of morning to satisfy every holidaymaker on every island in the Aegean; and after all, this was what they saved for, assiduously, all the year round. Responding to it, he smiled, counting his blessings, glad that he did not have to earn his living cooped up in an office for eleven months of the year. If this job had its drawbacks, then it also had its advantages, and moments like this were blessings indeed.

Spring, and the weather was beautiful; it must have been a day like this that saw the initial attack on Gallipoli. Anzac Cove, named for the Australian and New Zealand Army Corps, had passed into legend, and the debacle of the whole campaign faded to nothing beside the bravery of those men who endured it.

Transcribing Liam's diary, Stephen had begun by separating the notes relating to different years. Liam had dealt rapidly with 1914, while the memoranda for 1915 was fuller, but still frustratingly sparse on detail. With his eyes taking in the harsh skyline of mainland Turkey and the tip of the peninsula ahead, Stephen wondered whether Liam had made notes at the time of dates and places and particularly violent exchanges, or if, in that depressing return to the desert in early 1916, he had checked details with others who were on Gallipoli, entering noteworthy dates in his new diary sent out from York at Christmas.

It was difficult to say. Possibly it was a combination of both, since Liam seemed the kind of man who liked to keep a tally of what was happening. But if the notes for that period were disappointingly brief in comparison to the following year, they were also shocking in their terse accounts of attacks, gains, and casualties. Set against his own general knowledge of that campaign, the diary made him wince.

Studying the chart last night, he could see why the planners in London had thought it such a good idea. The Gallipoli peninsula, at the point where they had attacked, was only about four miles wide. With no firsthand knowledge of the terrain, and without taking into account the weeks of foreknowledge given to the Turks, London must have deemed it a great idea at the time. Capture the forts on either side of the Dardanelles, hold enemy shipping to ransom, and while you're at it, lads, just nip up and take Constantinople . . .

But those forts were never taken, and the troops were stuck there from April to December, lobbing homemade bombs into Turkish trenches, dying from the heat and flies in August, and frozen to death in November when it snowed. No fresh food or water, and everything had to come by ship from Lemnos.

The idea that ignorant men in comfortable offices in London could send other men across the world to die in conditions like that made him very angry. It made him angrier still to think that so little had changed.

His anger was so at variance with the beauty of the morning, it was unbearable. He went inside. An hour later, however, with the Dardanelles looming, he was back on the bridge, checking courses and radar projections, scanning the shoreline with powerful binoculars. The peninsula, low at its southern tip, rose in a series of ocher hills, in parts densely covered with evergreen scrub. From the sea it had a certain rugged beauty, but the vivid pictures in his mind's eye made him shiver. Although the Anzacs had landed way up on the seaward side, Stephen knew that what he was seeing now would have been seen by Liam as he took part in the second assault on Cape Helles on May 3, just a week after the original landings. In between the hideous fighting of the following few days, Liam noted that he had explored the ruined fort of Sedd el Bahr, had a swim in the sea, and chatted to a Commander Sampson about his airplane. It all sounded very cosy until the entry for May 8: *"Took part in the second attack on Krithia. Gained 800 yards, lost 2,000 casualties."*

By mid-May, however, Liam was back at Anzac Cove, landing during a concentrated shelling; and by May 20 he was fighting in the hell of Quinn's Post, where the trenches were no more than a few yards apart. In that small area the dead lay unburied in their thousands, so numerous and so offensive that an armistice had to be arranged for their interment. There seemed a dreadful irony in that. Although he had never remarked on minor injuries, considering the terrain and the intensity of constant warfare, Stephen could not imagine that Liam had remained unscathed. And if he had, there was always dysentery to contend with, which had been endemic, made worse by the lack of sanitation and the hordes of devouring summer flies. What amounted to a starvation diet had also taken its toll. For eight months those men had lived on the kind of iron rations meant to support a man in the field for no more than a few days. By the beginning of September Liam had been seriously ill. Not with dysentery—although he had probably had that too—but pneumonia. He left Anzac on a hospital ship for Alexandria, arriving at the Palace Hotel, Heliopolis, on the tenth. On that date, the tall, fine-looking young man noted that he had weighed only 130 pounds. In four months Liam Elliott had lost more than forty pounds.

Six weeks later, however, he was pronounced fit for action and, with a promotion to acting corporal, was returned to Anzac with a new uniform, which was one advantage many of the others would not have had. Winter came early to the peninsula that year, and the last two months were bitter, with temperatures well below freezing. In their pathetic holes in the ground, many of the emaciated troops died of exposure.

After that, just before Christmas, had come the evacuation. A creeping retreat so that the Turks would not realize it was over and that their foes were leaving. Liam, in the firing line to the bitter end, had watched stores and food being burned on the beach while those beside him went hungry. The next day, after a bombardment that lasted six hours, he and his compatriots left Anzac Cove without another shot being fired. Within twenty-four hours, he noted, they were back on Lemnos and drilling again three hours a day.

That terse comment was echoed, day after day, throughout the next three months. Egypt had not changed when they returned to it, but the men had. They were weary and depressed, had suffered an ignominious defeat, and had watched their friends die for nothing. That they themselves had fought like the Trojans of old, that they had endured and ultimately survived, was not enough to raise spirits which were crushed by the experience. That no one else seemed to care only added to the burden. The entries in Liam's diary for that period at the beginning of 1916 were short and monotonous and full of complaint, so indicative of malaise that Stephen's anger had been choking as he typed up days and weeks of the same thing. *"Drill again, food still scarce,"* was typical, as were complaints at lack of leave for the men, while officers were allowed plenty. Later, from an active post by the Suez Canal, Liam had written over several days: *"No food, nowhere to buy any . . . Digging gun pits and trenches . . . No issue of water for over 48 hours, one loaf of bread between three men . . . Lecture by our Colonel on whether we are fit to go to France . . ."*

Those entries in Liam's diary were, Stephen thought, a terrible indictment of all that had passed in the name of organization; all of it inflicted by those at the top, men of their own nationality, on their own side. That was the worst part: It might have been more forgivable had those deprivations been suffered under an enemy hand.

With the diary in his pocket and his eyes on that brooding neck of land, so intent was Stephen that he barely noticed the arrival of the Turkish pilot. It was with something of an effort that he brought his thoughts back to the present and the job in hand.

* * *

Some hours later they dropped the pilot at Gelibolu, where the Dardanelles widen into the Sea of Marmara. They passed much Soviet and Romanian shipping, most of it merchant trade, although there were a couple of naval vessels bristling all over with the latest military technology, that Stephen photographed just for the hell of it. Watching them slink past like greyhounds on a leash, he thought how ironic it was that Liam had fought, ostensibly, to release the czar's navy from the Black Sea. But the plan, ill-conceived and unprepared for such resistance from the Turks, had failed. At this distance in time, Stephen could not help wondering what difference it would have made to the war—and the world—had they succeeded. Probably not very much. Russia had been heading down the road to revolution even then.

After dark, Istanbul and the Bosporus slipped by like a jeweled stage set for the *Arabian Nights*; by comparison, Stephen thought, Odessa at noon was about as alluring as a banana republic on the eve of a coup. But it would have been all the same had their loading port been the best place on earth: He was too busy to go ashore, and except for Sparks, the Radio Officer, that went for his officers too. Not so the Filipino crew, however. Most of them managed to spend some time ashore, and while handing out rubles before they went, Stephen stressed the need to obtain receipts for everything purchased.

Two days later, eager to get away from the armed guards and that depressing townscape, before the ship sailed he called each of the crew to his office to collect the unspent currency.

"You may not keep any rubles," he explained. "All you have left must be returned to the agent. And I must have your receipts."

The first three shook their heads in some confusion. "But they do not give receipts, sir."

As the young steward outlined a female form with his hands, the two cooks dissolved into helpless laughter, and suddenly Stephen understood. But he could hardly credit it. "You mean *Russian* girls?"

"Oh yes, sir—*very* good!"

The situation afforded him the first hearty laugh for several days; nevertheless, he did wonder how to explain their purchases on the forms before him. He was left with a dual sense of admiration: for the crew's determination and obvious prowess, and also for the spirit of free enterprise at work in that grim Communist city. He was, however, glad to leave it.

Approaching the Bosporus on the return journey, he related the tale in a letter to Zoe, although with Liam still on his mind, the majority of what he had written was concerned with the diary and his enclosed transcript. Only as they anchored, awaiting the boat to collect the mail, did he feel the need to add lines that were lighter, and certainly more personal. With mosques and minarets reflected in the still water, and the fabulous dome of the Topkapi Palace facing him, it was impossible not to be touched by the romance of Istanbul. It was Byzantium and Constantinople, the seat of popes and sultans, a meeting place of past and present, sacred and profane, Europe and Asia facing each other across a narrow strip of water. The evening air was like velvet against his skin, perfumed and spicy, making him long for things which seemed forever destined, like the city itself, to remain just out of reach.

Describing both place and atmosphere, Stephen was tempted, suddenly, to make her smile. He had an ongoing sexual fantasy, he wrote, about sailing ships and warm wooden decks beneath the stars

> —and this would make the perfect setting. But then I look around me, and there are no tall masts and spars, no furled sails and smooth, scrubbed, wooden decks. Only functional painted steel, complete with squared-off afterdeck and bulbous bow—these days ships don't even *look* like ships!
>
> Why am I here? I ask myself that all the time. And if I have to be here, which it seems I must, why are you so far away? I wish we could be together again—here and now, with a good meal awaiting us at some candlelit restaurant, and my very comfortable, but oh so empty bed to return to. (And to hell with the warm wooden decks—better in imagination, I'm sure, than reality!)

Reading through the last few lines before he sealed the envelope, Stephen thought they came dangerously close to some kind of commitment, but he had no desire to retract them.

There had been moments in the past when he had longed to share the delight of an experience with someone else, but never before had there been a woman with Zoe's depth of understanding, a woman with whom he *could* share such things so completely. Most particularly, he could think of no other woman who would appreciate how he was beginning to feel about Liam Elliott.

His desire to talk to her on that very subject was underscored within the hour. The boat that came to collect their letters also bore a package of mail from London. As he sorted its contents into piles for different officers, Stephen's heart gave a pleasurable leap at the sight of Zoe's handwriting on two envelopes. Unable to resist opening them there and then, he quickly scanned the contents, gratified by her admission that life was not the same without him, that she missed him even more than she had anticipated. But as though that path was fraught with danger, she had rapidly abandoned it for safer ground. Disappointed, Stephen returned to those comforting few lines and read them three times. He skimmed the part about some new work and her agent's opinion, slowing as he reached a most unexpected piece of news. She had, she said, found among Louisa's letters a whole bundle from Liam written during the war. Addressed to Edward, they covered the period spent in Egypt, Gallipoli, and then France, the early letters full and vivid, the later ones terse with weariness, giving the impression that much was left unsaid, and not just for the censor's sake.

Her enthusiasm at this find sprang off the page, and also her sadness. Like Stephen himself, she was angered by the almost unimaginable horror of Liam's experience, a horror that led him to edit his own sentences before they were written, to couch all but the lightest moments in bland phrases.

"The strange thing is," Zoe had commented in her neat italic hand, "that despite his obvious attempts to hide things, I feel as though I know what it is he's hiding, and why he's hiding it. I feel as though I know him."

Me too, Stephen silently agreed, drawn suddenly closer to Zoe by that common awareness. In the next sentence, however, when she confessed that she had even begun to dream about Liam, Stephen's heart skipped a beat in apprehension. Despite the warmth of his office he shivered at that coincidence, wondering whether her dreams had been as disturbing as his own. He hoped not, but for the moment he was so unnerved, had she been there he would have told her to leave the letters alone. But she was in London and the mail had already gone.

With daylight and the return passage through the Dardanelles his reaction seemed extreme. He told himself that what they were investigating had very quickly ceased to be a mystery; identities and ambiguous relationships had been sorted out, providing clear motivation for both Liam's abrupt departure and Tisha's later eccentricities. In the peculiar feelings which had assailed him at the realization of Robert Duncannon's paternity, Stephen could well sympathize with those closest at the time. Even with two generations between, for him there had been an odd, almost drunken shift of perspective, which seemed ridiculous in retrospect, because he had never known Edward Elliott. He could only suppose that it was something to do with identity, with the assurance that came from knowing who you were, and where you had come from. It was not something people examined every day, but it was there, like childhood. And there must have been a world of difference, he reflected, between Edward Elliott, the poet, and Robert Duncannon, the professional soldier.

Unlike Stephen, Zoe had experienced no sense of shock at their discoveries. Having known nothing about the family, she had come to it clean with no preconceived ideas; yet when it came to Liam, her detachment crumbled. Just as his own did. Why?

It was a question to which there was no ready answer; or rather too many answers, all facile, none of them touching the heart of the matter, none of them explaining the long chain of coincidence.

Once out of the Dardanelles, however, Stephen made a concerted effort not to think about it. Knowing that Mac was growing anxious at what seemed an obsession, he dutifully accepted every invitation to darts in the bar and even organized a general knowledge quiz for Saturday night. At one time, he reflected nostalgically, social evenings had been organized by junior officers, with the old fogies invited along purely from courtesy. But for some reason, these days the youngsters organized very little. A diet of television and videos had apparently made them too sophisticated for old-fashioned parlor games, but the old games were more than simple entertainment, they made people *talk*. And social intercourse was vitally important, welding bonds between strangers, easing some of the strains of the working relationship with humor. Stephen needed to know his officers, needed them to know each other; the job itself was hard enough without the added stress of isolation and poor morale.

Initially, however, it was always difficult to promote enthusiasm; only afterward, having had a better time than any of them imagined possible did they suggest more. For the quiz, Stephen organized two teams, one headed by the Mate, the other by the Chief; Mac, as in all past quizzes, managed to raise hilarity by answering "Graham Greene" to every question on writers, and although there were some complaints from the younger end that Stephen had included too many questions on the First World War, the evening was a minor success. Stephen felt he had made a breakthrough when the Third Mate asked whether he might organize another quiz for the following Saturday.

"Providing we're not in port, you can. We'll get Saturdays organized yet—Board of Trade Sports in the morning, Quiz Night after dinner . . ."

The lad looked blank. "Board of Trade Sports, sir?"

"Boat drill, Marcus," Stephen explained with a grin, "and fire drill."

En route for Augusta, Sicily, Stephen's main concern became that of their next destination. He was not at ease when charters and cargoes were difficult to come by in London. With the war in the Gulf, he dreaded the kind of desperation for work that might send him and his ship running the gauntlet through the Strait of Hormuz. The cargo was discharged in Sicily without too many problems, but only as the last marine surveyor drank his beer and left did a telex come through from London. As though to keep them on tenterhooks, the instructions were simply to proceed in the direction of the Suez Canal.

"Oh wow," Mac said in an acid interpretation of a gleeful schoolboy, "haven't seen Port Said in years. Wonder if it's changed any?"

"One can always hope," Stephen responded, recalling too vividly his first trip through Suez, before the Six-Day War closed it: the boats clustered around every ship at anchor, the young boys with their cheap trinkets, and the constant demands for baksheesh. Remembering the girls of Port Said, he laughed suddenly. "Thank God we'll only be passing through. Can you imagine the crew ashore? They'd come back bankrupt!"

Mac gave a low guffaw of laughter. "After Odessa I think we should telex ahead to every port, telling them to lock up their women. Our lot might not speak the lingo, but they can certainly make themselves understood in any language! Mind you," he added slyly, "we didn't do too badly when we were younger, did we?"

"Not in bloody Port Said, though!" Stephen exclaimed with horror.

"Oh no, not Port Said. Singapore was the place then—and Japan. I remember a girl in Osaka-Ko who was the best—"

"Mac," Stephen interrupted, staring at the telex. "They're not telling us something. Why are we heading for Suez? Going through there costs money, and we're in ballast, earning not a brass farthing. Whatever they've got in mind for us east of Suez must be pretty bloody lucrative . . ."

Picking up that sudden, overwhelming conviction, Mac slowly shook his head. "No, no—come on, Steve, they wouldn't—"

"Wouldn't they bloody just!" He slammed the paper down and quickly lit a cigarette, pacing Mac's cabin like a caged tiger. "I bet you—I bet you any bloody thing you care to name that that's where we're going!"

Mac stroked his beard. "Indonesia?" he suggested hopefully. "Singapore? We are due for dry dock—"

"Stuff the bloody dry dock, Mac—we're going to the Gulf."

A few days later, it seemed that Stephen was wrong. Told to proceed toward Singapore for further orders, Mac was convinced he would get his dry dock after all; but as they cleared the Red Sea the telex came in that confirmed the worst of Stephen's fears. Not just a single trip in the Gulf but a charter which would have them in and out every week. *For a limited period*, the message said, but that could mean anything from six weeks to six months, as Stephen well knew. Furious that such orders had not warranted a personal telephone call via the satellite facility, he simply acknowledged the telex without comment. It was midday in London, so let them call him if necessary. If he spoke to the company now, in the heat of his anger, he might live to regret it.

Over the internal telephone, he called the Mate's cabin. He was off duty, and as expected, he was in bed. Mac and the Second were in the bowels of the engine room, but within ten minutes all four were gathered in Stephen's cabin with the outer door shut. The Radio Officer, with his professional commitment to keep the contents of telexes to himself, had already been sternly reminded of it. In deliberately neutral tones, Stephen read out the contents of the message to his senior officers. The Mate, unexpectedly, gave vent to a string of obscenities which were echoed, to a lesser extent, by the second; Mac simply stared, his brown eyes hurt, as though Stephen had personally arranged to prove himself right.

With a defensive shrug, Stephen skimmed the paper across the table so that they could read it for themselves. He went to the fridge for four cans of beer and set them on the table. It was hot in the cabin and he was sweating, his shirt sticking to his back like tissue paper.

"Technically speaking," he said slowly, "we are not obliged to carry on our occupation in what is officially termed a *war zone*. Technically, I could send a telex back, demanding reliefs for all of us—"

"And we all know what sort of a reaction you'd get to that!" Mac commented, red whiskers bristling. He took a long pull on his beer.

"True, but I can try. However, we need to anticipate a refusal, no matter how it's couched, and plan accordingly. Because no matter what pressure is brought to bear, certain people will want off, regardless."

"If they pay me enough," Mac growled, "*I'll* sail the bloody ship for them—right up the main street of Tehran!"

Laughter broke the tension, and for a few minutes they discussed money, and what should be demanded in return for their "loyalty" to the company. Stephen let them carry on, knowing that certain figures and percentages would be offered, and that it would be up to him to negotiate the best deal. He had few illusions about the attitude to reliefs.

Only the Mate seemed particularly unhappy. "I've got a wife and three kids, and as far as I'm concerned, they're more important to me than any bloody job. What's money if you're blown to bits?"

Stephen was inclined to agree with him, but forbore to do so. "I don't have a wife," he said, "nor do I have children. My objections are those of principle. I hate war and I loathe what they're doing." In the ensuing silence, his breathing sounded ragged, at odds with the chill in his voice. "However, what we have to face is our own economic reality. And I think—*before* we start telling the company where to get off—we have to consider our positions seriously.

"I also think," he went on a moment later, "that those of you who are married should try to get in touch with your wives. In a sense, they're just as involved as we are. But please, *not* until I've had a word with the office, and we have the official line on what the choices are."

Stephen took copies of the telex, had one posted in the bar, another on the bridge, while a third went down to the crew's quarters with a message for the bos'n to contact him as soon as possible. Part of him wanted to break his own rule and telephone Zoe at once, but although he had a good idea of what the official line would be, he felt he must await its confirmation. And when it came, shortly after seven that evening, the voice of his respected ship manager was hardened with a deliberate chill, like that of a 1916 officer informing his juniors of the next big push.

The slight pause inflicted by the satellite link distanced them further. We were friends, Stephen thought, united by many a previous difficulty mutually solved, and now we sound like enemies.

"I'm sorry, Jack, but feeling here is running strong. Nobody wants to risk his neck just to keep a bunch of Muslim fundamentalists in Exocet missiles!"

The voice, after a second's delay, was colder than ever. "This charter is to the *Kuwaitis*, Captain—the oil is *Kuwaiti* oil!"

"Balls!" he retorted, infuriated by that insistence on something they both knew was little more than a technicality. The oil might be coming through Kuwaiti pipelines—it might even be from their own fields—but the money it was earning, that was a different matter. In a biased neutrality, the Kuwaitis were feeding financial aid to their war-torn Iraqi neighbors, and the Iranians, knowing exactly what was going on, were intent upon stopping the trade.

Again the delay, but this time the voice had softened to a cajoling note. "Look, Stephen, I'm giving it to you from the horse's mouth. We *need* this charter, it's worth a lot of money to the company—we're on the edge, believe me, and it might just tide us over till things improve. *If* they improve." There was an eloquent sigh. "*We can't afford to turn it down.* Nor can we afford the delay while you and your crew pratt about making up your minds. If we have to do a complete crew change, I'm telling you the Filipinos will never work again—not at sea, anyway. And there'll be so many black marks on the officers' files, it won't be worth their while applying elsewhere. The company has long arms and much influence, you know that."

Stephen did know; nevertheless he could not believe he was hearing it stated so unequivocally. He had expected pressure, but not this deadly determination which was currently underscored by Jack's confidential tone. Had it come from anyone else, even the chairman himself, he knew he would have been tempted to lay down the gauntlet of challenge. But he knew Jack, and Jack knew the company inside out. In the intimate world of shipping and shipowners, these people were akin to the Cosa Nostra. How else had they survived when almost every other British company had gone to the wall?

Stephen knew, too, that however highly he was regarded, they would be prepared to fire him over this issue, and at the end of the day, when he needed a reference for something else, his file would be marked *unreliable*, and there would be a tactful disinclination to comment. They had him over a barrel and they knew it. Rage coursed through him. The iniquity of blackmail offended his principles and integrity even more than the nature of what he saw as being a very dirty job indeed. Biting back the urge to tell Jack what to do with it, Stephen shut his eyes and clamped his hand across the mouthpiece.

It took all his self-control to remind himself of the vow

made years ago: *When you pack it in, Elliott, it'll be when you are ready and not before.*

This was not the time to call the odds.

While Jack Porteous dotted the *i*'s and crossed the *t*'s of all he had said already, Stephen shuddered, as at a mouthful of bile. Releasing his cramped fingers, he said bitterly, "You know it's a pity the company can't use some of its fabled power to lobby the bloody government. If British shipping had more support from *that* quarter, Jack, maybe we wouldn't be in this situation in the first place. Tell that to the bloody chairman!"

It was, he felt, a suitable last word. Abruptly, he severed the connection, and it was some minutes before he had calmed down sufficiently to speak to anyone else.

In the radio room, Sparks was lounging like a disc jockey before the banks of electronic equipment. "So what are they going to pay?" he asked laconically. "Over and above, that is."

"Not enough," Stephen answered tersely. "And if it were a couple of million in a Swiss bank account, it still wouldn't be enough."

It was, however, a question asked by all the others. The bonus was to be a percentage of their monthly salaries, not ungenerous when considered in isolation, but worth little in the light of insurance policies made invalid by the war zone. Death or disability thus incurred was not standard cover.

The Mate was the first to use the satellite phone. His wife apparently echoed his sentiments, because he repeated his request for a relief. Wearily, Stephen nodded. The younger officers, however, were oddly exhilarated by the thought of danger and the chance of extra money; the older ones resignedly counted the weeks still to go before they could legitimately apply for leave. Mac and Stephen, having been last to join, still had something like four months ahead of them. The Third Engineer, with three months yet to do and a wife and baby at home, requested a relief.

"I'll get a job on the rigs," he said defiantly, "and stuff the bloody company."

Stephen rather admired the belligerency. Contrary to his expectations, the crew were quite unperturbed by the situation. He was not sure whether it was fatalism or greed on their part, but every one elected to stay. That should please Jack Porteous, he thought, returning to his cabin to make another call. With the receiver in his hand, however, he paused before dialing the London office, deciding to speak to Zoe first. He had some vague hope that she might persuade him otherwise, bringing forth a string of incontrovertible reasons as to why he should say, like the Mate and the Third, "Stuff the company, I'll find something else . . ."

But deep down, at the heart of him, he did not want to say that, not yet . . . Anyway, she was not at home. Envisaging the empty flat, he let the telephone ring and ring, willing her to dash up the stairs to answer it. Dejection gripped him; he had wanted so much to hear her voice. Then he was furious, wondering where she was, and what could be more important that she must be out when he needed her . . .

Still in that spirit of anger, with a sense of having all his exits cut off, Stephen called Jack Porteous, and their communication was terse and to the point. *Now we know where we stand,* Jack seemed to be saying, *we can organize with lightning speed.* As indeed they could. Nevertheless, Stephen did wonder whom he would be sent to replace the men he was losing.

It was not until he tried to call Zoe again, later, that he realized something was wrong with the satellite link. He tried the telex and that too was down. Impotently furious, he was further incensed when Sparks, having checked everything and risked his neck going up the mast, announced that it would take specialist engineers to cure the fault. For the next few days they were forced back to what seemed a prehistoric means of communication: Morse code over the short-wave radio.

The ship put into Fujairah, well outside the Strait of Hormuz, landed the two recalcitrants, and took aboard their replacements, together with the electronics experts. The only joyful moment for Stephen was in greeting the new Mate, that same John Walker with whom he had served aboard his last ship, the ill-famed *Nordic.* He had a feeling that Johnny's irreverent humor was going to be a tonic they would all savor.

"What the bloody hell made *you* agree to all this?"

"I dunno, Captain—I think my bank manager said I could do with the money. Mind you, I was a bit pissed at the time, so don't quote me."

Stephen laughed. "And what about the girlfriend?"

"No problem—last time I saw her, she said she'd like to see me in hell anyway."

"Oh. All off, is it?"

The long, lanky Mate shrugged, his nonchalance that of the seasoned campaigner. The new Third, unmarried, uncertificated, and well into his fifties, seemed to regard the situation as normal. Their combined attitudes put new heart into Stephen. They had been at home, living with the television news, and must know what they were getting into.

At noon Stephen went ashore with the agent, his chest struggling against heat which pressed like a hot iron. About to phone Zoe, he was apprehensive at the thought of having to explain where he was and why, and awed by the commitment he was about to make. This time, the need to tell her that he loved her had not come from outside himself, but from deep within; and it was suddenly the most important thing in the world. He wanted desperately to say so and to hear the same words from her lips.

The thought of dying, Stephen realized, clarified the mind wonderfully, identifying priorities with the speed of a computer. Having accepted the situation as unavoidable, all he wanted to do now was get on with the job. He was still angry, but he treasured the anger, like his love for Zoe, as a talisman against fear. And when the job was over, please God, he would go home, sort out his life, and make proper plans for the future. He had drifted too long; it was time to set a definite course.

Like a man with a terminal disease waiting impatiently for a lawyer to draft his will, Stephen drummed his fingers on the agent's desk, a telephone within reach, while the agent complacently sorted business of his own. At last the man left him alone to make his calls. Time demanded he contact the office first, and when that lengthy business was complete, he dialed Zoe's number. There was a silence, then interminable clicks and sighs; the phone rang four times and was then picked up.

A man's voice answered, light, cultured, faintly amused.

The unexpectedness of that stabbed like a knife in the breast, stopped his breath for a moment, made it difficult to speak. The voice at the other end was impatient, became peremptory. Almost stammering, Stephen asked for Zoe.

"And *your* name?"

"Elliott," he snapped back, barely controlling the urge to demand the other's name and the nature of his business at Zoe's flat at ten on a Saturday morning.

Muffled words, a voice—her voice—suddenly clear in the background; a rustle of movement which made him wonder where she had been, what doing; then flustered, breathy intensity.

"*Stephen*—where are you calling from? This *is* a surprise!"

Racked by the most painful suspicion, for a moment he almost hated her. It was with great difficulty that he controlled his words, his voice. "Just thought I'd ring—see how you were."

"I'm fine—just fine," she claimed while a nervous laugh escaped her. "But how are you? You—you sound *different*. Is anything wrong—or is it just this awful line?"

"I'm fine."

"Well, good, I'm glad to hear it. Where are you?"

"Some place you've probably never heard of. Fujairah—it's part of the United Arab Emirates."

There was a pause on the line. Stephen could almost hear her thinking, raking over world geography, trying to place it exactly.

"Zoe," he said with mounting urgency, aware of time passing as he was of the man in the background, and unable to ignore either, "we're going into the Gulf. We'll be in and out for the next few weeks, between Kuwait and Karachi. It's annoying, and I can't say it's something I relish—but frankly, there's nothing to be done about it. I just wanted to say"—he broke off—"I just wanted to tell you where we are—in case you don't hear from me for a while."

"The Gulf?" she repeated faintly. "Not the *Persian* Gulf?"

"The very same."

"But—there's a *war* going on. I keep seeing it on the news—missiles, minesweepers"—he could hear her breath coming sharp and deep—"Stephen—they *can't* send you there."

"Why not?" he demanded. "The rest of the world wants to buy what they're still selling—and fools like us have to do the dirty work!"

The muffled exclamation of her distress cut through his anger. The iniquity of his position, Stephen reminded himself, was not her fault. Apologizing, knowing the conversation was not going the way he had intended, he rubbed his forehead wearily. He would have liked to start again, but the presence of the other man in Zoe's flat was as tangible as the heat on the window behind him.

"I'm sorry, Zoe, I shall have to go. I'm phoning from the agent's office and it's a courtesy call. I'll write as soon as I can. By the way—did you get my letter from Istanbul?"

"Yes," she said eagerly, "I did, last week. And your transcript of the diary—"

"Good, well, I'll write again soon—let you know more about what's going on." For a moment he was tempted to end the conversation there, but his need to know about the other man was too great. Tersely, he said, "Who's your friend, by the way? Or shouldn't I ask?"

There was a short silence. Her response, when it came, was just a shade too dismissive. "Oh, it's only Philip. He—well, my car's playing up again, and he offered to give me a lift down to Sussex. It wouldn't have mattered," she added with a false little laugh, "but I've got an appointment this afternoon to see Tisha's old house, and—"

"I see." It sounded plausible and he would have liked to believe her, but not even the mention of Tisha's name could overcome a hot surge of jealousy. So Philip Dent was on the scene again. "Well, I hope he's a good driver. Have a nice weekend."

She seemed nonplussed by his acidity. "Stephen, it's not like that. Please don't—"

But he never could abide lies. Quite deliberately, he cut the connection, hating the false intimacy of telephones, the emotions stirred by the sound of a voice, the sheer impossibility of closeness that they underscored. And to the recipient, he thought sardonically, a call could be such an unwelcome interruption.

Standing by the window, with sunlight filtering through the young leaves of plane trees outside, Zoe listened to the empty hum of the line and knew the disconnection was not accidental.

Angry, hurt, disappointed, and most of all frustrated, she turned on Philip.

"There now—see what you've done!"

"Hey, just a minute, Zoe—you did ask me to answer it."

"I know—but now he's got entirely the wrong impression, and—" She broke off, slammed out of the room, and began to gather her things in a fury, dumping them in the tiny hall.

"Oh, *damn and blast!*" she ground out between gritted teeth. "Damn him—damn you, Philip—and damn the blasted car! If it hadn't been for that, this would never have happened. And if you hadn't been so ridiculously early, Philip—"

Severely put out, Philip of the perfect looks and elegant manner paced the room with less than his usual composure. "I'm beginning to wish I hadn't offered to take you down to Sussex," he declared huffily.

"Me too. But as you did, perhaps we'd better get going."

Without another word he picked up the lightest bag and set off down the stairs, keys jangling irritably between his fingers. Left behind to lock up, Zoe hoisted her bag, camera, and sketchbook, in that moment regretting everything to do with Philip Dent. Most especially, running into him again at the library two days ago. Sliding into the front seat of his red Ford Sierra, she reflected that it would have been far preferable to have caught the train to Brighton and had her mother collect her from there.

But after initial embarrassment he had seemed pleased to see her, so keen to talk about David and Clare—whom Zoe had met but once since that unfortunate evening with Stephen—that she was consumed by curiosity. Especially as he was obviously determined to treat her as a friend, and not an ex-lover. She wanted to know what was happening, and Philip seemed to need a willing ear, but the library was no place to talk and he had to get back to his office. He had mentioned a drink over the weekend, and she had mentioned Sussex, and here they were . . .

That Stephen should have chosen that moment to telephone! Half an hour earlier or later and he would have been none the wiser, and because there was nothing for him to worry about, she would have had nothing to explain. It really was *too* bad.

Fretting and fuming, she answered Philip in monosyllables, but it dawned on her at last that there was an edge of malice to his probing, and now that he had recovered himself, a certain smug satisfaction at her discomfiture. She was far too upset to be able to hide her feelings; wanting to hurt him too, she answered with brutal frankness.

"Yes, Philip—Stephen is important to me. He's the most vital man I've ever met. Being with him is like being alive to your fingertips—and yes, I'd dearly love to spend the rest of my life cooking his meals and darning his socks. Are you satisfied?"

"So much for feminism," he replied contemptuously. "I thought you wanted to be a free woman, devoted to your art."

"I've changed."

"All the nice girls love a sailor, eh?"

"Oh, don't be fatuous!"

"But he doesn't love you, does he? Or at least, the way I see it, he doesn't *trust* you. Not that I blame him—after all, you threw me over for him and now he thinks—"

"I did *not* throw you over for him! Clare's a liar if she said that—I hadn't even met him when I said good-bye to you!"

"But if he trusted you," Philip went on, regardless, "my being in your flat this morning wouldn't have meant a thing."

That hurt, because it was uncomfortably close to the truth; it hurt more because such lack of trust was unjustified. Stephen's wife had been unfaithful to him, and obviously, not knowing the facts, he suspected the same of Zoe. She could have wept with fury but would not give Philip the satisfaction.

"Do you have to be so hateful, Philip? So gloating? You've got your revenge on a plate—I hope it tastes good."

After that, neither of them spoke. In the glorious weather of early June, trees in full leaf made dappled patterns across the road. Zoe had glimpses of vivid color in cottage gardens and the forecourts of pubs and garages along the way, but they were traveling too fast for appreciation. Only as they slowed behind the massive, tubular bulk of a road tanker did she find her self-obsessed considerations suspended. With an anxious glance at the Sierra's speedometer, she realized that the tanker was doing something like fifty miles an hour, a good speed in two-way traffic along roads that were far from straight, but Philip was anxious to overtake. Zoe held her breath. The chemical symbols for petroleum spirit loomed large. Afraid to look at the road ahead, she glanced sideways, seeing massive double wheels too close for comfort and an unfamiliar logo, *Q8*, emblazoned on the tank above. Q-eight, Q-eight, Q-eight, drummed menacingly through her head until they were safely past. In relief she involuntarily murmured it aloud, and instantly the hidden meaning became clear. Not *Q-eight* petrol, but petrol from *Kuwait!*

"Kuwait," she repeated, stunned by the connection with Stephen. It was oil from Kuwait that he would be transporting out of the Gulf, and for which he would be risking his ship and his life. Guilt washed over her. Concerned by her own frustrations after that telephone call, Zoe had all but forgotten the reason for it. All but forgotten Stephen and the knife-edge of his situation.

"Yes," Philip said, obviously glad of a neutral topic with which to break the silence, "it's a new company. They've taken over another group—can't think who it was now. Prices seem reasonable, though."

"Reasonable?" she repeated, a shrill edge to her voice. She thought of the twenty-six lives aboard Stephen's ship, the hundreds, possibly thousands more who were engaged, at this very moment, in the same trade. "I suppose anything's *reasonable*, if you don't count the human cost . . ."

16

*S*he borrowed her mother's sports car to meet her appointment near Worthing and, despite the persistent anxiety of her thoughts, had to admit that it was fun to be driving the old Triumph Spitfire, its engine and gleaming red bodywork kept in excellent repair, and at enormous expense, by Marian's "little man" in the village. But it typified her mother. She loved anything with a smart label, preferably antique or vintage, and in prime condition. It was an expensive hobby, one that she had extended into a business, and most successfully. That element of perfectionism, however, also extended to her personal relationships, which were less obviously successful. With two failed marriages behind her and a number of relationships that had, at some stage, been *meaningful*, Marian seemed to have resigned herself to the fact that she was better off as a single woman. This was something of a relief to Zoe, who over the years had lost track of the different partners and the innumerable houses to which she had been invited during school holidays and vacations from college.

As women, Zoe and her mother were temperamentally opposed, although it was easier now to set differences aside and concentrate on the things they had in common. They both liked old things and had something of a fascination with the past. Where they diverged, however, was in this matter of family history. Marian found it hard to be rational about her own past and had a tendency to lay most of her considerable problems at Tisha's feet. She was bitter, too, about Tisha's relationship with Zoe, maintaining that she had managed to alienate Marian's only child. There was no point, Zoe had discovered, in repeating that one swallow did not make a summer or, in this case, that one summer did not make an alienated child, because Marian pegged all her guilt on that and did not want it shifted.

Nevertheless, she was to a certain extent intrigued by Tisha's past, wanting to know, if not to discuss, the reasons for the old lady's secrecy. But every time the subject came up, Zoe had to steel herself for the usual epithets "cruel," "paranoid," "mean," "selfish" when applied to Letitia Mary Duncannon Elliott. And every time, Zoe had to remind herself that her mother's story was both sad and unfortunate for all concerned.

So, it had been something of a surprise to receive a call from her mother last week to say that if she was interested, Tisha's old house was again up for sale.

"I was just glancing through the property pages, and I happened to see it. Gave me quite a shock, darling, but there we are. I rang the agents, by the way," she had added distastefully, as though it went against all her principles, "and they informed me that it's been for sale for some time. It's empty too."

If it had given Marian a nasty turn, the news provoked in Zoe a queer leap of the heart, bringing back memories of childhood, of that awful, uncertain time of her parents' separation, and the summer she spent with an eccentric old lady she hardly knew. Her father, she recalled, had protested at length, but as usual, Marian had had her way; and while the two adults sorted out their tangled emotional affairs, Zoe had been sent to that strange, ugly, Victorian house with its overgrown garden and empty rooms. It might have been the stuff of nightmares, but fortunately Zoe's disposition had always inclined toward the adventurous rather than the timid, and compared to the months which preceded that visit and the misery of boarding school immediately afterward, that summer had been heavenly.

Unable to resist a desire to see the old place again, Zoe had telephoned the estate agent and, trying to sound like a serious buyer, made an appointment to view. She hated lying, but knew that no self-respecting agency could afford to indulge a matter of idle curiousity. With her age and sex against her, Zoe hoped that the vintage sports car would give credence to her tale that she was looking at property on her father's behalf, and that his was a view to investment. It was so typically her father, she felt the tale was one she could carry off.

But she need not have worried. The young man who waited with the keys was singularly uninterested in who or why; so many had come and gone, it seemed that this was no more than another waste of a glorious Saturday afternoon. He did not even offer to show her around, but simply sat on the steps of the south-facing terrace with his sleeves rolled up and collar open, taking in the sun.

"If I really wanted to buy this place," Zoe remarked with a certain acid amusement, "I think I might report you for indolence."

He glanced up sharply, uncertain as to her meaning, and for a moment even looked faintly alarmed; then Zoe smiled, and he grinned back, relieved. "You mean you've no intention of buying? Well, I don't blame you—it's a heap. And it'll take a fortune to repair. But we live in hope . . ."

He was lazy and unprofessional and Zoe could have told him that he was in the wrong business, but he was not unlikable. She smiled again. "It might surprise you to know that it was not markedly different when I last stayed here, sixteen years ago. My great-grandmother had the house then, but she died the following winter and I haven't been back since. It passed on to my mother—I seem to recall she sold the place pretty quickly, but I don't know who bought it. Do you?"

"Fifteen years ago?" He pursed his lips. "Could be the people who are selling now. Same family, I mean. An old chap lived here—a widower. After his wife died, apparently he lost interest, let the place go, and his family were abroad. Actually, they still are. One son's in South America—he's the one we're dealing with—and the other's on an Antarctic expedition."

Zoe laughed. "So nobody's breathing down your neck?"

Beneath that attractive tan, he had the grace to flush. "Well no, I mean . . ."

"Never mind," she said easily, "I'm here under false pretenses anyway. I tell you what—you just sit here and enjoy the sun, and let me have half an hour or so to browse around."

Inside, so little had changed. Different wallpaper, perhaps, but sixteen years ago many of the rooms had been as empty as they were now, so nothing seemed strange. Although Zoe had said that the house had passed to Marian after Tisha's death, that was not strictly true; the house had never, in fact, belonged to Tisha. Her parents-in-law, the Fearnleys, had willed the house to their granddaughter, Edwina, with a lawyers firm and a distant Fearnley cousin as trustees. Edwina had grown up here and married young, a naval lieutenant, and they had a child, Marian, in 1940. Then Edwina and her dashing young husband were killed during one of the many raids on Plymouth, while their little daughter was safe at home in Hampshire with her nanny. Nanny had bestowed her charge on the closest relative—Tisha—and Tisha had been forced to don the mantle of motherhood for the second time.

There had been money from the naval officer's side of the family, but it had all been tied up for Marian, as was that rambling great house in Sussex. For years Tisha had been selling objets d'art to keep herself in little luxuries, and well before the war had closed up the house and taken a small flat in Pimlico, her old stomping ground. It had been such fun, she said, until Edwina's death, but London was no place for babies and nannies, so it was back to dreary Sussex and this insufferable old house.

Zoe could hear her saying it, hear Tisha's voice as plainly as though she had been standing there, gazing bitterly from the window. No, not bitterly—resignedly, Zoe thought. She might have been bitter once, but Tisha had outlived strong emotion, it seemed, and survived on a diet of cynicism. She had been allowed something from the child's inheritance, but it had never been enough; so when old man Fearnley's collection of objets d'art ran out, she had started selling larger pieces: paintings first, then furniture. By the time Zoe saw the house, there was little left, and Tisha was reduced to living in two or three rooms. Not that she cared. As long as she had enough to dress well, and to take a trip up to town once a week to meet a few cronies for tea at Fortnum's, she was happy.

She enjoyed playing the grande dame and did it on very little. Her immaculate outfits were always set off by one or two items of good jewelery and a mink stole; and she had enough handmade shoes to survive any fluctuation in fashion. "There's nothing new, darling," she used to say, "just the same old styles made over to look different. Keep a thing long enough, it comes back again."

And keep things she did. The furniture might have gone, but clothes remained, hoarded in trunks and wardrobes, packed between tissue and mothballs. Zoe had had a wonderful time with flapper dresses and feather boas, hobbling about in gilt and silver sandals, purple satin slippers, and velvet mantles fit for a queen. For a ten-year-old little girl, it had been paradise.

In the first-floor bedroom with its long windows and balcony outside, Zoe smiled, remembering. In those days this room had been stripped bare except for the wardrobes and a long pier-glass and an ancient chaise longue by the window. Excellent for dressing up. And Tisha had sat in the sun with the French windows open, watching her great-granddaughter through half-closed eyes, an almost feline satisfaction in her smile. She had never much cared for Marian, and seemed to derive pleasure in telling Zoe that she had not allowed her mother to rummage through those precious things when she was a girl; but as Zoe had not much liked her mother at that time, the pleasure was mutual. Only in retrospect did that seem shameful.

There had been added pleasure in the reminiscences the clothes provoked. Tisha might never had mentioned her early life in York, but she obviously enjoyed reliving the high points of her young womanhood, the parties, the people, the café society of the twenties and early thirties. And every outfit had a story—in one slinky black number by Schiaparelli she had danced with the Prince of Wales.

"He had a taste for slim, dark women even then—and in those days, darling, I was very slim and very dark." She had patted her short, chic, silver curls. "And of course people always said I had such marvelous eyes." She had peered closely at Zoe then. "A shame, darling, that yours lack color . . ." And then back to the original tack. "He should never have married that Simpson woman—she had hypnotic eyes, did you know that? She mesmerized him, like a stoat . . . Of course"—sighing—"I couldn't keep up with their set—didn't have the money, more's the pity. And with poor little Edwina to think of, here, in this place, with those dreadful Fearnleys—I had to keep coming *back*, you see . . ."

And while Zoe gazed at her, agog in childish innocence at this talk of princes and house parties and love affairs, she had suddenly grown sad.

"Edwina was a dear little thing. Very affectionate, very trusting, just like her father. Poor Edwin." Another deep sigh, and at Zoe's question, she said, "He died, darling, in the First World War—he was wounded, rather badly I believe, and then he died. We'd been married just over a year, and he never saw his baby daughter . . ." Gazing from the window into the sunny, overgrown garden, Tisha seemed lost in memory, and Zoe had been almost afraid to breathe; but then those thin shoulders shrugged, and with a smile she said, "What is it they say? 'Only the good die young' . . ."

There had been no need to ask about Edwina. Even then, Zoe had known that her mother's mother had been killed when Marian was too small really to remember her. But she had been sad and hugged Tisha, and her great-grandmother had wiped away a tear and said, "Well, darling, the tragedy is that I was never cut out for motherhood . . ."

But a moment later her eye caught the sweep of brilliant red silk spilling from one of the trunks, and she had launched into a tale of some exiled Russian count met in Paris just after the war.

Zoe smiled at the memory. For all its bareness, the house seemed full of her; she had impressed her forceful, independent spirit upon every red Victorian brick, giving a damn for nothing and nobody, least of all the remnants of her family. Vain, selfish, and egotistical by the standards of everyday society, Letitia Mary Duncannon Elliott had not been an admirable woman, and yet she had fascinated Zoe; beneath that carapace of cynicism, something in her had warmed to the child. Was it the recognition of kindred spirits, or a heavy measure of nonconformity passed down in the blood? Or was it simply a matter of lonely old age reaching out to a solitary and misunderstood child?

With a sudden flash of insight, Zoe realized that it was probably a combination of all three.

Certainly Zoe had enjoyed every minute of those summer weeks, loved the air of "camping out" within the house, the irregular meals and what her mother would have called "unsuitable" food. One day when the grocer neglected to call, they had lived entirely on strawberries from the garden; another time, after a trip to Fortnum's, it had been quails eggs for breakfast and pâté de foie gras with toast for tea. And the trips to town, after lengthy preparations the day before, had been the most exciting occasions of her young life. The three old ladies and their gentleman friend had gossiped unashamedly before her, stuffing her full of cream cakes and giving her sips of wine to drink. Witty and world-weary, dry and brittle as autumn leaves, they were relics of a time between the wars; how she wished she had been older, or that they were still alive.

It had been a fabulous, fantasy time: The weather had been glorious that summer, the towered and turreted house sleeping in the sun like a fairy-tale castle, the garden an overgrown mass of peonies and roses and wild honeysuckle. In the orchard a Russian vine had spread like a canopy through the trees, strangling everything with its winding tendrils and pretty, lacy blossoms. Despising gardeners and gardening, Tisha had said she preferred it like that.

A perfect place in a perfect summer, and for years it had been encapsulated in her mind as the idyll of childhood, with Tisha the benevolent white witch who made everything possible.

But the adult who looked at those great high rooms also saw rising damp in the kitchen quarters and dry rot in the attics; she shivered involuntarily, wondering what winter was like. The central heating looked prehistoric and the fireplaces were huge; Tisha would not have spent money on fuel. The winter following that idyllic summer had been harsh—Zoe recalled shivering every night in her boarding school dormitory and did not wonder at Tisha's sudden death. The certificate recently unearthed gave hypothermia as the cause.

Suddenly, needing the direct heat of the sun, Zoe hurried downstairs and out on to the terrace. Summoning a smile, she handed the keys back to the indolent young man.

"You can lock up now, if you like. I've seen all I want to
see inside. If you don't mind, I'll just have a wander through
the garden."

"I'll go then."

"Yes, you might as well."

He hesitated, gave her a practiced smile. "I don't suppose—you wouldn't care for a drink down at the village pub?"

Zoe shook her head. "No, thanks all the same. Another
day, I might have said yes—but right now I don't think I'd be
very good company."

"Sure?" He met her steady gaze and sighed regretfully.
"Oh well, never mind. Some other time, perhaps?"

"Yes, perhaps."

She watched him lock and test the doors, saw him stroll
back to his car and give Marian's little Spitfire a look of envious
admiration. With a final wave, he swung his modern saloon
around on the gravel drive and disappeared between the
shrubberies.

Like everything else, the gravel was overgrown with
weeds. In the orchard the vine had gone, while at some stage
the old trees had been pruned back to some kind of life, although it was impossible to tell whether they would ever bear
fruit. Zoe suspected not. Since Tisha's day, the garden had
obviously been cleared and tended, but more recent neglect
had again allowed the vigorous growth of climbers and creepers
to smother less hardy plants. There was a certain wild, ragged
beauty about it, but the place had lost its magic. She paced a
winding path through the shrubbery; as a child, this garden
had seemed endless, the paths like tunnels which went on for
miles.

Back at the terrace, Zoe sat down on the steps and glanced
up at the house. Afraid that it too might seem suddenly diminished, she averted her eyes, wanting to preserve the memory
as it had been. But the memory that was Tisha was crumbling
in the light of recent knowledge; secrets had been revealed
and personal traumas guessed at, clarifying motives hidden for
more than half a century. That happy, smiling family group
photographed in the garden of a cottage in York was no sham;
but Edward's face and the presence of Robert Duncannon presupposed tensions that were about to erupt into tragedy. How

the truth had come out, it was impossible to say; but that it had come out, and blasted them all in the shock, was certain. Letty Duncannon's correspondence with Louisa bore that out. She had stayed on at home for two more years, but Zoe gathered that it had been an uneasy truce, that her acceptance had been borne of necessity, as was so much else in her life. Never one to bemoan her situation, she had simply bided her time, like a half-wild cat awaiting its opportunities, and at the first opening of the door, she was gone.

The war provided her opportunity. With trained men off to the front or needed for training others, women had been taken on at the barracks as clerks; from York she had transferred to the War Office in London, and there, presumably, she had met Captain Edwin Fearnley, a regular soldier some years her senior. Had she loved him? Zoe wondered, gazing at the garden his parents had once so carefully tended. Perhaps she had, in her way, for she had spoken of him in affectionate terms. Perhaps he represented the security she had lost, the security destroyed by Robert Duncannon. And what, Zoe wondered, was her opinion of *him*?

As ever, the more questions were answered, the more others arose. It was a frustrating exercise, particularly when undertaken alone. Together she and Stephen had tossed ideas around, reasoning, speculating, sifting the evidence, and looking for logical conclusions to every question. And it was exciting because their minds complemented each other, hers quick and instinctive but not always leaping in the right direction, and his slower, but far more methodical, following the line of reason. Between them, they usually reached solid and satisfactory conclusions.

She missed him. Missed his company and his affectionate teasing, and most of all in that moment she missed the passion they had shared. Her body, as much as her lonely spirit, ached for him. If that lengthy and beautiful letter from Istanbul had perfectly expressed his yearnings, then Zoe could have echoed it here, in this garden, at the fall of evening. Across the lawn's soft grass, long shadows were creeping, indigo beneath the trees, dove-gray where they touched the rounded shape of a cherub in the dried-up lily pond. The past was no longer perfect, and the present less so; she wanted Stephen, needed him *now*, not in three or four months' time. She wanted him to be here, seeing all this, sharing her past, helping to exorcise the devils of memory which held her in thrall. It was hard to leave, because the last time she had done so it had been to discover that her own world was crumbling; like Tisha, she had had to face some very unpleasant truths. Her parents had parted and it seemed they no longer wanted her. James Clifford was in London and managed to see her only once before Marian was taking her to a huge, horrible place full of strangers. It was like a prison. That had been her first impression, nor had it changed, despite the beautiful grounds, the tennis courts and hockey fields, the neat village beyond the walls. After the freedom of this house and Tisha's own brand of magic, boarding school had represented endless years of punishment for some obscure crime she could never recall committing. And with Marian constantly moving around, the holidays were no remission. She saw little of her father, and Tisha was dead.

The drive back through summer twilight was not easy. Unfamiliar with these particular country lanes, Zoe had to force herself to concentrate on what she was doing and where she was going. When she finally arrived at her mother's cottage, Marian came out straightaway, as though she had been waiting by the door.

"Thank God you're back—I was convinced you'd had an accident, or worse. Picturing you locked up in that awful house with a madman, or something!"

"Oh, Mummy, I'm sorry. I should have phoned, I didn't think—"

Anxiety turned to anger. "Don't tell me you've been chatting up that estate agent in some pub, Zoe, or—"

"No—no, I haven't I—" On the verge of tears, Zoe dissolved instead into weak laughter. "But oddly enough, he did offer . . ."

Inside, with the lamps lit and a bottle of chilled wine on the low table between them, Zoe explained, as best she could, why she was so late; but the wine loosened her tongue, and for once she was not so well inclined to spare her mother's feelings and keep things to herself. Ignoring Marian's deepening frown and her occasional exclamations, Zoe let the whole day come pouring forth. She talked about Tisha and her relationship with the Elliotts and Robert Duncannon; she talked about the house and the summer she had spent there; and she talked about herself, the years at boarding school, the feeling she had then that her parents no longer wanted her. And the wine loosened something else, so that by the time she came to the end of the tale, which rested where it had begun that day, with a telephone call from Stephen, Zoe could no longer control the accumulation of grief. Huge tears poured down her face in silent rivers, running along her jaw and soaking the front of the thin blouse she wore. As Marian handed her a box of tissues, Zoe apologized again.

Marian seemed more confounded than upset, as though she were trying to sort out that mix of tragedies old and new, as though she could not find words to say or even a place to begin. Eventually she patted her daughter's shoulder and swept the damp hair from her face. Physical affection had never come easily to her, and it was almost as though she were afraid to embrace her grown-up child.

"I'd no idea you were so unhappy," she said at last, wonderingly, and it seemed to Zoe that she spoke no less than the truth. "You were always so self-contained—no tears, no tantrums, quite the perfect little girl in those days."

While Zoe sobbed afresh, recalling the tears she had shed in private, the secret world she had inhabited, Marian said, "I'd no idea I was such a poor mother. I liked school, you see, when I was a child. Everything was so ordered, so safe. There were rules and you obeyed them, and if you did well, people liked you. And I wanted to be liked, so I did well. But it wasn't like that at home. Home!" she repeated bitterly, "that great, empty mausoleum—you've no idea how I hated it, how unhappy I was in the holidays. No friends and nothing to do, and Tisha off gallivanting most days up to town . . .

"I only sent you there in utter desperation that summer," Marian went on. "I thought, well, the poor lamb will just have to put up with it for a few weeks—even that was better than the ghastliness of the separation. Rows, bickering, up to town to see lawyers—oh, it was awful. I had to spare you that.

"But you enjoyed being with Tisha, didn't you? I couldn't

understand it. And you were so difficult after that, Zoe, I'm afraid I blamed it all on her. I was convinced she'd turned you against me. We never did get on."

"I know," Zoe said bitterly, "that was obvious, even to a child."

"She resented me. Resented my existence. I dragged her back to Sussex and she hated it. She couldn't wait to get me off to school so she could resume her rounds of friends and men and parties. And in the meantime, she sold everything of any value in that house—things that should have belonged to *me*."

Zoe had heard it all before; nevertheless, she felt sorry for her mother. Tisha had managed to embitter her grandchild, and her selfish behavior had somehow managed to color Zoe's existence through Marian. There was a degree of blindness in them both, a limitation of spirit somewhere that made it difficult for them both to judge the effect of their behavior on others. Wondering whether that was, in part, everyone's problem made Zoe anxious. She was aware of wanting children, Stephen's children, and yet it frightened her to think that she might behave in the same blind, selfish fashion.

Nothing was resolved. Old bitternesses were raked up, which simply made Zoe more unhappy. Nor did her mother seem to understand about Stephen; and an awareness that she would *never* understand those special links forged by their common inheritance placed a clamp on Zoe's need to talk about him. Wishing she had not come, she took a train back to London immediately after lunch the next day.

Because so much had been said about her father, she found him still very much on her mind. Marian's claim that James Clifford was more interested in money than people was simply not true, although Marian would never believe that. Zoe supposed that belief eased her sense of guilt and rankled pride which, even after all these years, seemed still attached to their divorce. Although her mother had remarried within a very short space of time, and divorced again almost as quickly, Zoe's father had remained unattached, and she often wondered why. Perhaps, as he always claimed, his passion for business got in the way. But it was not money as such that interested him, rather the excitement of *making* it; and with his wide-ranging business interests, his time and attention were totally absorbed. When Marian said that he could not have looked after a little girl, even one at boarding school, Zoe knew she was right. It did not, however, ease her sense of regret, for she liked her father and there was a level of affection between them that she had never shared with her mother.

When he was not abroad, they met for dinner on a fairly regular basis, perhaps once or twice a month, and occasionally he would drop in to see her at the flat on his way home from the office. By and large she saw more of him than of Marian these days, but while he always inquired about his ex-wife, James Clifford never talked about the past. The present and the future were what interested him, not the whys and wherefores of a failed relationship, even one that had produced a daughter as dear to him as Zoe.

He knew about Stephen and professed regret that his daughter had not seen fit to introduce him previously; he was also rather intrigued by the blood relationship.

"Although I sincerely hope," he had said with a laugh when she had explained the connection, "that these Elliotts you speak of are nothing like their late and unlamented relative!"

Tisha had earned his grudging respect, if not his liking, for her nerve and sheer tenacity in clinging to a way of life that she had made entirely her own, and it amused him, in retrospect, to discover her origins. "Well, she always claimed a connection with the Irish gentry," he said, "and it seems she was telling the truth. I have to confess I didn't quite believe her at the time." But in the light of the Elliotts' position, and Tisha's illegitimacy, he was not at all surprised that she had been so secretive about the rest of her family.

But James Clifford was abroad again, and not even his sympathy could ease the problem of Stephen. Thoroughly miserable by the time she arrived home, Zoe sat and stared for a while at the ominously silent telephone, then went to invite her neighbor Polly for a drink.

Their friendship was one that had grown over the years, born of the fact that they were the only single women in the building, and, as far as they were aware, the only two regularly at home during the day. But if it had begun in the realms of convenience, their relationship had become a true one, with warmth and genuine honesty between them, and as a friend, Polly had proved to be more steadfast than others in more conservative professions. She was an actress whose rich, throaty voice was much in demand for radio plays and television voice-overs. Her vibrant personality masked an intensely practical nature, and her concern was generally expressed in forthright terms.

Faced with the problem of Tisha and the past, she said quite bluntly that nothing could change it, so worrying was a waste of time. "Look back if you must, Zoe, but only to check up on things. It strikes me that the mold was a pretty poor one, and the best thing to do is break it."

Which was virtually the conclusion Zoe had come to already, but it helped to hear it from someone else.

"And as far as your beautiful man's concerned," she went on later, "why don't you just write and tell him the truth about Philip?"

"But it might not be the truth," her friend protested. "I might be doing Philip a grave injustice. I mean, just because he wasn't very inspiring as a lover, doesn't mean to say that—"

"Oh come on, does it matter? All right, it obviously matters to him, and for his own sake, the quicker he gets himself sorted out, the better. *But*, as far as Stephen's concerned, I think you should be honest about your suspicions. It's all tied in with what you felt about Philip, right from the very beginning, and I'm sure Stephen's mature enough to understand that. Let's face it, he lives and works in an all-male environment—he must have seen it all before."

"But how did Philip strike *you*?"

Polly threw up her hands in despair. "For goodness' sake, why does everybody think, because I'm an actress, that I should be an expert on homosexual men? It doesn't say a lot for my reputation, does it?" She shook her head and laughed. "Anyway, you've asked me that question before—and as I said, he simply struck me as being not your type. Too quiet, somehow. I know you thought he had *hidden depths*," she reminded Zoe with a gurgling laugh, "but to me he was just plain *boring*."

Zoe chewed her lip. "You're sure?"

"No, I'm *not* sure. How do I know what turns him on, or what his hang-ups are? You went out with him for three months, and even *you* don't know! But I'll tell you this," she added firmly, pouring herself another glass of wine, "that man is getting out of all proportion. He's not important to you—Stephen is. So why don't you write him a searingly passionate letter, telling him how much you love and adore him, and you can't wait for him to get back to warm your lonely bed. That should cheer him up no end."

That was what Polly would have done. In and out of love with amazing regularity and unflagging enthusiasm, Polly was passionate about most things. Zoe's feelings, however, were more tender and, where Stephen was concerned, infinitely more vulnerable to pain. In her present mood of uncertainty, she was far from sure what it was that Stephen wanted to hear. It was all very well for Polly to maintain that he had telephoned simply because he cared, and that his sharp manner had been prompted by jealousy. It might be true, but he was so set against commitment, and in Zoe's book, a declaration of love was a serious matter.

In the end, having slept on the matter, she chose the lesser of two evils and wrote a letter explaining Philip Dent, from the circumstances of their first meeting to the moment of realizing it was all a waste of time. It was hard to be honest about the sexual side of their relationship, but even while she hesitated Zoe knew the words must be found and the truth expressed, whatever Stephen's reaction. He had to understand that Philip was in the past, and not likely to be resurrected by chance meetings and the offer of a lift to Sussex.

Suppressing a desire to tell him how much she loved and needed him, Zoe spent the best part of a day over the first half of that letter; the rest comprised a description of Saturday, almost from beginning to end. Despite her efforts to contain it, emotion crept in as she wrote about Tisha's house and the memories that visit had stirred.

> . . . I keep thinking I shouldn't have gone, although after a thoroughly miserable weekend, writing all this to you has somehow acted like a purge. And having raked over the ashes of those years and really looked at them, I find they are less dreadful than they appeared to be.
>
> And I think I must say the same about Philip. I'm sorry

I didn't tell you at the time—I wish I had, but I felt so badly about it. The silly thing is, Polly put it all in perspective for me when she said he was boring. He is, although I didn't realize the extent of it until I met you. Looking back on that episode, even talking to him the other day about Clare and David, I realize that I don't need that kind of thing in my life. And after the row we had in the car, I doubt I'll see him again. And as for Clare—well, I don't think I want to see her either. But I haven't any regrets.

Well, there is one. It was so wonderful to hear your voice the other day, I just wish we had been able to talk—really talk, I mean. But I was shocked by your news, and you were so obviously wondering about Philip . . .

Anyway, you have the truth of it now—I just hope you can understand what was a very peculiar situation . . .

Zoe paused and read her letter through. The more she wrote about Philip, the more she wanted to go over and over it, like a criminal obsessed by his crime. Which was silly, because, as Polly said, it was giving him an importance he did not deserve. There was no need to say more. Hesitating over how to close, instead of her usual "Love, Zoe," which was affectionate but casual, she wrote, "All my love to you . . ."

For a moment, its straightforward honesty made her feel better, but then uncertainty over his reaction attacked again, and she stared at it helplessly. She could hardly cross it out, and she did not want to write the whole page again, so in the end she let it stand, bestowing a sentimental kiss before she sealed it into the envelope and took it to the post.

It was a bright morning, invigorating, with a sly breeze that made her shiver a little as she returned from her short walk. She had a sense of fragile hopefulness, as after a brief but debilitating illness: not a conviction that things would turn out well, but an awareness that the only way forward was with one step at a time. Stephen's wrong impression the other day still bothered her, and she hoped that when he read her letter he would understand that the last thing she wanted to do was to play fast and loose with either his emotions or her own. She hoped too that he could sense the love between the lines, because she knew, more certainly than anything else, that he needed love, whether he was aware of that need or not. When he came home, they would have to begin again. It was as far as she could think, but it was enough. It had to be enough.

That letter, however, and the weekend's reflections on motherhood, brought something else to mind. In analyzing Tisha on paper, Zoe realized that in all Louisa's correspondence, she had so far come across nothing from her daughter.

In a large, strong cardboard box were all the as-yet-untouched bundles, now much depleted. In another were letters identified but still unread, and, filed in a series of smaller boxes, the ones already dealt with. Each envelope was numbered, each number corresponding to a series of notes Zoe was making in a large, stiff-backed notebook. It was a mammoth task and there were cross-references everywhere, but as she had so recently remarked in her letter to Stephen, it kept her occupied and interested, and left little time for anything else. Particularly a social life.

Not that she regretted it. Indeed, the task was becoming something of an obsession, since most of her spare time was spent reading and making notes, the rest of it searching for books in the reference library. Reminiscences, retrospectives, and official histories of the war had, together with the letters and Stephen's transcript of the diary, formed her staple diet for weeks—to the extent that she thought of little else. It was perhaps fortunate that she had no important commissions to undertake, for all her recent doodles were of crosses entwined with poppies and barbed wire, which seemed, like recent odd and disturbing dreams, to be the result of that extensive and often distressing research.

Now, eager to get back to Louisa's correspondence, Zoe was glad of a need to look for something else, something lighter that might provide a clue to Tisha's early life and form a bridge between the difficult girl referred to by Letty Duncannon and the sophisticated woman she had become.

That Tisha had been a source of much anxiety to her mother was evident in the replies Louisa received from her old friend Letty in Dublin, although once the girl had left for London, Letty's advice had been sound if unsympathetic: *"You really must stop worrying about her now. Robert will keep a discreet eye*

*upon her, and despite your present hard feelings toward him, he will
not allow her to come to any harm."*

And after that, Zoe recalled with much satisfaction, had
come the confirmation that she and Stephen had been seeking
for so long: *"After all, Robert is her father."*

Good old Letty, she thought with affection, having grown
fond of Robert Duncannon's sister with her quirky opinions and
eccentric interests, and that little tidbit would be an unexpected
present for Stephen when he received his letters in the Persian
Gulf.

That striking photograph of Robert, taken in full uniform
when he must have been in his early thirties, stood on her
bookcase along with several other copied pictures of the family.
It caught Zoe's eye as she crossed the room and made her
pause. Although the best part of a century stood between that
moment and this, she could feel something of the power of the
man. It was in his face, in the way he held himself—not the
arrogance at first suspected but confidence. He knew himself
very well. It seemed to her that he was a man who would make
few apologies.

Like Stephen.

That thought came unexpectedly, sending little shock
waves through her awareness. But after all, she reasoned, his
blood ran in Stephen's veins and genetic inheritance was a
strange thing, often skipping generations to reappear in unexpected quarters. Physically, except possibly in height and build,
they were not alike; Stephen favored Liam in looks, apart from
his hair, which was much darker, and Liam had favored his
mother more than Robert. Zoe was already aware that she bore
a strong physical resemblance to Tisha, even in height and
build, and unlike the rest of them, Tisha had not been very tall.
But who did Tisha resemble? Studying the gathered photographs, Zoe saw that her great-grandmother had Robert Duncannon's Irish coloring—dark hair, pale skin, and apparently
blue eyes—while the shape of her face was Louisa's—broad
forehead, high cheekbones, a round, determined chin. Only
Tisha's mouth was different: small and cherubic. How mis-
leading that was!—Louisa's smile had been both wide and generous.

And what was it that Stephen had said? That she had

Louisa's mouth. The memory pleased her, and made her smile even as she touched her lips with a fingertip. Perhaps she was not so much like Tisha after all; perhaps she had more of Louisa in her than she had suspected.

Poor Louisa. For the first time, in her own uncertainty over Stephen, in that longing for him which could not be assuaged, Zoe felt something of Louisa Elliott's pain. Robert could never be hers, not in the way she needed him to be, so she had turned her back on him and married Edward, and as far as anyone could know they had been happy together. But had she ever stopped loving Robert? In spite of everything, all the sadness and misfortune, all the terrible things that had happened over the years, could the ties be cut irrevocably? Zoe thought not. However much Louisa might have wished otherwise, the children held those links, and not even death could dissolve them.

In leaving York for London, Tisha had, willingly or not, been placed in the care of her natural father, which meant that by 1916 he had had two daughters to keep an eye on, one the dedicated nurse, the other perhaps already showing signs of what she was to become. Zoe wondered how he dealt with them, and in his apparently frequent absences from London, how he managed to supervise Tisha's life. Letty's confidence that her brother *"would not let her come to any harm"* gave rise to a wry smile. It was obvious to Zoe that Letty had not known her niece very well.

She had never been familiar with Tisha's handwriting, so her search through the box that day was for the unfamiliar, a difference of style that would declare itself. She knew Liam's hand at a glance, despite the variety of inks he had used, and Robin's too, while Letty Duncannon was characterized as much by the quality of envelopes and paper. In each beribboned package most of the outer envelopes had yellowed with age, and some were scuffed and faded which made identification difficult, but at last Zoe came to a bundle addressed in an ink that had paled to beige, in a hand that was not dissimilar to her own. Convinced by the London postmark that she had found what she was looking for, Zoe retired to the sofa, tucked up her legs, and prepared herself for an interesting hour or so. Very carefully she untied dusty ribbon which held perhaps a couple of dozen letters.

Unlike Zoe, Louisa Elliott had never, in haste, ripped open an envelope with her thumb. Each one had been slit with a paper knife, each letter carefully refolded into its original pattern, making every one look as though it had just arrived.

Opening the first letter, she glanced at the last page for the confirmation she expected. But this letter was not from Tisha. It was from Robert Duncannon's other daughter. Registering that it was Georgina's signature, Zoe was first disappointed and then annoyed; she almost thrust the pages back unread. But in the act of refolding them, an address, engraved at the head of the first sheet, leapt out at her. It was her own address. This house in Queen's Gate, London.

For a second she thought she had imagined it, that it was some kind of hallucination. She rubbed her eyes and stared at it; touched her finger to the lettering and felt its slight indentations. She looked again at the signature and then the heading. It sank in slowly. Georgina Duncannon was living here, at this address.

Feverishly, Zoe opened all the other letters, trying not to tear the pages in her trembling, fumbling haste. Not all were written from here; some were on cheap notepaper from a hospital in south London.

Was she nursing there? She must have been, Zoe thought, noting the irregular dates. Living in, while this was her real home. Or was it? A vague recollection of something Letty had written sent her scurrying for the thick notebook with its listed references. What was it that Letty had said about her niece?

Yes, that she was sharing her father's apartment in Kensington. And in brackets beside that note, Zoe had added a query as to the address. Well, now she knew. But which apartment? What floor? A sudden thrill of instinct told her that it had to be here, this floor, these rooms, and a dozen strange dreams slipped into place like pieces in a jigsaw puzzle.

But there had to be a way of proving it, of finding out who had owned this house at that time, and who were the tenants. Halfway to the telephone to speak to her father, Zoe stepped over scattered pages which had fallen to the floor. Guiltily, she scooped them up, noticing a date, *March 29, 1916*, and in that neat script that might have been her own, Tisha's name in the first paragraph.

17

*G*eorgina's bedroom was not very big. It contained a three-quarter bed, a small wardrobe, a chest of drawers, and a washstand, and those items almost filled it. Overlooking the mews at the back was a tall window draped with lace and a pair of gold brocade curtains, and on the floor, between one side of the bed and the wall, was a warm Turkish rug. The room was small and overcrowded, but compared to her Spartan quarters at the hospital, it was luxurious. The feather bed was soft, the eiderdown matched the curtains, there were pictures on the walls, and a triple mirror on the chest of drawers. It was a haven of comfort and privacy and Georgina loved it.

As always before making the effort to rise, she looked around, appreciating every item, the row of novels on a shelf, photographs of the family within reach, and, as always, blessed the day her father had insisted she make this place her home. At first there had been hesitation on her part, she had been unsure whether she wanted to commit herself to such an arrangement. But he had pointed out that his absences were frequent and often protracted, and Georgina had remembered the blessedness of escape from hospital life, even when she

was in York. Then, the cottage had been her haven, now the
refuge was her father's apartment.

Originally, before the army purchased it, the building had
been one house, tall and deep—a nightmare, Georgina often
thought, for the servants constantly up and down ten flights of
stairs from cellar to attic. This floor comprised two large rooms,
a hall, and two other rooms which might have been dressing
rooms or even part of the nursery quarters. One of the smaller
rooms had been converted into a sort of butler's pantry, with a
sink and gas oven and cupboards; it could hardly be called a
kitchen, although it served as such. And the other, which for
a few years had been her father's dressing room, was now her
bedroom. Robert's servant shared quarters two floors above,
and there was a communal bathroom on the floor below for the
use of the four staff officers who lived there. One had a wife
who stayed occasionally; the others were single men whom she
passed occasionally on the stairs.

There was no sense of community, but she had enough of
that at the hospital. Here was privacy, a peace and quiet that
reminded her of Dublin before the war, of home and luxury
and all the things she had then despised and since come to long
for with all the passion of nostalgia. Here were no bells, no
demands, no broken bodies to care for, no shattered minds to
soothe, no sudden deaths to sweep away before the next batch
of wounded arrived. Here was peace where she could write
letters, read books, or simply sleep the sleep of exhaustion,
gathering strength and wits in a brief respite from work.

It was pleasant, too, to see something of her father. She
found him much changed from the man who so vociferously
had opposed nursing as a career, and although there was often
anxiety in his expression when he looked at her, there was a
measure of pride too. He knew what she did, and while he
might regret the hours she worked, he saw its necessity. He
also seemed to appreciate how valuable her training had been
at the Retreat. Army doctors were not renowned for embracing
new ideas, but just occasionally one of the more enlightened
would, in a roundabout way, seek her opinion; and when it
was not sought Georgina did what she could within the limited
sphere of her time and influence. More and more often did it
seem to her that one day, when this war was over and there

was time to *understand*, special hospitals would have to be set up, or units within hospitals, simply to treat the injured minds. "Lacking in moral fiber" was no way to describe a volunteer whose spirit had been battered beyond endurance; and while "shell shock" was kinder, she was beginning to realize that it was more than just the sound of shells firing and exploding that destroyed a man. It was the sight and sound and smell of death, sudden and ever-present, sweeping down with a scream to gather friend and foe alike.

What astonished her, seeing the results of what was going on across the Channel, was the resilience of the human spirit. Not all succumbed to fear; most managed to thrust the horror aside, while some could still laugh and joke, still talk of excitement and comradeship and patriotism. They were the ones she found hardest to understand. Georgina was no longer patriotic. She did what she did because it had to be done and she was trained to do it; but from that well of compassion which refused to dry up, she thought of all the others in German hospitals, tended by German nurses who were as tired and stretched and heartsick as herself. The war for her had been reduced to exhaustion, an aching back, sore, calloused feet, and legs that continued to walk, stand, and bend far beyond what she considered to be their ability to do so. And her hands, constantly in and out of hot water, were like those of a maid-of-all-work, chapped and chilblained, their touch, she knew, like sandpaper on tender skin.

All winter Louisa had been sending pots of cocoa butter mixed with scented, soothing herbs, and while that preparation helped, it had no chance to cure. Robert joked about those little pots, made occasional acerbic comments when Georgina read Louisa's letters aloud, although he wanted to know what she said, what she had been doing, what life was like in York. And while his guilt was less acute these days, he always said, when Georgina was writing back, that she must enclose his love and sincere regards.

At Christmas, Robert had managed to use his influence with certain people at the War Office to obtain a week's leave for Robin. It had meant a lot of string pulling, but with the news so bad from Gallipoli, and Liam completely outside Robert's sphere, he had been determined to do something for Louisa, anything to lighten the load of their collective anguish. They had managed to see Robin on his return to the front, just an hour between trains in a dismal tea shop near the station, and it had been worth the effort involved. He was cheerful, but he was older, much less buoyant; and more than ever he resembled Robert Duncannon. Georgina remembered touching him, holding his hand, thinking of Liam.

Afterward, despite Robert's instructions to the contrary, Georgina wrote to Louisa, telling her that she had him to thank for Robin's leave; and although it was not directly acknowledged, since then Louisa had inquired after him in most of her letters. It warmed Georgina to think that her father was in some respect forgiven for that spilling of the truth.

Whereas Robin and Liam had both survived almost two years of war, her cousins from White Leigh—one older than Georgina, one younger—had both been killed at Loos. She had seen neither of them since her mother's funeral and it was hard to comprehend that she would never see them again. It seemed they would be preserved for ever in her memory as two young, thoughtless, high-spirited boys with whom she had played and danced and gone hunting. Like so much else, they were part of the past; only if she went back to White Leigh would she feel their absence and be able to grieve for them.

Glad of the impossibility, Georgina grieved now for her father who had just returned from there. His visit, which had coincided with official business, had distressed him. William, he said, had lost interest in everything: The estate was neglected, the tenants close to mutiny, the house no better than a mausoleum. His brother seemed set on drinking himself to death, while Anne, William's wife, had grown patriotic to the point of mania, working for the Red Cross, organizing sewing circles and knitting bees, and urging every man and boy within a twenty-mile radius to join arms against the evil Hun.

"She should be careful," Robert had confided last night over a large measure of brandy. "In spite of the war, public feeling in the south is not entirely pro-British . . ."

It was an informed comment, one that sent a chill through her as she stared at a photograph of her cousins on horseback taken in front of the steps at White Leigh. There was another of Robert as a young man, standing on those steps which led to the main entrance, with Georgina aged three or four in his arms. She was hugging herself close, her round cheek pressed to his, and he was laughing. One of the rare times that he had been at home . . .

That picture always aroused a plethora of memories, not all of them good: her mother, like a mad ghost at White Leigh, then the move to Dublin with Aunt Letty, and the happy years when Louisa lived with them. All too brief. And with Louisa's departure her father had abandoned them too, for a war in the Sudan. Then it seemed no time at all between that war and the next in South Africa, after which he had gone with his regiment to India, leaving his daughter to Dublin and Aunt Letty, and summers spent at White Leigh.

She had loved him, as one worships heroes, but she had never really known him; and until recently, what she had known about him—what had been revealed in the harsh glare of impatient youth—had been difficult either to like or understand.

Only in this last year had she grown closer to him, come to know him better. They talked together as adults, discussing her work and his, affording each other a respect born of new understanding. It seemed he was glad to have her there, and she wondered whether he was lonely. If he had women friends these days, Georgina never saw them, and with his life torn between London and Dublin, she thought he was probably too busy, never in one place long enough to form new relationships. It seemed, too, as though what had happened in York that summer of 1913, had killed something in him, a spark of willful carelessness perhaps; or rekindled a different flame, one that burned deeper than even he suspected.

He never spoke of it, so she could not be sure, and it was not a subject Georgina cared to probe. Instead they talked of Dublin and Letty, and his work, which, since 1910 and his return from India on half pay, had been largely concerned with Ireland. With his knowledge of the country and extensive family connections, the government had employed him in an advisory capacity pending the settlement of the vexatious Home Rule question. But the militant resistance of Ulster loyalists had managed to drag out negotiations interminably, and with the government's reluctance to come into conflict with the industrial north, public opinion, which had been favorable, waned yet again. Robert was sickened by a situation that seemed destined never to be resolved and, after four years' hard work, with all his arguments for Home Rule set aside, had wanted no more of it.

With the outbreak of war in August 1914, he had volunteered immediately for active service, but the War Office continued to refuse him, even as an administrator of Kitchener's new battalions. With what he saw as stubborn pigheadedness, his new masters insisted on sending him back to Ireland, using the connections he had renewed and built up to provide them with essential information on what was going on within Sinn Fein and the Irish Republican Brotherhood. Ostensibly, he was still employed on the Home Rule question, fostering the south's implicit belief that it would be granted with the cessation of hostilities. But the question had been debated during the whole of his lifetime, he had seen it come to Parliament twice and fail, and now no longer had faith in a third time.

Georgina knew her father loathed the duality of his role, the necessity for secrecy; she knew too that until recently he had felt most bitterly that his abilities and vast experience in the military field were being wasted. Only in the last few months had he begun to see the necessity for himself. England's other island might have largely set aside her antipathy during 1914's surge of patriotic fervor, and Irish mothers might still be sending their sons to die upon England's behalf, but as Robert had been at pains to explain to her, other, smaller, more determined forces were now at work.

Tension was in the air, and he was suddenly very much afraid that what could not be wrested from England politically would be attempted by force of arms. And that was something Robert could not condone. He held the king's commission still, and as a dragoon officer in Ireland before the Boer War, his role had always been to preserve law and order. Even now, to oppose the rule of the gun he would shelve his own ideals forever. What was alarming him now, however, was the realization that certain elements saw death and destruction as the only path to political freedom; and what frightened him beyond that was the potential reaction.

"The government won't stand for it," he had said the night before. "Not with a war going on. That's what these hotheads don't realize. They think they might just conceivably get their own way while our backs are turned—they don't believe me when I tell them what will happen."

"And what will happen?"

"Oh, my dear girl! Any such action will be regarded as treason—and it will be stamped on, quickly and effectively, no matter how many troops it takes to do it. The Fenians can't win—I've told them that in Dublin and in Waterford, and I've told them to pass the message on. But they don't believe me. And the stupid thing is, the ones I spoke to don't even think that anything's being planned! But I *know* it is—I can feel it in Dublin, brewing like a summer storm. I've told Letty to get down to White Leigh and stay there. Of course, she doesn't want to go . . ."

"You could be wrong," Georgina had ventured.

"No. Although I wish I could say I might be . . ."

Tired though he was by his journey from Dublin, her father had not wanted to go to bed. Knowing that mood, Georgina wished she could have sat up with him, but exhaustion had dragged at her eyes and limbs, and finally she had been forced to leave him to solitude and his bottle of brandy. Sighing now as she washed and dressed, she wondered how he was feeling, what reports he was composing, and how they would be acted upon.

Lost for a moment in a gloom of anxiety, the telephone's ringing startled her. She guessed it would be her father before she picked it up; apart from Tisha he was the only one who used it. The hospital had no idea that she could be reached by such instantaneous means, and she was determined never to reveal it.

He sounded weary and his message was brief. Knowing he was back, Tisha had called in to see him, wanting to come to tea; she wondered also whether she could bring someone with her.

"Who?" Georgina demanded, knowing she sounded ungracious and unable to control it.

"Oh, some young fellow from my department—Fearnley.

You know, the one who keeps pestering for active service. He's invited her out a couple of times, and now she wants to return the favor."

"Impress him, you mean."

"Well, perhaps so. But since he knows me well enough, he's not likely to be impressed. Do your best, Georgie, will you? Make some of those delightful scones of yours, and see if we can't be jolly for an hour or so."

"You don't sound very jolly."

"Nor do I feel it. Never mind—I'll tell you about it later."

Replacing the receiver, Georgina swore, softly and eloquently. Nursing soldiers had extended her education in many directions, not least those of language. No doubt her father meant well by Tisha, but Georgina resented her half sister's intrusion. Since her arrival in London at the end of January, life had not been the same. The thought of having to relinquish the novel she was enjoying, bind up her hair, and put on a pleasant company face was not one Georgina relished; and the idea of having to listen to an enthusiastic rendition of what a wonderful time Tisha was having in London was daunting.

Checking the contents of the little store-cupboard, she was thankful that enough was there to make a passable wartime feast. It would be pathetic by peacetime standards, but everyone was experiencing the same difficulties, so whatever was offered was praised. The scones were Louisa's recipe, which was why her father loved them, and even the blackberry and apple jelly had been sent from York the previous autumn and hoarded for special occasions. It was so difficult to buy anything good, and Louisa always remembered them.

Having prepared everything to her satisfaction, Georgina went to change her clothes, trying to find something smart, anything that might stand up to whatever modish creation Tisha would be wearing, but all her clothes were practical and well-worn. Eventually she settled on a gray skirt and pink silk blouse, and a string of pearls her father had bought for her twenty-first birthday. Not very exciting, but it was the best she could do.

They arrived just after five, cold after their journey by taxi from Westminster. Robert's servant had made up the fire and the room was welcoming in its dark, glowing colors. Outside, beneath a wild gray sky, it was more like winter than spring, with the window panes rattling and plane trees tossing in a blustery gale. Georgina drew one set of velvet curtains against a sneaky draft and sat down in her chair beside the fire, leaving Robert's servant to serve the tea she had prepared.

Fortunately young Captain Fearnley knew Robert well enough not to be overawed; had he known that the girl he escorted was Colonel Duncannon's natural daughter, rather than the niece she purported to be, Georgina thought he might have been considerably nonplussed. But Edwin Fearnley did not know. Along with everyone else in their respective departments, he had remarked upon a shared family resemblance, but Robert's relationship with Tisha had always been that of a rather distant relative, and her present attitude toward him—which Georgina always thought a shade too coquettish—did not appear to be amiss. Robert treated her now with the kind of fond indulgence which might be expected of a doting uncle, and only occasionally did Georgina detect a certain irony in the girl's response.

At such times she was possessed of a very unchristian suspicion that her half sister was using their father's affection and generosity to the utmost. She played up to him, just as she was playing up to Edwin now, exercising her pretty, kittenlike charm. But the kitten was growing up, she had claws with which to defend herself, and she could snarl and sulk with the rest. Robert had never seen that side of her, but Georgina had, and would never forget the wounds she had inflicted on others. For the moment, however, she was determined to be pretty and amusing, charming both men with her talent for mimicry, one minute a blustery old colonel from the War Office, the next a mouselike secretary.

And Robert, a colonel himself, though far from blustery, lapped it up, while young Edwin Fearnley was almost helpless with laughter.

"You're a very naughty young lady," Robert said with mock severity, while Tisha pretended contrition, called him "uncle," and passed him another of Georgina's scones.

Taking note of her half sister's stylish outfit and pretty shoes, Georgina experienced a twinge of jealousy that she knew was as silly as it was unpleasant. But it seemed that their father could refuse her nothing, that had she asked for the moon, he would have endeavored, somehow, to obtain it for her. He said, shamefacedly, that it was because his other daughter asked for nothing, that she refused him the chance to spoil her with pretty clothes and entertainments, and always had. There was, Georgina supposed, a certain amount of truth in that, but it did not cure the resentment. She felt so plain and dull beside Tisha, could not make witty conversation or make people laugh; even her funniest stories seemed out of place because they related to the hospital and brought the seriousness of war into the conversation, changing its tone completely. She laughed politely at Tisha's lively chatter, made the right comments, asked the right questions, and all the time wondered what was going on behind those bright but rather calculating eyes.

Edwin Fearnley, obviously smitten, spared barely a glance for Georgina. From observation and certain casually phrased questions, however, she did manage to elicit a few details. He was older than Tisha by some ten years, a regular commissioned officer who had been attached to the Staff College before the war in a minor administrative capacity. He claimed, jokingly, that every time he had applied for active service since then, they had promoted him and sent him elsewhere, so he was forced to the conclusion that his superiors thought he was not much good at anything and only wanted him out of the way.

"If they'd thought that," Robert chipped in, "you'd have been in France with the first wave—the second, anyway!"

Edwin grimaced at that and with a laugh said he was thinking of applying again for active service; that way, he would perhaps get his majority and a nice increase in pay if nothing else.

"Don't be too hasty," Robert warned. "They might accept your offer, and I would lose an excellent brain from my department!"

Wondering what it was he did, Georgina knew better than to ask; but he certainly had an intelligent face, and eyes which, when they were not looking at Tisha, were alive with shrewdness and good humor. He was not very tall or particularly good-looking, but a lively personality made him attractive. It came out in the course of conversation that his people lived in Sussex, his father having retired some years ago from lucrative business in the Midlands. It transpired, too, that he was an only son. Georgina began to see what it was about this man that made him so attractive to Tisha. For her, looks and personality would be important, but never quite enough.

Warming to his unspoiled, natural charm, Georgina felt a small stab of pity. He would probably make Tisha an excellent husband, but she was too young to appreciate good qualities in any man. She was a manipulator, out for her own ends. It was possible that she would ruin him.

It was also possible, Georgina told herself, that she was making too much of this visit. Tisha was busily enjoying a freedom she had longed for; Edwin Fearnley might be no more than a pleasant interlude. If he proposed marriage, she would probably drop him and move on to someone else.

But before they left, he was already talking of a run down to Sussex in the near future so that Tisha could meet his parents and see something of the beautiful coast and countryside. Robert was obviously pleased by this evidence of serious intentions, and even went so far as to pat young Fearnley on the back and address him as "my boy." Georgina could have kicked her father.

That antagonism, however, was put to flight minutes later by much stronger emotions, ones which were more difficult to hide.

"Oh, by the way," he said gently to Tisha as she stood to leave, "I heard something today about the Australians. They've left Egypt. Liam's on his way to France."

Georgina went cold. Her blood pressure fell so rapidly she thought she might faint. Wanting to sit down again, she clung to the mantelpiece while Tisha gave a tight little smile and said something to the effect that Liam would be pleased about that, he had never cared for Egypt.

Then, as a particularly violent gust shook the windows behind them, she indulged in a dramatic shiver. "But he won't like the weather much, will he?"

How Georgina controlled a violent response, she could never afterward imagine. But as she turned away, her father said with soft reproof, "I think he may find something more than the weather to worry about."

"Yes, I imagine so," Tisha agreed without interest. "Well, Edwin, we really must go, else we'll miss that concert at the Palladium—everyone says it's very good . . ."

Robert saw them out and, with a quick glance back at Georgina, said he would walk downstairs and see them to the front door. Startled by her expression, for a second he hesitated; then his eyes dropped away and he pulled the hall door shut behind him.

Georgina sank into her chair, as grieved by that news as she might have been by his death. France for her was no longer a foreign country, it was in her heart and on the hospital wards; it had become a place where men went to die. Only as she recognized that did Georgina realize how much she had depended on Liam being kept in Egypt indefinitely. Miserable for him perhaps, but so much safer there! By some unexplained miracle he had come through the hell of Gallipoli and survived; why must he come to France?

Her father's servant came in to mend the fire and clear away the tea things; with an effort she composed herself and picked up a book, pretending to read. When Robert returned she was almost her usual self.

He poured drinks for them both, handed her a sherry, and lowered himself into the chair facing hers. Under his security she felt exposed.

"I'm sorry," he said at last. "That was the news I've been sitting on all day. I thought I must tell Tisha. I didn't mean to shock you."

"He's my brother, too."

"I know. Sometimes I almost forget."

"I don't," she declared, looking straight into her father's eyes. "I never have."

"Good. I'm glad to hear it."

Aware that this was dangerous ground, she answered him with a certain amount of challenge. "But I do care about him—very deeply. Tisha doesn't. Robin perhaps—but not Liam."

Robert sighed and looked away. "Jealousy. Louisa made too much of him. Liam was her firstborn." After a long moment, he said, "She never wanted Tisha."

His honesty shocked her a little. "Why not?"

"Tisha was the end of our relationship," he answered painfully, "the result of conflict, not love. I've always blamed myself for that . . .

"Oh, I know you think I don't see how she really is, that I indulge her because she's pretty and amusing and knows how to flatter a man. You think I'm an old fool, Georgie," he went on, pouring himself another drink. "But I'm not in my dotage yet—and I've known enough women of that ilk to be able to spot another one. But she's young, and she's had a difficult time of it in recent years. I feel sorry for her—and I'm fond of her. She may change."

For some minutes, digesting those unexpected revelations, Georgina said nothing. She wondered at the nature of that conflict which he claimed had brought Tisha into being, but dared not ask. Instead she questioned him obliquely.

"Are you sure it's pity you feel? Or is it guilt?"

The question angered him. "She's my daughter, for heaven's sake—just as you are. Yes, I'm sorry for what I see in her—and yes, I do feel guilty. I can't help it."

"But she *knows* that, Daddy—and because of it, she's *using* you!"

He faced her squarely. "I know."

"And you'll let her carry on?"

"Yes. For as long as it's necessary."

"Why?"

"Because I don't think Louisa ever understood her. I do, in a peculiar sort of way. She needs fussing and spoiling for a while—and then, perhaps, a steady, level-headed man to love her. She could do a lot worse than young Fearnley—and if he stays put and keeps his mouth shut, he could see this war through. Which is more than can be said for most of the others out there."

Wincing, thinking of Liam—and Robin, she must not forget Robin—Georgina shook her head. "Oh, Daddy—I think you're wrong. She'll break Edwin Fearnley's heart—yours too if you're not careful."

He smiled and tapped his chest. "This old heart of mine's tougher than you think—but thank you for thinking of it."

They dined together at home, then spent a quiet evening, Robert studying papers at his desk, Georgina writing letters and thinking. Although she had long ago ceased in her attempts to communicate with Liam, she always mentioned him in her letters to Lousia. Detached, careful phrases, but they ensured a good response. And knowing that Tisha rarely sent anything more comprehensive than a postcard, Georgina included her father's news.

"No doubt you will soon be hearing from Liam. Indeed you may have done so already, from Egypt. The post is so peculiar these days. I've already written to Robin—you never know, they may meet up."

It was a feeble attempt to be cheerful, a single straw of hope in what she saw as a sea of despair. Addressing the envelopes, she laid them on her father's desk, ready for posting.

"Try not to worry," he said softly, squeezing her hand. As she turned away he rose to stand beside her. "Tisha's a born survivor, you know—and so, it seems, are your brothers. Perhaps it's something they inherited from me!" He smiled, then suddenly, impulsively, hugged her close.

"Oh, darling girl," he whispered against her hair, "you're the one I worry about. Do take care of yourself—I couldn't bear to lose you."

Tears welled for a moment and she clung to the unfamiliarity of her father's arms. He felt strong and safe and she wished she could have been a child again, just to have him go on holding her.

Eventually he let her go. Tucking back a stray lock of her long blonde hair, he said, "You'll be gone in the morning, I expect. If you have a free afternoon at any time, telephone the office. I'll send a car and we'll go out."

She nodded, clearing her throat. "When do you go back to Ireland?"

"I don't know. I dare say I could be there and back several times before they allow you another couple of days off. However, I'll keep you informed."

Reaching up, Georgina kissed his cheek. "Thank you, Daddy." Unable to risk another word, she hurried off to bed.

18

*T*he next morning, about the
time Georgina was setting out in wind and heavy rain for her
hospital in Lewisham, Liam was taking shelter from the
weather on the afterdeck of a Union Castle Line transport in
the Gulf of Lyons. He had been on submarine watch since four
and was cold and tired and thoroughly wet, but every now and
then he would cease his scanning of the seas on the starboard
quarter and glance forward, to where he could see land looming
on the horizon. It was probably the French coast: He knew
Marseilles could not be far away.

The thought of it was strange after all this time, not quite
believable after all the promises and diversions, after two
stretches of the purgatory that was Egypt and stoking the fires
of hell in between. It was almost two years since he had joined
up and he could still recall the names and faces of all those who
had been so desperate to get to France and who would now
never see Australia again. With the greater part of them gone,
he could hardly believe that he was still alive. For a long time
after Gallipoli his hands would indulge in a moment's automatic
exploration each time he awoke, checking all the vital parts of

his body before silently praising God for safe deliverance into another day, then praying for the guts to see that one through. He had abandoned the physical checks, but not the prayers—the prayers would always be important. When he thought of what he had survived, the narrow squeaks of every day on the peninsula—shells, bullets, shrapnel which always seemed to strike the next man, never himself, and the massive miracle of coming unscathed through battles that went on for days and in which thousands died—he could not take that survival for granted.

He should have died that August. He should have, everybody said so. From the dysentery that had racked his body for weeks, and from a bout of influenza that had turned to pneumonia within a couple of days. Everybody said how lucky he was to be alive, including the doctors in charge at Helouan and Heliopolis, and the nurses who had brought him through. For a while he had even enjoyed a certain fame, with even the oldest, toughest sisters beaming at him like head teachers with a particularly bright and well-mannered child.

But Liam had not needed to be told. There was a moment when he thought he had died, and the strange thing was that he was able to remember it as clearly as when it actually occurred. Memory had dimmed nothing of that gray mist and his sense of floating detachment, nor of the path which appeared between shrubs and trees of an unearthly, indescribable beauty. He had come to a meadow full of brilliant flowers, and beyond that a stream with a small bridge. Liam's sense of exaltation seemed complete when he saw Ned coming toward him with hands outstretched in welcome. A Ned no longer in uniform, but as he used to be, in boots and old moleskin trousers, with his shirt open and sleeves pushed back. No words were exchanged but they embraced; then Liam knew, looking at his old friend, that he must not cross the bridge. Ned took his arm and gently urged him back the way he had come.

And for a second, when he awoke from that dream which was not a dream, he was looking down at himself in a narrow hospital bed, surrounded by a sort of tent with which two nurses seemed to be struggling. His next awareness was of being in that bed, fighting for breath and to open his eyes. He saw the nurses, very hazily, above him, then slipped back into unconsciousness.

Meeting Mary Maddox when he was convalescing, talking of Ned's death on the beach at Anzac Cove, he had been aware of a need to comfort her, to give her something to hold on to in her loneliness and grief. During her third visit he tried to explain what struck him as being a glimpse of life beyond the physical present, but either she could not, or would not, understand.

Until that moment, Liam recalled, there had been something between them, sympathy and a shared love for Ned which might have drawn them closer still; sadly, afterward, she became a nurse again, assuring him with professional detachment that what he had experienced were no more than feverish hallucinations. She even told him that such hallucinations were quite common, which, far from weakening Liam's convictions, merely reinforced them. He wished he could have explained to her that Ned, who in life had always been so brusque and prosaic, was almost radiant with love. It was not, however, something Liam could put into words; it would have embarrassed him and she would not have believed him anyway.

He did not see her again. That she thought him foolish, even slightly mad, was a shame. He felt he had lost yet another link with Dandenong, and as each link parted, it seemed less and less likely that he would ever return.

Lewis visited, however. He was still in Egypt with the Light Horse and constantly on the move, but he did manage to see Liam a couple of times, and then again before the battalions left for France. He was much thinner, much harder, and sad at the loss of so many old friends. It was obvious, too, that he carried a sense of guilt at having missed Gallipoli. Egypt had been no picnic in the last year, but still it had been relatively safe.

"I should have joined up with your lot," he said as they were parting.

"Oh no," Liam had softly replied. "Somebody's got to go back to the farm, Lew, and you belong there. So take good care of yourself."

And watching him mount one of the sturdy Australian

walers, Liam had felt the pull of another parting, could not help feeling that they would never meet again, and that was upsetting. He liked Lewis, however briefly they had been friends.

Almost anywhere was better than the desert, and when it came to fighting, France could not be worse than Gallipoli. Promotion, however, had come quickly, and with two stripes on his shoulder Liam had tried hard, that next time in Egypt, to be worthy of the responsibility. There had been little opportunity for foolishness, anyway; reorganization, retraining, new recruits from Australia, new units with new tasks to perform, all required time and thought and care under a regime that was harsher than ever. Liam was in charge of a machine-gun team under an older and less-experienced sergeant, a man who very much resented the hero worship afforded to his twenty-one-year-old corporal. Keenan referred to him sardonically, in accents that still betrayed his Belfast childhood, as the "golden boy," or, "my blue-eyed Billy." Liam hated the sarcasm, and in the man himself found little to respect, even though he could understand what it was that so irritated Keenan, whose experience of Gallipoli was restricted to the last few weeks. Liam was one of the originals, a man who had survived the landings and illness and eight long months of fighting on the peninsula. He was a lucky man, a man to touch and stay close to, a man protected and revered by his companions. Keenan could lay claim to none of that.

The ancient port of Marseilles with its docks and factories and forts was a source of great fascination during the hours that elapsed between their arrival and disembarkation, but shore leave was not allowed. Guards patrolled both gates and gangways, keeping the ship's volatile cargo well confined and under constant surveillance. It was as though higher powers, remembering Cairo, were terrified of sudden outbreaks, drunkenness on a massive scale, and complaints of rape and pillage from the local population.

The Australian troops, however, had been well lectured before leaving Egypt and their finer feelings appealed to.

Most of them, Liam knew, would try to live up to those expectations, but for some it would always be difficult, especially where women were concerned. And the girls, lining the streets next morning as the troops marched through, were so appealing. Smiling, waving, pressing flowers into the men's hands, shouting encouragements in a musical but incomprehensible language, they were temptation personified. Laughing, his hand kissed by warm lips, Liam pushed a twig of cherry blossom into his rifle and thought it just as well that none of them had been let loose in this hospitable city, or few would have reached their destination. But that short, rapid march in close order was too short, even for the most determined straggler.

The train journey north from Marseilles took four days, not in cattle wagons this time, but third-class compartments with seats and windows. It was an unaccustomed luxury and the men were as lively as holidaymakers, waving and cheering to people at stations and in fields beside the track. Word seemed to have gone ahead and all along the line people were waiting to cheer or press gifts upon them at wayside halts. French soldiers were everywhere, some of them in red trousers and kepis, most of them wounded. Those Australians who had a smattering of French tried conversation, returning with an impression of fiery encouragement for what lay ahead.

From the rocky coastline they meandered slowly up to Avignon, halting at a siding for the night, then up the Rhone valley, a full day's journey with pauses at other sidings while express trains rattled past. They crossed the winding river on a series of girder bridges to enter Lyons early the next morning. It was frosty and clear and the air was very sharp, so evocative of England in the early spring that Liam exploited his rank to hug the open window, relishing the cold air, its smell and its taste, remembering so much and so clearly that it hurt. There were tears in his eyes as he regained his seat; it was a journey of new experience and old memories, sights and sounds that brought back his early youth, and other, small fascinations which underlined this country's difference.

It was a journey of such delight, he did not want it to end. He felt like a child traveling for the very first time, noting everything, wanting to ask questions, longing to stop the train, to walk and run across this field and along that dusty white road to where the woods were veiled in their first flush of delicate green. So different from Australia with its strong, dark evergreens, here he could identify many of the trees beside the tracks, silently repeating their names like a litany from childhood. He was very, very homesick.

Dozing as night fell, leaning into his hard window corner with his feet propped up on the opposite seat, Liam dreamed of home for the first time in months. He was in the kitchen with his mother, trying to make his peace, but she carried on baking, rolling out pastry with that familiar click click of her wedding ring, and did not seem aware of his presence. He spoke to her gently at first, then became agitated; when she did not turn around he shouted out . . .

He woke with a start to find the train stopped and in darkness, a man's weight against his shoulder and a body beneath his legs, stretched full-length along the floor. Aching and cramped, Liam tried to move without waking them. He wanted to move, to get away, to go home and leave all this behind. He wanted no more of these men, the weight of their lives, the press of their bodies. It was too much. He was no older than they were; too young to be responsible, telling them what to do, wiping their noses, and writing their letters—what would he do when they got themselves killed?

For a moment he almost panicked.

Flexing arms, fingers, a leg, he took a deep breath and reached for the window sash. With difficulty he lowered the glass, struggled to his feet, and amid moans and groans of protest, dragged sweet, cold air into his lungs.

There were some trees and the shapes of houses, dark against a less dark sky. Someone demanded to know where they were; Liam had no idea. Another voice suggested, forcefully, that he shut the window; he took no notice. Gradually the shuffles and protests subsided again into whistles and whimpers and heavy, stertorous breathing. Liam lit a cigarette and began to feel better.

In the stillness he heard the swish of steam, a reedy whistle, and the sudden grunt of power from their locomotive; the long line of carriages gave a convulsive jerk, waking everyone, and they were on their way again.

They passed through the dismal outskirts of Paris in the early hours, changing course again to head directly north.

Again it was a beautiful morning, hazy with a hard frost. In the hedgerows were partridge and pheasant, and across a whitened field he saw a fox make a furtive dash for cover. The land was rolling, heavily wooded, more like home than ever. He thought of the Wolds and the Vale of York and knew it was a lifetime past, that even if he went back now it would not be the same, because he was different.

All that—York, its surrounding countryside, the Wolds, the rugged sea coast beyond—was, he realized, an extension of home, part of his childhood, part of his mother. To go back now would mean facing *her*, letting her claim him again, letting the past claim him, and he was still determined to stand apart from that. If he was honest, too, Liam knew that in one small corner of his secret being, he was still afraid of what had happened three summers ago. He had not forgotten those wrenching, tearing, gut-churning emotions; nothing since had approached that pain, not even Gallipoli. The horror of that had been an external thing, which after a while lost its impact. Friends died, and if you could, you buried them; if not, you used their bodies as sandbags, knowing that even in death they would be pleased to protect you. He had come to terms with that; what he could not come to terms with were the facts of his own existence.

Approaching Calais in the afternoon, they passed it by, turned south again, then stopped for several hours on a siding at St. Omer, the old British headquarters, before continuing the final few miles of their journey. It was a strange route, east to Hazebrouck, then northeast toward Ypres. Finally, just after midnight, when they were convinced they were heading straight for that battered medieval city, the train stopped at a village just short of the Belgian border. The boom and flash of the guns at Ypres seemed horrifyingly close, and in spite of himself, Liam was afraid.

Ypres, however, proved not to be their destination. As one hard-bitten British Tommy informed them, they were not fit for Wipers yet; the nursery at Armentières was bound to be their destination.

Liam bristled at the older man's patronizing humor, felt his fists clench as Gallipoli flashed through his mind, but he bit back a scathing reply. In a way he was right: They were the new boys here and needed to learn how things were done. Already he was aware of differences, vast areas behind the lines that were untouched by war. Here was room to maneuver, whereas on Gallipoli once you landed, you were *in* it, right up to your neck. No time to learn the basic facts of life: You acted instinctively, and if you made a mistake, it was very likely your last. Here, in Flanders, the British were far more relaxed.

There was nothing relaxed about their first route march, however. Eight miles of cobbled roads on soft feet in relatively new boots was painful. Their journey was southeast this time, through the town of Bailleul to billets in a series of farmhouses off the Armentières road. With fifty other men Liam was directed to a walled enclosure of house and farm building. In the midst of the yard, assaulting their nostrils even in the crisp, cold air of that frosty afternoon, was a huge, sunken pit full of manure. It was something of a shock, as was their accommodation in the nearby barn, especially to those naïve enough to have expected beds and clean sheets in the farmer's best rooms. Whatever spare beds existed in the farmhouse were allocated to their officers.

Remembering Gallipoli, Liam laughed at the twitching noses around him. "Better than a hole in the ground," he declared, shrugging off his weighty pack, "and at least the straw's clean."

Although it had seemed a temporary resting place, they were at the farm for ten days, days that were given over to some very intensive training. There were lectures on gas attacks and an unpleasant but necessary exercise in the use of gas helmets. Tear-gas bombs were exploded to illustrate the effects on the unprotected, and then to give the inexperienced confidence in those hideous face masks, a cylinder of something more deadly was opened in a trench while the helmeted troops walked through it.

The machine gunners were put through a fresh series of courses on the stripping, mounting, and firing of the heavy Vickers machine guns, and their instructor was at pains to remind them, frequently, of the importance of care in filling the belts. Unless every cartridge was correctly in its place, the gun would jam; and as Liam well knew, that kind of carelessness cost lives. Once a gun stopped firing, and the enemy had its position, no quarter would be given. Machine gunners were not taken prisoner; they were killed.

In spite of the hectic activity, the lectures, demonstrations, and tests, Liam thought constantly of Robin and wondered where he was. It was some time since letters had reached him, and he was always listening for news of the Green Howards, hoping, too, to be posted to the same sector. He missed his brother, aware as never before of a need to see him face-to-face, to touch him, even hold him for a moment. It was, he supposed, a reflection of the loneliness he had felt since losing his companions from Dandenong. They had been like family, and since then he had had no particular friends. He was closest to the men of his machine-gun team, and his affection for Matt and Jack, Smithy and Carl—and even for Vic, the cocky youngster who made up the sixth member of the team—was general and undiscriminating. For any one of them he would have risked his life, but personal attachment was a thing of the past. Liam could no longer say, as he had once done of Ned, "This man is my friend." Since Ned there had been too many deaths.

His one frustration was Sergeant Keenan. Mostly, Liam tried hard not to provoke him because the older man had the power to retaliate in dozens of small, irritating ways, and small irritations were always the most maddening. The antipathy between them was strong, however, and much as Liam tried to contain it, Keenan seemed determined to draw it out. At times, Liam wanted to hit him hard, to drag him to his feet and tell him there was a war going on and they were supposed to be fighting on the same side, that if they could not pull together in a common cause, how on earth could they hope to win. But Keenan seemed to thrive on personal conflicts and certainly took pleasure in belittling those around him.

He was generally disliked, so much so that Liam began to wonder what might happen when they got into the trenches; in the heat of battle it was not unknown for old scores to be settled permanently, and who was to know whence the bullet came? Men who have fought and suffered together do not point accusing fingers at their friends. Despite his loathing, Liam was not even tempted. When the time came for Keenan, fate would decide his end, and if there was any justice at all, it would be sooner rather than later.

By mid-April they were on their way to billets nearer the front line. The weather, which seemed to have been warming up for spring, then changed its mind that day. Cart tracks and un-paved country lanes were quickly churned to mud while from a leaden sky the wind whipped cruel flurries of snow, stinging their faces, making what might have been a pleasant journey across country into a bitter slog.

Erquinghem seemed a haven of civilization after that march. It was a small but busy industrial town, all slate roofs and tall, red-brick buildings, its broad streets boasting a pleth-ora of small cafés and restaurants. As soon as the men were billeted they were out again, eager to sample whatever was on offer.

Gun drill and firing on practice ranges was interrupted only to familiarize the men with the trenches. Over the follow-ing week they went in small groups to view the front line in several places, and as a bonus also came to know the string of villages and small towns which followed the course of the meandering river Lys.

Easter came very late that year, not until the third week of April, but although Good Friday was wet and miserable, the Sunday dawned like a promise of summer. Liam had been one of very few to attend Friday's church parade, but on that glori-ous Easter morning, outside a ruined farmhouse on the edge of Fleurbaix, he was surrounded by most of the battalion. Ex-alted by the morning, by private meditations he wanted to prolong, not share, once the service was over Liam was aware of nothing more than a need to escape.

He had money in his pocket and the rest of the day free. With barely more than a glance and a wave at his companions, he crossed the bridge and set off in a westerly direction along the riverside. Somewhere there would be a place to eat and have a drink, and if he did not want to talk, he could always feign complete ignorance of the language. In fact the very basic French learned at school, had, with effort, come back to him and was improving daily. Although he did not always understand what was said to him, Liam knew enough to make himself understood among the French-speaking population, and his services as translator were much in demand among the men. It was sometimes funny, always a strain, and sometimes downright embarrassing, as their faith was stronger than his abilities, but he got by. Today, however, he wanted none of it. He wanted peace and quiet and time to reflect.

The weather was idyllic, and the sun was warm, releasing all the heady scents of spring. In his old life that yearly miracle had been taken very much for granted, but with the scorched, dry memory of Egypt still clear in his mind, Liam found a sensual pleasure in this subtle fragrance of earth and flowers and new leaves. In the midst of destruction it was like a blessing from God, a blessing he was not sure anyone deserved. After almost a month, it still amazed him to see fields like the one beyond the hedgerow, recently plowed and sown, and in meadows nearby cows munching contentedly while shells plowed fields just a few miles away. Here people lived on the brink of death, tending their farms with sandbags stacked against the direction of the guns, and windows shuttered against the blast. Just up the road to the east, half of Armentières was devastated, while in the other half lived families who still went to work, to school, to church on Sundays. It lent an incongruous air of normality to what was surely a highly abnormal situation.

After almost two years, he supposed the war had become no more than a fact of everyday life to these people, but there was danger in that acceptance, danger to the new soldiers among them. No matter how strongly they were urged to remember the close proximity of the German guns, and the keen eyes of enemy spotter planes crossing the lines, it was easy to be lulled into forgetfulness. In this lush land full of food and water and friendly faces, it was too easy to relax, to march, singing, down the center of a road to billets in nearby houses, to stand outside smoking and talking, and forget the eyes that watched and marked every movement.

Yesterday, Easter Saturday, two billets near Fleurbaix had been shelled to oblivion.

With his hat set at a jaunty angle, Liam had gone with his team for a meal in Erquinghem, had caught the eye of a pretty waitress and enjoyed some lighthearted banter. Teased and

egged on by his friends, and more than a little elated by the
wine he had drunk, he might have pressed his suit further, but
the girl's mother had not approved and, in complaining to
Keenan, had brought wrath upon the young man's head. Annoyed at the time, he could smile about it now. She was a nice
girl and he did not intend her any harm, but how to explain
that to an irate French mother? Thinking about it, he supposed
his grasp of the language was less than he had fondly imagined
last night; the girl had laughed but perhaps his words had
lacked finesse. Anyway, he reflected, there would be other
opportunities. They were not going anywhere just yet, and
when they did, it would only be to the trenches. Plenty of time
to renew the acquaintance.

He found himself in Sailly, among villagers returning home
from Easter services and idling soldiers from other parts of the
line. He nodded, exchanged the odd greeting, and continued
on his way. Beyond the village, where he had never been before, he found a small military cemetery beside the road. Most
of the graves were British ones, but there were already many
Australians buried there. It was warm and sheltered by trees,
and between the rows of wooden crosses were wild hyacinths
and narcissi growing by the older graves, and on some of the
most recent, bunches of daisies and anemones. Taking off his
hat, he walked the rows, reading every name, softly repeating
each one like a litany of prayer.

When he returned to Erquinghem it was late afternoon,
and the place where they had dined the night before, very
quiet. Two British soldiers were drinking themselves into a
stupor in the corner, and a group of Australians, having finished their meal, were preparing to leave. There was no one
behind the bar, and he did not really expect to see the girl this
afternoon; when she appeared to take his order, something
inside him responded instantly. Although he was very hungry,
he ordered a beer first, and with an insistence which was most
unlike him, begged her to sit at his table. For a moment she
hesitated, then, with a glance over her shoulder, poured herself
a mineral water and sat down.

He felt ridiculous then, with nothing to say. He could think
of plenty in English, but nothing that could be translated, tactfully, into French. So he drank his beer and looked at her.

Unlike most Flemish girls, she was fine-boned, with a delicate, pointed face and a certain pertness about the mouth and eyes which offered challenge. For the first time since those early days in Egypt, Liam was ready to accept it, was possessed of a need and a confidence that far outstripped anything felt before. He wanted her. His body was on fire with the need to know and touch and conquer; hard already to the point of pain, he wanted the ease of softness and release.

His desire was so violent that a corner of his mind, still coolly detached, was appalled; and knowing the impossibility of the here and now, he dragged his eyes away, shading them with his hand lest he terrify the girl into leaving.

But she was older and wiser than that. Protected though she might be, feminine intuition and two years of passing soldiery had ensured a certain loss of innocence. She took his trembling fingers between her own and made him look at her. Dark hazel eyes, which were striking against her fairness, had softened into sympathy. With a mixture of broken English and slow, clear French, she told him that she understood; she was sorry, it was not possible, but she understood.

"I'm sorry," he murmured, softer now, the violence abating, his desire for her still there but under control.

"No. No regret." Slim shoulders shrugged, and she smiled, eyes twinkling. "Beer?"

"Yes—please." He lit a cigarette, sucking the smoke in hungrily. It helped a little.

With the glass on the table she faced him, fingers interlaced, her eyes reading his expression more clearly than the words he longed to say.

"You are sad."

Liam almost laughed at that. "Am I?"

"Yes. Today—where?"

"Where did I go?" She nodded. "Walking—to Sailly." And then he remembered and his smile disappeared. "To the cemetery."

"Your friends?"

Liam shook his head, dragging more smoke into his lungs, aware, now that she had pinpointed it, of the utter desolation which had possessed him then. He knew now, as she probably did, why he had wanted her so violently, why, if he was truthful, he still wanted her now. It was to prove that he was still alive, and more than that, to know the joy of making love to a woman before he quit this world forever. Except he did not love her, he hardly knew her. She was just a pretty girl with a come-hither smile.

Monday was fine and devoted to training; Tuesday, the twenty-fifth, was the first anniversary of their landing at Anzac Cove. The brigade mustered that day for an inspection by General Walker, and as though to remind the Australians of what had been their fate a year ago, the German artillery shelled some billets outside Erquinghem, wounding ten men. A couple of nights later, after a gas alert, the Australian artillery opened fire for the first time, laying a barrage across the enemy parapets amid rousing cheers from their own side. Standing outside their billet, drinking vast quantities of the farmer's homemade beer, Liam and his companions whooped and yelled at every explosion, every flare that soared with a trail like a rocket and burst into a graceful, brilliant white star. With the red and yellow flashes of the guns it was like the celebrations of the Fifth of November; and Guy Fawkes, Liam thought with childlike joy, must be cheering from his traitor's grave.

"*Vive l'Australie!*" the farmer shouted in his ear, skipping like an ancient gnome as he hoisted a jug of beer and refilled all their mugs.

Drinking his health, Liam tried to explain, in French, the excitement of Guy Fawkes night at home; but the traditions of the eccentric British were lost on that son of Flemish soil, and the finer points of a Catholic plot to blow up Protestant King James as he opened Parliament in 1605 were seemingly appreciated only by a very small boy, who gazed up at Liam in open-mouthed amazement.

"And he was born in York, you know," Liam announced, reverting to English, "so he can't have been that bad, even if he was a traitor."

"Who was?" an Australian voice asked.

"*Guy Fawkes*—weren't you listening? And he might have had a point, at that," Liam went on, slurring his words slightly. Draining his mug, he held it out for more.

"Don't you think he had a point?" he demanded a moment later. "I mean to say, just *look* at all that—" he waved toward the brilliant sky, shouting above the din that was reaching them even here, three miles distant. "It's a wonderful fireworks display and—and I'm *sure* it's very good of them to put it on for us . . . But *what is it all for?*"

Swaying toward the man in front of him, Liam grabbed him by the collar. "Men are getting killed under that lot. Tomorrow—tomorrow, it might be *us*. I ask you, mate—what is it all *for?*"

The answer was briskly sober. "Shut up, Corp, you're plastered. Let that bastard Keenan hear you, and if he don't have you shot, he'll have them stripes off you right sharpish!"

"Bugger Keenan. We should take a leaf out of Fawkes's book," he declared in a confidential whisper, "and turn that bloody artillery on Haig and Walker. See how *they* like it!"

"Come on, mate, you're drunk—"

"Am I drunk?" Liam asked in surprise. He stared at his tin mug, empty again, although he did not recall drinking, and then up at the sky as a continuous volley rent the night in two. A great white star exploded and fell to earth in a sweeping arc, all the buildings and men around him seeming to move with it. Without the support of his companion, Liam would have keeled over into the mud.

"Yes," he mumbled, "I am drunk. What I was saying—stupid. Forget it."

"It's all right, Corp," the other man sighed, "if I'd been at the Landings, I might feel the same."

His hangover the next day was of Cairo proportions, made worse by the shame of recalling every single word he had uttered; what he could not recall was the identity of his companion. Not one of his own team, he was certain, and that was unfortunate. He felt a fool. What surprised him, however, was the realization that he could say such things when he was not even conscious of having thought them. At least, not for a very long time.

That, coupled with his reactions in Erquinghem on Sunday afternoon, conspired to worry Liam. He felt he was losing control. In an attempt to regain mastery, he threw himself into the tedium of their continued training with vigor and prayed for action soon.

They went, a few days later, into the trenches at Bois Grenier, and apart from the unpredictable weather and the brazen activities of their constant companions, rats, Liam was able to report in his letters home that he was quite enjoying himself. It was good, he said, to be in the thick of it again, to be doing something useful at last after months in Egypt and weeks of training over here. Even in the trenches, after a week or so, they were able to have their rest periods behind the lines. There had been no such thing on Gallipoli.

In his diary he recorded the events of everyday life, a sudden improvement in the weather in May, the welcome presence of a cat about the place. He described the many airplanes, the dogfights and daily bombardments, the sniping from enemy trenches which was an irritation, and his own satisfaction in returning fire. Their gun pit was in a ruined house beside a road that attracted constant attention from the enemy; and although they were living in a hut set into the ground and surrounded by sandbags, the Germans kept using the house as a target for their artillery. Supplies of food and ammunition could be obtained only at night, and at night machine guns played with devastating accuracy upon the road. Several times, bringing up ammunition, Liam had to run for shelter or simply lie flat in the mud until the enfilade ceased. The sniping at their hut, both with rifle and machine-gun fire, suddenly became less haphazard and more wickedly accurate, as though their own activities had finally stirred a crack shot into determined action.

He asked permission from Keenan to move. It was refused. The next day, however, Keenan left them to attend several days of an instruction course. After a few hours in which the hail of bullets had his men dancing every time they wanted to leave the pit, Liam decided to send a message up the line to their officer. He thought he would have to wait until after dark, but fortunately one of their own howitzers started firing into a wood on the German side, and under cover of the smoke, he was able to get out. With permission granted, they worked all

night to build a new gun pit a few yards up the road, and
the next day, during a bombardment of the German trenches,
moved out of the ruined house. None too soon as it transpired.
During the German return attack, four guns, firing as one,
managed to take off the sandbagged roof of their old hut; that
night, improving the new dugout, Liam piled eighteen inches
of earth across its top. The following afternoon, he watched
their old home disintegrate beneath a volley of high-explosive
shells.

"*Then they burst shrapnel overhead with the hopes of getting
anyone running about*," he jotted into his diary. "*As if anyone
could have survived anyway. But Fritz is very thorough. Thank God
we moved in time. If Keenan had been here, I suppose we would have
still been under that lot.*"

Bitterness and a certain amount of vindictive crowing
prompted Liam to keep up the fire from their new emplace-
ment. Having sighted the position of those four enemy machine
guns, he was determined to make them suffer; but his efforts
attracted the artillery again, setting all of them hopping as they
dashed back and forth to their tiny cookhouse, trying to get
something to eat. They were all laughing, but that afternoon,
when news came that they were to be relieved, Liam was more
than thankful.

After twenty-four days' subjection to shelling and machine-gun fire, it was good to be behind the lines, even if only
for a few hours. Liam and his team went to the baths at Sailly,
and then on to the battalion post office. Apart from one letter
from Australia, for some reason Liam had had no mail since
coming into action, so he was overjoyed to see a pile of letters
and two parcels of newspapers awaiting him. But he was cross
too—they should have been forwarded to the lines.

It was a pleasant afternoon and the six men ambled down
the road, reading their mail as they went. Liam flicked through
the collection of envelopes, mentally identifying each writer.
Three from York, one from his cousin Dorothy in Leeds, two
from Robin, and one with a blurred postmark and writing he
could not believe he recognized. He stopped in the middle of
the road, staring at that distinctive italic hand.

Georgina.

Although he had deliberately not thought of her for a long time, her face, smooth, fair, serene, appeared before his mind's eye as clearly as though she smiled at him.

For a minute or two his feelings were so jumbled he could not have said whether he was delighted or dismayed. He was certainly shocked. Why had she written? After all this time, why now? Was something wrong, had somebody died?

But no—he had letters from all who were important to him, it could not be that. Her father, perhaps? *His* father? He stared at the envelope as though it might tell him itself. Perhaps it was something else—perhaps she was getting married.

His jaw clenched on that thought. Liam slipped the envelope into his breast pocket. Whatever it said, he could not bear to read it now.

The others were already some distance down the road, seated outside a little estaminet, beers on the table in front of them. He lit a cigarette before joining them.

"All right, Corp?" one of them asked, glancing up with concern in his eyes. "Not bad news, is it?"

Liam shook his head. "No. Just something from somebody I never expected to hear from." He laughed a little shakily.

Another one grinned. "She's heard you're a hero, Corp—wants to know you now."

"Rubbish," he muttered, and stuck his head into a newspaper. The letters—all of them—would have to wait until he was alone.

The others read their mail and ordered more beers. Liam's newspapers were passed around. Lighting a fresh cigarette, he read the war news in the most recent paper and then immersed himself in York's more local tidbits. Although he was barely concentrating, the graphic description of a tragic drowning at Bishopthorpe caught his attention; and whether it was solely that or the effect of the letter in his pocket, he could not have said, but he was suddenly reliving the agonizing emotions of his last day at home. Robert Duncannon's voice, which he thought he had forgotten, surfaced unbidden banishing the flicker of hope that letter inspired.

A sudden exclamation from one of the others disturbed his anguish.

"Well, of all the dirty, low-down tricks! Have you seen

this? I never heard about this, did you? Where the bloody hell have we *been* for the last month?"

"In the trenches, mate—have you forgotten?"

They all wanted to see, but the newspaper was passed to Liam. Reluctantly he took it, scanning the headlines several times before the meaning sunk in.

In Dublin, a month ago, there had been armed rebellion on the streets. On Easter Monday a republic had been declared, and for several days the General Post Office on Sackville Street was occupied by forces opposed to the Crown; after five days of fighting the rebels were defeated, but British field guns had destroyed much of the center of the city.

It seemed incredible. A stab in the back. Like the others he was disgusted, on reading further, by the apparent connection with Germany. An ex-British consul, Sir Roger Casement, had tried to enlist enemy aid but had been arrested after landing from a German submarine. He was to be tried for high treason. The Irish rebels had been shot.

He stopped reading, handed the paper to someone else, and took a deep breath. Without that letter in his pocket, he knew he would have been frantic by now, wondering whether Georgina might have taken an Easter holiday to be with her aunt in Dublin, wondering whether she was still alive . . .

But where had that letter come from? And *when*? Oblivious to his companions, he whipped the envelope from his pocket and tore it open. The letter, dated April 30 and sent from a hospital in London, was almost a month old.

"Dear Liam . . ."

Dear God, he thought, closing his eyes, seeing her face, hearing her voice; how long since he had heard her speak his name!

. . . Just a few lines to let you know that we all are well. With the dreadful news from Dublin this week, I fear you may be wondering about us, and although I know your mother writes regularly, I wanted to be sure you were not anxious.

Father has been in Dublin since Monday. His letter today says the fighting is over, although he is deeply grieved by the destruction to the city. Not his responsibil-

ity, thank God, but he is bitterly angry with those who
ordered it, and now fears for the safety of all those involved. It will not stop here, he says.

The strange thing is that I applied for leave to go home
for Easter, it being so long since I saw Aunt Letty. Father
was against it, but in the end Matron could not spare me,
so it was just as well. Apparently Aunt Letty refused to
stay at home and came close to being arrested for trying to
help the wounded. All this in spite of her arthritis! What a
family we are!

I hope you are well, dear, and that things are not too
terrible for you in France. Your mother writes often and
keeps us up to date with your news, but it would be nice
to hear from you personally, if you have time to write. If
not, then I understand.

With affectionate regards—Georgina.

"Oh, you beautiful girl," Liam whispered, crushing the
page in his hand.

In June's early summer dawn, birds were warbling another
enthusiastic chorus from the hospital grounds. Roused from a
momentary reverie, Georgina stood before the open window
of her office, drawing soft, refreshing air into her lungs, and
wishing she could be as bright as they were at this hour. It had
been a long and wearisome night, not very busy but the last of
several weeks without a proper break. She could not wait to
have the next couple of hours over, to be away from here and
going home to sleep. Three days! Three whole days to relax
and do nothing. She needed it.

Voices were stirring on the ward. A young VAD nurse
knocked on the open door, demanding her attention. The amputee in bed four was severely distressed and would not be
quieted; would she come?

"*Names*, Nurse," Georgina repeated wearily. "He's not just
an *amputee*, he does have a name. Please remember that."

"Sorry, Sister—Private Hopkinson. It's just that—"

"I know—*when you were in France, they were in and out so
fast there was no time for names*." Georgina had heard that too

many times from this young woman and it annoyed her. "Here we have time—*here*, names are important."

The nurse bowed her head in acknowledgment but could not control an irritated sigh. Service in France had taught her much, and on a practical level she was very thorough. Georgina just wished she had more patience, could give some evidence of *caring* for these boys who were here, often for several months. They needed more than medication and clean dressings, they needed interest and reassurance and affection: She had learned that much from the Quakers and was determined to preach as well as practice that belief, particularly as, once the sheer relief of survival had worn off, many of them became depressed. Some had families close enough to visit, but too few knew what to say. It was as though the experience of war and terrible wounds had set insurmountable barriers between those boys and their loved ones.

Georgina was convinced that men who felt they were cared for recovered more quickly than those who imagined themselves a burden to the staff. For some nurses affection was hard to give without great personal cost to themselves, and the inexperienced sometimes erred by giving too much. It was a narrow, difficult line to tread, always with the danger of provoking passionate adoration from a patient; Georgina had found herself, from time to time, the object of both lust and fantasy as well as gratitude masquerading as love. And the young officers were far more susceptible for some reason than their men. But she explained to them all that what they felt was natural, if temporary, and that they would recover in a surprisingly short space of time. Few believed her, asking if they might write; some did so, in spite of her discouragement, from home, from convalescent hospitals, from France. But rarely more than once. She kept all their letters.

The ones who broke her heart were the ones who died.

It was perhaps because their future had been full of a potential which would never now be realized; or perhaps each death represented, to her, a personal failure. It was not something she could adequately explain. It might have been simply the sight of those young, beautiful bodies, which should have been warm and passionate and full of life, and were suddenly so cold and gray in death. She loved them all and grieved for them like children; only the detached nature of her love, the fact that she had never explored its physical possibilities, saved her from personal involvement and mental destruction. It was something she was only dimly aware of, yet she clung to it as a nun clings to her marriage in Christ.

Most of the medical officers were older, married men, too grossly overworked to indulge in more than the mildest flirtation. There had been one on temporary attachment, however, who had been attractive and single and barely older than herself. He was abrasive with the staff but unusually kind to the patients, and so Georgina had liked him—until in his odd way he had tried to court her. That he was doing so had not occurred to her until one morning over coffee, when he had declared with blunt frustration that she was one of the best nurses he had ever worked with, and by far the most beautiful. It was such a pity, he added, that she never raised her eyes to the level of whole, healthy, normal men; but if she did, he supposed she would not be the excellent nurse she was.

Dumbfounded by that declaration, she had not blushed but simply stared at him. Finishing his coffee, he had turned to leave.

"I thought you were perfect," he said from the doorway. "But you're not—you lack a woman's heart."

That had hurt. Thinking of it now, she wondered whether all that careful schooling of her emotions—so hard-won over so many years—had atrophied all feminine inclinations, leaving her as sexless as a machine. And yet, with her background, marriage would have been folly and as marriage generally followed love, she had always been careful not to love, not to look, not to encourage in any way the attentions of the opposite sex. Instead, like a nun, she had chaneled everything into her vocation.

But still, that accusation from a man—a man she had liked and respected—cut to the quick. By way of compensation she drove herself and her nurses even harder, trying to instill her philosophy into all of them. But it was not easy: Mostly they were too tired, too overworked, too desperately in need of kindness themselves, to be able to summon the necessary response.

Which was how she felt now. But the words would have

to come, the sincerity have to be found, the encouragement expressed.

Leaving the hospital at eight, Georgina was exhausted almost to the point of tears. When the porter called her back, she was tempted to ignore him. Even the small bundle of letters failed to lift her spirits. With a brief word of thanks, she pushed them into her pocket.

On the tram she fell asleep and had to be roused at the terminus. With a motor bus across the river, and yet another to take her to Kensington Gardens. She was home by half past nine. The flat was deserted, her father and his servant away, yet again, in Ireland, where executions were the order of the day, and rebels with whom few had previously sympathized were being raised to the level of martyrs. It was a bitter, heartbreaking situation, and like her father Georgina could see no sense in it. It seemed the crowning folly of years of mismanagement, years in which the famous English sense of fair play had been remarkable only for its absence. If only, she often thought, the government would not persist in treating Ireland like a recalcitrant child. Such arbitrary punishment was less likely to hammer evil out than temper it to greater strength for the next attempt. And there would be other attempts, of that her father was sure; his prognostications for the future were dire indeed, and the smaller tragedy was that his present sympathies were in direct conflict with his sense of duty. He had tried, yet again, to resign, but short of laying himself open to a charge of treason, it was impossible to reveal that depth of antagonism to his masters at the War Office. Georgina had never seen him so desperately low in spirit, and there was little she could afford in the way of comfort. Ireland was her country too.

Only one thing had cheered her father in recent weeks and that had been the arrival of the Australians in London. The first contingent had marched to Westminster Abbey on April 25 to commemorate the anniversary of the landing at Gallipoli, and since then others were to be seen everywhere about the town, handsome, muscular, sun-bronzed men on leave, engagingly friendly if curiously disinclined to salute the many British officers at large on the streets. That aspect afforded Robert Duncannon a certain amount of perverse satisfaction, and in the midst of his despair over what was happening in Dublin, he had related to Georgina a story that was currently being repeated in shocked tones throughout the War Office. While in Egypt, apparently, a young Australian officer had been accompanying a visiting brigadier on a tour of inspection. Coming upon a soldier on guard duty engaged in eating a pie, the horrified young officer immediately ordered him to present arms, whereupon the soldier calmly requested the brigadier to hold his pie while he did so.

True or not, that story amused Robert enormously, as did the legend of those rare salutes. These wild colonial boys were idiosyncratic when it came to one of the prime rules of British army life and would apparently only afford that civility to those officers known to them and respected.

"Which must cut out the entire general staff," Robert had commented with acid appreciation. "No wonder Haig loathes them—he was always so particular about his status!"

But when Georgina had gently teased him with the question of how he would feel if the Australian soldiers did not salute *him*, Robert had lapsed once more into bleak despondency.

"Well, as I don't have much respect left for myself at the moment, how on earth could I complain?"

That comment, Georgina felt, mirrored her father's attitude with disturbing clarity. She was anxious about him, on top of all the other constant, pressing anxieties that made up her life these days. Ireland, the war, her work, all intruded into every waking hour and often the sleeping ones as well. She dreamed often of Liam, a recurrent nightmare in which a faceless, mutilated body on her ward turned out to be him.

It was not necessary to ask her father whether any of the Australians currently in London included Liam. Robert Duncannon had made a contact on the Australian staff in London, who was primed to tell him the instant Liam's name came up either for leave or as a casualty. Nevertheless, that did not prevent her heart leaping every time she saw one particularly tall, fair soldier in the by-now-familiar slouch hat. But it was never him and the disappointment was always agonizing. Her need to see him, to have some word from him at least, grew out of all proportion, becoming for her a touchstone, the one thing that would relieve all other anxiety. She did not ask herself why that conviction had taken root, nor question its logic; she knew, quite simply, that it was so. She was also aware that Liam was unlikely, after all this time, to write to her. If she wanted to hear from him, she would have to be the one to break the silence. And by that time Georgina was incapable of weighing the issues involved.

But it was a month now since she had set pen to paper, using the flimsy peg of what had happened in Dublin as the excuse for writing, four weeks in which she had searched assiduously for his hand on every missive which arrived. Mornings of disappointment had given way to night hours in which she cursed herself for trying to break those silent years. She told herself that there was no reason why, after all this time, he should want to hear from her, or care whether she was in London, Dublin, or Timbuktoo; and in the greater hell of imagined rejection, it seemed to her to have been better to leave things alone.

Quite deliberately, a week ago, it being the only way to do her work and retain her sanity, Georgina had put him out of her mind. Now, glancing at the army-issue envelope, she assumed that it was from Robin, who wrote regularly, and dropped it on the bed. Unpinning her stiff white collar, peeling off the gray nurse's uniform, she peered down at the writing and realized it was different. Needing a better light, she hurried into the sitting room, thrusting back the heavy curtains to let in the morning sun. The hand was bolder, less consciously perfect than it had been before, but it was undoubtedly Liam's.

Hardly daring to believe it, she tore at the envelope with trembling fingers, her eyes running down the single page, taking in formal, stilted, uncharacteristic phrases. For a second she was torn between delight and pain; and then she smiled, remembering her own difficulties, the strain of finding words to overcome the years between. It must have been the same for him. He did not apologize, as she had not, for the years of silence, but simply thanked her for writing, saying he was glad to have her letter and relieved that she had not been in Dublin during the riots. Mail had been delayed, which was why he had not replied earlier. Life in France was even better than he had imagined, and they had not been involved in anything serious. The following sentence had been obliterated by the censor, so Georgina assumed it must have contained some reference to where they were or about to be, and although she held the page up to the light, that thick black line was all-encompassing. She swore with frustration. After all this time every word of his was precious to her; she could not bear to be so denied.

The letter ended on a note of hope, however. Liam said he looked forward to hearing from her again and would like to know something of what life was like for her in London. His signature, strong and forward-sloping, was underlined by a single flourish.

Pleased beyond all reason, Georgina burst into tears.

19

*A*t the end of June, three weeks after posting her letter to Stephen in the Gulf, Zoe was still waiting for a reply. The letter received the previous week was not in answer to any of hers, in fact it was little more than a note in which his reasons for telephoning were not given and the apology for his brusqueness was brief. There were few allusions to his own emotions, either with regard to her or the situation out there, although he did say in a postscript that she was not to worry about him, the media made far more of isolated incidents than was necessary.

Hardly knowing what to make of the letter itself, Zoe read that last sentence with grim disbelief. She took a respected daily newspaper and could hardly avoid the BBC news, either by radio or television. Misplaced or not, her faith in such institutions was not easily broken. Only a few days before, a journalist reporting from Dubai had helpfully analyzed the score of shipping hit in the preceding three years, and of those 227 ships, most were tankers, and most, like Stephen's, were registered in Liberia. The total of merchant seamen dead was equally devastating, especially when one considered that this was supposed to be a local war, the merchant ships unarmed and their crews "just doing a job." In the interests of world trade—and somebody's fat profit, Zoe thought bitterly—211 non-combatant merchant seamen had lost their lives.

The article did not list the numbers of maimed and wounded. It did, however, report that many ships' masters were breaking international law and the rules of safe navigation by running close into the coast of Oman and the United Arab Emirates, that two fully laden tankers had recently gone aground in their attempts to avoid attack by Iranian gunboats.

It did not make reassuring reading, and with those figures buzzing in her head as she pored over the latest international news, Zoe wished she had remained in ignorance. Pushing the newspaper aside, she cleared her breakfast things and set out the morning's work. The radio was playing a track from a Dire Straits album, one of Stephen's favorites, and she smiled, remembering; but at the following news announcement she felt herself tense, as always now, expecting the worst.

Another bomb had gone off in Belfast, killing two soldiers, and even as she winced, wondering whether Ireland's problems would ever be solved, the voice ran on, outlining Washington's plans for protecting American-flagged ships in the Gulf. And in the Gulf itself, Iranian gunboats had launched missile attacks on two tankers sailing out of Kuwait. The detached, unemotional voice of the newscaster went on to state that the Chief Engineer of one ship had been killed, two crewmen injured on the second.

Poised over her drawing board, listening with every nerve and muscle tensed, Zoe was still unsure of what she had heard. Doubt crept in. Had they really said *Scandinavian*, or was it *Liberian*? The news had been brief and no names announced. Perhaps they had made a mistake, perhaps only one ship was Scandinavian, and the other . . .

Abruptly, she pushed back her chair and reached for the telephone, got the number from inquiries, and dialed the BBC. Eventually she had the names of both ships, neither of them Stephen's. Trembling like an aspen, she set the kettle to boil and called her neighbor Polly.

"Oh God, I can't stand this," she whispered as her friend joined her in the kitchen. "I can't work, I can't sleep—after three weeks, I'm a nervous wreck. What am I going to be like after three *months*, for God's sake?"

"Stop listening to it—cancel the papers."

"*I can't.*"

"You must," Polly said practically, lighting a cigarette. "Put it out of your mind, Zoe, it's the only way."

"That's easier said than done! I'd have to be a stone wall, for heaven's sake, to ignore what's happening out there when Stephen's *part of it*." She hugged her body, rocking back and forth as though in physical pain. "Oh hell!" she exclaimed, "if anything was ever guaranteed to make me start smoking again, this is it!"

"Well, you're not having one of mine," Polly declared. "Have a glass of water instead—it's supposed to dull the craving." Turning on the cold tap, she doused her cigarette and opened the window. Filling a glass with water, she stood over Zoe until she drank it down. "There now—better?"

"No." Zoe paced the floor. "What if anything happens to him? What will I do?"

"Nothing will happen to him—and if, God forbid, it should, you'll help nobody by worrying yourself silly anticipating it. Look, why don't you ring that auntie of his? Or that couple you stayed with? You know—didn't you meet the wife aboard Stephen's ship? She must be worried sick too—maybe she'd appreciate a call."

Zoe nodded. "Yes, yes, I will—I've been keeping in touch with Joan, but I haven't spoken to Irene for weeks. I'll give her a call this evening."

"That's the thing. But in the meantime, turn off that bloody radio and listen to some tapes. Forget the news!"

An hour later, satisfied that Zoe was over the worst of her anxiety, Polly left. But Zoe could not get Stephen out of her mind, and while it was a comfort to talk to Irene that evening, to hear her calm, sensible voice saying much the same as Polly, once she had put down the phone, Zoe was racked by nerves. Worried for him, wanting him desperately, she almost wished they had never met; she certainly cursed herself for falling in love with such a man.

She spent a poor night and slept late the next morning. It

was with misery dogging every movement that she washed and dressed in jeans and an old shirt and went down to see whether there was any mail. The airmail envelope with *Karachi* on the postmark sent her spirits soaring.

Clutching the letter like a flower, she ran back upstairs, flicked on the automatic kettle, and reached for a chocolate biscuit; no matter how brief, letters from Stephen were a rare treat and deserved to be accompanied by the same. Had there been a box of chocolates in the flat, she knew she would have eaten the lot.

His letter was in answer to hers of three weeks ago, the first, stilted words of its beginning bending, almost reluctantly, she thought, into tenderness. Zoe's personal history seemed to have touched some chord in him that he could not disguise, as though having known a largely happy childhood, he could not bear to think of her endurance through unhappy years. His tenderness touched her, to the extent that she half regretted the outpouring of old sadnesses—he had the power, even with a word, of making her so happy she found herself wondering what all the misery had been about.

What he thought about Philip Dent, however, Stephen did not say. Other than to tell her to forget the incident, he made no reference to that half of Zoe's letter, and she was left wondering whether too much had been divulged. It was hard to judge if her honesty had caused him pain, or whether he was pleased to know that Philip no longer posed a threat. His reticence nagged at her, chilling the warmth she had felt initially. She read the letter again, looking for evidence of coolness, and managed to find something to chill her further in his suggestion that she should get out and about more often and spend less time on the past.

She wished so much that she could get through to him, that she could make him understand that a wholesale takeover of his life was not on her agenda, that she valued her own independence sufficiently to respect his. She wanted to share his life, not own it.

With his letter still in her hand, she slipped a tape into the machine, music she had copied from one of his records. It was the music from the sound track of *Far from the Madding Crowd*, and the introduction washed over her like the gentle rain it simulated, suggesting dripping trees and country lanes, and reminding her—as it always did—of the very first time she had heard it played, that night in Stephen's flat. They had stood together and looked out at the floodlit Minster, and they had talked about that battlefield in the mist. Remembering their closeness, then and afterward, she found herself longing for Stephen with a passion that shook her, and was suddenly tempted to write, at once, telling him all that she felt, that growing conviction that they were destined to be together.

Evocative of time and place, the music seemed to epitomize Hardy at his most poignant, gentle, plaintive melodies overlaying violent passion beneath, and interspersed throughout the score, the country ballads with their telling words. Laying Stephen's letter down, Zoe was about to set pen to paper when the words of one particular song stayed her hand.

> I overheard my own true love
> His voice did sound so clear:
> "Long time I have been waiting for
> The coming of my dear."
>
> Sometimes I am uneasy
> And troubled in my mind
> Sometimes I think I'll go to my love
> And tell to him my mind.
>
> But if I should go to my love,
> My love he will say nay;
> If I show to him my boldness,
> He'll ne'er love me again.

Old-fashioned words, she thought with a sudden surge of bitterness, but in spite of feminism and the lip service paid to equality, had very much changed between men and women since Hardy's day? She thought not. Let a woman talk of love and commitment—and by implication, children too—and most men would still run a mile. It was not selfishness particularly, nor was it immaturity, as Polly often maintained, it was simply the way they were made. Crawling up the ladder of civilization might have refined a few things, but the basic differences were still there, and all the education in the world would not change them.

On that thought she experienced a moment's pity for Stephen's ex-wife and knew that in spite of her own love of independence, basically she wanted the same sort of commitment from Stephen. She wanted to know that he loved her, that he wanted to father her children; because to Zoe the thought of children, of continuation, was becoming increasingly important. But not just any man's children: Stephen's.

Stephen, however, must come to her. He must be the one to speak of love and unity, he had to be willing to acknowledge the ties that bound them already. She was sure he was aware of those ties, but as yet they could be broken. He might prove to be the kind of man who was incapable of making a proper commitment to any woman—there were plenty of those about, and her first lover, Kit, was a prime example—or with such such physical distance between them, they might simply drift apart. And in this situation—oh God, *this situation*—death could intervene in one swift stroke, leaving her here, in Georgina Duncannon's flat, stranded and alone.

That thought chilled her.

Polly was right: She must not think of these things. Abruptly, Zoe switched off that haunting music and went out for a walk in the park.

Having loaded a mixed and highly flammable cargo of aviation fuel, diesel oil, and motor gasoline, the *Damaris* was ready to sail in the early afternoon. With no intentions of leaving before nightfall, Stephen left watchmen posted and told his officers to get some rest. He went below himself but found it difficult to sleep, and when he did eventually doze, it was to dream again of Liam Elliott, mud-spattered as ever, lurching toward him out of the mist, arms raised in some sort of begging plea. Although he had experienced the same dream two or three times before, it was no less disturbing for all that: Stephen woke in a cold sweat.

"For Christ's sake," he muttered into the gloom, "what are you trying to say to me?"

Glancing at the clock, he realized he had slept for not much more than an hour, but there was not much point in trying again: It would soon be time for dinner and he must eat. Lighting a cigarette, he went through into the dayroom to make a pot of tea. It was hot and sweet and refreshing, and with his second cigarette he began to feel a little better. A long, cool shower completed the process of dragging his reluctant body into wakefulness; as he dressed, his eye caught Liam's diary lying innocently on the bedside chest.

Sighing, he said aloud, "I can't think about it now. I haven't time."

Like an unexpected reply, the telephone rang, startling him. He snatched at it, his answer terse.

"Yes, I'm awake—I'll be down in a minute."

He reached for his clean shirt, fastening the epaulets with their four gold stripes to the shoulder tabs. For a moment he stared at the mark of rank, wondering whether ambition was worth it. Minutes later he was down in the saloon, sipping at a glass of iced water. Thinking of the long night ahead, Stephen ordered soup, a sardine salad, fillet steak and chips, and cheese to finish. He was not ravenously hungry but forced his way through everything; for the next twelve hours he would exist on black coffee and perhaps a cheese sandwich.

He exchanged a few words with the Mate and then they went together up to the bridge. It was Johnny's watch, but until they cleared the Strait of Hormuz in something like seventy-two hours' time, Stephen would remain on the bridge, resting in the sea cabin behind the wheelhouse during the necessary anchorages. Safe anchorages, supposedly, but in the Gulf safety was a relative term. Anchoring close to a neutral territory, center of population, or major oil installation simply made the risk of air attack by day less likely. In the daylight hours helicopters were buzzing around and Iranian jets screaming back and forth, while at night gunboats crept out, hiding among the fishing fleets of Arab dhows. Less than a month of running the gauntlet every week, and already the strain was making itself felt.

The tugs were away just before seven. Stephen telephoned the engine room. "Right, Mac, let's get this show on the road. Full revs as soon as you can." He gave a short bark of a laugh at the Chief's answering comment. "Too bloody right—we don't stop for *anything*. Particularly small boats wearing missile launchers!"

The last lingering glow of light over the desert was soon gone, and at full dark the ship was making sixteen knots away from the Kuwaiti terminal and directly out into the Gulf. Apart from the narrows at Hormuz, this was one of the worst stretches, the vast oil fields off the Kuwaiti and Saudi Arabian coasts making it impossible to hug the safety of neutral territory. At the farthest point, before turning south for Ras at Tannurah, they were only sixty miles from the Iranian coast, frighteningly close to the place where the Scandinavians had been attacked a couple of nights before. The gunboats were getting bolder.

Stephen checked charts and radar constantly, and with the changing of the watch at eight, had the Third Mate on the port bridgewing and a seaman to starboard. He moved all the time between them, every nerve stretched taut, carefully plotting every blip on the radar, identifying each approaching ship through night glasses. At mid-night, with the arrival of the Second Mate it was time to change course away from the center of the Gulf, back toward the Saudi coast. After that he took a short break for a sandwich and a cup of coffee before resuming his pacing. His mind was clear, concentrated totally upon that surveillance; he did not allow himself to wonder what he would do in the event of an attack. He had to trust himself and the years of experience behind him, had to trust that his reactions, which had never failed him yet, would be the right ones. To doubt that would be to fall apart.

With the Mate's reemergence at four, and Ras Tannurah no more than a couple of hours away, Stephen felt able to relax a little. Once Johnny had taken over the watch he eased himself into the high pilot's chair, aware of chronically aching knees and ankles.

Lighting a cigarette, the last of a pack opened just before dinner, he said, "Did you sleep?"

"After a fashion." Silhouetted against a faintly graying sky, Johnny was following the movements of three tankers, like themselves all running for the safety of the anchorage. He checked their courses against the radar plot, then said, "I kept thinking about those poor bloody Scandinavians."

"Mmm. Me too."

"Quiet night?"

"Plenty of tonnage going up, and we overtook a couple coming down."

"No nasty little men in boats, then?"

"Well, there were a bunch of fishing boats just before we changed course—made me sweat for a while, I can tell you. But nobody asked us to stand and deliver, so we just kept going."

Johnny grinned and continued his surveillance. Stepping down from the pilot's chair, Stephen made some coffee, relieved, after eleven hours of solid concentration, to let it lapse a little, to know that his senior officer was alert and capable. The worst of the night was over, and in the east the first glow of dawn was spreading like the fan of a peacock's tail. The sun rose rapidly, shooting a path of gold across the sea and casting long, dramatic shadows from the ships ahead. They were drawing closer to the three tankers now, with another, very slow-moving pair ahead of them. But were they tankers? Stephen wondered, trying to discern shape and form through the glasses. It was impossible, another ship was in line of sight. He studied the radar and thought it might be one ship under tow.

"Never mind, they seem to be heading for the anchorage—we'll see them soon enough."

He glanced at his watch. Six o'clock and he was hungry, more than ready for the breakfast that would be waiting once they were in position and securely anchored. One by one the ships ahead of him altered course and slowed for their approach, and as Stephen prepared to do the same, he noticed the farthermost vessel holding its original course. Once again he studied it through the binoculars and the thing, whatever it was—an enormous barge, Stephen thought at first—was attached to an oceangoing tug. It took several seconds for him to register what he was seeing, and as it dawned his hunger disappeared.

"Have you seen that?" Johnny murmured, and there was horror in his voice.

"I have indeed."

The two vessels were traveling so slowly, the *Damaris* was soon abreast of them, perhaps half a mile distant. With the glasses pressed to his eyes, Stephen was only dimly aware of Mac joining him on the bridgewing. The "barge" was a stricken tanker, her name and port of registry just visible beneath burned and blistered paint on the stern. Other than that, Stephen thought, she was barely recognizable as a ship, more an obscene caricature with plates ripped and curled, and pipes twisted across the remains of her foredeck. There was no super-structure, no accommodation, no bridge; only two bent up-rights that had once supported the wings.

In the Gulf these days, damaged ships were commonplace, most of them with holes in either bow or stern, temporarily crippled and waiting at every anchorage for their turn in the crowded repair yards, but Stephen had never seen anything like this. Whatever had hit her, either Exocet or high-explosive shells, had hit the aft accommodation, and presumably fire and a series of explosions had done the rest. Had anyone survived? Had there been time to jump clear? It seemed unlikely that there could have been chance to man the boats. When had it happened? And where? They had heard nothing during the night, and no word had come during their two days in Kuwait. It was a mystery but not one on which he wanted to dwell.

They were all subdued after that, and Stephen nosed his own ship's 870-foot length carefully between a motley collection of the world's shipping to find a comfortable space where the *Damaris* could swing around her anchor with ease. There were tankers of all sizes and all ages, Greek, Korean, Kuwaiti, Japa-nese, Norwegian, and at least a dozen carrying the Liberian flag. Some were in a sorry state, dented and battered, but none like that stricken thing on its way down toward Bahrain and ultimately the knacker's yard. All, without exception, were showing signs of wear, their hulls streaked with rust, decks and accommodation patchy. On runs like this Stephen was well aware that there was no time for cosmetics, no time to do any but the most essential maintenance. It hurt his professional pride that after only four weeks the *Damaris* was already begin-ning to look like an old tramp, but what was rust compared to structural damage and loss of life? And he could take comfort from knowing that Mac's engines were tuned like a Rolls-Royce, every valve and pump was in excellent order, fire-fighting equipment and breathing gear in a state of constant readiness. It gave him a certain grim satisfaction, too, to realize that he was right to insist so absolutely upon fire drill and boat practice.

Those activities were no longer exclusive to Saturday mornings, no longer a halfhearted effort to comply with regulations. Outside the Gulf Stephen insisted on a full drill every trip. He even had them blindfolded. Search and rescue were all very well in practice, but in reality, with generators gone, no lights, and the accommodation full of smoke, it would be hard to see anything. So he made them all pretend. To the crew it had been a great game occasioning much merriment. Having seen that blitzed tanker, he wondered whether they would laugh next time.

They spent the day at the northern holding anchorage, a day in which a hot, searching wind blew dust off the desert's face and the sun could have fried eggs on the steel decks, a day like any other, with the sudden, heart-stopping scream of low-flying jets and the more sustained anxiety of reconnaissance aircraft. Aboard the ships, however, nothing stirred until sunset, when there was a sudden flurry of activity. Like lizards that have been as dead as stone in the heat of the day, once the sun had gone those ships began to slip away, one after the other, on their various journeys through the night. It was another twelve hours of anxiety, with the safety of Das Island just after dawn; then another day of heat and inertia, of eating and dozing and reading in the sea cabin, while the officer of the watch paced back and forth across the bridge.

Stephen tried to write to Zoe, but there was so much that could not be said, it left little to describe. With the imprint of that stricken tanker still on his mind, it was hard to avoid mentioning the dangers, and an hour later, reading the letter through, he realized his observations of Kuwait sounded almost childishly resentful. In three pages he described the numbers of Soviet supply ships off-loading arms, presumably en route to Iraq, and went on to complain about the nit-picking levels of bureaucracy—worse than anything he had ever encountered—and the fact that no one from a foreign ship was allowed ashore in Kuwait. None of it endeared him to that tiny country, and the fact that he was risking his ship and his life to maintain the war and the oil sheiks' riches made him hate everything connected with it.

Anger and a sense of his own inadequacy depressed him. He would have liked to tell her how it felt, being here, but that was somehow too frightening to contemplate.

They left again after dark, part of a general movement of ships that clustered together for safety like an old Atlantic convoy, except that there were no corvettes or destroyers to protect them—only a bevy of little minesweepers doing their bit by the strait.

The air was heavy and close, visibility poor with dust in the atmosphere. In another few weeks the monsoon winds would be blowing in earnest, creating yet another hazard. He longed for news from London that would release him from this hellish contract, but he did not seriously expect it before his leave was due. This run was too lucrative. One thing was for sure, he promised himself: They could beg, plead, and threaten, but he would not accept another posting to this hellhole until every other Master in the company had taken his turn. And at that rate, Stephen calculated, he would be ready for retirement.

The anchorage at Dubai was a short stop, three hours before dawn to gather themselves for the final, nerve-shattering dash through the Strait of Hormuz in broad daylight. The strait was too narrow, too uncomfortably close to Iran and all those ferocious heroes of the Islamic Revolution for anybody to risk going through at night. With the thought of Exocet missiles for breakfast, however, Stephen was hardly comforted by the Radio Officer's news that three aboard that ravaged tanker had been killed and two injured. It was an improvement upon his imagination's score, but that was all. Unarmed men, part of nobody's war, they were victims of murder. And for what? Politics? Religion? Profit? Was the reason so important? He thought not. All that mattered was that they were dead.

And there but for the grace of God, thought Stephen, go I.

20

On July 1, 1916, on the slopes of rolling chalk hills north of the River Somme, more than twenty thousand British soldiers met their deaths in flower-strewn meadows, mown down by machine guns, trapped by giant caterpillar rolls of barbed wire.

At Fricourt, three miles from the little country town of Albert, Robin Elliott advanced with the Green Howards' 7th Battalion and watched his friends fall around him. In the shelter of a shell hole just before the German line, pinned down by a ferocious hail of bullets, he applied inadequate field dressings to the wounds of one man and a rough tourniquet to the arm of another. He comforted them, fed them sips of water, and waited for the day to pass. It was long and hot and cloudless, a day to sear the memory, the sun like a branding iron, the air thick with the smell of lyddite and blood. The cries of the wounded were harrowing. One of his companions, the one with abdominal wounds, died just before sunset; the other, with his hand a mangled mess of bone and tissue, moaned constantly. At full dark, which was not until after eleven that night, he hoisted the barely conscious man out of the shell hole and proceeded to crawl with him back to the point from where they had set off. It was not very far, perhaps a little over fifty yards, but it took him more than two hours to reach the safety of their own lines.

Under fire in the trenches opposite Messines in Belgium, Liam knew nothing of it. The Germans facing them were not only very alert but intensely serious about the business of killing. Here were none of the almost gentlemanly routine attacks that had so characterized Armentières; here the sniping was constant, the shelling unpredictable, and God help any man who did not think carefully before he moved. At the foot of a shallow slope, with no communication trenches behind them, it was impossible to leave by day; even by night the road, which meandered uphill and across six hundred yards of open country, was a challenge, being regularly strafed by machine gunners from across the valley.

It was a long time since Liam had been quite so nervous, and when, after ten days of noise and rain and squelching, stinking mud, the company was relieved, Liam could have kissed the incoming British troops. But one man was killed going out that night, and the fifth member of Liam's team, Jim Smith, was caught by the same scythe of fire. Half groaning, half laughing, with the fleshy calf of his leg in tatters, he hung on to Liam and Jack, the number two, while they dragged him through the mud to safety.

"The bastards got me," he kept saying, "the bloody bastards got me!" Then it seemed to dawn on him that he was wounded, and he said delightedly, "But it's a Blighty, this one—it's got to be Blighty! I'll be out of this bloody mess for a bit, won't I?"

"Oh, he's a lucky sod, this one," somebody else remarked. "Clean sheets for him, and angels with wings waiting on his every whim!"

"You're getting quite poetic, Vic—careful, they might give you a commission."

"Heaven forbid, Corp—I'm staying with you!"

But that wound put a slight dent in their feeling of invincibility. They had been together as a team since the early days at Bailleul, and as Smithy was handed over to the ambulance team it occurred to all of them that they were one less, that for the first time they needed a replacement.

Euphoria at leaving the line was further dampened by the weather. In the midst of an electrical storm they marched back to camp to find it flooded out. The morning was spent digging drainage ditches around tents and canvas bivouacs. Too tired to sleep and needing suddenly to get away from the press of other human beings, Liam went for a walk. The storm had cleared the air, leaving the sky pale and fragile, reflected like a string of pearls in puddles along the road. Beyond the woods that flanked the camp he heard strange noises, a hammering and tapping which bore no resemblance to gunfire. Investigating, he came across an army of engineers laying track-beds and rails at a tremendous rate. Fascinated by their activity, he stood and watched for a while, noticing as he did so that much horse-drawn artillery was moving south on a road close by.

Sauntering past a group of pioneers who had stopped to brew up, he asked what was going on.

"Don't you know, mate? It's for the advance. All that lot's going down to Amiens, and this track's for the armored trains."

"What advance?"

"Lord, son, where 'ave you been? Australia?" The old sergeant cackled at his own humor, while his men shook their heads. "Big push north of Verdun. Helpin' the Frogs out, we are—doing all right too. We'll soon 'ave Fritz on the run!"

Against a hard little kernel of disbelief, Liam's spirits lifted; because he wanted it to be true, he laughed, said it was tremendous news, and wished them well with their task. On the way back his step had a spring to it, and almost in spite of himself he repeated the story as though it were gospel fact. It certainly fitted with what they knew already, that the Germans locally had been rattled into vindictiveness, and probably by the news that they were being defeated elsewhere.

The next day the machine gunners were issued revolvers for range finding, it having been decided at long last that rifles were too cumbersome to carry along with gun barrels and tripods and heavy boxes of ammunition. They had some fun practicing with those, and even greater fun later at the baths in Neuve-Église. Cleanliness and a fresh change of clothes worked wonders; tiredness evaporated and suddenly life was worth living again. Pay and an issue of mail completed everyone's satisfaction.

Liam returned to their camp in the grounds of an old moated manor house, his disappointment that there was nothing from Georgina intensified by an awareness that his weeks-old request for leave was hardly likely to be granted now. Artillery was still moving down that road beyond the woods, and if the push was as big as was rumored, no doubt the Australians would soon be moving with it. On these somber considerations he settled down with his back against a tree trunk, lit a cigarette, and prepared to read his mail. Most unexpectedly, there was a letter from Tisha, which in her hurried scrawl announced the fact that she was married.

It had been very short notice, she wrote, because Edwin was about to leave on active service, something for which he had been applying regularly but not really expecting. At her description of his rank and background, Liam felt his lip begin to curl, and not even a vaguely lingering affection for his sister could prompt much sympathy for their situation. He knew already, from Georgina, that Tisha had landed on her feet in London and suspected she took as much advantage of people there as she had always done.

It was a shock, however, to read that Robert Duncannon had given her away at the short ceremony before a registrar.

"Mother and Dad weren't able to travel down, you see, as Dad's not been so well lately. I'm writing to Robin too, but if you should see him give him love from me and Edwin. Edwin is just longing to meet you both, but I don't suppose it will be until this dreadful war is over. We really must get together then, don't you agree?"

Liam swallowed hard, wondering why Tisha should still, after all this time, have the power to infuriate him. All those throwaway lines, no real news, just a series of "by the way's." *"Dad's not been so well lately."* What did that mean? There was nothing from Edward this time, only a brief note from his mother.

He scanned it quickly, looking for any reference to illness, but there was none. She said Edward was very busy at work, and what with that and the difficulty of traveling on short notice, they had not been able to go to the wedding. "But I don't expect that will have upset Tisha very much," was added in a telling statement, "and I gather the young man's parents were also unable to be present."

There was nothing surprising about the letter, yet for some reason it made him uneasy. Why should Tisha refer to illness, and his mother not mention it? If either of them suffered so much as a cold, she usually saw fit to remark on it. What was so wrong with Edward that it must be hidden? Or that—God forbid!—he was unable to write? Unpleasantly disturbed, Liam promised himself that he would ask some searching questions in his next letter home. And he would ask Georgina too. She communicated with his mother; she would know.

Suddenly, they had orders to pack up and leave. The fairy-tale beauty of the old manor house, reflected with such purity in the glassy waters before it, slept on in the morning sun, oblivious to all activity around it. The men packed limbers and field kitchens, hitched horses, filled in latrines, folded tents, and prepared for the lengthy march to Bailleul, their original base near Armentières. From there cattle wagons took them overnight to Doullens, where everything had to be unloaded from the train for a rapid march south through Picardy. It was beautiful country, a place of misty woods and hidden valleys, of winding country lanes and thatched, half-timbered villages. It was gentler than Flanders, more secretive somehow, and much less intensively farmed. It was also much poorer. The people had little to sell and nothing to give; two years of war had destroyed their harvests and the troops moving back and forth had eaten everything else. Bread was a luxury and fresh meat almost a legend. Liam had the impression at every halt that despite their forced smiles, the locals could not see much to choose between the marauding Boches and defending British. Their own sons were dead and dying at Verdun, and for those few who returned, a pathetic inheritance of shell holes and fallow fields would be all that was left.

That atmosphere of sadness seemed to color the landscape, beauty and tragedy mixed, as in some old romantic poem. Lovely but neglected châteaus, their gardens a wilderness of roses in full bloom, and picturesque old farmhouses whose quaintness hid emptiness and hunger within; ponds without ducks, barnyards without geese, water meadows by pretty rivers which supported no more than a wealth of wild flowers.

Standing outside one of those ancient barns at sunset, Liam heard the guns and imagined the destruction. He was a lover of beauty and solitary places, of land that was fruitful and lovingly tilled, and to him this march of men, of guns and battle and sudden, violent death was like rape. And he was a necessary part of it; that was what hurt, what made him long with a force that shook him for this battle to succeed.

The English newspaper he had bought in Bailleul claimed that it was going well, although as they came closer to the town of Albert, the sight of so many exhausted and dispirited British troops made him wonder at the truth of it. And the next day, with his first letter from Georgina in almost three weeks, Liam knew that much was being withheld.

Her note was little more than a brief apology. There was no time to write at length, little time to breathe with convoys of wounded coming in almost faster than they could be dealt with. All the staff were working ridiculous hours, the wards full with more beds being added every day. She prayed that he was still in Belgium and safely out of what was happening on the Somme. Had he heard anything from Robin? Louisa had received the usual printed card, circled where it said, "I am well," just three days after that first terrible day of battle. But other than that, nobody had heard a thing.

That first terrible day. Georgina's words had the ring of doom about them, flaring the ever-present embers of his anxiety over Robin. Sixteen days had passed since the initial advance, and the battle had not stopped. It was still going on, he could hear the boom of the guns like thunder just a few miles away. The whole of the Australian 1st Division was on the move, and the battered remnants of the British 29th, with whom they had fought at Gallipoli, were resting in the next village. The ones he questioned all told the same tale: that the Yorkshire regiments had taken the most dreadful battering, some battalions virtually wiped out. And his informants did not seek to shock; their words, like their eyes, were without any discernible emotion.

Recognizing the symptoms, Liam felt a chill enter his soul.

He did not ask what the battle had been like, there was no need. He had been there, at Quinn's Post and Lone Pine and a dozen other places on the peninsula. So he was gentle with them and shared his cigarettes and patted their shoulders when he left. Their band was playing that evening in the village street, but those rousing, popular tunes were as inappropriate as dance music at a funeral. The lament of a solitary piper would have been more fitting.

They were held outside Varennes until the nineteenth, and the move, when it came, was sudden. Kit was donned for fighting order, packs marked and handed in, felt hats exchanged for the new steel helmets. Marching through Senlis later that day, Liam saw a group of German prisoners unloading stores under guard and was astonished by their youth. Such boys they looked, their faces pale and bewildered; then he thought of his brother and pity evaporated.

Camp that evening was in the open, in a field outside Albert, beside the shell-pocked ribbon of the Bapaume Road. It was a broad path first built by Romans, not curving around hills but tackling them head-on without compromise. It climbed the long slope of "Tara Hill" like a smudged white line, disappearing over the crest to rise again in a series of small swells, beyond their immediate sight, to a high point some four and a half miles away, on which stood the village of Pozières. To left and right of the road, in an arc around the town, stood several other villages from which the Germans had largely been beaten back. In that bitterly defended action, however, they had retrenched themselves on the higher point of that rolling chalk downland from where they commanded views north to the ridge at Thiepval and south toward the valley of the Somme.

The aim of this push, their officer told them, was to make a break in the line—that never-ending line which ran from the Channel port of Ostend all the way to the Swiss border—so that the German forces could be outflanked at last, rolled up like a human carpet. The Australians' task, he revealed with awe and pride in his voice, was to dislodge the enemy from Pozières.

The 1st and 3rd Brigades would be going in first, with the 2nd, the Victoria Brigade, held in reserve. The young officer, who had joined them in Egypt, sounded regretful as he imparted that information; hearing it, Liam groaned with the rest. Like them he was keen to get in there and fight, keen to deal the swiftest, most lethal blow, so they could finish the war quickly and go back home. But it seemed they were destined to wait on the sidelines, dodging shells, chewing their fingernails, wondering when and if they would be needed.

The Roman road, bearing its evidence of craters, was too exposed for these latter-day legions; all approaches to the ridge were made via two shallow valleys, "Sausage" to the south of the road, and "Mash" to the north. The Division moved in stages to the southerly approach, through the ragged midsummer green of Bécourt Wood and along tracks that led into the shallow dip of "Sausage Gully." Once upon a time it had been good pastureland, but high on the ridge beside the Roman road was the chalky detritus of a massive crater, blasted by mines on the first day, and below it, crisscrossing the vale like the string of a cat's cradle, stretched dozens of tracks. The whole area was scarred by shell holes and old trench systems: white against brick-red earth and what remained of grass on the dusty slopes. It was a chaos of men and horses and transports, field ambulances, kitchens, and guns. Amid the intermittent blast of their own artillery came the distant crump of other guns, and at the head of the valley, where the stumps of Bailiff Wood stabbed the skyline, great gouts of smoke regularly obscured the cloudless blue beyond.

Over the next couple of days they were warned to be ready on several occasions. Liam's unit moved from field to wood to old German trenches overlooking the crater. Eventually the 1st and 3rd Brigades went in at midnight on July 22 after a terrific bombardment which had lasted five hours.

In the old, well-dug German trench Liam curled himself against the crushing reverberations, stuffing lint in his ears to block the din, but the roars and the shocks were continuous, like being bowled along in a steel drum hour after hour with no escape. It was worse than anything he had ever experienced and he could not imagine so much as an insect surviving beneath the impact. His pity went out to the attacking battalions, some of the men only a few hundred yards from where those shells were landing; he thought they must be going mad with it, wondered how they could gather themselves when the barrage lifted. And what about the Germans? Were they safe in their deep chalk dugouts, as they had been on July 1? Or were they being slowly pulverized to oblivion, dying, one by one, from concussion? Eventually his pity extended even to them.

Hour after hour through the long summer twilight it went on, great pink clouds of dust erupting over the horizon; and when darkness came, the night was lit by a continuous flickering band, with star shells bursting and shrapnel twinkling, and red and green rockets curving away into hell. And always the noise, the everlasting noise . . .

When it stopped, the silence was palpable, eerie; the only sound inside their heads, a dreadful, continuous ringing which each one had to shout against. The sharp ripping of machine guns, the crack of mortars, went unnoticed for a while, but eventually it came to them that the battle had begun, and then no one could sleep for wondering how it was faring.

It was a cold night with a heavy dew. Huddled inside a couple of old German overcoats, Liam dozed toward dawn, half an ear cocked for the call that would rouse them all to action. But none came. At sunrise he went down with three of the team for water and provisions and saw the stream of wounded coming in. Most of the injuries were slight, in legs and arms, and in spite of the pain the men were jubilant, the battle was going well, they had Fritz on the run. The claim was borne out by the numbers of prisoners being taken down the valley, most of them so dazed they looked like sleepwalkers.

"Poor buggers, I bet they were glad to surrender," the new man, Gray, remarked, and Liam was bound to agree. Their own walking wounded were singing.

It was a day of inactivity for the machine gunners in reserve. Liam obtained permission for his men to wander around the nearby deserted village of La Boisselle and went with them to explore the deep dugouts which had enabled the defenders to withstand that first bombardment three weeks ago. Flights of steps led deep into the chalk hill, with sizable rooms beneath, all fitted out with wire-sprung beds and dressing tables and electric lights. Awestruck by these creature comforts they were also ill at ease down there, feeling like voyeurs, intruders into a temporarily abandoned home. Tunics were still hanging on pegs, underwear in drawers; a broken powder compact beside a very feminine shoe gave shocking reality to the evidence of female names on a duty roster. Apparently they had worked here as telephone operators.

The men were shocked; having women in the front line seemed to verify the Germans' barbarism. But they were envious too. Perhaps this was the way to go to war, with pretty faces and trim ankles to alleviate the boredom, and a warm pair of arms to welcome you at night. But beneath the coarse jests were gentler longings, an awareness of home and their own women so totally out of reach.

It was damp and cold underground; the afternoon sun struck them pleasurably as they came out. For a good half hour the men lay sprawled on the warm grass, smoking and watching the clouds of dust rising and falling above Pozières. Passersby related the state of play as they would during a cricket match. The home team were pushing through the village, aiming for the cemetery at the northern end, the British 48th would meet them there; the artillery were pounding an isolated outpost of Huns on the western border. They sat up then to identify the spot, almost idly discussing tactics and positions. It seemed, disappointingly, that the reserves would not be needed. Above them planes were buzzing round like gnats, and behind the British lines Liam counted sixteen observation balloons like silver clouds against a cerulean sky.

Returning, they heard that the 8th Battalion had been called up to reinforce the 1st Brigade, which meant another night of anxiety, of wondering whether they would be called in support. They were not. By morning news came through that the village of Pozières had been captured, that the 8th had cut a swathe through enemy opposition and pressed forward to the cemetery. It was tremendous news; the men in reserve cheered and yelled, dancing like cannibals around the field kitchens. But it was by no means over. There passed another twenty-four hours of uncertainty, ferrying supplies up the valley, questioning every stretcher-bearer and runner whose anxious, gasping breaths would allow a reply. The Australians had the village, so why were they not pressing on? What was the holdup? But nobody seemed to know.

In the early hours of the morning of the twenty-fifth they

were woken by the din of a fresh bombardment, German guns this time, which seemed to be finding their marks. The wounded coming down that morning were in a poor way; it was rumored that 8th Battalion had lost two thirds in death and injury, the 5th even more.

All through that beautiful day a constant fume of fog hung over the ridge. The Germans were counterattacking, seeking to regain their lost ground, flinging everything at it in the attempt. The bombardment continued intermittently, intensifying at sunset, throwing back the most glorious colors to the watchers in the valley. Elsewhere the front line was quiet.

It seemed to Liam, moving up to Bailiff Wood with the rest of his company's machine gunners, that the world had paused to watch that duel on the hill. Although it was impossible to see Pozières, no more than a small field lay between the wood and the tiny village of Contalmaison. It was just a wreck, no longer inhabited by the living, its walls and rafters collapsed into paths and gardens, the orchards torn limb from limb. Like the dead. Unburied bodies, in the grotesque attitudes of death, lay strewn where they had fallen, Saxon and Yorkshiremen side by side among the rubble. Covering his mouth against the stench, Liam searched while the light allowed for any sign of his brother. Fricourt lay less than a couple of miles away down the valley; there the Green Howards had fought to a standstill and then came back a week later to try again. Had he been here? Was he among the dead?

But nothing remained that suggested the slender elegance of Robin Elliott. Alone, with one of the team watching out for the signal which might come any minute, Liam stopped for a moment in the shelter of a warm farmhouse wall. At his feet a few half-ripe apples were scattered among debris on the grass; a butter churn, undamaged, lay beside the mangled remains of a baby's high chair, while beneath it, staring up at him with bland, unblinking eyes, was a china doll with a broken face.

Suddenly, he was weeping uncontrollably, broken by this evidence of family life, the senseless destruction. This had been a man's home, the place to which he returned each night after work in the fields. War had made of it a charnel house.

Anger shook him then. He walked through the stink of death and raged at its indignities, seeing his brother in every distorted face. Why were they not buried? Why were they left here to rot?

He knew the answers to those questions well enough, but the anger sustained him. As he came back to rejoin the group in the wood, Sergeant Keenan strode up, angrily demanding to know where in hell he had been. Almost amused by the term, Liam turned away and was threatened by a charge. "Looking for my brother," he said, and something in his eyes quelled the other man.

Evening deepened into darkness, and from the valley behind them the British artillery opened up again. Watching red-hot shells passing overhead, Liam was sure the call would come soon. From time to time his body winced and shivered, but he was less conscious of fear than of physical tension, a coiled spring which when the order came released itself in a grunt of praise.

Of the two machine-gun sections to go up, theirs was the first. With his gear already strapped about him, Liam hoisted the fifty-pound weight of the gun's tripod and waited for the nod from Keenan. When it came he led his team down past the crossroads at "Casualty Corner" and along the partially sunken road that led eventually to the ridge. They had a guide, for which Liam thanked God; without him in the darkness they might easily have gone blundering on into the German lines. According to the directions, they were to take up a position at the southwestern corner of the village, relieving two sections of the 1st Brigade who were both undermanned and exhausted. They found the men they were to relieve in a shallow, crumbling trench, but of a village there was no sign.

With the sunrise they were able to distinguish bricks and rubble, the low remains of walls that roughly marked the line of the Roman road. In places where there should have been trees were uprooted stumps and splintered branches; the farmhouse on the corner which had been fortified by the Germans appeared as no more than another hump on a plateau piled with rubble. In its concrete cellars were the headquarters of the 7th and 8th Battalions.

It was very quiet for some time. Unnaturally so, without even the sporadic bursts of gunfire which always marked dawn and dusk. In the silence, the sound of birdsong carried clearly from woods behind the lines; a lark, unconscious of the tragedy below, went trilling up, up, up into the blue, praising the sun and its own ecstatic freedom. In their holes in the ground, the men sipped water and chewed on hard biscuits; Matt, the team's number two, had managed to procure a section of hard, dark-brown sausage which he pared into slices and handed around. It was spicy but satisfying, Liam thought. He had barely swallowed when with a sudden, head-splitting, synchronized crash the German bombardment began.

The new front line dug by the Australians in the past couple of nights had been located by artillery far to the east. On the stroke of seven those heavy guns exploded into action, firing salvo after salvo, rending the air with hurricane force, sucking up dust, lashing down grit, throwing out chunks of chalk and brick. The men were buffeted by the concussion; it pulled air from their lungs, squeezed chests and ears and noses; it made their hearts pound to the point of bursting. Overhead, shells screamed and shrapnel exploded like deadly rain; below, the earth groaned and shifted in protest.

It went on, with barely a cessation, for more than sixteen hours.

The Vickers, which had been set up against the parapet, was soon covered in rubble. Expecting an attack as soon as the bombardment lifted, which could have been any minute, Liam struggled to clear it. As he did so a shell landed not a dozen yards away, lifting two men like rag dolls and dropping them back, dead. A moment later another landed just short of the parapet, caving it in, burying several infantry-men close by. The team rushed to dig them out, scrabbling in the dirt with bare hands; four were alive, shaking and jibbering like idiots, but the fifth was dead, concussed or suffocated, no one could tell. Then young Vic caught a blast, knocked flat in the trench by a hundredweight of rubble; seeing it, Liam dived straight for the boy's head, digging like a dog until he had cleared a passage of air, then scooped dirt from his mouth. Alive and crying, choking on earth and grit, he was hauled free and Liam held him fiercely, rocking with the shocks, thumping his back while the boy coughed and sobbed and wept for his mother. With shoulders pressed to what remained of the parapet, and the team forming a protective arc around them, the two men clung together, and then that concentrated storm of death began to pass away to their left.

For a while Vic moaned with shock, burying his face against Liam's neck; then as realization dawned, there came the rising wail of hysteria, the desperate need to get away.

Clamping his arms, Liam held the boy and shook him. "You're all right! There's nothing wrong with you, Vic—you're *alive!*"

Twitching and shuddering, the boy still struggled. Liam slapped his face, hard and jammed a steel helmet onto his head. "It's moving—the barrage is *moving*—the shells are dropping somewhere else!"

Livid marks stood out against the bloodless cheek; the eyes were terrified but registered Liam's presence, the presence of authority. Before he could slip back into panic, Liam said harshly, "Pull yourself together, Number Six, and dig that bloody gun out. As soon as this lot lifts, we're going to need it! Now move yourself!"

They all jumped to it, entrenching tools clearing the dirt, experienced hands examining the barrel and mechanism for signs of damage. The boy, white-faced, still trembling, did what was required of him while Liam surveyed their position, tried to assess what was happening. Men were still alive, digging out caved-in sections of the trench, giving first aid to the wounded, and taking advantage of the lull just here to send messages back to base. He caught sight of Keenan, with another section facing the road, and had the satisfaction of watching him disappear as another salvo lifted clouds of dust behind him. With any luck, Liam thought, he too would know the terror of being buried alive. Moments later, however, his head was bobbing about again. Liam took a sip of water, swilled it around his gritty mouth, and spat.

Within minutes they had the Vickers stripped and cleaned, the tender mechanism oiled, and a fresh belt of ammunition locked into place. Liam aimed at a tree root two hundred yards away and fired off a few rounds; it was working perfectly. Moving farther down the trench they consolidated their position just as a fresh wave of heavy shells crept closer from the right. Supposed to stay apart during a bombardment, they all drew inexorably together, hanging on against the dreadful buffeting, needing the comfort of physical contact while the earth rocked and thudded beneath them. The noise was horrific. The boy who had been buried edged up to Liam and held his arm, his grip tightening convulsively with every ear-splitting explosion. Needing a hold on sanity himself, Liam started counting, totaling fifteen to twenty heavy 5.9s every minute.

Those concentrated bursts at the southwestern end of the village continued all day. The entrance to "Gibraltar," the fortified cellar on the corner, was blown in, and across the road the 6th Battalion's headquarters in a log hut was buried several times before taking a direct hit. Officers were killed and wounded; runners and stretcher-bearers traveling the sunken road ran races with death; the infantry in the line crawled out of it and took shelter in shell holes.

After sixteen hours the ground was pulverized, the trenches dug so painstakingly had ceased to exist; a thick fog of dust swirled constantly, obscuring everything; and those who survived were so dazed that the expected attack, had it come that evening, could not have been repulsed.

The attack did not come. That crippling bombardment was remarkable in that it was inflicted by the German artillery purely as a means of destruction, a terrifying punishment for the failed counter-attack of the day before. All the Australian positions held, and with the cessation of the barrage sometime after eleven that night, the 1st Division slowly gave way to the 2nd coming up from the valley.

Hardly able to believe they were still alive, hardly able to stand, Liam's company were relieved just before two o'clock in the morning of the twenty-seventh. Another bombardment was going on, this time by the British artillery, but the noise and reverberations were just the same. It took a couple of hours to reach their old billet near La Boisselle, two staggering hours weighed down by gun barrels, tripods, and equipment, on limbs which felt like jelly. On the point of collapse, longing for sleep, Liam could not believe what he saw. A row of massive sixty-pounder guns had been moved up from the wood, and their trench was just beneath them.

"Can't we go somewhere else?" he demanded of Keenan.

"There is nowhere else, sonny. All the billets are taken. You'll just have to put up with it."

In the end the team collapsed into dugouts just yards from those guns. The constant flash and crash and thudding recoil continued all night. Haggard, deaf to normal sounds, they emerged at first light to find the warm metal monstrosity of the battalion kitchen. Taking pity, one of the cooks brewed tea, which Liam accepted gratefully, cupping cold, shaking hands around the enamel mug. He felt like the walking dead, his heart beating erratically, limbs so heavy he could scarcely move. Inside his skull the noise was still trapped; he wondered whether it would ever go away.

Nobody said much. When he could raise enough interest, Liam looked at the faces around him, all gray, all filthy, all, like himself, unutterably weary. No jubilation this morning.

The tea was hot and sweet with condensed milk; after three mugs and several cigarettes, he began to feel a slight improvement, enough to respond to the smell of food. After twenty-eight hours of nothing but water and hard biscuits, he was suddenly ravenous. There was cold boiled meat and hot new potatoes, with bread and jam to finish. Breakfast at the Ritz, he felt, could not have been more satisfying.

21

After breakfast they moved down to Bécourt Wood at the mouth of the valley. From his issue of water, Liam drank long and deep, and then he washed as best he could before spreading out his greatcoat in the shelter of a grassy mound. He slept then, dead to the world and all its noise, for most of the day. As the sun was beginning to set in the peaceful west, the survivors of the 1st Division moved back to that field just outside Albert.

Most of them went down to the river to wash and swim. Stripping, plunging in, relishing the cold shock, Liam dived down into the cloudy depths, needing to rid himself of the filth of battle; and afterward he swam lazy strokes and floated, staring up at the pink-streaked sky, letting the water block his ears to noise. But it felt strange to be out in the open again, not to be grubbing for cover in some pathetic hole in the ground, and, despite the warmth of the evening, when it came time to settle down, he did not sleep well—his dreams were too disturbing, too well-connected to the thunder on the hill. Waking just after dawn he was glad to rise and move about. His insides still felt mangled, but as he lit a cigarette he was glad to see that the violent tremors of the day before had abated considerably. Forgoing breakfast, he sought out Keenan for permission to go into town. The sergeant looked sick, still too bemused by that pounding at Pozières to have the wit to question him closely, and with an admonition to be back before noon, permission was granted. Liam returned to his team only to tell them to cover for him should he be delayed.

"But what if we've moved on?" Vic asked anxiously; like a child he seemed afraid to let Liam out of his sight.

"I'll find you."

Albert at that hour of the morning was practically deserted, ruined buildings in dusty, shadowed streets the haunt of sparrows and starlings and stalking cats. On a sunny doorstep a brindled dog lay curled, muzzle between paws, too lazy to stir as Liam passed by. The town was extensively damaged, but people were still carrying on their lives and businesses. He wondered whether the inhabitants of the surrounding villages had migrated here or farther west, and what they would do when the war was over. Would they go back and start again? It did not seem possible.

The open, cobbled square was pocked by shell holes, the tower of its massive, Romanesque basilica badly knocked about. He stood and stared up at it, marveling at its size for such a small town, although he did not much care for the red-and-cream brickwork, which was too garish for his taste. He longed, suddenly, for the mellowed stone of English village churches, a game of cricket on the green, the faint rustle of applause from watchers outside the village inn. He could see it in his mind's eye: The inn was called The George, the landlord large and jovial . . .

Liam smiled, mocking himself. An illusion, a memory, a dream. Was England really like that anymore? Had it ever been so perfect, except on the surface? The image he conjured was a composite one, the product of his cycling tours through dozens of East Riding villages. The Saxon church with its square tower, the medieval pub, the village green; and the local squire in his manor, the tenants tipping their caps, the agricultural laborers living in ever-increasing poverty. That was a way of life from which he had escaped, a place where common men did not own the land but merely tilled it for the gentry. Even his parents, comfortably off though they were, did not own the cottage in which they lived, nor the land his mother utilized so productively. They paid rent to the man who owned it.

Reality. What was it? A place—a moment in time? This was real, this town square with its piles of rubble, its foreign-looking church, the Blessed Virgin knocked sideways, apparently throwing the Holy Child to his death . . .

And death was real, he could testify to that.

Was Georgina flesh and blood, he wondered, or just an idealized product of his imagination? He dreamed so often of leave in England, of seeing her, talking to her honestly with every barrier swept away. What would he do, though, if that opportunity was ever granted? He would have to remember, every waking moment, that he was her brother, not her lover. That thought seemed most daunting of all. Perhaps it was better that she remained the stuff of dreams.

And Robin, flesh of his flesh, blood of his blood, was here, somewhere in this small corner of France. He had to find him, dead or alive; he had to know, feel his reality, before he too became no more than a dream, a memory, an illusion.

Liam went into the church, trying to pray his English Protestant prayers among gilded frescoes and damaged plaster saints, but he was uneasy and not at all sure that the Almighty had ears left to listen. With all that noise at Pozières, all those men calling out from either side for Him to save them, God was probably weary or deaf or in retreat. And all the saints too.

Stepping over the rubble, Liam came upon an undamaged statue of Saint Anthony. He paused, clutching at a straw of memory, almost sure that someone—a Catholic boy he had been friendly with years ago—had once told him that Saint Anthony was the patron saint of missing things. Of course it might have been another saint entirely, but Liam felt it was worth a try. With a smile that was only slightly cynical, he took a candle, lit it, and set it in the sconce before the saint.

"Please," he whispered, "help me find my brother."

Leaving an offering in the poor box, he went out into the sunlight, feeling comforted. People were crossing the square, an old lady in black approaching the church for her morning devotions; shopkeepers were taking down shutters, and outside a small estaminet, the elderly *patron* was setting out tables and chairs. Liam strolled across and sat down, ordering coffee and rolls.

"Avez-vous du fromage? Un peu, s'il vous plaît."

The cheese was very strong, goats' milk, he guessed, but the bread was deliciously fresh and the coffee excellent. The luxury of the meal, as much as its sustenance, put new heart into him. Lighting a cigarette afterward, Liam felt better than he had for some time, almost relaxed, almost at peace. The *patron*, charmed by his attempts at the language, fussed a little, bringing fresh coffee, offering extravagant compliments as to the Australians' exploits over the past few days. Slightly embarrassed, knowing that he personally had done nothing to further the battle's progress, Liam was glad that the arrival of other soldiers demanded attention. They nodded to him and Liam peered at their regimental insignia, his heart twisting a little as he identified the arc of letters at the shoulder, KOYLI—the King's Own Yorkshire Light Infantry—which had always done much of its recruiting in York.

They were young and fresh, their uniforms too clean to have seen much action, if any, and they had about them all the excitement of youth. Beside them Liam felt old and weary and indescribably soiled. Their eyes were on him, noting the shoulder badge of crossed machine-gun barrels, his loose and comfortable Australian tunic with sensible bone buttons, the nonregulation leather gaiters he wore. He was big and blonde and tanned; he looked so absolutely a son of the outback that it always amused Liam to stress the flatness of his vowels in situations like this. With Australians, he could sound quite like them, but he could also revert to the broad, flat accent of his childhood. He thought he would surprise these youngsters.

Deliberately knocking the aitches off, he said, " 'Ave you seen any Green 'Owards about lately? I'm looking for my brother."

One started to answer before it dawned on him, then he laughed and said, "You're a Yorkie! Whereabouts do you hail from, then?"

Evasively, Liam gave a street name not far from his home.

"Oh, me auntie lives down there. Mrs. Dane, do you know her? Big woman, all mouth—everybody knows *her*!"

Liam laughed, shaking his head. "No, sorry—it's years

since I was last home." But it was so typically York, more an overgrown village than a city, full of friendliness, of people whose relatives never moved, that it brought a hard lump to his throat. He smiled and listened while the boys chattered on about people and places he might know. Eventually they got back to his question: Yes, they had seen reinforcements on the way down from Doullens; in fact they had traveled more or less together, overtaking each other through the villages between there and Amiens. If he hung about, he was bound to see them coming through the square.

Glancing at the sun, Liam said he had not much time to spare; thanking them for their information, he set out to look for those other reinforcements. They would know where they were heading, where the main body of the regiment was camped.

He crossed the square toward the Amiens road, intending to walk out in that direction in hopes of meeting them coming through, but within a few hundred yards he spotted the Green Howards' badge on a group of three NCOs. They were obvious veterans, with hardened eyes and uniforms that had seen better days, despite the brilliant brassware glinting in the sun.

He stopped, asked where they were camped, and did any of them know of a lad by the name of Elliott? He gave Robin's company, but they shook their heads.

"I'm his brother," Liam said, "and I haven't much time. We're moving out today—I don't know where—and I need to find him. If he's still alive," he added wearily.

"Aye, well, 'B' Company lost a lot of lads," one said flatly. "But I tell thee what, I'll come back with thee, show thee the way, like. And we'll look for him together. If he's alive, we'll find him, lad, never fear."

The old sergeant was from Rotherham, a miner whose wealth of blue scars told of years below ground and innumerable pit accidents. He looked hard, but his kindness was palpable. He had lost his eldest son, a regular soldier, at Mons.

"Didn't want him to go down the pit, see? Shoved him in the army—peacetime it was a good life. Bloody daft, eh?"

"But you joined up."

"Aye, well, felt I had to, somehow. Felt I owed it to my lad."

Liam sighed.

It was perhaps just over a mile to the camp outside Dernancourt; the sergeant inquired at headquarters for the company's location, and whether Liam's brother was still listed. His leathery old face was wreathed with smiles as he came out.

"He's all right, lad—fit as a fiddle, and should by rights be with the rest of 'em."

They went down together, past a forest of tents and canvas huts, to where "B" Company were camped. Liam's heart seemed to be performing somersaults, his eyes scouring every tall and slender figure, every man with crisp dark hair. In the end Robin saw him first, poised in braces and shirtsleeves, staring with openmouthed astonishment across a mess of kitchen fatigues. Meeting his brother's eyes, that beautiful open smile, Liam felt his own mouth curving, laughter swelling his chest as Robin bounded to him, swinging them both in a joyful embrace. Liam hugged him, lifted him off the ground, spun him around; and as he set him down again, met the broad, delighted grin of the old sergeant.

"Nice to 'ave an 'and in some good news, for a change," he said, turning away before Liam could thank him properly. He shouted his thanks to the retreating figure, and had the satisfaction of a wave. Then he turned to Robin and hugged him again.

"Why haven't you written home? They're worried sick about you!"

"I have written—last week and again, yesterday."

"Why didn't you write immediately—as soon as you came out of the line?"

Robin's eyes looked hurt, shifted suddenly away. "I—I couldn't."

"Why ever not?"

"Because," he admitted, shamefaced, "I *couldn't*. Didn't stop shaking for nearly a week."

Liam winced. "Oh dear God," he breathed, ashamed of his own lack of tact. "I'm sorry."

"Oh, I'm all right now," he declared, laughing. "And all the better for seeing you. What shall we do? Go into town? Come on," he said eagerly, "I'll just clear it with the Sarge, and we'll go and paint the town red!"

As Robin returned, pulling his tunic into shape, fastening buttons that gleamed with parade ground brightness and straightening his cap, Liam was amazed at the change in him. Even in his old, battle-scarred uniform he looked every inch the soldier, his bearing so upright he might have been a young officer in disguise. He had grown at least an inch, Liam guessed, and put on muscle, although his face was thinner, with the shadow of a dark beard along his jaw and upper lip.

"And you're a fine one to talk about writing," he said as they cleared the camp. "Almost a year, it was, before we heard from you. We were all convinced you were dead."

"Do we have to go into that?"

"No." He grinned, suddenly the boy again. "How strange it is, you turning up today. You won't believe this, but we didn't come back down here till Saturday, and we've only been in this place for a couple of days. I heard your lot were up at Poz when we arrived, and I've been looking for you ever since. Into town, morning and evening, hoping you might be passing through—but today I got stuck on fatigues."

"We came out of the line yesterday, but we're moving on this afternoon. I haven't got long."

"Were you in it? That lot at Poz?"

Liam nodded. "Twenty-four hours, that's all. The battalions were in for four days."

"We were watching it." A muscle twitched in his face. "I kept thinking about you. All the time."

"I was thinking about you too."

They walked on in silence, very close, arms touching, needing the reassurance of physical contact. Liam wanted to put his arm around his brother, and wanting to, eventually did, gripping his shoulder, not caring if they were seen or what might be thought. But it seemed strange that after three years apart, there should be so little to say. Or rather there was too much, and being so conscious of each other, it was hard to say anything at all.

They made for the estaminet in the square, the *patron*, delighted by their reunion, insisting on two beers on the house. It was nothing like English beer, but it was cool and thirst-quenching, and after two or three apiece, their tongues were loosened, the barriers down. They talked about home, about

Tisha and her marriage, and in a general way about Edward and their mother. Liam wanted to know if Edward was ill, but beyond recalling a certain frailty last Christmas when he had been home, Robin knew nothing more than his brother.

"I just thought he seemed very tired," he said. "And worried about the business and the war. Same as everybody else, I thought. I didn't think he was ill."

"Well, he may not be. Perhaps they just told Tisha that, as a sort of face-saver so they didn't have to go to the wedding."

"You could be right. Mother always did hate dressing up, having to put on a company face." After a pause, he said, "Did you know the Colonel gave Tisha away?"

Liam felt his face muscles tighten. "She said so in the letter." Under scrutiny he looked away, narrowing his eyes as he appeared to study the hanging Virgin across the square.

"You haven't got over it, have you?"

There was no need to elaborate; they both knew what he was talking about. With a shrug, Liam affected nonchalance. "Not entirely, but it's not something I want to discuss."

"I wish you would."

Briefly, Liam looked back at his brother and smiled. "All right, we will—one day. But not now. Don't let's spoil this time we have."

"There may not be another chance," Robin reminded him somberly. "Does that never occur to you? That each day might be your last?"

It did, but those sentiments coming from this younger brother caught Liam by surprise. Looking at him, really studying him, he could see how deeply the war had marked Robin. The joy of their meeting had covered it, given him the gloss of boyishness, but he was a boy no longer. He had seen too much of death, felt its brush too closely and on too many occasions. Liam thought how frequently he must have been under fire, and how much, very recently, he had taken of bombardments like the one at Pozières. Robin had seen too much, experienced too much, and it had taken his boyhood away.

The lines of his face, that bruised look about the eyes, were so common these days they generally went unnoticed; and because they were all of them in it up to their necks with no escape, it was no longer worth discussing. Gallows humor prevailed instead. It was the only way to survive.

So he was unprepared for this level of seriousness, felt exposed and horribly naked suddenly; for a moment he could have broken down and, like young Vic the other day, wept for his mother. But the moment passed. Blinking rapidly, he looked away.

"Yes," he said softly, "it occurs to me all the time."

"Then why don't you do something about it?"

"Like what, for heaven's sake? Dash home right now and tell them all is forgiven? That I'm sorry I rushed off like that and I won't do it again?" In the ensuing silence he fumbled for cigarettes and lit one, his fingers trembling over the match. "I do write, you know. I have, regularly, ever since that first letter I sent to you."

"But have you really made things up with Mother? That's what I'm talking about. You can write nice, cheery letters till the cows come home—or until this bloody war's over!—but until you say the words she wants to hear, she'll never rest. It's destroying her. Do you want that on your conscience?"

"Oh for Christ's sake, Robin! What words? What?"

His arm was gripped with painful urgency. "She wants to know that you understand—that you forgive her."

Liam looked at his brother's hand, then up into his face. He could have struck him. "But I *don't* understand," he declared in an undertone. "I never have and I doubt if I ever will. Now leave it alone, Robin, and get your hand off my bloody arm!"

Moving back, Robin downed the rest of his beer in one swallow, found his own cigarettes, and lit up. His hands were not quite steady. He ordered two more beers with a calm pleasantry for the *patron*, but there was tension in every muscle. With sweat standing out on him and heart racing, Liam felt as though he had just been under fire. He was distressed too, arguing with the only person he could love unreservedly, the one he had longed so desperately to see. On the point of apology, he heard the words from his brother.

"No." Liam shook his head. "I'm the one who's sorry. I'm sorry for this—I didn't want to talk about it because I knew what it would come to. And I'm more grieved than you can ever understand about the whole bloody sorry situation. Really I am. I do know what you're trying to say to me. I've thought about it so many times, don't think I haven't. But I can't resolve it." He sighed, shook his head. "It's impossible."

"But *why*? What is it you don't understand? I mean it happened—*years* ago—why can't you just accept it? What difference does it make? Especially *now*, with all this—" His gesture encompassed the whole of the shell-pocked square, the whole of the war. "How can it be important, in the face of all this?"

Liam turned away, afraid to show his pain, afraid that somehow, with that uncanny intuition of his, Robin would see and understand what it was that still gripped him. That he could not think of the man who was his father without loathing, or the woman who was his sister without desire.

Eventually, to deflect the subject, he said sardonically, "And our *father*—how is he? Where is *he* in all this? I don't see him in a sweat-stained, lousy uniform, do you? Where was he when we were sitting in our holes in the ground, going daft with the noise? He didn't sweat and tremble and cry, expecting death by the second! And when you stormed the trenches at Fricourt and saw all your mates mown down like grass, where was he?

"I tell you where he was," Liam added, stabbing the table with a finger that was scabbed and torn, "he was sitting in a comfortable office in Whitehall, or reading papers in his flat, or taking the boat train to Dublin. *That's* where he was. Not here. Oh no—not here."

"You're very bitter."

"He's a professional soldier, for God's sake! A fucking staff officer! He got medals for being so bloody clever in South Africa and the Sudan—he's an old mate of Haig's, did you know that? Oh, don't look so surprised," he added quickly, covering up for the source of that information, "I looked him up a long time ago."

"I don't think *mate* quite fits his relationship with Haig," Robin said stiffly. "He knew him, but they never got on. In fact I got the impression that he disliked him intensely."

"Oh, you did, did you? And when was that?"

"Last Christmas, when I was coming back from leave. He met me at King's Cross with Georgina."

Unable to trust his voice at that, Liam simply nodded, his mouth twisting into a travesty of a smile.

"I wish you could understand how deeply he cares, how bitter he is at being kept in Ireland. It's not his doing, you know."

"Isn't it?"

"No, it damn well isn't! I know you dislike him, but I wish you wouldn't despise him so. He doesn't deserve that. For all his faults he's very straight, and says what he thinks. Which is why he'll retire as a colonel, while Haig will probably end up with a bloody sainthood!"

"He's drawn you to his side, I see that."

"It's not a question of *sides*. I like the man, I admit it. I always have." He softened suddenly. "You know it's strange, but I remember him so well from when I was little. You don't, I know, although I can't imagine why. In fact one of my earliest memories is of sitting on his knee and eating humbugs. And then we had a game, and he let me slide down his legs—and I swallowed the humbug whole!" Robin laughed at the memory. "I suppose I must have been about two or three."

"And you've been swallowing humbugs ever since," his brother remarked acidly.

"Oh thanks! And what have you been doing that's so much better? Running away from things, burying your head in the sand, just like you always did! You can hurt other people, but nobody must hurt you. Is that it? Tisha always said you were spoiled—I'm beginning to think she was right."

Liam winced at that.

"You're my brother and I care about you. I'm taking nobody's side against you. But just because you're the eldest doesn't mean to say you're always right. In this case, I think *I* am. You can't change what happened, Liam, but you can change the way things are now." He paused and leaned across the table. "It would do Mother and Dad so much good. Get some leave, if you can. Go home and see them. Please, Liam."

How the old name affected him! It touched so many chords, brought forth a softness in him that could well have dissolved in tears. Was he really so selfish? Was that how it seemed to others? Had his behavior been interpreted as that of a spoiled, willful child? Surely not. His name, the thought of home, the memory of his mother placidly gardening, lovingly ruffling his hair, all flooded his mind and weakened that stony resolve. He wished with all his heart that he could go back, that the past with all its tragic mistakes could be wiped out, that truth could have come gently. Perhaps, if he went home, he might see things differently, perhaps the pain would ease . . .

Briefly, he gripped his brother's hand. "All right, all right. If it will satisfy you, I'll go home. If I get the leave I've applied for, I'll go."

There was joy in Robin's eyes and a sudden warm hand-clasp that said everything was all right again between them; what had been said was harsh, but they were brothers and it did not matter. It did, because Robin's words, despite their sting, had given Liam something to ponder over. But that ex-tracted promise left him feeling curiously relieved.

The atmosphere lightened, became rather silly. They or-dered more beers and something to eat; and more than a little drunk, with the hour of noon well past, decided to go and have their photographs taken.

"Looking like this?" Liam demanded. "I haven't even got a bloody hat—only this tin thing."

"We'll borrow one. Look—there's some of your mob killing time—go and ask."

Concerned that he should be on his way back to camp, Liam was reluctant to draw undue attention, but he knew why Robin wanted photographs, knew why he wanted them him-self. They were a kind of proof, something of this day, this meeting, to hold on to. Otherwise it would slip away, become dreamlike, unreal.

He borrowed a hat and stood the young soldier a beer at the estaminet. Half an hour later, with Robin promising to collect the photographs and send one on to him, they were walking back toward Liam's camp, when, rounding the corner on to the Bapaume Road, they spotted the whole contingent coming toward them. With a sharp about-face, Liam dragged his brother back to the square, to the shelter of a recessed doorway. There was no time for more than a hurried farewell.

As his company appeared, he slipped out to march along-side them; somebody moved over and he was roughly in place, two rows behind Keenan. Looking back to wave, he saw Robin

sprint forward, grinning from ear to ear as he kept pace alongside. His eyes were sparkling—with laughter or tears, Liam
could not be sure—but for a moment he looked so much the
mischievous boy, that Liam was disoriented, wondering what
on earth they were doing here.

They passed the church, but Liam's view was blurred; he
put out a hand to wave his brother away and felt it grasped in
an iron grip. Then Robin released him, said good luck, and fell
back.

At the corner, turning his head, Liam saw him shadowed
against the sunlight, tall and dark and straight, raising his cap
in a final wave.

22

*T*he photograph took just over a month to reach him. Holding it, Liam had the sense of a moment captured, preserved forever in time, a moment that seemed to have been amusing, although he could not imagine now what they had found to laugh about. Still, he was glad to have it; glad, too, to have Robin's letter despite its age. Was he still alive? He supposed so, he still had news of him from York, but it was one of the frustrations of war that letters took so long to cross a battlefield.

Knowing that he should write to him, Liam shied from the task; feeling as he did, he was in no fit state to communicate with anyone. Instead, he turned to his diary. *"Poperinghe. To-morrow, or the next day, Ypres. A sea of mud, probably, after a week or more of storms and torrential rain. Flooded out yesterday from the camp outside town, and today we are billeted in an old warehouse. Not much better, the roof leaks. Spent afternoon cleaning gun and filling belts. Had the usual silly orders read out, about smartness and saluting. As if it mattered."*

He sighed and tucked the diary back into his breast pocket, found his cigarettes, and went to the huge warehouse doorway to smoke. The rain was passing, a pale evening sun making high

drama of thunderclouds in the east. Across the canal everything
was sparkling, so green after the dearth of Pozières, so untouched. And so quiet, although that was probably deafness. He
felt as though his ears were permanently stuffed with cotton, and
it had been growing worse with every bombardment.

Swallows were swooping low over the water, and on a
sudden stirring of the air Liam caught the invigorating smell of
rain-washed fields. He felt his nostrils flare as he followed it,
drawing deep breaths into his lungs, filling his chest with clean,
ionized air. He had forgotten its intoxication, had imagined he
was filled forever with the sour-sweet smell of death and the
acrid reek of chemical explosives. Even now, with the freshly
washed streets of the little town before him, soldiers and black-
clad women passing back and forth, Liam still had a vision of
hell imprinted at the forefront of his mind. It was a wasteland
of shifting grit and ashes, a place so thoroughly obliterated
that no sign of human habitation remained. Only the dead
remained, only those rotting carcasses of men; and their mangled bits of arms and legs, sometimes attached to a piece of
khaki, sometimes tangled in strips of barbed wire, were thrown
up with horrifying regularity to remind those who were still
alive of those who had gone before. There were moments when
he thought that no one could convey the moonlit horror of
those journeys across the ridge, when the sudden explosion of
a flare or shell would send men flat, to come face-to-face in the
dirt with gnarled, disembodied hands, or the blackened eyes
of a rotting skull. Or the days of sweltering sun, lying in shell
holes that were alive with fat, buzzing flies and the sickening
miasma of corruption. Or the rain, which turned everything to
greasy, slithering mud.

In the four days that it took to take and hold Pozières, and
in the ten days which had just passed, the 1st Division had
lost almost eight thousand men. In between, the 2nd and 4th
Divisions had held the village and pressed northward a further
thousand yards to the stronghold of Mouquet Farm. Eastward,
they had taken the position at the windmill beyond the village
and pushed the Germans back a few hundred yards along the
Bapaume Road. But each attack had been on such a narrow
front, like driving a wedge into a hardwood log, each blow
less effective as the wood became harder, more dense with

resistance. Knowing what was coming, knowing too well the aim of those blows—which were to cut off the Thiepval ridge—the German commanders thrust all their reserves into that same small area. And the British Commander in Chief, Sir Douglas Haig, let the Australians get on with it. There was some assistance at Pozières, most notably, in Liam's experience, from the Black Watch, who managed to earn his wholehearted admiration; and the British artillery, alongside their Australian cousins, had kept those guns going night and day. But elsewhere on the front the attacks were no more than skirmishes. Haig's troops had taken a battering in those first two weeks of July; instead of flinging everything in, all along the line, he had held them back for rest and recuperation, and so was losing by the day any opportunity for following up that hard-won victory on the hill.

In bitterness they had all discussed it, all the amateur strategists repeating what this or that officer had been overheard to say; and it was all very well, Liam supposed, to know what to do in hindsight and with endless reserves. Talking to his brother, he knew how badly beaten the British troops had been, the difficulty of raising fresh reserves, the time it took to train them. And yet, had those good, brave men not been so utterly wasted—if that initial attack on July 1 had been at dawn, instead of in broad daylight, surely surprise would have been on their side! But at half past seven, attacking into dazzling sunlight, too long after the barrage stopped, they had not stood a chance.

And who was to blame for that?

The waste of it ate into his soul. And still it went on, still the Australian divisions were hammering at Mouquet Farm, trying to push through to Courcelette, trying to cut off the Germans at Thiepval. It was a lost cause; they had all been through it twice, and nobody wanted to go back again. Not there.

Heartsick to the point of illness, Liam could not summon so much as a sense of relief at being out of it; and after five days traveling on foot and by train from Pozières, they were relegated to rest and recuperation at Ypres, to take over from the Canadians, who were slowly moving down to the Somme. *Rest and recuperation at Ypres!* The Canadians laughed at that.

To be sure there was no big push to contend with, but it was hardly a place in which to sit and lick wounds.

In one explosion out of the millions that had churned the earth at Pozières, Liam had lost Jack, his number three. That big, cheerful, reliable man had fallen beneath a direct hit which Liam could still see in horrifying detail; there had been nothing left to bury, or rather, too many bloody pieces, and no chance, under that bombardment, to do the decent thing. That side of war, the impossibility of burial, of necessary prayers and time for grieving, could still hurt him; all the friends lost, and with no more than an indrawn breath, the business of war went on.

Young Vic, the railway clerk from Melbourne, had finally succumbed to horror and had to be sent out of the line, his reason gone completely. Liam prayed it was only temporary but did not expect to see him back. One burly sergeant had gone quite mad with the noise, attacking everyone in sight; it took four men to restrain and disarm him. Keenan, however, had survived, like the bad penny he was, twitching visibly by the end of it, but then they all were.

One night, after a relief of twenty-four hours, the team had carried up, between them, thirty-two thousand rounds of ammunition. It was all used up by morning. A bad night that, Liam remembered, in which the 2nd Brigade had attacked after a heavy bombardment, but by some mistake got into their own artillery barrage, losing many men. It was a bitter tragedy but understandable in that shifting sea of dirt, where there were no landmarks to establish, even from the air, the correct position of the line.

On a very trivial scale, that same night he had been struck on the heel by a flying shell splinter, which had sliced the heavy leather of his boot but not pierced it. Looking back, he was unsure whether to be happy or sad about that; like his old mate Smithy at Messines, he felt it might have sent him home.

Home. Strange word. Did he know where it was, could he identify it? When his mates said home, they meant Australia, but Australia had become, for him, no more than a distant dream. When he thought about it, which was less and less often since he had come to France, he could hardly believe that he had spent eight months there. It seemed so brief, a moment from another lifetime; while York, which he had left so bitterly, loomed tantalizingly on the edge of his awareness. Remembering his conversation with Robin, however, that extracted promise seemed to him no more than academic. Convinced he must die at Pozières, Liam found it hard to come to terms with his survival. He had no faith in the future, no belief in anything but death.

The guns were booming at Ypres. Was one destined to bring death to him? If so, he hoped it would be soon, direct, and instantaneous oblivion, not the drawn-out agony of disembowelment, or wounds that turned gangrenous, or the burning blinding retching end of poison gas.

It was a lovely evening, with people strolling here and there. Leaning against a wall, lighting a cigarette, Liam listened to the muffled thuds and wondered whether he was imagining them. Everyone else seemed quite oblivious, heads nodding in conversation, lips smiling. A sudden burst of laughter penetrated his deafness, and he could have turned and yelled at them to be quiet. He sauntered on, vaguely aware that he had missed a meal; he would have liked a drink but had no money. No pay since before Pozières. Had he been able to think where he might go to escape all this, Liam was aware that he would have gone. Just walked away. But he was beyond making any kind of decision. Nothing was left. He felt as empty and useless as a spent shell. There was not even enough in him to be afraid, although he had an uneasy feeling that he was not fit to carry out the duties of a corporal; and how he would deal with any new men coming into the team, he had no idea.

Having made a circuit of the town, and short of anywhere else to go, Liam supposed he should return to the billet and try to sleep. He was certainly very tired. Ambling back across the square, his eyes on the battered and uneven cobbles, he was stopped by a small man in the rather shabby uniform of a British officer. At first he tensed, expecting a dressing down for his lack of a salute, but the man was smiling. He was also wearing a clerical collar.

"Excuse me—you don't have a light, do you? I seem to have lost my matches."

As Liam fished in his pocket, the man produced a pack of cigarettes and held it out.

"Bet you could use a smoke, couldn't you?"

Liam hesitated, not wanting to be engaged in conversation, especially by a padre, but the man insisted and seemed determined to have his chat. Undeterred by monosyllabic replies, he turned and accompanied Liam, asking where he was billeted, and had he just come up from the Somme.

"Pozières," Liam answered, convinced it would mean nothing.

There was a noticeable silence, and then, very seriously, the padre said, "Come back with me to Talbot House. It's just along here. Have something to eat and a cup of tea. And if you'd like to just sit for a while and be quiet, you won't be disturbed."

There was such kindness in the man's face, such unspoken depths of understanding, Liam felt his resistance crumble. Clearing his throat of a sudden obstruction, he said, "We haven't been paid for weeks, I haven't any money to pay for food."

"No need. We ask only what a man can afford. And if he has nothing, we ask nothing—as simple as that."

The tall white house was on a street Liam had walked already; seeing the open door, the sign outside, he wondered how he could have missed it. In the depths of the house he could hear a piano playing and voices raised in song, but the padre steered him through to the garden, long and deep and still wet with rain. Shrubs and climbing plants made silent arbors, hiding seats and benches set back from the paths, and against the wall roses were still in bloom, nodding heavy heads, shedding drops like tears from their velvet petals.

It was a soothing, scented place, a million years, surely, from the shifting sands of Pozières. Hardly noticing that he was alone, Liam slowly lowered his numb, unfeeling body into a seat and closed his eyes. Not to sleep, just to breathe the perfumed air, just to feel its moist sweetness against his skin, to taste it on his lips. And when he opened his eyes it was to look at everything, each tiny leaf and tendril around him, the dazzling intensity of color in every bloom. It was so perfect it was almost unbearable.

A woman came with a tray of food, potatoes and tiny green beans and some sort of chicken stew, the whole meal a feast of delicate flavors, as perfect as the garden. He had barely finished when the padre came out to join him, smiling, bearing two hearty mugs of steaming tea.

"How was that? Good? We have an *excellent* cook—she can make something out of nothing, believe me!"

Watching him, almost lip-reading because of his deafness, Liam smiled. "I believe you, Padre. Thank you."

"No need. Glad to be of service. You know," he continued pleasantly, accepting one of Liam's cigarettes, "you never told me your name, or where you come from. I'd lay bets you're not Australian-born. Let me see now—don't tell me—you sound to me as though you might be from Lincolnshire, perhaps, or maybe farther north than that. East Riding of Yorkshire?"

"You've a good ear. I come from York."

"Ah, a *lovely* city—I know it well. The Minster, the walls, the river—what a combination. Some lovely churches too." He mused for a while, smiling. "I don't expect you've been home for a long while?"

"No."

"Have you applied for leave to England?"

"I have, but I shouldn't think I'll get it."

"Why not?"

The question was simple enough, but Liam could not answer it. He shook his head, words beyond him.

Very gently, the other man touched his arm. "My boy, if you'd rather I left you alone, just nod your head and I'll go. But if you'd like to talk, if you feel it would help in any way—and I think it might—then we'll go inside, where there's less chance of being overheard."

Confused, uncertain, almost against what he felt was his better judgment, Liam stood up, strubbed out his cigarette and followed the stockily built little man inside. He was not old—indeed Liam would have been hard put to guess his age—but there was a quality of fatherliness in him that drew a response, a warmth that was difficult to resist. He entered a room on the first floor and held the door for Liam; above it, there was a sign which read ABANDON RANK ALL YE WHO ENTER HERE.

Despite himself, Liam smiled. The padre chuckled. "Yes, some people do need reminding! But sit down—make yourself comfortable. You know," he added, settling himself into an easy leather chair, "you still haven't told me your Christian name. I don't want your surname, rank, and serial number, that doesn't matter, but I would like to know what to call you."

"My mates call me Bill, but my family always called me Liam. It's short for William."

"And what would you rather I called you?"

For a moment he hesitated. "Liam, I think."

To begin with, it was a terrible effort to speak, but the padre kept talking, facing Liam, lifting the pitch of his voice so that he could hear. With the odd question here and there, it soon became clear that this was a man who *knew*, who understood all the terrors to which Liam had been subjected, the effort it cost to stay calm under fire, the energy required to transmit that calmness to men who were on the verge of panic. He knew, too, of the terrible cost afterward, even to men who were otherwise strong, otherwise unmarked. And he understood the despair.

He neither defended nor condemned the war. Other than a gentle reminder that the general staff were men too, as fallible as the rest of humanity, he offered neither praise nor blame in that direction; but he did listen, and he did try to penetrate the despair.

To a certain extent he succeeded. Liam was unaccustomed to sharing burdens, and the enormity of what he felt about the war was difficult to express; but once the first words were found, the rest came tumbling out like water from a broken dam. The sense of release was curative in itself, and although the padre commented that he wished he could do more than simply listen, Liam was acutely aware that having such a listener was as much, at that point, as he needed. The suggestion that he should report sick, however, was dismissed with a sharp laugh.

"Begging your pardon, Padre, but that's a joke! I'm no more sick than any of my mates—and if I'm sick, they're all sick, every last one of them!"

The chaplain shook his head, insisting that Liam should continue to press for leave, that he needed time away from the war, time to recover his spirits.

Liam's response to that came without thinking and it shocked him. "I don't want to go home."

There was a long silence. "Do you want to tell me why?"

He shook his head, aware of a hard lump in his chest. "Not really."

"Is it to do with why you left home in the first place—why you went to Australia?" At Liam's abrupt nod, he said, "Was it a crime you committed?"

Laughter released the hard lump inside him, but it threatened to get out of hand. With an effort, Liam calmed himself and apologized. On a deep breath, he said, "I discovered, in a very shocking manner, that my father was not who I thought he was. That is, not my mother's husband. I have a brother and a sister, and the man who fathered us was someone I thought was just a distant relative."

For a moment, it was impossible to say more. He tried to light a cigarette, but the trembling which had begun with talk of the war had gone beyond his control; the padre lit two and passed one across to him. Liam smoked in a short, angry fashion, leaning forward, forearms pressed against his knees.

"It wouldn't have been so bad," he said, "but I'd fallen in love with his daughter. I thought we were no more than—oh, I don't know, second cousins, I suppose, the relationship was never clear. She was older than me, and I never really thought it would come to anything, but—" He coughed sharply and shook his head. "Oh God, I was eighteen years old and I was in love . . ."

"Was she aware of it? Did she encourage you?"

"No. No, she knew what the relationship was—she was just fond of me, I suppose." With a short, sardonic laugh, he added, "Like a sister should be."

For a while, digesting that, the other man said nothing. Then, "What about your mother?" he asked. "And the man you thought was your father? I presume he raised you?"

"I can't forgive her. I've tried, but I can't. Oh, I write home, I write to them regularly—and I've even promised my brother that I'll go home when I get some leave—but I dread seeing them. I dread having to see my mother again."

"Were you very close to her? Before all this, I mean?"

Liam's voice failed at that. Eventually he nodded. "But

still I can't forgive her for what she did to me. The lies, the deceit—letting me think—" He broke off. "I can't tell you what it was like . . ."

"You don't have to. I can imagine." After a little while, the padre said, "And what about this sister of yours—the one you love. Are you afraid of seeing her too?"

"Yes. But I want to see her, that's the terrible thing." Inhaling deeply, stubbing out the remains of his cigarette, Liam sat back, aware, now that he had given voice to the core of it, of a sense of exhaustion. There was nothing to be done, however, just as there was nothing to be done about the war; but he felt so much lighter, the trembling had abated, and, quite suddenly, he could have slept.

They talked on for some time, but after that the conversation seemed at one remove, and Liam could not recall afterward what he had said. A great deal, he suspected, since he was in that quiet little study for almost two hours. He did remember the chaplain saying to him that he should press for leave, should see his mother, that only in facing her would he be able to achieve the forgiveness he was looking for. And then, perhaps, he would be able to see his sister in the proper light. The chaplain's kindness, and his sense of conviction, penetrated that haze of tiredness and stayed with Liam. He made his promises and gave his thanks, then, with a short prayer and blessing, was sent on his way.

In the doorway, however, that same doorway which insisted that before God and in this room all men were equal, Liam paused for a moment.

"Padre, why did you stop and speak to me this evening? You didn't really need a light, did you?"

The round, cheerful face beamed. "Not really, no, but it's a way of getting into conversation. Most soldiers smoke, most will accept a cigarette even from a man of the cloth!"

"Why me, though?"

"Why not you? God hears us, even in our despair. *Especially* in our despair."

Liam hesitated. "And do you really hear His voice?"

The other man chuckled. "Well I don't know about a voice—not like yours or mine, anyway. But quite often He gives me a nudge—a little prompt, if you like, to do or say something.

I don't always know why, and I certainly don't think it's exclusive to me. Perhaps you've felt it yourself—that urge to do something out of the ordinary, or against what you think is your nature?''

With a regretful sigh, Liam shook his head. ''No, I can't say I have.''

It was only when he was outside and alone in the darkness that realization dawned. He *had* done something extraordinary; he *had* acted against his nature. In following the little padre, in listening to him, and most especially in *talking* to him, Liam had stepped aside from his usual path; he had listened to the prompt and obeyed it. And it had been to his benefit.

But there was trouble to pay when he got back. The remaining three members of his team were on guard duty outside the warehouse, their faces eloquent as he approached. He remembered instantly and his heart sank; how on earth could he have forgotten that it was his section's turn to stand guard that night?

''Keenan's hopping,'' Matt hissed from a corner of his mouth.

''Where is he?''

Carl jerked his head. ''In the office. What're you going to do, Corp?''

''Get it over with, I suppose.''

Squaring his shoulders, Liam marched inside. At a temporary desk inside the old foreman's cubbyhole, Sergeant Keenan was going through some papers, cigarette burning, a mug of greasy tea beside his hand. He looked up as Liam entered, gooseberry eyes narrowing dangerously.

''Oh, *Corporal* Elliott—you're back! This is a surprise—thought you'd gone for good this time.''

''Not me, Sergeant—you know me better than that. I went out for a walk—and completely forgot it was my guard tonight. I'm sorry.''

''Forgot? You *forgot*? That's no excuse! Corporals aren't paid to forget, corporals are paid to *remember*. And why? It's so they can round up all the skivers and lead-swingers and get them to the bloody church on time. Or in this case, the picket line! Oh, your mob turned up all right, ten minutes late, half-dressed, and no credit to you!''

He paused for breath, but Liam knew better than to interrupt. Better to let the flow go on until Keenan had worked the ire from his system.

"I could have your bloody stripes for this, Elliott. It's not the first time you've wandered off, God knows where, and taken your bloody time about coming back. You're not here on a Cook's bloody tour, you know—you're here to fight a bloody war, and somebody's paying you over the odds to do it!"

He strode around the desk, coming up short a foot away from Liam. "And let me tell you this," he declared, emphasizing each point with a jab of his finger, "if it wasn't for the fact that we're going back into the bloody line the day after tomorrow, with about half the men we should have, I'd have you up on a charge right now!"

Knowing the truth of that, Liam stiffened his jaw and stared over Keenan's head. On the wall opposite was pinned a map of the trenches in the Zillebeke sector, southeast of Ypres. Concentrating on that, he winced as the sergeant's voice rattled his ears again.

"One more little stunt like this, Elliott, and I *will* have you, good and proper, you see if I don't!" With a final jab into Liam's chest, he returned to his seat, eyes gleaming maliciously. "Tomorrow you're on fatigues, sanitary, along with the rest of your team. I want those bloody latrines filled in like they were never there—and new ones dug at least six feet deep!"

It was a disgusting job, but not one to which Liam was a complete stranger. It always amazed him, however, how much mess could be made by several hundred men in just over twenty-four hours. The latrines were perhaps a hundred yards from the warehouse in an open field. They had been dug hurriedly the day before, and were not very deep; owing to the storm and the already saturated nature of the land, the pits were half full of liquid, which overflowed as they were being filled in. The stench was unbearable, and Liam waved his men away from it, knowing that this punishment was entirely his fault, brought about by his absentmindedness, not theirs. He had left them sleeping.

Getting the turf back was no easy matter, and beneath that deceptive greenness the filled-in pit squelched like a quagmire.

"Maybe we should get Keenan to come and take a look," Gray suggested, leaning wearily on his spade. "If he tries to tamp that little lot down, he'll end up in it—up to his flaming neck!"

The others laughed. Liam was less amused, anxious to get them away and cleaned up, now that the job was done.

"I wonder what he'll find for us to do this afternoon?"

"I don't give a damn what it is," Matt declared, "the other poor buggers are off on a bloody route march. Anything's got to be better than that!"

There was more heavy rain that afternoon, which made a joke of Matt's convictions as the punishment detail was set to unloading heavy boxes of stores from a series of trucks. Within half an hour they were all soaked to the skin, aching, and in no better state than the rest of their company taking foot exercise. The only consolation was that they were finished well before the others returned, their clothes drying over a feeble stove in the drafty warehouse while they sat huddled in blankets, trying to keep warm.

That chill, northeasterly wind had veered around to the west by the next morning, and having been warned to be ready by two o'clock, Liam had the gun stripped and cleaned first thing, damp overcoats set out to air in the morning sun. Dinner was a nondescript stew consisting mainly of vegetables in a grayish liquid and a small portion of matching potatoes. He ate it, could have eaten more because he was hungry, while thinking of the delicious meal he had been given at the Talbot House and wondering how it was that army cooks could destroy food so thoroughly.

By midafternoon the battalion with its supporting company of machine gunners was ready to move to the station at Poperinghe; a short rail journey took them to the outskirts of Ypres to a little halt near an asylum. Hanging around, waiting for orders, Liam had plenty of time to remember the Retreat and the evening he had cycled up to meet Georgina. It was the last time he had seen her, spoken to her: the last hour of innocence. Odd snatches of conversation returned to him, no longer painful, thank God, but curiously poignant. He recalled giving voice to his dreams, so broad, so ambitious, and the joy of her understanding, her encouragement. Remembered, too, that he had said he would write a book one day when he settled down, when he had done all that he wanted to do. There was irony in that when he thought how little he had managed to achieve; how, without knowing it, time had been loaded against him.

It still was. Not one man on this battlefield could look forward with any reasonable expectation to a comfortable old age; *if I get through it* was as far as it went. Forty-eight hours ago Liam had been in despair, preferring death to life; back on the side of the living, he was still weary, still unsure of himself, full of vague apprehensions which seemed to be making themselves felt in a physical way. His stomach was churning unpleasantly, and it was hard to tell whether it was simple fear or the greasy stew he had eaten earlier. In an effort to divert his mind, he kept thinking about Georgina, about what they had talked about that evening. It seemed important, suddenly, not to lose sight of those old ambitions.

Above the western horizon, rain clouds threatened, rising, gilt-edged, to swallow the sun before it set. Its disappearance was like a signal from HQ; moments later orders were given for the troops to form up and proceed. Within the first mile the rain began, drenching packs and overcoats, turning already muddy roads into glutinous slime. Treachery lurked with every footfall; shell holes gaped, full of the detritus of war, rain spattering like shrapnel fire from the surface of every puddle. In the fading light, the bloated carcasses of horses loomed hideously by the wayside, twisted bits of guns and limbers their permanent companions. Up ahead, the ruined towers of Ypres formed stark silhouettes against the flickering glow in the east. It was a place of gothic horror, a place to strike a chill even on the warmest night. With rain seeping through his greatcoat, Liam shivered, wondering what it must be like in winter. If this was the end of August, what would January bring?

By the shattered ruins of the great medieval Cloth Hall, the battalion turned right to leave Ypres by a gap in the ramparts known as the Lille Gate. They crossed a battered bridge over an ancient moat, ran the gauntlet of shell and mortar fire at Shrapnel Corner, and found their way, eventually, to the Canadian trenches north of the Ypres-Comines Canal. The line, what they could see of it in occasional illuminations, was a boggy, meandering maze of duck-boards and sandbags, shallow com-

munication trenches and battered parapets. The dugouts such as
they were were shallow and in poor repair. Apart from defending
this particular sector, it seemed the Division would also be making
some extensive alterations to its physical aspects.

It was past midnight when they arrived, some five miles
from that little railway halt; limbers were unpacked, stores,
guns, and ammunition carried a further three hundred yards
to the front line. With the Vickers and fourteen boxes of ammunition, Liam's team were directed to a muddy, sandbagged gun
pit still containing all the litter of previous occupation. Chilled
to the bone, shivering despite his exertions, Liam set about
clearing the mess of empty tins, cigarette packs, and used car-
tridges. Warned not to move or light fires by day, and desperately in need of something warming now, he ordered a brew
of tea and, from their store of rations, took a tin of Maconochie's
meat and vegetables. It seemed to take an age to heat through,
and his stomach felt hollow and queasy, but he thought it might
improve with food. Carl and Matt shared it, the three of them
huddled in the confined space of the gun pit with barely enough
headroom to sit up. It seemed strange, being reduced to three;
with no reinforcements as yet, Gray had been sent to make up
numbers in another team. It made Liam feel very vulnerable.
With one man filling belts, another feeding them into the feed-
block, and himself firing the gun, three was the necessary minimum. Looking at these poor defenses, and with the Canadians'
warning about sniper fire still ringing in his ears, Liam could
find no comforting thoughts on which to sleep.

With his stomach issuing painful threats after that meal of
Maconochie rations, Liam offered to take the first watch, but
Matt was concerned about him and said he should rest. He
tried to, but the pain grew worse, sending him out to find a
latrine. In the hour before dawn, he was up and down several
times, crawling along the shallow trench, wondering what he
would do in daylight with no-man's-land a flat stretch of two
hundred yards, and every bobbing head a sitting target like
wooden ducks at a fair.

After periods of short relief, in which he shivered and
shook and felt as weak as a baby, the cramps intensified; he
drank water and was violently sick, munched hard biscuits in
an attempt to absorb the fiery liquid in his guts, and was forced

by daylight to crouch just outside the dugout, using a makeshift
latrine the others had dug. Even lying down he was in agony,
trying not to moan as the fever gripped and chills racked his
body.

Bursts of gunfire from the German trenches kept the others
busy. They dared not abandon the position or cease to keep up
a sporadic response. From time to time mortar bombs flew
across, exploding with deadly crumps up and down the line.
It was a nerve-wracking place in which to rest after all they had
been through at Pozières, and it was no place in which to be
ill. In between filling belts, Carl, the broad-shouldered, slow-
talking Dane, wiped Liam's face with damp cloths and murmured reassuringly. They would get him out at nightfall, get
him to the medics, and make sure he got some treatment; he
mustn't think of staying in the line, he wouldn't be letting them
down, they'd find a replacement from somewhere.

But by midafternoon, when he was passing nothing but
blood, and vomiting even on sips of water, Liam was beyond
protest. He thought he was dying. Slipping in and out of delir-
ium, he lost track of time; lucid for a while, he was aware of
lying in his own filth and being unable to move. All he could
do was apologize. From his position crouched over the gun,
Carl was suddenly brusque, telling him to save his breath; Matt
sponged his face and tried to persuade him to drink.

As soon as it was dark, they got him to the 8th Battalion
HQ, carrying him between them and bundled in greatcoats.
The MO was busy dealing with a series of both major and
minor injuries; Liam had to wait. Eventually he was seen and
diagnosed as being just another victim of dysentery, albeit an
unusually virulent case. In a painfully conscious moment, Liam
wondered whether the MO was right; on Gallipoli, in company
with almost every other man, he had suffered from dysentery
most of the time, but never to this extent. Never before had it
attacked with such ferocious speed.

On Gallipoli he would have been given arrowroot and left
to suffer; here, blessedly, he was ordered to the 2nd Field Ambulance Dressing Station, but as there were no more stretcher-
bearers available, his friends had to accompany him, staggering
over the duck-boards and through the mud in pitch darkness.
They found the place eventually, just behind the second set of

lines; there he was offered the comparative comfort of a stretcher. About midnight, along with two others, he was bundled into a horse ambulance. Matt and Carl pressed his hands, said good-bye, and set off back to the front line; the horse ambulance trundled off on its rough journey to Ypres.

A motor ambulance conveyed him from there to an Australian Clearing Station, where someone had the sense to mark him *infectious* and keep him apart from the wounded. Only partially conscious, he stayed there for the rest of the night.

Morning brought another journey, this time as far as Poperinghe, to a Canadian Clearing Station which could offer the facility of a clean bed and a vast amount of pills. A nurse offered him a cup of milk to drink, but that started a bout of vomiting which continued on and off all night. Next morning brought a doctor who paused to ponder at the foot of his bed, and that afternoon Liam was on his way again, this time by hospital train to the base at Boulogne.

He was there for a week, seven days and nights of pills and blood tests, medicines and various liquid diets. As the cramps and vomiting lessened, Liam slipped into natural, healing sleep. He slept for hours each day, woke to be washed and fed and dosed, and slept again. On the evening of September 11, which Liam remembered was his mother's birthday, the doctor returned to mark his card with just one word: ENGLAND.

23

*P*eople were kind. Extraordinarily kind. He kept thinking that all the way home. Home, that word again; but England was home, even if London was not. While British troops were afforded the choice of hospitals in their native countries, the Australians had but one destination, London, and for that Liam had no real regrets. Despite advice and entreaties and promises made, for the moment he felt less than able to face his mother, and more desirous of Georgina than ever. She was somewhere in London and, as soon as she knew where he was, would probably come to see him. With the decision made for him, he allowed anticipation to outweigh all else.

Of his old uniform, only his hat remained. He had managed to hang on to that while everything else had gone to an incinerator. The new uniform was fine, if a little stiff, but he was glad of the hat, it had been with him since Gallipoli. To lose that would have been like losing a friend. It was good, however, to feel clean and smart again, to meet smiling faces on the dock at Portsmouth, to accept small gifts and blessings, to feel kindly hands assisting him from place to place. Although he was classified as walking wounded, he was still very weak, and standing for more than a minute or two produced debilitating waves of nausea. But hospital trains, at least in England, seemed to run more on schedule, and they were soon on their way to London and Waterloo.

What looked like a fleet of private cars awaited them. While the stretcher cases were transferred to another train, those who could walk were directed to the cars. A middle-aged lady in black drove Liam and two companions to the Australian hospital at Wandsworth. She chatted amicably, requiring little in the way of serious replies, which was just as well, Liam thought, because he felt sick and one of the other men was close to passing out; and had she asked what the problem was, he would have hated to embarrass her by telling the truth.

She pointed out various places of interest along the way: Lambeth Palace and, across the river, the Houses of Parliament; Vauxhall Bridge, and, farther on, Clapham Junction, nerve center of London's railways.

"The zeppelins keep trying to bomb it," she announced in her well-bred, penetrating voice. "Oh yes, we've had some fireworks in Wandsworth, you haven't had it all to yourselves over there, you know!"

The very sick man looked at Liam and managed a feeble smile; the other muttered something about it making them feel at home. In spite of the fresh air whipping into his face, Liam knew that if they did not see the hospital soon, he would have to ask her to stop, his stomach was threatening to disgorge itself.

"How far to the hospital?" he managed to ask.

"Not far—we're almost there." She indicated the broad green common ahead of them, and beyond the trees the great sooty mass of Hospital No. 3, London General, which had been set aside for Australian soldiers.

Apart from the blackened stonework, which seemed standard here, Liam thought it looked out of place with its turrets and towers, like a grand French château standing on its own grounds, with the dip of a railway cutting for its moat. Through the waves of nausea, he had a moment of wondering what it might have been before, and as they drove bouncily through an imposing gateway, their lady driver informed them that it had been a school, a girls school, the pupils now evacuated to the safety of the countryside.

In the warm, early afternoon sun, convalescents were patrolling the grounds in the company of nurses, friends, and volunteers. Mildly curious glances were cast in their directions as they pulled up, close to two other cars, at the main entrance. A bevy of young nurses, all bearing red crosses on their aprons, all looking like angels, were waiting to assist them inside.

"This is more like it!" somebody was heard to declare, and a little ripple of laughter touched the gathered arrivals. They were ushered into a vast assembly hall, where names were taken and wards allocated, and then, at last, a ward with long rows of beds, a hot bath, clean towels, and the soft blue cloth of hospital uniform.

But to his consternation the nurse who handed him these things insisted on staying.

"We don't want you passing out in the bath, now do we?" she declared briskly, and with that proceeded to unfasten his tunic.

"I can manage," he protested feebly as her fingers reached his waist.

"I'm sure you can, but I haven't got all day."

After that, he let her get on with it. At the base hospital in Boulogne, he had been given sponge baths, in bed, and the nurses there were stony-faced, far too busy to give more than perfunctory attention to basic needs. It seemed very strange to be standing naked in front of a pleasant young woman of his own age, one who helped him into the bath and stood over him while he soaped himself, and stranger still to feel those firm hands scrubbing his back and neck and the base of his spine. But it felt very good. Sinking back into the water, all embarrassment gone, Liam was aware of faint relief that he had not disgraced himself, although with towels wrapped around him and her hands rubbing him dry, he was thankful that she left the intimate parts of his anatomy to himself.

With a bed assigned to him at last, it was bliss to crawl into it, feeling the cool, fresh linen surrounding him and the softness of pillows beneath his head. Within minutes he was sleeping.

He was woken for tea, and again for supper, both meals consisting of toast and a hot drink, and then he slept again, ten solid hours until six the next morning. Another nurse came to check his pulse and temperature, bringing water and a towel so that he could wash, and later, a lightly boiled breakfast egg with tea and more toast. A man from farther down the ward brought over a selection of books but, beyond introducing himself and a few others, did not stay to talk. Liam was grateful for that. He glanced through the books, read a little, and dozed again. The doctor came, asking the usual questions, giving the usual answers that he was in good hands and recovery was just a matter of rest and time. The problem of his deafness, however, was something that would be attended to just as soon as Liam was fit to be out of bed for a few hours. It was probably nothing more than a severe buildup of wax, the body's natural defense against noise. Reassured about that, for he had no pain in his ears, Liam thanked him and settled back against his pillows. The doctor, with the ward sister in tow, moved on to the next patient.

The Sister was a buxom, middle-aged Australian woman with a weather-beaten face and a map of lines that suggested great good humor, but enough steel, he guessed, to keep a firm hold on the motley collection of men beneath her rule. Liam tried to picture her in civilian life and imagined her nursing at some small medical station in the outback, at a mine or logging camp perhaps, or serving a vast area of small settlements. She was not a city woman, he was sure of that, and wondered how she coped with the confinement of London.

The ward, once the doctor had gone, erupted into its usual buzz of chatter with bursts of laughter from men who had been ill and were recovering well. It was a medical ward with none of the hush and incipient tragedy attached to surgical cases. Of the thirty beds, not all were occupied, and most of the men were up and dressed. Liam's bed was nearest the door, and he recalled from his previous spell in hospital that as he improved he would move farther down. The man next to him had come in two days previously, and a couple of others across the way had arrived by the same train as Liam. All bore the same hollow, dark-eyed look, a look he had come to associate with utter exhaustion. He supposed his own face must tell the same story and no longer wondered at that overwhelming urge to sleep.

He managed to stay awake until lunchtime, looking out of

the opposite window at a hazy blue sky above the line of slate roofs and chimneys, and down the center of the ward an array of lacy ferns stirring in a slight breeze from the open window at his back. It was a warm and pleasant day and he was aware of nothing more than a feeling of absolute rest and contentment. He had been terribly ill, but the worst of it was over and now he would get better. He had all he required and could ask for nothing more. When he felt a little stronger, he thought before slipping off into sleep, he would write and let people know where he was.

Visitors arrived that afternoon but Liam was only dimly aware of them; rolling over onto his side, protected by his partial deafness, he listened to the regular sibilation of his own breathing and drifted back into comfortable dreams.

Something stirred him. Not a sound but a touch, light and cool, against his wrist. Through half-open lids he saw the outline of a nurse beside his bed, stiff white wings of a headdress, a short gray shoulder cape of gray edged with scarlet, starched cuffs above a hand which held his own. Another nurse came to check pulse and temperature, he thought, closing his eyes again, wishing they would leave him alone. He drifted for a moment, expecting the brisk word, the sharp prod of a thermometer against his lips, but a minute passed and none came. The fingers against his hand tightened perceptibly, then relaxed and lifted.

He opened his eyes more fully, but the nurse had not moved away, she was still sitting there, head bent, her fingers busy with a handkerchief. She was dabbing her eyes.

Frowning, he blinked several times, trying to muster sight and sensibilities trying to find a logical reason why a fully fledged sister of the military nursing reserve should be *sitting* beside his bed, crying. The answer came to him even as she glanced up, even as he recognized the pale oval of her face and met the deep, dark blue of her eyes. Like cornflowers, he thought, noting the wet, spiky lashes; and her hair, what little he could see of it, was still the color of summer wheat. He saw her lips curve into a hesitant smile, and he felt his own mouth responding, broadening as he whispered her name.

"Georgina?"

She nodded and he pressed her hand, not really believing

it, sure the image was just a dream and that in a moment he would wake to emptiness and disappointment as had happened so often in the past. But he felt her responding pressure, heard a little sound, between a sob and a laugh, and experienced the wonder of seeing two fat tears escape her eyes and roll unchecked to her chin. Was she really crying for him?

She said something that he did not catch, shook her head, and dabbed again at her eyes, more forcefully this time. Although he could have watched her contentedly for the rest of the afternoon, he realized she was asking questions, but apart from an odd word, he was at a loss.

"Come closer," he begged, with a little tug at her hand. "I'm still very deaf."

Concern clouded her eyes, and she edged the chair forward, leaning her elbows on the bed. She was close enough, almost, to kiss.

"Can you hear me now?"

"Oh yes," he breathed, knowing that if he raised himself even a little, he could press his mouth to hers, and who would object?

She would. She most certainly would. But the idea delighted him, that she should be here, close enough for him to touch, to hold, to kiss. And so *soon*! With a little laugh in his throat he glanced away, pressed his lips together in a smile, and looked back into those beautiful, concerned, compassionate eyes.

"How did you *know*?"

"Casualty list." She glanced down at the scars on his hands, the trimmed but badly damaged nails. "I got to hear about it this morning."

There was a vague question in his mind as to how she had come by the information in her hospital at Lewisham, but he was too enthralled by her presence to express it. "What time is it now?"

"A quarter to four. I managed to organize an early break. I usually get a couple of hours from four till six, but I changed it."

"And came straight here."

She laughed softly. "I wanted to be sure you were all right."

"I'm fine, just fine." Although his hands were a mass of

scars that he tried to hide, she seemed to find some fascination there, smoothing the rough and dented knuckles with her fingers. He was supremely conscious of her touch, every tiny movement sending echoes into his heart. For a while he watched her fingers, long and fine, whiter than he recalled from her days at the Retreat, but still those of a working woman. The nails were trimmed short, neatly filed to cause no pain, the skin across her knuckles slightly rough from constant washing. He wanted to touch them to his lips, which suddenly, like his throat, seemed terribly dry.

Huskily, he said, "It's wonderful to see you," and she smiled then, shyly, and said it was wonderful to see him, too; everyone had been so worried.

But Liam did not particularly want to know about *everyone*, just her.

"How are you? I know you've been very busy, I had your letters—"

A bright smile dismissed her own problems. "Oh, I'm very well—really. Looking forward to a break soon, but otherwise all right. Things have calmed down a little, I'm glad to say."

"Not before time."

"Mmm. But I know they've been busy here."

"Still are, I should think," he murmured, and felt the tension along his jaw. "But I'm out of it for a while, thank God. Just so pleased to be here, you've no idea."

A smile touched the corner of her mouth, and he wanted to touch it too. "Oh, I think I have," she said.

Dark, ash-gray lashes cast flickering shadows beneath her eyes as she looked away, and along her cheekbones, he noticed, was the faintest blush of color. It seemed to deepen even as he watched, but he could not tear his eyes away: She was so beautiful, even the tiny frown lines between her brows seemed perfect to him.

That she could tear herself away from great responsibility just to see him, and that she could care, even a little, was a thought that swelled his heart with such love, such gratitude, it was overwhelming.

She seemed to sense it anyway. Her fingers tightened and she bowed her head, and when she looked up her smile was a little too brave, her eyes a little too bright.

She whispered his name; tears sprang to his eyes then. Blinking them away, he was aware of nothing more than a need to tell her how much he loved her, how much he had *always* loved her, and how much the fact of her presence emphasized it. He had not been wrong; he had not harbored false illusions; his youthful sense of her kindness, her deep affection for him, was true. Time had changed nothing.

Time had changed nothing. The words went through his mind again, but with a different meaning, and even as he raised his hand, touching blunt fingers to the softness of her cheek, he knew that what he felt went too far beyond what could ever be acceptable to her. She was his sister. She was also older than he was, and in the past three years, who knows what loves and loyalties had developed? He knew men, knew that a beauty as remarkable as hers could not have failed to attract attention, and anyone who knew her well must surely love her. Whom did she love? Was there a man somewhere, a young officer, probably, whose life she had saved? Or a doctor with whom she worked? That sounded more likely. But he did not ask.

She held his hand to her face, then, very gently, took it away. "Is there anyone," she asked, "that you'd like me to get in touch with? Tisha, perhaps, or your mother? I'm not sure either of them know yet."

The question brought him back to reality with something of a start, setting different considerations running like hares; and like hares they scattered, leaving him empty-handed and confused. Slightly panic-stricken too, although he could not have said why.

He shook his head. "I don't want anybody to know. Not just yet."

"Well, dear, I'm afraid that as next of kin, your mother will be informed soon, if she hasn't been already."

He closed his eyes, imagining his mother distraught, flying to his side instantly now that she knew where he was. "I don't want to see her. Not yet."

He heard Georgina sigh. "Very well, don't worry about it. Would you like me to write to her anyway, putting her off for the time being? I know traveling can be difficult these days—detours, endless delays, changes in the middle of the night—she might be quite pleased not to have to rush the visit."

"Would you do that?" He was immensely relieved. "Tell her I'll write to her myself, very soon."

"I'll do that. And I won't say anything to Tisha until you feel more up to seeing her. How's that?"

"That could be a long time," he muttered in an attempt at a joke, but he was thankful. Having thought of no one but Georgina for days, he was beginning to realize that the ramifications of being in hospital in London were endless.

The sudden ringing of a bell out in the corridor rattled his eardrums. Wincing, he saw Georgina glance at her watch. At the far end of the ward, some visitors were standing up, pushing chairs back into place.

"I've got to go."

"So soon?"

She smiled. "It's the end of visiting time. I was late arriving. Anyway," she added, patting his hand like a nurse, "you've had quite enough talking for one day. Time to rest."

"That's all I do," he protested with a little laugh.

"And all you should be doing," she said firmly, but she was smiling too. "Don't worry, you'll soon be on the mend—soon be up and around, chasing all the nurses!"

He laughed at that. "Is that part of the cure?"

"It certainly seems to be," she admitted ruefully. "I can usually tell when a man's feeling better by the blushes on my girls' faces!"

Laughing, feeling good because of it, he inquired teasingly, "And what about you? Do they make you blush too?"

"Oh no! They don't try anything with me—I'm the one who cracks the whip!"

"I don't believe it."

"It's true," she insisted. "I don't stand any nonsense."

Although she was laughing, Liam believed her. It cheered him immensely.

"I really must go, or Sister will have my head for outstaying my welcome. But I'll come again soon, if I may. Is there anything you need? Anything you'd like me to bring?"

He shook his head. "Just yourself."

Her lips parted, and he thought she was about to say something else. With sudden warmth, however, she pressed his hand and bent, quickly, to kiss his cheek. Brief, light, the touch of her lips was hardly there; but once she had gone he pressed his fingers to the place and then, lingeringly, against his mouth.

Coming off duty later that night, still basking in the afterglow of that reunion with Liam, Georgina had to force herself into professional briskness before telephoning her father. It would not be wise, she thought, to reveal the depth of happiness and relief occasioned by that visit.

Robert Duncannon's first concern, as it had been that morning, was for his son, and his sigh of gratitude, followed by a lengthy silence, was eloquent indeed. Having given him a factual report on Liam's condition, Georgina could not hold back on the satisfaction that he was looking much better than she had expected, and sounding quite cheerful.

"And how long before he's well again?"

His question jarred, driving her thoughts ahead to where they did not want to go. "Before they can send him back again, you mean?" It was bitterly said, but she made no apology. "I don't know. He's back, he's safe—can't you be satisfied with that for the moment?"

"I need to know."

"Well, I can't tell you. It depends on the severity of the infection and the constitution of the patient. The germ has a nasty tendency to linger, even when to all intents and purposes, the patient seems quite well. It could be two or three months. It could be more. Why do you want to know?"

"Then there'll be convalescence," her father said, ignoring the question, "followed by retraining. I suppose," he mused over the crackling line, "that we're talking about five or six months. That should give us plenty of time."

"For what?"

"Why to get this mess sorted out, of course. It's been impossible so far, and this is the first chance anybody's had to get that young idiot on one side and really *talk* to him. I'll be honest, Georgie, now I know he's all right, and not about to peg out on us, I'm bloody glad he's ill. It keeps him in one place, and for long enough, to try and get him to see some sense. It's bothered me, you know," he added gravely, "all these years it's bothered me. Perhaps now we can take steps to resolve it."

Georgina sighed again, hearing it echo over the intervening

miles, and for a long moment said nothing. She understood what her father was saying and sympathized greatly. He was concerned, mainly, for Louisa. If he could effect a reconciliation between Liam and his mother, it would also expiate some of his own guilt. Not a bad aim, and one with which she concurred, but she had other loyalties too, and other sympathies; and as a nurse she was concerned for the well-being of a man who needed to recover mental as well as bodily strength. After all he had recently undergone, she could quite understand why Liam felt unable to cope with the emotional problems his family represented.

"I think we're going to need a lot of patience, Daddy. We're going to have to give him *time*. Yes, I know he's had three years," she said quickly, in response to Robert's exasperated gasp on the line, "but I'm not talking about that. I'm saying he needs time to get over these last few weeks. He's been through *so much*—if you'd been able to talk to the boys on my ward, you'd know how much—and he's been very ill. He needs time to get over that."

There was a long sigh. "All right, I understand. Louisa isn't going to be able to get here straightaway, so perhaps it's just as well." On a note of weary resignation, he said, "I know you said you'd write to Louisa, but I'm beginning to think I should go to York myself, before they get an official envelope and think the worst. That might finish poor Edward completely. And that wouldn't help at all."

"Oh Lord." In the excitement of the day, Georgina had barely considered that aspect. "But what if they've heard already?"

"I doubt it. The wheels of bureaucracy turn slowly, my dear, and that list I received this morning from Horseferry Road had only just come in from Boulogne." After a short pause, Robert said heavily, "I'll go to York first thing in the morning. Break the news gently and persuade Louisa to stay where she is for the time being."

Assuring her that he would also speak to Tisha, he told her that she must leave the family matters to him and get some sleep; she worked far too hard as it was. On a grateful farewell, Georgina replaced the receiver and stood for a moment, thinking about him. Although her concern was primarily for Liam, her father's, genuinely, encompassed them all, even Edward, of whom he was not inordinately fond. But as he said, to lose Edward now would only complicate matters, negate even further what small chances there were of settling things.

The indisposition which had prevented the Elliotts from attending Tisha's wedding, and which Liam had inquired about in his letters, was more serious than Louisa cared for her sons to know. Her attitude was that they could do nothing, and knowing would only make them worry, so she had asked Georgina to keep the information to herself. But Edward had suffered two minor heart attacks already, and any major shock was likely to be detrimental to his precarious health. Possibly even fatal, so it was important to play things down. Important, too, for Liam, who needed to regain his balance.

If her presence was a comfort to him, Georgina thought as she made her way back to her room, then she would do her best to visit regularly, even if it meant changing shifts and begging favors. That way she could keep a check on his progress and, as soon as he was in better health, press him to apply for temporary home leave. It seemed to her that it would be preferable to have Liam meet them again on old familiar home ground rather than have Louisa trailing here to London. But that would be something to discuss later with Liam. Much later, she told herself sharply; for the time being it was enough to have him safe.

And *accessible*, she thought with warmth and pleasure later when she was in bed. Despite his illness, despite the exhaustion written into every line of his face, it had been so good to see him. That same pleasure would draw her back, no matter how she tried to disguise it as something that was beneficial purely to him, she knew it and felt guilty about it, and realizing that, admonished herself. Devotion to duty, to other people's needs, the habit she had acquired over a period of years of always putting others first, was not a bad thing, except where it divested her of the ability to please herself. In the course of the war, her own self, her own happiness, had been neglected, if not altogether forgotten; it seemed strange now, to look forward to something so mutually enjoyable.

By Friday, however, warned to expect three more serious cases, Georgina realized that Sunday afternoon visiting would be out of the question. Disappointed, she wrote to Liam what she hoped was a cheerful letter, saying that she had managed to exchange her rostered day off for visiting day on Wednesday, which would make the journey to Wandsworth so much easier. And in October she was due a short break of three days, which with any luck would enable them both to have at least one pleasant day out. By then, he should be feeling well enough to enjoy it.

It was all very vague, but she felt it important that he should have things to look forward to; the mundane routine of hospital life could so easily become depressing. She did not tell Liam that her father had decided to pay a visit to York on his behalf, nor did she mention its successful outcome. Robert had telephoned her from the hotel to say that Louisa was tearfully relieved by his news, and that Edward, on his feet at last but still having to take it easy, had actually thanked him for coming to tell them.

It seemed that Edward, unlike her father, felt very strongly that the boy should take his time. "He'll come to us when he's ready," was a phrase that had apparently been repeated several times. Georgina loved him for his wisdom and was immensely relieved that Edward would keep some sort of rein on any wild impulses of Louisa's. Robert's, she would have to restrain herself.

Although Wednesday was her day off, she was awake as usual at six. Ordinarily, she would have tried to sleep again, but a flutter of excitement set her mind rushing over the day ahead, thinking of Liam, how he would look, what he might say, what she would say to him, and within minutes further sleep was impossible. Pulling on a dressing gown, Georgina went down to the kitchen to make tea and toast. Another sister was fumbling through the same routine, only half awake and bitterly resenting the beginning of another day. She greeted Georgina grumpily and stomped off down the corridor. Watching her go, smiling a little, Georgina suddenly realized that she was like that herself most mornings, and most days off, unless she had shopping to do, she stayed in bed. It was rather a surprise to find herself so bright and breezy, feeling not at all tired and looking forward to the day ahead.

It was a pleasure to bathe and wash her long hair, to sit by the window in the sun, drying it; the only annoyance was having so little choice of clothes. Apart from her uniform, she kept only one other outfit here, and that for emergencies, a navy blue skirt and jacket and matching hat, and a pink silk blouse. It was smart and serviceable for most occasions, and yet she would have preferred something more frivolous, a pretty pastel dress, a hat trimmed with feathers, and silly, high-heeled shoes. It was that kind of day. And then she smiled at herself; even in her wardrobe at Queen's Gate, she possessed nothing of that description. Most of her clothes were plain and practical, tailored to fit her personality; her shoes were good, with small, neat heels, handmade by her father's bootmaker.

"While Tisha buys hers ready-made on Bond Street," she muttered aloud to the caretaker's cat. "Perhaps I should do the same. What do you say, Puss?"

The cat purred and nodded, settling herself down on Georgina's knee.

"Or am I being foolish?"

She lunched early and alone in the communal dining room, then went along the High Street to buy something for Liam. Although the boys newly arrived from France loved nothing better than fruit, she suspected that Liam's diet would not yet allow for pears and plums, and that confectionary would be more acceptable. After trying several shops, Georgina eventually found what she wanted: a little box of Terry's peppermints and another of chocolate neapolitans, both made in York. She hoped the memories evoked would be happy ones.

The journey by public transport to Wandsworth took longer than expected, and it was almost a quarter past the hour for visiting when she arrived outside the hospital gates. People were still streaming in, however, and being met by convalescent patients, many of them heading straight out again and up the road for town. Expecting Liam to be on the ward if not actually in bed, Georgina paid little attention to those passing faces and had covered perhaps twenty yards when her name and the touch of a hand on her arm stayed that eager progress.

She turned and he was there beside her, so much taller than memory served, with his hat set at a rakish angle and laughter dancing in his eyes.

The hat was swept off in greeting. "I was waiting by the gate, and you walked right past me . . ."

Standing so close, looking up into that open smile which seemed to embrace her with such welcome and delight, Georgina could have sworn her heart turned over. Unprepared for the impact of his physical presence, she suddenly felt quite weak. A little breathlessly, staring up at him, she laughed and shook her head. And had to look away.

"What on earth are you doing out of bed?" she demanded.

Shrugging, laughing, spreading his hands in a gesture of innocence, Liam said he was fine, that he had been up and about for the last three days and allowed out that very morning.

"You've never been out since this morning?" She thought it far too soon and would have ushered him back to bed had he been her responsibility.

"Well, not entirely," he admitted, taking her arm and walking with her along the gravel path. "I had to see the ear specialist first thing, to have my ears syringed." He made a face. "It wasn't pleasant, but it seems to have done the trick. My hearing's improved already—I can hear the birds singing, and trains chugging up the incline, and people's *voices*. It's amazing, everything was so muffled before, I hadn't realized how bad it was—as though my ears were stuffed with cotton."

His pleasure was infectious. With a little squeeze of his arm, she said she was so pleased for him, so glad that there had been no permanent damage. With small, shy, darting glances, Georgina felt it necessary to reassure herself that he was indeed whole and physically undamaged; she saw so many injuries, both small and horrific, that it seemed no less than a miracle to have this beautiful, unmarked man walking beside her.

The evidence of physical injury, however, was all around. As they came to a vacant seat and moved toward it, Liam's eyes followed the passage of a legless man in a wheelchair, and suddenly all his euphoria disappeared.

"Deafness isn't much to complain about, though, is it? I'm here and I have my limbs and my sight intact—and, please God, a couple of months of peace ahead of me." He looked at her intently. "What more could I ask?"

"What more indeed," she murmured. There were men

hobbling on crutches, others with bandaged heads and arms, although by the smiles and light voices it seemed everyone that day was conscious of the joy of being alive. It would be stifling on the wards, even with all the windows open, and Georgina found herself thinking of all those still confined to bed, those who were dying slowly, by inches, like the boy with gangrene on her own ward at Lewisham. Three operations already, but he was not likely to survive.

With a sudden frown, knowing that Liam could so easily have been that boy, she pressed his hand. "You've been so lucky."

"I know."

He would have kept hold of her hand, but she withdrew it, too conscious of his closeness, his adult masculinity, to be entirely at ease. It had been easy to relegate Liam, like the boys on her ward, to the role of *patient*; but fully dressed, sitting beside her with his knee almost touching hers, he seemed so very different. In her memory he had still been a boy, and although his recent letters had prepared her for a certain maturity, Georgina had forgotten the extent of a young man's development between the ages of eighteen and twenty-one, and not allowed for the toughness induced by military training.

Dark shadows beneath his eyes told their own tale, however, and her professional glance discerned pallor beneath that weather-beaten skin, a paring of the flesh which lent the lines of nose and cheek and jaw a harshness they had not possessed before. That boyish softness which had made the resemblance to his mother so pronounced before was now entirely gone. He was very much his own man, she thought, and only he knew what experience had shaped his thinking.

For a while they sat in companionable silence, but he kept glancing at her, frowning a little then smiling, as though something about her intrigued him. She was on the point of asking what it was, when he said, "You don't seem to have changed a bit. Seeing you out of uniform reminds me of how you looked the last time we met—do you know it's more than three years ago?" He smiled. "It seems like yesterday."

Surprised, because her own thoughts had been concerned with change and the passage of time, Georgina shook her head. Half-tempted to make some flippant remark about how old she felt, she discarded it and said gently that a lot had happened in the interim.

That made him frown. "I know." A moment later, he said, "But I can't quite believe it. It seems so unreal." His eyes, very shadowed, moved away from her, ranging beyond the gardens to a place of his own imagining. "I don't think I know what reality is anymore."

Alerted by that change in tone, she searched his face and saw the fear within. She knew it well but in him it frightened her. She bit her lips and clasped her fingers tight, fighting the urge to drag him back from whatever brink of horror claimed him.

But he brought himself back. "I can't believe I'm here with you," he said softly, and with a gesture that encompassed the neatly trimmed lawns, the tennis courts, and shrubberies, he added, "It seems no more than a dream . . ."

She placed her hand in his and felt warm dry fingers close over hers. "I'm real enough—does that help?"

He nodded. "It's strange, though. From here the war seems so far away. I find myself wondering whether it really happened—if it's still going on. And that's the thing you see—" he turned to her and his glance was painful in its intensity—"I can't believe it's going on *without me* . . ."

Georgina swallowed hard. "It does, I'm afraid."

With a bitter smile he turned away. "That sounds like vanity, I suppose."

"No. It's a very common feeling. It goes after a while."

He said nothing to that, but she saw his eyes were suddenly brimming. He rubbed a hand over his face. "I'm sorry. I was so happy to see you, and yet . . ."

Hurt for him, aware that his whole body was trembling, Georgina clasped his arm and tried to find the right words to comfort him. She thought perhaps it was time to be professional and wished she had worn her uniform after all.

"I'm a nurse, Liam," she reminded him, "as well as your—your friend." But there was a tight constriction in her throat and it was so hard to express cool detachment when all she wanted to do was hold him in her arms and let him weep. Clearing her throat, she said, "Give it time. You're still not well—at least not as well as you think you are. And you're still suffering from reaction . . .

"There's nothing to be ashamed of—it happens to *every-one*—you must have seen it yourself on the battlefield. The bravest suffer most when the danger is past." Unsure whether he was really listening, she tightened her grip and gave his arm a little shake. "But you will get over it. *You will.* It just takes time."

Pausing, softening her voice, she added, "And don't think you have to apologize—I've seen enough, believe me, to know something of what you're going through. It's a little like grief, coming in waves—fine one minute, in tears the next." The swings in mood could be alarming, Georgina knew that; what he needed was her reassurance. Stroking his hand, she said, "And don't try too hard to bottle things up. Whatever you want to say, say it—I'm not likely to be shocked, Liam, I promise you that."

"Thank you," he said gruffly, not looking at her, "I appreciate that. But you see, I don't want to hurt you."

What should have been the nurse's bright, confident answer—*you won't hurt me*—was in this case neither appropriate nor true. She wanted to say, *your pain is my pain, and for you I'd suffer willingly,* but that, too, was out of place. In the end she said softly, "I think it's more important that you tell me than that you worry about how I feel."

As he turned to look at her, she was rewarded by the faintest curve of his lips; he was regaining his equilibrium, for the moment, at least. With a little sigh she patted his arm and judged that it was time to change the subject. "Anyway, tell me about Australia. That's something you didn't mention in your letters to me. Was it all you expected it to be?"

"Oh yes," he murmured, and the warmth of his response set her wondering, as it had three years before, how many young women had longed to see him smile for them. But he seemed charmingly unaware of his own appeal as he talked, describing the young, growing city that was Melbourne, and the richness of the country beyond. His words painted a vivid picture of Victoria's hills and forests, exotic birds and animals, and revealed a deep admiration for the people. Georgina wondered—could not help wondering—whether there was one special person among them.

"And when the war's over," she said slowly, "will you go back?"

His answer seemed a long time coming. Like a sudden shadow, pain passed over him. He shifted position, drawing slightly away from her. "I don't know. I'd like to, yes." His tone had an edge to it, suddenly, and his eyes were distant. *"When the war's over . . .* We keep saying that, you know. We all say it. Or we did. But nobody quite believes it anymore. You look back, and war is all you can remember—the blokes talk about Gallipoli as though it was ancient history—and you try to look ahead, but all you can see is more of it. And no matter what you do, how hard you fight, how many men you lose, that's all there is ahead of you."

Georgina winced. "It will be over one day. We have to believe in that." But she heard the desperation in her own voice and wished she had never mentioned Australia.

"I'm sure it will—one day. The question is, will we be there to see it?"

It was cynically said, and searching his pockets for cigarettes, Liam did not notice the pain it caused. A moment later, finding them, he said, "If I come through it, yes, I'd like to go back. It's a wonderful country—paradise. You'd love it," he added with a quick glance into her eyes as the match flared into life. He cupped broad fingers around the flame, drew deeply, and released a cloud of blue smoke.

A moment later, with a soft smile for her, he said, "And you, Georgina—what will you do when the war's over? Will you go on nursing, or what?"

"What else is there?" The words came out bleakly, unexpectedly, and frightened her a little. She had never before been aware of a lack of conviction, but it seemed to be there nevertheless. She wondered whether Liam had released it with his talk of that clean, new land.

Catching the bleakness, he shot her a quizzical glance. When he spoke, his words had the air of being carefully chosen. "You've never thought of marriage, then?"

The question was so unexpected, the idea so unlikely, that she was torn between laughter and astonishment, but something in his tone brought color to her cheeks too, and she had to look away. "Marriage?" she repeated, laughing and shaking her head. "No, never."

"You say that as though it's never occurred to you. Surely it must have, at some time?"

"No," she said seriously, glancing up and seeing the bafflement in his eyes. "It's always been out of the question."

He doesn't know, she thought, or has never considered it. But why should he? His life and experience did not encompass madness. Although it was not something she wanted to talk about, it suddenly struck Georgina that the truth of her own background might shed light for Liam on so much more.

She stood up. "Shall we walk a little way? Do you feel up to it?"

As they strolled across the lawns, skirting tennis courts where a couple of desultory games were being played, Liam slipped off the jacket of his blue hospital uniform and loosened his tie; and in the hot sun Georgina removed her gloves and hat, aware as she did so of a sense of freedom, and a lifting of that oppression that thoughts of her mother always incurred. Somehow, being with Liam made things easier, and suddenly she wanted him to know about her mother, about the past and a childhood that was so inextricably involved with his own.

They had talked about Charlotte Duncannon that last evening, when he had insisted on coming to meet her at the Retreat, so he knew that she had died in a similar place in Ireland. What he did not know was the history of that illness, its insidious progress through the years, and she felt instinctively that Liam's antipathy to her father might be alleviated to some extent if he knew what Robert Duncannon had suffered because of it. Putting together what she had gleaned over the years from various relatives, and adding to that her own knowledge of mental illness, Georgina described her mother from adolescence to grave, the girl who had seen her parents murdered in Ulster, been adopted by her uncle's family in Dublin, and introduced into society at the age of eighteen. She described a young woman of extraordinary, ethereal beauty, whose aloof, mysterious personality had attracted her father from the start. Robert Duncannon's suit was favored, but not until after the two were married did he discover why his wife's wealthy, titled relatives had been so eager to promote the match, to arrange the wedding so rapidly. Charlotte's mysterious attitudes became downright odd, even bizarre as time went by: She heard voices and conversed with people who were not there, and ultimately her strangeness degenerated into hatred and violence.

Anxious about his wife, unable to leave her alone, Robert had left her with his brother and sister-in-law in Ireland while he moved to England with his regiment. After Georgina was born, Charlotte became much worse, one of her most obsessive delusions being that Robert Duncannon was the spawn of the devil and that it was her duty to kill him.

Georgina glanced sideways at Liam as she said that and saw him start. "It wasn't easy to be on the receiving end of all that hatred, especially when he cared so much. And he did care, Liam, I'm not just saying that. He always did his best for her, and he tried so hard to keep her out of an asylum. He didn't want her abused and ill-treated, which was the norm in those days, so he insisted on her staying at White Leigh. But he was away most of the time, so that was hard on my uncle and aunts . . ." She sighed, remembering those days more by repute than reality, for she had been very young at the time. One incident did stand out, however, and that she related to Liam—the Christmas when they had returned from church to find her father prostrate on his bed and covered in blood.

"I thought he was dead. I screamed and screamed, and they tore me away, shutting me up, alone in my room. I had nightmares for years after that."

With a stifled exclamation Liam shook his head, muttering something derogatory about the wisdom of adults. Lighting a cigarette, he said, "She'd attacked him, I suppose?"

"Oh yes. He'd gone to see her while we were out, and she went for him with a pair of scissors. He wasn't badly hurt, as it turned out, just bleeding profusely and in a state of shock—but as I say, I thought he was dead." She paused, glancing at him sideways, before going on to tell him that sometime after that—she did not know how long it was—her father had met Louisa, and when he returned to Ireland with his regiment, had persuaded her to accompany him. "It was the beginning," Georgina said briefly, "of three very happy years. I always think of those years as my childhood."

She waited for Liam to take her up on that, to ask questions about that time, about when he was born and the early years they had spent together as brother and sister, but he did not. Instead, after a minute or two's silence, he went back to the subject of her mother. "What I don't understand," he said slowly, "is why your mother agreed to marry him, if she hated him so much."

Georgina sighed. "I shouldn't imagine she did hate him, not to begin with. But I'm not saying she loved him either. People like that are very strange, often devoid of ordinary human affections, totally wrapped up in themselves. Things happen around them, and half the time they don't seem to notice. How she took to being married, I've no idea, but she couldn't ignore childbirth, could she, poor woman?" Half to herself, she murmured, "She must have been terrified, wondering what was happening to her. Perhaps she blamed him for that . . ."

Her own birth, and the effects of it, ever since she had been old enough to understand had never ceased to horrify Georgina. That she had gained life at such an expense was a hugely sobering thought. Had Charlotte Duncannon died then, it would have been better, more just, easier to bear; but to know that she had lived on, suffering in her insanity, bringing constant anguish to so many other lives—including her own and Liam's—was a hard cross to carry. Nor had it ended with Charlotte's death. Within her, Georgina carried the seeds of her mother's insanity. Or that was how it felt. Seeds which might never come to fruition in her own life, but which might be carried on into her children's lives, and the lives of their children after that. Like fair hair, or blue eyes, or a birthmark on the hip.

If she ever married.

She never would, of course. That decision had been made many years ago, before men as potential husbands had entered her awareness. And having made the decision, she had cut herself off emotionally, halting any advance before it became necessary to explain herself. How odd that she should be faced with explaining it now, and to Liam.

"So you see," she went on, matter-of-factly, "that I could never consider marriage. Once upon a time I thought I might end up like that myself." She gave a kind of laugh, as though the matter was one for joking, but it was the only way not to shudder. "However, it seems unlikely now. After all I've seen and done in the last two years, Liam, I'm sure that if I were about to lose my reason, I'd have lost it already. But I might pass it on, you see. If I married and had children," she repeated quietly, not laughing now, "I might pass it on . . ."

He stopped suddenly and turned toward her; and when she looked up at him, his face was taut and hard with suppressed emotion. All the diffidence was gone from him. She thought he was about to speak, to utter some fierce denial, but he raised his hand to cup her face and bent to kiss her forehead. It was a warm, firm kiss, not at all loverlike, yet it expressed so absolutely his love and compassion, Georgina felt her own heart leap in response. She was at once both humbled and exalted, feeling like a child in the presence of some tremendous wisdom, a warmth that longed to encompass and hold her safe. She could have clung to him and wept.

They had walked on a small distance when he said tersely, "I didn't know. I remember you telling me about your mother, but I never realized—I mean, that side of things never occurred to me. I am sorry."

She tried to make light of it and found herself almost stammering. "Don't be. I mean, well—well, it's one of those things, isn't it? Unfortunate, but one accepts it—that's the way things are, after all . . ."

"But is it? Do you know for certain that the illness is inherited?"

"It hasn't been proved, if that's what you mean. But I *feel* it. I know it's there." Confused in the face of his intensity, she felt herself reduced to emotion rather than fact. "I can't really explain," she finished lamely, "I just know it and it frightens me."

He regained her hand, and she was aware of its hard dryness, the callouses on the palm, and a warmth flooding between them. It seemed to take away all the pain. Instead of arguing, he asked bluntly, "So you've never been in love? Never wanted to marry?"

"No, never. It was always—well, something I avoided."

"I don't think people *choose* to fall in love," he remarked, and something in his expression as he looked at her made

Georgina feel very gauche, very vulnerable. Too conscious of his hands and his smile and that tingling, spreading warmth, she eased herself away, suggesting a halt.

On the far side of the trees, where it was sheltered and sunny, he sat down, spreading his jacket for her on the grass. Kneeling beside him, she remembered belatedly the little gifts she had brought, and as he opened the wrapping, tracing the trademark of palm trees with his finger, she saw him smile with wondering pleasure. He leaned back, stretching himself full length on the grass, holding up the little packets before him.

"So," he murmured, "they're still making these, are they? My old favorites—how did you know?"

She was able to laugh then. "I must have remembered."

Not consciously, she was aware of that, but once said, it did come back, like so many other things. Seeing him there, lying on the grass, long legs looking longer still in the narrow blue trousers, shirtsleeves pushed back over brown forearms, she was reminded again of that last evening before the storm broke, when he had talked, so innocently, about leaving. She had thought him beautiful then, a lovely boy with all the world at his feet . . .

And now he was a man.

The realization made her shiver, as did the thought of all that had gone between. He had changed and matured, she could see that, but despite a weariness and bitterness bred by the war, he was still, miraculously, the same person. A little wiser perhaps, and with less-polished ideals, but a gentle man for all that, not brutalized, as some were, by the hard school of experience. Sensitivity was still there, and that he still cared for her, very deeply, was evident by all that had passed between them today.

But perhaps, she reflected, that was less good than it seemed. For a moment she experienced a faint twinge of unease, and then he smiled at her and it was gone.

$\mathcal{L}$iam had good days and bad, bursts of energy that led him to believe he was quite well, often followed by several days in which he shivered with weakness and misery. His nights, too, were mixed, sometimes tense and wakeful, and as often full of nightmare and horror as they were of relaxed, health-giving sleep. The ward sister who had been in charge when he first arrived moved back to her regular night slot, which Liam had cause to be glad about. Often when he woke in fear, unable to sleep again, she would make him a hot drink and let him talk for a while quietly until the anxiety passed. She did that with all of them. She was very kind.

He imagined Georgina doing the same, and he would think of her, years hence, wondering whether she would always be devoted to the suffering of others, living for them, never having a life of her own. Nursing was a noble vocation, if an excessively demanding one; no doubt it had its rewards, although as a mere patient suffused with gratitude, he could not imagine them. Each of these women could marry and leave the profession, but that choice was not open to Georgina. Although she could leave, and no doubt live comfortably in idleness on the income from her mother's inheritance, he could not imagine her doing so. No, she would carry on probably for the rest of her life, never knowing a man's love, which seemed a tragedy to him, a sin against the natural order of things. She was a woman who deserved to be loved and cherished. Yet he could not deny the surge of relief when she declared that love and marriage were not for her. Although the reasons were tragic, in a strange way they eased his conscience; he felt less selfish in loving her, less guilty in looking for her affection. With the surety that he was detracting from nothing and no one, it seemed to Liam that he might freely enjoy her company and give whatever degree of love she might accept.

Despite the obvious and insurmountable barriers, he felt there was no real reason why they should not share a tender friendship and the comfort of knowing that each cared about the other. It was not a love which could be consummated, but then he had never expected it to be, so experienced no particular sense of loss. There was even a strange comfort in it, a sense of knowing, without being told, exactly where he stood. It was one of the few things in his life with any sure foundation.

What caused him some unease, however, was the image she had presented of Robert Duncannon as a loving father and tormented young husband. It sat awkwardly against his own fixed impression of a middle-aged philanderer who cared everything for his own passions and little for his offspring. What age had he been then? Mid- to late-twenties, Liam supposed, not much more than he was himself now, and hotheaded, inexperienced in the ways of the world . . .

No, it would not do. If he stopped hating Robert Duncannon, everything else would fall apart. If he stopped hating the man who had brought all this about, then who was there left to blame? And it must be somebody's fault, this crazy situation, it had to be somebody's fault.

He stopped thinking about it altogether and wrote his mother and Edward a few bland missives, saying he hoped they were well and he would see them as soon as he was fit to travel. There was no point, he argued, in their coming to London; he would travel free on a rail pass as soon as he could obtain leave, which was bound to be quite soon.

As the September days shortened with fog and rain, he spent much time in the library, a place of endless fascination.

The hospital had been a school, an orphanage the history of which he read one dark afternoon when the ward was crowded with visitors and Georgina unable to come. It had been built on a wave of patriotism after the Crimea for the orphaned daughters of veterans of that campaign. Public subscription had raised more than a million pounds for its erection, and it was grand indeed, the great hall decorated with banners and arms of the great cities of Britain and the Empire. Like the whole building, it had something medieval about it, an air of masculine romanticism, upon which several hundred little girls had failed to leave an impression.

Although the present wards had been dormitories and school-rooms, they were built around quadrangles which reminded him of cloisters. Often, hanging around the rear entrance on wet afternoons, smoking, he would look back across the brick-paved cloister and watch the passage of nurses up and down, up and down, and the men, hundreds of them, whom except in a professional capacity, they must never meet. There was an otherworldliness about it, romantic, medieval, monastic, which fitted the place exactly. With its high, Gothic walls, quaint arched windows, and communal living quarters, it seemed part of Chaucer and Mallory and the romantic poets of old, and that sense of celibacy, enforced and upheld, seemed natural rather than irksome. He was not, he was sure, the only one to feel that; it seemed to affect the other men too, even the ones on his ward, who were by and large less ill than the rest. Each new nurse had her followers, men who fell romantically in love with amusing regularity, but there was less coarseness than might have been expected. Worship, adoration, and respect were the order of the day, and in that atmosphere Liam's relationship with Georgina seemed not at all strange.

He was teased, of course. Georgina was referred to as his *private nurse*, and he was asked several times whether he was going to do the decent thing by her and name the day. All the men were convinced she was in love with him and just waiting for Liam to pop the question. If it was flattering, it had also been highly embarrassing initially when he was less practiced at fending them off. Two of the men had asked the same question. "Is she your sister, or what?" To which he had said they were cousins, a point which had been agreed, early on, between himself and Georgina. But each response had been similar, words to the effect that his answer explained the close family resemblance. "Mind, she's a bloody sight prettier than you!"

Liam took the teasing in good part, while finding much irony in those comments. Except in coloring, and possibly something about the eyes, they were not alike. He was heavy-boned, while she was as slender as a willow; and if he had inherited his fairness from the Elliott family, she had hers from her mother. Robert Duncannon had passed on nothing of his dark Irish looks to either of them. Robin was the one who seemed to have inherited the coloring and bone structure, and Tisha, who was not tall, bore her resemblance in hair and eyes. It was odd too that when his sister did arrive on a brief visit, no one recognized her as such.

Liam was more pleased to see Tisha than he had expected to be, but they had so little to say to each other that the visit was something of an embarrassment. The only matters they had in common were York, home and the past, and as each had private reasons for not wanting to discuss these things in depth, it left little to talk about.

Tisha did, however, manage to shock him. She revealed the fact of Edward's illness in such a casual way that at first he thought he had misheard. When pressed for details, she said airily that he was quite well again, there was nothing to worry about, and their mother had everything well in hand.

More upset than he could say, Liam was aware of his own heart pounding painfully, that erratic, uneven beat that had become more pronounced since those last bombardments at Pozières; he was sweating too, drenched down chest and back although it was not a warm day.

"Have you seen him?" he demanded. "Did you go home?"

"Well no. I've been very busy since I got married. Edwin went off training and then he came back on embarkation leave, and I knew Mother couldn't do with visiting when Dad was ill, so I thought it better to leave it for a while."

"But he might have died!"

She clicked her tongue. "Oh, Liam, you always did exaggerate! They were only mild attacks, and Mother particularly impressed upon me that I was not to worry."

"So you didn't?" he asked sardonically, resisting a frightful urge to smack her. "But do you think you might? Go home, I mean?"

"Not just yet," Tisha replied, smoothing the seam of her stockings."Mother's got enough to do without looking after guests."

"You're hardly a *guest*—you're her daughter, for heaven's sake! Or doesn't that mean anything to you?"

His sister looked up, fixing him with a cold stare. "Since you ask—not a great deal, no."

He was stunned. Almost stammering, he said, "But, Tisha, you *should* go home."

"And so should you," she retorted. "And maybe when you've been and settled your differences, maybe I'll go. Maybe. Until then, dear brother, don't try to tell me what to do. I'm a married woman now, and I can please myself."

With that, she swept out, as elegantly as she had come in, on a wave of French perfume and a swirl of silk.

Guilt washed over him, and a helpless feeling of frustration. Three years! What had happened to her in that time? She had been just a child when he left, and now she was every inch a woman, smart, hard, and sophisticated. On the surface at least. What was she beneath, though? A childish, vindictive little monster. Married woman, indeed! Liam pitied her husband.

When he had eventually calmed himself, he wrote to Edward, a letter less carefully phrased than usual, expressing his deep concern and need for assurance. He would come home, he said, just as soon as he was able to do so.

It was several days before he saw Georgina, and by that time his anger had abated; nevertheless, at the first opportunity he took her to task on the matter, demanding to know why, since she was aware of Edward's illness, she had neglected to tell him.

"You were in France," Georgina said stiffly, "facing rather more immediate dangers. Louisa knew—and I agreed with her—that a matter of a mild heart attack did not mean that Edward was at death's door, although you and Robin might have jumped to that conclusion. And if you had, what good would it have done? Could you have obtained leave at that time? I doubt it. And when you arrived here, and the opportunity to tell you arose, it was my considered opinion that you were too ill to be faced with it."

"I don't agree with you!"

"Liam, I *know* how ill you were." She touched his arm gently. "And the worry of knowing would have held back your recovery. Please believe me."

"So when did you plan to tell me?"

"I didn't," she said honestly, "I was leaving it to your mother to do that. But I think it's time you understood how much she and Edward care for you. It was a joint decision not to tell you, even when they knew you were here in London. They didn't want any undue pressure put upon you—they were, and are, longing to see you, on your terms, and in your time. You see, in spite of everything, they still love you very much."

It was too much to bear; he turned away, aware of a hard lump in his throat. Because he did not want to accept that, he said brusquely, "But there they go again—keeping things from me, as though I were still a child! When are they going to start being honest? All this secrecy and deceit makes me so angry!"

She said nothing, and he knew she was waiting for him to calm down; making a supreme effort, he stood up and walked away, leaving Georgina sitting in the shelter of the chapel wall. When he had half smoked a cigarette, he came back and apologized.

"I suppose Tisha should have kept her mouth shut."

She smiled wryly. "I think perhaps she should. But that's Tisha."

"Yes, isn't it?" He sat down, feeling cold and shivery; it was a poor day. "Do you want to go inside?"

"Not unless you do. It's quieter out here."

After a while, thinking about York, thinking about his sister, he said, "What's happened to her, Georgina? We never had much in common, but I don't remember her being quite like that."

"I don't know, she was never easy to understand."

But a sudden sigh made Liam look into her face; there was much sadness and a small frown. "Tell me," he said heavily, "whatever it is. I don't like to think of you keeping things from me." Nor did he. It was hurtful when he wanted so much to be part of her, when he wanted to understand the things that grieved her as well as those that made her happy. "Tell me."

But there was little to tell. Small incidents, small cruelties that Georgina had witnessed during the less frequent visits made after his departure, a moment of revelation for Liam when she admitted feelings of guilt at that time, and the bleak atmosphere which had prevailed at the cottage with both boys gone.

Wanting to question her about the guilt, he let it pass, needing to know, initially, about Tisha. But Georgina's assessment of what ailed the girl was not easy to listen to; most of it only served to increase his own sense of unease, to promote a growing suspicion that perhaps his own actions had much to answer for.

"Something happened to Tisha about the time you left. Don't ask me what, because I don't know—I honestly don't know. I can only assume that what she heard, what she discovered, was as great a shock to her as it was to you. Except she didn't have your avenue of escape. And I think Edward and Louisa were so shattered by what you did, so absolutely devastated, they ignored her. They didn't realize how much she needed them.

"And Tisha," Georgina sighed, "was always the one who wanted to be important, who wanted an audience for every trick. Particularly a male audience. Edward doted on her—but suddenly he wasn't paying much attention anymore—Louisa absorbed most of his time and affection. And she did need it, Liam—she was like"—breaking off, Georgina shook her head—"she'd lost you, her eldest son. She didn't know where you were. You might have been dead. The *not knowing* almost killed her."

He bowed his head against that. But he had asked, had demanded to know, could not now beg her to stop, unsay the words that spoke the truth.

"Once Robin had heard from you—once you'd written to Edward—all that changed, of course. Louisa was much better, more able to take notice of what was going on around her. But it was too late where Tisha was concerned. In a way, I think they were both quite relieved when she left to come to London. And since then, she's been more or less as you describe her. I don't think she cares for anyone very much. Edwin, perhaps, but he's gone away too. I don't think she expected that."

Liam shook his head at the folly of it all, scarcely able to believe the extent of destruction caused by one man's hasty words. He supposed he should have been feeling pity for his sister, but all he could think of was that afternoon when he returned from work, that moment when the truth assaulted him.

"If you only knew . . ." Fumbling for his cigarettes, lighting one, he was aware that his hands were trembling, but the pain, curiously enough, was less than it had ever been. In the face of his mother's suffering it seemed somehow pathetic, even selfish, to have nursed it so long. Three years! For God's sake, in war that was a lifetime!

"I never meant . . ." he began again, then stopped, feeling inadequate and very guilty. He felt Georgina's hand on his arm and turned to look at her. She seemed so stricken by his anguish that he wanted to draw her close, enfold her in his arms, and tell her nothing mattered. But it did matter, and he could not hold her, and there was very little comfort elsewhere. Certainly not in his own thoughts.

"What is it? Can't you tell me?"

Her voice was gentle, persuasive, but in spite of his need to respond, the words were still locked behind a barrier of remembered pain. Pathetic though it was, he knew it would hurt even more to break that seal, to let the torrent of bitterness go. Among it lay the jewel of his love for her.

"I can't," he said miserably, "not now."

"That's all right," she whispered, "I understand."

"I wonder if you do?"

Pressing her hand, he rose to his feet, and with the ringing of the bell they went inside.

Throughout most of September he had spent mornings in bed, rising for the main meal of the day, staying up until six or seven in the evening, when he was glad to return. By the end of the month, feeling stronger, he was often up and about from breakfast till supper, filling his days in library or grounds, and occasionally performing small tasks in the ward kitchen. When six of the men left for one of the convalescent homes, Liam found himself helping on a fairly regular basis. He rather liked it, enjoying the informality of the kitchen, the young nurses' company and the way they good-naturedly teased and bullied him. The work gave him something to do, and stopped him from brooding.

Nevertheless, Tisha's visit and that conversation with Georgina had brought to mind an awareness that kept returning. During all the time he had been away from home, beyond the contentment of Australia and the blind intensity of the war, beyond the seclusion of hospital life, time had not stood still. Although in his mind it had been frozen at the point where he left, he was faced now with reports of change, truths it was difficult to avoid. Like having an uncorrected map of no-man's-land, he thought, and with an order to go over the top, suddenly being told of fresh saps and gun pits and an acre of barbed wire.

Although he had wanted to hurt them, intended it and obviously succeeded, from this distance it seemed a childish, petty thing to have done. Since that promise to Robin he had imagined going home, his mother begging his forgiveness, and he, reluctantly, granting it, like some medieval pontiff; but it seemed to him now that he should be the supplicant, his mother the one dispensing grace.

It was not a comfortable awareness, and one he tried to ignore, pushing it to the back of his mind against the day when he would have to do something about it. What he could not ignore were his feelings toward Georgina. In the beginning it had not been a problem; his relief at being safe, at having the joy of her company at regular intervals had amounted almost to euphoria, a sense of such well-being that for long enough it carried him happily along; and while they met within the rarefied atmosphere of hospital and grounds, it was sustained. But they had begun to go out. Once or twice up to town for the afternoon, seeing the sights of London from the open-topped deck of a bus, and amid the bustling, workaday world he was aware of wanting to behave like any other young man with his sweetheart, drawing her arm through his, kissing her cheek as they said good-bye, or like the soldier and his girl spied in the shadow of trees at twilight, indulging in a long, passionate embrace.

It was becoming a struggle to remember his obligations, a

constant battle to quell the physical desire that seemed to be increasing in direct proportion to his good health.

His twenty-second birthday fell at the end of the first week of October, and Georgina had endeavored to organize her three days' leave to coincide with it, and also to borrow her father's car, a dark green, open-topped Ford. Liam had reservations about that, but as the weather promised to be good, it would have been churlish to refuse. Once he had recovered from the unease of sitting in Robert Duncannon's car, he began to enjoy the sensation of speed and freedom, and to admire the way Georgina handled such a complicated piece of machinery.

Pink spots of color enlivened her cheeks, the chiffon scarf that anchored her hat blowing back gaily in the breeze. A beige dust-coat covered her clothes but her skirt beneath it was a shade of old rose, echoed and deepened in the colors of her swathed velvet hat. He thought she looked not just beautiful—she was always that—but extraordinarily pretty. That impression was reinforced when they reached their destination. Removing the dustcoat and scarf, she left both in the car and turned, a little flirtatiously, he thought, to ask what he thought of her new outfit. The plum velvet jacket, with its deep lapels and high waist, was very flattering, like the gabardine skirt which ended several inches above a pair of very pretty ankles. He thought she looked wonderful and said so, but he had to swallow hard first.

In the golden shades of early autumn, Hampton Court was a delight, old stone and brick lending a mellow grandeur to the day, a sense of timelessness, as though nothing in life could be too tragic when something so lovely had withstood it all. They wandered through the grounds and talked about Cardinal Wolsey, the man who had built this great palace, and they took a boat on the river, and talked about Bishopthorpe, Wolsey's other palace outside York. While Liam rowed, Georgina was full of reminiscences, asking did he remember this and that, and particularly the afternoon he had taken her across the river to the fair on St. George's Field. He did remember, he remembered everything exceedingly well, but even as he smiled and nodded, his heart was breaking for the loss of innocence. He had loved her then with a boy's romantic adoration; he adored her still, but he wanted her too, and that was very hard to bear.

At Bishopthorpe, looking up at that great palace from the river, he had discovered that Georgina was to be forever denied him; at Bishopthorpe, on that lovely late summer afternoon, he had come face-to-face with the truth.

Those memories colored everything, lent the afternoon a sad, ironic air and spoiled his enjoyment. He was glad to leave, to get back in the car and be driven on. They went to Richmond and walked in the park, and the sun was still shining through a faint autumn haze. Liam knew that he should have been happy, but everything that afternoon was tinged with a sense of loss.

Aware of his sadness, although not, he was sure, under-standing it, Georgina strolled beside him, remarking softly on the sights and sounds and smells of autumn. He was conscious of her perfume, roses, overlaying the scent of dying leaves, and he listened to the sounds their feet made rustling through golden carpets beneath the trees. She looked soft and warm in her velvet, in those dusky, muted colors that somehow blended with the falling afternoon. He wanted so much to touch that softness, to draw her close and taste the sweetness of her lips, that he dare not even brush her hand.

Back at the car he held the door for her but did not offer to help her in. Drawing the dustcoat around her knees, she glanced up, inquiring tentatively whether anything was wrong, whether she had said something to upset him. Cut by the knowledge that he had pained her, Liam shook his head, wretchedly unable to explain.

"I'm just a bit tired, I think," was all he could say.

The afternoon was deepening to dusk as they drove back, and there was no time to stop elsewhere. Outside the hospital gates, while he sat for a moment unspeaking, reluctant to leave her, she reached into her bag, drawing out a small slim package.

"I intended to give you this over tea," she said in that soft, low voice of hers, "but we ran out of time. It's nothing really—just a small gift to mark your birthday. I wish you could have had it last year, for your twenty-first."

Mystified, saying with a little laugh that it was the first present he had been given in years, Liam opened the wrapping to find a beautifully chased silver cigarette case. Inside it was inscribed with his initials and the date. For a minute he could not even look at her; turning it over and over in his hands, he felt crass for having spoiled a potentially perfect day, and with the date engraved he knew he would never forget it. And for what? All for the want of something he could not have. He felt selfish and ashamed.

"I'm so sorry," he managed at last, "for the stupid mood I've been in today. You've given me so much, and I . . ." He broke off, shaking his head. "Can you forgive me?"

"For what?" she asked lightly, smiling into his eyes. "It's been a lovely day."

"Yes," he said quietly, "it has. And you looked so lovely. Thank you."

She was half turned toward him, her mouth slightly parted in expectancy or puzzlement, he was not sure which. Wanting to express his feelings, wanting to make up for all those silent, brooding moments, he searched for words and found none. With his heart pounding crazily, he leaned across and kissed her very gently on the lips. There was a soft, momentary response, one that made it hard to draw away; with his blood on fire, he forced himself not to kiss her again.

It seemed to take an eternity to move. He would have liked to step out of the car, to utter a casual farewell, but he was trembling quite badly and his breath seemed to be stuck somewhere deep in his chest. Watching her face, her eyes, he thought he saw surprise mingled with both pleasure and confusion before she turned away. With her hands on the steering wheel and color heightening her cheeks, she murmured something breathlessly about it being rather late.

Taking his cue from her, Liam said yes, it was, and he really must go. A voice he hardly recognized as his own added that he hoped to see her again soon, and that he would drop her a line tomorrow.

The next morning, still enthralled by an inner vision of lustrous eyes and lips, Liam began a letter to Georgina which was full of warm recollections. With gentle self-parody he described pausing on the drive before going in, and that because his hands were so unsteady it had taken three matches to light one cigarette.

Musing for a moment, picturing himself, Liam smiled, and

as one of the young nurses passed by with a pile of linen, she grinned at him. It was the one who had scrubbed his back that first day, and it was she who had seen him come in last evening, hissing in an undertone that he should wipe the silly smile off his face before Sister wondered what he had been up to.

She knew, or had a good idea, what had taken place, but oh God, he thought in the next second, if she *really* knew, she wouldn't smile.

Sobered, he turned back to his letter, and all the silly, romantic, loverlike things he had said and still wanted to say, about the softness of her lips and not sleeping a wink, were suddenly inappropriate. Aware of his own foolishness, he tore the page into shreds and stared moodily from the window. That kiss must never be mentioned, not even in apology. If he wished it to remain the casual, friendly, brotherly gesture it just might have seemed, then it must be allowed to pass unremarked. He knew full well, however, that brotherly or not, it could never be repeated.

In a fresh beginning after lunch, Liam confined himself to safer topics, to repeated thanks for a lovely day out, and most especially for a gift he would always treasure. His words were sincere but dreadfully bland. Her reply, when it came by return post, was almost equally so.

Part of him—the sensible, practical part—was considerably relieved by that, but the lover in him was frustrated. Over the next few days, longing to be with her again, he was plagued by subtle torments. What did she think of that kiss? How did she feel? How would *he* feel when next he saw her, tantalized by closeness, by her perfume and the temptation of her smile? How could he look at her yet refrain from touching the perfection of her cheek, the softness of her smooth blonde hair? Turbulent emotion gripped him whenever he recalled that parting kiss and the way she had looked at him afterward. His dreams were full of unsatisfied desire.

Although they corresponded regularly by letter, Liam did not see Georgina again for more than two weeks. One visit had to be postponed due to pressure of work, and then he was laid low by a couple of antidysentery injections and would not have seen her even if he could. On her next afternoon off, the day that he was looking forward to taking her up to town, all passes were canceled. The entire hospital seethed with resentment and Liam was furious.

Amid an indignant, vociferous crowd at the gates, there was little opportunity for awkwardness. To clear a path it was necessary to keep her close to his side, but in holding her he also wanted to caress her, and that made him angrier still. Curtly, in answer to her query, Liam related the reason for the ban: Two men had gone out for an afternoon and neglected to return for three days. To his further annoyance, the tale seemed to amuse her.

"Where did they go?"

"Oh, nowhere in particular—just on a bender in town. Got so roaring drunk they couldn't remember where they were—or even *who* they were!"

With a mischievous smile, she said, "They'll be in for it!"

"We all are," he responded grimly, "confined to barracks for the rest of the week. As if that will deter anybody! The ones that are ready to go convalescent can't wait to get out of here." He paused to light a cigarette. "I'm starting to feel like that myself. In fact I asked about home leave the other day, but it doesn't seem likely until I'm clear. It's ridiculous, I feel fine."

"Don't rush things," she said gently, "it'll take its course."

"Yes, but when you start straining at the leash, you know you're getting better."

Because he was also thinking of other restraints, the words came out sharply, and Georgina's smile froze. He saw the pain he had caused before she glanced away, and could have bitten his tongue. Instantly contrite, pressing her hand, he quickly changed the subject. But Liam knew as well as she did that once declared fit he would be moved away from London, to the south coast probably, which was where most of the convalescents were sent.

It was not an easy afternoon, and when she had gone Liam was left with a bitter taste of regret. With the matter of home leave still on his mind, he was torn between a desire to spend as long as possible within reach of Georgina and a natural anxiety about Edward. Although letters from York continued to be reassuring, he had the feeling that time was running out, that he should make every effort to get home, if only for a couple of days.

The arrival of a new medical officer prompted him to ask again. There was sympathy when he explained why, but the doctor said that further tests would have to be taken before a decision could be made. Another specimen was sent down to the laboratory, and, two days later, on accosting the day Sister, Liam was told that the officer in charge of the lab wanted to know whether the patient was still in bed, as evidence of colitis was still present. Although she made no further comment, her expression said quite clearly that if he wanted to retain his current degree of freedom, he must press no further.

Downcast and frustrated, Liam kept the news to himself. Gloomy weather did nothing to lighten his spirits, and his letters to Georgina reflected it. She wrote to suggest a trip to the theater on her next day off, but the idea was less appealing than it might have been. Concert parties came to the hospital frequently, some good, most very amateurish, and sometimes organized trips went from Wandsworth to the Palladium at Stockwell just up the road. Liam thought he had had enough of that brand of hearty cheer, but it seemed churlish to refuse. He arranged to meet Georgina in a tea shop they had visited before just off Leicester Square.

It was a miserable afternoon, cold with the rawness of winter, a misty rain driving up from the river, the streets bobbing with umbrellas. There was a leaden yellowy cast to the sky, and someone had said it might be foggy later, so be sure to get back early, but Liam had no desire to cut short his time with Georgina. Waiting for her outside, with his hat pulled well down and the collar of his newly issued sheepskin jacket turned up to meet it, he still felt the cold. Seeing the queue for tables, he thought it more prudent to wait inside. Just as one was being allocated, Georgina arrived in a brimmed hat and belted mackintosh, shivering as she furled her umbrella.

He wanted to warm her against his heart, instead he held her hands across the table and smiled at her. It seemed to have the desired effect and she relaxed visibly, although with the arrival of the tea she drew her hands back to herself. They stayed longer than they intended, and the popular revue they meant to see was packed when they arrived, with people still waiting on the pavement. Although it had stopped raining, Georgina said she was too tired to walk, she wanted to sit down and relax. Liam glanced down at her then, and the pinched look he had attributed to the weather seemed more pronounced in that gray, unforgiving light.

"Come on," he said, taking her arm, "we'll go into the first empty theater we find, and if you like, you can fall asleep on my shoulder!" He laughed and she responded with a smile, but she seemed a little distracted. He wondered whether she was worrying about work or about her father who was presently in Dublin.

Within a few yards, he said, "Are you sure you wouldn't prefer to go home? You look to me as though you should be tucked up before a nice warm fire, not traipsing about town like this."

"No," she said quickly, "I'm fine, really I am. I'll have an early night, though, I could do with a good sleep."

"Let me call you a cab—"

"No, Liam—really." She tucked her arm in his and he felt the intimacy of the gesture like a warm glow. On a corner, a few yards down the street, was another little theater, advertising yet another amusing variety performance. Georgina suggested going in there.

The show had already started but seats were available. Paying for two in the stalls, Liam sighed as they went in: The place was half empty, which did not augur well for the quality of the performers.

He was right, they were not very good. In fact he had seen a far superior ventriloquist at a hospital performance the week before, and it seemed to him that there were better jugglers among the nurses. Muttering that to Georgina, he made her laugh, but the audience, comprising mainly soldiers, was becoming restive. After half an hour, disturbed by some of the coarser catcalls, Liam was about to suggest leaving, when a soubrette came on rather fetchingly dressed in male attire.

The British Tommy's uniform, with its breast pockets and breeches and neatly wound puttees, fitted her better, Liam thought, than any man. She was a neat, curvaceous girl with an angelic face, and as soon as she appeared the jeering died down, giving place to a series of whistles and handclaps. When she started to sing, her voice silenced the house.

It was a sweet, rich soprano, eminently suited to the series of sentimental ballads she had chosen to sing. "Home, Sweet Home!" was followed by "Roses Are Blooming in Picardy," so currently popular that the choruses were taken up by the audience; then, when the applause had died down, she began to sing Liam's favorite, sections of which were so well known to him that he was almost tempted to sing the words with her.

> Far ahead, where the blue shadows fall,
> I shall come to contentment and rest,
> And the toil of the day
> Will be all charmed away,
> In my little grey home in the west.

> There are hands that will welcome me in,
> There are lips I am burning to kiss;
> There are two eyes that shine
> Just because they are mine,
> And a thousand things other men miss.

It seemed to express everything he felt for the woman at his side: that longing for the war to be over, a comforting fantasy that one day she might make a home for him, be there every evening when he returned . . .

On a warm, natural impulse, he reached for her hand, stealing a sidelong glance at her downcast eyes; she seemed as moved by those words as he was, her fingers clasping his in sudden emotion. His heart leapt in response, and he thought how long it had been, weeks in which he had tried very hard not to touch her at all. Except for that fleeting kiss and the warmth of her linked arm this afternoon, he had kept apart from her, and he wondered whether she knew how difficult it had been.

Georgina's hand, imprisoned for a moment, opened to his, palm to his palm, the fingers slowly—oh so slowly—entwining with his. Wanting to lock her to him and never let go, Liam was suddenly conscious of his own strength, the breadth of hands thickened by constant use, and a fear of hurting her. Very gently, he drew her fingers through his in the most intimate caress, while her light, responding touch sent waves of rapture coursing through him, catching the breath in his throat,

fusing love and desire so totally he was only marginally surprised by the sudden heat in his loins. The contact between
them was so restrained yet so sensual, it seemed there were
but two points in the whole universe, linked by a line of acute
and exquisite pleasure; it was almost like making love. Or how
he imagined it should be.

Did she feel it too? For a moment he was convinced she
must, convinced by the sensuality of her caress, by her closed,
fluttering lashes, the soft, partly open mouth, the distinct rise
and fall of her breasts. She seemed as deep in thrall as he was
himself. And then as desire mounted overwhelmingly, as the
fire in his loins became more pain than joy, he thought no, she
can't be aware of this, it's impossible. If she was she would
stop, withdraw this instant before we fall on each other without
a care for who or what surrounds us . . .

But even as he moved to slip an arm around her shoulders
and draw her close to him, on an indrawn breath Georgina
pressed her fingers to her mouth and shook her head, like one
bemused or waking from a dream.

Paralyzed, he watched her rise abruptly and push her way
out down an empty row of seats.

The encore came to an end. The soubrette bowed to a storm
of applause and stamping of feet. Galvanized into action, Liam
grabbed his jacket and mackintosh and followed at a run for
the side exit. Coming out into the dismal street, he saw her
hurrying away, heading not for the main thoroughfare but into
the side streets of Soho.

"Georgina!"

He ran, his heart pounding, catching at her arm as he came
up with her, but she would not stop. He pulled her around,
quite roughly, to face him. Trembling still, she kept her eyes
averted. At a loss for words, he knew, with heart-stopping
certainty, that her emotions, her desires, echoed his. In the
dark warmth of the theater, that thought had been exciting;
here, in the cold and foggy daylight, it seemed a huge, terrible
knowledge, as though on discovering he could swim, he found
himself faced with the sea from the top of a cliff.

Instantly sobered, murmuring inadequate apologies, he
slipped the mackintosh around her shoulders.

"Let me take you home."

25

Although she protested, it was in a vague, halfhearted way. Liam had no difficulty at all in guiding her toward the main thoroughfare and finding a taxi to take them to Queen's Gate. Leaning back into the corner with her eyes closed, she said nothing all the way there. He held her hand in a comforting fashion, feeling both anxious and chronically guilty every time he looked at her.

His intentions were to drop her at the door and make his way back to Wandsworth, but even as he paid the taxi and prepared to say good-bye, Georgina asked him to come up to the flat. "I think it's time we talked, don't you? Have you time?"

He looked at his watch. "A couple of hours."

She smiled slightly at that, a wan, resigned sort of smile that seemed bleaker than the afternoon. "Time for a cup of tea, at least."

While she searched for her key he glanced down the broad, tree-lined avenue to where it disappeared into driving mist, finding its elegance as daunting as the moment. With a deep breath he mounted the steps, following her into a wide, marble-floored hall. The broad staircase was carpeted, but she lifted a finger to her lips as they began to climb the first of several flights to the Duncannon's door. In the tiny hall she took his hat and sheepskin jacket and laid them across a chair, and without raising her eyes led the way into a large, comfortably furnished room which obviously answered several different functions. There was a fine dining table and chairs before the windows, and in one alcove a large mahogany desk; a tall bookcase graced the far side of the chimney, while a large leather sofa and chairs faced the fire. It was a room with a masculine air and a faint smell of cigars; the colors, mainly dark greens and golds, were restful, and the sofa well used. Nevertheless, Liam sat down gingerly, very much aware in those initial seconds that this was Robert Duncannon's home.

But it was also Georgina's and she was his first priority. With an effort he forced himself to ignore his surroundings and to concentrate on her. Putting a match to the neatly laid fire, she asked him to tend it while she went into the kitchen to make some tea. He wanted to say that tea was not important, but she seemed to need the bustle and the movement. Nursing the fire into reluctant life, he wondered what it was she wanted to say and dreaded being told that they must not see each other again.

And yet if she said that—and she would, she was bound to say it—Liam knew he could not disagree. With regard to this afternoon, the most he could say in his own defense was that it was a miracle it had not happened before. Wanting her was hell, nevertheless he knew he would promise anything just to be able to go on seeing her.

He went and stood by the window, staring out at the plane trees, their soot-stained yellow leaves hanging limply from blackened boughs. Below, he could see the dark hood of an old hansom cab waiting by the curb, and, less clearly, across the street a line of forecourt railings; but the light-colored buildings were becoming difficult to make out. Twilight was deepening with the encroaching fog, and he was anxious, suddenly, about making his way back to Wandsworth. In mounting desperation, he went through into the kitchen. She was setting a tray. Hesitantly, very much afraid that she would flinch or back away, he laid a gentle hand on her arm.

"Please, Georgina, come and sit down. I can't bear this—I need to talk to you, but I don't know what to say . . ."

She was very silent for a moment, very still. Looking down

at her bowed head, he sighed and touched a loose strand of hair, smoothing it back from her face. It was very fine and soft between his fingers, like silk; he would have liked to loosen the thick coil, see it fall around her shoulders, but did not dare. He let his hand rest against the warmth of her neck. "I didn't mean to hurt you . . ."

With a sudden shiver she turned toward him, bending her head to his chest; hardly daring to breathe, he held her very lightly, his whispered plea for forgiveness barely more than a sigh.

"It wasn't your fault." The words did not come easily, he could tell that, there was a certain bitterness about them, as though she had conducted battles of her own and this surrender went against every principle.

"Oh, I think it was," he said manfully, preparing himself for the worst. "After all, I—"

"Liam, stop. Listen to me." She looked up, searching his face with those bleak, hurt eyes. Her arms came up around his neck, and she stroked the soft hair at his nape. "I love you." But she frowned as she said it, and he knew the admission pained her, even while it set his own heart aflame with joy. "I know it's wrong and so do you—but I can't bear it any longer . . ."

His arms went around her then, fiercely, possessively, and he held her hard because he thought he might weep with relief at not having to pretend any longer. He told her that he loved her too, that he had always loved her, that all through the beauty and tenderness of these last weeks he had been longing to tell her so, and that it was for love and love alone that he tried so hard not to touch her, to give no cause for regret.

The words came out brokenly, a jumbled mix of past and present that miraculously she seemed to understand. "I know, I know," she said over and over while her hands touched his face and caressed his shoulders, and her lips returned those tender, hesitant kisses.

"I missed you so much—all those years I missed you and longed to hear from you. It was so cruel of you to leave like that, without a word—I thought you hated me."

"I did, I did," he whispered against her hair, "but only for a little while and only because I loved you so much, because you knew and I didn't and you didn't tell me—"

"I *wanted* to—oh, my darling, I wanted to tell you, but I couldn't, I—"

"Hush now, it doesn't matter, it really doesn't matter . . ."

And in the joy of her, the bliss of her slender, pliant body pressed so passionately to his, Liam let go of the past, forgetting all the things that should have been remembered, all the things that until now had kept them so carefully apart. He was lost in the scent of her hair and skin, in the soft pressure of her breasts and the touch of her fingers against his cheek. She moved even as he moved, turning her face, her mouth, to meet his. He tasted salt on her lips, and in those spent tears seemed to rest so much love, more than he ever expected, far more than he deserved. With the warmth and passion of her response, all restraint vanished; she set fire to the hunger in him, and he sensed no reservation, no withholding, but rather an eager taking of every caress, and a need to respond in kind.

In his inexperience, Liam might have hesitated, but she seemed to understand so much, to know his body as well as he did; and when he pressed his lips to her throat, she unfastened his shirt and ran her fingers beneath it, sending shivers of delight with every touch. After that, with his hand welcome at her breast, it seemed the most natural thing in the world to release a few tiny buttons, to push back flimsy straps and know the rapture of her firm and naked breasts against his skin.

With senses reeling they clung together, searching, exploring, gasping at each unexpected discovery, at the escalating riot of need. Wanting to be part of her, to quench his desire in the warmth and softness of her most secret place, he was conscious only of its necessity, of that strange act of fusion that would release and make them one. Lifting her up, he carried her into the other room, laying her down before the hearth. With her eyes half closed she took him to her, making no defense of her virginity. But her virginity was in part its own defense; he was too reluctant to force that tender place, and in the end movement brought its own release. Too soon to bring joy, but too soon, mercifully, to cause lasting regret.

In those seconds which followed, before remorse or apology or thought could take hold, the telephone rang, startling them both with its loud, insistent ringing. Tense, horrified, still as statues they held each other, conscious of half-nakedness,

the terrible intimacy of what had just occurred. It was as shocking as though someone had walked into the room.

Georgina recovered first, scrambling to her feet, pulling at
her open blouse and the crumpled folds of her skirt. Almost
staggering as she crossed the room, she left open the door to
the hall, and Liam saw her stand for a moment before picking
up the jangling instrument.

Then she looked at him, straight at him as she was speaking, alarm in her eyes, her strained voice struggling for clarity.
"No, Tisha, he's still in Ireland . . . I'm not very well at the
moment, nursing a cold . . . yes, it is a nasty one, you wouldn't
want to share it . . ." Liam cringed. ". . . in fact I've just woken
up, I've been sleeping most of the afternoon . . . No, Father
won't be back for another ten days or so, you must have misunderstood . . ."

Not knowing whether to laugh or cry, as Georgina answered questions about Robert Duncannon's trip to Ireland,
Liam went into the kitchen to rescue his cigarettes. As she
finished the call at last, he caught hold of her, supporting her
across the room to the sofa. Holding her close in the crook of
his arm, he lit a cigarette and expelled a great cloud of blue
smoke, aware that all he wanted to do was find a bed and take
her to it, and just go on holding her.

"Did she want to come and see you?"

"Not me particularly—she was simply hoping someone
might be at home. I managed to put her off."

"Thank God for that."

He held her close and stroked her hair, no longer bound
in its neat coil. Releasing the last of the pins, he smoothed it as
best he could, kissing her all the time. Gradually, her trembling
subsided, but his nerves were still raw from reaction, his mind
just beginning to grasp the full implications of what had taken
place between them. He did not know whether to apologize for
attempting to make love to her, or for failing so abysmally; in
the end he confessed to severe fright.

"But I wanted you to," she admitted in a very small voice.

"I know. That frightens me too." He hugged her closer,
kissing the crown of her head as she pressed her face inside his
open shirt.

"I love you, Liam."

"And I love you," he whispered, caught again by the torment of their situation. "What are we going to do?"

It seemed an unanswerable question. They talked for a while and Georgina made some tea. While she went to change her crumpled clothes, Liam coaxed the fire back to life and soon had it blazing merrily. He was sitting cross-legged on the hearth rug when she returned in a blue velvet dressing gown, her hair brushed loosely in soft waves around her shoulders. Watching her in the firelight glow, Liam thought she looked like a princess in a fairy tale, more beautiful than he had ever seen her. With no more pretense between them, she was softer, gentler, so infinitely giving that it seemed his love for her doubled each time they touched, each time his glance met hers.

Nevertheless, that sense of joy was not entirely unfettered. They talked about love and loving each other, about its beginnings and its heartbreaks and uncertainties; and they discussed—albeit with some constraint—that sudden, overwhelming culmination. Georgina said that the wrong of their situation was as nothing compared to what was going on across the English Channel, which made Liam realize that she had been thinking about this for some time. His view, however, was more specific and personal. It was also very difficult for him to put into words. Concerned for her vulnerability rather than those abstract and relative concepts, he simply said that it must not happen again; he was prepared to exercise restraint if she was.

His bluntness made her smile. It was a soft, indulgent, admiring smile. "I don't deserve you," she said.

The dark afternoon had closed in early with a thickening blanket of fog. Sometime after six, when he should have been thinking of leaving, Liam went to the window to stare out at the murky darkness. Even the plane trees had disappeared. Beside him, echoing his thoughts, Georgina voiced the opinion that neither of them stood much chance of reaching their destinations tonight: Trams and buses would be stopped, and it would be far more sensible to stay put.

"Well." He smiled. "I can't pretend I'm sorry. For a night with you, I'd happily be shot at dawn. But what about your matron? What will she say?"

"What can she say? She can't argue with the weather."

Georgina patted his arm. "I'll telephone, tell them I'm stuck here. And it might be as well for you to get in touch with Wandsworth, then they won't be worrying about you. Say you're staying with relatives."

Laughing, Liam blessed the weather.

Georgina woke about six. For the first time in her life, however, she did not wake alone. In her soft feather bed, she and Liam were curled together like a pair of spoons, the length of his body pressed to her back, his arms, warm and heavy, around her. It was a strange but intensely pleasurable sensation, as though her very skin came alive in the instant of awareness, and as memory flooded back she had to stir, had to recapture the tingling thrill that came with every tiny movement against him. Last night she had been dizzy with it, as though intellect had ceased to exist, her only awareness being of him and with him, where his limbs touched hers, where hands and mouth aroused and explored, driving her to the edge of ecstasy and beyond. He had taken such delight in her, needing to look and touch, a little shy at first, unfamiliar with women, uncertain of what was and was not permitted. Inexperienced herself, Georgina had simply known, deep inside, that she wanted him to touch her in all the ways she longed to caress him.

There was advantage for her in that she knew men's bodies, every basic function, every hidden sensitivity; and years of nursing had blunted neither her wonder nor her deep sense of respect. There was also an odd, half-realized feeling that in making love to him she was in some way expressing all the tenderness she had felt for other men, men who had passed into and out of her care, men who had recovered, or died, or simply returned to the front without ever knowing a woman's love. And in remembering them she also recalled the young doctor who had so surprised her with his bitterness, his accusation that she had no heart, no soul.

If only you knew, she thought then; and that thought repeated itself now, making her smile a little. But he had frightened her with his vehemence, made her half believe he was right. After that she had thought too much about the curse of nursing, the fear that in seeking protection against suffering, the heart eventually shriveled completely, so that in the end feeling was gone. It happened to some. But Liam had saved her from that, proved to her, right from the beginning, that love and compassion were still there, that she was capable of happiness as well as pain.

After years in which even the acknowledgment of love had been suppressed, these recent weeks had been fraught with conflicting desires. Watching him recover in health and strength, the need to fuss and touch and bestow a thousand kisses had crept up inside like yeast fermenting in a stoppered jar. She had wanted him so much and been so afraid of showing it.

If his kiss that evening in the car had loosened the lid, then the touch of his hand yesterday had released raw physical desire in such torrents that she had been appalled, unable to reconcile such intense physical need with the tender, romantic fantasies she had previously entertained. Knowing, bleakly, that their relationship could not go on in that false, frustrating manner, she had been aware of a need for honesty, a desire to put all cards on the table and say, however baldly, *this is how I feel about you—what must I do*? Rights and wrongs that had kept her awake at night seemed suddenly immaterial; the one remaining fear was for the consequences. Yet even that—yes, *even that*, she repeated to her shocked other self—she had been prepared to risk for the joy of knowing his embrace. It was shocking, and in the warmth of his arms, Georgina felt she did not deserve the depth of his love, or the extent of his consideration.

Turning, stretching out slowly, pressing her lips to the smooth muscle of his upper arm, she luxuriated in his presence, hearing him sigh, feeling him stir against her as he woke from sleep. She had switched off the lamp beside her bed hours ago, but the hall light was still burning; by its dull glow through the open door she was able to see his face, the beginnings of a sensual smile touching his lips. He had changed, she thought, watching the curve of his mouth, just as their relationship had changed, all hesitancy gone in those hours of intimate exploration, hours in which they had discovered each other. He had brought her to pleasure with gentleness, but he had done it roughly too, with a kind of urgent desperation she understood, even while it made her writhe and gasp. That first time, driving his fingers into her, she had arched and cried out, and he had moaned at the sight of blood on his hands, for a moment not understanding that it was virginal blood, her cry the cry of all women invaded for the first time. It had, however, deepened the bond between them, subtly altering some delicate balance in their relationship. Prior to that she had been the one to encourage and reassure; afterward he was more dominant, and also, oddly, more protective.

"I love you," he said sleepily, nuzzling her neck, burying his fingers in her tangled hair. He ran a hand over her body, over breasts and belly and thighs, teasing her gently. She turned to him and he kissed her with slow, languorous pleasure, murmuring against her lips, "I shall probably wake up in a minute, in that bloody hard bed in Wandsworth."

His words, regrettably, broke the spell. As she shivered, Liam wrapped his arms around her and held her close. "There'll be other times—we'll find ways of being together, you know we will . . ."

But with a mass of impossibilities flooding her mind, Georgina could only cling to him in disbelief. Loving him, wanting to keep him close forever, she could see only the perfection of what they had shared, and the future's bleak uncertainty. Her father might be away for another ten days, which presupposed one more meeting; but after that . . .

There had to be ways, even if it meant meeting in hotels for a few stolen hours; she had money, more than enough, and was prepared to do anything, anything at all, to be with him.

The fog was still thick, but a sense of duty made it incumbent upon them both to attempt a return to their rightful places. After laying out her own spare uniform, Georgina set the iron to heat and gathered up Liam's clothes for pressing. She fetched a razor from the collection in her father's room, together with a brush and a keg of sandalwood shaving soap, laying them down before a small mirror on the washstand in her room.

"There we are—all new. But if you want to brush your teeth, my darling, you'll have to borrow my toothbrush. I haven't got a spare one."

"Oh, I think I can bear that," he responded with a grin.

Bringing a jug of hot water from the kitchen, Georgina left

him to it. With a towel wrapped around his waist, Liam washed quickly in the early morning chill, hesitating only briefly before attacking the stubble along his jaw. He had to shave, it was a matter of necessity, and it was stupid to be so finicky about using Robert Duncannon's things, even if they were new. But he disliked it, performing the task with as much speed and efficiency as he could muster. Satisfied, dabbing his face dry, he went in search of Georgina and his clothes. Shirt, jacket, and trousers were all pressed and ready to wear, in keeping with his story of staying with relatives as an overnight guest.

While she prepared breakfast for them both, he returned to her room to dress, noticing that the other bedroom door was open to reveal a large bed with a maroon quilt, and on the bedside chest, facing him, a collection of photographs.

He glanced away, was on the threshold of Georgina's room when recognition swept over him in a wave of guilt. He turned back to look again.

From a silver frame his mother's face regarded him. It was a familiar photograph, one taken when she was young, with cropped, curly hair and such a proud tilt to her chin. In his surprise at finding it there, that sense of being caught in something shameful disappeared. He was fascinated by her youthful loveliness which it seemed he had never before noticed: In his memory she was much older, her face softened by time and experience. But even as he stared at it, the photograph blurred and he had to sit down, almost unmanned by images of childhood, his mother's constant, reliable affection, her care and gentleness. Assailed by sorrow and regret, he asked whether she deserved the cruelty he had meted out and knew she did not. His behavior toward her had been unforgivable. He thought of the war and the dozens upon dozens he had had killed in the heat of battle; but he had pitied German and Turkish prisoners, even sharing food and water and cigarettes when necessary. It struck him then, and very bitterly, that he had been kinder to sworn enemies than he had been in recent years to his own mother.

He picked up the polished silver frame and looked at that lovely young face, and for the first time he was able to view her, not as his mother, but as a contemporary, with thoughts and feelings akin to his own. Like Georgina, about her age, full of life and passion, with the same needs, the same yearnings, reaching out, crossing barriers, taking what love had to offer whenever it was offered.

Like Georgina. Just like Georgina.

And he thought of Robert Duncannon, whose room this was, a young man then, not much older than himself; and he thought of that tragic marriage doomed to misery and failure.

He looked at his mother's photograph, still beside the bed after all these years, and understood the love that must have been between them then, that need to grab hold of happiness before it could slip away . . .

And Liam thought about himself loving Georgina, knowing it should not be, yet almost committing the unforgivable. Carried away in the heat of the moment, they had both wanted that consummation, both intended it, despite its incestuous nature and regardless of the consequences. If degrees of wrongdoing were to be considered, Liam knew full well that in the scheme of things, adultery was far less culpable than incest.

It made him shiver. He had blamed his mother and Robert Duncannon for heinous sin, yet it seemed to him now that what they had shared was no more than the folly of loving unwisely. Previously, he had imagined that his love for Georgina was greater and purer and more magnificent than any man had ever felt before. But in the light of sudden revelation, he wondered whether all men felt like that. All women too. And passion itself, once tasted, was self-perpetuating; being with Georgina, seeing and touching the beauty of her nakedness, he wanted more, always more.

He would always love her. Always.

Was that what Robert Duncannon felt? Did he, a man well into his fifties, still love Louisa Elliott? Did he still long for her in the lonely hours of the night, still regret that parting?

Liam shivered again. That longing seemed present in the room. It clung to the photograph of his mother, to the other, smaller ones that stood beside it. He looked at them for the first time and, with a terrible lurch of the heart, recognized himself as a child. One was very familiar, taken with Robin and Tisha some ten or twelve years before, possibly for Robert Duncannon's benefit, and sent to him in India or South Africa or wherever he had been stationed at the time.

There was another, one Liam had never seen: three children again, but much younger, and not the same three. A little girl of perhaps seven or eight years old, with long blonde ringlets and a pretty dress, holding a baby, awkwardly, on her lap, and beside them on the chaise longue, a chubby toddler in a sailor suit, stiff and frowning as though told to sit still.

Recognizing himself in the sailor suit, recognizing Georgina, his throat constricted. It was true then; it was all true. He remembered the house, the house in his dreams, and knew the little girl as he had always known her in his secret memories. It was Ireland, where his mother had been unhappy and cried such a lot; where Father was a big man on a beautiful horse, who had once lifted him up, miles it seemed, to view the world from the height of his saddle.

Lost in that secret world, he never noticed Georgina come to him, became aware of her only as she slipped an arm around his shoulders and pressed her cheek to his. He tried hard to compose himself, but the flashes of memory were disconcerting, unconnected, and incomplete. Turning to Georgina, he buried his face in the crook of her shoulder, against the silkiness of her hair. It was impossible to speak, impossible to express the anguish he felt, the riot of emotions to which those sudden revelations gave birth. He was beginning to understand what he had never been able to grasp before, and it was painful, in a deep, wrenching, physical way.

Like a wounded man, he clung to her. "Hold me," he whispered, "don't ever let me go . . ."

The sister on duty that day was on relief from another part of the hospital. Not knowing her, Liam was able to report with a series of half-truths which seemed convincing enough. Having the previous evening's record book before her, she accepted his explanations with no more than an expression of sympathy at the state of the weather. Another Australian, she loathed these London fogs herself and dreaded the coming winter.

With a sigh of relief, Liam let his stiff facial muscles relax, going into the kitchen to see whether he could beg a cup of tea. It had taken him more than two hours to get back, almost an hour since leaving Georgina at Vauxhall Bridge, and he had just missed the usual midmorning drink. Breaking off what she was doing, one of the young nurses put the kettle on the stove to boil.

"Heavens," she exclaimed, peering up into his face, "you look a bit peaked this morning. Did you have a bad time getting back? Wasn't it *terrible* last night? I got lost, just trying to find the nurses' home! Did you set off from your relatives' house, or not even try?"

"Didn't even try," he said, clearing his throat. "We were having tea and talking, and never noticed it getting worse. Then I went to the door, and everybody said it'd be folly to set off and I'd better stay the night. I'm glad I did, otherwise I don't think I'd have made it. It was bad enough this morning."

"Very wise. Kelly and McLaren didn't get back till half past ten from Stockwell—they'd been wandering around the back streets for nearly three hours! And the terrible trio spent the night on the floor at Horseferry Road—found their way that far, but couldn't get any farther. Awful."

Liam sipped his tea and listened to a few more horror stories, glad to know that he was not the only one missing from the ward last night. Now that they were returning to the fold, the wanderers would relate and embellish their stories with gusto, while his tale of a night spent with relatives would be far too dull to provoke interest. It was a relief: Not only was he incredibly tired after not much more than three hours' sleep, the emotional upheaval that followed seemed to have drained his mind completely. He felt incapable of rational thought, and had only one idea in his head: to escape to the library as soon as he had eaten, find a quiet corner and a comfortable chair, and *sleep*.

Feeling much improved by suppertime, Liam turned in to bed early, making a good book his excuse for not wanting to share in a game of cards or billiards. The concert which had been booked that night for the Great Hall was canceled due to the continuing fog, and there was an air of restlessness about the ward, raised voices that had the night sister out of her office on several occasions, telling them all to remember those less fortunate. But there was nobody really ill among them; in fact their number had been reduced to eighteen, most of them fitter than Liam and just waiting for their cards to be marked *convalescent*.

Keen though he had been to elicit some leave, he was now back where he had begun: uncertain as to his feelings and praying for a little time to adjust. Although he read for more than an hour, the subject matter provoked rather than settled his mind, and it was difficult to sleep. He was beset by too many new impressions not least of which being that sense of things *coming together*, which had gripped him so forcibly that morning. Loving Georgina, he had been concerned primarily to avoid unpalatable consequences for her, and while his physical need was great, the very last thing he wanted was to leave her with a child. Had it not been for that consideration, he knew he would have made love to her fully with no compunction whatsoever. He loved her and, had it been possible, would have married her; the fact that they were brother and sister had no real meaning for him. That was the trouble: He had never been able to accept it. If he had, Liam reasoned, that innocent, boyish passion would have died years ago.

But it was hard to avoid the parallels between making love to her last night and being brought face-to-face with other realities this morning. Love and pain, past and present, York and Dublin, had all made themselves felt in a peculiarly harsh way, as though two rusty, long-unused parts of his life had suddenly meshed together with a great grinding of cogs and levers, jerking him forward to a point of new perception.

It was not a comfortable sensation. He had moments of gratitude and others of intense irritation when he wished it would all go away and leave him in peace. In bed he wanted to think about Georgina, idly to dream about the hours they had spent together; he wanted to savor each precious moment, every new discovery. Yet as soon as he relaxed, it seemed something else came into his mind, like the visits Robert Duncannon had made to York when Liam was very young, or the occasion of his fifth birthday, when his mother and Edward had been married.

Because that memory was so clear, he gave in then and let his mind settle on that for a while: the party, the surprise at coming home from school to find Aunts Emily and Blanche gathered there, everyone's bubbling happiness. Having always thought that party was for him, Liam had felt betrayed when he found out; yet now it seemed a necessary deception, the only way to explain the celebration to three innocent, talkative young children. People must have assumed, for long enough, that Louisa and Edward were married, just as he had assumed that Edward was his father.

When had that happened? He could not recall when or how or why he had abandoned his memories of Dublin and Robert Duncannon, but in the light of Georgina's recollections, he wondered whether at two years old the shock of being wrenched away from things known and loved had had anything to do with it. That dawn parting on a bleak quayside had marked her very deeply; and although he did not recall clinging to her and being dragged away by her aunt, Liam had suffered with her as she told the story. What he did remember, very vaguely, was arriving in the dark of a winter's night at a strange house, and strange people whose accents he did not understand. He remembered crying with fear and loneliness. But another incident much later stood out very clearly, and it was a memory which had returned that day at the Maddox farm, when Ned bent to examine the horse's legs. Even now Liam could see Robert Duncannon doing the same thing, and as he rose, saying wistfully, "You don't know what to call me, Liam, do you?"

How true! he thought painfully. Standing before that imposing man, the child had been so frightened, so guilty in the knowledge of his own disloyalty, so confused by that sudden and unlooked-for return.

Did I know then who he was? Liam wondered. But he could not be certain; only emotion remained, and even that was fading fast with this strange new ability to accept old truths. And he could accept them now only because he had begun to understand.

But truth, as ever, was a double-edged sword. If memory had at last consented to show him the indissoluble link which existed between himself and Robert Duncannon, then it had also revealed the connection between himself and Georgina. There was suddenly less pleasure in recalling that long night of love and mutual exploration, and the arousal it produced was tinged, very definitely, with unease.

When he did sleep, it was not to dream of any of those things, but to experience again, for the first time in weeks, another terrible nightmare about Pozières.

26

*I*t was a strange, unsettling week. For three days the fog lingered in a claustrophobic blanket that did nothing to ease his introspection or sense of guilt. When he was not hugging the stove on the ward, Liam was in the library searching for fresh books to read, and when he was not reading, he was busy writing letters most of which he destroyed.

To whom could he confess, to whom turn for advice? No one, that was the short and simple answer, and yet he had never felt more in need of help. There was no escaping the fact that what he felt for Georgina, what they had already shared, was incestuous; and the matter of incest was taboo, with church and state and society unanimously sweeping the whole subject beneath a dusty carpet of ignorance. He looked back on the hours spent with Georgina in this ward, these grounds, under the eyes of both authority and friends, and knew he could never, ever, confess what was between them. Not to anyone.

It would have helped if he could have seen her, to talk over the things that kept going around in his mind, but the weather resolutely prevented that. He found himself praying, with the fervor of a fanatic, that Sunday would be clear enough for them to make their planned assignation.

Another nightmare about Pozières woke him in the early hours, but in the trembling, sweating aftermath, he heard the steady drumming of heavy rain on roofs and windows. It cleared the sulfurous fog, leaving the morning bright and new-washed, raising everyone's spirits like a breath of spring. There was almost a fight for passes that afternoon, but Liam was lucky, and a little after one he was on his way to meet Georgina at Vauxhall Bridge. Within the hour they were climbing the stairs to her apartment, and despite his creeping feeling of guilt, very shortly after that he was again making love to her.

The bedroom smelled of roses from a bowl of potpourri on a chest near the window, and her skin gave off a similar fragrance, as though she liked to wear, and be surrounded by, a constant memory of summer. She reminded him of summer days, of those last glorious weeks he had spent at home before the war—open cornfields beneath a wide blue sky, the warmth of gentle sun, and larks singing with blithe unconcern. She was warm and happy and giving, allowing nothing to mar their brief time together, allowing nothing to intrude. Relaxed, breathing gently, she lay along the length of him, her long and beautiful legs entwined with his, face hidden in a curve of his shoulder, hair lying in glinting strands across her back. He wound the long, silky hair through his fingers, heartbreakingly aware of her beauty and the love they shared. But for him the innocence was gone. He knew the depth of his desire and he knew it should have no place here, felt it like a weight at the core of his being. Yet he could no more stay away, he thought, than sprout angel's wings and he would go on seeing her, go on loving her like this, for as long as it was permitted.

Sensing that difference in him, Georgina stirred and asked what was wrong. He shook his head, said it was nothing, but she was not convinced. Eventually, with much hesitancy, he did manage to put into words what he had been trying to write without success for days. Going back to the moment of awareness, that moment when he had finally been able to accept the truth of who his father was, he tried to explain this sudden sense of guilt; and in the telling of it, it seemed to Liam that they had been shown a glimpse of paradise only to have it snatched away.

He found himself thinking of that book he had found the other day in the library. Not a child's book, that translation of the *Rubaiyat*, with its references to wine and love and all-powerful destiny; a man's probably, left behind in sudden departure and no doubt much missed. It was not new to him; he had first come across a copy years ago at home and read it with interest but little understanding. As he read those lines again, however, they rushed back like old, familiar music, pulsing with meaning and fresh significance, doing their best to defy the sense of guilt. What they could not defy, indeed what they underscored, was the fleeting passage of time, brief moments of beauty lost forever in death and decay.

Was that why he dreamed of the war?

"What is it?" Georgina murmured. "What else is bothering you?"

Liam shook his head, reluctant to upset her further, but again she pressed him until he quoted the one line that kept repeating itself over and over in his mind like a haunting refrain.

"One moment in annihilation's waste, one moment of the well of life to taste . . .

"And it makes me think of you, and a place on the Somme that doesn't even exist anymore. It's just a name—Pozières—that's all it is, a name, and a shifting wasteland of grit and ashes. It used to be a village on a hill . . ." He closed his eyes. "I dreamed about it again last night . . ."

She did not speak, but hid her face against his chest while Liam stroked her hair and the smoothness of her back. "*Annihilation's waste,*" he repeated, "that's what it was. A wasteland. Nothing. Pounded to oblivion, with men beneath it. And every time another shell landed . . ." He shuddered, unable to give voice to that vision of burial and disinterment, the shifting shell holes and mind-shattering noise, the dust and ashes blowing in the wind.

With suddenly trembling fingers he reached for his cigarettes and lit one, drawing smoke deep into his lungs, releasing it slowly as tension disseminated throughout his body. He continued to stroke her hair, finding consolation in its warmth and softness, and something of healing in her tears.

"But you, my love," he murmured with bleak simplicity, "are like that *'well of life'* to me. You've given me so much, restored me, made me whole again—and I love you so much, it *hurts*."

Back at the hospital that night, Georgina spent a long time staring into the darkness, her cheeks wet with tears, her heart aching for him. His memories and regrets bit deep, and it seemed painfully ironic that he should have come to awareness so suddenly, and through loving her.

What he needed was time to assimilate these things, but time was something they had so little of. That was her one, lingering regret, although unlike Liam she had been aware of it all along; and that sense of time running out had pressed her most dreadfully, contributing—she could see it now—to the urgency of physical need. That, she did not regret—it seemed to have been essential to them both—and in thinking about it, Georgina had no sense of guilt, only grief that it could not go on forever.

On the Thursday, which was her day off, Liam telephoned to say that he could not get a pass to come up to town, and without one he would have to report in by half past four. Although he wanted to break the rules and take the risk for an hour of her company, Georgina felt bound to dissuade him. Anxiety had dogged all day, inexplicable and without apparent foundation, yet very real. It was with some difficulty that she persuaded him to stay where he was, and let her come to him.

Saying little, they went out for a walk, each terribly aware of the other, wanting so much more than the chaste kiss of greeting and the respectably linked arms that propriety demanded. More than ever did Georgina realize that they would have to find a meeting place, somewhere within easy reach of both Lewisham and Wandsworth, sufficiently anonymous for them both. It was the last day of October and they had, perhaps, a few more weeks in which to be together; it seemed very important not to waste them.

It was beautiful across the common, very cold and still, with a faint blue haze of woodsmoke drifting through the trees. On the way back, they sat for a while by the old windmill,

watching an elderly gardener raking up leaves, savoring between them an air of sharp nostalgia, of the last days of autumn,
with winter waiting on the threshold. The trees were bare and
the sky had a strange, translucent beauty; everything seemed
clear and poised and not quite real. Georgina felt it echoed in
herself, in a heightened awareness of the falling dusk, her own
stillness, and Liam's quiet presence. Catching his glance and a
slow, intimate smile, her eyes lingered on the lines of his face,
the sweep of heavy lashes, the firm chin, and well-shaped
mouth; and within her came a stirring that was at once both
deeply sexual and deeply grieving. Knowing his strength, she
had a sense too of his fragility, and that exquisite, momentary
happiness that he had talked about, moving on to realms unknown, horizons unseen.

It hovered on the edge of agony, that blend of spirit and
sensuality; and the moment of awareness seemed like a threshold, a pause between day and night, autumn and winter, perfect past and uncertain future. But as the shadows lengthened
and uncertainty took hold, a sudden, violent shiver dispelled
it. Liam took her hand and caressed it, and he was warm and
vital and full of concern.

"You're cold," he said gently, "and I think we
should go . . ."

She had to go back to the flat for her uniform, and as she came
up the stairs she was astonished to see the door standing open
and her father's servant coming out with what looked like an
empty trunk. Too astonished to speak, she simply nodded and
gave a feeble smile as he passed and said her father was inside.

Pausing, she had a frantic moment. Imagining the scene
had she been in bed with Liam when her father made his
unannounced arrival, her breath caught, then she wondered
whether the place was truly tidy, whether Liam had left anything behind to raise awkward questions. Still puzzled by the
fact that her father was back today, instead of next Monday,
as yesterday's letter had indicated, she stepped across the
threshold.

They both uttered their surprise together but neither
laughed. After a brief embrace, Robert commented again on
her arrival at such a time, and Georgina was forced to give a

somewhat convoluted account of her day, including the fact
that she had been to Wandsworth to see Liam.

"And how is he?"

With the uneasy feeling that her father could see right
through her, she tried to appear nonchalant. "Well, he seems
quite well, but I suppose the doctor must think otherwise, or
else he wouldn't still be there."

"And what about you?" he asked. "Are you home for the
night or going back to the hospital?"

Because she was rostered for an early duty the following
morning, she had intended to return that evening, but something about her father's eyes—something in his whole de-
meanor—prompted her to say that she could stay if he wanted
her to do so.

His glance, as it rested on her, softened into gratitude.
"Yes, Georgie, I'd like you to stay." He pressed her arm, became suddenly brisk, pouring drinks for the two of them even
while she removed her coat and hat and went into her bedroom
to check swiftly that all was well. An empty matchbox in the
wastepaper basket seemed the most damning evidence and she
snatched it out, thrusting it deep into her pocket. Nothing else
was out of place.

Accepting a glass of sherry, Georgina went to sit down
beside the freshly lit fire. When Robert's servant had left them,
she said, "And what brings you home so early, Daddy? Your
letter said Monday."

She was part prepared for something unpleasant, but
oddly enough she never thought of Robin. When her father
said that he had been injured, it was a great shock.

"How? I mean, how badly is he injured?"

"Leg wound—I don't know any more than that." Robert
drank most of his brandy in one gulp, splashed some more into
the glass, and came to stand before the fire. "Some bloody place
on the Somme—I forget the name of it. A raid on enemy lines,
apparently—company commander bought it, and another officer, and a couple of men."

"Including Robin." She felt sick, thinking of the mud, already notorious on the battlefields, all that ghastliness infecting
an open wound. Much would depend on how rapidly he had
received attention, how close they were to a field hospital; but

even so, he would be lucky to escape without the complications
of gangrene. Too familiar with the results of that, she took a
deep breath and released it slowly. "When did you find out?
Where is he?"

"Still in Boulogne, I think, and I gather he'll be there for a
while. I imagine they'll send him to one of the Yorkshire hospitals, but I don't know. I'll try to establish what's happening,
tomorrow. I got the message yesterday morning and managed
to get a letter off to Louisa straightaway—then spent most of
the day trying to organize my affairs so that I could come home.
However, I'd planned to take Letty down to White Leigh on
Friday . . ." His voice tailed away, his eyes staring, unfocused,
on the fire.

"How is she?"

"Oh, you know—her arthritis playing up again, but otherwise all right. William seems set on drinking himself to death
though—and God knows what's happening to the estate.
That's why I wanted to go down. But he's lost interest, Georgie,
lost interest completely. And as for Dublin . . ." With a great
sigh of weariness and despair, he lowered himself into the chair
facing her.

Looking at him, at his hair which was now almost white,
and the lines of sadness in his still-attractive face, she was
struck by sudden guilt. Since Liam's return, she had given
Ireland barely a passing thought. With a sigh to almost match
his, she said, "I am sorry—it's all such a terrible mess, isn't it?
Everywhere you look. What's happening to the world, I often
wonder . . ."

Robert shook his head. "I don't know, Georgie, and that's
the truth. I can't see any hope at all—that's the tragedy. As you
say, Ireland's in a shocking mess and I can't see it getting
better—and the world's in a worse state, but what can any of
us do? We're just a bunch of old men," he rumbled grimly,
"trying to rein in a team that's bolted. We're old and feeble,
and all the young men—all the ones who might have saved
us—they're all dying. Every last, decent one . . ."

He was bitter and despairing, and it showed in his face.
Hurt by her father's pain, unable to offer any consolation, Georgina looked away.

For a while they both stared into the fire, occupied by

miseries collective and individual. She was thinking about Robin when her father expressed the dismal hope that the injury might act as a catalyst.

"How do you mean, *catalyst*? I don't understand."

He sighed. "I mean that I hope it will act on this ridiculous situation—drag Liam out of his self-imposed exile, put him on better terms with his mother."

That stabbed to the heart. For a moment Georgina sat very still, torn between two very distinct loyalties. The matter of Liam and his mother had weighed on Robert for years, and Georgina had promised—an age ago, it seemed—to act as conciliator. Although she had done little to persuade Liam, if her father were looking for catalysts, then he need search no more.

"I don't suppose you've got any further with him, have you?"

The choice of phrase, she felt, was unfortunate. While she bit her lip, wondering what to tell him and how to explain it, the heat of guilt grew in her breast and spread to her face.

On a deep breath, struggling for equanimity, she said, "I think I told you in the beginning that it would be a long process, and that you'd have to have patience—but yes, I think the message has finally gone home."

Robert stared at her, his blue eyes suddenly bright and full of wondering hope. "Good God Almighty," he murmured, "how on earth did you manage that?"

That too was a phrase that jarred, and tiredness made her sharper than she intended. "I didn't manage anything," she retorted. "I told you he would come round to it in his own good time—and that's more or less what happened."

Irritated by her father's scrutiny, she went to pour them both another drink.

"Well? Aren't you going to elaborate? I'd like to know what he said—"

"At the time," she declared crisply, "he didn't say very much at all." Needing to think, playing for time, she handed Robert his glass and took hers over to the window. It was dark outside, and for a minute she watched the feeble lights of passing traffic, wondering how much she should tell him, balancing loyalty to Liam against her father's need, which at the moment was great.

"He brought me home one afternoon last week—my last day off. We'd been up to town and I was tired—not feeling very well. So he brought me home in a taxi and came up with me to make sure that I was all right." She frowned and rubbed her forehead. "It was as he was leaving—your bedroom door was standing open, and he saw that portrait of Louisa by your bed. He went in to look at it—I didn't try to stop him—and he saw the other photographs too. He seemed most upset."

"And?"

"I don't know—it's difficult to explain. It just seemed to bring things home to him, that's all. We didn't talk about it then. Later, when I saw him, I had the impression that he was viewing things differently."

Turning, looking back at her father, Georgina said, "He had already come round to the idea of seeing his mother again, and was talking about the possibility of getting some leave—although that still seems doubtful. But you see, what he couldn't accept—what he didn't want to accept, for some reason—was the fact that you were his father. He has accepted that now. I don't know what he thought before, but until he saw that photograph, I don't think he ever understood how much you loved Louisa . . ."

Robert glanced away, cleared his throat, made quite a play of searching for his cigars. A moment later, from behind a fragrant cloud of blue smoke, he said huskily, "I'd dearly love to see the boy. All these years, Georgie, and we've never had the chance to talk . . .

"Do you think we might get together?" he asked. "Do you think he would agree?"

In that moment, she had a sense of something being over. Those precious weeks, which circumstance had decreed should be theirs alone, would never be repeated. The demands of family, halted until now, were about to press forward over Liam's horizon. If only for Robin's sake, he would allow himself to be drawn back into the family circle, which of late appeared to include her father; and she, Georgina, would have to relinquish him.

Shaking her head, blinking away the tears, she said with difficulty, "I never asked him that. But I'm sure you'll see him sooner or later. It's inevitable, really . . ."

27

*L*iam was in the library the next morning, not reading but gazing absentmindedly from the window and thinking about Georgina, when a messenger came looking for him.

"For God's sake, smarten yourself up," he hissed, "you've got a visitor—a full bloody colonel from the War Office. What the hell have you been up to?"

He felt the blood rush hot into his face and then drain slowly, leaving a clammy chill in its wake. For several seconds, while his mind worked overtime, calculating and discarding facts and suppositions, he could not move. His companion from the ward nudged him, none too gently, and thrust a comb into his hand.

"Here—rake that thatch of yours. And do up a few bloody buttons!" He twitched at Liam's jacket, glancing over his shoulder. "I'm sure he was following me down the stairs . . ."

An icy calm settled over Liam. The Colonel was supposed to be in Ireland, and whatever had brought him back and prompted this visit, it was hardly likely to be good news. And he had seen Georgina yesterday—thank God, not at the flat, but still . . .

Feeling like a man awaiting execution, he smoothed his hair, straightened his tie, and slowly fastened his jacket. Vaguely aware of other men in the room, browsing along shelves, quietly reading, Liam took comfort in the thought that he could hardly be hauled over the coals in here; if the colonel wanted to reduce him to the level of a naughty child, he would have to choose a different venue from this.

The thought was barely formed when the door opened, and for the first time he looked on Robert Duncannon knowing that he was his father.

It was a strange feeling. There was apprehension and a certain amount of dread, an involuntary knotting in the pit of his stomach, residue of the hate with which he had lived for so long; but there was, too, a sense of recognition. The last few days had opened Liam to so much, and he was aware now of things in himself that had their origins with this man and no other. It was fleeting, but it quelled the antagonism, leaving part of his mind free to register other things.

The past three years had left their mark. Robert Duncannon looked very different from the man Liam recalled. Hair that had been iron-gray had now turned almost silver, and, like so many others, he was thinner. But if the uniform and that loss of weight made him seem taller, it also struck Liam that he had lost his air of invincibility. Despite the marks of rank, he was a man like any other, not an ogre, not an enemy, but a human being as fallible as himself.

From his position against the window, Liam watched him stand for a moment, scanning every face, then he turned and their eyes met. Almost in spite of himself, Liam came to attention, as did the man at his side; but then a slight smile softened those stern features, and the Colonel approached to extend a hand in friendly greeting.

"Well now, Liam—how are you? It's been a long time."

As they shook hands, from a corner of his eye Liam was aware of a startled glance before his companion ducked away. Robert Duncannon seemed not to notice but continued to clasp his son's hand for a long moment. Had his life depended on it, Liam could not have spoken and, like any good soldier, left it to his senior officer to suggest that they sit down and talk.

Even in those first seconds, although there was tension

between them, it was apparent that there was no antagonism on his father's side, and with Georgina at the forefront of his mind, Liam released a slow breath of relief. For a while, too, it seemed the visit was no more than a social one, an impulse long delayed by circumstances and pressure of work. It was almost credible. They talked of this and that, the weather, the war, Liam's state of health, nurses in general and Georgina's working hours in particular. As the coiled spring in Liam unwound, and he began to respond more naturally, his father gradually brought the conversation around to family and the real reason for his visit.

The news of Robin's injury was put with tact and restraint; nevertheless, it was a shock. The lack of detailed information left him imagining too much.

"Come on," Robert said briskly, "let's take a walk outside. We can smoke, and that will do us both good, I think."

It was a relief, anyway, to be moving. Hunched against a cold, easterly wind, the two men paced the gravel paths and smoked Robert's cigars. The situation struck Liam as so unlikely that he wanted to laugh. There were very few men about, but when they came upon a couple of his wardmates, having a quiet smoke in the shelter of the chapel wall, Liam could contain his amusement no longer.

"I'm sorry, sir," he laughed, "but if anyone had told me that I would be taking a walk in these grounds with a British army colonel, and smoking his cigars, I'd have thought they were mad."

To his surprise, Robert laughed too, and for a moment there was such closeness between them, they were almost like friends.

"Considering our collective reputations," Robert remarked, "the situation does have its elements of farce. But I would hazard a guess," he added dryly, "that when you return to your friends, you may have to suffer for this meeting . . ."

"Perhaps so. I shan't mind it."

"No?"

Shrewd eyes looked him over, and Liam laughed again, ruefully this time. "I've suffered worse."

"Yes," his father softly remarked, "I'm sure you have."

They walked for a while in silence until Robert broke it with a suggestion that Liam might like to visit his brother once he was settled into a British hospital. "I know you've applied for home leave and been refused—but give it another couple of weeks and apply again. By that time we should know what's happening with Robin, and you may well be fit to travel, of course."

"I feel fit enough now."

"And to me you look it," Robert agreed. "But you know what these medical chaps are—like to have the whip hand. If they still want to be awkward, I shall have to see what I can do—and if it comes to it," he added with smile, "I dare say we can always wangle some leave for Georgie and get her to travel with you . . ."

Liam's heart leapt, and he could not meet his father's eyes. He was almost abrupt in his dismissal of the idea, and yet the thought of traveling with her, of spending two or three days in her company, filled him with guilty delight.

"Well, we'll see what transpires. I may even take some time off, too. I haven't had any leave to speak of for the last couple of years . . ."

There was awkwardness, but it was mysteriously ironed out. Liam was granted forty-eight hours' home leave and released into the care of a trained nursing sister—Georgina—and her father, Colonel Duncannon.

Ready and waiting for them just before midday, he was subject to the kind of ribbing he had endured at the time of Robert's first visit—and more than a few sneers. "It's all right for some" seemed to be the general tone of it, issued in varying degrees of envy. Although it set him apart from the others, he could tolerate that; what he could not ignore were the slanders heaped upon Robert Duncannon because of his rank. Liam was astonished at the level of anger they provoked in him; even more so to hear himself defending his father in much the same way as Robin had done some four months previously. Yet it was not that he saw him as being suddenly perfect—he was still aware of the other man's shortcomings and an arbitrary manner that took little account of other people—but Robert

Duncannon was his father, and Liam had accepted that, and it made all the difference in the world. He might still criticize the man himself, but he would not have others do so.

Of course, he could not admit to the relationship. As far as anyone else was concerned, they were uncle and nephew, and Georgina was still his cousin; but with her connections revealed, he was no longer teased about her devotion to him.

The journey north was a trial, however. Liam was so afraid of betraying the intimacy between them that he spent most of the journey staring out of the window or pretending to be asleep. His uncommunicative mood was taken for natural anxiety about his brother and apprehension at the forthcoming reunion. Despite the Colonel's assurances, and a letter from his mother saying she was overjoyed at the thought of seeing him soon, Liam could not help worrying. He kept thinking, too, about his last few hours at home, about reactions that had sent him fleeing to the far side of the world. Now the pain had gone, it all seemed so extreme.

He was rather surprised not to have been interrogated about that. In a subsequent meeting with his father at Queen's Gate, the past had been referred to, but although Liam had steeled himself, the questions never came. Indeed, it was with uncharacteristic difficulty that Robert Duncannon broached the subject at all. And it seemed he had done so only in order to apologize.

"We must all of us," Liam remembered him saying, "seem so inadequate—your mother, Edward, and myself. And yet we only did what we thought was best at the time. Other than being totally frank with you all from the beginning—and given the circumstances, Liam, that was very difficult—I can't see what else we might have done. None of it was intentional—and I know your mother well enough to say that she was only trying to protect you. She didn't want you—any of you—to suffer the slur of illegitimacy. And whether it was right or not, Edward and I went along with that.

"But still, I haven't forgiven myself for calling on your mother that afternoon. I'll be honest—I wanted to see her, and for no other reason than the pleasure of her company. But she was not pleased to see me, and ultimately, we argued. And that was the argument you overheard. I'm sorry. Believe me, I am very, very sorry for that . . ."

And with a swift glance at his face, Liam had believed him. It was impossible not to. But in that moment he had dreaded any reference to the subject of that quarrel and, in order to deflect it, broke in with acceptance of that apology, and his own assurances that he understood.

For a moment he had endured a very searching glance, but the only questions that were asked were with regard to his mother. How did he feel about seeing her again, and had he forgiven her?

He had, of course. Having now added the sin of deceit to all his other crimes, Liam was no longer standing in judgment on even the smallest omission. The thing that still hurt was his blood tie with Georgina; had it not been for that, he could have loved her without deceit, taken her as his wife, and looked forward to some kind of future. With her beside him, nothing else would have mattered. But—and his practical mind always came back to this—had his mother never met Robert Duncannon, he, Liam, might never have been born. And even if he had, his world and Georgina's were so far removed, it was unlikely that they would ever have met. And try as he might, Liam could not regret the joy of her, would not willingly have lived without knowing that.

For much of the journey, his mind was a vortex of conflicting emotions, and the only thing that he was truly glad about was the absence of his other sister. Tisha had gone up to York the week before but would be staying with Aunt Emily in Leeds while Liam was visiting. That, at least, was a blessing. He did not think he could have coped with her sharp eyes and tactless observations. Robert and Georgina planned to stay at a hotel in town.

It was dark well before they approached their destination, and after what had seemed an interminable time, Liam was surprised to feel the pull of that long curve, and to hear the guard shouting, "York—this is *York*—change here for Scarborough, Whitby, Harrogate . . ."

As those old familiar names caught him, Liam rubbed the window. The train slowed to a squeaking halt. Through the grime he could just make out dim lights and bobbing heads along the platform. Then Robert lowered the window and hailed a porter, and Liam saw the bold sign on a vacant seat—YORK.

Home. It affected him more deeply than he would ever have believed. He took in the cast-iron railings of the barrier, the wooden stationmaster's office, and the clock by the steps. It was after six, and that slow journey via sidings and wayside halts had taken five and a half hours. Cold, sooty air assailed his nostrils as he stepped down onto the platform; behind her father's back, Georgina pressed his hand and he smiled at her briefly.

They took a taxi to Harker's Hotel, and ignoring all protests, Robert paid the driver to take Liam on to Clementhorpe. "Nonsense," he declared, "we're supposed to be looking after you—and if I thought you wanted our company, I'd have insisted on seeing you to the door."

Liam was grateful. "I'll see you both tomorrow, then?"

"Yes, make it about half past ten—that should leave us time enough to get to Leeds and have something to eat before we go on to the hospital."

They shook hands. For a second, Liam was nonplussed, wondering how to part from Georgina, but she squeezed the hand he held out to her and reached up to kiss his cheek. "Best of luck," she murmured, and waved as the taxi left the curb.

By the feeble light of gas lamps, York seemed no different from the city he had left, but it disturbed him nevertheless. Needing to find his emotional bearings, he dismissed the taxi by Skeldergate Bridge and walked the last few hundred yards along the riverside. The scent of the river was the same, dank and cold, racing along with winter rains, carrying with it the mustiness of flour mills and sawed timber from warehouses on his right. Winter-naked trees reached up into the night, and a chill wind increased the tension within him. Too soon, it seemed, those ancient elms gave way to a line of spearlike railings, railings that he had painted in that summer before the war . . .

It was too much. Shivering, he stopped to light a cigarette, absorbing the dark mass of the cottage against the night sky, two downstairs windows lit, and the half-perceived forms of shrubs beside the path. It seemed he had lived a lifetime since that summer dawn, changed beyond recognition from the boy he was then. What changes would he find within?

The kitchen curtains were not quite drawn. Caught by a movement, his eyes studied the gap. He moved close, paused by the railings, and on an impulse, climbed over them, not trusting the gate. Edging carefully between the shrubs, he reached the side of the house and the path that ran around to the kitchen door. As he expected, the rear curtains were not drawn at all, and he could see his mother in profile, bent over the stove. She looked anxious for a moment, closed the oven door, set down her cloth, and pushed back a strand of hair. It was a gesture he remembered well. Flushed by the firelight glow, her face seemed just the same, the cheekbones a little more noticeable, perhaps, but she had not really changed at all.

A great wave of relief swept through him, releasing the tension, leaving him weak as a child. He leaned for a moment against the wall, eyes closed in silent gratitude; only as he moved did he realize that his lashes were wet. He brushed at them roughly and took a deep breath; like going over the top, this would have to be done quickly or not at all. Passing close to the window, he tapped lightly on the door and then walked in.

Although he was expected, a look of incredulity swept over her. For a second she clung to the edge of the table, swaying a little, then, as he took a step toward her, she moved. He thought she was going to embrace him, but she stopped short above a yard away, stiffly, just looking at him, every conceivable emotion chasing across her features. Then she burst into tears, hiding her face as those great, heaving sobs racked her body.

"Mother . . ."

Equally distraught, for a moment he was afraid to touch her, and when he did, she was so stiff in his arms he thought she would never unbend, never forgive him.

"Please—don't—I'm *sorry* . . ." He kept repeating the words, over and over, while the harsh sobs shook him. She felt so small to him and fragile; he could feel the bones of back and shoulders hunched beneath his hands and it frightened him. He had never known her to weep like this. To him she had always been so calm, so strong.

But just as he thought the sobs would never stop, they did. She hugged and kissed him, and hugged him again; her tears wet his face, but she was smiling, her sobs more like little laughs as she struggled for control. Liam hugged her to him, then, burying his face against her shoulder, for a full minute he wept like a child. She soothed and petted him, and he was vaguely aware of a door opening, then quietly closing again.

His mother sat him down in her chair, close to the stove, and as he searched his pockets, handed him a handkerchief. "Here—take this—you always did lose every handkerchief I ever gave you . . ."

He laughed weakly. "No, I have got one somewhere . . ." but he took the one she gave him, wiped his eyes and blew his nose, and everything was suddenly all right, the kettle was on, tea was being made, and his mother was smiling, telling him that she had made his favorite, a shin beef stew with lots of vegetables; the savory dumplings were ready to go in . . .

"Go in and see your dad," she said, arranging things on a tray. "He came in a minute ago but didn't want to intrude. I'll bring the tea."

In Edward he did see changes, saw them instantly in pallor and slowness of movement as the older man rose to greet him. He was a year or two over sixty, and for the first time looked that and more. As they embraced, Liam was aware that time, for his adoptive father, was running out, and the awareness stabbed at him.

"It's so *good* to see you." There were a couple of betraying tears, brushed hastily away.

"And you, Dad . . ." For a while they just clasped hands and looked at each other. "How are you?"

"Oh, not quite as tough as I used to be—but all the better for seeing you!"

Liam glanced around. As he came in he had noticed the single bed, standing at the back of the room where Edward's desk had always been.

"Yes, it's a damned nuisance, but we had to bring Tisha's old bed down here for me to use. I don't seem able to manage the stairs these days . . ."

That weakness evidently annoyed him, but in the next

moment he was praising Louisa's care, saying she should have been a nurse; and that despite the chronic wartime shortages, she worked wonders with fuel and food. "And she works so hard—out in the garden all weathers, digging and planting, hoeing out weeds. The way she goes at them, you'd think each one was a German with a gun!" He laughed. "But she seems to thrive on it, I don't know why."

"She always did love her garden," Liam said, smiling.

"And you," Edward said. "She always loved you . . . I'm so *glad* you've come home . . ."

What threatened to be another emotional moment was saved by his mother's arrival. The tea was sweet and strong, its freshness an exquisite pleasure after the stewed and adulterated brews he was used to; and although there were more vegetables than meat in the meal they shared later, it was the best food he had tasted in months.

Afterward, they sat by the fire, talking, until Edward's eyes began to droop, then Louisa boiled the kettle again and put hot-water bottles in all their beds while Liam volunteered to do the dishes. Once Edward was settled, however, the two of them sat in the kitchen until well after midnight, discussing his illness and Robin's wounds, and the girl to whom he had become quite seriously attached.

Liam remembered her well, a pretty girl of about his own age, with striking, red-gold hair. Before the war, Robin had been a particular friend of her brother, Freddie, but like so many others, he was dead now, killed on the first day of the Somme. Robin had been writing to Sarah Pemberton since he joined up—or rather, his mother pointed out dryly, she had been writing to him—but since his leave at Christmas, it had become more than just a casual friendship.

"She's been visiting him, which I'm glad about, because I haven't been able to get to Leeds more than once a week. With your dad not so well, it's been a bit difficult, but they say they'll be moving him over here, to the military hospital once he's a bit better."

"And how is he? What do the doctors say about that knee of his?"

"Well, he's made good progress, apparently—he's had a

couple of operations already, as you know, but it's healing well. He won't lose the leg," she added tersely, "although he may never walk properly again."

"If you ask me," Liam remarked, "that can only be a good thing. If he can't march, Mother, the army won't want him back."

"But—"

"But *nothing*—he's done his bit, he's been in it since the very beginning, and after what his lot went through, he's lucky to be alive. But if he could march with the best of them, Mother, they'd drag him back tomorrow." With anger inside him, Liam shook his head. "Just be thankful."

"I am. I am thankful—most particularly to have you here, and in one piece." She pressed his hand. "I was so *afraid*—so afraid . . ." Unable to finish the sentence, she looked away and dabbed hurriedly at her eyes.

"I'm all right," he said gently, "I'm the lucky one." With a confidence he did not feel, he added, "If I could come through Gallipoli without a scratch, then I can survive anything. The proverbial bad penny . . ."

His grin provoked a smile. "You can be as bad as you like—just stay alive!"

But that made him think of Georgina, and his eyes slid away. His mother knew of occasional visits and had expressed gratitude as well as concern. She knew, she said, just how wearing were the journeys, particularly on top of hard work and other responsibilities; and it was a pity that Tisha could not have stirred herself more often. But it seemed his sister was expecting a baby, which excused much. The news was a surprise to Liam, and an obvious pleasure to his mother, so the topic of Tisha and her husband and the forthcoming child occupied them for some time.

But just as he was yawning and saying that he really must go to bed, his mother returned to the subject he had been trying to avoid all evening. After a brief inquiry as to the arrangements for next day, she said, "By the way, I do hope you managed to get over that—well, that fancy you had for her once. You did, didn't you?"

She almost caught him off guard. Only because he had been expecting something like that, did he manage a light laugh. "Oh, Mother—that was years ago. I've known a lot of girls since then."

There was relief and approval in her smile. "Well, I thought you must have, but I had to ask." With a teasing twinkle in her eye, she asked, "Nobody serious, then?"

Liam stood up, taking their cups to the sink. "If it's marriage you're talking about—no. Time enough for that when the war's over."

Edward had been to the hospital to visit Robin the week before with Tisha; the tiresome journey and the fact that several were going made him glad to bow out this time. Or so he said. Liam knew that had he been able he would have gone to see Robin any day of the week, but it was neither practical nor sensible. Aware that he had so little time in York, Liam promised to spend the evening at home and found himself concentrating very much upon the leave he would have once he was declared fit.

"It may be no more than a week, I don't know, but I should get something—I haven't had leave as such since I joined up in 1914. Anyway," he promised, "whatever I get, I'll spend here, with you."

Edward tried to be dismissive but he was grateful, Liam could see that. It reminded him most painfully of years that he had to make up to them both.

At last, his mother was ready. She was wearing a hat and coat that he did not recognize, not fashionable by Tisha's standards but smart. As she pulled on her gloves and checked the furl of her umbrella, he said how attractive she looked; his comment produced a little flush of pleasure from her and a smile from Edward. Before they set off, the older man cupped her face between his hands and kissed her tenderly.

"Give Robin my love. Tell him I'll try to see him soon . . ."

She hugged Edward, kissed his cheek. "I will, dear. Have a rest this afternoon—we were all up too late last night."

On the way to the hotel, it struck Liam that it would be the first time that he had seen his mother and father together since that afternoon before the war. For a moment he wondered about their present relationship; Robert Duncannon was the one person she had not talked about last night, and he wondered what she felt for him now. It occurred to him that perhaps she was suffering a certain embarrassment, trying to compose herself before meeting her ex-lover under the eyes of her son. Just as he was trying to compose himself before meeting Georgina. That idea suddenly amused him, so that he, at least, arrived in a more relaxed frame of mind.

If there was any constraint on his mother's part—and Liam was far from sure that there was—then Robert Duncannon was singularly unafraid of showing his affection. He kissed her warmly on the cheek, held her for a moment, and smiled at her as though she were the only woman in the world; then he told her that she was looking wonderful. Her response to that was not a blush but a glance of amused irony; and while she was prepared to walk beside him, she refused his arm. Far from being put out, Robert simply laughed. They seemed to know each other very well, which given the years between rather surprised Liam. What surprised him more, however, was the realization that it was such an exclusive knowledge. Robert could not resist trying to tease and charm her, while she, with the benefit of past experience, constantly strove to put him in his place. Something about this exercise—albeit reluctantly on his mother's part—amused them both, so that they both seemed so much younger and more alive. Liam thought it extraordinary, until he recalled that other occasion, when he had been angry and jealous, rubbed all the wrong way because of a vibrancy between them that he simply did not understand. Now, he saw that it was involuntary, and was no longer embarrassed. He was even a little amused by it.

Walking behind, he glanced inquiringly at Georgina and saw that her thoughts echoed his. "Have they always been like this?"

She suppressed a smile. "Not always, no. But when Father is happy, he can charm the birds from the trees . . ."

"Yes," Liam murmured dryly, "I'm beginning to understand that."

"And when he isn't . . ." For a moment she left the sentence unfinished, then glanced up at Liam. "You haven't seen the other side of him. When the mood's on him, he can be impatient, overbearing—quite insufferable." She shook her head. "So different from Edward."

Liam nodded. "I was just thinking that." Pondering the strangeness of life, he shook his head. His mother had been happy with Edward, he knew that. Looking back, he could see the richness of contentment and knew it was not just a hazy, childhood memory, but truth indeed. Even recently, when she had obviously shouldered several burdens, there was still a tenderness between those two that spoke of limitless understanding.

And yet, watching her now, she almost sparkled. It caught at him, and without wishing to be disloyal, he could not help feeling . . ."It's a shame, isn't it?"

"What is?"

He shrugged. "Well, that they never married."

But Georgina could not agree. "Oh, Liam, don't be misled. Father's a bachelor—always has been and always will be. He likes his freedom and being on the move. He was never happy in one place for long. But Louisa—well, you know her, she loves her home and her garden and having family around her." She shook her head, sadly. "He never really wanted that . . ."

As they came to the bridge, the open vista of the river caught his attention and he paused, musing for a moment. "Was that it then? What made them part?"

"Essentially, yes."

"So you don't think . . ."

She shook her head. "No, I don't. Not really."

They moved on, and with a safe distance between themselves and the older couple, Georgina said, "If Louisa were free—which she isn't, and has no desire to be—I could see them coming to some sort of *arrangement*, eventually."

"But not marriage."

"No, I can't see them marrying. They know themselves and each other too well." A little later, she said, "Does that bother you?"

Liam smiled and pressed the hand on his arm. "No. Nothing like that bothers me anymore."

Relaxed in the knowledge that his parents were largely too taken up with each other to spare keen eyes for their offspring, Liam enjoyed the journey and his lunch. Georgina was smiling too, chatting to Louisa as though it were no more than a convivial day out. That changed, however, as they drew near the hospital. His mother became rather taut and brisk, explaining that Robin was still confined to bed, still in a lot of pain, and that they would probably have to go into the ward in twos.

"Perhaps if Liam and I go in first . . . ?"

Robert was in full agreement. "Of course. We don't want to overwhelm him . . ."

Wooden, temporary structures had been built adjacent to the main hospital, and Robin was in one of those, a good five or six beds down from Sister's office, which was a good sign. Or should have been. Laid back against the pillows, with his ruffled hair no more than a charcoal smudge against the surrounding whiteness, he seemed barely there. The little mountain of a protecting frame beneath the blankets dwarfed him. Remembering his last sight of Robin in the square at Albert, Liam was shocked; and his brother's smile, such a pale imitation of that other smile, was almost more than he could bear. Blinking rapidly, for a little while Liam had to let his mother do the talking.

Robin pressed his hand. "You look disgustingly fit for a sick man," he said with an echo of his old spirit. "How are you?"

Still wearing hospital blues, Liam felt like a malingerer in this surgical ward, where the majority were so obviously ill. Forcing a smile, he said shortly, "As you say—disgustingly well. I just wish I could persuade the MO of that fact. I might get some proper leave then."

"Don't rush it," his brother said, echoing Georgina's sentiments. "It'll come soon enough."

Liam knew what he meant, but their mother's presence precluded talk of the war. He wanted to know about his injury, the action that had led to it, but did not like to ask. He would, later, when he had more than just this day and could visit Robin on his own.

They stayed for about half an hour, then left to allow the others in. With an eloquent gesture to Georgina as he strode past her in the lobby, Liam went straight outside. His mother came to stand with him for a while, but it was cold, and he was too upset to speak. She went inside, and a little while later Georgina came to join him.

"It didn't seem fair to take up so much visiting time—I thought I'd let Louisa go in again."

Liam lit another cigarette. "What did you think?"

"I had a word with Sister before we went in—he's doing all right."

"But you—what did you think?"

She pressed his hand and looked away. "It was a shock—seeing him like that, yes, it was a shock. Dear Robin . . ."

He wanted to hold her, needed the physical comfort she always gave. The impossibility of it made him swear, eloquently, under his breath. Abruptly he turned away, pacing afresh the few yards between hut and railings. Georgina stood quite still, watching him.

"Father's taken a week's leave," she said as he returned to her side. "He wants to stay on in York for a few days."

His heart leapt at that. "But I thought we were all going back to London together?"

"Apparently not. We shall have to make do with each other's company . . ."

"Then for heaven's sake," he murmured huskily, "let's take an early train."

The general uncertainty of traveling times made an early start advisable. They were at the station by half past six, but so were a great many others. Despite the First-Class tickets purchased by Robert Duncannon, when the train pulled in from Newcastle, they could not find an empty compartment.

"We're going to have trouble with me in this uniform," Liam muttered, spotting several staff officers in the forward section of the train. There had been a few quizzical and disapproving looks on the outward journey, but the Colonel's presence had forestalled comment.

"We won't get a seat anywhere else, though," Georgina pointed out. "Standing room only, by the look of things."

In the end, they found a compartment with two elderly clerics and an iron-faced lady whose sweeping glance would have withered a sergeant major. Georgina's youth and nursing sister's uniform attracted benevolent nods from the elderly gentlemen, but they were obviously not quite sure what to think about Liam. The distinctive hat with its rising sun emblem had, thanks to the British press, become synonymous with bravery, and had he worn officer's insignia, they would have been delighted to welcome him. The corporal's stripes on his heavy jacket threw them a little, however; apparently he was in the wrong section of the train, but they were too polite to say so.

Not so the lady with her feathered toque and fur stole. With her umbrella, she tapped him, none too gently, on the knee. "Young man—this is *First Class*."

Her attitude annoyed him. For her, and people like her, his friends were dying, his brother injured. He considered the polite reply and then discarded it in favor of colonial innocence. While Georgina smothered a smile, he glanced round at plush seats and linen headrest covers, the beveled mirrors below the luggage rack, and nodded approvingly. "Yes, ma'am, I'd say it is and no mistake. 'Fair dinkum,' as we say back home."

With that he took a seat facing Georgina, maintaining a poker face.

"You'll know about it, young man, when the guard comes round!"

Liam nodded politely and stared out of the window. It was still dark, but as the train jerked and shuddered its way out of the station, he saw the first fingers of a gray dawn above the city walls. A savage amusement prevented any feelings of deprivation, however, and he knew he would soon be back for a longer stay.

A few minutes later the guard arrived. For the benefit of the female dragon next to him, Liam went through a mime of alarm while the others had their tickets checked and clipped, even kept the guard waiting in weary impatience before producing that precious piece of card.

"Jeez, thought I'd lost it. Here we are, mate—clip that!"

With stony indifference, the guard did so, tipping his cap perfunctorily as he moved on to the next compartment.

Abandoning that strong Australian accent as soon as the door closed, he leaned confidentially toward Georgina and, in a very passable imitation of a British officer, said, "You know, for a minute there, darling, I really thought I'd lost that ticket."

He had the satisfaction of seeing one clergyman's shoulders shake, and the other hide his smile behind a copy of *The*

Times. He did not turn his head to look at the woman next to him, but he could feel her indignation.

Georgina said under her breath, "You're very wicked." But her eyes were dancing as she said it.

It was impossible to conduct an intimate conversation, so they said very little, but after the strain of guarding even their eyes, it was a relief to be able to look at one another without concern for other people. Liam wanted her so much he ached with it, and by her eyes she wanted him too. During the whole of that journey they were alone for no more than a few minutes, but it was time enough to say what was in both their minds. When they arrived at Kings Cross they headed straight for the nearest hotel. It was more awkward than before because Georgina was in uniform. This time she made the booking and, with the excuse of a train to catch later that night, paid in advance; Liam went into the bar, sidling up the stairs when the clerk's back was turned. On the third floor she was waiting for him, anxiety and impatience written into every line.

He reached for her even before the door was closed, crushing her into his arms, raining hungry, demanding kisses onto face, hair, and mouth, while she struggled to unfasten her cape and his jacket, and close the door behind them. In privacy at last, she gave up, opening her mouth to him, responding to that fierce hunger with a need of her own. He loved kissing her, loved the feel of her teeth and the honeyed sweetness of her tongue; but the soft interior of her mouth made him want to enter her in other ways and that need was becoming very difficult to control.

As he began to tug at the stiff collar of her dress, she forced herself away from him. "Liam—we have to arrive looking as though we've just stepped off a train—" She paused, gasping a little, holding a firm hand against his chest. "Let me take off my own clothes—let me *fold* them, please."

He laughed, a little shakily, pecked at her lips, and began to undress. Folding his own uniform, he watched her do the same, knowing she was teasing him a little now, and loving it. She came to him and he kissed her breasts, running his hands down over hip-bones and haunches to cup the soft flesh beneath. His words, as he pressed himself against her, were explicit as were hers in reply, but it was becoming part of a ritual, a sort of vicarious satisfaction, and he did not want that. Almost roughly, he pushed her onto the bed, kneeling over her before she could rise. "I mean it," he said.

But it seemed his intensity killed something. Her desire seemed to evaporate before his eyes. "All right then, go ahead . . ."

Her acquiescence was feigned, he knew that, and he could no more have forced her than slapped her face. With a defeated sigh he collapsed on the bed, cradling her in his arms. "Darling, I'm sorry . . ."

She was more upset, kissing him, fondling him, despairing at the lack of time and the need they both shared.

That despair tinged the rest of their lovemaking, bringing them closer in anguish than in joy. Afterward, holding her, Liam found himself thinking that it would always be like this: stolen moments in anonymous places, longings that turned to ashes, and a love that was set to break both their hearts.

28

Queen's Gate, SW.
November 28th

My Dear,

What a pleasure it was to see you again and, despite the circumstances, to know that you are happier than when last we met. Robin is improving and in such good hands will continue to do so, of that I have no doubt; and to see Liam again was for me a pleasure, so for you—well, I could see the happiness in your face.

He is a fine young man. You have every reason to be proud of him, you and Edward both. I had so little to do with his upbringing, I claim no praise at all. As his mother, you will, I dare say, see changes in him that I have missed, but I do not think he is the worse for them. If he has suffered from the war, then I am sure that it has also matured him, and it strikes me now that his willingness to understand is a direct result of that. I know that war altered my perception, all those years ago in the Sudan—but it came a little too late, didn't it? I thank God that it was not too late for Liam.

I was pleased to have Tisha's news too. Rest assured
that in the absence of young Fearnley, I shall keep an
eye on her as much as I can. It will be strange to have a
grandchild. Here I am, approaching fifty-five years old and
yet—at the moment, anyway—feeling no more than half
that.

Yes, it was good to see you, and this run of good
news and good luck is uplifting after all the gloom and
despondency of this year. I hope and pray that it continues,
and that Robin makes a swift recovery. He will, I am sure,
and although the army is unlikely to want him back, that
strikes me as being the best part of all. I never thought I
would live to say a thing like that, but I am truly sick of all
this death. We need our young men, but I have my moments of wondering whether Sir Douglas realizes that.

I may be talking treason, my dear, so perhaps I had
better close. My regards to Edward—he seems much better
for seeing Liam, and I'm glad to have been instrumental in
that—

Ever yours,
Robert

It was hardly a love letter, yet its warmth touched Zoe. Since
1900 he had written infrequently, and nothing survived of his
correspondence before that date, but what Louisa had kept
glowed with affection and regard. Reading those letters had
changed Zoe's view of him entirely.

"You really loved her, didn't you?" she said to the photograph on the bookcase. "All those years—she must have been
quite a woman."

Not for the first time, Zoe regretted the lack of anything in
Louisa's hand. It was like being party to only half of a fascinating conversation, and always there was the desire to hear the
other voice, share the full exchange. As it was, Louisa Elliott
remained a partly perceived, enigmatic figure, while the only
living person to have known her remembered her best in old
age, when the temperament and passion of youth had faded.

Sighing, Zoe studied her collection of photographs, all copied from those Stephen had let her bring to London. They had become so familiar, it sometimes seemed they were more alive than members of her immediate family, scattered across the south coast. That sense of living presence worried her occasionally, making her wonder whether the obsession was becoming unhealthy; but the intimacy of those letters, their verve and individual style, made the writers seem so very much alive.

Had she been a contemporary, such glimpses into their private lives would never have been allowed; nor would Zoe have desired it. It would have been like reading her father's correspondence or invading her mother's private life. And whereas she had no desire to know such intimate details, she did want to know what had driven Robert and Louisa apart in the mid-1890s, and what had really transpired between Liam and Georgina. More and more was she sure, despite the lack of hard evidence, that those two had been lovers.

Two dates in Liam's diary, at the end of October, were underlined, along with four more in November and December; yet they contained no more information than the initial G. On previous occasions he had noted that *"G visited today"* or *"Went up to town with G."* The lack of detail was significant in a diary that contained references to food, weather, the quality of a concert, and places he had visited. Only during that two-day visit to York was there a similar lack of comment. *"Went to Leeds to see Robin. He seems in a poor way just now"* was the sum of it. No mention of the reunion with his mother and Edward, nor of the journey north with Georgina and Robert Duncannon. It was as though he could not bring himself to write about emotional matters, or that he was for some reason afraid to do so; instead there was just an *aide de memoire*, a brief comment, or a solitary initial.

Had he come here, to see Georgina? Zoe was sure he had. Why else the dreams?

Basically it was the same dream, with variations, many times repeated. Always Liam, always in uniform, always here. To begin with she had hardly recognized the flat with its dark furniture and old-fashioned decor, and it was a long time before she realized that the setting of the first dream was in fact her bathroom. That long room with its single tall off-set window, had contained a single bed, shelves full of books and photographs, and a washstand with a rose-patterned bowl and ewer. In the dream she paused in the doorway, surprised to see Liam stretched out on the bed, fully dressed in uniform and boots. His hat was on the bedside chest, and his attitude was one of immense sadness. He did not speak, simply lay there, head back against raised pillows, eyes watching her, following every movement she made.

Zoe was herself in modern clothes, and she knew that this was her own time, seventy years on from his, despite the heavy Edwardian decor of their surroundings. Her initial astonishment and dismay turned to a need to comfort and reassure; but her most powerful awareness was of love flowing between them.

That sense of loving was present in every subsequent dream; together with his silent presence, it never changed. What did change was the flat itself, and the change was coincident with the spine-tingling discovery that Georgina and Robert Duncannon had lived here during the First World War. After that, the rooms in the dream became recognizably her own, even down to the spacious bathroom with its airing cupboard and shower cubicle, and matching, biscuit-colored suite. The old fittings had been ripped out before Zoe moved in, and her father had asked her advice on color and layout. At the time, neither of them had given a thought to what the room had been originally.

She knew now. When Georgina had shared this flat with her father, that tall, off-set window had sported elegant drapes, with a chest of drawers beneath it, a bed to one side, a washstand at the foot, and a wardrobe behind the door. It had been the room where Georgina slept.

Had Liam slept there too? It was a question which came frequently to mind, and no amount of rationalizing on Polly's part could sway Zoe from the conviction that Liam was trying to tell her something about his relationship with Georgina. She constantly reminded Polly, whenever the subject came up, that she had dreamed of Liam in the flat *before* she discovered Georgina's address. But as Polly pointed out, she had been obsessed with Liam long before that.

Was it wish fulfillment? Or did the essence of the man live

on, enabling him to enter her sleeping mind, flooding it with certain images, leaving clues for her to follow?

If that was so, then Zoe had to admit that the clues were obscure. She wished he would say something, but he never did; he simply watched and appeared to listen to the incongruous nonsense she uttered. She had seen him in her kitchen as well as the bathroom, standing there smoking, and looking vaguely lost; she had seen him by her desk, gazing out of the window into busy Queen's Gate.

Waking that morning at the beginning of August, Zoe retained an image of him sitting on the edge of her bed, staring at a photograph in a large silver frame. He was partly turned toward her, head bent, fair hair falling forward across a furrowed brow; and the image was so clear, his distress so real, she had reached out to touch him even before she opened her eyes.

As ever, he eluded her. The image went, and as she opened her eyes she saw only the empty, familiar room, the large wardrobe, the matching Victorian chest, a couple of Pre-Raphaelite prints on the wall, and her favorite photograph of Stephen in a wooden frame on her bedside table.

She had taken it herself, on the city walls near his flat with the Minster in the background. He was smiling at her, as though trying to remind her of happier times they had spent together in York. But it all seemed so long ago, so unreal, even less substantial than the dream which had just faded from her grasp.

York. Stephen was no longer there, but the city was. Glancing back at the photograph, just for an instant it seemed to Zoe that Liam was smiling, beckoning her away.

Telephoning Joan Elliott, Zoe hoped that she would suggest Stephen's flat as an overnight abode, but apparently some old-fashioned sense of propriety prevented that, and she was forced to contact the hotel on Gillygate, keeping her fingers crossed that it would not be fully booked at the height of the tourist season. She was lucky, Mrs. Bilton had a single room available, the same one Zoe had used before; and after that friendly conversation, she found herself more pleased than sorry. After all, Gillygate had been Louisa's home for some twenty years before

she and Edward moved out to Clementhorpe, and knowing so
much more about the family gave the small hotel even greater
significance.

With her ancient Renault recently serviced and running
sweetly for the first time in months, Zoe decided to drive up to
York, taking the A1 as far as Stamford, then motoring at a
leisurely pace through the sleepy country lanes of Lincolnshire.
It was not an idle choice: In a village south of Lincoln, Louisa's
mother had been born, and from another village nearby, Louisa
had received letters from a cousin, John Elliott. Zoe felt it was
a fair assumption that the Elliotts had spent at least a couple of
generations in that part of the country, probably farming, and
wanted to see the area for herself. It was the day to do it too:
good harvest weather, with an arc of blue above and billowing
white clouds along the horizon. The fields were gold with
wheat and barley, acre after acre rolling away across gentle dips
and rises, marked by crumbling walls and ancient hedgerows,
the towers and spires of village churches standing clear from
dark pockets of trees.

The roads wound tortuous routes round woods and fields,
became village streets, and returned to leafy lanes. Fortunately
the traffic was light, and she was able to drive slowly, pulling
in whenever another car nudged impatiently from behind. She
wanted to absorb it all. A minor road took her from Sleaford to
Metheringham, the place of Mary Elliott's birth, but just before
it she had the surprise of Blankney, a model village of quaint,
neo-Gothic cottages set either side of the main road. From here,
John Elliott had written to his cousin in York. It gave her a
strange feeling. The church, heavily restored, was still in occasional use, but the Hall, to one side and at the head of a curving
drive, was in the process of being demolished. Wondering why,
and hating the sight of those broken walls, she turned her back
on it, staring out across the road at what must have been a
sweep of parkland and was now the rising slope of a golf course.
A patch of woodland on the crest caught her eye, and she stood
looking at it for quite some time, although she could not have
said what it was about it that made her want to go there.

She glanced at her watch: Past one o'clock already, and she
had to have lunch and make her way to York. There was no
time to go strolling across the golf links just to explore a belt of

trees that was no different from all the other woody thickets she had passed on the way here. Nevertheless, she had a strong feeling that she must bring Stephen here; then, with a shrug, Zoe went back to her car, parked at the junction of a small side road.

A signpost indicated that the little lane would bring her into Metheringham, which it did, into the village street itself, with the church set back on one side and a couple of inns punctuating the curve of cottages, shops, and small businesses that seemed to form the heart of a spreading community. Although it was quiet here, with a hot, noonday stillness, Zoe sensed the presence of natural, homogeneous life, so different from the sterile precision of Blankney only a mile away. And the small pub facing the church boasted upward of a dozen customers, most of them with plates as well as glasses before them. She ordered a smoked mackerel salad, which was both generous and good, and a glass of orange topped up with ice and soda. Considerably refreshed, and with a little time to spare, she decided to have a look at the church. It was locked, a sad reflection of the times, and the exterior told her very little. In some disappointment, Zoe walked around it, studying gravestones here and there, looking for the Elliott name but by no means expecting to find it. Under the east window, however, were a whole row of them, dating from the 1870s back to the beginning of that century, their names engraved on crosses and arched stones, "In Loving Memory" and "Sacred to the Name of . . ." interspersed with biblical quotations.

Her knowledge of village burials and rituals was virtually nonexistent, yet as she gazed at other stones, their positions and styles, it came to her that to be buried so grandly, and in such a prime place, these Elliotts must have been people of some substance. Were they Tisha's family, and Liam's? Were they the grandparents and great-grandparents of Edward and Louisa? It was impossible to prove, just looking at these monuments, but she had a powerful feeling that they were her people, and Stephen's, and that one day, perhaps when he came home, they must return here together, and search the parish records.

She left them in their undisturbed peace, left them to the sun and the birds and the gentle rustling of the breeze in tall trees, and something of that peace settled with her as she headed out on the Lincoln road.

The city, topped by its magnificent cathedral, climbed the ridge before her, dominating the broad agricultural plain in a far more dramatic way than York; and yet there were similarities enough to catch her eye, to make her think of Roman legions building major defensive strongholds on that ridge, and then again, seventy miles to the north, in the fork of two rivers at Eboracum. Norman overlords had seen the same advantages as had medieval merchants and the princes of the Church; and in the last century, something had prompted at least two members of the Elliott family to leave one cathedral city for another.

The landscape changed around Scunthorpe and Goole, becoming markedly industrial, but then she was into the Vale of York, flatter than Lincoln, but not so different. Ripening wheat fields stretched out on either side of the road, and the fields and hedgerows were riotous with scarlet poppies.

She arrived in York just before five, amid the bustle of homebound workers and a crawl of cars and bikes down Gillygate. There was a long-stay car park beyond the junction with Lord Mayor's Walk fortunately remembered from her last visit, and with a sigh compounded of relief and pleasure, Zoe stepped out onto the tarmac, fished her overnight bag from the Renault's backseat, and gave the little black car a pat for not letting her down. The smile stayed all the way down Gillygate as she joined the hurrying feet, feeling part of the city's life, part of its people, its solid stone pavements, and its air, which was golden with dust. It was, Zoe, decided, unbelievably good to be back.

Mrs. Bilton greeted her like an old friend, made her a pot of tea, and sat with her for a few minutes in the front parlor. When she had gone, Zoe found herself staring at the fireplace, thinking of Edward and Louisa, and Mary Elliott who had left her home in the Lincolnshire countryside to live and eventually die here. She thought of the children too as she climbed the stairs, passing rooms any one of which might have been their nursery; and then there was Robert Duncannon, to whom this house must have been very familiar.

So many coincidences. And in the beginning they had been

astonishing, but as time went on they began to seem almost normal, part of a distinctive chain that had forged its original link at her meeting with Stephen Elliott. But was that really so? Zoe asked herself as she paused on the landing. It was the first in *her* life, but the links in the chain seemed to have been forged long before that. Perhaps the first one was made in this house.

It was an idea which seemed to come from nowhere, an idea that took root as she stood before an open door and gazed into a spacious bedroom with two long windows and a pretty Victorian fireplace on the far wall. The windows were open and looked out on to Gillygate; she could hear the passing traffic and snatches of conversation from people in the street. This had been Mary Elliott's home, but it had also been a hotel. Had Robert Duncannon stayed here? Was this the place where Louisa met him for the very first time?

It was a warm evening, but Zoe was suddenly cold all over; hairs pricked at the back of her neck and along her arms. Rubbing them, she hurried up to the next floor, dumped her bag, and went straight down again, pausing only long enough to note that the door which had been open was now closed.

Refusing to entertain the thought that it had opened and closed of its own volition, she hurried out into the busy street, and following the directions Joan Elliott had given her, headed straight for Walmgate.

Away from the town center it was quieter, with Fossgate practically deserted. The elegant span of Foss Bridge crossed a narrow river which boasted nothing busier than a flotilla of ducklings bobbing their heads beneath the still green waters, while farther on Walmgate itself sat peacefully behind a façade of respectable shops and offices, now closed for the evening. In one guidebook Zoe had read that a total of twenty-six inns and alehouses were doing business during the street's notorious heyday in the last century when the area was a mass of medieval slums. That disease-ridden, cheek-by-jowl poverty was hard to imagine now with the slums cleared years ago and many of the shop fronts being renovated to the same standard as Gillygate; but here and there stood ancient, sagging buildings, apparently untouched for a century or more.

The public houses, she noticed, were reduced to two, and while memories of the area's unsavory reputation still lived on—Joan Elliott had been eloquent on the subject before she moved—much new building had taken place within the city wall. Joan's new flat was on the first floor of a three-story block, small but practical, and with a view of the inner face of Walmgate Bar.

She apologized to Joan for the unexpected visit and, explaining why, said they would meet, as planned, for lunch the next day. For the time being, however, she was anxious not to stay very long.

"I don't know if you recall, but in one of those trunks you gave Stephen, there was a large, leather-bound visitors book. We only glanced at it and put it back with all the other books, but I seem to think it covered several years, and I'd like to have a look at it. Really, I'd like to look at it now, if I may, that is, if you don't mind me having Stephen's keys for an hour or so. Or if you have time, perhaps you'd like to come with me?"

"Oh, I don't think so, dear. Not this evening—it's a bit warm for me to want to trail up there. Besides,"—she smiled, a little guiltily—"I like to get my feet up after tea and watch *EastEnders*! No, you take the keys—bring them back tomorrow when you come—I'm sure Stephen won't mind. After all, if he didn't trust you, he wouldn't have given you the letters to sort out, now would he?"

Zoe suppressed a smile at Joan's belated logic, realizing that it had never occurred to her to offer the facility of Stephen's flat for the night. Had she asked, Zoe might have stayed there. But in Stephen's flat would she have thought to check the old visitors book? Probably not.

At half past seven, the warmth radiating from mellow brick walls in Bedern was still considerable; Stephen's flat was hot and airless, and the first thing Zoe did was to open all the windows. For some minutes, however, she stood looking out at the evening light and lengthening shadows, the play of rich color across stone and brick and tile. She was reminded of that first evening spent with Stephen, how they had talked while sitting here and looking from this very window. They had watched the colors change and the shadows fall, and seen the last of the light reflected in each other's eyes.

Abruptly, she turned away. Moving from room to room, she was aware of how strange the place felt without him, like

a time capsule, she thought, finding one of her earrings on the
bedside chest. And suddenly she was reliving that last evening,
the harsh words and the tears, and that brief hour of passion
before the mad dash to Teesport. Three months ago, and it felt
like forever; yet every word, every gesture, was etched indelibly
upon her mind. If she lived to be ninety and never saw him
again, Zoe knew that last, long night would remain with her,
together with the sight of him waving from the deck of the
Damaris.

She mooned around the bedroom, touching his belong-
ings: a bolas from South America, a Japanese earthenware bowl
holding shells and bits of coral; a carved ebony mask and a
framed batik print from Africa, which she had always admired,
and a laughing Buddha in jade that had been given to Stephen
as a parting gift by a Chinese crew. With his tremendous rolls
of fat and all-embracing grin, the Buddha was symbolic of happiness and good fortune, and even in her presently dejected
state, he managed to raise from her a small, wan smile. No
wonder Stephen kept him.

In a long, built-in wardrobe, a row of suits and shirts and
jackets still retained a faint scent of their owner, and Zoe gathered them toward her, laying her face against the fine, soft wool
of a black doeskin jacket. Only as she opened her eyes did she
notice the row of solid brass buttons, and four shiny gold rings
on the sleeve.

She dropped the uniform as though the thing had bitten
her, in that moment hating all it represented: his job, the war,
the danger in which he stood. Anguish and longing fused into
instant rage, and she swept everything back with a curse, hating everything that had taken him away, accusing him, cursing
him, demanding of his possessions *when*, when would he be
coming back . . .

Giving way before her fury, several things fell off their
hangers; she sank down after them, bundled on her knees in
the bottom of the cupboard. Rage was pursued by an acute
sense of futility, and hot, angry tears flowed for some time.
Sniffing noisily between muttered pleas and accusations, Zoe
eventually pulled herself together, replaced the clothes in their
proper places, and went to wash her face. Dragging a comb
through tangled hair, she braided it back and told herself there

was work to be done. It might well take all night and she had no idea as yet whether she was chasing an illusion.

Putting Stephen and his bedroom behind her, she made a pot of tea and took it into the spare room. She found what she was looking for straightaway, among books and albums and bound Victorian journals. The visitors book was large and heavy and had the name of the hotel engraved and gilded on the cover. Probably Edward's work, she thought, remembering the albums and Liam's diary with its gilded initials on the cover. Somehow that realization calmed her, as though Edward's reassuring personality was imbued in the things he had touched.

Deciphering other people's handwriting was a lengthy task, but eventually, working back through the entries, Zoe found what she was looking for. At the beginning of 1892, a full two and a half years before Liam was born, Robert Devereaux Duncannon had stayed at the hotel on Gillygate. The how and why of it eluded Zoe, but as she stared at that entry, she was convinced that that was the date of Robert and Louisa's first meeting, the beginning of an affair that had led to love and children and parting—and the dreadful combination of circumstances that drove Liam and Tisha away, and Liam and Georgina into each other's arms.

The tragedy of it oppressed her. As she packed the items away and straightened the bed on which she had been sitting, Zoe wondered whether she really wanted to know these things. Looking into those trunks had been like opening Pandora's Box, with all the joys and miseries of the past released to obsess and engulf the present. If she had been lonely in her ignorance, Zoe felt that knowledge had not brought happiness. Indeed, the brevity of what she had enjoyed with Stephen, which had seemed so right to begin with, now struck her as being no more than a tantalus with which to torment herself.

Closing the windows, taking a last look around, she wondered whether she would ever see the flat again. Of course she would write to Stephen, tell him of her latest discovery, but would it matter to him? On the knife-edge between living and dying, how could any of this matter?

Back at the hotel, Zoe went straight to her room, but it was a long time before she slept; next morning, feeling lethargic but in need of fresh air, she headed for the riverbank, intending to take a quiet stroll away from the crowds before meeting Joan Elliott for lunch at one. The pleasure boats moored near Lendal Bridge were a tempting diversion, however; when she saw that their excursions lasted an hour and included a view of Bishopthorpe Palace from the river, it seemed an excellent way of spending the morning.

Several people were already gathered on the upper deck, and within ten minutes the boat was ready to sail. An occasional but not intrusive commentary from the helmsman pointed out buildings of interest, which between Lendal and Ouse Bridges rose sheer from the waterline. Arched and gated entrances, with steps leading up into blackness, were all that remained as evidence of once-extensive river traffic.

Converted warehouses reared beyond Ouse Bridge, and facing them on the left, the open staithes and fine houses that had so pleased her on her last visit with Stephen. Then there was Skeldergate Bridge, flanked by trees on one side and a rise of new buildings on the other. In trying to place for her the approximate position of Louisa's cottage at Clementhorpe, Stephen had described the line of factories and warehouses that had formerly stood on this spot. Beyond, the riverside opened out into a tree-lined path which now led to the Rowntree Memorial Park, created after the First World War.

"Unfortunately," he had said that afternoon as they strolled along the path, "in buying up the land, I gather from Joan that they also bought the freehold of Edward and Louisa's cottage. Edward didn't own it, you see—he only rented it from a landlord. But it was virtually the only habitation down here—the rest was allotments and open fields, with a tendency to flood in winter . . ."

Zoe had assumed from that that Rowntrees had forced Louisa to move from her house of some twenty years' standing; to her it had seemed a blot on the Quaker reputation, but in logging dates and addresses of all Louisa's letters, she had seen, thankfully, that Louisa had moved out of the cottage in the summer of 1918 to a house just off Lord Mayor's Walk, where she had continued to live for many years. That house was down on her list of things to ask Joan about.

The boat chugged quietly downriver, past the park on the right and New Walk on the left, "*New*" the helmsman informed

them laconically, "about two hundred and thirty years ago."
Elegant Georgian and early Victorian terraces sat back behind
the trees above that riverside path, but gradually the houses
petered out, giving way to open farmland beyond the new
ringroad. She found herself thinking of Louisa's children growing up here, and most particularly of Liam as a young man,
knowing these paths and fields and woods, the land so similar
to that of Lincolnshire. Perhaps that feeling for the land, for
farming, had always been in his blood, inherited from the Elliott
forebears. And Louisa, of course, had always had her garden.

Liam had enjoyed swimming too. His diary, she thought,
revealed two prime concerns throughout the war: food and
water. Water to drink, water in which to wash, and always the
joy when he found a place to swim. He must have known this
river well, enjoyed its cool, green depths on hot days like this.
She could just imagine him stripping beneath those trees, div-
ing in from the bank there, and surfacing, flinging back the
wet hair from his forehead, striking out with a long, powerful
stroke toward the far bank or floating downstream with the
current.

The currents here must be quite strong, she thought suddenly, noticing the bend ahead; and there, where the trees
overhung the bank, just before the rise of the Palace wall, there
would be weeds below the surface . . .

She shivered. Quite dangerous really; whoever swam here
would have to know the river, have to know his own powers
of endurance. He would have to be young and strong and very
fit. As Liam was.

Was. Had been. More than seventy years ago, before
that war.

Strangely, she had such a sense of his presence here, and
a sense of sadness too. It was so very beautiful, the river, the
trees, the mellow stones of the Palace; it must have been hard
to leave for a new world, an unknown land, a future apart from
family and friends and those he had come to love. And what
had it felt like to return? When he came back with Georgina
and Robert Duncannon in the November of 1916, and then
again for Christmas, how had it seemed to him then?

There must have been changes, particularly at home, with
Edward ill and the restrictions of wartime. Food and fuel would

have been in short supply for everyone, and in the December gloom York must have seemed a sad, gray place, a city of mourners, with all those boys of the Yorkshire regiments killed on the Somme . . . No, Zoe thought sadly, it would not have been the place he had left, any more than wartime York bore much resemblance to what she saw now.

That imagined gloom seemed to shadow the sun; a chill breeze sprang up as the boat turned for home, and within minutes Zoe was cold, glad of the light jumper she had brought but had not expected to need. In sight of the concrete road bridge, she thought it singularly ugly, and the noise of cars drumming over it acted like an insulation against the power of the past. After that, the return journey had a bleakness about it. She looked at the landscape, listened to the desultory commentary, and felt nothing at all.

Joan was pleased to see her, and in the warmth of her welcome, Zoe lost her strange mood. Objectivity returned, and with it, a sense of urgency. Her time here was limited and it was easier to glean information face-to-face in natural conversation than by letter or over the telephone. One subject led to another, prompting memories that refused to come under direct questioning; and Zoe was sure Joan knew far more about the past than even she suspected. Little things, unimportant by themselves, added up to form—if not a full picture—then a shadow, an outline, on which to base further investigation.

Over lunch she introduced the topic of Louisa and her move from the cottage to Lord Mayor's Walk. Joan was surprised by the date of it.

"Do you know, I always thought she'd moved because of Rowntrees' wanting the land. Whenever Dad took us to the park when we were little, he always said they'd lived there . . . Still, if you're right—and I'm sure you must be by the dates of those letters—then she must have left not long after Edward died. Perhaps that's why—it was very isolated in those days, and I remember Dad saying they were flooded out two or three times when he was young. Maybe she couldn't face it on her own."

"Yes, I wondered that. She must have moved out about a year later."

"I suppose she must—he died in 1917, April I think it was, the date's on the headstone."

Zoe had a sudden, overwhelming desire to see that stone. "Could we go to the cemetery?" she asked. "I'd like to see his grave."

"It's her grave too," Joan said.

An hour later, on their way to the old cemetery off Fulford Road, Zoe returned to the subject of Louisa and her move to Lord Mayor's Walk. Joan said the house had been at the Monkgate end, just behind St. Maurice's Church; but both house and church were gone now, demolished in the early seventies.

"Of course, it wasn't more than a few minutes from where we lived, which was quite handy, especially when Dad was ill. Gran often came and helped look after him—sitting up at nights, that sort of thing, so Mother could get some rest. Then, at the beginning of the war—just after Dunkirk, it was—my brother, Bill, decided he was going to join up, and after he went so did I. That left Mother on her own, and it seemed stupid the pair of them rattling around in separate houses, so Gran sold her place and moved in with Mother. They didn't always see eye to eye—two women never do, do they?—but it solved a problem and they were company for each other."

"Louisa *sold* the house? You mean she owned it, didn't rent the place?"

"No, she owned it."

"How strange—I mean because they rented the cottage, didn't they? Still, I suppose Edward must have left her quite well-placed."

"No," Joan said emphatically, "he didn't. He sold the business during the First World War—*for a song*, Dad always said—and after that there wasn't much at all."

"Are you sure? She must have had money from somewhere, if she bought that house . . ."

There was a long silence. "Well, I'm sure you're right, but I don't think it can have come from Edward."

"How on earth did she afford it?" Zoe asked, and in the next instant knew the answer. "*Robert*," she breathed. "I bet you a pound to a penny, Joan, that Robert Duncannon bought it for her!"

"Do you think so?"

"I most certainly do."

In a small, hesitant voice, Joan Elliott said, "We owned our house too. And Dad had his own business. It never occurred to me before to wonder who set him up. And somebody must have, because after the First World War it was hard for everybody. Most people didn't have two halfpennies to rub together. And Dad's business—photography—was a luxury, not a necessity, so he didn't make much." She sighed heavily. "But he always said we were fortunate, that we should count our blessings, and as children we tried to. But Mother always set her mouth at that, and I often wondered why . . ."

"Perhaps she didn't approve of Robert Duncannon?"

"Maybe she didn't. She certainly never spoke his name to me."

In the midst of an affluent society, it was hard to imagine the levels of poverty prevalent after the First World War, poverty which continued throughout the twenties and thirties with the General Strike and the Depression. Those returning soldiers, so many of them with severe disabilities, had found work difficult to find, if not impossible. The *land fit for heroes* had been more concerned with larger matters, leaving them to beg or starve in an economic wilderness. The more she thought about Robert Duncannon, the more logical it seemed that he would have done his best to provide a home and a means of livelihood for his son.

"Maybe she resented the generosity," Joan went on. "My mother was a proud woman, she didn't like to feel beholden to anybody. 'Neither a borrower nor a lender be,' was her maxim, but it was a hard world in those days, and she didn't have it easy. After Dad died she brought us up on her own, on a war pension, which was ten shillings a week then. No, it wasn't easy for her."

Remembering the stiff, disapproving old lady she had met, Zoe tried to envisage her early life and the world that had made her. It was difficult, and that memory of being disliked for no good reason did not promote the sympathy she no doubt deserved. Yet Stephen had been fond of her . . .

"Yes, I know she was funny with you, but she was old then, and the past, I suppose, was starting to be more important than the present. But she was a good mother and a good wife—she adored my father, and he felt the same way about her. When she was ill, she nursed him—and his heart was bad, you know, it wasn't just the leg. The doctor said it was the effect of all those bombardments, weakened the heart, wore it out. He was only thirty-six when he died."

Aware of her own inadequacy, Zoe murmured something sympathetic, while Joan Elliott simply shook her head, said yes, it was tragic, but many fared worse, and at least her father had known happiness with the wife and family he treasured.

"He's buried here too—with Mother."

Just inside the cemetery gates, Joan filled a plastic bottle with water for the flowers she and Zoe had bought in the market. It was pleasant in the sun, a slight breeze disturbing long, feathery grasses between graves in the old section, rustling the leaves of massive chestnut trees near the derelict chapel. Scaffolding around it signaled the beginning of work on the chapel's restoration, and Victorian monuments were obviously in the process of being cleared of encroaching brambles. In the newer sections, long grass had been cut and wildflowers encouraged to grow. Although Joan extolled the past beauty of the place, its roses and arbors and neat delineations, Zoe found its present state not unattractive.

Robin Elliott's grave moved her. He had written many letters to his mother from France, and she felt again the desperate loneliness of that young man, the forced cheerfulness of his words masking fear and horror and a million things he could never tell the people at home. But he had found his love in Sarah Pemberton, and had been happy with her. They had shared twelve years of marriage until his death in 1931, and now, as the inscription said, they were reunited. He had never disturbed her dreams, and Zoe felt he was as truly at peace as the atmosphere around his grave suggested.

She watched Robin Elliott's daughter perform a ritual that over the years had obviously been repeated innumerable times. Dead flower stalks were removed from the urn and set to one side; unwrapped, the fresh flowers were then shortened and arranged, the old stalks wrapped up with several long ends of grass tugged from around the headstone. The damp, scrunched-up parcel was used to wipe the marble base, leaving all admirably neat and tidy.

She said as she straightened, "I must remember to bring some shears next time. That grass is getting long, and they don't cut it very often."

Joan stood quite still for a moment, and Zoe suspected that this was part of the ritual too, and as meaningful today as it had always been.

"Now," she said briskly, taking Zoe's arm, "we'll go and find Granny's."

"What was she like? When you knew her, I mean. Was she very sad?"

"Oh goodness me, no. Well, I should say, not *generally*. I do remember her being sad, of course—anniversaries and Armistice Day, particularly. When Dad was alive we always went together—Dad with his walking stick and his medals, standing ever so straight with Granny in black by his side. He wouldn't march with the veterans, but he always went to the service. Mother hated it, she usually stayed at home, to see to the dinner, she said. But I think," Joan added, "it was mostly that she refused to be seen crying in public. She lost a brother, you know, at the Somme . . .

"Then, after Dad died, Granny took us. She was even sadder then, but though she cried, she said it was our *duty* to go, to remember all those who gave their lives in the war to end all wars." With a shuddering sigh, Joan shook her head.

"Twenty years—it didn't take long, did it? The second war upset her—I think, like so many more, she'd have had peace at any price. She'd been so *content*, you see, with her little house and a couple of friends she'd made who lived nearby. And my brother and I used to call from school, and then from work, two or three times a week. And she came to us on Sundays. We loved her, you see, and she spoiled us—we could always take our friends there.

"But then the war came. She couldn't believe that it was all starting again, and it's only now, when I look back, that I realize she must have imagined it being just like the first one. When my brother, Bill, joined up, it almost broke her heart—I'm convinced she thought she'd never see him again. She did, thank heavens, because he didn't go abroad until 1944. But I remember her saying to me that I mustn't let them send me to France—I must come home immediately if that was so much as suggested!" Joan laughed. "We didn't go to France, of course, but I can just imagine my officer's face if I'd told her what my Granny said!"

"Stephen told me she was a bit confused toward the end."

Joan sighed. "Well yes, she was, but not until the last few weeks. Of course she worried about everything, and as I say, I'm sure it was the war. Shortages, the blackouts, everybody in uniform. And the air raids! The sirens themselves were enough to frighten anybody to death. They had an incendiary bomb down the chimney one night—it didn't go off, thank God—Mother picked it up with the fire tongs and doused it in a bucket of cold water! It sounds funny now," she said with a laugh, "but it can't have been at the time, especially with an old lady who flatly refused to go into an air raid shelter. In many ways she was tougher than she looked, but the strain of it told in the end.

"I saw a big difference in her that last week. I had some leave not long before D-Day and came home. Granny was in bed most of the time, and obviously failing. Mother said she was always talking to Edward, and the sad thing is, when I arrived, she seemed to think I was *her* mother. Her voice was different too, lighter, younger . . ." She paused. "It was a bit unnerving."

"What did she say? Can you remember?"

Joan's kindly face seemed distressed. "Yes, I can remember. She said—'*But I loved him, Mamma, what else could I do?*'"

Zoe studied the gravel path. "No names?"

"No. Not then. I didn't know who or what she was talking about. I was young and upset for her, because whatever it was, it was upsetting her. Tears were streaming down her face."

Zoe blinked and swallowed hard. "Poor Louisa . . ."

"Thinking about it now, I suppose she must have been talking about Robert. I don't recall her ever mentioning his name, though. What I do remember is that just before I went back—the last day, in fact—she suddenly turned toward the door and said, with real surprise—"*So they let you have some leave, after all. I didn't expect to see both of you here.*"

"She seemed so lucid," Joan went on, "I honestly thought my brother had walked through the door. I turned round, expecting to see Bill, but there was nobody there and the door was shut. That did frighten me, because I thought it was Bill that she'd seen—you know, Stephen's father—and that he'd been killed."

"How awful for you," Zoe murmured. "But he was all right?"

"Yes, right as ninepence as we found out later—he came through without so much as a scratch." With a deep sigh, she said, "But my man was killed in Normandy, and although Granny never met Joe, I did wonder whether it was him she'd seen."

"Do you still think that?"

"I don't know, Zoe—I don't know what to think, after all these years. I know what you're thinking, though—that it was my father and his brother she saw."

"Robin and Liam—yes."

"Well, you may be right. She died sometime that night while I was on my way back to camp in Dorset. Just slipped away in her sleep. I never got to go to the funeral, so there was only Mother and a few neighbors and an old lady who was a friend of Granny's, somebody she used to have tea with once a week." Joan smiled. "When she came to us, you'd hear the pair of them in the front room, laughing away like girls." With a shake of her head, Joan laughed again. "I don't know what they talked about."

"The past, probably. When they were young." It was a thought that made Zoe smile, two old ladies reliving the years of their youth before the turn of the century, when the world must have seemed a different place.

As they walked the long avenue where Joseph Terry, the chocolate manufacturer, was buried, Joan pointed to his grand memorial before leading the way to Edward and Louisa's grave. It was set back from the main path, and by comparison with the Terry monument, that carved headstone of an open book was modest indeed.

Here lies Edward Elliott
Bookbinder and Poet
died 7th April 1917
aged 62

On the other page was Louisa's memorial, equally simple, giving her name and date of death, her age as seventy-seven years, and the fact that she had been Edward's widow.

As Zoe arranged her flowers before their names, she offered up a prayer for Louisa, that warm, generous woman who had loved her family and friends so much that she could not bear to part with her memories, nor the evidence of their affection. And they had loved her, that much was obvious from their letters; and if love survived—which Zoe was beginning to think it did—then why should it not be that they returned to comfort her in those last anxious days?

But she was with them now, and at peace, of that Zoe was convinced. Only her correspondence remained, revealing insights into a long life that had contained more than its fair share of anguish and upheaval. Even so, Zoe thought, Louisa didn't give in; and that awareness was reassuring somehow, and strengthening.

She gazed at the headstone, remembering the mass of correspondence relating to it: She knew how much the plot had cost and the stone itself, and had a fair idea which members of the family had attended the funeral, how crowded the service in the cemetery chapel had been. Well-known and obviously well-liked, Edward Elliott had come to his last resting place accompanied by the respect and affection of many people.

However devastated Louisa had been by his death, Zoe hoped that she was comforted by that show of affection, and most particularly by the presence of her sons. Amid the dreadful abnormality of war, fortune had decreed that both of them should be there.

29

They stood either side of her, Robin in hospital blues, resting heavily on a walking stick, Liam in Australian khaki, tunic pressed, puttees wound tightly above polished brown boots, his hat held respectfully against his chest.

The weight he had gained latterly while convalescing, had, Georgina thought, been refined during the last month's training in Lincolnshire. He looked fit, if very pale, the last vestiges of French and Egyptian sun having disappeared long ago. His hair was darker too, its sun-bleached fairness cropped by a succession of barbers and quelled today by the rain. She watched a wayward lock fall forward, as it inevitably did when he lowered his head, and almost smiled, expecting him to brush it back; but he seemed unaware of it, his thoughts reflected in strain around his mouth and jaw, and in shadows beneath his eyes.

Sadness touched her own heart too, but it was for them, that little group by the open grave, rather than for herself or Edward. She had seen so much of tragedy that it was hard to grieve for a man who had died peacefully by his own fireside after sixty good years of life. He had known the joy of reunion with Liam, the relief of knowing that Robin's war was over, and he had Tisha's news of another generation about to be born—for Edward there was no sadness, only contentment and peace.

Although she hoped Louisa felt something of that, Georgina suspected not; that was a comfort that would come with time; now she was simply bereft, cast adrift without the husband who had always loved and supported her. The future, for her, must seem bleak indeed.

That thought was not, however, one Georgina wished to pursue. If she thought about the future at all, she knew she would weep. For the moment it was enough to gaze at Liam, to feast her eyes on the sight of him after five long weeks of separation. That short February leave, spent with him in Bournemouth, had created its own particular hell, but she could not regret it. Now that the worst anxiety was past, she was glad things had happened as they did. If it had to be the last time . . .

She shivered and, with an apprehensive glance at her father, tried to discipline her thoughts. Desire, as she had so often said to Liam, showed in the eyes, and her eyes were liable to give her away. But it was so hard not to look at him; knowing she should not devour him so, Georgina blessed the rain, the essential umbrella that shielded her eyes from all those immediately facing. And they were behaving correctly, studying the crushed grass and the mud, and no doubt the state of their boots, while a surpliced parson intoned the prayers for the dead. There had been only the briefest note from Liam the other day to say that he would be here for the funeral, and that while he had expected this, it was still a great shock. It showed in his face, she thought, in a sort of frozen calm. He would be strong while it was required of him, she knew that, but still Georgina longed for the chance to offer comfort, to be somewhere private and alone where they could talk and hold each other, where the world could not intrude. The sheer impossibility of that was painful.

Someone was holding an umbrella over Louisa, high enough to shelter Liam bending toward her; and another covered Tisha and Robin. They were all very close, and as Tisha began to weep, Robin transferred his stick to the other hand, slipping an arm around his sister's shoulders. He looked close to tears himself, and the strain of standing showed so plainly in his expression, Georgina was suddenly anxious. As soon as this trial was over, he would need the wheelchair that had brought him from the chapel.

Louisa seemed composed, and alone of the group held her head up, although her eyes were closed as though in prayer. Someone moved and Georgina caught a glimpse of her hands, locked around Liam's, her arm entwined with his as though she would never let him go.

The crowd began to move, slowly and discreetly, away from the grave; the parson went to utter a few words of consolation, then reached out an arm to lead the grieving widow away. She seemed reluctant, and beside her, Georgina was aware of her father shifting uncomfortably. He wanted to go to Louisa just as much as she wanted to go to Liam, and it was very hard not to, hard to pretend no claim, no special love, hard to have to walk away.

But as Robert took her arm, Liam looked up, his glance encompassing them both; with an almost imperceptible nod he seemed to be thanking them for their presence, and acknowledging the arrangement to meet later. Someone brought up the wheelchair and Liam moved then, assisting his brother into it; Louisa turned too, and as Robin was settled, his head bent with obvious pain, she leaned down to embrace him. A moment later she embraced her daughter as well, but Tisha, stiff with her eight-month pregnancy, accepted rather than returned it. Georgina bit her lip, wishing her half sister would be kinder, but that attitude seemed to be her defense, and not even their father could penetrate it. She found herself praying that Edwin Fearnley would be granted some leave, and soon; Tisha was in need of comfort, and from him it might be acceptable.

Stealing a final, backward glance at the family group, she saw that Robin's fiancée, Sarah Pemberton, had joined them. Tall, like Louisa, but thin almost to the point of gauntness, she was nevertheless a fine-featured girl with striking hair. Although they had met only once before, and briefly, Georgina had the feeling that she was regarded with a certain suspicion. It was a shame, because she wanted to like the girl, for Robin's sake and also to build foundations for the future. Robin was important to her, and she did not want Sarah Pemberton—his future wife—to set barriers between them.

But that, Georgina reflected sadly, might have been done already. She was unsure how much had been said about their complex relationships, and if Robin, in love and trust, had revealed the truth of his background, then it might be that Sarah would find it difficult to understand. Their situation was not, after all, a conventional one, and while she could not blame him for an accident of birth, she might not wish to be reminded of it.

The antipathy between her and Tisha was mutual and obvious, but as Liam had been at pains to explain, that was a personal thing and went back a long way. They had known each other as girls and found nothing in each other to like. Tisha was younger, articulate and sure of herself; she could play to the crowd and have everyone hanging on her every word, while Sarah would stand apart, looking both regal and disdainful, until a barb from Tisha sent her away.

"And is she disdainful?" Georgina had asked.

"I don't think so," Liam had replied, laughing. "In fact, I would say the reverse. As I recall, she was always rather shy and unsure of herself. She used to come down to the cottage to buy fruit and vegetables, and sometimes she'd stay a while talking to Mother. But if Robin arrived, she'd blush scarlet and hurry away. We all knew she had a fancy for him even then."

That she loved him now was in no doubt, and that was probably the best thing about her, Georgina reflected. There was no mistaking the tender solicitude with which she cared for him, and if they married—which they would eventually, when Robin was discharged from the army—then she was sure that Sarah would protect and support him for the rest of his life. Right now he needed that strength, that sense of security, and probably always would. In that sense, he was lucky; the survivors of this war, however many there were at the end of the day, would need a brave generation of women to take up the load on their behalf, of that Georgina was convinced.

Watching her walk away, Liam took a deep breath, steadying himself against an almost overwhelming urge to call her back. He wanted Georgina beside him, needed her calm strength to bolster the fragile remains of his own ability to cope. Nor would the Colonel have been unwelcome, yet because of propriety and his mother's concern for what her sisters might think, Robert Duncannon and his daughter were relegated beyond the pale of family, and must only be seen to pay their last respects among a crowd of other acquaintances. Aunts Blanche and Emily, and that crowd of female cousins from Leeds—who had barely seen Edward for years—must come back to the cottage, partake of the funeral tea, murmur their platitudes, and be tolerated until boredom finally took them away.

Liam hated it, hated them. Pointed looks from Blanche told him he must expect a pious lecture on past sins; and even Emily, whom he had met twice in recent months, would no doubt find reasons to repeat all the unasked-for advice she had given already.

All he wanted was Georgina and a place to be alone with her. It seemed so long since her visit to Bournemouth, and since that sybaritic few days of luxury and love, he had suffered three weeks of hell at Wareham, retraining. The machine gunners' course at Belton Park, which he had just joined, was joy by comparison; the only snag was that it would not be for long. In a couple of weeks, maybe less, he would be on his way back to France, and the possibility of further leave was very doubtful. He had hoped for a day, or that she might be able to make the journey up to Grantham, but Edward's funeral made that hope remote indeed. They had both used up what days they might have begged from respective authorities. For him there had been eighteen days at Christmas between leaving Wandsworth and being admitted as convalescent near Bournemouth; and since then, after being discharged as fit, he had had six further days, three of which he had spent in an hotel with Georgina.

Looking back, he realized that only the thought of seeing her again had kept up his spirits. York was a city dressed in mourning, a sad and gloomy place where the sun seemed afraid to shine, and its depressing shabbiness was only accentuated by the pinched look of people in the streets. Middle-aged women, hardly recognizable as the cheerful mothers he had known, stopped to speak, but their initial smiles quickly faded, conversation turning solely upon absent sons and husbands. Many of his old acquaintances, it seemed, were dead; and his good fortune was so often remarked upon that Liam began to feel guilty, began to feel that he should not have come home to flaunt himself. When he mentioned it to his mother at Christmas, she said the same: that people seemed resentful that she should have two sons in uniform and both of them in one piece. Robin's injury hardly seemed to count.

Lately even the cottage had depressed him. The dankness of the nearby river, a raw wind, and a chill in the house that carefully hoarded fuel could not defeat, all conspired to dull his spirits. After years away from it, he had forgotten how bleak a northern winter could be. Warmth and brightness, which was what he remembered most about his childhood home, had been defeated by the war, but knowing that did not alter the situation. There had also been the feeling that Edward's days were numbered. Over Christmas, particularly, they had talked for hours on a multitude of subjects, and Liam was left with the realization that his adoptive father had been both kind and shrewd, the possessor of a keen intellect and a generous heart; no businessman, to be sure, but a better father would have been hard to find. It did not take long to conclude that as children they had been immensely fortunate in having Edward to guide them, and Liam's one abiding regret was that he had taken himself away from that benign influence in a fit of unjust rage. Their knowledge of each other as adults had been far too short.

That, however, appeared to be one of the penalties of war. Everything good had come and gone far too quickly, while seeming to possess a concentrated power that lingered in the memory like a warm afterglow. But happiness, it seemed, must go hand in hand with sorrow and regret. Nothing was unalloyed. But after the slow death of emotion in France, even sorrow was welcome. The words of the funeral service had elicited tears, shed as much for those comrades left behind at Pozières and Gallipoli as for Edward; and with the interment of the coffin, Liam had mentally buried all those friends who would never have a grave.

But if those boys had missed the proper obsequies, those who mourned them had also been spared the ghastliness of the funeral tea. In this case, being just after one o'clock, it was more of a luncheon, but it was as bad as Liam had envisaged. He suffered a lecture from Emily, disapproval from Blanche, and simpering smiles from two young female cousins. Robin was so unwell within the hour that he had to be taken up to bed. Returning, Liam found his ire further aroused by the fawning of his aunts upon Tisha, their whispered advice and secret, womanly nods infuriated him while his sister seemed to preen beneath their attention like a cat.

Only with her sisters' departure did Louisa drop the fixed half smile she had worn all afternoon; slumped in a chair beside the fading fire, she looked worn and tired. There were no tears, however; only once last night had she wept, and that was at his arrival. For several minutes she had clung to him and sobbed, and again it had seemed so strange to be holding and comforting her, instead of his mother comforting him.

Kneeling beside her chair, Liam placed a hand over hers. "Why don't you go up to bed for an hour? I'll make a cup of tea and bring it to you."

A faint smile brightened her eyes. "I'd like the tea," she said softly, patting his hand, "but I think I'll stay here."

Liam reached for the footstool and lifted her ankles, and when he saw that she was comfortable, went through to make some fresh tea. Sarah was washing plates and cups; there was no sign of his sister, who had apparently gone up to bed, not feeling well.

Not wanting to spoil her hands, Liam thought, and with a sigh returned to the parlor with tea that Sarah had made. The future bothered him, the idea of his mother alone in this isolated cottage, with Robin in hospital and incapacitated for months to come. Compared to that, his own illness had been trifling.

The future. Tisha had her own life now and could hardly be relied upon to give their mother a second thought, while Robin had his Sarah, and despite that dreadful injury to his knee, Liam knew he envied their future happiness. But with a wife and family, how would he survive financially? That worried Liam. Edward had left so little from the sale of the business, barely enough for his mother to live on, there would not be enough to provide for Robin.

While his mother poured tea for both of them, stirring plenty of rationed sugar into his, Liam lit a cigarette and tried to put those anxieties into words. The money he had sent home, which Edward had placed in a separate account, was to be used, he said, in whatever way she thought fit. It was no use to him, he could manage very well without it; he just wanted to be sure that his mother had all she needed.

She frowned at him and, in an attempt to be stern, said she was adequately provided for. "I don't need that money—you do. You will, anyway, once the war is over. You'll need it to set yourself up, buy that bit of land you were talking about. That's what Edward wanted for you. And so do I. I shall be all right—with a bit of careful managing, I'll be fine. You mustn't worry about me."

Her confidence brought a lump to his throat. He forbore to tell her that he had willed the money to her, anyway, and that his own estimates of survival were not very high. On a surge of emotion he stood up and went to the window to look out over the garden. After a long winter, it was in need of attention.

"Will you stay here?"

"Oh, I imagine so." She paused, wearily. "But I don't know . . . it's not something I've thought about, dear. Why do you ask?"

"I think you should move into town, get somewhere smaller, more manageable. All this"—and he gestured toward the muddy, rain-drenched garden—"will be too much for you."

There was the smallest strip of grass close to the house, a skeletal frame of rose stems against the fence, and naked trees struggling to come into bud. Apart from a few dejected daffodils in the orchard, all else had been turned over to vegetable production and was now a bare expanse of rutted soil.

"Well, I don't know about that," Louisa said with some asperity, "I'm only forty-nine, you know—not quite decrepit!"

He smiled then, cheered by her sharpness. "I'm sorry, I tend to forget. Dad was so much older, wasn't he?"

"Yes. Yes, he was. But he never seemed so . . ."

Glancing back, Liam saw her distress and blamed himself for a clumsy fool. He went to her and she leaned against him, taking comfort from his solidity.

"I'm so glad you were able to be here," she whispered. "I don't know what I'd have done if I'd been alone."

Her words expressed his own anxieties. "I know. That's

what worries me. I can't bear to think of you being here all alone."

"Oh, I shall manage, I expect. People do, you know. I shall get used to it, eventually . . . No, what I meant was—today—I was glad you and Robin were here with me today. And Tisha, of course," she added as an afterthought. "I wasn't sure whether she'd come, whether she'd be able to travel, I mean."

Liam knew quite well what she meant. Tisha was not predictable, and even Robin had been surprised to see her. But he did not want to talk about his sister. Returning to his main anxiety, he said; "What will you do when we've gone?"

"Keep busy," she said firmly, drawing away from him, "as I've always done. You mustn't worry about me, Liam—I've never been a clinging vine, and I don't intend to start now. And I won't be entirely alone, you know. There's Robin to think about, and even when he comes home, it'll be a while before he's fit enough to get married. But when he is, I'll let him go. I won't interfere."

That statement, however, did not reassure him. His mother was a proud woman and might hold off from her family when she needed them most. Thinking about his father, he said, "And there's the Colonel. I'm sure he'll be in York from time to time, to see Robin."

"I'm sure he will," she said with just a hint of asperity. And then she smiled, suddenly. "Oh, I shouldn't speak of him like that, should I? He's been very kind. He always was, Liam, and very generous—the thing is, I never wanted him to be . . ."

"Well, I hope you won't spurn his kindness in the future. I'd like to think there's one person you can rely on for help and advice, should you need it."

"I'll remember that," she said gently, touching his hand.

"Do. I don't want to be worrying about you." Reassured, he dropped a kiss on her cheek. "I'd better go and see how Robin's faring. And Tisha—Sarah said she wasn't feeling very well."

But at the foot of the stairs he paused, considering the changes in their relationship. Now that Edward was gone, he was very much aware of shouldering an elder son's responsibility, not only for his mother but for the rest of the family too. It worried him, however, that the war prevented him from fulfilling those obligations. Ordinarily, as his mother had been, he would have been too proud to ask the Colonel for help; but these were not ordinary times, and his mother needed someone to care for her. And after all, the Colonel was family, whatever Aunts Emily and Blanche might think.

He went upstairs. Sarah was sitting with Robin, who was looking much brighter, and in her old room Tisha was reading a fashion magazine, feet propped up on pillows on the bed. She said she was hungry, so Liam knew she must be feeling all right. With a sigh he went down again, wondering what was to be prepared for the evening meal, and whether he should make an attempt at it. He was tired more than hungry, yet a sense of restlessness made it impossible for him to relax. There was so little time, he felt he should be doing things, although precisely what eluded him. Standing there in the middle of the kitchen, he lit a cigarette and glanced at the clock. Almost five and Georgina would be here about seven. Two hours. And then what? An hour or so of family company, of guarded eyes and studiously bland exchanges between them. He needed to be alone with her, needed to talk, needed to be able to reach out and touch her. Letters were not enough; and besides, it might be the last chance he would ever have.

The thought of having to pretend a commonplace friendliness drove him to distraction. If only he could think of a way of seeing her alone!

Liam was still wrestling with the problem when Tisha appeared and, to his great surprise a moment later, started peeling potatoes. She demanded to know whether Sarah was staying to eat with them, and when he said not, expressed voluble relief.

With a nervous, upward glance, Liam begged her to keep her voice down.

"Let her hear me, I don't care. I tell you what, though—if Robin marries her, he can kiss the rest of us good-bye. She wants him for *herself*, you mark my words, and when she gets him, she'll *smother* him."

"I think you're wrong, but why should that matter to you?" Liam asked equably. "You haven't bothered much about Mother or Dad since you left York, so why bother about him?"

There was a long silence, followed by a suppressed hiccup

that might have been laughter or tears. In some amazement, he realized she was crying. He had thought her incapable of tears. Real ones, anyway. But this grief seemed genuine enough. He moved to comfort her, but she shrugged him off, fighting to control that sudden, wayward emotion.

At last bitterly she said, "Because he's the only one of this bloody selfish family who ever cared about *me*."

"How can you say that?"

"It's true. Even Dad—even *he* didn't give a damn what I did . . ."

"Oh, Tish, that's not true. He did care—he did. Mother too." Distressed for her, weighed down by sudden guilt, Liam tried to take her in his arms, but she was stiff and awkward, and the swell of the baby she carried felt very strange to him. Pressing his cheek to hers, he patted her shoulder while trying to think of something convincing to say. But there was nothing that did not sound hollow. In truth, she had always been the odd one out, hard to understand, impossible to reason with; ultimately, when she kicked, they let her carry on. Perhaps that was a lack of caring . . .

"It's all my fault," he murmured wretchedly. "I didn't understand then—and when I went, I certainly didn't mean to hurt *you* . . ."

"It was her, wasn't it?" she sobbed. "If it hadn't been for *her*, you wouldn't have gone, would you? It's not fair, it shouldn't have been like that . . . why did she have to come and spoil things?"

He stiffened, released his hold on her. "What are you talking about?"

Tisha felt her way to a chair, sat down, and cried for a while. When the tears eventually subsided, she managed to say with passable control, "I know why you went. It was Georgina, wasn't it? I heard Mother and Dad talking about the two of you one night. It was just after you'd gone. I didn't understand then. Not until that first time I saw you together in London. It was the way you looked at her." She paused to wipe her nose and eyes. "Are you lovers?"

Liam sat down. He thought he was going to be sick. It took him a minute to find his voice, and when he did, it sounded foreign to him. "Not in the sense you mean, no."

If she was unconvinced by that outright lie, she did not say, and he dared not look up. As he fumbled with a pack of cigarettes, she took it from him, lit one and then another, with hands that were steadier than his.

"Shocked you there, didn't I? Oh, don't look so worried, I won't say anything." She puffed inexpertly at the cigarette, picking bits of tobacco from her lower lip. "Does Robin know?"

Liam shook his head, trying to gather his scattered wits. "I don't think so. Anyway, it's over, I shall be going tomorrow."

"Just as well. Sarah might drag it out of him, and she would *never* approve."

"Don't tell me you do."

Tisha shrugged. "I'm not shocked and stunned, if that's what you mean. It doesn't matter now. In fact," she admitted, narrowing her eyes through a haze of blue smoke, "it makes me like you a little better. You were always so bloody pure and perfect, weren't you? Quite priggish, really. It does me good to realize you're no better than I am."

"Did I ever claim to be?"

"Not in so many words. But you always *thought* you were better, always acted that way."

"If I did, then I'm sorry," he said sincerely, responding to her pain and quelling his innate distrust of both words and motives. "I am sorry, Tisha. I wish you'd believe me."

"Oh, I do," came the weary reply, "but it's a bit late now, isn't it? I mean we've all made such a bloody mess of things, haven't we? And you can't go back. What a family! I don't know about cigarettes, Liam, but I could do with a drink. Still," she sighed, "I don't expect Mother keeps strong liquor in the house."

"There's some sherry . . ."

"No thanks."

A moment later, while Liam was reflecting on their various situations, Tisha said bleakly, "I hope I never fall in love. It's just a shambles, isn't it? Look at Mother—look at you! God, what a mess. And I can't say those two lovebirds upstairs fill me with confidence either. If that's what love does to people, fawning all over each other, I don't want it."

He was shocked. "But what about Edwin? Don't you love him?"

Again that eloquent shrug, as though Edwin was of no moment. "I'm fond of him, yes. In love—no."

"But—how? I mean, *why*? Why marry him?"

Her glance was pitying. "He was the best offer I had. The best I was likely to get, what with everybody going off to the war and getting killed. Quite young, nice-looking, plenty of money . . . kind too. And madly in love with me. Trouble was," she added with devastating candor, "I never counted on him getting called up. I thought he was safe, secure, and ensconced in the bloody War Office for the duration! He used to joke about it, about volunteering and being promoted every time." She sighed heavily. "But they called his bluff. Now I expect he'll end up with some dreadful wound, like Robin, and I shall have to be a nursemaid for the rest of my life . . . The thing is, I can't see myself being very good at that."

Words failed him.

"Oh, don't look so grim," she said with affected lightness. "What does it matter? What does any of it matter? We all die in the end, don't we?" But her voice broke there. "Like Dad—just like Dad . . ."

On a flood of grief, she hurried, as fast as her bulk would allow, for the stairs.

Liam felt as though he had been mangled. Remembering the sherry, he poured a generous measure and downed it in one gulp. Tisha was right: It was a mess, and likely to remain so, but with regard to himself, he wished only that he could trust her. If it suited her ends, she was quite likely to blurt out his secret to whoever would listen. And if she did—oh God, the people it would hurt!

Then another thought struck him. If she had guessed so accurately then others might have done the same. But no, surely not. If anyone else had guessed, he would know from their attitude toward him. Only Tisha could be as nonchalant as that.

Although the thought of food nauseated him, Liam put together a meal of sorts: boiled potatoes and carrots—which with a box of withered apples were the only things to have survived Louisa's winter storage—to go with what remained of the sliced cold meats prepared for the funeral luncheon. There was some cold apple pie to finish with. Apart from Tisha, it seemed no one had eaten much earlier, so Liam's basic meal was much appreciated, especially by Louisa. To his surprise, with the return of a little color to her cheeks, she announced that she would stay on at the cottage, for the summer at least.

"My garden has provided food for us and helped out a lot of families besides. So I'll do what I did last year—plant vegetables that can be stored—and it will give me something to do. Edward would have wanted it."

It seemed the last word on the matter, and although Liam would have preferred to think of her in a less isolated place, his mother's determination was heartening, and perhaps the satisfaction of growing things was a good antidote to grief.

While the women cleared up, he helped his brother into the parlor, propping him up with cushions on the sofa. He was in constant pain, and the day's strain and activity had made it worse. In a silent gesture of sympathy, Liam reached out and held his hand.

"It's good to see you again, despite the circumstances."

Robin nodded and pressed his hand. "I'm so glad you came home and made it up with Mother and Dad."

Liam smiled. "So am I."

It was good to see him up and about again. In the hospital Liam had wondered whether his brother would live. Well, he had, and strength would return, he was sure of that. Robin was possessed of will and determination to overcome both pain and disability, but he would never again be that carefree boy. None of them would.

He shivered, and Robin looked up to read the bleakness in his eyes; there was a flash of understanding between them, and then his brother's fingers gripped with surprising force.

"You'll be all right," he whispered. "You haven't come this far to go down now. I always thought you were a lot tougher than me, only I seem to have spent most of my life trying to prove otherwise." He smiled wanly. "Anyway, it doesn't matter anymore. The point is, you're one of life's survivors—you'll come through, I know you will."

Grateful for that vote of confidence, although by no means certain he deserved it, Liam smiled. "Well, if you say so . . ." he remarked lightly, and the moment dissolved in soft laughter.

With the squeak of the garden gate his heart leapt. Two shadowy figures hesitated for a second before advancing down the path, and as they did so he rose, with deliberate lack of haste, to open the front door.

The Colonel shook his hand, his eyes urgently questioning even before the words were on his lips. Liam said that his mother was taking things very bravely, although he suspected she was more upset than she allowed herself to appear.

"I shouldn't think she's taken it in yet," the older man said softly as Liam took coats and hats and hung them on the hallstand.

"Probably not." He frowned, wanting to say more, but it was impossible, here. His father went into the kitchen, and Georgina reached up with a chaste kiss for his cheek. At close quarters, his earlier impression that she was thinner was confirmed, and there was a tension about her that was echoed in himself. He ached to hold her, to feel that tight anxiety dissipate in the warmth of her embrace; he must see her alone, he *must* . . .

But as he began to frame the words, Tisha joined them, and Georgina turned to greet her with a solicitous inquiry. Still talking, they all moved through into the parlor. Liam thought his sister's quick, glancing smile was dangerously conspiratorial, but no one else seemed to notice, and in the sun of Georgina's greeting, Robin beamed, assuring her that he was quite well, really, and in only slight discomfort. Although it was a patent lie, she did not dispute it, passing on to lighter matters, including Tisha in her conversation. She did it so very well, only Liam knew the effort it cost.

As Robert and Louisa joined them, there was a necessary rearrangement of seats. Liam stood up to offer his chair, but Robert declined it, preferring the end of the sofa to what had traditionally been Edward's place, while the two young women elected for dining chairs, and Louisa took her usual seat by the fireside. There was a further exchange of inquiries after everyone's health and subdued comments on the funeral, all quite normal under the circumstances; but Liam, listening, looking, experienced a particular feeling of dislocation. The room was much the same as it had always been, with pictures and ornaments shining in the soft lamplight; the delft tiles framing the fireplace were the same, and the embroidered velvet mantelcloth; the spoon-backed chairs and the table and heavily carved sideboard were all as he recalled, only the people were different. He was sitting in Edward's chair, something he had not been allowed to do as a boy, and Edward was no longer here.

His absence left an enormous gap, yet that was only part of it. Another awareness dominated, shuttling thoughts back and forth between this gathering and a similar one in the summer of 1913, when they had all sat down in this selfsame room for tea. Then, hostility and unformed suspicion had been uppermost in Liam's mind: He had noted the resemblance between his brother and Robert Duncannon, and his mother's unusual gaiety, and that lively repartee across the table had seemed somehow improper, especially in the shadow of Edward's quiet watchfulness. He understood it now, but ,at the time he had thought Robert Duncannon to be taking far too many liberties.

He could not be accused of that now, however. His affection for them all was palpable but subdued, and if there was any corner of his heart that was relieved by Edward's death, it was not apparent. Rather, to Liam, it seemed that he grieved for them all in their loss as any caring father would.

The oddness lay in Liam's awareness that for the first time they were all gathered together as a family, round one fireside, knowing the truth of their situation. Mother, father, children, all together for the first time. It was odd enough to send a tingling shiver down his spine. He wondered whether the others were aware of it too, and whether it crossed their minds, as it did his, that this one occasion might well be the last. Tisha was married and would soon return to London, presumably to bear her child and greet Edwin on his return, making a family of her own. Sooner or later, Robin would be in a similar position, while Georgina would always be Georgina, full of compassion for others, making her life with them and for them. As for himself, well, with first light he would be away, and once he returned to France, his fate would lie in other hands.

Remembering Bournemouth, he felt that it was just as well. The war would roll on, and if he survived, Liam knew he must return to Australia. There could be nothing for him here, and with Georgina close enough to reach yet more than ever forbidden, it was impossible to contemplate. If there had been hopes and fantasies before, then those stolen days together had revealed all the impossibilities to both of them. Their relationship could go no further, not without the direst of consequences, not without destroying the already fragile threads that held this family together. Liam had done enough damage and, in his struggle to repair it, would not willingly blast them apart again. Nor could he bear to think of Georgina's fear made reality. Bad enough if he should be here to support her; but intolerable for her alone.

If the death of innocence had killed their high ideals, then weeks of separation had finally broken all the curbs. It had not been intentional. In the joy of reunion it had simply happened, almost before either of them realized it; and once joined, there could be no going back. Nor had there been. The physical sense of being part of her was too seductive, and the emotional sense too comprehensive not to repeat it. And with that awareness of impending separation the wanting had been equal, so that they had made love far too often. Oh, he had been very careful, particularly after the first time; and, looking back, he thought how strange it was that he should have been so calm, so absolutely sure of himself and what he was doing. It was as though he were saying to her, as he had longed to do in the beginning, that in this they were one and could never be divided.

In the heart of the flame, pain did not exist, there was only a sense of calm, of being insulated and protected against all else. They were loving and tender with each other, perfectly content for the first time; they did not discuss what was happening between them, there was no point, no need. It simply *was*; and in a short time, it would be no more. They both knew that.

They had parted at the station, Georgina to return to London, while Liam traveled the short distance to the training camp at Wareham.

That was where reality took center stage, leading torment with burned and blistered hands. Compared to what was going on in his mind, the physical hell of retraining was almost a pleasure. When he finally received the letter, two days before he left Wareham, to say that all was well and she could not possibly be expecting a child, he was light-headed with relief.

Georgina made it clear that they must never tempt fate in such a way again, and with that Liam heartily concurred. Only afterward, however, with all the ramifications clear to him, did he realize what she was saying. It was over, it had to be; they could never meet like that again.

As things were, it was no longer possible, and for that he had a small measure of gratitude. But it was no match for the pain that overwhelmed him every time he thought about saying good-bye.

She was sitting close to Robin, her hand resting lightly on his shoulder, part of the family circle which at that moment was almost a physical entity. Slightly apart from the rest, Liam was aware that in some strange way the break lay with him, that he was the odd one out, divided by thought and consciousness and the nature of his love for her.

Exhaustion broke into the group, and as Tisha went upstairs, Liam helped his brother to bed. As in the old days, they were sharing a room again; knowing he would see Robin later, Liam went down, wondering how he could contrive to speak to Georgina alone. As he hesitated at the foot of the stairs, it came to him that if he offered to make a pot of tea, she would probably come through to the kitchen to help. But as he set the kettle to boil, it was his father who came in to speak to him.

"I wonder would you see Georgina back to the hotel? It's been a long day, and she's tired, and I'd like to stay with your mother for a little while." For a second he hesitated, then went on, "It won't take long, but there are a few things we need to discuss."

Liam prayed that his expression betrayed none of his relief and only a fraction of his willingness to obey. "Of course, sir," he murmured, allowing himself a small smile. "I'll see her safely back."

Robert closed the kitchen door behind him. He seemed unusually tense. "What time is your train, by the way?"

"Half past six—that is, if it's not delayed. They usually are."

"And a slow journey back to Grantham, I've no doubt. Would you like me to come to the station, see you off?"

Liam's heart lurched. "No, sir, really, I'd rather be alone. Much rather, but thanks all the same."

His father's level gaze met his, regarding him somberly. "Don't worry about your mother. I'll take good care of her—in fact I shall insist on doing so," he added with a small, dry smile, "whether she wants me to or not."

As he tried to express his thanks, Robert cut him off. "No, it's the very least I can do. In the meantime, if we don't manage to meet before you go—take great care of yourself. No foolish heroics, promise me that?"

"I promise. I got these stripes for long service, not heroics!"

"In that case, let's be seeing another one next time you're home."

"I'll do my best, sir."

There was a silence, and apprehension suddenly struck Liam, he could not say why. His father frowned and looked down for a moment, and although he had his hand on the door, it seemed the interview was not over. "By the way," he said at last, and his voice was suddenly sharp with accusation, "did you know about Georgina's plans? That she's volunteered for service abroad?"

The question caught him completely off guard, as afterward he was sure it was meant to. Liam felt the blood drain from his face, and when he found his voice, he stammered. "A-abroad? No—no, she—she didn't tell me . . ." On a vision of casualty clearing stations, often under fire, he closed his eyes.

"I'm sure," Robert continued heavily, "that you have a better idea than any of us just what that might mean." There was a repressed anger in him that in spite of shock, set every sense on the alert.

"I'm counting on you, Liam, to dissuade her. She's done enough already, for God's sake—I don't want her risking her life out there." He paused. "I shouldn't imagine you do, either."

There was an additional edge to his voice as he said that, and his glance, steady and penetrating, told Liam that he knew—or suspected—the true state of affairs. It was worse—far worse—than Tisha's confrontation earlier, because no accusations were leveled, and there was nothing for Liam to deny. Instead of the dressing-down he might have expected, there was just this terribly restrained civility.

"I've discussed the matter with Georgina, and I realize that there is no point in taking it further. With *anyone*." His voice was hushed, deceptively so, because every word had the sharpness of an incision. "You're going away tomorrow, and it seems it's just as well. You know the folly of what you've done as well as I do, and only because I blame myself more than anyone else do I beg you—*beg you*—to be sensible. You cannot expect—"

"The decision has already been made," Liam said gruffly, forcing the words through trembling lips. His whole body was shaking; he found himself clinging to the back of a chair, wanting to apologize, wanting to explain to his father just how it had come about. He wanted to be forgiven. But there was no time. "I'm sorry . . ." he whispered, and the words were grossly inadequate.

There was a momentary brilliance in his father's eyes. "So am I," he breathed, "so am I." With a sudden compression of his mouth, he looked away. "Do something useful, Liam—stop her from committing another folly."

"She's not—not volunteering *to be close to me*, is she?"

"No, oddly enough. She seems to think that active service will remove her entirely from your sphere of influence. When you come home on leave, she won't be here. It will also make communication difficult."

The truth of that was like a hammer blow. He could give no more than a puppet's nod in answer to it.

"But staying away from each other is one thing—getting yourselves killed is quite another. I don't want to lose either of you—and if your mother knew, she'd say the same. In our separate ways, we care—very much—about both of you."

"I'll do my best," Liam said.

Robert glanced at his watch. "Shall we say an hour?"

"If I had a week," his son responded bitterly, "I'm not sure it would be long enough. But I'll try." He moved toward the door and Robert opened it for him; as he donned his heavy overcoat, he said, "Tell Georgina I'll be waiting outside."

The rain had turned to a fine, drenching mist that obscured everything, even the river. The only light was that from the cottage doorway, and like a blanket, the night absorbed it. Seeking support rather than cover, he stood beneath the first tree beyond the gate and shivered like a man with palsy. April, and it felt like January, and the shocks and miseries of the day gave him no warmth, no comfort.

A couple of minutes later she followed him out, pausing only to raise her umbrella. He called to her and she hurried to his side; she was upon him before his expression could halt her eagerness, reaching out to embrace him as he grasped both arms and shook her, angrily.

"Why didn't you tell me? Jesus Christ, I walked straight into that! Why didn't you tell me he knew?"

He saw the shock on her face, saw too the sense of betrayal. She glanced back over her shoulder, then up at Liam, and then she hung her head. "He said—he promised—that he wouldn't say anything to you. I'm sorry—I didn't—didn't want to tell you . . . and in a letter, how could I?"

"*When* for God's sake? How did he find out? What did he say?"

She leaned against him, touching her forehead to his shoulder. Almost against his will, Liam embraced her. "Tell me," he whispered urgently, "I have to know—*all* of it."

Time was passing but he could not move until he knew. The umbrella provided shelter as he lit a cigarette and listened to her brief, staccato explanation. Those stolen few days in Bournemouth had been their undoing. Georgina had arranged her leave with the hospital but neglected to tell her father; he had needed to speak to her on an urgent matter, telephoned, and been told she was on leave. When she came back, he had, quite naturally, wanted to know where she had been.

"It was a risk, of course, and I'd worried about it for days before I came to you. And the trouble was, I couldn't think of a convincing lie to cover the situation . . ."

"You should have told me—I thought he was in Ireland!"

"I didn't see the point of worrying you too." After a moment, she went on. "Anyway, as soon as I saw his face, I realized that lying would have been a waste of time. He knew, Liam, he knew full well where I'd been. He'd had plenty of time to work it out, and he'd even checked with the convalescent home and been told you were on leave too. Only the fact that he didn't want to believe the worst made him accept my abridged version of the truth."

"And what, for God's sake, was that?"

"I said we'd taken separate rooms, that I went down to Bournemouth simply because we wanted to spend some time together before you went away . . ." Her voice broke on that. "And that, as God's my witness, is the truth, isn't it?"

"Except I never slept in mine." He threw the stub of his cigarette in the direction of the river and took her arm. "We'd better get moving—I'm supposed to be seeing you back to your hotel, and we haven't got long."

"I told him we loved each other. God, he was so upset, and so *angry*—I thought at one point he was going to hit me, and he's never done that in his life. I had to go back to the beginning, to that summer before the war, and tell him *everything*. It's just as well that I was so naïve in those days—he knew I was, and so he was able to believe me when I said I thought we were just good friends. I told him," Georgina went on, "that it was being together—visiting so regularly when you were in hospital—that made us both realize it was something more than friendship. That was what hurt him—because he *wanted* me to see you, to keep in contact . . ."

"Why?"

Her voice dropped so much that Liam had to strain to hear her next words. "He wanted me to explain the past. He wanted you to understand what he did and why he did it. He wanted your forgiveness. And he knew you wouldn't listen, or even agree to see him, so he sent me instead."

There was something so familiar in that, it made Liam sigh. "So he blames himself, does he? Well, he needn't. I just pray to God he doesn't say anything to my mother. She won't take it the way he has."

"He won't. She's had enough grief, he wouldn't do that to her."

"He promised—you said—not to say anything to me!" But the bitterness waned as Liam went over what had been said by Robert Duncannon. Nothing direct, nothing specific; it had all been contained in the eyes, in the tone of voice as he dropped the bombshell of Georgina's plans.

Liam faced her with that as they walked through town, as deserted streets echoed to every footstep, and a driving mist chilled their faces. Few gas lamps were lit and most of those were dimmed. They found their way less by sight than familiarity, realizing with some surprise that they were not far from the hotel. The matter, however, was far from over, a long way from being settled to Liam's satisfaction. For a moment he thought of her private room, its warmth and seclusion; but there was too little time, and he had no desire to compromise her further.

They walked on past the Minster, its looming mass shadowed and silent, suggesting an emptiness within that made a mockery of existence. Shivering, Liam drew Georgina toward him, seeking the shelter of a little archway he recalled off Goodramgate. Mist and smoke and fine, drenching rain made a blanket of the night, cutting them off, in that dry place, from the probing eyes of passersby. Not that there were many. At the sound of muffled footsteps they dropped their voices, huddling against a dry wall, its ancient bricks warm from some interior chimney.

"You might be sent anywhere," Liam murmured against the softness of her cheek. "And I don't just mean Boulogne or Flanders or places behind the front lines. There are British nurses in Egypt and Malta, and the seas, my darling, are *crawling* with German submarines. Didn't you see that report in the paper? More than fifty ships went down last week, including a troopship with nurses aboard. Why risk that when you can do so much good *here*?"

When she did not immediately answer, he drew away. "Look, you're being silly about this. You know how impossible it was for me to get leave before—and after six months off, God knows when I'll get leave again." With an exasperated sigh, he added, "Do you want me to make that promise again? I won't try to see you—and if you don't want to hear from me, I won't even *write*."

"What use are promises?" she whispered brokenly. "It wouldn't be any use. If I knew you were home on leave, I'd want to see you, and if I thought we could keep in touch easily, I'd always be looking for your letters. Or writing to you."

"Georgina," he got out bitterly, "you're making this so difficult . . ."

"But don't you see why I want to go away? Can't you see that if I stay, where you and I were together and happy, I'll never forget? Everything in London—the places we went, even the numbers of the buses we took—in the kitchen, the drawing room, by the window, in my bed. God, in my *bed*. I never sleep. I doze and I dream of you beside me. I wake and search for you. I even run my hands over my body and pretend they are *your* hands." She clung to him, sobbing. "I can't bear it, Liam. I *cannot* bear it. All this time, and it doesn't get any easier. I want you more, not less. I have to get away—I have to."

He held her, and he thought his heart was breaking.

"But I just want you to be *safe*. Don't torture me with that kind of worry. I *have* to go—you don't. Stay, please, where I can think of you in safety . . ."

"I don't want safety," she said harshly, pulling back from him. "I want a place where the work and the danger, and the sheer hell of existence, take my mind off the worse hell of living without you."

"You're being childish. You haven't the faintest idea what it's like."

She turned on him then, and even in the darkness he saw the flash of fury in her eyes. "Don't, please, accuse me of that! Have you any idea what it's like living in a place of safety, and *worrying*—day in, day out, week in, week out—about the people you love in constant danger? You don't know what's happening, you haven't the remotest idea whether they are alive or dead, and you live for the letters while you dread the telegram. And the newspapers tell of glorious victories while every other page is full of casualty lists. I *nurse* those casualties, Liam—I know about the lies!"

"I don't want you to go," he said quietly. "There's killing enough, and your life's too precious."

"And so is yours, to me! But I can't beg you to stay, and you couldn't if I did!"

In great agitation she paced their little square of shelter, and through the darkness he watched her, bent against the pain, her face a pale oval of anguish. He lit another cigarette and, aware of the trembling in his limbs, leaned back against the wall. The truth of everything she said was undeniable, and it cut him deeply. It hurt more because they were arguing, because these might be the last minutes they would ever have together. That much had been agreed already: that when he left England this time he would never try to see her again.

He might have said, in answer to her harrowed distress, that the future seemed just as meaningless to him, that without her he did not even want to live. There was nothing left for him, and he had nothing more to give; all that he had, had been given, already, to her. It was unbearable to think of it being thrown away like this, on such an empty gesture.

But he said none of those things. Instead he took her arms, calming her resistance, soothing her toward the bitter release of tears. She clung to his strength, touching his face and hair and neck with passionate, feverish hands, as though needing to impress the feel of him forever. That almost destroyed him, and when he found his voice, it was low and husky with grief. It hurt to tell her that pain was a thing to be borne, that there was no escaping it in flight.

He kissed her then, a deep, tender, loving kiss, and against the silkiness of her hair he murmured that it was time to go, they had to go, it was already late.

Together they moved out from beneath the archway and into the Minister Yard, heads down against the swirling mist. The blank windows of St. William's College watched them pass, and the great sweep of the Minster's east end looked down as they paused in the triangle of space before it. They embraced again, and there was passion and desperation in the way their lips met, a feverish longing in the clinging of hands at the parting.

He took a step or two toward her but she stayed him with a gesture, backing away, hurrying, turning, running, her skirts caught up, cape flying into the darkness.

"Pray for me . . ." he whispered, but she could not possibly have heard.

He stood there for some time, sheltered by the night and the mist, and the air was like a cold, wet shroud against his face. Then, blinded by grief, he stumbled forward to cling to the support of a great buttress in the wall. He raged then, and cried out, beating his head against the stone, demanding in the name of all that was holy, why this agony should have to be . . .

There was no answer, no consolation at all, not even of knowing he had done the right thing.

Eventually that storm of anguish passed, and he was able to move on leaden feet toward home. He followed a meandering route which took him nowhere near the hotel, but was back at the cottage within the hour. A note on the kitchen table said his mother was tired and had gone to bed; she would see him in the morning. Liam set his damp clothes to dry in front of the stove and went to bed.

30

*I*t seemed at first that he could not go on without her. The animus was gone, and all that remained was unfeeling flesh.

He stumbled through the days, earned a dozen reprimands and suffered the ensuing bitter weather without complaint. The shooting ranges at Grantham were under several inches of snow, fuel was scarcer than ever, and the activity of German submarines on British shipping meant that rations were very short. For ten days he was cold and wet and hungry, yet it seemed no more than a fitting match for the chill in his soul. The news of another big push near Arras touched him in only one way: He prayed that his return to France would come soon, and that death might erase the terrible emptiness of his existence.

The former prayer was answered quickly enough. By the third week in April he was on his way to join a large batch of reinforcements heading initially for Folkestone. The journey to Kings Cross was cramped and cold, but he was pleased to be moving, pleased to be on his way to that other life he hated but knew so well, the life that had nothing whatever to do with Georgina. As he left the huge, echoing station behind, however, and set forth with a score of others to cross London, his bitter pleasure withered before an agony he had failed to predict. He knew then what Georgina meant, knew exactly the level of torture she must suffer in her journeys back and forth across the city: Oxford Street, where they had wandered in and out of little shops and massive stores; Hyde Park, bleak beneath a gray shroud of snow; Buckingham Palace, where they had stood and watched the changing of the guard one sunny day last October . . .

The wait at Victoria was interminable. On a walk round the station precincts he found a public telephone and was tempted to use it. Forcing himself away, he went to the bar and drank two pints of beer in quick succession, but instead of numbing the pain, the alcohol only blunted the fine edge of his decision, and within the hour he was back, demanding the hospital number from the operator. Georgina, however, was not on duty, and the ward sister was too new to be able to tell him anything. There was no reply from Queen's Gate.

They spent five hours in Folkestone before boarding the transport for Boulogne, but that was all right: Georgina had never been to Folkestone. Huddled in overcoat and sheepskin, Liam took the chance of rest in a corner of the great cargo shed where hundreds were waiting. Some were playing cards, others writing letters, while a few were singing to the plaintive strains of a harmonica. It reminded him of the night before Gallipoli, except it was a damn sight colder and he did not wish to be part of it. He dozed for a while, to be woken by an anxious group of youngsters as soon as there was a rumor of boarding. They were excited and jumpy, eager to stay close to him with his veteran's experience of war. Like the boys who had accompanied him to France from Egypt a year ago, they regarded him as some kind of oracle, pouncing upon every utterance and repeating it in hushed whispers among themselves. That he said little seemed only to make each word more significant.

His shrug of unconcern regarding submarines was observed with awe, and his words, "Well, you take your chance, don't you?" went down the line with the speed of an express train. Their involuntary straightening gave him a certain bitter amusement; he wondered whether they would have been so keen to worship had they realized he genuinely did not care one way or the other whether a German torpedo sent him to the watery depths, or an explosion from hell scattered him across the mud of France.

Any wild acts of heroism or aggression he might have been tempted to perform were foiled initially by further training near Armentières, which was so familiar it seemed he had never been away. Exactly a year, and little had changed, even the weather was the same, bitter winter clinging on, then suddenly giving way before a wild outbreak of sun and green leaves. In a week, blossoms were everywhere, and the old Flemish faces in shops and bars were starting to smile again. But they were thinner and grayer and more weary, and in his walks along the Lys, he saw that the cemeteries were fuller, and new ones had been created.

He found himself thinking often about those stolen few days in Bournemouth, the scent of the pines in a narrow ravine close by the hotel, and the salty tang of the sea. With a pale sun glistening across the waves, it had seemed in those few days that even winter was being kind. They had strolled along the beach beneath the cliffs, dodging incoming waves and skimming pebbles out to sea, and happiness had been theirs—not a wild excitement, but a calm, sure awareness of contentment and each other. He had never been so relaxed, so absolutely himself, as in those days with Georgina. And for her it had been the same. Perfection, but perfection is such a fragile thing; they were aware of that too. That last evening, as they returned at twilight along the promenade, the frosty air had been disturbed by a low, continuous rumbling, like thunder in the distance. Georgina, bemused, had asked what it could be, while Liam, knowing, had shivered in recognition.

The beginnings of another massive bombardment across the Channel had seemed to herald the end of things, not just that brief escape from reality, but the end of everything.

Here, the rumblings, if not particularly intense, were more or less permanent, and he had learned not to wince with every explosion, learned to school his expression into blank acceptance while his heart pounded and stomach turned to water at the memories each one invoked.

There was no word from Georgina, despite resurrected hope. What did arrive was a short, sad letter from his father, saying that she had been accepted for service in Egypt and had left London within a couple of weeks of his departure for France. Later, came a further missive, confirming her safe arrival. Unless Liam requested specific news of her, his father wrote, he would leave the situation at that.

No address, and Cairo had several hospitals. It was a relief, however, to know she was safe, not in France where her presence might tempt him to go looking for her, or in danger of being blown to pieces by stray shells or a sudden German advance. In Liam's opinion, Egypt was not a pleasant place to be, but the officer status of nursing sisters would no doubt ensure a better standard of food and accommodation than he had ever enjoyed. Also, the ancient history of the place would appeal to her; she had been fascinated by his descriptions of the tombs and monuments and museums. But even as he remembered those conversations, Liam was struck by a certain irony: If London had been unbearable because they had enjoyed it together, how would she feel about Egypt, where he had spent more than eight months of the war? Would she watch the moon rise over the pyramids and see his shadow in the sand? While she wandered through the gardens and the palaces, would she feel his presence beside her?

He would imagine her there, see the flaming desert sunsets again through her eyes, smell the orange blossoms in the courtyards of Heliopolis and watch the fountains playing in their marble pools. All the hospitals were grand hotels or former palaces; he had convalesced at the summer home of the German crown prince, and that particular irony had given him a vast amount of pleasure at the time.

That memory made him think of the last time he had seen Mary Maddox, now nursing at Harefield, another Australian hospital outside London, and by association her brother Lewis. According to the last letter Liam had received from him, Lew was still in Egypt with the Light Horse, full of verve and confidence now that he had been promoted to captain. That he had continued to keep in touch was warming, a testimony to the reality of those months immediately preceding the war, and to the odd friendship which had sprung up between them. Liam might have let it lapse, particularly during the worst periods of the war, when Australia had seemed no more than a passing dream, but Lewis had kept on writing. Liam wondered now whether it was something more than friendship that prompted him. It seemed there was a need for reassurance there, a need to know that he was not the only one left of those boys from Dandenong, that someone other than himself was still surviving. Perhaps he felt guilty, or slightly freakish in his ability to dodge death. Liam had known moments like that himself, especially when all were falling around him.

He was saved from guilt, however, by a strong streak of fatalism, and by an inner conviction that for every man there is a time to die. It had not been his destiny to catch a burst of shrapnel on Gallipoli, or to breathe his last with pneumonia at Heliopolis, and that strange dream of Ned had as much as told him so. In London he had mostly been too happy to think about it, but the subject had arisen once with Georgina, and she, surprisingly, had not disputed it. Nor had she entirely agreed with him; for her, the sense of appalling, unjustified waste was too strong. But she had seen the calm that came over dying men, as though old friends beckoned them away from pain and into peace. She did not think it was hallucination and did not doubt the veracity of his experience.

But she had no explanation for it either.

Since then, there had been too many other, more pressing matters for him to dwell on it, and now, looking back on his friendship with Ned and at the love he still bore for Georgina, he had to wonder *why* such things came about, and why they had to end. In the midst of what he recognized as the pain of bereavement, it all seemed so pointless, and a small part of him wondered whether it might have been better to know none of it. Without love, could that sense of loss exist? But with Georgina there had been such happiness, such ecstasy; laughter and closeness and that sense of being one person, with the same thoughts and feelings, desires and despairs. Through her, he had come to understand so much, and he was aware that in giving her up he had lost far more than could ever have been imagined four years ago.

What made it worse was knowing that she suffered too.

That deep, constant ache, and the bouts of misery which continued to sweep over him, made communication with his family difficult. He had to force himself to write, force himself to express what he hoped was a natural level of concern, when in effect he was experiencing both envy and resentment toward them all. Robin had Sarah, and Tisha had her baby, a little girl. Although he was pleased for her, he loathed her cynical attitude, which took such precious things as marriage and children for granted. Even his mother, about whom he had been so worried before leaving, seemed more blessed than himself. She had known twenty years of happiness with Edward, and five before that with Robert Duncannon. Even now, whether she wanted to accept it or not, Liam knew she need do no more than say yes to have her former lover permanently by her side. It seemed grossly unfair.

Communication with Georgina, however much he might wish it, was not only forbidden, but impossible. Against the setting of Egypt, however, she was constantly in his thoughts, and in the end, coming across that three-month-old missive from Lewis, Liam wrote to him. Toward the close of a letter, which briefly recounted the least personal of recent events, he mentioned Georgina—"*a close relative of mine*"—and made a casual request that Lewis look out for her, should he be in Cairo.

It was not quite the long shot it might have seemed. Officers, particularly in the Middle East, managed a fair amount of leave, and the military community in Cairo was a close one. Georgina might be reluctant to make herself known to him, but on a specific request, Lewis would most certainly inquire after her. Knowing someone, even at one remove, might just ease things, and Lewis was a decent sort. There was also the added advantage, Liam decided, that if he did come across Georgina, Lewis would write and say so.

The simple act of writing and posting the letter made him feel slightly better, and the news that he was to rejoin his old company provided a further lift to his spirits. There had been some savage fighting at Bullecourt—twice in recent weeks—and in many ways he was sorry to have missed it; he was looking forward to seeing familiar faces again but traveled down by train to Amiens with mixed anticipation. Among the men with him were reinforcements for the 1st Division, some still raw, others, like himself, lately recovered from wounds or sickness. The word was that three Australian divisions—the

1st, 2nd, and 5th—were to be pulled out of the line for a long and much-needed rest. Everyone else latched on to this news with an enthusiasm that might have greeted a great victory, but Liam was a little unsure. It was hell in the line, even on a holding front; in the line, however, there was little time to think and none to brood. *Rest* was also a comparative term: What it meant was weeks of retraining, moronic exercises to grind the new boys into the machine. It was boring and soul-destroying and left too much time to ponder the pointlessness of things.

Nevertheless, for his old comrades-in-arms, he was greatly relieved. Since July the previous year, the Australians had been involved in almost continuous fighting on the Somme and at Ypres, followed by a return to the Somme for the winter, where they were then sent in pursuit of the sudden German withdrawal. Liam was glad that those men who had slogged so hard to break the German line on the Bapaume Road in August should then have been allowed to take Bapaume itself in March. But that success had come after a savage winter in which sleet and snow and glutinous mud were far worse enemies than good old Fritz. In hospital in London, and convalescing on the south coast, he had been spared the constant physical misery of the trenches, although he had read the newspapers and shivered. Recalling November on Gallipoli, when men had died of frostbite and exposure, he could hardly imagine how they had survived the depths of a continental winter. But survive they had. They deserved their rest.

The old Somme battlefield was oddly silent, a barren, windswept heath that at night seemed to moan with the souls of the dead. A blasted heath indeed, a fitting stage for tragedy beneath a climbing moon, although the worst of it had come and gone. Only memory was left, and those days and weeks at Pozières paled beside more recent tragedy.

By day, however, as a riotous spring settled into glorious summer, the first green shoots of growth appeared, and all along that barren line the poppies bloomed, bright pools of scarlet among the gauzy white of mayweed. *Blood and Bandages*, he thought, like the shoulder patch of the 8th, his old battalion; but the patch he wore now was a solid square of red above crossed machine-gun barrels.

Within a few miles of the old front line, in little, sheltered valleys, crops started to appear, tended only by women and children and very old men, and for Liam they were a sign of hope, a sign of life. And meanwhile, the decimated battalions began to replenish themselves, absorbing new men, new equipment, new strategies. Gradually the grayness disappeared, and the sun made them brown again, and laughter was heard in the camps at night. They drank and gambled, drank and brawled, and some of them looked up old girlfriends while others found new ones. The bars and brothels of Amiens did excellent trade with the Australians that summer, and Liam had enough twenty-four-hour passes to roister with the best, but his vow to make the most of wine, women, and song was only partly successful. The songs and the wine he could manage very well, it was the women he had no real taste for. It was not that they were unattractive, but what they offered was a poorly degraded currency, worthless after the gold he had possessed.

He would look at that old photograph of Georgina and he would compare it with the other he treasured, taken of the two of them in a studio off Oxford Street. There was still sweetness in her smile but the serenity had gone; her eyes were sad and full of knowledge, shadowed by the suffering she had seen and the ridiculous hours she worked. It was a woman's face, not a girl's, and every time he looked at it his heart bled for her.

His father wrote to say that she was well, working fewer hours and enjoying something of the life in Egypt. Liam hoped that was true. There was still nothing from Lewis.

His old friend Matt went on Blighty leave for three weeks and came back full of himself, having painted the town red, seen every show worthy of the name, and cut a swathe through all the girls. Liam smiled and took it with a pinch of salt. Promoted to lance corporal, his friend was now with a different team, and Carl had gone too, after being gassed at Ypres. Not badly, but he was still in hospital. Somebody said Liam must have just missed him at Wandsworth, and wasn't that a shame. But the shame was that so many old mates had gone, to be replaced by unfamiliar faces. Even his sergeant, Keenan, had recently lost an arm at Bullecourt. Liam could scarcely believe how much he missed seeing that repulsive, gooseberry glare.

Their new sergeant, however, was younger, fitter, and more able, and Liam both liked and respected him. He was a veteran of Gallipoli too but had recently been transferred from one of the infantry battalions, and although he had done the requisite courses, he seemed glad of Liam's experience with the Vickers guns.

In June, the 3rd and 4th Divisions had a great success at Messines, although the casualties were horrifying, and as at Bullecourt in April and Pozières the previous year, the British commanders failed to follow up that success. The bitterness among the Australian troops was wholehearted and universal, the only consolation being that they as soldiers had not betrayed themselves.

Haig's plan for another great push in Flanders struck dismay into every heart. The artillery were moved up in July, the infantry and their supports in September.

August had been a month of storms that year, but September came in like an Indian summer, hot and fine and dry, as though determined to set the scene for their success. Infantry and artillery that had been bogged down earlier found the quagmire to the east of Ypres drained by the heat, and by the time the Australians were ready to take their part in the second stage of the Third Battle of Ypres, that shallow depression in the landscape resembled a cracked and rutted bowl.

The planning was incredibly detailed and thorough, and secrecy for once was paramount. The care with which every man was prepared for the coming battle largely dispersed their initial dismay, and after four months' rest and a fine season's training on the Somme, the men were fit and raring to go, ready to pull the British army out of the mire and crack the German defenses once and for all. It was generally felt and often said that with all these new strategies and any luck at all Sir Douglas might actually remember to follow through this time.

Physically, Liam was feeling particularly good, conscious of professional pride and satisfaction, and delighted that the battle plan, with maps and models, had been the subject of detailed lectures for days. Every man was aware of the aims and objectives and how these were to be achieved; and for the first time not one Australian division but two were to be fighting side by side, as the central spearhead of a push to take the ridge from Gheluvelt to Passchendaele.

The first major objective was Polygon Wood with its huge butte, the long, high mound of the shooting range once used by the Belgian army; but before that were two more woods, Glencorse and Nonne Bosschen, and dozens of concrete pill-boxes from which the worst danger would come during the advance. There was, however, to be no hours-long bombardment, rather a creeping barrage behind which the attacking troops would hide; and the danger there, of course, lay in the inevitable short-falling shells. In that situation there was always a chance that a man might be dispatched by his own side, although the majority of them had a touching faith in the accuracy of their own artillery.

They moved up from the Somme on September 12 and settled in small villages southwest of Ypres with orders to keep out of sight. On the eighteenth, the battalions moved in attacking order to within easy reach of the front line. They were due to march to their jumping-off positions at midnight on the nineteenth.

Ypres, Liam decided, was no more beautiful than it had been a year ago, but at least the sun was shining on its shapeless brickwork and battered, crumbling towers. The medieval streets were no more than tracks between piles of rubble and gaping shell holes, littered with charred oak beams and faceless, broken statues of saints and kings and merchants. They lay like the dead beside the shattered wheels of limbers and the gleaming metal of modern artillery, and they made him think of York with its churches and its carvings and its people. But there were no people here, only soldiers, and this medieval town was dead.

Military police with clipboards stood at every intersection, directing that stream of human traffic; the atmosphere was taut, voices sharp with prebattle nerves, everybody keyed up and anxious to be off. The machine-gun companies were attached in supporting positions to their respective battalions, and on that glorious afternoon there was little to do once they were in position but to check the guns and wait. And waiting was the hellish part, when doubts attacked in force and fear screwed the intestines into a fierce, hard knot. In an attempt to relax, Liam climbed the mound of the old ramparts, settling himself beneath the stump of a tree to look out along the Menin Road. It was no more than a rutted, pockmarked track in an ocher wilderness dotted with the detritus of war. In the heat haze, the slight rise of the ridge seemed an impossible distance away, with little puffs of smoke appearing here and there, to be followed by the inevitable series of dull thuds. On the still air, the chatter of gunfire occasionally intruded upon the buzz of voices from below.

Beneath him, on either side of that gap in the fortifications known as the Menin Gate, men were packed like sardines along the battered face of the wall, doubled by a perfect reflection in the still waters of the moat. There was an overplayed joke about this place that sprang to mind as he watched: "Would the last man through please shut the Gate?" But there was no gate to shut, and the streams of men were endless.

Many went out and few returned. Would he? It was hardly a new thought, but eternity had lost its attraction, and as in every other battle, Liam simply wanted to survive. With Georgina very much on his mind, however, he wondered whether he should write to her. A year ago, with death a constant companion, the idea of penning a final word would have seemed faintly ridiculous, but this coming confrontation would be the first for him since last September, and death had become a stranger whose face he might not recognize.

Still, he hesitated. From a crumpled pack, he took out a cigarette and lit it, and then he found the silver case in which he kept, not cigarettes, but those two precious photographs and a single letter of hers—a short note, loving but less erotic than the ones he had felt bound to destroy. If he should die, if his things were sent back home, he did not want that degree of intimacy revealed to others. It would have been unendurable for Georgina and hurtful to his family. Reading that well-thumbed note again, he supposed he should destroy that too, but he could not bear to have nothing of her; he needed just this one reminder that she loved him, and that their love had been true.

The past few months had brought acceptance of a kind,

but it had been hard-won. Since April he had scraped the barrel of despair before anger reached out to save him, a petty, illogical fury that was directed mainly at himself; and since then he had settled down to a more tolerable level in which the craving was occasional rather than constant. Looking back on the pain he had already endured, Liam had no wish to open those wounds afresh, and he knew it must be the same for her, but still he ached for news. In the past few months he had torn up innumerable letters to his father, begging for her address, and he imagined her doing much the same.

But still, if she knew what was facing him tomorrow . . .

As shadows began to lengthen over the moat, he could stand it no longer. With indelible pencil on a scrap of paper torn from his notebook, he wrote: *"I haven't forgotten, and I know I never will. I love you and I'm always thinking of you. I wish it could have been different. Yours, always and forever, Liam."*

He penned a note to his mother too and, with a covering letter to Robert Duncannon, instructed him to use his discretion about forwarding both; then, glad of a need for action, he hurried to find an orderly who might take the letter to a battalion post office. He was one of many with last-minute missives, and there was much grumbling and passing of cigarettes as bribes. It was more than his life was worth, the orderly said, to leave the massing point, but he went in the end.

By early evening the sky was clouding over, and after dark a fine drizzle of rain began. Spirits sank; it seemed the fates were determined to make life hard. By midnight, although the rain had ceased, the cross-country tracks leading off the Menin Road were slippery with surface mud, making the going slow indeed. Flanked on both sides by British troops, almost thirty thousand Australians moved up to their markers in silence. Intermittent shell fire from a nervous enemy lit their way as dawn's first fingers touched the sky, but the rain proved to have been a friend, creating sufficient mist to shroud the advancing armies from view.

On the left, by Glencorse Wood, battalions of the 3rd Brigade were caught by a sudden barrage of fire, suffering heavy losses. The feeling of vulnerability increased. Then the 8th, one of the last battalions to find their places on the far right, ran into another barrage, losing a company commander and several men. Coming up on the flank, the youngsters in Liam's company were suddenly nervous.

For a moment, catching sight of their officer's anxious face, Liam knew what he was thinking: that the plan was blown. But it seemed no more than a random strike, and as the shelling stopped he found himself craving a forbidden cigarette. In that final ten minutes, sighs and muffled coughs could be heard, and the sounds of men furtively relieving themselves. Liam set the range on the gun and counted the seconds. At 0540 all hell broke loose, the heavens rent by the flash and crack and ear-splitting thuds of heavy artillery. Firing the Vickers, Liam hardly noticed it. One man fed belts through the gun, another lit two cigarettes and placed one between his lips. He drew deeply as the belt was changed but did not take his hands from the mechanism, smoking and firing with savage pleasure as the barrage held its curtain 150 yards away. Four minutes later, as it began quite visibly to move beyond that point, the signal came to stop firing.

The German bombardment came even as they were dismantling the Vickers, and their sergeant was shouting at them all to get a bloody move on, their officer urging them forward, out of the line of fire.

Liam hoisted the heavy tripod, his number two slung the barrel across his shoulder while the others grabbed boxes of ammunition, running with the surge of men following the curtain of their own barrage. They were horrifyingly close, obscured by smoke, lit up as shells burst in front, deafened by explosions, punched by the blasts; it was a taste of hell on earth but they were beneath the arc of the counterbombardment and heading for the first objective.

As German pillboxes came to light through that dense cloud of dust and smoke, they were bombed and captured. Glencorse Wood was taken and Nonne Bosschen on the left; on the right the Victorian Battalions also took Fitzclarence Farm, capturing an officer and forty men. Moving forward, fighting as they went, the Australians reached that first line, almost six hundred yards away, within half an hour. All was in precise accordance with the timetable.

Possessed by a wild sense of elation as they dug into a shell hole, Liam could scarcely credit the success, the timing.

Stunned by that barrage and the speed of the attacking force, the Germans were giving up without much of a fight—it was unbelievable.

There was to be a halt of three quarters of an hour to allow for assessment and reorganization. It had seemed excessive beforehand, but in practice it proved essential. Men from the different battalions had been mixed up in that surge to escape the German shelling, and now they were sorted out and dug in to await the next stage of the advance. The barrage continued to provide cover, and to the minute it began to move forward. Again the Vickers was dismantled and hoisted, the men shouldering forward over rutted, slippery ground to reach the next objective.

If there had been little resistance to the first attack, there was less with the second. The next three hundred yards were covered according to plan, and the second line was reached by 0745.

On the right flank, struggling to keep ahead of the battalion, and gasping a little from the weight he carried, Liam led his men from shell hole to shell hole, keeping an eye on the officer in front. From the rim of one old crater, he directed Matt's team to another, and Liam's to a third where they dug in and set up the gun. What little rain had fallen the previous evening was mainly absorbed into cracks in the clay, but there was old mud in the bottom and the surface was greasy. With a wait of two hours ahead of them, it was worth digging a decent firing step and ledges to hold the ammunition.

Months of practice made short work of the job; and while the barrage moved up to strike the farther German lines, the team lit cigarettes and took turns with the binoculars, eager to know the state of play.

It was full daylight but misty with dust and smoke. The far left of the line was perhaps five hundred yards away, almost touching the southern tip of Polygon wood. A mass of stumps rather than trees, it looked like a skeleton army standing in a sunlit haze with the massive hump of the butte like a shadow behind. Much closer was the point known as Black Watch Corner; there a blockhouse was still in frantic action, bursts of fire playing havoc with the 5 Battalion. Nearer still, at Lone House, stood another pillbox; and most worrying of all to Liam, a line of six to the right stretching away above the Reutelbeek. He was instructed by the sergeant to cover that sector, while Matt, some twenty yards away on the next gun, would work in conjunction with him, providing covering fire for the attacking infantry. He hoped they would get going soon; the occupying Germans might be stunned for a while, but they would soon recover . . .

Excited chatter from the rest of the team told him that an attack was being made on Black Watch Corner by a company of the 5th. Trying to concentrate, he told them to shut up, but they were too wound-up, too concerned with what was going on. An officer was shot; his men were going mad, slaughtering the Germans who were trying to surrender; other officers were intervening . . . it was stopped, prisoners were being taken . . . the 5th were digging in . . .

"They can take care of their bloody selves," Liam muttered, his concern closer to home. A platoon of the 8th were moving out toward the nearest pillbox when a sudden blaze of fire revealed a German machine-gun team still very much on the alert. Rattling off a burst of bullets, he swore viciously as two men went down.

He heard the echo of Matt's supporting fire, then the eager demand of a young voice on his left. A head popped up beside him, binoculars raised. He yelled at the boy to get down, out of the way, dragged hard at his collar . . .

For a split second he heard and felt the violence of a massive explosion, and for that split second the heat and noise and pain were unendurable. The violence erupted into a great, deafening display of rockets and shells and bursting flares, lighting the black sky . . . it seemed to go on and on forever . . .

As the mist cleared, he looked about to see who was hurt. For a moment he thought he was alone, but a man beside him murmured his name. Liam turned and saw the face of his friend. His uniform was torn and bloody in places, but it was Ned, all right, it was definitely Ned . . .

The bullet that killed Liam also injured the boy he had saved. Hit in the hand, all he could do was stare at the inert body beside him, at the bloody mass that had been the side of his corporal's face. Matt saw it all and in a break in the firing, came dashing across to give assistance. Seeing his old mate was dead, he simply unfastened the useless steel helmet and held him for a moment, not caring about the blood.

"He was one of the originals, you know," Matt said softly to anyone who cared to listen. "He was there at Anzac . . ."

When their officer came, crouching in the mud at the crater's foot, the number two gave a whispered report on what had happened. The boy with his injured hand lay back, tears streaming down his white face. Matt emptied the pockets. A crumpled pack of cigarettes, a silver case, matches, notebook, a stub of pencil, letters in dog-eared envelopes, and a diary . . .

"Were you his friend? Then you'd better hang on to them," the officer said. He sighed, glancing anxiously at his watch, then peered over the crater's rim. "Bury him. Mark the grave as best you can. We can't take him back."

Beneath that superficial covering of mud, the ground was hard. Digging enough of it to bury a man was far from easy, but they managed it. Matt, who was not religious, could think of nothing more than to bid farewell to a brave man and a good mate. He concluded those few words with a prayer that he might rest in peace, although at that moment, and even to him, the words had a hollow ring.

They fashioned a rough cross from pieces of an ammunition box and gouged his name and number with a bayonet in the hope that the grave would later be found, the body reinterred in a proper place.

But the ground they won that day was swamped by autumn rains. Polygon Wood was taken, and later—much later—the combined forces also took Passchendaele. That winter their Russian allies made a separate peace, and the following spring the German armies recaptured the Ypres Salient and almost forty miles of Allied territory.

Along with so many more, Liam Elliott's grave was lost.

31

Opening an unusually thick envelope, Stephen rapidly scanned the single page of Zoe's letter and was disappointed by its brevity. In a futile search for more, he flicked through the accompanying wad of photocopied army forms and headed letters, his attention caught by a typewritten sheet with Liam's name and serial number and *2nd M.G. Coy. A.I.F.* listed at the top.

Almost in spite of himself, he let his eyes run down the page.

> *. . . on Sep 20th, 1917, Cpl. Elliott was . . . advancing with the infantry . . . made a halt and took cover in shell holes to the left of Northampton Farm . . . waiting for your barrage to lift . . . lot of German snipers . . . while Cpl. Elliott had his head exposed . . . a bullet struck him in the right side of the head . . . He died instantly, he suffered no pain, before he had time to realize the first shock he was dead . . . bullet that killed him also wounded another . . .*

As though to staunch a sudden wound, Stephen pressed those pages back together and held them, tight, within his hands. It was several seconds before he drew a cautious breath, and when he did the pain flooded in on a hot, unwelcome wave. The news might have been recent, intensely personal, the death of a close and much-loved friend; the scene of grief and compassion was overwhelming.

With bowed head he sat quite still, unaware of his surroundings, contemplating that death, its suddenness, the years snatched away by one stray bullet.

Footsteps, a tap at the door. Stephen averted his head and stood up, peering from the office window as though something vital had caught his attention. He addressed the man without looking at him, and only when he had himself under control again, did he turn and apologize.

The problem was soon solved. A moment later he was alone again, the papers still in his hand, rolled now like a baton. With great care he returned them to their envelope, all the time wondering at the power of those words. He had known, Stephen kept telling himself, all the time he had known that Liam was dead, and that date, September 20, 1917, was not news to him. Knowing should have lessened the impact, but it didn't. Having come to know Liam Elliott more intimately than his closest friend, Stephen felt bereaved.

Mingled with sorrow was a sense of needless waste; anger too that the world seemed so unchanged. Suddenly vulnerable, he wished that Zoe might have kept hold of that information rather than sending it on. It made him all too aware of the transient nature of human life, and remembering the dreams, he began to wonder whether sudden death was his destiny too.

He thrust the idea away. That was depression working, and tiredness, and the knowledge that he was sick to the heart of this endless stress.

Even Karachi was no improvement. After forty-eight hours, Stephen was more than usually glad to be leaving. The inevitable barrage of port officials had descended at unpredictable times to deliver their various assults upon his patience and ingenuity, and had departed, weighed down with cigarettes and paperwork and duty-free whisky, leaving nothing but the memory of their gleeful smiles.

As he jammed on his hat and adjusted the chin strap, the pilot wished him a pleasant voyage, but there was a glint in his eye as he turned to leave. The southwest monsoons were blowing, and he knew as well as Stephen that the next couple of days and nights were going to be far from pleasant.

Lurching in the swell in the lee of the *Damaris*, the pilot boat hovered, its engines growling over the noise of the wind. Stephen leaned over the starboard bridgewing, watched the pilot down the ship's side and his nifty leap onto the boat; with a full-throated roar, it surged away, bouncing as it caught buffeting wind and waves beyond the ship. Envy clutched Stephen's heart as it disappeared into the evening murk: He wished he was on it and going home, not facing his tenth trip through the jaws of Hormuz with no specific date for relief. Both Second Mate and Second Engineer had been relieved last time around in Kuwait, and watching them go had been hellish. Until then, he had not realized just how much he wanted to be off. Ah well, he was getting to know the new men, and they seemed all right.

He watched the Bos'n and a seaman hoist the pilot ladder inboard and, with a bitter sigh, turned and closed the bridge door behind him. It was cooler inside.

With the anchorage astern of them and a force-eight gale on the port bow, Stephen ordered the speed kept down to ten knots. With no cargo the ship was light and high in the water, yet tanks had to be cleaned and freed from flammable gases; and in spite of the weather that meant men on deck, working throughout the night. The Mate, who had been up for most of their forty-eight hours in Karachi, supervising the discharge of cargo, had grabbed a couple of hours' sleep and something to eat and was about to go on deck to start washing the dregs of gasoline from numbers one and two tanks up by the fo'c'sle. It was not a particularly arduous task, but the pumping of inert gas into all the cargo tanks was long and tedious, with valves and pressures to be constantly monitored. Altogether, it would take approximately twenty-four hours, and with this weather to contend with, Stephen did not envy the job.

Still, he had done it often himself, and without an understanding master to split those hours on deck. Remembering the utter exhaustion of discharging a cargo, then getting to sea and having to tank-clean without chance to sleep at all, was something that could still give him the horrors. He had once worked a straight forty hours without sleep, a nightmare that he was determined never to impose upon any of his own officers. What hardship was it to do a bridge watch occasionally to enable a sensible relief system to work on deck? Stephen could not understand the masters who still insisted, in this era of reduced manpower, that their watch-keeping days were over.

His standard arrangement with his officers required no more than the briefest acknowledgment. With the arrival of the Third Mate, Stephen handed the watch over to him, told him to speak to the Mate on deck—via the walkie-talkie radio—if he needed advice, and meeting Johnny in oilskins and hard hat, simply said that he would be relieved on deck at midnight.

He checked his watch: twenty-five minutes to seven and it was time to have his dinner and go to bed. At midnight he would take over the bridge watch for six hours while the Second Mate took over the tank cleaning. They would each work six on, six off until the job was finished. Nor could the engineers go to bed and rest; after working around the clock in port, they must continue to man the engine room until the job was done. Not an easy time for anybody, and Mac's men were as tired as his own.

Stephen ate with Mac in the saloon, and mostly in silence. They were both too weary for small talk, too used to the harassment of Karachi even to comment on it. As though by mutual consent they made short work of the meal and rose from the table together. The ship was rolling heavily, and the climb up several flights of stairs was something of an effort. By the time Stephen reached his cabin he had the beginnings of a headache.

He lifted the heavy typewriter from his office desk and set it on the floor, then sided his paperwork away, locking drawers and cupboards for safety. In his dayroom, he retrieved a handful of music tapes that had already found their way to the deck, and having made sure nothing else could wake him with bangs and crashes, he switched on some music, dimmed the lights, poured himself a large measure of whiskey, and raised the blind on the forward window. It was too dark to see very much, but he could just make out white-tipped spray rising in sheets from the port bow, and a glimmer of torches on the starboard side. With a sigh he lowered the blind, dragged off his damp shirt, and sat down to read his mail.

Joan's letter was full of Zoe's visit to York, and the fact that there had been a reply, at long last, from the Australian War Memorial. Months ago, Stephen had persuaded her to write to Canberra regarding Liam's war record, and the reply apparently had been well worth the wait. Very sad, Joan's letter said, and she had shed a few tears over it—Stephen felt his own heart lurch again at that—but Zoe thought he would be pleased by the detail and was sending on copies.

Pleased was by far the wrong word, he thought, but he turned again to Zoe's letter, as disappointed now as he had been earlier. The account of her trip to York was much briefer than Joan's, expanding only to mention the hunch which had led her to check the old visitors book at his flat.

"But I didn't stay long, the place felt very empty and strange without you . . ."

For some reason that disturbed him. It seemed to stress his current sense of unreality and made him more aware than ever that his life was lived in separate boxes, that each journey between the two required him to assume another identity. There was always an awkwardness about that, particularly going home, a feeling of dissociation until he found again the requisite color and character to blend in with his surroundings. From here, in this situation, he could scarcely recall the man who lived in York, the man who for a few short weeks had been so absolutely happy in the company of a young woman named Zoe Clifford. And he had been happy; she had made him feel lighthearted and young, as though the world still had something to offer, something worth striving for. It seemed so strange looking back, he began to wonder whether he had imagined it; worse, that this other half of him had sunk without trace.

He read the letter through again and sighed over it, over the change in tone, the change in her. Originally, she had written in an easy, conversational style that evoked voice, humor, enthusiasm, and yes, her affection too, which came through the lines to warm him in a silent embrace. Of late, however, her letters had become rather stilted, very much confined to the research she was doing. The rest of her life was barely mentioned. He wondered why. Perhaps she thought he was no longer interested, perhaps there was someone else after all. Zoe had closed a door somewhere, and the view was now restricted.

But perhaps, Stephen reasoned, the fault was not all hers. He had a suspicion that he was equally to blame, that in his dogged determination to stick to his own rules, he had managed to alienate her affection. And anyway, he asked himself, what did he write about these days? Not his own emotions, that was for sure; they were shackled to a wall in some remote dungeon of his soul and would not be released until he was home and free. The lacerating stress of these weekly voyages between Kuwait and Karachi was another topic he avoided, which left his correspondence as unadorned as extracts from the logbook.

Even his response to the research was lacking in vitality, and yet he would read her letters, logging opinions and assumptions along with every new discovery, and feel a tingle of excitement. When it came to setting it down on paper, however, his enthusiasm seemed to wane. It was a new and unwelcome phenomenon to one who had always enjoyed writing as a form of communication, and the weary thought "I'll tell her when I see her . . ." had become a habit.

He felt as dry and barren as the desert, and across the harsh landscape of his inner vision, Zoe appeared with no more substance than a mirage.

Glancing at the first page of those photocopied sheets, he saw the heading "Australian War Memorial" and knew a deep reluctance to read further. His eyes were dry with fatigue, head aching with the increasingly violent motion of the ship. He should get to bed, get some sleep. And yet . . .

The letter stated that there were five eyewitness reports of Corporal Elliott's death in the Red Cross files, which made Stephen think that someone must have queried the facts, either because his body was never found or someone did not believe the manner of his death. Perhaps it was Robin, to whom that tale of a bullet through the head must have sounded exceedingly suspect; yet despite being a convenient fiction for the poor souls who were literally blown to bits, *some* men had to die like that, cleanly, with all their limbs intact. But his body was never found, *ergo,* the Red Cross inquiry.

What a hell of a job, Stephen thought, his mind unable to

grasp the extent of such a task, if all the thousands upon thousands of missing were investigated to that extent. Tracing five eyewitnesses for *one man's death* . . . and from the dates of those statements, taken up to eighteen months later, from Grantham in Lincolnshire to the State of Victoria, the size and scope of the investigation was incredible.

After that, he had to read the statements, just to see how well they tallied with that first account given by a sergeant at Grantham in March 1918. Apart from one, who seemed to be out with regard to location, they tallied very well, too well to be making things up for the benefit of anybody's sensibilities. But even though he had steeled himself to read those accounts, Stephen found himself unbearably moved by the personal detail.

He was a tall man, well-built, fair, about 25 years of age . . .
He was known as Bill . . .
I knew him—I saw him killed . . . I have already written to his people about it . . .
I was 20 yards away at the time—I saw his body a few minutes later . . .
He was buried on the battlefield . . .

It was enough; he did not want to read more. The rest could wait for another time. Bracing himself against the motion of the ship, he poured himself another drink, knowing it must be the last, he really had to get some sleep. He sipped the measure of twelve-year-old malt slowly, savoring its smoothness, letting his mind drift on the question of Liam's death and the enigma of his relationship with Georgina. What must she have felt? he wondered; and in the next moment he was thinking about Zoe, trying to imagine what her reaction would be, if . . .

That made him shiver. There were too many similarities for comfort, too many coincidences that would never be explained, and he did not want to make one more. Please God, let there be no stray bullets for him!

He drank the rest of the whisky in one gulp, tucked the empty glass against a protecting cushion, and lurched across to his bedroom, not even slightly drunk. From a cupboard he

rescued his bright orange life jacket and, lifting the mattress of
his double bunk, stuffed it underneath, making a well between
the raised edge and the wall.

His bunk ran fore and aft, a bad design, but wedged into
that small valley, Stephen was prevented from rolling side to
side. It did not prevent the other motion, though, that tipping
from head to toe, like some fairground swing-boat, as the ship
pitched and lifted with every wave. It was an unpleasant cork-
screw motion made worse by the lack of cargo. With weight in
those massive tanks, the *Damaris* was not a bad old girl, but
light, she could perform somersaults on a wet facecloth, of
that Stephen was convinced. He tensed, listening as the bow
plunged into those heavy seas and the stern lifted beneath him,
right out of the water. The noise rose to a scream as the propeller raced, then came the unearthly groan and shudder as the
stern slammed down and the prop bit deep. Everything quaked
and trembled, steel decks and bulkheads, interior walls, cupboards, fittings, and in the darkness the noise and vibration
seemed worse, as though the ship were being physically
wrenched apart.

The ship surged across to port, forcing his back against
the wall, pitched forward with a rising shriek, rolled again to
starboard and slammed back with a particularly violent shuddering groan . . . a bad one, that.

Searching for the rhythm, trying to relax with it, Stephen
found himself thinking of Ruth. Storms had always unnerved
her, even at home, and the typhoon they had met off Japan
that time had seen her in a state of terror, convinced with every
pounding wave that death was no more than minutes away.
When the corrugated awnings were torn off the aft accommodation, she had dissolved into helpless, hysterical tears, and the
sight of the foredeck bending under the strain of wind and sea
finished her completely. It availed nothing to explain that the
ship was designed to bend, that if it did not, it would break in
two . . . Ruth had been huddled in a life jacket, deaf to all
reason.

Stephen had been ashamed of her. He could admit that
now. He had been Mate at the time, and she had been the only
wife aboard; he would never forget the pitying glances of the

other officers. They had tried to be kind, but he knew what they were thinking, and the Master had rapidly lost all patience, ordering her below, off his bridge where she was starting to unnerve him. It had been a humiliating experience, made worse by the fact that it had been a genuinely worrying situation. With the true unpredictability of typhoons, that one had turned and caught them in its new path, just as they were running away from it. And it had been particularly violent, force-twelve and more.

And then he thought of another such incident, off Cape Hatteras a few years later, and the Mate's teenage daughter giggling with glee as enormous turquoise seas broke over the foredeck, swamping the fully loaded ship. For all the world, it had looked as though they were sinking, but she had known otherwise. Laughing with her, he had remarked on her bravery, whereupon she had admitted to being scared at night but loving it during the day, when it was so *exciting*. "I used to be frightened of the *Bomb*," she had told Stephen, "you know, nuclear holocaust, and all that. But living through a storm at sea, thinking all night that you're going to die any minute, it sort of *cures* you, doesn't it? You know you can't escape, so you just have to accept it. I'm not scared of dying anymore . . ."

How old had she been? Thirteen, fourteen? No more than that. *Out of the mouths of babes*, he thought, admiring her guts and her wisdom, and knowing she was right. Living with the thought of dying made the idea lose all its terrors, inducing a certain fatalism, a readiness to accept the worst.

Had Liam felt like that?

Or had he felt, like Stephen, that it was not the idea of death that was frightening, but the endurance required to survive?

He finished his watch at six in the morning, as the pitch-black murk became gray, then pink and orange, and finally a sickly yellow, like thick industrial pollution. The dust was so fine it was almost the texture of talcum powder, collected by winds blowing with the force of hurricanes across North Africa and the Arabian Desert, and it found its way through every crack and crevice, leaving its evidence across charts and instruments,

blearing the windows with muck and salt, so that it was necessary to peer through spinning, clear-view screens and consult
the radar every few minutes.

The *Damaris* was still punching those seas, sending up
great walls of water over the port bow; as she rose, they came
tumbling back over the foredeck to swirl against the accommodation. Standing on the central catwalk, Johnny and the Second
Mate were soaked by spray. Stephen watched them shouting
against the wind, bright yellow oilskins glistening as they
turned and parted. Clinging to the rails, the Mate made his way
forward, while young Paul, after six hours on deck, staggered
inside to breakfast and his bunk.

Stephen went down to his office, timing his descent of the
steps with the roll of the ship. He made half a cup of coffee,
spent an uncomfortable hour at his desk in an attempt to make
some impression upon the paperwork, then went down for
breakfast in the saloon. After that he retired to his bunk, sleeping solidly for four hours before returning to the bridge at
twelve. The gas freeing was completed by eight that evening,
but the weather was still too bad to increase speed. By the time
they reached the vicinity of Fujairah, just before five in the
morning of the third day, it was too late to reach Hormuz with
any degree of safety.

As though gunboats and helicopters were not enough to
contend with, Stephen had received warning by telex of mines
in the approaches to the Kuwaiti terminals; and only a few
days before on the BBC World Service had come reports of an
American supertanker, the *Texaco Caribbean*, hitting a mine in
the Gulf of Oman, eight miles off Fujairah. It was thought to
be a stray, drifting down from the strait, but no one could be
sure. It was a daunting prospect, but as Stephen had said to
his senior officers at the time, a tanker is a very difficult vessel to
sink. With buoyancy retained by all those sealed compartments,
providing the vessel was hit in the bow—the most obvious
place under way—then little damage would be sustained. A
hefty claim on the insurance, into Dubai for repairs, and with
any luck at all, the company would fly most of them home.

Brave words, cheerfully said. But in the teeth of that still-
howling gale, with visibility down to a couple of hundred yards,

Stephen's nerves were twitching. Never yet had he damaged a ship, and he did not intend to start now. Damage was damage, however slight, and there was always the unnerving possibility of someone being in the wrong place at the wrong time. He could do without that on his conscience.

In the predawn darkness he was glad they were late, glad of those necessary hours at the deep-water anchorage off Fujairah during which they could all take a much-needed rest. As they came slowly within the shelter afforded by the land, the wind lessened appreciably. In the wheelhouse, studying the charts, it was possible to stand without clinging on and to move about with some degree of ease.

The broad sweep of the radar revealed dozens of ships at anchor and the protecting ridge of land to the west. With their speed reduced to a half, he found a suitable area, checked it against the radar, and plotted a position where it was possible to swing with ease. While the Third Mate watched, he marked the place on the chart and gave directions to the helmsman at the wheel. As he checked the depth of water—forty-five fathoms—against the echo sounder, the crackle of his walkie-talkie radio told him the Mate was out on deck with the anchor party. Stephen responded, picking up the engine room telephone to ask the duty engineer for Dead Slow Ahead. A few minutes later, as the ship's speed came right down, he spoke on the radio to the Mate.

"She's down to three knots, walk the anchor back to one shackle . . ."

He could see the flash of torches on the fo'c'sle, hear the creaks and groans of the port anchor being slowly lowered by winch, the dull clunks of that massive chain going out over the side. In this depth of water, just to let go would be to burn out the windlass brake, or worse, to drag the chain bodily from its housing. Slowly, slowly was the trick . . .

A couple of minutes, and the Mate's voice came back, "One shackle and holding . . ."

"Hold till we're in position." He glanced back at the helmsman on the wheel, and the Third Mate moving between chart and radar. On his signal, Stephen rang down for Slow Astern, then hurried out to the bridgewing to watch the action of the propeller-wash against the ship's side. When it was just coming back and passing him, he knew the ship was stopped in the water.

"Okay, she's stopped. Just walk the anchor out and let me know how she's leading."

He listened to the Mate's voice over the walkie-talkie, counting each shackle off as it descended those forty-five fathoms to the seabed below. After three shackles, he said, "Cable starting to lead astern . . ."

"Okay." The anchor was down, the cable starting to lie along the seabed.

"Four shackles, cable leading astern . . ."

Stephen turned and shouted to the Third Mate. "Stop engines."

"Five shackles, cable up and down . . ."

He waited, while the wind whipped at his hair and the night was still full of those creaks and groans from the windlass. It might be time to give that cable a bit of assistance, rather than let it fall in a heap around the anchor.

"Six shackles, cable beginning to lead ahead . . ."

"Okay, we'll pull her back a bit"—he turned to the Third Mate—"ring down for Slow Astern."

"Slow Astern it is, Captain."

He leaned over the port side, watching those flickering torches on the fo'c'sle. The weather was clearing, ahead and to port he could see the misted lights of other ships. He glanced at his watch: almost half past five, not long to daybreak.

With the familiar crackle that preceded the Mate's regular report, there was suddenly an almighty flash from somewhere below and astern, and a simultaneous explosion that knocked Stephen sideways.

Stunned, deafened, his ears ringing from the blast, for a second or two he lay on the deck wondering why the night should be glowing like November 5, and what the hell had gone wrong in the engine room.

He tried to get up, pushing with his right hand against the step of the compass—and cried out as pain shot like red-hot steel through his shoulder to his chest and spine and wrist. For a moment, he almost passed out. Fending off the Third Mate's assistance, he took a deep breath, which hurt horribly, and demanded to know what had happened.

"I don't know, sir!" His voice was high, panicky. "I think something's blown in the engine room . . . the alarms went, then stopped—"

"Well then, press the manual alarms, for God's sake—and pass me that bloody radio!"

"Are you all right, Captain?"

"No, but I can *manage*," Stephen insisted, hauling himself to his feet and shouting above the ringing in his head. "Alarms, Marcus—*now*!"

As the young man ran to obey, Stephen pressed the transmit button to answer the faint, crackling voice of the Mate. "No, Johnny, I don't know for sure—might be the engine, more likely a fucking mine. Start the fire pump for'ard, and get yourself back here, sharp as you can. Out."

He leaned for a moment on the bridge front, dragging air into his lungs, fighting to conquer the nausea coming in waves. His right arm hurt like hell, and he did not seem able to move it. With it hanging like a useless appendage, he forced himself back to the wheelhouse and ordered the Third Mate to his emergency station.

As he clattered away down an outer ladder, the inner door opened to admit the Chief Engineer and Radio Officer, and a blast of ringing from the alarms. Sparks was only half dressed, his boots and boilersuit trailing, while he dragged on his gear, Mac fastened a life jacket and listened to Stephen's very brief report. His red beard bristled as he set his jaw.

"So both of them were down there? Second and Third? I'd better get down and investigate."

"Keep me advised, Chief."

Armed with torch and radio, Mac went back the way he had come. Watching him descend into darkness, for the first time Stephen realized that all the lights were out, even those that should have been powered by the emergency generator. Familiar with the unlit bridge, he had not noticed before. It was obviously bad down there, whatever the cause. He switched off the manual alarms, and in the ensuing silence could hear the rattling of feet on steps and steel ladders, and the excited, slightly panicky chatter of the crew rising from the stairwell.

Everything was echoing around the accommodation, and it was a weird, unnatural sound, accentuating the deadness of the ship, its lack of a heartbeat.

For a second, it almost unnerved him; he thought about the anchor and thanked God the cable was out, enough to hold at least. Then his radio crackled, and Mac's voice was reporting that he had met the Electrician on the stairs—he had tried to get to his emergency station in the engine room, but all he could see were flames . . .

"Second and Third Engineers? Have they turned up?" The reply was negative and Stephen's heart sank. "Okay—get to Emergency HQ right away. I'll be in touch."

He turned to Sparks, hovering by the VHF. Thank God that thing worked off its own batteries, everything else was down, radar, computers, direction finder. "Put out a Mayday, all frequencies, with present position—on fire, request immediate assistance."

The Second and Third Mates reported in. With the exception of the anchor party, all crew were present and correct at boat stations. Stephen bit back a curse.

"Well, get them to their *emergency* stations—and tell them to stop panicking. We're in no danger of sinking, but the engine room's on fire, and two engineers are missing. The Chief and Mate are on their way to you now . . ."

Where *was* the Mate? "Did you hear that, Johnny?"

"I heard you, Captain—I'm on my way—coming around the accommodation now." He left his radio on and Stephen could hear his breathing, slightly ragged, as though he were running. It was a long way from the fo'c'sle . . . "I tell you what, it's bloody hot out here . . ."

Stephen glanced at his watch. Twenty-three minutes to six, just seven minutes since he had last glanced at it, seconds before the blast. It seemed an eternity. He steeled himself for what he had to say next.

"Chief, when the Mate gets to you, I want him and Lecky geared up—flame suits, breathing apparatus—to search the engine room for the missing men."

"Captain, I'm all geared up already—let me go down."

It was as he expected. "*No*, Chief. Absolutely not. I know

how you feel, but you're the only engineer I've got just now, and I need you."

"It's my engine room."

"And it's my ship. Stay out, Mac—and that's an order." Stephen took a deep breath, and winced at the ensuing pain. "You'd better go around and trip the fuel shutdowns."

"I've done that." He sounded furious.

"Good. Stay where you are and keep me informed."

He glanced again at the time, urging a response from Fujairah. He thought about the missing men, realizing medical aid would be essential, if only to treat victims of shock and smoke. Please God, nothing worse. As he turned to Sparks, a loud, heavily accented voice startled them both. A port control officer from Fujairah announced that fire-fighting tugs would be with them in thirty minutes; Sparks responded, requesting the assistance of a doctor. Moments later, there was another call, this time from a salvage tug from Hormuz, offering to come and stand by; the offer was followed by several more.

"The vultures are gathering," Stephen murmured bitterly, aware that an abandoned ship was a rich prize for the salvage companies. Well, they could gather; he had no intention of abandoning anything, least of all his ship.

"How's that arm, Captain?"

He shook his head. "It'll do for the time being." He was more concerned for those men in the engine room, envisaging the different levels from propeller shaft up to control room, and trying to relate that mental map to the blast. The control room was on the port side, and the loss of power could be attributable to a wipeout in that area. At least one of those men must have been there when the explosion occurred.

He felt for his cigarettes and realized they were missing. Sparks passed one of his own across and left the pack within reach. Stephen inhaled on a shuddering breath and went out to peer over the port bridgewing. A dull glow lit up the surrounding area and was reflected by the dancing waves. In the east, a pale band of lighter cloud streaked the horizon. The sun was coming up, and would soon add to the heat traveling up through steel decks and bulkheads.

Wondering what was happening down there, praying for

a miracle, he found himself questioning, illogically, the safety of the cargo tanks. How thoroughly had they been inerted? And to what point of destruction did theory apply? If those tugs didn't get here soon, they might all be blown to kingdom come.

His walkie-talkie sparked into life. "Emergency HQ to bridge."

"Go ahead, Chief."

"Lecky and the Mate have found the Second. He's got a gash on the head and he's not too good—only half-conscious. But he's out, he's alive. No sign yet of the Third . . ."

Oh thank God. One of them alive at least . . . But what of the other man? "Let me speak to the Mate."

Johnny's voice was hoarse, his report staccato. "Tried the port entrance—full of smoke and flame. We just shut the door on it. Starboard side—smoke but no flame." He paused for breath, and Stephen could hear it rasping in his throat. "Went in, down ladder—couldn't see a damn thing. Stuck together. Halfway down on starboard side—found the Second crawling along the plates toward us. Practically unconscious. Dragged him out. He's got a bad gash on his head, but I think he'll live . . ."

"Well done, Johnny. Pass that on to Lecky too." For a second Stephen paused, thinking about the missing man, recollecting his whiskery grin and a cheery greeting as they passed on the stairs. When was that? Yesterday? He tried to keep his voice steady. "Do you feel able to go back? To search again?"

There was another pause, as though the men at the other end were consulting. Then the Mate's voice again. "Affirmative, Captain. We're going down now."

"Be careful, Johnny—no heroics. From either of you."

Something like a laugh came back at him. "Heroics? Us? We're more like Laurel and bloody Hardy."

Stephen smiled at the image: the tall, lanky Mate and Lecky who was short and very round . . . He pulled himself up short and asked for Mac. "Detach the Second Mate, Chief, and get your man to the hospital."

Back in the wheelhouse, Sparks lit him another cigarette; a few minutes later, Mac was calling with the news that they had managed to get some sense out of the injured man. He had answered a generator alarm, and as he left the control room to check it out, the explosion occurred. The Third Engineer was still in there.

"Not good."

"No. Especially as he's almost sure that something hit the ship from outside, just by the control room."

"A mine."

"Sounds like it."

"The *bastards* . . ."

It struck him again how fortunate they were to have got the anchor laid out before the blast; otherwise the ship would have been drifting, helpless and on fire, a danger to half the ships in the anchorage. And there were plenty. All tankers.

In the unnatural silence he could hear the wind buffeting the funnel, flapping the radio aerials and stays; the sea was making a shushing noise to windward, as it did when they were under way . . . and he suddenly became aware that the deck beneath him had a tilt to it; water was rushing into the engine room, pulling the ship down by the stern.

The Mate's voice intruded upon that consideration. "It's no-go, Captain. Everything's on fire down there. We managed to get pretty close, though—spotted a clear space around the hole, water flooding in just there—" He broke off, sniffed audibly, and seemed to be having difficulty getting the next words out. "The body was in bits. I've told the Chief—no chance of getting near it."

Hearing those words, Stephen realized that while he had not consciously framed the thought, it was no more than he had expected. Nevertheless, an image sprang to mind of Jim Stubbs, Third Engineer, short, thickset, with wild gray hair and always a couple of days of stubble on his chin. An unkempt, scruffy Liverpudlian, unmarried, uncertificated, and wedded to the job. His humor was abrasive, and he was a bit too fond of the booze, but he was reliable and a bloody good engineer.

What a way to die.

And for what?

Sorrow and pity washed over him, together with the vaguely consolatory thought that it must have been instantaneous. That was the only decent thing about it.

With an effort he found his voice and forced it to remain

calm. "I understand. You've done all you could. Thanks for that. Is Lecky okay?"

"He's wheezing like hell, but he'll be all right."

"Good." Now, back to business. "Right, Johnny, in your considered opinion, is it now time to batten everything down and flood with CO_2?"

"It certainly is, Captain."

"Right, Johnny—put me on to the Chief."

He ordered Mac to close all openings and ventilators and to release the carbon dioxide gas, then he called the Third Mate to see to the boundary cooling.

"Get those fire hoses through the accommodation, leave them running, and *get out*. Make sure the crew are away from the area. Get them up for'ard and on to the fo'c'sle—and give the Bos'n a radio, we'll need to keep in touch. Then come to the bridge."

Over the starboard bow he could see the tugs approaching, bright orange hulls standing out in the soupy daylight; behind them, coming up fast, was a pilot boat. Stephen spoke to the Second Mate in the ship's hospital with the injured man. "Get your party up for'ard, Paul, with the crew. The pilot boat's on its way with a doctor."

From the bridgewing he watched the crew, bobbing about in twos and threes as they hurried along the main deck, followed at a more sedate pace by the stretcher-party. The injured man's face was dappled, white patches against the black where the Second Mate had cleaned his cuts and dressed them. Still, a couple of days in a proper hospital and he should be all right. Be up and chasing the nurses in no time . . .

The Mate and Lecky, both haggard and disheveled, joined him, Lecky collapsing onto the compass step as though his chubby legs would not hold out another instant. He looked in poor shape, trembling visibly as Sparks lit him a cigarette. Johnny was gray with strain but bearing up.

"Well, here we are, smoking on deck . . ." He gave a weak little laugh, but suddenly his mouth was working. He turned away to watch the activity on deck while Stephen studied his back and decided to be brisk.

"I think you should go with them, see a doctor. Both of you," he added, turning back to the other man. He really did look bad; Stephen felt guilty, thinking about what he had put them through. Weakly, Lecky nodded his agreement; it was clear he wanted to be off the ship, and who could blame him.

Johnny, however, shook his head. He was staying, he said, and would be fine once he had rested and had something to drink. "Any chance of liberating a few cans of Coke? I've got a mouth like the bottom of a birdcage."

It was something Stephen had not had chance to think of. His cabin was nearest, however, and had a recently restocked fridge of soft drinks and a cupboard full of spirits for entertaining. Sparks volunteered to go while Stephen manned the VHF. Calls were still coming in from other ships and tugs eager to offer assistance, and on the port quarter, the fire fighters were busily hosing seawater over the afterdeck and into that gaping hole below.

Mac came up to join them, his steps dragging like an old man's. His face was ashen, and as he propped himself up against the pilot chair, he seemed incapable of speech. He glanced at Stephen and away, and simply shook his head.

"Mac, I'm sorry . . ." For everything, he might have added—that shocking death, the ruin belowdecks, and most of all for having to forbid his friend the opportunity to search his own engine room for his own men. It felt like a betrayal, and yet Stephen's first duty was to the ship.

"No, you did what you had to . . ." He lit a cigarette and smoked in silence for a while. Then, noticing Stephen's useless arm, asked what had happened.

"The blast knocked me over—I fell against that bloody thing"—he indicated the compass repeater on the bridgewing—"and must have hit the deck awkwardly. I think it's dislocated."

"Could be broken—you'd better get the doctor up here, let him have a look at it."

But Stephen for the first time was indecisive, torn between the pain he was suffering and the need to stay aboard. While he debated what to do, Mac took his radio and called up the Second Mate, asking him to escort the doctor up to the bridge once the injured man was safely off the ship.

Twenty minutes later he was with them, a small, dapper Arab in a smart linen suit, only slightly soiled by his climb up

the pilot ladder to the fo'c'sle. His English spoke of several
years' training in an English hospital.

Slender fingers examined the injured arm, and a pair of
dark, unsmiling eyes studied Stephen's face as he tried to answer questions and avoid too many grunts of pain. Behind and
to one side of the doctor, the Second Mate, as ship's medical
officer, hovered uncomfortably. Grimy and sweat-stained,
wearing a ragged boilersuit open to the navel, and with his hair
plastered to his head, he was not the average nurse. Meeting
his anxious gaze, Stephen managed a lopsided grin.

The doctor said, "I think no break or fracture, but a dislocation of the shoulder. I can manipulate it back into position now,
but it will be very painful. You should come to hospital. There
we can give anesthetic. And also X-ray for possible small frac-
tures in the wrist."

"I'm not leaving the ship."

There was an eloquent shrug. "You wish me to perform
the operation now?"

Stephen glanced at his medical officer. "Get Sparks. Tell
him to bring the whiskey."

A slight curl of the lip expressed the doctor's disapproval.
"Alcohol is not good for shock."

"I know that. But it's bloody good for pain."

He reached for the bottle, removed the cap, and took a
hefty slug. Then he took another. It caught his breath for a
moment and made his eyes water, but he still held the little
doctor's gaze. It felt like a battle of wills, one that Stephen was
not at all sure he would win. Never mind, he would go down
trying. And he would not leave the ship.

"Lie down, please. On the floor, on your side."

He felt the knee in his back, one hand against his shoulder,
the other at his wrist. There was a sudden wrench and agonizing pain, and a grinding crack that seemed to explode in his
skull . . .

The reek of ammonia brought him around. Wafting the smelling
salts beneath Stephen's nose, the Second Mate looked as
though he were the one about to faint. The doctor was checking
the contents of his bag.

"You should rest," that cool voice advised. "Go to bed."

"Don't be bloody silly . . ."

Standing over him, with surprising gentleness the doctor eased him forward; between them, he and the Second Mate got Stephen to his feet and through the open door of the sea cabin. Sparks had folded the sheets back and stood beside the bunk like a hotel manager.

As though instructing a child, the doctor said, "Here is a bed—rest in it." To the Second Mate, he added, "He will need the arm supported by a sling. There will be much bruising, much pain. You should give him something to relieve it."

Stephen sat on the edge of the bunk, nursing his arm; he felt sick and shaky and took several deep breaths to control it. As the doctor glided out towards the bridgewing, he glanced at Sparks, who rolled his eyes and sagged with sudden relief. Sweat dripped off his unshaven chin.

"What's he doing now?"

"Giving the Mate and Lecky a once-over. The Chief asked him to."

"Right. As soon as he's gone we'll have to try and raise the office." His watch said it was ten minutes to seven. In London, his ship manager would be in bed and asleep. "Four in the morning—Jack Porteous'll love that."

"Five," Sparks reminded him, "it's Summer Time."

Fatigue dragged at him, and pain that throbbed through his ribs and shoulder right down to the wrist; the thought of all those office wallahs being dragged out of their beds, however, gave him a certain perverse satisfaction.

With the second mate in tow, the doctor returned, giving Stephen to understand that in his opinion all the officers were suffering from some degree of shock and exhaustion and should by rights be taken off the ship; only one, however, had agreed to go.

"Well," Stephen explained, "as we don't have any electricity to speak of, we can manage without our electrician . . . which he is well aware of. Everybody else is essential."

"I see." He glanced around like a prince finding himself in the unfortunate surroundings of a labor camp. Then he smiled. "Well, Captain, I must go. I wish you good luck."

"Thank you."

As soon as he was away, Stephen went outside, fighting

dizziness and nausea on his way to the bridgewing. The pilot boat was still alongside, the crew hanging hopefully over the fo'c'sle. One of the fire-fighting tugs had stopped its hoses and was coming in. The VHF crackled, the tug master asking permission to put a crew aboard. Stephen acknowledged and agreed, passed on instructions to the Third Mate, and watched the half dozen men scramble up the ship's side.

Within half an hour the fire was reported to be under control; with that news he felt able to breathe easier, able to give a constructive report to his ship manager in London. He raised Fujairah and requested a call to be put through via the local radio station. It took some time, but eventually he had Jack Porteous's sleepy voice over the static on the line.

"Jack, it's Stephen Elliott—on the *Damaris*. Sorry to wake you, but we're in an emergency situation . . ." He went on to report the events in brief, reassured by the calm, unemotional response.

". . . I'm getting good reports from the fire-fighting team, so once it's out I'll need a tow to a repair yard. I think Dubai—that's nearest. Also I'll need to appoint agents in Fujairah to deal with the injured and the crew . . ."

"Okay—go ahead. I'll do the necessary at this end—I'll get in touch with next of kin myself, and get your engineer superintendent on the first available flight. Do you need any reliefs at this stage?"

"No, we'll get her to the repair yard ourselves—we can talk about reliefs later."

"What about you, Steve? Are you all right?"

"I'm okay now, but I've got things to attend to, Jack. I'll call you back as soon as I can."

"Or I'll call you. The media are bound to get onto this . . . can you cope?"

"As long as they don't want to come aboard."

"If they get too pressing, just refer them to us."

"Okay, will do."

It was not until a representative of ITN news called him up that Stephen gave a thought to his own next of kin. While he demanded assurances that names and ranks of casualties would not be used without contacting the shipping company first, he suddenly remembered his sister, Pamela, and prayed she would have the sense to phone Joan before the news hit television and radio broadcasts. And that Joan would be able to contact Zoe . . .

32

*F*or some time, Zoe had not been sleeping well, but she woke that night with the impression that someone or something had disturbed her. Instantly alert, for a moment her eyes scanned the darkness while she listened for unaccustomed sounds. Nothing, not even a disturbance of the air, and yet her heart was hammering against her breast, every muscle tensed as though for flight.

She glanced at the clock, its small, illuminated hands pointing to half-past three. Not even light yet. Swallowing hard, she slipped out of bed, dragged on a light cotton bathrobe, and tiptoed through the tiny hall to her sitting room. The blinds were up and she saw at once that nothing had been disturbed. The kitchen was empty. More confident now, but still anxious, she opened the door to the staircase and crept out on to the landing. Listening, looking up the stairs and down, she waited a couple of minutes until a sudden shiver drove her back inside. With her door locked again and bolted, Zoe went back into the kitchen to make some coffee.

The hot drink restored her nerve, yet anxiety lurked, indefinably, at the edge of her mind. Eventually, she came to the

conclusion that she must have been dreaming, something disturbing but elusive disappearing from consciousness at the moment of waking. The trouble was that she was now far too alert
to sleep. She picked up a novel, but it was too bland to hold
her attention. It seemed a better idea to utilize the time by
working; if nothing else, work could always absorb her concentration.

With no more than a quick wash, she dragged a brush
through her hair, braided it back, and pulled on an old pair of
jeans and a paint-stained khaki shirt. She switched on the
angle-poise lamps above her worktable and studied the piece
of work in progress. From an imperial sheet of fine paper colors
glowed, rich dark reds and blues, muted grays and greens in a
stylized pattern of leaves and branches against the carved stone
of an ancient monument. Tendrils of ivy curled around the page
and into the picture, while the climbing stem of a velvety,
bloodred rose wound sinuously over the stone, its petals lit-
tering the grass. In the distance, between the leaves, was a
glimpse of open meadowland bisected by a path.

The illustration had been inspired in part by that visit to
the old cemetery in York, which was one of the reasons she
had chosen that particular verse as one of the six she was
commissioned to paint. The other reason was that the lines
reminded her so strongly of Liam and those sleepy villages in
Picardy that he had described so evocatively in his letters: roses
running wild over ruined walls, and a long white ribbon of
Roman road . . .

> I sometimes think that never blows so red
> The Rose as where some buried Caesar bled.

Had Liam known those lines from Edward Fitzgerald? Remembering that Victorian edition in the trunk of books at Stephen's flat, Zoe thought he must have done. And therein lay
another coincidence, that out of this new, illustrated series of
major Victorian poets, Zoe should have been chosen to work
on the *Rubáiyát*. When first approached by the publishers, she
had remembered that slender volume and been tempted to
suggest that they produce instead a facsimile edition. Econom-

ics sealed her tongue, however, that and a burning desire to work on such a sumptuous project. But although she had seen that old book only once, Zoe had coveted it, impressing the illustrations on her mind.

They were hard to forget, so she used memory as her inspiration, deliberately choosing different verses to illustrate. And anyway, it was difficult to be truly original; the brief was that it should *look* Victorian, which meant following the symbolism so beloved of the age. Eminently quotable though it was, however, the *Rubáiyát* must have seemed anarchy to those brought up on duty and the principle of suffering being good for the soul. Zoe could find no merit in that idea, or imagine anyone relishing agony against the promise of a place in heaven. Although by that yardstick, she felt the last few months should have earned some worthy spiritual reward. Nevertheless, she had hardly relished it. Acceptance was not her strong point, and the worst part of those months had not been the loneliness, which she had thought she was used to, but the suspense of not knowing about Stephen. Not knowing from one minute to the next whether he was safe, and not knowing what he felt about her.

"If I thought you loved me . . ." she often murmured aloud to his photograph, but there was no reply, not even from his letters, which had become as barren as the desert he described. Only the research kept her going, and the thought of Liam, to whom she felt closer than ever. Enthralled by his diary and letters, and even by the bureaucratic comments that comprised his army record, she sometimes felt his presence behind her, as though he were drawn by what she was reading. But she was no longer alarmed by that slight tingle down the spine and the sense that he was leaning over her shoulder. It had come to the point where she sometimes spoke to him, as though to a friend determined to play hide-and-seek, but he kept his silence and never showed himself, and she wondered, occasionally, whether her obsessions were getting out of hand.

With this most recent commission, however, it seemed that the tangled emotions of love and doubt and longing were at last finding a means of outlet, and with feverish inspiration she had rapidly outlined ideas and sketches for a dozen illustra-

tions. If there was death, there was life too, in vines and lus-
cious grapes, in the brilliant reflection of sun from carved
Moorish arches, and in the shadowed figures seated beneath
exotic, floral bowers.

The hard work came in translating those rough color
sketches to the formal, intricate patterns demanded by the style
of the period, which in itself was allied to medieval forms, and
which Zoe was attempting to combine with a suggestion of
Byzantine opulence. While freshness lasted and her hands were
steady, Zoe applied color in small sections to the first of her
chosen pieces. It was detailed, painstaking work that required
absolute concentration. At this stage, the most she could do
was a couple of hours; after that, fatigue set in and the hand
started to wander. Usually she took a break then, continuing
for a while with trial pieces, working out patterns to be used
later or experimenting with colors. This morning, however,
after two hours Zoe had had enough.

Tired, shaky from tension and too little sleep, she made
some coffee, slipped another tape into the stereo, and tried to
relax. For a while she considered going back to bed, but the
sun was up and it promised to be a beautiful day; it seemed a
sin to waste the best part of it either in bed or indoors.

That thought reminded Zoe that she had been trying to
arrange a suitable day to go with Polly to Wandsworth, but her
friend had been inundated with work prior to her holiday and
could not spare the time. Although it had been vaguely agreed
that they would go later, Zoe suddenly thought that today was
as good a day as any, and there was absolutely no reason why
she should not go alone.

The decision cheered her considerably. She snapped off
the stereo and strode into the bathroom. A hot shower banished
the gloom and a hearty breakfast put strength into her sense of
purpose. With her hair freshly washed and wearing her preti-
est summer dress—a soft, floaty thing in shades of peach and
palest sea-green—she set off to join the morning rush-hour
crowds.

Zoe had made her inquiries about the hospital at Wandsworth some time ago, and had been longing to see the place
where Liam had spent almost four months of the war. Consid-

ering the damage done during the London Blitz in the Second World War, however, it seemed incredible that the place was still standing.

The man she had spoken to at the Imperial War Museum had declared she was fortunate in catching almost the only local person working there, and to prove it, he had gone on to give her the name of an acquaintance, a historian with a particular interest in Battersea and Wandsworth. Correspondence with that gentleman had proved worthwhile; not only was he able to tell her that the building was still standing in its entirety, but he also provided photocopied pictures, a map, and a potted history of its origins. The old school had recently been bought and renovated, he said, after years of standing derelict, and now housed some very attractive flats, studios, and a small bistro.

Recalling her excitement at the time, Zoe almost hugged herself with renewed pleasure and anticipation. For weeks she had been promising herself lunch at that little bistro, finding it astonishing that after years in which the place must have been forbidden territory, the presence of a restaurant now gave any member of the public a legitimate entry. If that was coincidence again, then it was fortunate indeed; and if it should be more than mere coincidence, she thought, then somebody's sense of timing was impeccable.

Just beyond the station she left the bus to walk down Windmill Road. Here, everything opened out, with pretty Victorian houses facing the tree-lined common, and the black tower of an ancient windmill over to the left. Children were playing on the grass, women pushing prams and walking dogs; an old gentleman out enjoying the sun raised his panama as she passed by, and Zoe was aware of a sense of timelessness, as though in outward terms at least nothing here had changed very much. That, she acknowledged, was an odd feeling in London, where things seemed to be changing all the time.

Her first sight of the building was partially obscured by trees; needing a clearer view, she walked across the grass to a point where she could see it properly, a huge place standing in solitary grandeur, like a castle, overlooking the common: honey-colored brick and stone, raised in a mid-Victorian Gothic that was so restrained it might have been genuinely medieval, with turrets and towers, pointed arches, ornate windows, all perfectly balanced and restored.

It was so unexpected after the blackened photocopies she had received, she sent up a silent message of thanks for whichever obsessive philanthropist or entrepreneur had paid for the restoration. May you thrive and prosper, she thought, making her way back to the road.

The sight of two hideous sixties accommodation blocks, just inside the main gates, halted her for a moment. Glaring at them as though they had absolutely no right to be there, she wished upon them concrete fatigue and a rapid, crumbling death. For a fleeting moment she even considered writing to Buckingham Palace; Prince Charles was known to be of a like mind where architectural monstrosities were concerned.

But one step inside those gates, all such considerations fled. A tingling thrill from scalp to fingertips, from the tips of her toes to her face—especially her face—possessed her, banishing thought, defying logic, filling her with unexpected and unlooked-for joy. It took her so completely by surprise that she wanted to laugh, to say, "Hang on a minute, let me get my bearings," but her unseen companion was laughing, impatient, tugging at her hands, bearing her up as he swept her along.

It was like arriving at a party and being swept immediately into the dance by an exuberant admirer; and she knew him this time, she was no longer afraid.

And he was aware of that, drawing her with him as though he simply could not wait to show her this place. For a moment he allowed her to stop before the main entrance, but the sense of physical lightness continued, even while she took in a wealth of architectural detail, that carving of St. George and the dragon in its niche above the door.

"Of course the whole place would've been black when you were here," she said softly, "especially with that railway line so close and all the soot and smoke. Yes, I imagine it was a bit forbidding in those days, especially in the last quarter of the year . . ."

But it was impossible to feel that, even while she thought of all the orphans who had passed through those portals and spent their days within its walls, even when she pictured the sick and wounded who had been Liam's companions here. She felt light and happy, full of astonishment and wonder as she toured the precincts, remarking softly on the chapel which stood at the far side, knowing from the diary that Liam had sometimes worshipped there. For a little while she stood in a sheltered alcove, every instinct telling her that there had once been a seat here, where Liam had regularly spent part of the afternoon.

He let her stay for a while, touching her face and hands with that gentle, tingling caress, invading her heart and mind with joy, and then he led her on to a rear courtyard and a low doorway which bore directions to a craft studio. But Zoe ignored them, following her guide down a stone-flagged passage and into a half-glazed walkway which bordered three sides of a quadrangle. A vaulted ceiling and cast-iron pillars gave it the look of a cloister; at the corner, hesitating for the first time, she had the feeling he was about to leave her.

She wanted to say, "No, don't," but even as the words formed, she saw him quite distinctly, in uniform, his hat tipped at a rakish angle, striding toward her with a smile of love and triumph, as though he were saying "Look, just see what I can do when I really try . . ."

She gasped in astonishment. He looked so real, so physically solid, so full of warm vitality that her heart leapt with the urge to run to him, to be swept up in those strong, loving arms; rooted to the spot, all she could do was gaze at that happy, purposeful approach.

He was almost within reach when he disappeared. Staring at the empty corridor, for a second Zoe was stunned, then her spine was tingling, the fine hairs on her arms and at the nape of her neck stirring at his caress. She wanted, desperately, to reach out and hold him, half turned, with her arms raised, before realizing its futility. He was with her and he was touching her, but he was no longer flesh and blood; she could not clasp him to her breast the way her physical self longed to do, and he could love her only by bringing with him this sense of joy.

Suddenly, her eyes were wet. It was too much. So brief, so elusive, as fleeting as a dream and just as insubstantial.

Breathing deeply, she leaned against an open window,

looking out on ancient brick setts in the courtyard and trying to contain her emotion.

Why me? she silently asked. Had she lived before as Georgina Duncannon? But a firm *no* came into her mind at that, and Zoe was left with the impression that she was loved for herself. She tried framing other questions, but no answers came, and she began to feel the waning of Liam's presence, as though the power he had summoned to be with her was now beyond his control to retain. She sensed regret, and a final, lingering touch on her cheek; and then he was gone, taking with him every anxiety, every petty frustration. A feeling of well-being remained, of calm and peace and absolute contentment. He was alive. What else mattered?

On the way home, she realized she was hungry. The fine lunch that she had promised herself had been set before her just after midday, but her appetite had been sadly lacking, even after a second stroll in the grounds—this time alone. The bistro was quiet, and Zoe had spent most of the time chatting to the owner, whose passion for the old building led him to show her around and air his knowledge of its history. And after she had seen the great hall with its newly refurbished coats of arms, the man had let her wander around the upstairs restaurant alone, looking at his collection of prints and photographs of the hospital era. It had been strange, viewing those pictures of coy nurses and grinning soldiers, knowing that Liam had been here then, and that she had just seen him walking toward her in the corridor. Half tempted to ask whether the place was haunted, Zoe had desisted, knowing that it was unimportant to her. Liam was not a ghost imprisoned by place or a moment in time; he had simply chosen that moment to show himself, to share with her the joy he felt at her visit. At least, that was how it had seemed. Instinct said that he had been happy there, away from the war, and with thoughts of Georgina to counter his bleakest days.

And if Georgina had given him solace when it was most needed, then Liam had brought ease and comfort to Zoe at a time when misery and chill depression had threatened to swamp her completely. She was immensely grateful for that, and it seemed to Zoe that even if Stephen had ceased to care,

Liam had not. Perhaps he had always been there, on the edge of her awareness; she began to think that he had wanted her to find him again, to get involved with his life, that the interest in the Elliott family had been in some way instigated by Liam, not Tisha, as it first appeared.

But why? There seemed to be no rhyme or reason to it. It was extraordinary, and her experience of him that morning was something she would never forget. His love was almost palpable, and that sense of peace afterward was still with her. It was as though he were trying to tell her that everything would be all right . . .

The telephone was ringing as she struggled to unlock her door, but just as she dashed across the room to answer it, it stopped. Trying to think who her caller might have been, she looked at her watch. Almost five-thirty. She stood for a moment wondering, then shrugged and went to make herself some coffee and sandwiches, returning to the sitting room for the early evening news.

The ITN headlines were being announced as she sat down. ". . . from Northern Ireland, and in the Gulf, a Liberian tanker hits a mine, killing one British officer and injuring another. More about that later, and now to . . ."

Oh God. With a sickly feeling of apprehension, Zoe sat down, her heart lurching with every change of topic, willing the newscaster to hurry up, ignore the rest of the world's tragedies, and just get to the Gulf. The suspense was agonizing.

"Oh, bloody get on with it!" she muttered ferociously as the Prime Minister was pontificating on a new atmosphere of cooperation between London and Dublin. At any other time she might have been interested, but right now . . .

"And now, to the Gulf of Oman, where Jeremy Brown reports on the latest casualty in the Gulf War . . ."

Squinting against the glare, a sunburned young man faced the camera, while behind him stretched a dazzling sea dotted with ships. "Behind me you see the Fujairah deep-water anchorage, favorite stopping place for tankers on their way into and out of the Gulf. Here, just before dawn today, a Liberian-registered oil tanker, manned by British officers, struck a mine while anchoring . . ."

The young man's face on screen was replaced by an anonymous aerial photograph of a large ship, while his professionally flat, unemotional voice went on, "The tanker—the *Damaris*—was hit in the stern, causing an explosion in the engine room where a British engineering officer was killed, and another injured. The ship's master was also slightly hurt by the blast, but he was able to speak to us over the ship's radio . . ."

Icy with shock, Zoe heard Stephen's voice, terse and distorted by the VHF, giving a brief account of events, including the fact that the fire had been rapidly brought under control and the ship was now under tow to Dubai. Only toward the close of the report did the reporter interject with a question.

"But I understand that you too were hurt by the blast, Captain?"

"Very slightly. A dislocated shoulder which has been attended to."

"Are you anxious about returning through the Strait of Hormuz?"

"Not at all. The damage has been done, another tanker is incapacitated, and that's what it's all about. The fact that one of my officers is dead and another injured is purely incidental to the people who direct and carry out these attacks on international shipping."

He sounded so bitter.

The interview ended, the picture faded, and with the usual cryptic question about what this new turn of events might mean, ITN's man in Fujairah signed off and returned the picture to the studio.

Zoe stared blankly at the screen, taking in nothing of the following summary of who was doing what in the Gulf, and to whom—or anything else. Eventually, the jolly jingle of the local news magazine penetrated her consciousness and she rose to switch the television off. Her body felt like lead, her brain paralyzed. She stood, poised, by the telephone, knowing she had to speak to someone, had to find out what was going on . . .

Who?

She thought of Irene, then recoiled from the idea. What if Mac was the one who was killed? She had to find out before she spoke to her.

"Joan . . ." Reaching for her address book, she dropped it, had great difficulty retrieving it, fumbling as she searched for the right page. Dialing the York number, first her hands, and then her body, started to tremble. She sat down, but by the time Joan answered on the third or fourth ring, Zoe was almost incapable of speech.

"Oh, *Zoe*—I've been trying to get you *all day*, since just after nine this morning. You've been out, obviously—did you see the news?"

"Yes—just now."

"Yes, ITN—wasn't it dreadful? It was on at lunchtime too. Now listen, Zoe, you are *not to worry*. He's all right. Somebody from the London office telephoned Pamela this morning. It's a terrible thing that's happened, I know, but Stephen is *all right*, and that's the main thing."

"But he was *hurt*—and Mac, what about Mac?"

"He's all right," Joan assured her firmly, adding on a softer note, "it was the Third Engineer, poor man. I don't know if he had any family, but he wasn't married, which I suppose is a blessing . . ."

"Oh God . . . And poor Stephen, having to cope with all that . . ."

"He's very capable, love—*very* capable. And he won't die of a dislocated shoulder. I telephoned the ship manager myself this morning, just to make sure Pamela had everything straight—she was dashing off to work when they got in touch with her, and she's a born worrier, you know, panics at the slightest thing, just like his wife. Sorry, just like Ruth used to do . . ."

Zoe closed her eyes, feeling the words wash over her. Finally, Joan caught herself and returned to the matter in hand.

"Anyway, it seems they're going to do their best to get everybody home from . . . oh Lord, where is it now? Abu Dhabi? No, *Dubai*, that's it. As soon as they get to Dubai, the company will get things sorted out and fly him home. Shouldn't be more than a few days, a week at the most—he was most insistent about that. And Stephen is *fine*, Zoe. If he wasn't, he wouldn't still be aboard, now would he?"

Although Joan sounded very convincing, Zoe was not at all sure about that. A man with Stephen's determination would probably need to be taken off in a stretcher . . .

With a repeat of all those assurances, Joan advised her to
make a good strong cup of tea with plenty of sugar in it and to
call in a friend to stay with her.

Zoe found it hard to think of anyone she wanted to be
with. Polly would have been ideal, but Polly was at the moment
sunning herself in Marbella with a man friend.

"Well, why don't you call your mother?"

There were dozens of reasons why Zoe preferred not to
call either of her parents, the least of which being the time it
would take for them to get there. Finally, however, she said
that she would.

Joan repeated her instructions about that cup of tea and
said she would call Zoe back in an hour. But before she could
say good-bye, Zoe interrupted.

"Joan—I saw Liam today."

There was a short silence. "Sorry, dear—what did you
say?"

"I went down to Wandsworth, to the old hospital—remember I told you about it? That's why I was out all day.
Anyway, Liam was there. I saw him, clear as day, coming down
a corridor toward me . . . Funny isn't it? And now this . . ."

She was not at all sure that Joan believed her. She thought
she did, but it was hard to tell over the phone. Perhaps she
did. Anyway, what did it matter? The point was that she had
seen him and had felt his presence beside her for some considerable time; she would defy anyone to tell her it was an illusion.

What she could not understand was *why*. None of it made
sense, particularly today of all days, when this terrible thing
had happened to Stephen. It was beyond her.

Trying to follow Joan's advice, Zoe opted for coffee instead
of tea, which she disliked, and two chocolate wafer bars in
place of sugar. Chilled to the bone, she changed her dress
for trousers and a warm sweater, and gradually the trembling
abated. Her thoughts remained a jumble, anxiety for Stephen
vying with confusion over Liam, and a pressing need to find
out more about the situation aboard the *Damaris*. Longing to
speak to Stephen, or to someone who *had* spoken to him, she
cursed the impulse that had led her to Wandsworth today. If
only she had been at home, it would have been possible to

telephone the shipping company, speak to the manager Joan had mentioned.

She picked up her address book. Irene, Mac's wife, might know more . . .

But even as she reached for the telephone, it rang.

The clicks and sighs of a distant connection met her ears; then a man's voice, foreign, asking her to stand by for a call from a ship.

For a moment she did not fully understand what was said. Hardly daring to breathe, she gripped the receiver like a lifeline, and then suddenly Stephen's voice, faint but unmistakable, was miraculously speaking her name.

Incredulous, thankful, overjoyed to the verge of tears, she could do no more than utter his name in response, while in her heart she thanked God for this minor miracle.

"Zoe, darling, are you all right? I'm so sorry I wasn't able to call you earlier—it really has been chaos here, so much to organize, you wouldn't believe it . . ."

"Oh, Stephen, I'm fine, it's just so good to hear your voice—but how are *you*?"

"A bit tired, but otherwise all right. We seem to have got most of the problems ironed out now, and there's not much more I can do until we get to Dubai, so I should be able to get my head down for a few hours. Anyway, what about you? It must have been a bit of a shock—did Joan or Irene manage to get in touch?"

"No, I was out all day. I didn't get back until just before the news came on—and that *was* a shock, believe me." Zoe paused and swallowed hard. "Anyway, I phoned Joan right away, and she said she'd been trying to get hold of me since first thing this morning—and I was just about to phone Irene when you called."

"Oh, love, I'm sorry about that—sorry you had to hear it on the bloody news—that wasn't the idea at all. I'm just glad I managed to get through to you now—we've had one or two problems during the day with calls. Anyway, not to worry. The thing is, we're all right, and we should be in Dubai sometime tomorrow. I expect it'll be a dry dock job, and it's bound to be lengthy—the engine room's virtually destroyed. Mac's really sick," he added with a short laugh, "we always used to joke about it being so clean down there. His little ice-cream parlor, we used to call it . . . Well, we won't be saying that anymore, I'm afraid . . ."

Zoe was faintly shocked. How could he joke at a time like this? And anyway, a man was *killed* . . . "Stephen, what happened? I didn't really take in what you were saying in that interview."

There was a silence before he answered her, and when he did, the strain in his voice was quite audible. "We hit a mine, love. Backed into it while we were laying out the anchor. It blew a bloody great hole in the port quarter and wiped out the control room, including one of the engineers." He paused for a moment. "The irony is, Jim joined us in Kuwait after the original Third demanded off. He volunteered for the job. Sick, isn't it?"

Wincing, Zoe could think of no words of consolation. "What about the other man—is he all right? And you—you haven't told me about yourself . . ."

"Well, the Second's in hospital now. He got a bash on the head, but I think he'll be all right, and we put Lecky ashore as well. I was daft enough to be hanging over the bridgewing at the time, so I took a bit of a knock as well—dislocated my shoulder, but it's been put back."

"Was that terribly painful?" she asked tentatively.

She heard him laugh. "Yes, you might say that . . . but not to worry, I keep taking the tablets! Actually," he confessed. "I was bloody lucky not to do worse. I had a look afterward to see where I'd fallen, and how the hell I missed cracking my head open on the compass repeater, I do not know. There's a metal ridge and locking nuts on either side, so I'm really thankful I didn't hit that on the way down. The damage might've been permanent . . ."

Zoe winced. "But you're all right?"

"Fine, honestly. It's been a hellish situation, but I'm still here . . . hard to believe, but true . . ."

As his voice tailed away, she said impulsively, "I've missed you, Stephen—missed you dreadfully . . . and I've been so *worried* . . ." Her voice broke at that, and for a moment she had to struggle hard not to be more specific, or worse, burst into tears. Eventually, she said, "Do you think they might send you home?"

The lengthy pause that followed made her wish that she had not given voice to those sentiments.

When it came, his reply was suddenly softer and deeper, as though for some reason he had stopped shouting into the telephone. She had to struggle to make out his words, something to the effect that he was not alone on the bridge, and that he would try to contact her again from Dubai, which would make conversation easier.

"And I'll know more when I've had chance to talk to the super—the troubleshooter from the office. But it may be quite a while before we get home, Zoe—Masters and Chief Engineers usually stay with their ships in dry dock. I'm sorry, but that's the way it is."

His brusqueness hurt her, silencing the challenge she might have made; the line was crackling, and anyway, that promise to get everybody home was probably no more than a placebo to keep the relatives quiet. Nevertheless, acute disappointment almost choked her.

"I'll phone you from Dubai—give me a couple of days, all right?"

"Yes—yes, of course. I'll be waiting . . ."

"Must go, love—take care."

"Yes—you too . . . Stephen—"

But he was gone. The empty line hummed, stressing the distance between them. Very slowly she replaced the receiver, while two large tears rolled down her cheeks. She was unsure whether it was anxiety, disappointment, relief, or just the release of tension that made her cry, but she let them run, mopping them with tissues as they dripped off her chin. One way and another, she decided, it really had been one hell of a day. Eventually the tears ceased and she poured herself a brandy, which restored both heart and reason.

He was all right. He had telephoned. He had called her *darling*, which took Zoe back to the passionate days of their first acquaintance; but he mostly called her *love*, which she had long ago come to realize might mean all or nothing. It seemed that most Yorkshiremen and women called everybody *love*. A term of endearment akin to the Cockney *ducks* and West Country *m'dear*, apparently applicable to anyone short of the totally obnoxious.

And to think that only a massive lump in her throat had stopped her from blurting out that she loved him, wanted him, couldn't bear to go on like this a moment longer . . .

She felt a fool, a weak-kneed, lovesick, adolescent *idiot*.

On the other hand, she thought with the second tot of brandy, while it had taken him a moment to respond to the emotion in her voice, there had been something approaching emotion in his . . . and she had a suspicion that he had been about to say something important, something halted by the fact that he was not alone.

Ah well, perhaps when he called again from Dubai, on a more private line, perhaps then he would sound less impersonal.

She picked up the telephone and dialed Irene's number in Northumberland.

33

*Z*oe did not stir from the flat. There was no call from Dubai, but on the morning of the third day, Jack Porteous telephoned with flight details.

"But I thought . . . I mean, Stephen said he would have to stay for the dry dock," she said foolishly, torn between disbelief and a desire to kiss the man on the other end of the line.

There was a short bark of laughter. "Well, that's Steve for you. We've just about had to prise him free, but a relieving master is on his way out there at the moment. They'll hand over as soon as he arrives, and Steve will be on his way home in the morning, along with all the others. He wanted me to let you know, as he thought you might like to meet him at Heathrow."

"Oh yes—yes, of course I'll be there . . ."

"There's only one slight problem. With Steve and the Chief Engineer, Mr. Petersen, living so far away, we'd like them to come into the office immediately for a firsthand report on the accident. It saves them going home and then having to travel back to London later in the week—I hope you understand?"

"Of course—that sounds sensible to me."

"Good. So there'll be someone from the office at Heathrow

tomorrow—a Mr. Goodall. He knows them and they know him, so there shouldn't be any problems about meeting up. He'll have transport arranged into the city . . . I hope a journey to the office and back won't disrupt your day too much?"

"Oh no, not at all. I'm sure it will be very interesting . . ."

"Good. Well, Miss Clifford, I look forward to meeting you tomorrow—until then, try not to worry. Steve's fine."

"Thank you—yes, I'm sure he is . . ."

Her sense of relief was so vast, Zoe hardly knew whether to laugh or cry. With Polly home from Marbella the previous evening, she now had someone to celebrate with; in a dizzy whirl of delight she dashed up the stairs and almost fell through her friend's door. They hugged each other and did a little dance around the kitchen, then Polly grabbed a bottle of Spanish bubbly from the fridge and they toasted Stephen and each other, Jack Porteous, Polly's man friend, and the glories of Marbella. Then they toasted Stephen again.

Half an hour later, silly with champagne and relief and sheer, unbridled joy, Zoe remembered her obligations and left to make a series of telephone calls. She shared her joy with her mother and Joan, and very briefly with her father's secretary—as usual, James Clifford was in a meeting and could not be disturbed—and then she contacted Irene, making arrangements to meet up at Heathrow the following day.

"It's going to be quite a party," Irene said, "I wonder if the company will treat us all to lunch?"

They were both a bundle of nerves waiting by the barrier for the men to arrive, trying to distract themselves by guessing possible identities among the crowd. The man from the office could have been one of several, and there were so many other women it was impossible to know which ones might be the wives or girlfriends of the other officers.

The flight had landed some time ago, and Zoe's eyes were torn between the clock and the exit from the Customs area. To begin with a thin trail of passengers carrying hand luggage came through, followed in ones and twos by those with carts and babies; eventually a whole bunch emerged together, among them three particularly tall men, whose eyes seemed to scan the crowd with some anxiety. She and Irene spotted Mac's red hair and beard in the same instant, and Irene was gripping Zoe with one hand and waving madly with the other. Mac grinned and edged around the carts, dropping his suitcase and scooping up his wife in a bearlike hug. Behind them, Stephen was hidden for a moment, then another man, laughing, was telling Mac and Irene to clear a path there, other people wanted to get through. He pushed past them to be grabbed by a glamorous blonde who brushed Zoe out of the way in order to get to him; that he was astonished to see her was obvious.

Zoe turned her head to see Stephen edging toward her, still blocked by the crush of passengers in that narrow space. His hair was much longer than was usual for him, and surprisingly curly; like his deeply tanned skin, it seemed at variance somehow with the immaculate pale gray suit and tie. His face looked thinner, etched with sharp lines of exasperation; then he glanced up and saw her, and for a moment his eyes held hers with such longing, Zoe thought she might explode with frustration. Then he was free, and smiling, and in the same moment she moved forward to greet him.

But shyness seemed to catch them both; for a second they hesitated, then he opened his arms and she kissed his cheek and he was hugging her as though he would never let her go. Breathless, on tiptoe, she clung to him while he buried his face against her hair; and then he found her mouth and kissed her with warmth and gratitude and undeniable relief.

"It's so good to see you," he said huskily, "you've no idea . . ." And then he laughed to cover his emotion, hugged her and kissed her again. "There's a man we have to see—and business still to attend to," he added ruefully.

"Yes, I know—Mr. Porteous told me."

Glancing around, Stephen spotted the man from the office, already talking to Sparks and the Third Mate.

"Come on—we'd better get this over with. I must introduce you to the Mate—and the others too; they've been a great bunch of lads, I don't know what I'd have done without them."

They were surprisingly shy, Zoe found, apart from the Mate, who bent to kiss her cheek as though he had known her for years. He was even taller than Stephen, but less stockily built, and his girlfriend was obviously determined not to let him go, clinging even while he was talking to the man from the

office. Keen not to do likewise, Zoe stood with Irene while the
men talked and laughed, and finally organized themselves for
the next moves in their separate journeys. She had been under
the impression that all the officers would be going together
for the debriefing, but Irene told her that it would only be Mac
and Stephen. Watching as they all shook hands and said their
good-byes, Zoe did not miss the respect and affection with
which they parted from Stephen. Only the Mate addressed him
by his Christian name, and that seemed to be a mark of special
friendship between them; the others gave him his title along
with their thanks, and that depth of sincerity touched Zoe as
much as Stephen. Almost bursting with love and pride, she
could not have spoken had her life depended on it. How Stephen managed to voice his farewells, she had no idea.

Mr. Goodall saved the day for all of them, moving in at
just the right moment to whisk his group away to a waiting
taxi. Along with him, Stephen took one of the tiny seats, while
Mac squeezed between Zoe and Irene on the long one, tucking
both their hands in his, and saying he had by far the best of
the bargain.

It was a journey full of jokes and hilarity, the repartee
between Mac and Stephen flying back and forth with unremitting mirth. Zoe felt she had never laughed so much, her sides
aching by the time they arrived at the office on Leadenhall
Street. She knew this part of the city well; her father's business
premises were just around the corner on St. Mary Axe, but she
neglected to point that out. She always had a fear that people
might think she was boasting, but Stephen remembered, and
as they stepped out of the taxi, mentioned it to her.

She blushed and nodded. "I spoke to him the other evening—he said if you were staying a few days, he'd like to take
us both out to lunch. But you don't have to," she added quickly.
"I didn't say for sure that we would."

"No," Stephen said, "I'd like to meet him. In fact I'm
looking forward to it . . ."

That pleased her enormously, buoying her up through
what seemed an interminable wait while the men were being
interviewed. A receptionist brought them coffee, and Zoe and
Irene gazed uncomprehendingly at shipping journals while
catching up on each other's news. Having had an early start,

Irene was ravenous and longing for something to eat. Eventually, just before two o'clock, Mac and Stephen reappeared with Jack Porteous and another man to whom they were introduced. Only afterward did they discover that he was one of the directors.

It was a good lunch that they had in a nearby restaurant, but that interview seemed to have quelled the hilarity of their journey from Heathrow. Jack Porteous kept the conversation away from the Gulf and behaved with gallantry toward the ladies; but the other two were showing signs of strain, both of them drinking more than they ate during that hour at the table. Zoe was suddenly very keen to get away, and Irene kept glancing at her watch; at last politeness was satisfied and Jack said he had to get back to the office, while Irene confessed she was anxious not to miss the four o'clock train from Kings Cross.

They collected their baggage from the office, and thankfully two taxis arrived in quick succession. With a promise to meet again soon, Stephen waved Mac and Irene away, shook hands with Jack, and handed Zoe into the cab. He pushed his luggage into the space beside the driver and joined Zoe on the rear seat, slipping an arm around her shoulders and pulling her close beside him.

"I am *exhausted*," he said.

"Do you want to go straight to bed?" Zoe asked as soon as they arrived. "To sleep, I mean."

He smiled. "No, I'll be fine. I just want to sit and talk to you."

So they sat and talked and drank coffee and tried to pretend that there was not a wall of diffidence between them. Zoe told herself that four months was a long time, so the feeling of strangeness was only natural. So much had happened in the interim, to him, particularly. Nevertheless, that he did not immediately want to sweep her off to bed was a disappointment; and although she was not sure she could have coped with that, it did seem to her the best cure for an awkwardness that seemed to be growing rather than receding.

It was not that he was silent; indeed, he talked a great deal about Kuwait and Karachi, the red tape at one end and the corruption at the other, but when she asked direct questions about those journeys through the Gulf, he sidestepped every one, returning to the idiosyncrasies encountered at either end. Noticing—as she had since meeting him that morning—that he was using his left hand most of the time, she asked about his shoulder, but he was dismissive about that too, saying that it was badly bruised but otherwise all right. That he did not want to talk about the accident and the subsequent journey to Dubai was obvious. Although he asked what Zoe had been doing, about the research and her latest commission, she found it oddly difficult to explain those esoteric connections. It did not seem the right moment to be talking about Liam.

And then the flow of conversation suddenly dried up. She went to make more coffee and when she returned, Stephen was slumped into a corner of the sofa, jacket off, staring blankly at the empty fireplace. He looked so exhausted that her heart went out to him, overriding the awkwardness, the awful suspicion that they were strangers, with nothing at all in common. Leaning across the sofa back, she kissed the lobe of his ear and his cheek and stroked his hair.

"I think you're very tired," she said as he loosened his tie and unbuttoned his shirt. "I know it's only six o'clock, but why don't you go to bed for a couple of hours? I'll make a chicken casserole and put it in the oven, and it won't matter whether we eat it or not. But if you have some sleep, Stephen, you might feel better."

For a moment she thought he was about to protest, but he gave in, pausing only to collect his shaving things from the suitcase in the hall. A few minutes later, going into the bedroom to turn down the sheets for him, Zoe heard the shower running; when he came out, wrapped in a towel, she saw the bruising around his shoulder. It was black-and-blue and alarmingly extensive; with an involuntary gasp she reached out to touch him, but he drew her into his arms, kissing her tenderly before she could speak. He smelled damp and sweet and his mouth tasted of toothpaste, and that combination was suddenly the most erotic thing she could imagine. When he kissed her again there was an urgency about it, and in that mounting passion it seemed that all the strangeness fell away. They were together, and everything was going to be all right.

"Come with me and lie down," he whispered, "I don't want to sleep alone."

She ran her fingers over his shoulder, touched the bruised flesh lightly with her lips; as though he felt her unspoken question, he said, "It looks worse than it is. Although," he added with a twinkling grin, "I don't think it would stand up to twenty push-ups just now. Still, never mind, perhaps I should just lie back and think of England . . . what do you say?"

She laughed. "Well, if you will make these offers I can't refuse . . ." She kissed him lingeringly and smoothed the damp hair from his brow. "But if you want to eat later, just let me pop that casserole into the oven—two ticks, I promise!"

It was almost ready for the oven, prepared while Stephen had been soaking away his exhaustion beneath a hot shower. She added chopped vegetables to the chicken breasts and covered them with a creamy sauce; with the lid secure she checked the oven temperature, slipped the dish inside, and shut the oven door. There, that was that. The salad and new potatoes could wait.

But a tremor of nerves caught her as she crossed the sitting room, making her pause and wonder why she felt so much like the mythical bride on her wedding night. She had never felt like this before . . . But then again, she had never been in this situation before.

She opened the bedroom door. The westerly sun flooded the room, and Stephen was lying back against the pillows, an arm across his eyes. He seemed to be asleep, yet that was strangely more of a relief than a disappointment, and with a sigh she undressed quickly, her back to him. Only as she slipped between the sheets did she realize her mistake: He was not asleep, and had been watching her.

"You're so lovely," he whispered, folding his warm limbs around her, and she melted to him willingly, giving herself up to hands and lips and the gentleness of his caress. She wanted him so much, could hardly wait to be joined with him, to banish this sense of separateness and relegate the last four months to the nature of a distressing dream.

But she sensed very quickly that something was wrong, and was suddenly threatened by panic. Irrational fears, prompted by more than one similar experience with Philip, left her incapable of thought or action. With a plummeting heart she tried to pretend that nothing was amiss, but the last few months rose mockingly before her, the bleak letters, the lack of any genuine endearment. All had been wonderful before, with the excitement of novelty and that instantaneous attraction; but that was then, and the attraction had waned, it was just that he did not know how to tell her . . .

For a moment or two she felt humiliated; with an effort she summoned rational thought and told herself that he was tired, that he had suffered an incredible amount of stress, and just because he could not make love to her right now, did not mean that he had stopped wanting her.

But she was not entirely convinced, and the fact that he drew away from her before apologizing did nothing for her self-esteem. Had she possessed sufficient courage to look into his face, she might have seen that he was equally distressed, but Zoe was too concerned with hiding her own emotions, her face buried in the crook of his good shoulder while she prayed he would not notice how deeply she was hurt.

For a long time, neither of them spoke. She lay with her face against his chest, while his hand rested slackly against her neck. At last, in a soft, flat voice, Stephen said again that he was sorry, that he was very tired, and that she mustn't think that it was anything to do with her; and with a similar lack of joy she said that she understood, of course he was tired, and it was silly to imagine otherwise . . .

He held her gently and stroked her hair, and after a while the tension in him relaxed. When she dared to lift her head, Zoe saw that he was asleep.

Very gently, she eased herself away from him, and when she was sure that he would not stir, crept out of the bedroom with her clothes. It was a ridiculous situation. She had the strongest urge to walk out, leave, put all this behind her and never set eyes on him again; and yet this was her flat, and Stephen Elliott was asleep in *her* bed. And if she wanted to get any rest tonight, she would have to creep in again beside him, and try to sleep.

When the casserole was cooked, she turned it off and made a sandwich, which she ate while watching an old film on television. When that was over she read until eleven, until her eyes would no longer focus, and crept back to bed. He stirred slightly, murmuring something about fuel lines, but did not wake.

Zoe slept badly and was awake before six. Eager to avoid a repeat of the previous evening, she found her jeans and a cotton shirt and escaped to the bathroom. By the time Stephen was stirring she had already been working for an hour. Not wanting to discuss that commission, however, she quickly covered it and, in a breezy imitation of normality, offered to make him some breakfast.

Whatever else was amiss, she decided, there was nothing wrong with his appetite. He consumed eggs and sausages and bacon, several slices of toast and marmalade, and two cups of coffee, and said that it was the best meal he had eaten in months. Gratified, she allowed herself to unbend a little, but when he reached for her afterward, the inadvertent stiffening was back. With a faintly hurt expression, he let her go and lit a cigarette. While she clattered about, clearing the kitchen table, he managed to startle her by saying that he felt he should return to York.

Turning sharply, she caught his gaze, illumined by full sunlight, and in those astonishing blue eyes was something cold and accusatory.

"You don't have to go . . . surely?"

"Oh yes," he said quietly, stubbing out his cigarette, "I think I do."

Chilled, for a moment she could think of nothing to say. Then, foolishly, she remarked, "But I thought you were planning to stay for a few days."

"There are things I should attend to," he said, rising from the table, "and people I ought to see. And I really do think I need some time to sort myself out . . ."

Instantly, she felt guilty, as though she had let him down in some way; but although she said she did not want him to go, and almost begged him to stay, Stephen simply pointed out that he had three months' leave due to him. He was going to take all of it, he said, come hell or high water, so there would be plenty of time to see each other later.

He was outwardly pleasant, but there was something so

implacable about him, it froze every argument, every persuasion. Short of flinging herself at his feet, there seemed no way
of denting his decision. Watching him zip up his suitcase, she
felt weak and ineffectual, a fair match for that ex-wife of his.
But if she had this sort of thing to contend with, Zoe thought,
then I feel sorry for her.

In the end, all she could do was insist upon taking him to
the station, overriding all his objections. She drove atrociously,
swearing at every driver to cross her path, but apart from a few
sharply indrawn breaths, he made no comment.

At Kings Cross there was nowhere to park. He leaned
across, kissed her briefly, and said he would be in touch. "And
if you need me, you know where I am."

But I need you now, she almost wailed, watching him drag
the suitcase, left-handedly, from the Renault's backseat. Taxis
were pipping their horns; she had to move the car. Helplessly,
she glanced up at him, but he simply smiled and waved. It was
a taut smile, and the salute was abrupt.

Blinking away tears, Zoe gritted her teeth and swung out
into the traffic.

If Zoe was miserable, then so was Stephen. The difference was
that he was more angry with himself than with her, and too far
beyond rational thought to be able to react other than instinctively; and his instincts were to escape and lick his wounds in
private. Which was what he should have done in the first place,
he kept telling himself, cursing the fantasy that had led him to
think he could bury the past four months in the peace of her
arms.

The trouble was, he had wanted her so much—too much,
he supposed—expecting everything to happen brilliantly, just
like the first time. Initially, there had been a moment's promise,
and then—nothing. And how to explain that while the spirit
was willing, the flesh was flatly refusing to respond? He had
been too appalled to explain *anything*, too bitterly aware of
disappointment on both sides, and too demoralized to utter
more than a word of apology. Vaguely, as he drifted unwillingly
into oblivion, he had thought that things might be better in the
morning; but she had deliberately avoided being there when
he awoke, and that was what hurt most of all.

The journey north passed in a blur, the sight of golden fields ready for harvest making no more impression than a flat expanse of ocean. Normally he took great delight in his first view of England after months at sea, but this time nothing could lift his spirits. Even his first sight of the city walls failed to stir more than a bleak glance, and it was with no pleasure at all that Stephen returned to his flat in Bedern.

He opened windows, turned on water and electricity, and made a cup of black coffee. There was no milk, no food laid in for his return. Joan, obviously, was not expecting him for several days. The thought of having to contact her, to answer questions about his speedy return from London, was too much. He unpacked, phoned the garage about his car, then went to the pub for several pints and a sandwich. In the afternoon he slept. His car was delivered just before six, and immediately afterward he went to Sainsbury's to do some shopping. That evening he ate out.

At a loss the following day he took the car out for a drive through Helmsley and Farndale and over the North York Moors, returning in a wide arc via Thirsk and Ripon. There was pleasure in pushing the Jaguar around snaking bends, feeling the surge of power with which it conquered every hill. With Harrogate in sight and feeling slightly better, Stephen thought he would drop in to see his sister and brother-in-law.

Pamela was just back from school and on her own, but within half an hour he knew that the visit had been a mistake, that he should have waited until his mental faculties were better prepared for Pamela's particular style of interrogation. She was pleased to see him so unexpectedly, but piqued by the idea that he had stopped off in London for a few days to see his girlfriend rather than coming straight home to his family. Especially after what had happened.

"I stayed there one night," he said, "and that was largely because I had to go into the office. I got back to York yesterday lunchtime."

"Joan never said."

"I haven't spoken to Joan yet."

"Why not?"

He answered vaguely, while Pamela's eyes seemed to rake

his face for the truth. She changed tack then, wanting to know about this girlfriend of his, the one he had said so little about.

"Oh for God's sake, she's more of a cousin than girl-friend—didn't Joan tell you? She's involved with family history—I was helping her for a while, that's all."

"Yes, I can imagine," she remarked sardonically, pouring boiling water onto instant coffee. "Poor Ruth was so upset, you know. When that piece came on the news about your ship, she had to come over here straightaway. She was in tears—it brought it all back to her . . ."

"Brought *what* back?"

"Oh, you know—that awful trip she did with you, the storm and everything."

"Don't be ridiculous—that must be all of ten years ago."

"So? You don't forget things like that, you know." Her voice dropped, and she glanced up at him over her coffee cup. "Ruth still cares about you."

For a moment he held his sister's gaze. "I'm impressed. If I recall, she had a lovely way of showing it."

Pamela glanced away, chewed her lip for a moment. "I don't think it's working out with Dave . . ."

"Tough."

"God, you're so bloody hard, Stephen—doesn't anything touch you? She was your wife, for heaven's sake—doesn't that mean anything?"

"*Was* my wife, Pam. Isn't anymore. Hasn't been for six years. And even when she was my wife, it didn't seem to mean a lot. She met somebody else, somebody she preferred to me—and if it ain't working out, sis, well pardon me for saying so, but that's *her* problem. Not yours, and certainly not mine." He drained his coffee and stood up. "I'm going to tell you something now, something I should have said a hell of a long time ago. I don't know why I didn't, except for the fact that you're my sister, and I didn't want to cause a breach between us.

"But I'm sick to death of hearing about Ruth—I'm not interested anymore. She was neurotic and unstable, and she made a big bloody mess of my life—and it doesn't sound as though she's changed very much. It's time she grew up—and it's time you stopped sympathizing with her. Next time she comes here, crying her eyes out, kick her backside for her and tell her to sort her own bloody problems.''

Had he slapped her, his sister could not have appeared more stunned. Her small mouth was agape, her eyes wide with astonishment.

Stephen turned by the door. ''You know, I used to think it was my fault—that I made her so unhappy. I've labored under that delusion for years—and you, Pam, managed to keep the guilt alive. Well, you've just wiped it out. I'm glad it's not working out with *Dave*—that makes me feel one hell of a lot better. Maybe it *wasn't* all my fault after all.''

He drove far too fast back to York, and when he slammed the door of the flat behind him, Stephen realized he was sweating. He lit a cigarette and poured a drink and then he realized that he had better call Joan before his sister managed to upset her.

She was pleasantly surprised to hear from him, and if something in his voice alerted her to trouble, she made no comment. She did, however, invite him around for something to eat.

''What, now?''

''Yes, why not? I think there's enough for two, and I've baked today . . .''

It was a much more comfortable reunion. With Joan Elliott, Stephen could be himself, and he managed to relieve some of his frustrations by telling her about Pam and the fact that he had finally said what he thought on the subject of his ex-wife.

''Well, that's Pamela for you—she could never leave a thing alone, even when she was little. She would never be told, somehow, at least not until you'd got really cross with her.'' Joan sighed over the vagaries of human nature. ''Still, there's one blessing, love—it's made you realize about Ruth. I never much cared for her, myself—too much the clinging vine, particularly for you.''

He was surprised at that. ''You never said.''

She laughed. ''You weren't after my opinion in those days! Anyway, you wouldn't have liked it, if I had said . . .''

''I wouldn't have believed you,'' he admitted. ''But you know, Pam scared the life out of me when she said things weren't going too well for Ruth, and that she still cared for *me*—God! I thought the last thing I want is to get involved again with *her*."

Joan gave him an old-fashioned look. "I shouldn't worry about *that*. It'll have been the high drama of what happened—especially with it being all over the news—and then Pam making mountains out of molehills as usual. Anyway," she said briskly, "You've got bigger fish to fry, unless I'm very much mistaken."

"Have I?" He was puzzled. "What do you mean?"

"Zoe."

Avoiding his aunt's penetrating gaze, Stephen was very noncommittal.

"Well, I'm not going to ask for details, love, but if there's something wrong between you and her, I suggest you try and get things sorted out. She thinks a lot about you, and she's a good girl—too good to lose for the sake of a petty argument."

"We didn't have an argument."

"Well then—it might have been better if you had."

That raised a dry smile. Before he left, she said something else that gave him something to think about on the way home. It was to the effect that bottling things up never did anyone much good; if he could think about what had happened, and talk about it, then he would recover more quickly from its effects.

"Is it that obvious?"

She nodded. "You're not yourself just now."

"Mmm. Well, you might be right, at that . . ."

When he got home, Stephen poured himself a large whisky and spent a long time just looking at the telephone. Part of him was desperate for the sound of Zoe's voice, but the rest of him was very reluctant to expose itself to more pain. And he was tired. Perhaps he would call her tomorrow.

He switched on the television for the late news, but there was something on about the Gulf, so he switched it off again and went to bed. Unlike the previous evening, he fell asleep straightaway, but at about two he woke again, shaking and sweating, having had a horrifying dream about the *Damaris*. There was an explosion, and there was fire, spreading rapidly throughout the accommodation; and the anchor was unsecured, the ship drifting closer and closer to another tanker full of motor gasoline . . .

It was so real, so vivid, every time he closed his eyes the images came back. In the end he forced himself out of bed and went to make a pot of tea. Two cups and several cigarettes later, he had managed to come to terms with his fear and to clear his mind of it. How odd, he thought, that he had never been particularly afraid of drowning, yet the thought of being burned alive could always terrify him. The worst thing he had ever had to do was send the Mate and Lecky down into the engine room, while in his mind seeing all too clearly what they would have to face. Some years ago he had been on a fire-fighting course in Liverpool, and having to climb into those protective suits with the breathing apparatus strapped on, then crawl through a blazing room full of flames and smoke—that had been fear. If it were the last job on earth, Stephen knew he could not fight fires for a living.

And poor old Jim . . .

Stephen had written to his next of kin, a brother and sister-in-law in Wallasey with whom he stayed when on leave. It had been a terrible task, made only slightly easier by the fact that Mac had also offered to write to them. But however well-phrased those letters, nothing could alleviate the shocking manner of his death, its pointlessness, and the terrible irony that Jim had volunteered for the job. The company would pay a considerable sum in compensation—that much at least had been established during that visit to the office—but what was money in exchange for a life?

The more he thought about it, the more convinced Stephen became that he was lucky to be alive. They all were. If things had gone wrong—if that fire had taken hold in the accommodation, it would have swept through it in no time . . .

Enough. Don't think about it, he told himself; go back to bed.

But passing the half-open door of the spare room, Stephen's eye caught sight of the old trunk full of books. It reminded him of Zoe's latest commission, the one she had been strangely reluctant to talk about. Out of curiosity he thought he would take a look at that old edition of the *Rubáiyát*, which she had so admired when they first found it in the spring.

Its beauty struck him more forcefully now—at the time his mind had been concerned with other things—and he could see why she was so taken with it. He remembered then that he had intended to give the book to her as a sort of farewell present, a good intention forgotten in the unexpected haste of his departure for Teesport. Well, he could still give it to her. She was, he decided, as much entitled to own it as anyone else in the family. More so, really, because of her ability to appreciate its value as a work of art. The illustrations were more intriguing than he had realized, and as he studied them, he began to read the verses alongside, and then other verses seemed to leap out at him.

> Ah, make the most of what we yet may spend,
> Before we too into the Dust descend;
>   Dust into Dust, and under dust to lie,
> Sans wine, sans Song, sans Singer, and—sans End!
>
> There was a Door to which I found no Key:
> There was a Veil past which I could not see:
>   Some little Talk awhile of Me and Thee
> There seemed—and then no more of Thee and Me.
>
> One Moment in Annihilation's Waste,
> One Moment of the Well of Life to taste—
>   The Stars are setting and the Caravan
> Starts for the Dawn of Nothing—Oh, make haste!

The images were dazzling, the message unmistakable; that last verse particularly sent chills running up and down his spine. He stared at it for some time before gently setting the book down. His eyes were drawn to the smaller trunk, empty now of its letters, with just the treasured bits and pieces in the tray at the top. But there was something else . . .

His fingers touched and lifted little shoes, opened an old envelope containing locks of hair in tissue paper; there was a small leather box containing two gold rings, and another with—my God, a diamond and sapphire brooch! Where did *that* come from? Stephen sat back, holding up that brooch, seeing lights wink through the dust. Did Joan know about this?

It must be worth . . . well, a lot. He put it back, bemused for a moment, knowing that none of these things were what he was looking for, and yet he could not have described what it was.

With the tray empty, he turned to the base of the trunk, carefully feeling along the corner, wondering whether it contained a false bottom. The soft leather lining was torn in a couple of places, bulging a little where it was loose. Running his fingers down the sides, he suddenly felt the ridge of something hard. Very gently, trying to raise it without tearing that fragile lining, he finally extracted a slim cigarette case. The silver was tarnished, and it had been closed so long the catch was stiff, but even before he opened it, Stephen knew that this was what he was looking for.

Running the edge of a thumbnail down the edge, he managed to prise it open and out fell a couple of photographs and a square of folded paper. Engraved on the case were Liam's initials and the date of his twenty-second birthday. Remembering an entry in the diary, Stephen guessed that this had been the *"birthday present from G."* which Liam had felt bound to record.

There was no mistaking her, Stephen thought as he retrieved the photographs: Georgina Duncannon, with smooth fair hair swept back from the classic beauty of her face. She really was very lovely, he thought, feeling a strong pull of sympathy as he glanced from one to the other, recognizing the possessive pride in Liam's eyes.

It was a little while before he remembered the worn piece of paper, and as he opened it, Stephen was very much aware that his heart was beating that little bit faster. More than any of the others, this letter both touched and awed him. It was a direct communication to Liam from Georgina; probably the only one still in existence. And her neat italic script reminded him, sharply, of Zoe's.

My Dearest,

How I miss you! From here, Barton-on-Sea seems a whole world away, despite your wonderful, loving, precious letters. How good you are, writing to me every day, keeping up my flagging spirit, giving me such an amusing

picture of your fellow convalescents in that little seaside
hotel! I do so wish that I had time just now to send you
more than just these few lines.

I refuse to make excuses about the ward and
work—but, my darling, you know how and why it is, none
better. Remember always that I love you, that my spirit
loves you even when my hands and mind are occupied,
and that I think of you in my quiet times, and especially
during the lonely nights.

Soon, my dearest, soon. We will be together, come
what may, and then these lonely weeks will be forgotten—

My love, my heart—
G.

The words became a blur. Overwhelmed for a moment,
Stephen bowed his head, heart and eyes both aching at the
sadness and the waste.

The note shivered in his fingers, sending a tingling shock
right through him; the air was suddenly charged with urgency,
and he looked up, startled, half expecting to see Liam standing
there before him, arms lifted in supplication, the way he had
seen them in so many dreams.

For perhaps a minute he could do nothing, and then as
the urgency faded, he slowly nodded in understanding and
acceptance. "All right," he said softly, "I'm not entirely stupid,
I know what you're trying to say. I'd just about worked it out
for myself anyway."

He refolded that fragile paper, placing it with the photographs inside the cigarette case where they belonged. While he
dressed and shoved a change of clothes into an overnight bag,
he laid it on the bed, hardly taking his eyes from it. When he
was ready to leave, he slipped it into the breast pocket of his
shirt, picked up a warm sweater, and went down to the garage.

34

$\mathcal{H}$e stopped once on the motorway for petrol and was approaching the outskirts of London as the sun came up. It had been a fine, dry night with little traffic, and he could not recall when he had enjoyed a drive so much. The Jaguar performed on the open road as it was meant to do; he saw two police cars before they saw him, slowed to an acceptable speed, then returned to a steady ninety-five as soon as they were gone. And everything, but everything, was crystal clear in his mind.

The only doubt at all was whether Zoe would still be there. As he drove through London, wending a tortuous route through already thickening traffic, he prayed that either from anger or misery she had not abandoned the flat in favor of her mother's cottage in Sussex, or worse, gone to friends elsewhere. The anxiety grew stronger with every passing mile, and he cursed the indecision that had prevented him from calling her last night. Then he began to worry about where he might leave the car, but as he came down Queen's Gate from the park, he saw one of the residents pulling away from the curb and pulled neatly in before the space could be taken by anyone else. No doubt he would be in trouble with somebody for leaving it there, but in that moment it was the least of his worries. Climbing out of the car, he stretched and flexed his long legs, took a long look at Zoe's window, and with a deep breath crossed the road. For a moment at the front of the steps he was daunted; then he thought of Liam and pressed the bell.

It rang in Zoe's flat as a sort of crackling buzz, and that buzzing continued, on and off, for more than a minute before she became aware that the noise was real and not part of a dream. In a pale blue, sleeveless nightshirt that skimmed her knees, she staggered to the intercom in the hall, wondering why the postman always rang her bell when he needed to leave a parcel.

"Yes?"

"Zoe? It's me, Stephen."

Stephen? What time was it? What was he doing here?

"Zoe? Look, I'm sorry I was such an idiot the other day . . . won't you let me in so we can talk?"

"Oh. Yes. Push the door." She pressed the button, gave him a second or two to enter, then shook her head as though to clear it. Panic set in.

She flew to the bathroom, grabbed a toothbrush, scrubbing furiously at her teeth while she surveyed the mess in the mirror. Yesterday's mascara smudged beneath her eyes, her hair looking like an untrimmed hedge . . .

Her face was washed, hairbrush dragging at the last of the tangles as he knocked at her door. Startled gray eyes set in a somewhat shiny face stared back at her from the mirror. The well-scrubbed look with a vengeance, she thought, but it would have to do.

The cool, nonchalant image that she had cherished, on and off for the last forty-eight hours, would have been satisfying had she been able to carry it off, but Zoe's heart was beating a wild tattoo, and besides, she was too utterly thankful to dissimulate. As soon as she saw him, tall and tanned and slightly crumpled from the journey, all the heartbreak disappeared. She wanted to hate him, but the only thing in her heart was love.

His eyes, long-lashed, so brightly blue, were softened by a discernible amount of shame and a lot of love. "Forgive me?"

he murmured, while Zoe was too overcome to speak. She wanted to say she was sorry too, but all she could do was nod and let him in. The door swung to of its own accord.

Between sighs and kisses and little sobs of laughter, she managed to say that she had tried to telephone him yesterday several times; and between her eyes and mouth and throat he managed to tell her where he had been.

"But then I woke about two, and I couldn't sleep for thinking of you and . . ." He found her mouth again. "I knew I *had* to see you, I couldn't tell you how much I love you over the telephone . . . I tried twice before, and each time—"

For a second, Zoe wondered whether she had heard correctly. With a quizzical little smile she looked up at him. "What did you say?"

He was very serious. "I love you, Zoe. Will you marry me?"

Bubbles of happiness seemed to explode inside her; her smile broadened into a grin and seemed to go on forever. Laughing, she said, "You are *incredible*. After all you've put me through, and you turn up at seven in the morning, when I'm not even *awake*, and ask me to *marry* you. I ought to turn you down and throw you out!"

"But you won't?"

She shook her head. "I love you." For a long moment she looked at him, the desire to kiss him battling with an urge to return some of the pain she had suffered, particularly in the last two days. The kiss won, by a narrow margin. It was fierce and hard and very passionate.

"Enough to marry me?"

"Oh more than enough," she whispered as the anger evaporated. "It's been more than enough for a long, long time."

She looked up, at his eyes and his mouth, and was caught for a second by that uncanny resemblance to Liam. Remembering his touch, she felt it again; and at her sudden shiver Stephen hesitated, as though he sensed something too. His eyes searched her face, then very tenderly he traced the outline of her mouth. "I've loved you," he said softly, "almost from the moment I first saw you, that night in the fog. I just wish that I could have believed it . . ."

With his words, her awareness of Liam intensified; she

answered abstractedly, while little shocks ran through her at every movement of his hands.

"It was meant, wasn't it? Our meeting—everything since . . ."

"Yes," she whispered, wanting him, needing him, a little afraid of what else was happening. He touched his mouth to hers with a tenderness that quickly flared to passion; at the invasion of his tongue it seemed an array of shooting stars arced across a midnight sky, and she clung as he lifted her up and carried her back to that rumpled bed.

In a daze she watched him undress, her own fingers fumbling with tiny buttons until she was naked too, reaching out to hold him as he came toward her. She pressed her face against his body, kissing him, hearing him gasp at every touch. He was trembling and so was she, the shocks between them so exquisite they were almost unbearable. With the lightest touch he pushed her back, and slowly, as though performing part of a ritual, entered her with such gentleness it seemed no more than an extension of a light caress.

One flesh, joined but barely moving, the center of awareness not deep in the womb but spreading from the mind, encompassing them both. Slowly, he began to move, with steadily mounting urgency driving sighs and moans of pleasure from her lips, while she felt her soul expanding, drifting somewhere on a sea of rapture, tied to bodily sensation, but only just. She heard her own voice, and his, through the pulsing of a heartbeat, a beat that rushed and swelled like the booming of the sea, taking her with it in huge waves that curled and broke against an unfamiliar shore. Her soul was the sea and the cry of a bird, and his was the unrelenting force that drove her on; the night and the stars were Liam's.

She was borne up, lifted, broken in a vast cascade of shimmering light; and from somewhere came a long drawn-out cry that could not have been hers, but it was, it was, and so far away . . .

The aftermath lingered like the wash of the tide when the storm is over, and they clung together like half-drowned castaways, speechless, blinded, deafened, aware of nothing but each other and the fact of being alive. Inert, locked as one, it seemed that time and place had ceased to be; everything was shimmering and echoing, the smallest movement such torture that even breathing brought its pain. It was like being bathed in a burning light, and the silence and the stillness were alive with Liam's tremendous power.

Slowly, very slowly, the intensity waned, and as he finally left them, tears seeped unbidden from Zoe's eyes, silent at first, and then in great, heaving sobs that were impossible to control. Stephen moved then, cradling her like a child, drawing up the sheets around her shoulders, murmuring soft words of comfort against her hair.

"I know, I know . . . darling, I know." He kissed her wet cheeks and her lips, tasting the saltiness of her tears, and he knew what it was that racked her, because he had felt it too.

It was not a thing that either of them wanted to talk about, particularly at first; words seemed a desecration, but the awareness was in their eyes, in every touch. Over the next couple of days, Stephen referred to it only once, and that was after he had made love to her again. "That was beautiful," he said softly, a smile lighting his eyes, "but it didn't blow my mind. And I think that's how I prefer it."

That was true. Exaltation was one thing, but in that coming together they had not been alone, he would swear to it; never, in the whole of his life, not even in the most abandoned of lovemaking, had he experienced anything like that. And that lovemaking had been far from abandoned. It was controlled, but not by him, and certainly not by Zoe. From that moment in the doorway, everything seemed to have been orchestrated, like a symphony played many times before.

Stephen did not pretend to understand it. It was not something that worried him exactly, but it stayed in his mind and he often thought about it, and so, he suspected, did Zoe.

There were, however, a vast amount of other things to talk about, and it seemed they never stopped, memories, facts, discoveries, moving constantly back and forth from Zoe's research here to the Elliotts in York, and Stephen's experiences in the Gulf. Once that subject had been seriously broached, he found it easier than he had imagined, and to talk about his own experience in relation to Liam's during the First World War helped to set much of it in perspective. He found Zoe's attitude practical as well as sympathetic, and the fact that she was interested in his job rather than resentful of it not only eased the stress but reinforced his confidence in her. Artistic she might be; it also seemed that she was far tougher than he had previously given her credit for, and Stephen was happy to acknowledge his mistake. If, in the future, he had to leave her, he knew full well that she would not buckle at the first crisis. The Gulf, for her as much as himself, had been a baptism of fire; if she could withstand that, then she would probably weather most things.

She was honest enough not to spare him the worst of her anguish during those dreadful weeks, just as he was honest enough to admit that he had been wrong in keeping silent; but with love and trust between them, there was no longer any room for foolish pride.

"Either yours or mine," he gently reminded her.

They were in Kensington Gardens when he mentioned, casually, the idea of Zoe traveling with him. It was a beautiful afternoon, the manicured expanse of London's parkland as far from the barren expanse of oceans and deserts as it was possible to be; but the sheer contrast of what was still so close behind him reminded Stephen of what would, eventually, have to be faced again. Not the Gulf: he had played his part for the company and had told them he was not going back there; but life at sea was something different. He hoped Zoe understood that.

Her eyes were shining as she glanced up at him. "Do you mean it? Could I really come with you?"

Stephen laughed. "All the time, if you wanted to."

"But I thought—didn't you say before that you were thinking of giving it up?"

On a deep breath, he said, "If you wanted me to, I would . . ."

With a sudden, fierce hug, she shook her head. "I don't need that kind of sacrifice. It's you I want, and your work is part of you, just as what I do is part of me—and we'll make it succeed together."

"I suppose your work's portable?"

"I'll make it so," she said fervently.

It was not until they returned to Queen's Gate that afternoon that Stephen remembered the things he had brought from York. He gave her, first of all, that illustrated copy of the *Rubái- yát*, and watching her face as she opened it, full of wonder and delight, knew he could not have given her anything better. All at once she started to talk about her commission, to show him the work already done, explaining the symbolism and the ideas that had inspired every illustration. Stephen was fascinated; he knew practically nothing about art, and less about the history of design, but her enthusiasm was catching and the subject held them even while she was preparing dinner.

It was something of a scratch meal, but they had lunched out, and neither of them wanted more than the other's company. Settling down afterward, with lamps lit against a falling dusk, Stephen refreshed their glasses and lit himself a cigarette, then he reached into his pocket and brought out the little silver case. It was strange to realize, as he handed it to Zoe, that Georgina's gift was no stranger to this flat.

"I haven't cleaned it, and it's difficult to open, but I'd rather you tried it for yourself . . ."

She was intrigued, and while she felt for a way to spring the catch, he told her where he had found it, and about the inner certainty that had led to the search. "Somebody had obviously hidden it. Probably Louisa, but I dare say it might have been old Sarah."

"Oh, I don't think so, Stephen—those letters hadn't been disturbed for years. You could tell—the ribbons were still tied as Louisa must have left them, and if you recall, the oldest letters were still at the bottom. I think the most Sarah did was add to them—you know, the letters she had from Robin during the war. I don't think she wanted to know about the rest . . ."

The cigarette case suddenly opened, its contents falling into Zoe's lap. As he had done, she looked first at the photographs, and as she saw the one of Liam and Georgina together, her frown faded into a small, sad, compassionate smile. "Together," she whispered. "I'm not at all surprised, are you?"

He shook his head, unable to speak, tenderly pushing back a lock of hair from her face. She stared at that photograph for a long time before opening the little square of cheap paper on which Georgina had penned those few lines to Liam all those years ago. For a long time she said nothing.

Seeing the tears in her eyes, Stephen drew her close. "You know, I might have written those words," he whispered, "while I was away. I wish I had, because that's exactly how I felt."

For a while they clung together, and Zoe wept a little. When she was calmer, she said, "But we were right, weren't we? They were a lot more to each other than brother and sister. No wonder Louisa hid the evidence."

"It's a wonder she didn't destroy it," he murmured, trying to envisage the depth of shock.

"Perhaps she knew, deep down. Maybe she felt guilty . . ."

"Maybe she did. We'll never know."

They were lost for a while in contemplation: There had been neither a time nor a place for Liam and Georgina, and never a chance of happiness. Whatever it was that they had shared, that affair could never have been resolved, no matter how long Liam lived. As lovers, they were doomed from the beginning.

"By an accident of birth," Zoe said softly.

"It all goes back to Robert and Louisa, doesn't it? If he hadn't been married, or if they'd never met . . ."

"Well," she sighed, "if they hadn't met, we wouldn't be here, would we?"

That gave him a strange feeling, akin to his old suspicion that somehow his life was linked to that of Robert Duncannon, as much as to his son Liam; that somewhere old accounts were being rendered and old scores settled, and that Zoe was part of it too. It struck him that Robert and Louisa had never married, and he wondered why, when both of them were free. Had Liam and Georgina's affair rebounded on them, made it impossible to marry?

Zoe voiced his thoughts, and for a while they discussed the many different facets of that lifelong relationship, and certain parallels began rather chillingly to emerge.

"You say he didn't die until 1923, six years after Edward's death. Well, even granting the fact that they were both in late middle age by then, they *could* have married. Why didn't they?" He tapped Georgina's letter. "Imagine it—and if you think of where we stand today, it shouldn't be too difficult to put ourselves in their shoes.

"I'm unhappily married, but I can't get a divorce. We meet, fall passionately in love, and at some stage or another, I persuade you to become my mistress. For a while, life's wonderful, but I'm away a lot with my job, and after a few years it all starts to fall apart at the seams. We eventually go our separate ways. You, as Louisa, marry the cousin who's always loved you, and to make life simpler, our three children are brought up as his. Then, years later, *our* eldest son and *my* grown-up daughter fall in love . . ."

Stephen paused to let that sink in, and as it did so, he saw the mounting aversion in Zoe's eyes. "It's a horrifying thought, isn't it? We'd blame ourselves, wouldn't we? We'd be saying we should never have met, never given in to that overwhelming passion, and certainly never had children. Even if they weren't hung up on sin, Zoe, the guilt must have been like a lead weight, no matter what else they felt for each other." As her gaze slid away from his, he touched her cheek. "I don't wonder the rest of the family never knew about the Duncannons."

He woke early the next morning, thinking about Robert, and about the years in which this flat had been a base for him and a refuge for Georgina. In the dim light, Victorian furniture and elaborate cornices fostered the illusion that little had changed; and when Stephen considered world upheavals and the bitter continuation of struggle in Ireland, it seemed to him that progress was no more than superficial gloss, a coat of paint on the rusty old tub of human nature, making its journey between the same old ports. Tolerance tried very hard to cure it, but religion and politics were as corrosive as ever, and while the crew battled on, the brokers sat on a sunny quay, totting up the profits.

During the last ten years of his life, Robert Duncannon must have seen plenty of that, Stephen reflected, particularly when he was approaching his sixtieth year and treading a fine line between government expediency and his own sense of what was just. Judging by his letters, the Easter Rising and its bitter aftermath had broken Robert's faith in a peaceful settlement; with the advent of the Black and Tans he had resigned his post, given up this War Office flat, and become something of a nomad, dividing his time between Dublin, Waterford, and

York. Stephen wondered briefly whether he had become involved in any anti-British activity then, but it seemed unlikely,
except perhaps to turn a blind eye from time to time, or with-
hold information from those arrogant thugs, the Black and
Tans. Robert's attitude, it seemed, had been one of contempt.

It seemed, too, that as a professional soldier he had resented being kept from the war in Europe. Since he was a man
who had been decorated twice for bravery, in the Sudan and
South Africa, Stephen could understand the depth of Robert's
frustration caused by his enforced involvement with the holding operation in Ireland. It was false diplomacy, a papering
over of the cracks, until a burst of madness that Easter of 1916
tore everything apart. And in his own country.

Reading again, last night, Robert's description of the devas-
tation, Stephen mentally substituted York for Dublin and understood exactly how he must have felt. He could understand,
too, why Georgina had never wanted to go back.

The war in Europe, conducted over a strip of land ex-
tending from the North Sea to the Swiss border, had destroyed
a generation, taking with it Robert's eldest son, his two nephews, and Tisha's husband, Edwin Fearnley, and leaving a legacy of illness for Robin. A generation, a way of life, was gone
for ever, and the face of Europe was irrevocably altered. Bitterness and grief, Stephen reckoned, must have been standard
baggage in every family, from the steppes of Russia to the Isle
of Ushant, but for a man who had been prevented from doing
what he was trained and qualified to do, there must also have
been a large measure of self-recrimination.

In the summer of 1921 he had gone abroad for two months,
on a motoring tour of the battlefields, sending Louisa letters
and postcards from all the places mentioned by his sons in their
correspondence. That journey seemed to have been something
of a catharsis for him, a means of coming to terms with the
unalterable truth of Liam's death.

And toward the end of the following year, he had followed
Georgina, via Egypt, to Australia.

Thinking about her, Stephen looked at Zoe as she slept.
He gazed at her for a long time, aware of an inexpressible
tenderness, a love for her that went far deeper than the sexual
desire which had initially drawn them together. In retrospect,

however, it struck him that even then there had been something else, a mutual sympathy and understanding, a sense of
recognition, somehow, that he could only think was inspired
by shared blood and a common inheritance. It had acted like
an emotional shortcut, obviating the need to discover things
like background and social interests, and going straight to the
heart of the matter.

The full extent of that other relationship could only be
guessed at, but he was convinced the emotions were shared to
every last nuance; and just as he wanted more than anything
that Zoe should be safe, and cared for, and happy, so he knew
that Liam would have wanted the same for Georgina.

He had only heard about those final letters of hers, never
seen them, for they had been pushed down among earlier bundles, as though Louisa wanted nothing to leap out and remind
her of that illicit affair.

After breakfast, Zoe set aside the letters from Robert that
had occupied their attention the evening before, handing to
Stephen those written by Georgina. There was a note of sympathy, posted from Cairo almost a month after Liam's death, and
in its terse, wrung-out phrases, it was almost possible to hear
the heartbreak. With what both of them now knew, it required
little imagination to transport themselves back to that date in
October 1917 and envisage a young woman's agony at the death
of her lover. The worst nightmare realized, dread made fact,
and the added anguish of being so far from home without the
comfort of being able to grieve with others who had loved him.
Zoe thought that it must have near killed Georgina to write that
note, to sympathize without being able to beg for sympathy,
while Stephen felt her isolation, that sense of being cut off and
in exile.

Remembering the sudden deaths of his parents, he also
knew how emotionally crippling distance could be, how hard
it was to believe that they were gone, how lengthy the period
of grief. He had not fully understood his own sense of loss until
his wife's betrayal released it, and then the bereavement pain
had been almost unendurable.

He understood very well the course of Georgina's pain,
could follow it so easily in those widely spaced letters to Louisa.

That heartbreaking note was not the first she had written

from Egypt, however. In an earlier missive, she had described
the strangeness while confessing a liking for it. After the bleak,
unremitting years in London, Cairo was exciting and the ba-
zaars compulsive, constantly tempting her to buy things for
which she had no earthly use; and there was a sybaritic splendor in the shady halls of those great, converted palaces in which
she spent her days. Off duty, Georgina wrote, as long as there
was shade to cling to, she found she rather liked the heat; it
made her feel like a cat, content with nothing to do, which was
a luxury she could not recall enjoying before.

Even allowing for the fact that she was deliberately telling
Louisa only the best part of her experience in Egypt, it was
possible to read a lot of truth in those lines, to understand
that for many years Georgina's life must have been a long,
exhausting round of activity, always busy learning things and
putting them into practice, with latterly a constant struggle
to overcome weariness and fear and the effects of the war.
Compared to London, and York and Dublin before that, Cairo
was obviously a relief; and after the additional stress of her
affair with Liam, and an agony of parting that Zoe and Stephen
could only guess at, it seemed those first few months in Egypt
were like balm to her soul.

But there was more. Her remarks on the loneliness of the
desert, and the eeriness of the pyramids at sunset, seemed,
even after all these years, to be alive with thoughts of Liam.
For her, his memory was there even if he was not.

In a postscript, she mentioned that a friend of Liam's,
Lewis Maddox from Dandenong, had very recently surprised
her by introducing himself.

> . . . I thought it an odd coincidence until he said that he
> had had a letter from his old friend Bill—as he calls
> Liam—asking him to look out for me here. It was kind of
> him to do so, and we spent a pleasant hour talking about
> Dandenong and our mutual friend . . .

That was in August, and after October's letter of condo-
lence there was nothing more until June 1922, in which she
pressed Louisa to join her father in coming out to Australia for
a holiday.

* * *

. . . I would dearly love to see you again, Louisa, if only to talk as we used to do so long ago. Surely the time has come for us all to put the past behind us—the saddest things, anyway—and work toward a better future. That is what I have spent the last few years trying to do. Liam has not been forgotten, and here among his old friends in Dandenong, you would be touched and surprised, I think, by the reverence accorded to his memory. It's not a morbid thing, but a deep sense of respect for all those who made Australia's name in the world, particularly at Gallipoli.

I have found it a deep and lasting comfort, and am so glad that I came here. There was nothing for me in either England or Ireland, and the impulse to come here, to see what it was that had so inspired Liam, was more deeply felt than I can ever describe. It was as though I *had* to come, and I have not regretted it.

Lewis sets great store by the fact that Liam virtually introduced us, and he has used that fact unashamedly in all his attempts to persuade me to marry him. He asked me first a long time ago—before he left Egypt in fact. But I could not answer him then. I am sure you understand why. Fortunately, Lewis also understood that it had nothing to do with the injuries he sustained at Beersheba; and after all, what are they to me, after all these years of nursing? But a strong will and great determination has made his recovery far better than anyone expected, and I think we know each other well enough by now to be assured of a happy future together. There will be no children, of course, but that is a relief to me rather than a sadness, and anyway there are children enough about the farm, a multitude of nephews and nieces, all delightful enough to satisfy us both.

His elder brother served with the 5th Battalion in France and returned some time after Lewis, reasonably sound in mind and limb, but less well disposed to company. He and his family live out at Warragul, but the children stay often with their grandparents, so I am getting to know them well. Lewis's widowed sister lives here too, with her three children, so it is quite a little commune, or will be when we settle in the new bungalow being built near the old homestead.

Mary—do you remember Liam writing about her?—has married and is living now in Sydney. We became quite friendly when I was working with her in Melbourne, but she rarely spoke about Ned. Lewis still talks about him, and Liam of course. We talk about Liam a lot.

I think you would like Lewis; he is very frank and open and cares so passionately about growing things. Too much, probably, to be a very successful farmer, but he listens to his father these days, which he apparently did not, before! His family are good, honest people, and they have accepted me very well. I know my father is looking forward to meeting them, if only because they were so good to Liam before the war and have been good to me since.

I wish you would come with him, Louisa. Just being here would be so good for you, and the journey out and back would be a wonderful experience.

If it should be entirely out of the question, I do hope that the reason is not because you still blame me—or yourself—for what happened. I think we have all punished ourselves enough, and all the tears in the world won't bring him back, or undo the circumstances in which we found ourselves.

Write to me, please, and tell me you understand. That is all the blessing I need before my marriage to Lewis.

> My love to you, as always—
> Georgina.

It was a letter that could not have failed to strike some chord in a woman whose life had contained more than its fair share of tragedy. And it seemed the letter had provoked a sympathetic response because Georgina had written again, thanking Louisa for her generosity and expressing regret only at her inability to accept the invitation to Dandenong.

Although Louisa had apparently used Robin's uncertain health as her excuse, Zoe was of the opinion that embarrassment lay behind her refusal. Louisa was not, after all, married to Robert Duncannon, and whether the Maddox family were aware of that unconventional relationship or not, it seemed unlikely that she would want to advertise it, or subject herself to questions about the connection between her son and Robert's daughter.

So Robert had obviously set off alone. It was clear from his letters to Louisa that he planned to be away for up to six months. The wedding was set for the beginning of January 1923, and his last missive was full of that homely little ceremony in Dandenong, descriptions of the family, and his admiration for his new son-in-law. The fact that Lewis had always been a horseman, and had served with the mounted Australian forces in Egypt and Palestine, had given the two men much to talk about. The impression of that last letter was of a man cheered considerably by his daughter's happiness and full of hope for the future.

He died, three weeks later, of a sudden seizure, while out riding with Lewis.

35

*T*here was a letter from Lewis Maddox, written in a strong, upright hand, but nothing apparently from Georgina for several months. she had, it seemed, been devastated by her father's death.

With personal experience to draw on, Stephen could imagine only too well the effects of that second blow, releasing all the shock and grief she had probably been unable to express after Liam's death; and so, it seemed, could Zoe.

"Nursing in the midst of war, surrounded by the dying—it would be impossible, wouldn't it? It was the era of the stiff upper lip," she remarked sardonically, "when they all pretended they were just fine, and carried on regardless." With an exasperated sigh she shook her head, then said, "But yes, I can see she would go to pieces when Robert died. She thought the world of him, didn't she? I think, too, that it would be like letting go on all the other deaths, all that stress and anguish she'd suffered—not to mention losing Liam."

"Poor girl," Stephen murmured, drawing Zoe close into the crook of his arm.

"Yes. Thank God she wasn't alone. He sounds to have been a pretty decent sort, that guy she married."

"And a decent family, from all accounts." Turning over the Australian correspondence, Stephen recalled something his aunt had said months ago about Louisa receiving letters from Australia. "Do you remember? Something about her always having kept in touch with the people Liam had worked for before the war. It never struck me, because—"

"Because at that time we didn't know about Georgina!" Zoe interjected. "But *then* she said—"

"That her mother, Sarah, hadn't bothered after Louisa died, because she was never much of a letter writer anyway."

Zoe laughed. "Sarah wouldn't have known Georgina, anyway. I mean, if she met her once or twice, it wouldn't have been more than that, would it? And she was in Egypt when Sarah and Robin got married."

"And I doubt whether Sarah would have known about the relationship between Georgina and Liam—Louisa wouldn't have advertised *that*, would she?"

"No." After a moment's thought, Zoe said, "I don't think old Sarah wanted to know about the Duncannons. I can imagine Robert's death must have been, for her, anyway, the end of an embarrassment. And Georgina was far enough away not to be an intrusion. No wonder she kept quiet about that half of the family!"

"And it wouldn't be the sort of complication that Louisa could explain to my father and Joan," Stephen added. "Not when they were young, anyway."

They were both struck by the roundabout route they had pursued to reach that conclusion, and by the years that had elapsed between those final letters from Georgina, written mostly before 1939, and interrupted by the war. Although it was hardly likely that she was still alive, Zoe felt that Georgina Duncannon would still be remembered by someone in Australia.

"Strange, isn't it? She lived here for no more than a couple of years, and yet for me she felt a lasting impression. She welcomed me when I first came here, I know she did."

At her dreamy, slightly speculating expression, Stephen could not restrain a smile. "You've got something on your mind. What is it?"

"Oh, nothing, really," she said vaguely; but a moment

later, watching him return letters to envelopes, she said, "You
know, I think I might try writing to them . . ."

"Who?"

"The Maddox family. There sounds to have been enough
of them, and I bet somebody's still running that farm . . ."

He was unconvinced. "Listen, the last time I was in Melbourne was twenty years ago, and it was growing fast. Whoever
owned the Maddox farm probably sold out and made a fortune—it's probably a housing estate now."

"Oh, don't be so defeatist! Dandenong's miles from Melbourne—"

"It's not that far—"

"—and *anyway*," she continued, silencing him with a kiss,
"nothing ventured, nothing gained. Look what I got when I
wrote to all fifty-two Elliotts in the York phone book . . ." She
kissed him again passionately.

"In that case," Stephen murmured minutes later, "I think
I should forbid you even to try. Lord knows what you might
come up with next time."

"A handsome hunk of an Australian?" she inquired
wickedly.

"Guzzling Fosters and grunting *G'Day*," he retorted,
laughing. "Be warned—in my day, Australian women were
third-rate citizens. Which is why," he added, "we Brits were
so much appreciated . . ."

For a while the teasing continued, but a couple of days
later, determined to prove a point to Stephen, Zoe put together
a letter inquiring about Georgina Maddox née Duncannon,
posting it to that old address. Even the longest shots, in her
opinion, were worth attempting; and as she remarked to Stephen, there had been so many beneficial results already, perhaps the letter would produce one more.

With that he could not disagree.

They were invited by Zoe's father to a lunch which lasted most
of the afternoon, and on another evening to dinner with Zoe's
mother at her cottage in Sussex. Although the former meeting
had initially caused him much apprehension, Stephen found
James Clifford much as Zoe had described him, of medium

height and build, in his early fifties, pale eyes that missed nothing even while he laughed. Affable but sharp-witted, his smiles and good humor helped to disguise, along with much conversational padding, the most pertinent questions. Although Stephen was quite familiar with interview techniques, he had to admire Zoe's father for his expertise, while being thankful that he had nothing to hide. Afterward, he was able to smile only because he knew that he had passed the test; James Clifford had, quite literally, given them both his blessing before they left.

"Not that it would have mattered a jot," Zoe assured him. "I'd have married you, my darling, whether my father approved or not. But still"—she grinned—"it's nice that he liked you."

"I liked him," Stephen said frankly. "And yes, it is a relief to know he thinks me capable of taking care of you." And flattering, he thought but did not say, to think he had the older man's respect.

His reaction to Zoe's mother, however, was far less clear-cut. Although Marian was taller and heavier than her daughter, she was a very elegant woman whose looks belied her age. Stephen found it disconcerting to realize that just as he was ten years older than Zoe, her mother was a mere ten years older than him. He remembered then that he and Marian were second cousins and technically of the same generation; to quell the feeling that he was cradle-snatching, he had to remind himself that at twenty-seven, Zoe was no child.

He was the only one feeling ill at ease and callow as he was introduced to the proud and rather brittle Marian. Everything about her had the high gloss of perfection, and the cottage she owned was such a showplace of furniture and objets d'art, he was almost afraid to sit down, and terrified of lighting a cigarette.

Sensing that momentary panic, while her mother poured sherry from a crystal decanter, Zoe went in search of an ashtray, pushing it ostentatiously toward him as she flopped down on luxurious cushions.

"Stephen smokes, Mummy. You don't mind, do you?"

The challenge with which this was said would have credited a far braver man than Stephen; but by the answering glance he knew that Mummy would mind, and very much. Despite her gracious acquiescence and several nudges from Zoe, he managed to hold out until after dinner, when his nerve had relaxed sufficiently to persuade him that just one cigarette might be forgiven.

On the drive home, he chain-smoked while Zoe giggled, telling him that Marian would now be rushing around opening windows and squirting the dining room with fresh-air spray.

"I do hope you're exaggerating."

"I'm not. She used to do that before, when I indulged in the odd cigarette. She's got a fetish about it."

"After we're married," he said heavily, "I shall do my best not to offend her—but if she visits us in our own home, I'm afraid she'll have to put up with my obnoxious habits."

"Have you noticed something? People keep asking us when we're going to get married, and where we're going to live—and giving us some very odd looks when we say we haven't discussed it yet!"

"Well, they're two very good questions," he replied, stubbing out the last half of a cigarette, and shaking his head as Zoe, laughing, offered him another. "When and where?"

He glanced at her while she was considering that, not exactly dreading her reply but hoping that she would want to marry soon. Marian's references to bridesmaids and guest lists had given him a sinking feeling; big weddings took time to arrange, as he knew from past experience, and in his job, dates were practically impossible to guarantee. And there was, of course, the major problem of his divorce: not a point that could be overlooked by the average man of the cloth.

The maturity of her reply took him by surprise.

"Well, my darling, I would have liked to be married in church—*in the sight of God and before this congregation*—but I suppose that's because of all those years at school. I don't think it's going to be possible, though, is it? At least not without an unseemly touting around for somebody willing to perform the ceremony. Anyway, as far as I'm concerned, it's the rest of our lives that matter, not just the place and the number of bridesmaids and a guest list as long as your arm. Which is what Mummy's envisaging." The sigh that followed, was, he realized, inspired by thoughts of her mother. "She'll hate it, of course. Me being an only daughter and all that. But quite honestly, I can't think of more than half a dozen people I'd like to be there, so what does it matter?"

Stephen said nothing but gently squeezed her knee.

"It's you and me that matter, isn't it? Our promises to each other? I'm sure God will hear us, whether it's in church, in the middle of a field, or in the local registry office . . ."

"I'm sure He will," Stephen said quietly, thinking of nights far out at sea, the vastness of the ocean and the endless stars. Amid all that mystical beauty, it was possible to feel closer to God than in the most fanciful or familiar church. One day he wanted Zoe to experience that, to understand that naked sense of solitude and humility, in which the slender division between flesh and the spirit seemed so very fragile.

But, perhaps he thought, she understood something of that already.

36

*T*he question of place and date was easily disposed of. Zoe said she could not envisage any-where else but York, and as they were both keen to set the seal of legality on their relationship, the date was set for a Thursday in the middle of September.

It left little time for the final detail of other arrangements, and Zoe's mother was both furious and panic-stricken. September was always a busy time in Brighton, and how could she possibly leave the business at such short notice? There would be clothes to buy, a wedding dress to arrange—"Off the peg, darling? Oh, how *awful*"—and other essentials such as flowers and a reception. "Although how on earth you expect me to organize that, from *here*," she had wailed to her daughter, "I really do not know!"

Stephen sent a bouquet of flowers to his future mother-in-law by way of apology and reassurance. "Leave everything to me," said the enclosed card, which she might not like, he thought, but at least she could absolve herself of any connection should the arrangements be less than she expected. Zoe's fa-ther, however, had been far more amenable. "Use your discretion," he had said when they met at his home by the Thames at Sunbury, "and just send me the bills."

While Zoe did her best to organize her work and a certain amount of shopping in London, Stephen returned to York to enlist Joan's help. Delight at his news was not spoiled by thoughts of Marian's celestial standards. "Well," she said firmly, "we'll just have to make sure we don't let the side down, won't we?" And with that she set about making inquiries as to a suitable venue for the reception.

She had a surprising amount of friends and acquaintances. Stephen had not realized the extent of her connections until she announced that an old friend from her ATS days, who lived in a glorious Georgian mansion just outside the city, would be willing to place her house at their disposal. "She does it regularly for charitable functions," Joan explained, "and always uses the same caterers. And I can vouch for their excellence. I don't think we could do better."

"You're a wonder," he declared, kissing his aunt roundly. "It sounds just right."

And it was. Meeting Joan's friend and viewing the house the week before, he was able to assure Zoe that even her mother would be impressed. "It's a beautiful old place with a long drive and fabulous windows. You'll love it. And the trees in the park are just beginning to turn—we should get some great photographs."

Leaving his flat to Zoe and Polly, Stephen moved out the afternoon before to stay with Mac and Irene at the old family hotel on Gillygate. Mrs. Bilton, it seemed, could not have been more thrilled, feeling a certain proprietary interest in this forthcoming marriage. She insisted upon giving Stephen the best room, the large double that fronted Gillygate, with its own private bathroom. Across the corridor, Mac and Irene had an excellent view of the ramparts. The next morning, serving breakfast, she was quite fluttery with excitement, fussing over Stephen like a mother as he tried without much success to eat.

While Mac tucked into an old-fashioned English breakfast, and Irene's brown eyes sparkled with laughter, Stephen picked at scrambled eggs before giving up in favor of coffee and cigarettes. In honor of the occasion, Mac had trimmed his beard,

which transformed him from rampaging Viking to distinguished Rear Admiral, especially once he had changed into his
best uniform.

He complained long and loudly, however, about the necessity for it. "If I'd known square rig was the order of the day,
you bloody con-merchant, I'd never have agreed to be best
man!"

"Oh, do be quiet, Mac," his wife ordered as she reached
up to brush his jacket. "I've not seen you looking so smart in
years." She turned to Stephen, who was struggling with the top
button of a new white shirt, and managed to fasten it for him,
watching through the mirror as he anxiously adjusted his black
tie. "For goodness sake, *relax*, Zoe's not going to bite you!"

"No, but her mother might," he declared pessimistically
as Irene held out his jacket.

She laughed. "You're not marrying her mother."

"I'm pleased to know that."

He stood still while Irene brushed away a few clinging
specks of dust, fastened his jacket, and glanced in the long
mirror. Hair neat, no shaving cuts, tie in a perfect Windsor
knot, and the old uniform looking as good as ever. Brass buttons gleamed, gold braid shone against the near-black doeskin,
and after almost eight years, it still fitted perfectly, which was
just as well, he reflected, since there would have been no time
to have another one made, and the uniform had been a specific
request from Zoe.

Irene handed him his cap with its starched white cover,
and as he brushed at the gold oak leaves on the brim, he stared
for a moment at the anchor of the Merchant Navy badge. Remembering that other anchor, the one that held when it was so
vital, Stephen felt his tension miraculously lift. He was here and
very much alive, and today, he realized with heartfelt gratitude,
was the first day of the rest of his life.

Glancing up, meeting Mac's eyes, there was a sudden flash
of understanding between them, on an impulse, they embraced, brief emotion finding release in laughter as Irene
hugged them both and, with a long, happy sigh, stood back to
look at Stephen.

"Oh, Robert Redford, eat your heart out! You look so good,
I could marry you myself!"

"That's the best offer I've had all day." He grinned, kissing her warm cheek. "And I must say, you look pretty tempting . . ."

"Now just a minute," Mac interrupted, taking his wife's arm, "*I'm* supposed to be the best man around here!"

They went out, laughing. About to close the door of his room, Stephen turned, on the impression that someone had called his name. It was so clear he even went to look in the adjoining bathroom, but no one was there. A shiver touched his spine as he remembered Robert Duncannon and his Elliott forebears, and he was aware, as he had been on his first visit to this house, of links stretching back into the past. Then he glanced around, noticed that the long windows were slightly open, and he told himself that what he had heard was no more than a man's voice rising from the street. But it had sounded so close . . .

He shrugged and went downstairs. Mrs. Bilton was waiting in the hall. She kissed him and wished him luck, saying that she would follow them down in a few minutes; she wanted to see Zoe and congratulate them both as soon as the ceremony was over.

They went on foot to the Registrar's on Bootham, causing several female heads to turn during that short walk. Mac's mutterings of discontent were echoed as soon as they arrived by Johnny, who was waiting for them on the steps.

"Jesus, thank God you're here—I've only been waiting five minutes, and already three people have stopped to ask me the time of the next bus!"

"You're a lying hound, Walker—and you look smarter than I've ever seen you, so stop complaining."

"Let's get inside," Mac muttered, "we look like the three bloody musketeers, standing here."

"You're enjoying every minute," Irene declared, linking arms with Johnny, "and I'm having the time of my life."

During the next ten minutes, the other guests assembled, Stephen making a few introductions while they all waited for the bride. Pamela arrived with her husband and Joan, and a moment later Zoe's mother came in with a tall, distinguished man in a dark suit. She seemed unusually tense and flustered, and Stephen had a panic-stricken moment wondering what could have gone wrong; but hard on her heels came Polly, all smiles and vibrant color. She shot him a beaming smile and a discreet thumbs-up sign, which enabled him to breathe again, and immediately made a beeline for Johnny. They seemed quite taken with each other, he thought, remembering the laughter of the night before, and unconcerned by the absence of current partners . . . Moments later, alerted by a sudden hush, all such considerations vanished.

Holding her father's arm, Zoe seemed to drift toward him, layers of chiffon stirring as she slowly crossed the room. Although the dress was of a style and material reminiscent of the early twenties, looking at her, Stephen was reminded of one of her own illustrations, *Titania* perhaps, or the *Spirit of the Rose*. Her hair was as fine and flyaway as the chiffon bandeau she wore, sunlight catching a skein of tiny flowers nestling among the curls. He had always known she was beautiful, but in that moment she was breathtakingly so; had his life depended on it, he could not have spoken.

With an effort, he tore his eyes away, laid his hat on the Registrar's desk, and took hold of Zoe's hand. She was trembling slightly, and that surprised him. He glanced down at her and met a tentative smile that immediately restored his confidence. Squeezing her fingers, he felt a responding pressure as the Registrar cleared his throat to begin.

The ceremony was very short; within minutes it seemed all the formalities were complete and two single people had been joined as one. They stared at each other in happy amazement until a nudge from Mac reminded him that he was supposed to kiss the bride. Almost hesitantly, he bent his head, but Zoe flung her arms around his neck and hugged him, and in the joy of that embrace, Stephen swept her off her feet and swung her around, his kiss raising cheers from the gathered company.

"We couldn't have done that in church!" she said with a giggle as he set her down.

"Start off as you mean to go on," he replied, and kissed her again.

The reception was a great success, the guests few enough to limit the need for constant circulation; before long, the wedding breakfast had become a party.

Afterward, Zoe's mother was almost effusive in her praise, raising a dry smile from Stephen only as she intimated that she had not thought him capable of organizing things so well; but James Clifford's compliments were untinged by any such qualification. And he said, succinctly, that he liked Stephen's friends. It was tantamount to a seal of approval. Zoe nudged him later, pointing out Marian and Joan deep in conversation, and said that his sister, Pamela, had seemed both friendly and sincere when they had talked earlier.

"Don't let this go to your head," Stephen told her, "but Pam actually confessed that she liked you . . ."

"So she might accept me, yet?"

"She might indeed," he said warmly, squeezing her waist. He glanced at his watch, "I hate to break up the party when they're all getting on so well, but it's time we were shedding all this finery and getting on the road."

Zoe ran her fingers beneath the soft doeskin lapels of his jacket. "That's a shame," she said, "because I must confess to rather liking you in that uniform. I think it's incredibly sexy . . ."

He chuckled. "Go on—get up those stairs."

They emerged, some twenty minutes later, in clothes that were considerably more suited to traveling, to find that their presence had scarcely been missed. For a moment they were both tempted to simply creep away, but Mac drew everyone's attention, demanding to know, unless it was a state secret, where they were going for their honeymoon.

"We're going to France," Zoe said brightly, glancing up at Stephen.

"To look at a few vineyards and châteaus, and sample the food," he added with a disarming smile.

For some reason, no one seemed inclined to believe them. He had to produce the ferry tickets, Hull to Zeebrugge, before anyone was remotely satisfied, yet even then an air of suspicion lingered.

"I know," Johnny declared, "you're going for a dirty weekend in Amsterdam—Canal Street and naughty things by candlelight!"

"No, we'd have taken the Rotterdam ferry for that," Stephen said, keeping his face straight.

Zoe's father erupted into laughter, while his ex-wife looked faintly shocked.

A few minutes later, Marian said wistfully, "I thought you might have taken Zoe to the Caribbean."

"Oh, not at *this* time of year—the weather's appalling. Hurricanes, you know. No, Zoe and I have a taste for something a little closer to home. France will suit us fine."

"They didn't believe a word of it, you know," she said happily as the Jaguar took them out of sight and hearing.

Grinning, Stephen changed gear and let the car pick up a little speed. "Well, they wouldn't have believed the truth, that's for sure. Anyway, we didn't tell any lies."

Her smile broadened and broke into laughter; glancing at her, Stephen was caught again by her beauty and high spirits. She looked so gorgeous when she laughed, all he wanted to do was kiss her. Laughing at himself, he turned his eyes back to the road. "Can you imagine . . ." He shook his head, unable to finish the sentence.

"They'd have thought us so *eccentric*."

The idea continued to amuse them all the way to Hull.

The cabin was small but beautifully fitted out, and with its own tiny bathroom; the only drawback, as far as they were concerned, being the single tiered bunks.

"Ah well, never mind," Stephen muttered, inspecting everything with an expert's eye, "where there's a will, there's a way . . ."

"You've got a one-track mind," Zoe observed as he reached for her.

"Are you complaining? Or even surprised?"

She laughed. "No."

"Good. Because," he informed her between kisses, "this is our wedding night, and despite the . . . somewhat . . . *cramped* conditions . . . I've always had this erotic fantasy about . . ."

But he never did manage to tell her; banged heads and elbows and snatches of conversation from cabins either side reduced them both to near-hysterical laughter. In the end they gave up in favor of drinks and dinner.

The wine was good, the food forgivable, and the lounge

bar had a resident pianist. He was charming and played requests. Stephen and Zoe decided that perhaps "The first time ever I saw your face," ought to be their song; it was that kind of evening, with a calm sea shushing past and stars appearing in the twilight. They even took the requisite stroll on the deck.

But it was chilly and they told each other that it had been a long day.

Ensconced in that narrow lower bunk, holding each other close after making love with more urgency than finesse, it seemed to strike them both, very suddenly, that they were married.

Raising her left hand to his lips, Stephen kissed the palm and the base of her third finger with its pair of slender rings. "So tell me, Miss Clifford—how does it feel to be Mrs. Stephen Elliott?"

Zoe's pretty mouth curved into a smile. "I think the word, Captain Elliott, is *loved*—and amazingly *secure* . . ."

"I'm glad," he whispered, "because I do love you, so very, very much."

"I know. And I love you. I always will."

That word, *always*, seemed neither strange nor impossible on her lips. It seemed to him that love in the Elliott family was like that.

Zeebrugge at eight in the morning was a gloom of rain drizzling from a leaden sky, and streams of cars with glaring headlights, their drivers fighting through to factories and offices for a day on the treadmill.

"God, I couldn't do this every day," Stephen swore as he dodged traffic, searched for the right lane, and struggled with the initial strangeness of driving on the other side of the road.

"Never mind, you don't have to," Zoe observed equably, a map on her knee. "Just think, most of these people couldn't bear to do what you do either."

"Look, spare me the philosophy just now, darling, and tell me what road we should be on."

"Keep following the signs for Ostend."

"Right."

Once clear of Zeebrugge, it was simple enough, dual carriageway to the seaside town of Ostend, with the Jaguar nicely eating up the miles, then south on a minor road to Dixmude toward Ypres and Armentières. Their plans were flexible, the main idea being to follow Liam's footsteps from Flanders down to the Somme and back to Flanders again for September 20, which coincidentally was also the seventieth anniversary of the Battle of the Menin Road. They had been warned that the town would be very busy that weekend, so had booked an hotel in advance; but for the rest they were easy enough, content to take choice and chance as it came. They had Michelin guides with maps, a book of battlefield tours, and even an ancient guide complete with photographs that Stephen had found among the books in the trunk. Published in 1920, it had Robert Duncannon's signature scrawled across the flyleaf.

Zoe had invested in a waxed jacket and green wellies in case of mud and bad weather, while Stephen had boots and sea-boot socks, and said his old Burberry would have to do. They were both rather looking forward to tramping through woods and across plowed fields in the rain, but as they turned inland the weather improved, the sun struggling through a hazy autumn mist over countryside that appeared not unlike the Vale of York.

Bypassing Ypres, the first town they came to was Poperinghe. Parking the car off a cobbled market square, after lunch they found themselves wandering around, rather as Liam once had, and being drawn toward Talbot House. The tall, white town house, where a British chaplain called Tubby Clayton had set up a home-from-home for weary and distressed troops, was now a place of pilgrimage for battlefield travelers but not a museum. When Stephen and Zoe called, the door was open to visitors and a friendly young man with perfect English invited them in. He explained how the Everyman's Club had come about, and what a refuge it had been in the darkest days of the war. The garden was still there, and the chapel beneath the rafters, its chairs and the little altar ready for the next service. Below it was the study with its instruction to ABANDON RANK ALL YE WHO ENTER HERE.

There was a sense of peace and solace in that room, and affected by the knowledge that Liam had been there, at what was probably the lowest point of his war, neither of them wanted to leave. It was, however, late afternoon, and both Stephen and Zoe were aware of sudden fatigue, a need for baths and rest and a quiet meal before turning in for the night. They found a comfortable hotel just off the square which provided all their requirements.

Pouring the last of the wine as they finished their meal, Stephen said, "You would say, wouldn't you, if you didn't want to go on?"

"Of course I would. Why, don't you?"

"Oh, I want to go on, no doubt about that. It's just"—he broke off, drank some more wine, and finally shook his head—"this afternoon—you were on the verge of tears a couple of times, and so was I. It made me think that—well, there's going to be a lot more of it, and we are going to be sad, maybe even very upset at times. Is this a good idea for a honeymoon? I know it's what we said we'd do, but there's no shame in changing our minds—we could drive on down to the Côte d'Azur, if you'd prefer . . ."

"And come back another time?"

Stephen nodded, toying with his glass. He saw her eyes darken before she glanced away, watching diners at other tables, and waiters passing.

"I know what you're saying," she said at last, "but no, I don't think so. We talked about this, didn't we, before we finally decided. And if you recall, we both had it in mind that this was what we wanted to do, honeymoon or not." A sudden smile dispelled the shadows. "We just decided to get married first."

Relieved, he clasped her hand across the table. "So you want to carry on?"

"Yes. I think we have to."

"That reminds me," Zoe said as they reached their room, "I had a letter before I left London. Can't think how I forgot to tell you," she added, glancing up at him with an ironical lift of her eyebrow, "unless it was that wedding we attended the other day . . ." She fished in her capacious shoulder bag and produced, with a flourish that would have credited a magician, an airmail envelope bearing the Southern Cross emblem of Australia.

"The farm's gone—most of it, anyway. But the old house

and the bungalows are still there, on a few acres of land, and guess what? The family still own it."

"You're kidding." He took the envelope and opened it, scanning the contents quickly before settling down to read properly. The writer was a Mrs. Laura Maddox, widow of David, son of Lewis Maddox's elder brother. She was sixty-seven years old, and remembered Uncle Lew and Aunt Gina very well. In fact, since her husband's death some six years previously, she had moved into their old bungalow, leaving the farmhouse to her son and his wife.

Although she was not sure exactly what it was Miss Clifford wanted to know about the old lady, Mrs. Maddox felt she could say without fear of contradiction that Aunt Gina had been one of the kindest people it had ever been her pleasure to know, and much missed after her death in 1973.

. . . and Lord knows how old she was. In her eighties, I'm sure, but she always kept her age a secret. Bright as a button, though, right up to that last week or so. Then she suddenly faded, like old people do, and got a bit muddled. She took a chill that turned to pneumonia, and died at the end of September. Uncle Lew went in 1949. Nice old bloke he was, frail when I knew him, but always had a joke for you, in spite of being a sick man. She was a nurse, though, did a lot of good for the folks around here, especially between the wars. Delivered I don't know how many babies, people always sent for her before the doctor. Uncle Lew said if it hadn't been for her, he would have given up years ago.

Lew and her brother were best friends in the war, and I seem to think he worked here before that. She had a lovely picture of him on the mantelpiece, a nice portrait photo taken in uniform. I still have it, couldn't bear to throw it away, but I don't think it would interest anybody else. If you would like it, I could send it on, you being related to the other brother . . .

Stephen looked up at Zoe, who was standing over him, and his happy smile gave way to a laugh of appreciation and amazement. Her luck, he felt, was phenomenal, and it would have been hard to say which touched him most: the fact that yet another of her shots in the dark had reached its mark, or the contents of that letter from Mrs. Maddox.

On balance, he thought, drawing Zoe close against his shoulder, it was the latter. Knowing that Georgina's marriage had been a happy one, that she had gone on to enjoy a long and apparently fulfilled life, eased much of the tragedy attached to her affair with Liam. Louisa and Robert, he felt—and Edward too—should have been able to rest in peace knowing that.

But what of Liam? The more Zoe told him, and the more he thought about it, the less Stephen understood. Having come to accept Liam Elliott's presence in their lives, and his inescapable influence, it was increasingly apparent that in his case, the term, *at rest*, was simply not applicable. Zoe's experience that day at the hospital served only to underscore it; yet belief and understanding were still miles apart. It was one thing to acknowledge Liam's power, to look back and realize, thankfully, that all his efforts so far had been to the good; but it was quite another to chart a definite pattern and to see what it was that he was trying to do.

Part of it, they were both by now convinced, was to do with themselves, the love they shared, and in that love the resolving of problems which had remained outstanding for more than seventy years; but that was not all, that was not everything. And whatever else it was that Liam was trying to say, the only way to understand it was to be open to him, to subdue logic and reason, and give him access to instinct. As far as either of them could tell, that was the way in which he worked best. So however hard reason might argue against subjecting themselves to the sadnesses of this journey, instinct said to carry on.

Next morning they were on the road shortly after nine, heading directly south for Bailleul and the area which had been the training ground for most of the troops arriving in France. Driving between hedges along narrow country lanes, it was possible to ignore the broad new swathe of *autoroute* over to the left, and to imagine Liam seeing this rich farmland for the very first time. Even the villages had a sleepy, timeless atmostphere, as though nothing much had changed in the years between, and it was easy to pretend that nothing had. Within just a few miles, however, they had a rude awakening to reality. The string of hamlets and small towns that followed the meandering River Lys between Estaires and Armentières were almost one, with industry crowding out what few farms and fields remained.

Stephen had no desire to be embroiled in the maze of a busy city center. On a sharp decision he turned right, away from the river and the factories, along a less busy but much narrower road that seemed to serve a string of farms and hamlets. Here, at last, in that flat land divided by hedges and fences, was it possible to visualize the lines of waterlogged trenches, barbed-wire entanglements, and the sand-bagged ruins of barns and houses. Somewhere along here had been the front line; in the region of this road Liam had spent a couple of months with his company of machine gunners, learning to cope with the mud and the rats and the terrifying moments, learning to live with the deadly business of war.

They followed the road back to Estaires, and thence in a meandering curve away from the industrial areas of Béthune and Lens and Arras. Liam's route south had been via St. Pol and Doullens, and that was the way Stephen intended to go. It was an unexpectedly beautiful drive, past shorn wheat fields and woods ablaze with the first tints of autumn. Having lunched early and simply in Estaires, they stopped again at a wayside café just after four, and then continued south into Picardy.

On the Michelin map, Zoe had marked all the villages mentioned by Liam in his diary; they stretched in a broad, horizontal sweep either side of the main road between Doullens and Amiens, from the wide valley of the Somme near Abbeville in the west, to Albert and the valley of the Ancre in the east. The distance was perhaps some thirty miles, which was, Zoe thought, a lot of marching, particularly after the stress and exhaustion of battle. Much easier by car, she decided, even while they debated which route to take. Stephen said it had been a long day, even in the comfort of the Jaguar. He thought it advisable to head directly for Amiens and a bed for the night.

The following day, after a morning spent motoring through the wealth of tiny villages, taking photographs of ancient, timber-framed barns, and wondering in which ones Liam had slept on those journeys to and from the front, Stephen and Zoe arrived in Albert at lunchtime. The basilica with its massive red-and-white brick tower was visible for miles, the sun glinting from the gilded Virgin and Child which crowned it; so easy to see what a gift that had been as a marker for enemy artillery, so easy to cringe at the thought of shells landing with such accuracy in the square below.

There was a café in the square; sitting at a pavement table in the warm September sun, they both wondered whether it was the same estaminet where Liam and Robin had met in the summer of 1916. In a sentimental gesture, Stephen ordered two beers, and while they were waiting for the *omelettes et frites*, he gazed up at that massive edifice across the way, comparing it to the postcard reproduction of a 1916 photograph. The barred church with its famous statue poised like a diver had been completely restored, so well that it was hard to believe that it had not always looked so solid. The town itself was prosaic with no pretensions to grandeur, but they took a walk around before driving out to Fricourt, where Robin Elliott had survived the carnage of 1 July.

The village nestled in a dip of those rolling chalk downs beyond Albert, a pretty enough place in an attractive setting. It was horrifying, however, to view the field of combat from the Green Howards' memorial. The granite cross stood inside the wall of the British cemetery, and beyond it lay a small field bounded by a dense copse of trees to the left and a low ridge which curved from the right. At most, the ridge, which now bore a line of modern bungalows, was no more than a hundred yards away, a twelve-second sprint to a fit young athlete keen to gain his objective; yet the young men of the 7th Battalion had been mown down by the score as they attempted to take the German guns.

Looking out over that little field, Zoe shivered in the sun, knowing that what had happened here had, that very same day, been repeated along a front that extended for eighteen miles.

Stephen left a small wooden cross bearing a scarlet poppy and his grandfather's name by the granite memorial. Robin Elliott, as much as the men who died here, had been a victim too. Thinking about all those ordinary men, the clerks and the laborers, artists, miners, and scholars, it seemed no more than an echo of his thoughts to find that someone else had written in the visitors book 'There are no politicians buried here . . .'

A short distance away was the German cemetery, as neatly kept but bleaker somehow, lacking the gentling effect of flowers. Simple black crosses set among trees looked out from higher ground over the battlefield. Here and there an arched stone bearing a Star of David marked the last resting place of a Jewish soldier. In the light of that other war, a mere twenty years later, there was a dreadful irony about that.

Through a drift of fallen leaves they made their way back to the car. With a deep sigh, Stephen picked up the maps and guides and made quite a show of studying the various routes to Pozières. Zoe looked out over the battlefield and said nothing at all.

He turned the car, going back the way they had come, through the village and right toward Bécourt. By that deserted roadside lay another cemetery, row upon row of white headstones against a stubble field, with woods, gold and green, crowning the rise beyond. Within a few hundred yards, where the road curved into the next village, a large white crucifix stood at the junction of two cart tracks, one leading into the wood, the other skirting it, leading to open fields above.

"This must be Bécourt Wood," Stephen said, looking again at the enlarged map in the battlefield guide, "and the track, if I'm not mistaken, must lead to Sausage Valley—or Gully as the Aussies called it." He glanced at Zoe and she smiled. "Do you want a walk?"

"Better get the wellies," she replied, stepping out of the car. "I've a feeling that chalk uplands, after rain, will be greasy and muddy."

She was right, and Stephen knew that it would take more than these few days of fine, sunny weather to dry out the plowed fields that rose gently to either side. It was too warm, however, for wet-weather gear, and in scarves, sweaters, and jeans they walked hand in hand along Sausage Gully. Hugging a raised hedge part of the way, the track swept up the center of that shallow bowl before curving away to the left toward a crown of trees and shrubs that Stephen thought might be close to the village of La Boisselle. Straight ahead of them, a slender stand of trees indicated Contalmaison, while beyond that, according to the map, lay Pozières.

Distances were deceptive, and the stiff climb to La Boisselle took longer than they thought. They were both breathing rather heavily by the time they reached the crest, but what struck each of them with equal force was the time it had taken to climb one side of that shallow valley, and the sense of absolute exposure. There were no hedges to conceal them from watchers on that horseshoe ridge, and it seemed fair to assume that any hedges pre-1914 had been dug up or blasted out of existence long before the Australians arrived. There had been trenches, of course, but still, to traverse that place in journeys to and from the forward line seemed hazardous in the extreme.

Looking back the way they had come, in the midst of those newly plowed acres, they could see white lines meandering across the earth, and large white patches, roughly circular, that marked the position of old craters and shell holes. After seventy years, there was something faintly chilling about it, as though the earth itself was determined to keep its own memorial to those bitter days. More chilling still was the little pile of rusty, unexploded shells propped against a stone where the track became a road.

"Seventy years," Stephen murmured, "and they're still digging them up." He looked down, and among the bits of chalk spotted a shrapnel ball, a heavy lead pellet the size of a child's marble, just one of the hundreds packed into every shrapnel shell, designed to burst in midair like deadly rain. Weighing it in his palm, he imagined it biting through tender flesh, breaking bones with the force of its impact . . .

He slipped the small thing into his pocket, joining Zoe as she rounded the shrouding line of shrubs at the crest. There before them stood a wooden cross, right on the lip of a massive crater, the size and depth of which took Stephen's breath away. So this was the crater of La Boisselle, blown by mines before the Australians arrived, part of the British attempt to dislodge the German forces from their position on the ridge of the Bapaume Road. Once, there had been trenches here, and deep dugouts; the rest had gone, but the crater remained, a deep well in the chalk some sixty feet deep.

Stephen gazed into it and fingered the tiny lead ball in his pocket: From the large to the small, the opposing forces had tried everything to annihilate each other. Little had been achieved, barring the waste of a generation, and the land continued to tell the story.

A car with British plates drew up before the cross, the occupants two middle-aged men in overcoats. They smiled and nodded, looked up at the memorial and down into the crater, and proceeded to walk the rim. Watching them for a moment, with a blustery wind sharpening the air, Stephen and Zoe debated what to do. The village of La Boisselle was a couple of fields away down the asphalt road, with the main Bapaume Road immediately beyond it; Pozières was perhaps another two miles. In the end, neither of them wanted to walk that distance along a main road, and as the afternoon was drawing on, it was decided to return to Bécourt for the car.

Zoe's research into the action at Pozières had turned up enough to make them realize that nowadays there was little to see beyond a single main street, the Australian Memorial, and the base of the old windmill beyond the village; with a glance at his watch, Stephen decided that there was still enough daylight to do that before returning to their hotel in Amiens for a well-deserved dinner. Both of them were hungry, but Albert's cafés seemed modest places, and without a thorough search, their chances of a decent meal with all the trimmings looked slim. So, a look at the rebuilt village, a visit to the memorial, and back to Amiens for the night.

Old photographs reprinted in a modern account of the battle revealed that Pozières had been a singularly plain French village of mainly one-story houses hugging the arrow of the Roman road; its gardens and orchards, according to the old maps, were all to the rear. Nothing seemed to have changed. Driving up the hill from the direction of Albert, the village appeared as a short stretch of unpretentious dwellings, the kind of place to drive through, at speed, on the way to somewhere infinitely more interesting. Talking to Zoe, Stephen did just that before realizing where they were. As luck would have it, he slowed and turned the car by the old windmill. Again, it was so modest as to be hardly noticeable. Along a strip of mown grass, a white path led to a flat memorial stone and the rough mound where the windmill had once stood; the old concrete fortifications were now well sunk into the ground.

How many lives had it cost to take this place? Stephen did not know, could not even guess; but with its commanding view of the countryside to the north and east, he could understand why the Australians wanted it. From there it must have been possible to see the German guns.

At the other end of the village, by Fort Gibraltar—a bramble-covered mass this time—stood the obelisk erected to the memory of those men of the 1st Australian Division who had fought so doggedly and endured so bravely throughout three long years of war in France. There was a plaque naming the legendary places of those engagements, from Pozières to Passchendaele, and a dozen more between Bullecourt and the Hindenburg Line. Above it, bronze against granite, rose the rising sun emblem with its imperial crown and curl of motto beneath, striking and instantly memorable. Zoe called it a brilliant piece of design, but there were tears in her eyes as she said it, and Stephen knew she was thinking of Liam in this place, and trying not to cry.

In the west the sun was setting in a hazy, azure sky; to the north a lilac mist wreathed the woods of Thiepval and its huge memorial, while night clouds gathered over Pozières. All around were the gentle slopes of cultivated land, a sense of peace accentuated by the twitter of birds settling down for the night, the murmur of a passing car, and a distant buzz from a homebound tractor. It was hard to believe that this place had been obliterated, reduced to a naked, barren, ash-strewn heath; that earth and sky had been riven, night and day, by the constant thunder of the guns. Hard to believe, until the eye caught the glimmer of light on the tall crosses between the trees, until the number of cemeteries were counted.

37

*T*he lights of a small café caught Stephen's attention as they returned to the car, and thoughts of hot coffee were suddenly more pressing than anything else. They were both chilled, so he ordered cognac to accompany it, Zoe responding in careful French to Madame's warm and friendly welcome.

She was a plump, middle-aged, cheerful woman, the personification of her cosy and old-fashioned establishment. Delft racks and huge, dark dressers lined the walls, filled with an assortment of meat plates and jugs and the myriad examples of wartime memorabilia. There were regimental insignia, photographs and flags, caps and helmets, polished brass shell cases from the enormous to the minute, nose-cones, water bottles, and bayonets; it was a collector's dream and a place of endless fascination for anyone even remotely interested in the battlefields. Glass in hand, Zoe wandered around peering at everything while Madame bustled in and out of the kitchen with plates of food for a group of travelers in the corner. The aroma was tantalizing, the presentation enough to capture a gourmet. Catching Zoe's eye, Stephen shot her an inquiring look, and instantly she smiled and nodded. Why trail back to their hotel, when there were feasts to be had right here?

The paté was rich, the chicken delicately flavored, and the cheese excellent. They drank a recommended wine and exclaimed over it, then finished with a colorless liqueur *on the house*. With her other visitors gone, Madame was pleased to talk about Pozières, her little café and its museum, and the people who regularly stopped to eat, drink, and say *bonjour*. On July 1 the previous year, which had been the seventieth anniversary of the Battle of the Somme, she said she had served hundreds of meals to Australians, Canadians, Irish, Scots, and English: a memorable day for her family and the people of Pozières.

Some might have said, cynically, that the old war was obviously good for business, and yet despite the difficulties of language, it was easy to understand that business was secondary to the fact that Pozières was not forgotten. The young men who died here might have been foreigners, but Madame's forebears had suffered too; to the north and the south they had died under arms, and here their lives had been wrecked by the destruction of their village and the land itself. The Gallic shrug said, "Well, that's how it was, you have to accept it," yet this woman cared too much for the living not to be affected by that senseless waste. Zoe did not think she was unusual.

What struck her particularly—and Stephen too, as they discussed it on the drive back to Amiens—was the tenacity of these people, their brave determination to come back and start again. Not only to return, but to rebuild their village as it had been before.

It must have taken years to clear their lands of the detritus of war, to reclaim those fields from the dead, but they had done just that, and done it with courage and respect. Here, it was impossible to forget the past; the young men who had given up their lives in one of the bloodiest wars the world had ever known were part of these people's present. They could never be forgotten, not here, not in Albert, not in the hundreds of towns and villages that had formed the battlegrounds of seventy years ago.

That same thought, having taken root, continued to grow as they eventually made their way north, back to Flanders and the medieval town of Ypres. Its wealth, accrued in the thirteenth and fourteenth centuries from the wool trade, had given birth to a series of fine Gothic buildings, most notably the massive Cloth Hall, whose tower dominated a grand marketplace. Parking the car in that cobbled square, Stephen and Zoe stepped out in noonday sun to be faced by a dazzling array of medieval architecture, steep roofs and stepped gables, tall, narrow houses, tiny shops and cafés, and the glowing sandstone of the Cloth Hall itself. Here, the best of the past had been re-created to shine for the future; everywhere, datestones from the 1920s proclaimed a new beginning after the holocaust. The whole town was a monument to endurance and determination.

Crossing the road to their hotel, Stephen and Zoe were, without realizing it, in line with the Menin Road. Glancing each way for traffic, they suddenly saw the memorial, massive, white, bridging the narrow street before it like a classical version of one of York's ancient gates. They both paused, a car slowed, but neither of them noticed; astonished and mesmerized, they wandered to the far pavement and then along the street, unable to concentrate on anything else.

"I don't know why, but I always imagined it standing on its own, like the Arc de Triomphe but out in the countryside."

"Yes, me too," Stephen murmured, thinking of the memorial at Thiepval, grim and isolated among its woods and fields and cemeteries. This was just as imposing, but somehow far more pleasing, integral with the town's old defenses and overlooking a peaceful moat. There were trees on the ramparts, shedding golden leaves into the water below, and traffic passing back and forth beneath the enormous tunnel of the archway itself. Like the city of York, Ypres formed the hub of several main roads, and the one to Menin was as busy now as it had ever been. There was something reassuring about that, a sense of life and continuation in a place that had seen so much of death, and it seemed singularly appropriate that Liam's name should be here among the living, in a place that had so much in common with his childhood home.

Almost every regiment and unit of the Empire had seen service here, passing along a *via dolorosa* of Ypres' ruins to front lines that straddled the Menin Road, and those who passed through and did not come back, those who fell and were denied the privilege of a marked grave, were remembered here. Fifty-five thousand names. Australians, Canadians, South Africans, Indians, and West Indians, with more than forty thousand British soldiers among them.

Stephen and Zoe stood beneath the great vault of the central arch, gazing up at those high walls, smooth blocks of white stone, each bearing so many names, so many regiments. Above them, sunlight streamed through open roundels, while to either side twin arches faced each other across the road, with steps leading up to more walls, more names.

They found the Australians at last, and among the Machine Gun Corps, Liam's surname and initials carved into the stone. Familiar, yet strange, and as Stephen reached out to trace those fading letters, he was possessed by a sharp sense of his own mortality. Embracing Zoe with sudden need, he realized more sharply than ever how fortunate he was to be alive, to have her love, and, just as important, her understanding. And what they shared, which seemed so much a part of Liam's gift to them both, was a living, growing thing that had its roots embedded firmly in the past and its branches reaching out toward the future. For Robert and Louisa, who began all this, time and fate had decreed something other than natural fulfillment; and the legacy bequeathed to Liam and Georgina cast a blight that but for Liam's untimely death might well have gone on to ruin both their lives. For Stephen and Zoe, however, sharing the same blood, the same inheritance, there were no such tragedies, no such impediments.

With arms around each other, they went back to the hotel. A couple of hours later, as a beam of sun picked out the chestnut lights in her hair on the pillow, he said softly, "I feel so much at peace, as though everything at last is right. Not just you and me, but everything to do with us—even those odd coincidences seem to have slipped into place. He wanted us together, didn't he? And he wanted us to come here."

"Yes, of course he did."

Kissing the fingers she raised to his lips, he smiled into her eyes. Dark, curling lashes cast shadows against her cheek, and it seemed to him that she knew so much, understood with greater depth the things he was just beginning to see. Yet she did not try to tell him, did not attempt to push him down roads with which she was already familiar; she was content, instead, to let him discover things for himself. Wondering whether she was fey or simply very wise, he smiled again, remembering his first impression of her, that she was like a misty Irish morning, soft, gentle, and slightly mysterious. And when the sun shone through, she sparkled, as her eyes were sparkling now, full of light and love and an uncanny knowledge of what was in his mind.

"And do you know what I want?"

She tried to suppress a smile, but her eyes gave her away. "No, tell me."

"I want us to have children."

That was something Stephen had never said before because as a man who lived very much in the present, he had never wanted to look that far ahead, or in that particular direction; but here, with Zoe, he was beginning to see the importance of the future. Their future, his and hers, with a family of their own.

"But not this very minute," he said laughingly a few minutes later. "I'm selfish enough to want you to come to sea with me, a couple of times at least—"

"And I want to enjoy living in your flat—"

"*Our* flat," he reminded her.

"—with that glorious view. I want to enjoy that for a little while, before we have to think in terms of a house and garden, and domestic bliss!"

"You're sure you won't miss London?" It was a question he had asked several times, and when he asked it, he did not really mean London but her flat on Queen's Gate, the one that had belonged to Robert and Georgina.

"I won't miss London at all, I've told you that, and as for Queen's Gate—well yes, I will miss it, but it's not something I want to cling to at the expense of my life with you. It's part of the past," she said softly, "like Robert and Georgina. But I won't ever forget it, just as I won't forget them." With a sudden warm smile, she said, "Anyway, it doesn't belong to me, it was only on loan, so to speak . . ."

"At the right time," he murmured.

"Oh yes—like everything else, it was at the right time . . ."

They ate a very satisfying meal that evening in a tiny restaurant across the square, a place that like their hotel seemed full of English visitors here for the following day's anniversary. At the next table they spotted the same two middle-aged men they had seen previously at La Boisselle. Recognition and warmer greetings led, eventually, to a very fruitful conversation. The two men were battlefield pilgrims of some twenty years' standing: one an ex-soldier whose grandfather had died leading his men on the first day of the Somme, while the other's great-uncle had been killed at Passchendaele. Their knowledge of both areas was astounding.

Zoe asked what it was that drew them back time after time, and for a moment they both seemed quite nonplussed; between them they provided all kinds of reasons, from a pair of understanding wives to the beauty of the countryside and the welcome of local people. Ultimately, however, they both agreed that what really brought them back year after year was the very special atmosphere.

"There's something about the place—here and on the Somme. I don't know whether you've noticed it yet, but you probably will in time. It's not the sadness you'd expect—far from it. It's a sense of tremendous *peace*. Very healing, somehow," the ex-soldier said unexpectedly, and without a trace of embarrassment. "I often come here feeling as though I've got the weight of the world on me, but I go away again quite restored."

The other man nodded, while Stephen and Zoe glanced at each other. "Yes," she said, "we have noticed it."

As Stephen squeezed her fingers, she knew what he was thinking, that after the shocks and the stress of almost three months in the Gulf, he had not truly recovered himself until the last few days. He was more relaxed and at peace now than she had ever know him. So was she; and in her heart she knew that it was not simply because they were married and happy with each other. It went far deeper than that. It was both curious and reassuring to realize that other people felt it too.

Stephen talked about their particular interest in the initial

stages of the Australians' advance, and in return received clear
instructions on how to approach the area. The ex-soldier, with
his appreciation of aims and strategy, was able to clarify the
separate objectives and achievements, and to indicate roughly
the place where Liam must have met his end.

Next morning, after an early cup of coffee, Zoe stuffed
their pockets with chocolate and biscuits before setting off at
first light to drive out toward Polygon Wood.

Against a brightening sky streaked with pink in the east,
that great, dense stand of oaks and conifers loomed dark and
brooding across a landscape wreathed in low-lying mist. It was
eerie and beautiful, and also faintly chilling to realize that on a
morning such as this the battalions had formed for their advance. To their left, mist clung in tattered shrouds to the shivering green and gold of Glencorse Wood, while isolated
farmhouses appeared like ghostly mirages across the fields.
They parked the car and walked along a narrow country lane
toward what had been marked on their map as the second
objective. The line came down at an angle, just beyond another
lane that joined this one between Nonne Bosschen and Polygon
Wood, and led back toward the Menin Road.

The junction of the two lanes formed the apex of a triangle,
and as they came to the corner the sun came up in all its glory,
flooding sky and mist with light. Polygon Wood seemed to float
before them, a dark island on a milky sea, while they waded
waist deep through the clinging, shifting fog. They passed an
isolated dwelling, and farther on, a group of houses with barns
and outbuildings, some quite new, others that might have been
rebuilt on or near the fortified remains of old farms. From the
information they had, it was hard to be sure of even an approximate place, but somewhere close to this lane, probably between
it and the modern, high-speed road running parallel a hundred
yards or so away, a sniper's bullet had caught Liam as he raised
his head. Somewhere near here he had been buried.

It doesn't matter. The words came into Zoe's mind even as
she dwelt on the tragedy, even as the pair of them looked
around at fields and farms and back at the looming darkness of
Polygon Wood. *None of this matters.* It came again, so clearly
that she looked up at Stephen, almost convinced that he had
spoken. For a moment his blue eyes, catching the sun, were

brilliant; and then he smiled and shook his head and slipped an arm around her shoulders.

"No," he said huskily, "I don't suppose it does matter anymore. Not to him, anyway."

She knew what he meant. Seventy years ago today, as the sun rose over these autumn woods and misty fields, Liam had met his death; but for him it had been the beginning of a life that ranged far beyond these Flanders fields. That, she felt sure, was by far the greater part of what he had always been trying to tell them: that life was important, but death was by no means the end. And if love in all its forms was the most essential part of life itself, then love was eternal, all-powerful, and it was with love that he had come to them.

His power was unmistakable, although whether it was exceptional was a question neither could answer; and whether their love and remembrance of him increased that power, or whether through them he was fulfilling a destiny denied to him in life, was another imponderable. The only thing of which they could be sure was that he was near them now, communicating in his own inimitable fashion.

A sense of lightness, akin to that Zoe had experienced at the Wandsworth hospital, possessed them both: calmer, less heady, but equally unmistakable. Although they were conscious that he had left them before they reached the car, there was, as before, that lingering sense of clarity and peace.

Stephen stopped the car before the Menin Gate and they stood quietly for a while, watching a pair of swans among the drifting leaves, both very conscious of past and present and the changes seventy years had wrought. Above them were the old brick and earth walls of the ramparts, and dominating the Menin Road, that great triumphal arch. And it was triumphal, despite the names of the dead—or even, perhaps, because of them. A triumph of the spirit was invested here, as dazzling as the morning sun, as glowing as the love and hope and blessedness in their hearts.

Together they placed their wreath of remembrance poppies on the steps beneath Liam's name and, with hands locked, felt his presence encompass them like a loving embrace. After a moment or two they climbed those broad steps to the ramparts above, and from there the world seemed a blessed place, full of light and love and perfect clarity. A great surge of spiritual joy came then, and a tingling of the blood; and in each other's eyes and faces was a radiance that owed much to what had so long been denied, and what could be fulfilled. Stephen looked at Zoe and saw for a moment Louisa's smile and Georgina's serenity, and in her, he knew, was combined the legacy of the past and all his future promise.

And Liam knew that too. Liam had always known it.

Awareness flooded through him then, like a great tidal wave, so clear and absolute that Stephen could only wonder afterward at the completeness of that vision. It was all here, in the lives of Robert and Louisa and Edward, in that diary which was written like a series of notes for the book Liam intended to write when the war was over; and it was tied in with his life, and Zoe's, and the shared experience of this past astonishing year. Stephen knew what Liam wanted, he wanted it written down for the living to read. It shook him so much that all he could do was reach for Zoe and hold her very close against his heart.

"I'll do my best," he whispered as he raised his face to the light. "I'll do my very best."